PENGUIN BOOKS

THE THIRD RUMPOLE OMNIBUS

John Mortimer is a playwright, novelist, and former prac-
ticing barrister. During the Second World War he worked
with the Crown Film Unit and published several novels
before turning to theater. He has written many film scripts
as well as stage, radio, and television plays, including *A
Voyage Round My Father*, the Rumpole plays—which won
him the British Academy of the Year award—and the
adaptation of Evelyn Waugh's *Brideshead Revisited*. He is
the author of ten collections of Rumpole stories and two
volumes of autobiography, *Clinging to the Wreckage* and
Murderers and Other Friends. His novels *Summer's Lease,
Paradise Postponed*, and its sequel, *Titmuss Regained*, have
been successful television series. His latest novels are *Dun-
ster* and *Felix in the Underworld*. John Mortimer lives with
his wife and two daughters in Oxfordshire, England.

John Mortimer

THE THIRD

Rumpole

OMNIBUS

Rumpole and the Age of Miracles

Rumpole à la Carte

Rumpole and the Angel of Death

PENGUIN BOOKS

PENGUIN BOOKS
Published by the Penguin Group
Penguin Putnam Inc., 375 Hudson Street,
New York, New York 10014, U.S.A.
Penguin Books Ltd, 27 Wrights Lane,
London W8 5TZ, England
Penguin Books Australia Ltd, Ringwood,
Victoria, Australia
Penguin Books Canada Ltd, 10 Alcorn Avenue,
Toronto, Ontario, Canada M4V 3B2
Penguin Books (N.Z.) Ltd, 182–190 Wairau Road,
Auckland 10, New Zealand

Penguin Books Ltd, Registered Offices:
Harmondsworth, Middlesex, England

This volume first published in Great Britain by Penguin Books Ltd 1997
Published in Penguin Books (U.S.A.) 1998

1   3   5   7   9   10   8   6   4   2

Rumpole and the Age of Miracles first published in
Great Britain in Penguin Books 1988
Published in Penguin Books (U.S.A.) 1989
Copyright © Advanpress Ltd, 1988
All rights reserved

Rumpole à la Carte first published in Great Britain by Penguin Books Ltd 1990
Published in the United States of America by Viking Penguin,
a division of Penguin Books USA Inc. 1990
Published in Penguin Books (U.S.A.) 1991
Copyright © Advanpress Ltd, 1990
All rights reserved

Rumpole and the Angel of Death first published
in Great Britain by Penguin Books Ltd 1995
Published in the United States of America by Viking Penguin,
a division of Penguin Books USA Inc. 1996
Published in Penguin Books (U.S.A.) 1997
Copyright © Advanpress Ltd, 1995
All rights reserved

We Were Dancing copyright 1935 by the Estate of Noel Coward,
quotation on page 177 by permission of Michael Imison Playwrights Ltd.

ISBN 0 14 02.5741 1
CIP data available

Printed in the United States of America
Set in Plantin

Contents

Rumpole and the Age of Miracles

To Penny

Rumpole and the Bubble Reputation

It is now getting on for half a century since I took to crime, and I can honestly say I haven't regretted a single moment of it.

Crime is about life, death and the liberty of the subject; civil law is entirely concerned with that most tedious of all topics, money. Criminal law requires an expert knowledge of blood-stains, policemen's notebooks and the dark flow of human passion, as well as the argot currently in use round the Elephant and Castle. Civil law calls for a close study of such yawn-producing matters as bills of exchange, negotiable instruments and charter parties. It is true, of course, that the most enthralling murder produces only a small and long-delayed Legal Aid cheque, sufficient to buy a couple of dinners at some Sunday supplement eaterie for the learned friends who practise daily in the commercial courts. Give me, however, a sympathetic jury, a blurred thumbprint and a dodgy confession, and you can keep *Mega-Chemicals Ltd* v. *The Sunshine Bank of Florida* with all its fifty days of mammoth refreshers for the well-heeled barristers involved.

There is one drawback, however, to being a criminal hack; the Judges and the learned friends are apt to regard you as though you were the proud possessor of a long line of convictions. How many times have I stood up to address the tribunal on such matters as the importance of intent or the presumption of innocence only to be stared at by the old darling on the Bench as though I were sporting a black mask or carrying a large sack labelled SWAG? Often, as I walk through the Temple on my way down to the Bailey, my place of work, I have seen bowler-hatted commercial or revenue men pass by on the other side and heard them mutter, 'There goes old Rumpole. I wonder if he's doing a murder or a rape this morning?' The sad truth of the matter is that civil law is regarded as the Harrods and crime the Tesco's of the legal profession. And of all the varieties of civil action the most elegant, the smartest, the one which attracts the best barristers like bees to the honey-pot, is undoubtedly the libel action. Star in a libel case on the civilized stage of the High Court of Justice and fame and fortune will be yours, if you haven't got them already.

It's odd, isn't it? Kill a person or beat him over the head and remove his wallet, and all you'll get is an Old Bailey judge and an Old Bailey hack. Cast a well-deserved slur on his moral character, ridicule his nose or belittle his bank balance and you will get a High Court judge and some of the smoothest silks in the business. I can only remember doing one libel action, and after it I asked my clerk, Henry, to find me a nice clean assault or an honest break and entering. Exactly why I did so will become clear to you when I have revealed the full and hitherto unpublished details of *Amelia Nettleship* v. *The Daily Beacon and Maurice Machin*. If, after reading what went on in that particular defamation case, you don't agree that crime presents a fellow with a more honourable alternative, I shall have to think seriously about issuing a writ for libel.

You may be fortunate enough never to have read an allegedly 'historical' novel by that much-publicized authoress Miss Amelia Nettleship. Her books contain virginal heroines and gallant and gentlemanly heroes and thus present an extremely misleading account of our rough island story. She is frequently photographed wearing cotton print dresses, with large spectacles on her still pretty nose, dictating to a secretary and a couple of long-suffering cats in a wistaria-clad Tudor cottage somewhere outside Godalming. In the interviews she gives, Miss Nettleship invariably refers to the evils of the permissive society and the consequences of sex before marriage. I have never, speaking for myself, felt the slightest urge to join the permissive society; the only thing which would tempt me to such a course is hearing Amelia Nettleship denounce it.

Why, you may well ask, should I, whose bedtime reading is usually confined to *The Oxford Book of English Verse* (the Quiller-Couch edition), Archbold's *Criminal Law* and Professor

Ackerman's *Causes of Death*, become so intimately acquainted with Amelia Nettleship? Alas, she shares my bed, not in person but in book form, propped up on the bosom of She Who Must Be Obeyed, alias my wife, Hilda, who insists on reading her far into the night. While engrossed in *Lord Stingo's Fancy*, I distinctly heard her sniff, and asked if she had a cold coming on. 'No, Rumpole,' she told me. 'Touching!'

'Oh, I'm sorry.' I moved further down the bed.

'Don't be silly. The book's touching. Very touching. We all thought Lord Stingo was a bit of a rake but he's turned out quite differently.'

'Sounds a sad disappointment.'

'Nonsense! It's ending happily. He swore he'd never marry, but Lady Sophia has made him swallow his words.'

'And if they were written by Amelia Nettleship I'm sure he found them extremely indigestible. Any chance of turning out the light?'

'Not yet. I've got another three chapters to go.'

'Oh, for God's sake! Can't Lord Stingo get on with it?' As I rolled over, I had no idea that I was soon to become legally involved with the authoress who was robbing me of my sleep.

My story starts in Pommeroy's Wine Bar to which I had hurried for medical treatment (my alcohol content had fallen to a dangerous low) at the end of a day's work. As I sipped my large dose of Château Thames Embankment, I saw my learned friend Erskine-Brown, member of our Chambers at Equity Court, alone and palely loitering. 'What can ail you, Claude?' I asked, and he told me it was his practice.

'Still practising?' I raised an eyebrow. 'I thought you might have got the hang of it by now.'

'I used to do a decent class of work,' he told me sadly. 'I once had a brief in a libel action. You were never in a libel, Rumpole?'

'Who cares about the bubble reputation? Give me a decent murder and a few well-placed bloodstains.'

'Now, guess what I've got coming up?' The man was wan with care.

'Another large claret for me, I sincerely hope.'

'Actual bodily harm and affray in the Kitten-A-Go-Go Club, Soho.' Claude is married to the Portia of our Chambers, the handsome Phillida Erskine-Brown, Q.C., and they are blessed with issue rejoicing in the names of Tristan and Isolde. He is, you understand, far more at home in the Royal Opera House than in any Soho Striperama. 'Two unsavoury characters in leather jackets were duelling with broken Coca-Cola bottles.'

'Sounds like my line of country,' I told him.

'Exactly! I'm scraping the bottom of your barrel, Rumpole. I mean, you've got a reputation for sordid cases. I'll have to ask you for a few tips.'

'Visit the *locus in quo*' was my expert advice. 'Go to the scene of the crime. Inspect the geography of the place.'

'The geography of the Kitten-A-Go-Go? Do I have to?'

'Of course. Then you can suggest it was too dark to identify anyone, or the witness couldn't see round a pillar, or . . .'

But at that point we were interrupted by an eager, bespectacled fellow of about Erskine-Brown's age who introduced himself as Ted Spratling from the *Daily Beacon*. 'I was just having an argument with my editor over there, Mr Rumpole,' he said. 'You do libel cases, don't you?'

'Good heavens, yes!' I lied with instant enthusiasm, sniffing a brief. 'The law of defamation is mother's milk to me. I cut my teeth on hatred, ridicule and contempt.' As I was speaking, I saw Claude Erskine-Brown eyeing the journalist like a long-lost brother. 'Slimey Spratling!' he hallooed at last.

'Collywobbles Erskine-Brown!' The hack seemed equally amazed. There was no need to tell me that they were at school together.

'Look, would you join my editor for a glass of Bolly?' Spratling invited me.

'What?'

'Bollinger.'

'I'd love to!' Erskine-Brown was visibly cheered.

'Oh, you too, Colly. Come on, then.'

'Golly, Colly!' I said as we crossed the bar towards a table in the corner. 'Bolly!'

So I was introduced to Mr Maurice – known as 'Morry' –

Machin, a large silver-haired person with distant traces of a
Scots accent, a blue silk suit and a thick gold ring in which a
single diamond winked sullenly. He was surrounded with empty
Bolly bottles and a masterful-looking woman whom he introduced as Connie Coughlin, the features editor. Morry himself
had, I knew, been for many years at the helm of the tabloid *Daily
Beacon*, and had blasted many precious reputations with well-
aimed scandal stories and reverberating 'revelations'. 'They say
you're a fighter, Mr Rumpole, that you're a terrier, sir, after a
legal rabbit,' he started, as Ted Spratling performed the deputy
editor's duty of pouring the bubbly.

'I do my best. This is my learned friend, Claude Erskine-
Brown, who specializes in affray.'

'I'll remember you, sir, if I get into a scrap.' But the Editor's
real business was with me. 'Mr Rumpole, we are thinking of
briefing you. We're in a spot of bother over a libel.'

'Tell him,' Claude muttered to me, 'you can't do libel.'

'I never turn down a brief in a libel action.' I spoke with
confidence, although Claude continued to mutter, 'You've never
been offered a brief in a libel action.'

'I don't care,' I said, 'for little scraps in Soho. Sordid stuff.
Give me a libel action, when a reputation is at stake.'

'You think that's important?' Morry looked at me seriously, so
I treated him to a taste of *Othello*. 'Good name in man or woman,
dear my lord' (I was at my most impressive),

'Is the immediate jewel of their souls;
Who steals my purse steals trash; 'tis something, nothing.
'Twas mine, 'tis his, and has been slave to thousands;
But he that filches from me my good name
Robs me of that which not enriches him,
And makes me poor indeed.'

Everyone, except Erskine-Brown, was listening reverently.
After I had finished there was a solemn pause. Then Morry
clapped three times.

'Is that one of your speeches, Mr Rumpole?'

'Shakespeare's.'

'Ah, yes . . .'

'Your good name, Mr Machin, is something I shall be prepared to defend to the death,' I said.

'Our paper goes in for a certain amount of fearless exposure,' the *Beacon* Editor explained.

'The "*Beacon* Beauties".' Erskine-Brown was smiling. 'I catch sight of it occasionally in the clerk's room.'

'Not that sort of exposure, Collywobbles!' Spratling rebuked his old school-friend. 'We tell the truth about people in the public eye.'

'Who's bonking who and who pays,' Connie from Features explained. 'Our readers love it.'

'I take exception to that, Connie. I really do,' Morry said piously. 'I don't want Mr Rumpole to get the idea that we're running any sort of a cheap scandal-sheet.'

'Scandal-sheet? Perish the thought!' I was working hard for my brief.

'You wouldn't have any hesitation in acting for the *Beacon*, would you?' the Editor asked me.

'A barrister is an old taxi plying for hire. That's the fine tradition of our trade,' I explained carefully. 'So it's my sacred duty, Mr Morry Machin, to take on anyone in trouble. However repellent I may happen to find them.'

'Thank you, Mr Rumpole.' Morry was genuinely grateful.

'Think nothing of it.'

'We are dedicated to exposing hypocrisy in our society. Wherever it exists. High or low.' The Editor was looking noble. 'So when we find this female pretending to be such a force for purity and parading her morality before the Great British Public . . .'

'Being all for saving your cherry till the honeymoon,' Connie Coughlin translated gruffly.

'Thank you, Connie. Or, as I would put it, denouncing pre-marital sex,' Morry said.

'She's even against the *normal* stuff!' Spratling was bewildered.

'Whereas her own private life is extremely steamy. We feel it our duty to tell our public. Show Mr Rumpole the article in question, Ted.'

I don't know if they had expected to meet me in Pommeroy's

but the top brass of the *Daily Beacon* had a cutting of the alleged libel at the ready. THE PRIVATE LIFE OF AMELIA NETTLE-SHIP BY BEACON GIRL ON THE SPOT, STELLA JANUARY I read, and then glanced at the story that followed. 'This wouldn't be *the* Amelia Nettleship?' I was beginning to warm to my first libel action. 'The expert bottler of pure historical bilge-water?'

'The lady novelist and hypocrite,' Morry told me. 'Of course I've never met the woman.'

'She robs me of my sleep. I know nothing of her morality, but her prose style depraves and corrupts the English language. We shall need a statement from this Stella January.' I got down to business.

'Oh, Stella left us a couple of months ago,' the Editor told me.

'And went where?'

'God knows. Overseas, perhaps. You know what these girls are.'

'We've got to find her,' I insisted and then cheered him up with 'We shall fight, Mr Machin – Morry. And we shall conquer! Remember, I never plead guilty.'

'There speaks a man who knows damn all about libel.' Claude Erskine-Brown had a final mutter.

It might be as well if I quoted here the words in Miss Stella January's article which were the subject of legal proceedings. They ran as follows: *Miss Amelia Nettleship is a bit of a puzzle. The girls in her historical novels always keep their legs crossed until they've got a ring on their fingers. But her private life is rather different. Whatever lucky young man leads the 43-year-old Amelia to the altar will inherit a torrid past which makes Mae West sound like Florence Nightingale. Her home, Hollyhock Cottage, near Godalming, has been the scene of one-night stands and longer liaisons so numerous that the neighbours have given up counting. There is considerably more in her jacuzzi than bath salts. Her latest Casanova, so far unnamed, is said to be a married man who's been seen leaving in the wee small hours.* From the style of this piece of prose you may come to the conclusion that Stella January and Amelia Nettleship deserved each other.

One thing you can say for my learned friend Claude Erskine-Brown is that he takes advice. Having been pointed in the direc-

tion of the Kitten-A-Go-Go, he set off obediently to find a cul-
de-sac off Wardour Street with his instructing solicitor. He wasn't
to know, and it was entirely his bad luck, that Connie Coughlin
had dreamt up a feature on London's Square Mile of Sin for the
Daily Beacon and ordered an ace photographer to comb the sinful
purlieus between Oxford Street and Shaftesbury Avenue in
search of nefarious goings-on.

Erskine-Brown and a Mr Thrower, his sedate solicitor, found
the Kitten-A-Go-Go, paid a sinister-looking myrmidon at the
door ten quid each by way of membership and descended to a
damp and darkened basement where two young ladies were chewing gum and removing their clothes with as much enthusiasm as
they might bring to the task of licking envelopes. Claude took a
seat in the front row and tried to commit the geography of the
place to memory. It must be said, however, that his eyes were
fixed on the plumpest of the disrobing performers when a sudden
and unexpected flash preserved his face and more of the stripper
for the five million readers of the *Daily Beacon* to enjoy with
their breakfast. Not being a particularly observant barrister,
Claude left the strip joint with no idea of the ill luck that had
befallen him.

Whilst Erskine-Brown was thus exploring the underworld, I
was closeted in the Chambers of that elegant Old Etonian civil
lawyer Robin Peppiatt, Q.C., who, assisted by his Junior, Dick
Garsington, represented the proprietor of the *Beacon*. I was entering the lists in the defence of Morry Machin, and our joint solicitor
was an anxious little man called Cuxham, who seemed ready to
pay almost any amount of someone else's money to be shot of the
whole business. Quite early in our meeting, almost as soon, in fact,
as Peppiatt had poured Earl Grey into thin china cups and
handed round the *petit' beurres*, it became clear that everyone
wanted to do a deal with the other side except my good self and
my client, the Editor.

'We should work as a team,' Peppiatt started. 'Of which, as
leading Counsel, I am, I suppose, the Captain.'

'Are we playing cricket, old chap?' I ventured to ask him.

'If we were it would be an extremely expensive game for the

Beacon.' The Q.C. gave me a tolerant smile. 'The proprietors have contracted to indemnify the Editor against any libel damages.'

'I insisted on that when I took the job,' Morry told us with considerable satisfaction.

'Very sensible of your client, no doubt, Rumpole. Now, you may not be used to this type of case as you're one of the criminal boys . . .'

'Oh, I know' – I admitted the charge – 'I'm just a juvenile delinquent.'

'But it's obvious to me that we mustn't attempt to justify these serious charges against Miss Nettleship's honour.' The Captain of the team gave his orders and I made bold to ask, 'Wouldn't that be cricket?'

'If we try to prove she's a sort of amateur tart the Jury might bump the damages up to two or three hundred grand,' Peppiatt explained as patiently as he could.

'Or four.' Dick Garsington shook his head sadly. 'Or perhaps half a million.' Mr Cuxham's mind boggled.

'But you've filed a defence alleging that the article's a true bill.' I failed to follow the drift of these faint-hearts.

'That's our bargaining counter.' Peppiatt spoke to me very slowly, as though to a child of limited intelligence.

'Our what?'

'Something to give away. As part of the deal.'

'When we agree terms with the other side we'll abandon all our allegations. Gracefully,' Garsington added.

'We put up our hands?' I contemptuously tipped ash from my small cigar on to Peppiatt's Axminster. Dick Garsington was sent off to get 'an ashtray for Rumpole'.

'Peregrine Landseer's agin us.' Peppiatt seemed to be bringing glad tidings of great joy to all of us. 'I'm lunching with Perry at the Sheridan Club to discuss another matter. I'll just whisper the thought of a quiet little settlement into his ear.'

'Whisper sweet nothings!' I told him. 'I'll not be party to any settlement. I'm determined to defend the good name of my client Mr Maurice Machin as a responsible editor.'

'At our expense?' Peppiatt looked displeased.

'If neccessary. Yes! He wouldn't have published that story unless there was some truth in it. Would you?' I asked Morry, assailed by some doubt.

'Certainly not' – my client assured me – 'as a fair and responsible journalist.'

'The trouble is that there's no evidence that Miss Nettleship has done any of these things.' Clearly Mr Cuxham had long since thrown in the towel.

'Then we must find some! Isn't that what solicitors are for?' I asked, but didn't expect an answer. 'I'm quite unable to believe that anyone who writes so badly hasn't got *some* other vices.'

A few days later I entered the clerk's room of our Chambers in Equity Court to see our clerk, Henry, seated at his desk looking at the centre pages of the *Daily Beacon*, which Dianne, our fearless but somewhat hit-and-miss typist, was showing him. As I approached, Dianne folded the paper, retreated to her desk and began to type furiously. They both straightened their faces and the smiles of astonishment I had noticed when I came in were replaced by looks of legal seriousness. In fact Henry spoke with almost religious awe when he handed me my brief in *Nettleship* v. *The Daily Beacon and anor*. Not only was a highly satisfactory fee marked on the front but refreshers, that is the sum required to keep a barrister on his feet and talking, had been agreed at no less than five hundred pounds a day.

'You *can* make the case last, can't you, Mr Rumpole?' Henry asked with understandable concern.

'Make it last?' I reassured him. 'I can make it stretch on till the trump of doom! We have serious and lengthy allegations, Henry. Allegations that will take days and days, with any luck. For the first time in a long career at the Bar I begin to see . . .'

'See what, Mr Rumpole?'

'A way of providing for my old age.'

The door then opened to admit Claude Erskine-Brown. Dianne and Henry regarded him with solemn pity, as though he'd had a death in his family.

'Here comes the poor old criminal lawyer,' I greeted him. 'Any more problems with your affray, Claude?'

'All under control, Rumpole. Thank you very much. Morning, Dianne. Morning, Henry.' Our clerk and secretary returned his greeting in mournful voices. At that point, Erskine-Brown noticed Dianne's copy of the *Beacon*, wondered who the 'Beauty' of that day might be, and picked it up before she could stop him.

'What've you got there? The *Beacon*! A fine crusading paper. Tells the truth without fear or favour.' My refreshers had put me in a remarkably good mood. 'Are you feeling quite well, Claude?'

Erskine-Brown was holding the paper in trembling hands and had gone extremely pale. He looked at me with accusing eyes and managed to say in strangled tones, '*You* told me to go there!'

'For God's sake, Claude! Told you to go where?'

'The *locus in quo*!'

I took the *Beacon* from him and saw the cause of his immediate concern. The *locus in quo* was the Kitten-A-Go-Go, and the blown-up snap on the centre page showed Claude closely inspecting a young lady who was waving her underclothes triumphantly over her head. At that moment, Henry's telephone rang and he announced that Soapy Sam Ballard, our puritanical Head of Chambers, founder member of the Lawyers As Christians Society (L.A.C.) and the Savonarola of Equity Court, wished to see Mr Erskine-Brown in his room without delay. Claude left us with the air of a man climbing up into the dock to receive a stiff but inevitable sentence.

I wasn't, of course, present in the Head of Chambers' room where Claude was hauled up. It was not until months later, when he had recovered a certain calm, that he was able to tell me how the embarrassing meeting went and I reconstruct the occasion for the purpose of this narrative.

'You wanted to see me, Ballard?' Claude started to babble. 'You're looking well. In wonderful form. I don't remember when I've seen you looking so fit.' At that early stage he tried to make his escape from the room. 'Well, nice to chat. I've got a summons, across the road.'

'Just a minute!' Ballard called him back. 'I don't read the *Daily Beacon*.'

'Oh, don't you? Very wise,' Claude congratulated him. 'Neither do I. Terrible rag. Half-clad beauties on page four and no law reports. So they tell me. Absolutely no reason to bother with the thing!'

'But, coming out of the Temple tube station, Mr Justice Fishwick pushed this in my face.' Soapy Sam lifted the fatal newspaper from his desk. 'It seems he's just remarried and his new wife takes in the *Daily Beacon*.'

'How odd!'

'What's odd?'

'A judge's wife. Reading the *Beacon*.'

'Hugh Fishwick married his cook,' Ballard told him in solemn tones.

'Really? I didn't know. Well, that explains it. But I don't see why he should push it in your face, Ballard.'

'Because he thought I ought to see it.'

'Nothing in that rag that could be of the slightest interest to you, surely?'

'Something is.'

'What?'

'You.'

Ballard held out the paper to Erskine-Brown, who approached it gingerly and took a quick look.

'Oh, really? Good heavens! Is that me?'

'Unless you have a twin brother masquerading as yourself. You feature in an article on London's Square Mile of Sin.'

'It's all a complete misunderstanding!' Claude assured our leader.

'I'm glad to hear it.'

'I can explain everything.'

'I hope so.'

'You see, I got into this affray.'

'You got into what?' Ballard saw even more cause for concern.

'This fight' – Claude wasn't improving his case – 'in the Kitten-A-Go-Go.'

'Perhaps I ought to warn you, Erskine-Brown.' Ballard was being judicial. 'You needn't answer incriminating questions.'

'No, *I* didn't get into a fight.' Claude was clearly rattled. 'Good heavens, no. I'm doing a case, about a fight. An affray. With Coca-Cola bottles. And Rumpole advised me to go to this club.'

'Horace Rumpole is an habitué of this house of ill-repute? At *his* age?' Ballard didn't seem to be in the least surprised to hear it.

'No, not at all. But he said I ought to take a view. Of the scene of the crime. This wretched scandal-sheet puts the whole matter in the wrong light. Entirely.'

There was a long and not entirely friendly pause before Ballard proceeded to judgment. 'If that is so, Erskine-Brown,' he said, 'and I make no further comment while the matter is *sub judice*, you will no doubt be suing the *Daily Beacon* for libel?'

'You think I should?' Claude began to count the cost of such an action.

'It is quite clearly your duty. To protect your own reputation and the reputation of this Chambers.'

'Wouldn't it be rather expensive?' I can imagine Claude gulping, but Ballard was merciless.

'What is money' he said, 'compared to the hitherto unsullied name of number three, Equity Court?'

Claude's next move was to seek out the friend of his boyhood, 'Slimey' Spratling, whom he finally found jogging across Hyde Park. When he told the *Beacon* deputy editor that he had been advised to issue a writ, the man didn't even stop and Erskine-Brown had to trot along beside him. 'Good news!' Spratling said. 'My editor seems to enjoy libel actions. Glad you liked your pic.'

'Of course I didn't like it. It'll ruin my career.'

'Nonsense, Collywobbles.' Spratling was cheerful. 'You'll get briefed by all the clubs. You'll be the strippers' Q.C.'

'However did they get my name?' Claude wondered.

'Oh, I recognized you at once,' Slimey assured him. 'Bit of luck, wasn't it?' Then he ran on, leaving Claude outraged. They had, after all, been to Winchester together.

When I told the helpless Cuxham that the purpose of solicitors was to gather evidence, I did so without much hope of my words stinging him into any form of activity. If evidence against Miss Nettleship were needed, I would have to look elsewhere, so I rang up that great source of knowledge 'Fig' Newton and invited him for a drink at Pommeroy's.

Ferdinand Isaac Gerald, known to his many admirers as 'Fig'

Newton, is undoubtedly the best in the somewhat unreliable band of professional private eyes. I know that Fig is now knocking seventy; that, with his filthy old mackintosh and collapsing hat, he looks like a scarecrow after a bad night; that his lantern jaw, watery eye and the frequently appearing drip on the end of the nose don't make him an immediately attractive figure. Fig may look like a scarecrow but he's a very bloodhound after a clue.

'I'm doing civil work now, Fig,' I told him when we met in Pommeroy's. 'Just got a big brief in a libel action which should provide a bit of comfort for my old age. But my instructing solicitor is someone we would describe, in legal terms, as a bit of a wally. I'd be obliged if you'd do his job for him and send him the bill when we win.'

'What is it that I am required to do, Mr Rumpole?' the great detective asked patiently.

'Keep your eye on a lady.'

'I usually am, Mr Rumpole. Keeping my eye on one lady or another.'

'This one's a novelist. A certain Miss Amelia Nettleship. Do you know her works?'

'Can't say I do, sir.' Fig had once confessed to a secret passion for Jane Austen. 'Are you on to a winner?'

'With a bit of help from you, Fig. Only one drawback here, as in most cases.'

'What's that, sir?'

'The client.' Looking across the bar I had seen the little group from the *Beacon* round the Bollinger. Having business with the Editor, I left Fig Newton to his work and crossed the room. Sitting myself beside my client I refused champagne and told him that I wanted him to do something about my learned friend Claude Erskine-Brown.

'You mean the barrister who goes to funny places in the afternoon? What're you asking me to do, Mr Rumpole?'

'Apologize, of course. Print the facts. Claude Erskine-Brown was in the Kitten-A-Go-Go purely in pursuit of his legal business.'

'I love it!' Morry's smile was wider than ever. 'There speaks the great defender. You'd put up any story, wouldn't you, however improbable, to get your client off.'

'It happens to be true.'

'So far as we are concerned' – Morry smiled at me patiently – 'we printed a pic of a gentleman in a pin-striped suit examining the goods on display. No reason to apologize for that, is there, Connie? What's your view, Ted?'

'No reason at all, Morry.' Connie supported him and Spratling agreed.

'So you're going to do nothing about it?' I asked with some anger.

'Nothing we *can* do.'

'Mr Machin.' I examined the man with distaste. 'I told you it was a legal rule that a British barrister is duty-bound to take on any client however repellent.'

'I remember you saying something of the sort.'

'You are stretching my duty to the furthest limits of human endurance.'

'Never mind, Mr Rumpole. I'm sure you'll uphold the best traditions of the Bar!'

When Morry said that I left him. However, as I was wandering away from Pommeroy's towards the Temple station, Gloucester Road, home and beauty, a somewhat breathless Ted Spratling caught up with me and asked me to do my best for Morry. 'He's going through a tough time.' I didn't think the man was entirely displeased by the news he had to impart. 'The Proprietor's going to sack him.'

'Because of this case?'

'Because the circulation's dropping. Tits and bums are going out of fashion. The wives don't like it.'

'Who'll be the next editor?'

'Well, I'm the deputy now ...' He did his best to sound modest.

'I see. Look' – I decided to enlist an ally – 'would you help me with the case? In strict confidence, I want some sort of a lead to this Stella January. Can you find how her article came in? Get hold of the original. It might have an address. Some sort of clue ...'

'I'll have a try, Mr Rumpole. Anything I can do to help old

Morry.' Never had I heard a man speak with such deep in-sincerity.

The weather turned nasty, but, in spite of heavy rain, Fig Newton kept close observation for several nights on Hollyhock Cottage, home of Amelia Nettleship, without any particular result. One morning I entered our Chambers early and on my way to my room I heard a curious buzzing sound, as though an angry bee were trapped in the lavatory. Pulling open the door, I detected Erskine-Brown plying a cordless electric razor.

'Claude,' I said, 'you're shaving!'

'Wonderful to see the workings of a keen legal mind.' The man sounded somewhat bitter.

'I'm sorry about all this. But I'm doing my best to help you.'

'Oh, please!' He held up a defensive hand. 'Don't try and do anything else to help me. "Visit the scene of the crime," you said. "Inspect the *locus in quo*!" So where has your kind assist-ance landed me? My name's mud. Ballard's as good as threatened to kick me out of Chambers. I've got to spend my life's savings on a speculative libel action. And my marriage is on the rocks. Wonderful what you can do, Rumpole, with a few words of advice. Your clients must be everlastingly grateful.'

'Your marriage, on the rocks, did you say?'

'Oh, yes. Philly was frightfully reasonable about it. As far as she was concerned, she said, she didn't care what I did in the afternoons. But we'd better live apart for a while, for the sake of the children. She didn't want Tristan and Isolde to associate with a father dedicated to the exploitation of women.'

'Oh, Portia!' I felt for the fellow. 'What's happened to the quality of mercy?'

'So, thank you very much, Rumpole. I'm enormously grateful. The next time you've got a few helpful tips to hand out, for God's sake keep them to yourself!'

He switched on the razor again. I looked at it and made an instant deduction. 'You've been sleeping in Chambers. You want to watch that, Claude. Bollard nearly got rid of me for a similar offence.'*

* See 'Rumpole and the Old, Old Story' in *Rumpole's Last Case*, Penguin Books, 1987.

'Where do you expect me to go? Phillida's having the locks changed in Islington.'

'Have you no friends?'

'Philly and I have reached the end of the line. I don't exactly want to advertise the fact among my immediate circle. I seem to remember, Rumpole, when you fell out with Hilda you planted yourself on us!' As he said this I scented danger and tried to avoid what I knew was coming.

'Oh. Now. Erskine-Brown. Claude. I was enormously grateful for your hospitality on that occasion.'

'Quite an easy run in on the Underground, is it, from Gloucester Road?' He spoke in a meaningful way.

'Of course. My door is always open. I'd be delighted to put you up, just until this mess is straightened out. But . . .'

'The least you could do, I should have thought, Rumpole.'

'It's not a sacrifice I could ask, old darling, even of my dearest friend. I couldn't ask you to shoulder the burden of daily life with She Who Must Be Obeyed. Now I'm sure you can find a very comfortable little hotel, somewhere cheap and cosy, around the British Museum. I promise you, life is by no means a picnic, in the Gloucester Road.'

Well, that was enough, I thought, to dissuade the most deter-mined visitor from seeking hospitality under the Rumpole roof. I went about my daily business and, when my work was done, I thought I should share some of the good fortune brought with my brief in the libel action with She Who Must Be Obeyed. I lashed out on two bottles of Pommeroy's bubbly, some of the least exhausted flowers to be found outside the tube station and even, such was my reckless mood, lavender water for Hilda.

'All the fruits of the earth,' I told her. 'Or, let's say, the fruits of the first cheque in *Nettleship* v. *The Beacon*, paid in advance. The first of many, if we can spin out the proceedings.'

'You're doing that awful case!' She didn't sound ap-proving.

'That awful case will bring us in five hundred smackers a day in refreshers.'

'Helping that squalid newspaper insult Amelia Nettleship.' She looked at me with contempt.

'A barrister's duty, Hilda, is to take on all comers. However squalid.'

'Nonsense!'

'What?'

'Nonsense. You're only using that as an excuse.'

'Am I?'

'Of course you are. You're doing it because you're jealous of Amelia Nettleship!'

'Oh, I don't think so,' I protested mildly. 'My life has been full of longings, but I've never had the slightest desire to become a lady novelist.'

'You're jealous of her because she's got high principles.' Hilda was sure of it. 'You haven't got high principles, have you, Rumpole?'

'I told you. I will accept any client, however repulsive.'

'That's not a principle, that's just a way of making money from the most terrible people. Like the editor of the *Daily Beacon*. My mind is quite made up, Rumpole. I shall not use a single drop of that corrupt lavender water.'

It was then that I heard a sound from the hallway which made my heart sink. An all-too-familiar voice was singing *'La donna e mobile'* in a light tenor. Then the door opened to admit Erskine-Brown wearing my dressing-gown and very little else. 'Claude telephoned and told me all his troubles.' Hilda looked at the man with sickening sympathy. 'Of course I invited him to stay.'

'You're wearing my dressing-gown!' I put the charge to him at once.

'I had to pack in a hurry.' He looked calmly at the sideboard. 'Thoughtful of you to get in champagne to welcome me, Rumpole.'

'Was the bath all right, Claude?' Hilda sounded deeply concerned.

'Absolutely delightful, thank you, Hilda.'

'What a relief! That geyser can be quite temperamental.'

'Which is you chair, Horace?' Claude had the courtesy to ask.

'I usually sit by the gas fire. Why?'

'Oh, do sit there, Claude,' Hilda urged him and he gracefully agreed to pinch my seat. 'We mustn't let you get cold, must we. After your bath.'

So they sat together by the gas fire and I was allowed to open champagne for both of them. As I listened to the rain outside the window my spirits, I had to admit, had sunk to the lowest of ebbs. And around five o'clock the following morning, Fig Newton, the rain falling from the brim of his hat and the drop falling off his nose, stood watching Hollyhock Cottage. He saw someone – he was too far away to make an identification – come out of the front door and get into a parked car. Then he saw the figure of a woman in a nightdress, no doubt Amelia Nettleship, standing in the lit doorway waving goodbye. The headlights of the car were switched on and it drove away.

When the visitor had gone, and the front door was shut, Fig moved nearer to the cottage. He looked down at the muddy track on which the car had been parked and saw something white. He stooped to pick it up, folded it carefully and put it in his pocket.

On the day that *Nettleship* v. *The Beacon* began its sensational course, I breakfasted with Claude in the kitchen of our so-called 'mansion' flat in the Gloucester Road. I say breakfasted, but Hilda told me that bacon and eggs were off as our self-invited guest preferred a substance, apparently made up of sawdust and bird droppings, which he called muesli. I was a little exhausted, having been kept awake by the amplified sound of grand opera from the spare bedroom, but Claude explained that he always found that a little Wagner settled him down for the night. He then asked for some of the goat's milk that Hilda had got in for him specially. As I coated a bit of toast with Oxford marmalade, the man only had to ask for organic honey to have it instantly supplied by She Who Seemed Anxious to Oblige.

'And what the hell,' I took the liberty of asking, 'is organic honey?'

'The bees only sip from flowers grown without chemical fertilizers,' Claude explained patiently.

'How does the bee know?'

'What?'

'I suppose the other bees tell it. "Don't sip from that, old chap. It's been grown with chemical fertilizers."'

So, ill-fed and feeling like a cuckoo in my own nest, I set off to the Royal Courts of Justice, in the Strand, that imposing turreted château which is the Ritz Hotel of the legal profession, the place where a gentleman is remunerated to the tune of five hundred smackers a day. It is also the place where gentlemen prefer an amicable settlement to the brutal business of fighting their cases.

I finally pitched up, wigged and robed, in front of the Court which would provide the battle-ground for our libel action. I saw the combatants, Morry Machin and the fair Nettleship, standing a considerable distance apart. Peregrine Landseer, Q.C., Counsel for the Plaintiff, and Robin Peppiatt, Q.C., for the Proprietor of the *Beacon*, were meeting on the central ground for a peace conference, attended by assorted juniors and instructing solicitors.

'After all the publicity, my lady couldn't take less than fifty thousand.' Landseer, Chairman of the Bar Council and on the brink of becoming a judge, was nevertheless driving as hard a bargain as any second-hand car dealer.

'Forty and a full and grovelling apology.' And Peppiatt added the bonus. 'We could wrap it up and lunch together at the Sheridan.'

'It's steak and kidney pud day at the Sheridan,' Dick Garsington remembered wistfully.

'Forty-five.' Landseer was not so easily tempted. 'And that's my last word on the subject.'

'Oh, all right,' Peppiatt conceded. 'Forty-five and a full apology. You happy with that, Mr Cuxham?'

'Well, sir. If you advise it.' Cuxham clearly had no stomach for the fight.

'We'll chat to the Editor. I'm sure we're all going to agree' – Peppiatt gave me a meaningful look – 'in the end.'

While Landseer went off to sell the deal to his client, Peppiatt approached my man with 'You only have to join in the apology, Mr Machin, and the *Beacon* will pay the costs and the forty-five grand.'

'"Who steals my purse steals trash,"' I quoted thoughtfully. ' "But he that filches from me my good name . . ." You're asking my client to sign a statement admitting he printed lies.'

'Oh, for heaven's sake, Rumpole!' Peppiatt was impatient.

'They gave up quoting that in libel actions fifty years ago.'

'Mr Rumpole's right.' Morry nodded wisely. 'My good name – I looked up the quotation – it's the immediate jewel of my soul.'

'Steady on, old darling,' I murmured. 'Let's not go *too* far.' At which moment Peregrine Landseer returned from a somewhat heated discussion with his client to say that there was no shifting her and she was determined to fight for every penny she could get.

'But Perry . . .' Robin Peppiatt lamented, 'the case is going to take two weeks!' At five hundred smackers a day I could only thank God for the stubbornness of Amelia Nettleship.

So we went into Court to fight the case before a jury and Mr Justice Teasdale, a small, highly opinionated and bumptious little person who is unmarried, lives in Surbiton with a Persian cat, and was once an unsuccessful Tory candidate for Weston-super-Mare North. It takes a good deal of talent for a Tory to lose Weston-super-Mare North. Worst of all, he turned out to be a devoted fan of the works of Miss Amelia Nettleship.

'Members of the Jury,' Landseer said in opening the Plaintiff's case, 'Miss Nettleship is the authoress of a number of historical works.'

'Rattling good yarns, Members of the Jury,' Mr Justice Teasdale chirped up.

'I beg your Lordship's pardon.' Landseer looked startled.

'I said 'rattling good yarns', Mr Peregrine Landseer. The sort your wife might pick up without the slightest embarrassment. Unlike so much of the distasteful material one finds between hard covers today.'

'My Lord.' I rose to protest with what courtesy I could muster.

'Yes, Mr Rumbold?'

'Rum*pole*, my Lord.'

'I'm so sorry.' The Judge didn't look in the least apologetic. 'I understand you are something of a stranger to these Courts.'

'Would it not be better to allow the Jury to come to their own conclusions about Miss Amelia Nettleship?' I suggested, ignoring the Teasdale manners.

'Well. Yes. Of course. I quite agree.' The Judge looked serious and then cheered up. 'And when they do they'll find she can put together a rattling good yarn.'

There was a sycophantic murmur of laughter from the Jury, and all I could do was subside and look balefully at the Judge. I felt a pang of nostalgia for the Old Bailey and the wild stampede of the mad Judge Bullingham.

As Peregrine Landseer bored on, telling the Jury what terrible harm the *Beacon* had done to his client's hitherto unblemished reputation, Ted Spratling, the deputy editor, leant forward in the seat behind me and whispered in my ear. 'About that Stella January article,' he said. 'I bought a drink for the systems manager. The copy's still in the system. One rather odd thing.'

'Tell me . . .'

'The logon – that's the identification of the word processor. It came from the Editor's office.'

'You mean it was written there?'

'No one writes things any more.'

'Of course not. How stupid of me.'

'It looks as if it had been put in from his word processor.'

'That is extremely interesting.'

'If Mr Rum*pole* has quite finished his conversation!' Peregrine Landseer was rebuking me for chattering during his opening speech.

I rose to apologize as humbly as I could. 'My Lord, I can assure my learned friend I was listening to every word of his speech. It's such a rattling good yarn.'

So the morning wore on, being mainly occupied by Landseer's opening. The luncheon adjournment saw me pacing the marble corridors of the Royal Courts of Justice with that great source of information, Fig Newton. He gave me a lengthy account of his observation on Hollyhock Cottage, and when he finally got to the departure of Miss Nettleship's nocturnal visitor, I asked impatiently, 'You got the car number?'

'Alas. No. Visibility was poor and weather conditions appalling.' The sleuth's evidence was here interrupted by a fit of sneezing.

'Oh, Fig!' I was, I confess, disappointed. 'And you didn't see the driver?'

'Alas. No, again.' Fig sneezed apologetically. 'However, when Miss Nettleship had closed the door and extinguished the lights, presumably in order to return to bed, I proceeded to the track in front of the house where the vehicle had been standing. There I retrieved an article which I thought might just possibly have been dropped by the driver in getting in or out of the vehicle.'

'For God's sake, show me!'

The detective gave me his treasure trove, which I stuffed into a pocket just as the Usher came out of Court to tell me that the Judge was back from lunch, Miss Nettleship was entering the witness-box, and the world of libel awaited my attention.

If ever I saw a composed and confident witness, that witness was Amelia Nettleship. Her hair was perfectly done, her black suit was perfectly discreet, her white blouse shone, as did her spectacles. Her features, delicately cut as an intaglio, were attractive, but her beauty was by no means louche or abundant. So spotless did she seem that she might well have preserved her virginity until what must have been, in spite of appearances to the contrary, middle age. When she had finished her evidence-in-chief the Judge thanked her and urged her to go on writing her 'rattling good yarns'. Peppiatt then rose to his feet to ask her a few questions designed to show that her books were still selling in spite of the *Beacon* article. This she denied, saying that sales had dropped off. The thankless task of attacking the fair name of Amelia was left to Rumpole.

'Miss Nettleship,' I started off with my guns blazing, 'are you a truthful woman?'

'I try to be.' She smiled at his Lordship, who nodded encouragement.

'And you call yourself an historical novelist?'

'I try to write books which uphold certain standards of morality.'

'Forget the morality for a moment. Let's concentrate on the history.'

'Very well.'

One of the hardest tasks in preparing for my first libel action was reading through the works of Amelia Nettleship. Now I had to quote from Hilda's favourite. 'May I read you a short passage from an alleged historical novel of yours entitled *Lord Stingo's Fancy*?' I asked as I picked up the book.

'Ah, yes.' The Judge looked as though he were about to enjoy a treat. 'Isn't that the one which ends happily?'

'Happily, all Miss Nettleship's books end, my Lord,' I told him. 'Eventually.' There was a little laughter in Court, and I heard Landseer whisper to his Junior, 'This criminal chap's going to bump up the damages enormously.'

Meanwhile I started quoting from *Lord Stingo's Fancy*. ' "Sophia had first set eyes on Lord Stingo when she was a dewy eighteen-year-old and he had clattered up to her father's castle, exhausted from the Battle of Nazeby," ' I read. ' "Now at the ball to triumphantly celebrate the gorgeous, enthroning coronation of the Merry Monarch King Charles II they were to meet again. Sophia was now in her twenties but, in ways too numerous to completely describe, still an unspoilt girl at heart." You call that a *historical* novel?'

'Certainly,' the witness answered unashamed.

'Haven't you forgotten something?' I put it to her.

'I don't think so. What?'

'Oliver Cromwell.'

'I really don't know what you mean.'

'Clearly, if this Sophia . . . this girl . . . How do you describe her?'

' "Dewy", Mr Rumpole.' The Judge repeated the word with relish.

'Ah, yes. "Dewy". I'm grateful to your Lordship. I had forgotten the full horror of the passage. If this dew-bespattered Sophia had been eighteen at the time of the Battle of Naseby in the reign of Charles I, she would have been thirty-three in the year of Charles II's coronation. Oliver Cromwell came in between.'

'I am an artist, Mr Rumpole.' Miss Nettleship smiled at my pettifogging objections.

'What kind of an artist?' I ventured to ask.

'I think Miss Nettleship means an artist in words,' was how the Judge explained it.

'Are you, Miss Nettleship?' I asked. 'Then you must have

noticed that the short passage I have read to the Jury contains
two split infinitives and a tautology.'

'A what, Mr Rumpole?' The Judge looked displeased.

'Using two words that mean the same thing, as in "the enthroning coronation". My Lord, t – a – u . . .' I tried to be helpful.

'I can *spell*, Mr Rumpole.' Teasdale was now testy.

'Then your Lordship has the advantage of the witness. I notice
she spells Naseby with a "z".'

'My Lord. I hesitate to interrupt.' At least I was doing well
enough to bring Landseer languidly to his feet. 'Perhaps this
sort of cross-examination is common enough in the criminal
courts, but I cannot see how it can possibly be relevant in an
action for libel.'

'Neither can I, Mr Landseer, I must confess.' Of course the
Judge agreed.

I did my best to put him right. 'These questions, my Lord, go
to the heart of this lady's credibility.' I turned to give the witness
my full attention. 'I have to suggest, Miss Nettleship, that as an
historical novelist you are a complete fake.'

'My Lord. I have made my point.' Landseer sat down then,
looking well pleased, and immediately whispered to his Junior,
'We'll let him go on with that line and they'll give us four hundred thousand.'

'You have no respect for history and very little for the English
language.' I continued to chip away at the spotless novelist.

'I try to tell a story, Mr Rumpole.'

'And your evidence to this Court has been, to use my Lord's
vivid expression, "a rattling good yarn"?' Teasdale looked displeased at my question.

'I have sworn to tell the truth.'

'Remember that. Now let us see how much of this article is
correct.' I picked up Stella January's offending contribution.
'You do live at Hollyhock Cottage, near Godalming, in the
county of Surrey?'

'That is so.'

'You have a jacuzzi?'

'She has *what*, Mr Rumpole?' I had entered a world unknown to
a judge addicted to cold showers.

'A sort of bath, my Lord, with a whirlpool attached.'

'I installed one in my converted barn,' Miss Nettleship admitted. 'I find it relaxes me, after a long day's work.'

'You don't twiddle round in there with a close personal friend occasionally?'

'That's worth another ten thousand to us,' Landseer told his Junior, growing happier by the minute. In fact the Jury members were looking at me with some disapproval.

'Certainly not. I do not believe in sex before marriage.'

'And have no experience of it?'

'I was engaged once, Mr Rumpole.'

'Just once?'

'Oh, yes. My fiancé was killed in an air crash ten years ago. I think about him every day, and every day I'm thankful we didn't –' she looked down modestly – 'do anything before we were married. We were tempted, I'm afraid, the night before he died. But we resisted the temptation.'

'Some people would say that's a very moving story,' Judge Teasdale told the Jury after a reverent hush.

'Others might say it's the story of *Sally on the Somme*, only there the fiancé was killed in the war.' I picked up another example of the Nettleship *œuvre*.

'That, Mr Rumpole,' Amelia looked pained, 'is a book that's particularly close to my heart. At least I don't do anything my heroines wouldn't do.'

'He's getting worse all the time,' Robin Peppiatt, the *Beacon* barrister, whispered despairingly to his Junior, Dick Garsington, who came back with 'The damages are going to hit the roof!'

'Miss Nettleship, may I come to the last matter raised in the article?'

'I'm sure the Jury will be grateful that you're reaching the end, Mr Rumpole,' the Judge couldn't resist saying, so I smiled charmingly and told him that I should finish a great deal sooner if I were allowed to proceed without further interruption. Then I began to read Stella January's words aloud to the witness. ' "Her latest Casanova, so far unnamed, is said to be a married man who's been seen leaving in the wee small hours." '

'I read that,' Miss Nettleship remembered.

'You had company last night, didn't you? Until what I suppose might be revoltingly referred to as "the wee small hours"?'

'What are you suggesting?'

'That someone was with you. And when he left at about five thirty in the morning you stood in your nightdress waving good-bye and blowing kisses. Who was it, Miss Nettleship?'

'That is an absolutely uncalled-for suggestion.'

'You called for it when you issued a writ for libel.'

'Do I have to answer?' She turned to the Judge for help. He gave her his most encouraging smile and said that it might save time in the end if she were to answer Mr Rumpole's question.

'That is absolutely untrue!' For the first time Amelia's look of serenity vanished and I got, from the witness-box, a cold stare of hatred. 'Absolutely untrue.' The Judge made a grateful note of her answer. 'Thank you, Miss Nettleship. I think we might continue with this tomorrow morning, if you have any further questions, Mr Rumpole?'

'I have indeed, my Lord.' Of course I had more questions and by the morning I hoped also to have some evidence to back them up.

I was in no hurry to return to the alleged 'mansion' flat that night. I rightly suspected that our self-invited guest, Claude Erskine-Brown, would be playing his way through *Die Meistersinger* and giving Hilda a synopsis of the plot as it unfolded. As I reach the last of a man's Seven Ages I am more than ever persuaded that life is too short for Wagner, a man who was never in a hurry when it came to composing an opera. I paid a solitary visit to Pommeroy's well-known watering-hole after Court in the hope of finding the representatives of the *Beacon*; but the only one I found was Connie Coughlin, the features editor, moodily surveying a large gin and tonic. 'No champagne tonight?' I asked as I wandered over to her table, glass in hand.

'I don't think we've got much to celebrate.'

'I wanted to ask you' – I took a seat beside the redoubtable Connie – 'about Miss Stella January. Our girl on the spot. Bright, attractive kind of reporter, was she?'

'I don't know,' Connie confessed.

'But surely you're the features editor?'

'I never met her.' She said it with the resentment of a woman whose editor had been interfering with her page.

'Any idea how old she was, for instance?'

'Oh, young, I should think.' It was the voice of middle age speaking. 'Morry said she was young. Just starting in the business.'

'And I was going to ask you . . .'

'You're very inquisitive.'

'It's my trade.' I downed what was left of my claret. '. . . About the love life of Mr Morry Machin.'

'Good God. Whose side are you on, Mr Rumpole?'

'At the moment, on the side of the truth. Did Morry have some sort of a romantic interest in Miss Stella January?'

'Short-lived, I'd say.' Connie clearly had no pity for the girl if she'd been enjoyed and then sacked.

'He's married?'

'Oh, two or three times.' It occurred to me that at some time, during one or other of these marriages, Morry and La Coughlin might have been more than fellow hacks on the *Beacon*. 'Now he seems to have got some sort of steady girl-friend.' She said it with some resentment.

'You know her?'

'Not at all. He keeps her under wraps.'

I looked at her for a moment. A woman, I thought, with a lonely evening in an empty flat before her. Then I thanked her for her help and stood up.

'Who are you going to grill next?' she asked me over the rim of her gin and tonic.

'As a matter of fact,' I told her, 'I've got a date with Miss Stella January.'

Quarter of an hour later I was walking across the huge floor, filled with desks, telephones and word processors, where the *Beacon* was produced, towards the glass-walled office in the corner, where Morry sat with his deputy Ted Spratling, seeing that all the scandal that was fit to print, and a good deal of it that wasn't, got safely between the covers of the *Beacon*. I arrived at his office, pulled open the door and was greeted by Morry, in his shirtsleeves, his feet up on the desk. 'Working late, Mr Rumpole? I hope you can do better for us tomorrow,' he greeted me with amused disapproval.

'I hope so too. I'm looking for Miss Stella January.'

'I told you, she's not here any more. I think she went overseas.'

'I think she's here,' I assured him. He was silent for a moment and then he looked at his deputy. 'Ted, perhaps you'd better leave me to have a word with my learned Counsel.'

'I'll be on the back bench.' Spratling left for the desk on the floor which the editors occupied.

When he had gone, Morry looked up at me and said quietly, 'Now then, Mr Rumpole, sir. How can I help you?'

'Stella certainly wasn't a young woman, was she?' I was sure about that.

'She was only with us a short time. But she was young, yes,' he said vaguely.

'A quotation from her article that Amelia Nettleship "makes Mae West sound like Florence Nightingale". No young woman today's going to have heard of Mae West. Mae West's as remote in history as Messalina and Helen of Troy. That article, I would hazard a guess, was written by a man well into his middle age.'

'Who?'

'You.'

There was another long silence and the Editor did his best to smile. 'Have you been drinking at all this evening?'

I took a seat then on the edge of his desk and lit a small cigar. 'Of course I've been drinking *at all*. You don't imagine I have these brilliant flashes of deduction when I'm perfectly sober, do you?'

'Then hadn't you better go home to bed?'

'So you wrote the article. No argument about that. It's been found in the system with your word processor number on it. Careless, Mr Machin. You clearly have very little talent for crime. The puzzling thing is, why you should attack Miss Nettleship when she's such a good friend of yours.'

'Good friend?' He did his best to laugh. 'I told you. I've never even met the woman.'

'It was a lie, like the rest of this pantomime lawsuit. Last night

you were with her until past five in the morning. And she said
goodbye to you with every sign of affection.'

'What makes you say that?'

'Were you in a hurry? Anyway, this was dropped by the side of
your car.' Then I pulled out the present Fig Newton had given
me outside Court that day and put it on the desk.

'Anyone can buy the *Beacon*.' Morry glanced at the mud-
stained exhibit.

'Not everyone gets the first edition, the one that fell on the
Editor's desk at ten o'clock that evening. I would say that's a bit
of a rarity around Godalming.'

'Is that all?'

'No. You were watched.'

'Who by?'

'Someone I asked to find out the truth about Miss Nettleship.
Now he's turned up the truth about both of you.'

Morry got up then and walked to the door which Ted Spratling
had left half open. He shut it carefully and then turned to me. 'I
went down to ask her to drop the case.'

'To use a legal expression, pull the other one, it's got bells on it.'

'I don't know what you're suggesting.'

And then, as he stood looking at me, I moved round and sat in
the Editor's chair. 'Let me enlighten you.' I was as patient as I
could manage. 'I'm suggesting a conspiracy to pervert the course
of justice.'

'What's that mean?'

'I told you I'm an old taxi, waiting on the rank, but I'm not
prepared to be the get-away driver for a criminal conspiracy.'

'You haven't said anything? To anyone?' He looked older and
very frightened.

'Not yet.'

'And you won't.' He tried to sound confident. 'You're my
lawyer.'

'Not any longer, Mr Machin. I don't belong to you any more.
I'm an ordinary citizen, about to report an attempted crime.' It
was then I reached for the telephone. 'I don't think there's any
limit on the sentence for conspiracy.'

'What do you mean, "conspiracy"?'

'You're getting sacked by the *Beacon*; perhaps your handshake is a bit less than golden. Sales are down on historical virgins. So your steady girl-friend and you get together to make half a tax-free million.'

'I wish I knew how.' He was doing his best to smile.

'Perfectly simple. You turn yourself into Stella January, the unknown girl reporter, for half an hour and libelled Amelia. She sues the paper and collects. Then you both sail into the sunset and share the proceeds. There's one thing I shan't forgive you for.'

'What's that?'

'The plan called for an Old Bailey hack, a stranger to the civilized world of libel who wouldn't settle, an old war-horse who'd attack La Nettleship and inflame the damages. So you used me, Mr Morry Machin!'

'I thought you'd be accustomed to that.' He stood over me, suddenly looking older. 'Anyway, they told me in Pommeroy's that you never prosecute.'

'No, I don't, do I? But on this occasion, I must say, I'm sorely tempted.' I thought about it and finally pushed away the telephone. 'Since it's a libel action I'll offer you terms of settlement.'

'What sort of terms?'

'The fair Amelia to drop her case. You pay the costs, including the fees of Fig Newton, who's caught a bad cold in the course of these proceedings. Oh, and in the matter of my learned friend Claude Erskine-Brown . . .'

'What's he got to do with it?'

'. . . Print a full and grovelling apology on the front page of the *Beacon*. And get them to pay him a substantial sum by way of damages. And that's my last word on the subject.' I stood up then and moved to the door.

'What's it going to cost me?' was all he could think of saying.

'I have no idea, but I know what it's going to cost me. Two weeks at five hundred a day. A provision for my old age.' I opened the glass door and let in the hum and clatter which were the birth-pangs of the *Daily Beacon*. 'Good-night, Stella,' I said to Mr Morry Machin. And then I left him.

*

So it came about that next morning's *Beacon* printed a grovelling apology to 'the distinguished barrister Mr Claude Erskine-Brown' which accepted that he went to the Kitten-A-Go-Go Club purely in the interests of legal research and announced that my learned friend's hurt feelings would be soothed by the application of substantial, and tax-free, damages. As a consequence of this, Mrs Phillida Erskine-Brown rang Chambers, spoke words of forgiveness and love to her husband, and he arranged, in his new-found wealth, to take her to dinner at Le Gavroche. The cuckoo flew from our nest, Hilda and I were left alone in the Gloucester Road, and we never found out how *Die Meistersinger* ended.

In Court my one and only libel action ended in a sudden outburst of peace and goodwill, much to the frustration of Mr Justice Teasdale, who had clearly been preparing a summing-up which would encourage the Jury to make Miss Nettleship rich beyond the dreams of avarice. All the allegations against her were dropped; she had no doubt been persuaded by her lover to ask for no damages at all and the *Beacon*'s Editor accepted the bill for costs with extremely bad grace. This old legal taxi moved off to ply for hire elsewhere, glad to be shot of Mr Morry Machin. 'Is there a little bit of burglary around, Henry?' I asked our clerk, as I have recorded. 'Couldn't you get me a nice little gentle robbery? Something which shows human nature in a better light than civil law?'

'Good heavens!' Hilda exclaimed as we lay reading in the matrimonial bed in Froxbury Mansions. I noticed that there had been a change in her reading matter and she was already well into *On the Make* by Suzy Hutchins. 'This girl's about to go to Paris with a man old enough to be her father.'

'That must happen quite often.'

'But it seems he *is* her father.'

'Well, at least you've gone off the works of Amelia Nettleship.'

'The way she dropped that libel action. The woman's no better than she should be.'

'Which of us is? Any chance of turning out the light?' I asked She Who Must Be Obeyed, but she was too engrossed in the doings of her delinquent heroine to reply.

Rumpole and the Barrow Boy

In the dog days of life at the Criminal Bar, when my tray in the clerk's room seems to be filled with communications from the Inland Revenue and hardly a brief offers its pink tape to my eager fingers, it's as well to have some more or less constant source of income, some supply of regular customers to fall back on. Such support and comfort has, for many years, been furnished for me by the Timsons, an extended, intricate and perpetually expanding family of South London villains, whose turnover of crime, though never of a sensational or particularly ambitious nature, shows commendable industry. Armed robbery, murder, mayhem or serious fraud are out of the Timsons' league. The most simple breaking and entering, burglary, and the taking and driving away of clapped-out Cortinas are their bread and butter; receiving stolen jewellery their occasional slice of cake. If your telly, your video and your microwave mysteriously leave home while you are away for the weekend, ten to one some Timson has got it and is disposing of it at a knock-down price in the saloon bar of the Needle Arms. Working for the Timsons is not exactly blue chip litigation; it is not much like being retained by I.C.I. or the Chase Manhattan bank. All the same it provides steady and fairly honourable employment and for many years I have been content to act as the Timsons' Attorney-General with Mr Bernard as my solicitor. Many a time, although this is not a fact She Who Must Be Obeyed cares to face up to, we have sat down, in our kitchen in Gloucester Road, to chops and mash bought as a result of the Timsons' endeavours. The pleasant thing about the Timsons was that they were never, to use the favourite expression of contemporary politicians, 'entre-preneurial' and they seemed quite uninterested in 'extending their market share'. They were not, in the smallest degree, 'upwardly mobile'. And then, much to my surprise, a new breed of Timson was born. Out of a docklands comprehensive school, Shepherd's Bush market and the Big Bang on the Stock Exchange, a certain young Nigel Timson came to prominence in the City and was able to introduce me to the world of high finance.

I first heard of Nigel when I was in Brixton prison visiting Fred Timson, the undisputed head of the family, who was awaiting trial as a result of an activity for which he was far too old and not nearly nimble enough – warehouse-breaking by night. Try as I would to discuss the ins and outs of this offence with him, he was only anxious to solicit my help for Nigel.

'Cousin Andy's boy, Mr Rumpole, what went into the City. Works cheek by jowl with lads from Eton and Harrow College.'

'This prodigy is in some sort of trouble?' I asked.

'I'd like to have his trouble. Rides around in a C-reg. Porsche. Girl-friend's the boss's daughter. Luxury flat on the Isle of Dogs. Funny that. Old Andy spent his whole life working his way up from the Isle of Dogs to Shepherd's Bush and now his boy Nigel's gone back to live there. Anyway he wants for nothing; even gets a smashing view of the river from the jacuzzi. And all got on the legit, Mr Rumpole.'

'Then what can I do to help him?' Cousin Andy's boy seemed to need an accountant and not an Old Bailey hack.

'Young Nigel got himself arrested. By the Fraud Squad.'

'So he hasn't entirely let down the honour of the Timsons.'

This was the first I heard of my future client, but later I was able to piece together, in further detail, the history of the rise and fall of Nigel Timson. He was clearly a bright boy at school with a quick head for figures. Released on the world he worked on a cousin's greengrocery barrow, and his instant calculations of the highest price for apples the market would tolerate provided admirable training for his subsequent brilliance in a stockbroker's office. He was an ambitious boy who went to evening classes in computer technology and business studies. When he felt ready he answered an advertisement for a job at the old-established firm of Japhet Jarroway which had just installed roomfuls of new technology to take the temperature of recovering, ailing or simply hypochondriac businesses around the world. Nigel remained, even when he rose rapidly and took out a mortgage on his part of a converted docklands warehouse, the bright and pleasing boy who had always gladdened the hearts of old ladies out to buy half a pound of Granny Smiths. The ex public-school boys he worked with found him ever ready to come to the help of their faltering mathematics, and Rosie Japhet, only daughter of the firm's Chairman, who occupied the next computer on the dealing floor, fell in love with him. Nigel became the first Timson to relieve the punters of their money in a way which was not only legal but considered, in the strange times in which we live, far more worthy of reward than teaching in schools or nursing the sick. It goes without saying that he received salary and commission which sounded like a prince's ransom to an Old Bailey hack.

The facts of Nigel's arrest came out in the numerous statements obtained by the police. It was his birthday. Bottles of champagne were opened on the floor of the dealing room during a brief lull in business. Nigel's computer was festooned with streamers and birthday cards. His girl-friend, Rosie, presented him with a pigskin Filofax and a pair of boxer shorts decorated with dollar signs. His health was drunk by his closest friends – Rosie and three other young stockbrokers, Hugo Shillingford, Katie Kennet and Mark Marcellus. And then a Kissogram girl equipped with fishnet tights, high heels and a bow in her hair appeared to speak the immortal lines, clearly recollected by those who attended the joyous occasion:

> Greetings to you, Nigel,
> Whose happy birthday this is.
> We wish you all you wish yourself,
> That's money dear and kisses.

The Kissogram lady had just implanted her sticky lipstick on Nigel's cheek when two anonymous gentlemen in dark suits and mackintoshes entered to announce that they were members of the Fraud Squad and asked for Nigel Timson. The birthday party took them to be part of the show, hired with the Kissogram to entertain the company, until one of them introduced himself as Detective Sergeant Arbuthnot come to arrest Nigel for certain offences contrary to the Companies Act.

'I think,' Hugo Shillingford said in the ensuing silence, 'that he's seriously serious.'

At the end of the day when I visited Fred Timson in Brixton and had young Nigel commended to my care I was snoozing in front of the gas fire in Froxbury Mansions. Sleep was, in fact, knitting up the ravelled sleeve of care when 'Methought I heard a voice cry, "Sleep no more!"' It was She Who Must Be Obeyed telling me that I didn't need the gas fire in the middle of March and turning it off with a definitive plop. There was, I pointed out to her, as I struggled to regain consciousness, a bit of a chill wind blowing. 'I'm not going to let you waste the gas now that I own it.' She had bought ten pounds' worth of shares in British Gas; it was a time when practically everything was being auctioned off on the Stock Exchange. Her investment, she clearly felt, gave her a proprietorial interest in the entire North Sea production. I managed to light a small cigar with freezing fingers, mainly for the purpose of keeping warm. 'Please don't buy the electricity, Hilda,' I begged her, 'or we'll all be stumbling around in the dark.'

'I'm not likely to be buying anything,' Hilda said darkly. 'I went to the bank today to cash a cheque on our joint account.'

'And I hope you went to the little lady at the third window.' I had considerable experience of the Caring Bank. 'She's the most merciful.'

'I went to the Head Cashier, the one with the small moustache. He went to look things up behind the scenes.'

'I should have warned you about that fellow with the moustache, can't keep his nose out of other people's business.'

'As a result, Mr Truscott, the Manager, asked me in for a little talk. It was not a pleasant experience.'

'Oh, I know. Not much of a conversationalist, that Truscott.'

'We'll cash this one now,' he said, 'but tell Mr Rumpole he's scraping the bottom of the barrel.' Why're you scraping the bottom of the barrel, Rumpole?'

I gave her a brief rundown on my somewhat precarious financial position; it was the old, old story. The Government didn't believe in spending out too much on Legal Aid and anyway the time it took for me to get paid for any case was about equal to the gestation period of the giant turtle. The small amounts of cash that filtered through to our account in the Caring Bank get frittered away on such luxuries as income tax and sliced bread and washing-powder and Brillo pads and . . .

'Why don't you make fifty thousand pounds a case, Rumpole, like Robin Peppiatt?'

She mentioned the most fashionable Q.C., a smooth talker, who does big commercial and smart libel actions. 'I'm not Robin Peppiatt.' I had to point the hard fact out to her. 'And I'm not a Q.C.'

'Why aren't you?' Hilda remained unsatisfied by my argument. 'Phillida Erskine-Brown's a Q.C.'

'You may not have noticed this,' I did my best to explain. 'But I bear practically no resemblance at all to Mrs Phillida Erskine-Brown. To start with, I'm not a woman.'

'What's being a woman got to do with it?'

'Lawyers feel so awful about the way they've treated women down the ages, not letting them into Chambers, not giving them the key of the loo, they push them into silk gowns as a sort of compensation.'

'What about the Head of your Chambers; why is Samuel Ballard a Q.C.?'

'It is not for us to question the inscrutable ways of Providence,' I told her devoutly.

'He's a silk, Rumpole.'

'In my view, a highly artificial silk.'

'Why don't you do something to get on in the world?'

'Because it's getting rather near the time when I should get off. Probably at the next stop.'

I felt a great temptation to return to sore labour's bath, balm of hurt minds, great nature's second course – sleep. The possibility of asking the Lord Chancellor for a silk gown, entitling me to sit in the front row and to be called a Queen's Counsel, had sometimes crossed my mind, but such a promotion would deprive me of such bread and butter as dealing with the little problems the Timsons might leave in their wake. I was also not at all sure I could find a judge to back my claim, as I had enjoyed differences of opinion, often dramatic, in open Court with most of them.

'I've been thinking about you, Rumpole,' Hilda announced after a prolonged pause for reflection. 'And I've decided that if you don't do something about getting on in the world . . .'

'You want to be upwardly mobile?' I asked her. 'You want us to improve our lifestyle and move to the Isle of Dogs?'

'I want you to pull your socks up, Rumpole. That's what I want.' I looked down at the woollen tubes concertinaed round my ankles. 'And if you don't, well, you're quite likely to find yourself alone in your old age.'

'Promises, Hilda,' I muttered, and, when asked to repeat myself said, 'I'd miss you, Hilda.'

Further discussion on the Rumpole career was stopped by the fact that Hilda discovered from her *Daily Telegraph* that we were missing the television programme 'City Doings' which, in view of her new holdings in public utilities, She now found essential viewing. As the television screen flickered into life, the distinguished, aquiline features of Sir Christopher Japhet, crowned with beautifully brushed iron-grey hair and surmounting an equally distinguished old-school tie, entered our sitting-room. Sue Bickerstaff, the eager interviewer, was asking him why we heard so much, nowadays, of crime in the City. Was it the after-effect of the Big Bang? Sir Christopher, shaking his head sadly, was very much afraid that the City wasn't what it was when he first joined Seymour Japhet in the firm now known as Japhet Jarroway. He then made a short speech which I can recall, as I had a subsequent use for it.

'In the old days,' Sir Christopher told us, 'a stockbroker's word was his bond. No doubt about it. You had your rules and you'd've no more thought of breaking them than you would've failed to offer your seat to a lady or eaten peas with a knife. Insider dealing? We never heard of insider dealing, and *why*? Not because there were laws against it, but because it just wasn't on. Now we've got a flood of young men working in the City. "Barrow boys", "spivs", I call some of them. "Wide boys". No wonder you get trouble.'

The next item was how to raise money on half paid-up Granny bonds for investment in a Grannyflat, and I was about to tuck in once more to great nature's second course when Hilda asked piercingly, 'Why aren't you *Sir* Horace by now, Rumpole? After all he was *Sir* Christopher and he looked a great deal younger than you.'

Hilda had murdered sleep. 'Do you really want to be a lady?' I asked her.

In due course I defended Fred Timson and, much to my surprise, owing to the failure of the security guard to identify my client as the leader of the posse who escaped after an unsuccessful attack on the warehouse, I got him off. When I went back to Chambers, triumphant from the Bailey, I found our clerk, Henry, reading a glossy publication liberally illustrated with portraits of kangaroos and suntanned bathing beauties. Lifting it from his desk in idle curiosity, I read: *Come to the land of the Koala Bear and the Kookaburra. Sport topless on Bondi and bet your bottom dollar at Surfers Paradise. Watch the crickut at Melbourne and take the family to the footie.* All this led me to ask, as I handed the brochure back to Henry, 'Do I deduce from this that you're planning a holiday in the Antipodes?'

'Not a holiday, Mr Rumpole.' He changed the subject. 'Anyway, your con's upstairs. It's another Timson.'

'Oh yes. So it is.' I remembered young Nigel.

'Don't *you* ever get tired of it, Mr Rumpole?' Our clerk, I thought, looked somewhat stricken. 'Doesn't it ever occur to you, sir, that there must be more to life than saving various members of the Timson family from their just deserts. Don't we all long for a new life, Mr Rumpole, in a new world, perhaps?'

'Henry! Whatever's happened? It's not like a barrister's clerk to feel the call of the wild.'

'I told you, sir. Mr Bernard's upstairs and he's got another Mr Timson with him.' The man avoided my eye. 'You'd better not keep your con waiting, had you?'

So I left Henry to his Australian brochure and went upstairs to meet young Nigel. He was, I knew, charged with a mysterious commercial offence known to the financial cognoscenti as insider dealing. Now I am an acknowledged expert, perhaps *the* acknowledged expert, on bloodstains, gun-shot wounds and disputed typewriting, but insider dealing was a closed book to me. I thought of how I might manipulate my conference so that I could receive instruction without betraying my ignorance. Then I entered my room and the waiting presence of Nigel Timson and Mr Bernard, the Timsons' regular solicitor.

Young Nigel, in his dark blue suit and clean white shirt, looked exactly the kind of personable yet dependable young man with a future every mother would like her daughter to marry. When he spoke he had lost all but a hint of that accent in which he used to call the price of apples in Shepherd's Bush market. I sat down, lit a small cigar, and asked him how his business was doing. A slight shadow fell across those features which I recognized from a couple of generations of Timsons. 'Things aren't what they were with the Big Bang, Mr Rumpole,' Nigel admitted. 'Not since the market's been falling. There's people losing their jobs and their cars and their cottages round Newbury. Everyone's complaining.'

'Less a big bang than a big whimper?'

'The Prosecution will say you needed money.' Mr Bernard brought us sharply to the business in hand.

'Of course, I'm only the marzipan at Japhet Jarroway.' Nigel gave me my first taste of the strange tongue spoken by young, upwardly mobile persons. 'I come above the stodge but definitely under the icing-sugar.'

'So they say you supplemented your income with a bit of insider dealing.' Bernard seemed to be quite *au fait* with this mysterious offence.

'And you know what insider dealing is, I suppose?' I thought it best to challenge Nigel.

'Of course, Mr Rumpole.' He looked at me strangely. 'Don't you?'

'Don't I know what insider dealing is? Of course I do. It might just be helpful, to all of us, if you explained it in your own words.' I sat down to listen and take notes if necessary.

'Explain it to *you*?'

'Yes, please.'

'But you know.'

'I know I know.' I was starting to lose patience. 'But the Jury won't know I know. I just want to hear how you'd explain it to *them*. Regard me as twelve honest citizens with nothing between them except a few shares in British Telecom. Explain what you're supposed to have done.'

'Don't the Prosecution have to do that?' I wasn't getting maximum cooperation from the client.

'Come on, Nigel. We can't leave everything to the Prosecution.'

The boy, being naturally eager to please, began an explanation which I found obscure. 'Well, there's this little fish swimming along.'

'A fish?'

'This little company. Cornucopia Preserves and Jams Ltd.'

'First-class marmalade.' I was on home ground now. 'Adorns our breakfast table in the Gloucester Road.'

'Undervalued stock. Big factory. Lots of old shops on street corners. It seemed W.G.I. was about to make a Dawn Raid.'

'W.G.I.?'

'Worldwide Groceries Incorporated.'

'Of course. Dawn Raid.' The words echoed down the years. 'Puts me in mind of my old days in the Royal Air Force, ground staff.'

'Takeover bid.' Once again Nigel translated. 'Sudden jump to buy the stock before anyone has quite woken up to it. Well, a week before that happened I bought sixty-eight thousand pounds' worth of Cornucopia shares for a client. And then Cornucopia went soaring up.'

'They say you'd got to know about the Dawn Raid.' Bernard put the prosecution case.

'Which was being planned . . . Where?' This seemed to me, in my extreme ignorance, the vital question.

'In the Corporate Finance department of our firm, Japhet Jarroway.'

'So you could have easily got to know what was afoot,' I assumed.

'No, I couldn't.' Nigel was positive. 'It was in another department, Corporate Finance. Behind a Chinese wall.'

'Behind a what?'

'You know, a wall of silence. Between departments in the
same building. We call them Chinese walls.'

'Of course I know,' I lied shamelessly. 'I just wanted to see
how you'd explain it for the benefit of the Jury. But not everyone
keeps to their side of these imaginary walls?'

'Everyone in our firm does.' Nigel suddenly sounded like a
public school prefect explaining what is, and is not, cricket.

'Are you sure?' Was there really honour among young stockbrokers?

'You'd be out on your ear if you broke the rules.'

'Really?'

'Sir Christopher Japhet is our Chairman. Very keen on the
sanctity of the Chinese walls is Sir Christopher.'

'A bit of a Mandarin?'

'You could say that.'

'And this client you bought the shares for?' I remembered one
of the more comprehensible passages in my client's statement to
the police. 'This Mabel Gloag. You never met her?'

'No. Apparently someone had recommended us. She had a bit
of money and I moved it around for her. Then she rang up and
said she'd had a legacy. Sixty-eight thousand pounds. She
wanted to put it all into Cornucopia.'

'And after the Dawn Raid?'

'I sold her shares. She doubled her money.' A handsome profit,
I thought. And the Prosecution would say it was a handsome
profit for Nigel, got as the result of information illegally obtained.
In all probability they would cast doubt on the very existence of
Miss Mabel Gloag.

'What was she like?' I started to cross-examine the client.

'I never met her.'

'You talked on the telephone?'

'Yes. She sounded a nice old lady. It surprised me.'

'What surprised you?'

'I suppose, that she was dealing on the Stock Exchange.' I
took another look at my brief, particularly at those points of it I

could understand. 'The cheque was sent to her at a P.O. box number in Harrogate, Yorkshire,' I reminded Nigel.

'I suppose that's where she lived. She never gave us an address.'

'But her letters were collected, presumably by someone calling herself Mabel Gloag. And when the transaction was over some anonymous well-wisher paid twenty thousand into your account at the National Wessex in Cheapside.'

'I can only think . . .'

'What?'

'That was Miss Gloag. Showing her gratitude. I never got a chance to thank her.'

'You never heard from her again?'

'No.'

'Had you told her where you banked?'

'That's the strange thing. I never did.' He looked at me then, with the simple faith which all the Timsons happily feel for their regular brief. 'They speak very well of you, Mr Rumpole. They say you can work miracles.'

'Where do they speak well of me? In Brixton prison?'

'Well, I suppose so.'

'They speak well of you there, too. It seems you know Sir Christopher Japhet's daughter.'

'We've been going out together for about six months.'

'I suppose that means staying in together?'

'Well, yes. We make up a Dink.'

'Oh, do translate.'

'Double Income No Kids. That's what we call it.'

'How quaint.'

'And now it seems I'm a Yid.'

'Really?'

'Young Indictable Dealer.' He looked at us and his eager anxious-to-please smile died slowly. 'It's not really funny, is it?'

'Not very.'

We were silent for a moment and then he said quietly, 'Knowing my family as you do, you think I must be guilty.'

'I don't think you'll find that Mr Rumpole has ever let the Timson family down,' Mr Bernard rebuked him, and I said,

'That's entirely for the Jury to decide.' That was all I could do then except to tell them both to concentrate on the search for Miss Mabel Gloag, whose exact role seemed to me to be the main point at issue in the case. Bernard told me then he had written several times to the P.O. box number, but it seemed her letters weren't being collected any more.

When they had gone, I sat down to read my brief in detail. For the case of *The Queen* v. *Nigel Timson* I had to start learning a new language. I could forget about tea leaves and shooters. I was in a new world of Dawn Raids and Dinks and Chinese walls. It all made me homesick for the simple days when you just smashed a window, grabbed the money and ran. Times and the Timsons had changed and God knew how I was going to get used to it.

The search for Miss Mabel Gloag, during the next week or two, produced no tangible results. Nigel Timson did find a Harrogate number jotted down on the corner of an old cheque book. That, he told Bernard, was, he was sure, the number Miss Gloag had given him when he was busy when she telephoned him and she had asked to be rung back. Bernard called the number in some excitement, which evaporated when he got through to the Old Yorkshire Grey pub in Harrogate. No one in that establishment admitted to ever having heard of a Mabel Gloag.

All was not sweetness and light among the band of barristers who shared our Chambers in Equity Court. Not only was Henry discontented and apparently planning emigration down under, Claude Erskine-Brown came to me with a peculiar woe. It seemed he nursed a strange ambition to join the club where actors and judges, publishers and journalists, meet to shelter from their wives and enjoy shared reminiscences and nursery food.

'I want to put up for the Sheridan,' he told me.

'Isn't that rather a frivolous ambition for a fellow who can sit through *Tannhäuser* without laughing?'

But Claude was not to be dissuaded. 'I've wanted to belong to the club for years,' he confessed, 'but the trouble is that Ballard's on the committee. He's going to remind them of that unfortunate incident when I was photographed in the Kitten-A-Go-Go.'

'But it **was** clearly established' – I defended the suffering

Claude – 'that you only went there to inspect the scene of the crime.'

'Ballard says members of the Sheridan Club should be like Caesar's wife, above suspicion. And if he decides to blackball, the others on the committee might follow his lead. The blackballs would be all over the place, like . . .

'Sheep shit?'

'Think of it, Rumpole.'

'Unpleasant, I agree. My God, what did we ever do to get Soapy Sam Ballard wished on us as a Head of Chambers?'

The soundness of that last remark was born out by the behaviour of Soapy Sam at our very next Chambers meeting. When we were all assembled he addressed us in sepulchral tones, so that I thought that at least one of our best solicitor clients had shot himself in the clerk's room. 'I have called you all together,' Ballard told us, 'because I have reason to believe that a crime of major proportions has been committed in Chambers.'

'Someone has nicked the nail-brush from the downstairs loo again?' I remembered the last horror story in our Chambers history.

'I received a fee of fifty pounds for an opinion in a breathalyzer.' Ballard opened his case without condescending to answer my question.

'Come a bit cheap, don't you, Bollard, as one of Her Majesty the Queen's Counsel?' I sounded, I hoped, genuinely concerned at the fellow's rate of reward.

'I signed the receipt, of course. In the usual manner.'

'Hardly worth all the trouble of becoming a Q.C. for that.'

'Do any of you remember how old Pelham Widdershins became a Q.C.?' Uncle Tom, the briefless barrister who is the oldest inhabitant of our Chambers, a friendly figure most often to be seen practising putts along the carpet in the clerk's room, was in reminiscent mood.

'Please Uncle Tom!' Ballard did his best, but, once started, no one could stop the old fellow's flow.

'Oh, all right, then,' he said. 'I'll tell you. The Lord Chancellor had two lists, don't you see? One for chaps he was going to make Q.C.s, and the other for chaps he was going to ask down for a spot of shooting. Well, he got a bit fuddled, it seems, and mixed the two lists up. Old Widdershins was absolute death to a woodcock but he didn't dare open his mouth in Court. All the same, he was handed a silk gown, and put Q.C. after his name, to everyone's amazement.'

'I still don't understand.' I looked at Ballard in some bewilderment. 'You don't shoot, do you?'

'Perhaps, Rumpole' – Sam was displeased – 'I got silk because I don't regard the criminal law of England solely as a subject for jokes about nail-brushes and suchlike matters. If we might be allowed to return to the subject in hand.'

'Of course. You were telling us about your little breathalyzer.'

'I signed the receipt and gave the cheque to Henry to bank. That cheque, it is my painful duty to tell you, never reached the National Wessex. And I have yet to receive a satisfactory explanation.'

'Eaten by mice?' I tried to make a helpful suggestion, but Ballard wasn't having it.

'I don't think I heard that, Rumpole.'

'No. But perhaps Rumpole's right.' Uncle Tom weighed the evidence carefully. 'There *are* mice in that old cupboard in our clerk's room. Sometimes I get a strange feeling that they've been at the digestive biscuits.'

'I have told Henry that he has to give me a satisfactory account of the matter.'

'What was it? Fifty quid?' I asked. 'He'll probably retire and live on that for the rest of his life.'

'Come to think of it,' said the grey-haired barrister named Hoskins, obsessed with getting his fingers on enough crime to maintain his four hungry daughters, 'I have seen Henry reading a brochure about Australia.'

Ballard was grateful for this and other evidence he took as strong indicators of our clerk's dishonesty. Erskine-Brown contributed the information that Henry now arrived at work in a bright red *Triumph D-reg. sports car*, a clear sign of sin when coupled with the fact that he habitually left this motor holding hands with Dianne, our plucky but not always accurate typist.

'His marriage is on the rocks,' Ballard said severely. 'And

when a fellow's marriage is on the rocks he can't be trusted with
a cheque.'

'Oh, really?' I tried to sound interested. 'How's your marriage,
Ballard?'

'You know perfectly well I'm a bachelor.'

'Then aren't you rather like a life-long vegetarian giving us his
recipe for steak and kidney pud?'

'Let us try and keep to the point, shall we? Is it the feeling of
the meeting that I tell our clerk, Henry, that he must account for
the missing cheque or else . . .'

'Or else what?'

'Or else he will have to look elsewhere for employment. I
assume we want to avoid the embarrassment of a prosecution?'

'I support the Head of Chambers.' Erskine-Brown was filled
with a sudden enthusiasm for the Ballard cause. 'I think we in
Chambers should support each other. I will be behind you in
this, Ballard. Just as I expect you to be behind me on another
matter.'

'Another matter?' Ballard was puzzled until I enlightened him.
'He means his election to the Sheridan Club.'

'I can't promise you that, Erskine-Brown.' Soapy Sam was at
his most judicial. 'Each case, I feel, must be decided strictly on
its merits. Now. How many in favour of an ultimatum to Henry?'

I regret to say that all hands but mine were raised in condemnation. What they all failed to realize was that Henry's comparative
prosperity was due to his having the intelligence to be a barrister's clerk and not a barrister. He could sit in comfort taking
in ten per cent of our earnings while we slogged out to do breath-
alyzers on the cheap. However, the vote went overwhelmingly
against him. Ballard announced that the resolution was carried
and we could all go home by train as he didn't suppose we all had
red 'Triumphant' sports cars like our clerk. 'And alas,' he told
me, 'my train will be taking me to my bachelor establishment in
Waltham Cross. We're not all blessed with the warmth and loving
companionship of family life as you are, Rumpole.' Like so many
of the pronouncements of our learned Head of Chambers this
proved to be misinformed.

*

When I returned home, travel-worn and weary, having ab-
breviated my time at the bar in Pommeroy's for the sake of
propitiating She Who Must Be Obeyed, no voice challenged me
on my entry into the mansion flat with a suspicious 'Is that you,
Rumpole?' A cursory inspection of the premises showed me that
they were devoid of life – bare, ruined choirs where late sweet
Hilda cooked. At last I found, on the living-room mantelpiece,
one of those notes, sometimes known as a 'Dear John', familiar
to practitioners in divorce cases: *This may bring you to your
senses, Rumpole*, she had written, ever economical, on the back of
a used envelope. *If I leave you alone you may have time to think
seriously about your career. Try not to use too much gas. Hilda.*

I must confess now, and long after the event, that I didn't
obey her orders. In fact I turned the gas fire up to a companionable roar, opened the bottle of Château Thames Embankment I
had brought home from my brief visit to Pommeroy's and started
to knit up the ravelled sleeve of care with my eyes shut.

About an hour later the telephone rang. This time it was Fred
Timson who had murdered sleep. I had forgotten that he was
now at liberty and he told me that he was anxious to do all he
could to help young Nigel. Were we, for instance, in need of an
alibi? If so, he could undoubtedly supply any number of witnesses from the Needle Arms to say the lad was in the saloon bar at
the time in question.

I told him that it wasn't that sort of a case. What we wanted
above all was to find a Miss Mabel Gloag who had a P.O. box
address in Harrogate and a telephone number which connected
us to the Old Yorkshire Grey pub, where Miss Gloag had never
been heard of.

'Right you are, Mr Rumpole. My cousin Den moved up to
Yorkshire. I believe he's at liberty at the moment. I'll get him to
make a few inquiries relative to the bird in question. Every little
helps. The Old Yorkshire Grey, was it?'

'Yes. And she's not a bird, Fred. She's an elderly lady who
makes a habit of investing on the Stock Exchange.' At the time I
put too little trust in the Timson information service and was
soon soaking again in sore labour's bath.

*

Life continued uneventfully over the next few weeks and I must say I rapidly became used to my solitary existence in the Gloucester Road. I spent little time brooding on the upwardly mobile possibilities of my becoming a Q.C., a title which I have long held stands for 'Queer Customer', and I was able to stay late in Pommeroy's without encountering icy blasts of disapproval on my return home. One night, when Jack Pommeroy was calling 'last orders' in a half-hearted sort of way, I found myself at the bar with our clerk, Henry, who was trying to drown his sorrows.

'Mr Ballard, Q.C., thinks I robbed him of fifty quid, does he?' Henry challenged me as I drew my large Château Fleet Street up alongside his double gin and Dubonnet. 'He wants me out on my ear, does he? He's welcome! That's all I can say. He's very, exceedingly, welcome! He can say what he likes. Because if I'm sacked for thieving, how could I face my wife and the neighbours in Bexley Heath? Quite frankly, Mr Rumpole, a new life beckons. My marriage would be over!'

I bought another round of drinks for us, which Jack agreed to put on the slate until the next Legal Aid cheque came through, and then sought to comfort our clerk by saying, 'Surely, your wife would stand by you?'

'My wife,' Henry shook his head decidedly, 'has gone into public life. She has taken her seat on the Council. She is Chair of the Disabled Toilets Inquiry. She is also Chair of the Senior Citizens Ways and Means and the Equal Opportunities in Catering. These responsibilities keep her out every evening. Do you know what I return home to now, Mr Rumpole? Quite frankly, I return home to cheese on toast.' He drank and I followed his example. Then he asked bitterly, 'Have you any conception of what it's like, Mr Rumpole, to find yourself married to a Chair?'

'You thought you had married a woman, and you find yourself tied to an article of furniture?' I saw his difficulty.

'Oh, too true that, Mr Rumpole. Too very true. And I'll tell you something else . . .'

'Feel free, Henry.'

'Now she's that active in local government nothing can stop her getting "Mayor" eventually. In due course of time, Mr

Rumpole, I am likely to serve out my year as her Lady Mayoress.' My heart bled for the fellow as he added, 'Only one way out, quite frankly. Only one means of escape as I reads the situation.'

'What's that?'

'Could my wife appear with a Mayoress sacked from his job in the Temple for petty theft, Mr Rumpole?' he asked rhetorically and I had to admit, 'I suppose that might cause a bit of embarrassment at the function.'

'Too true, Mr Rumpole. Once again, too very true. And to spare her that I would start a new life in the Dandenong Mountains in the State of Victoria.'

'Well, I suppose they have barrister chambers, even in the Dandenong Mountains.' I tried to imagine it.

'I'm not clerking any more. I'm taking up a new career.'

'You want to be a barrister?' Henry, it appeared, was prepared to face a steep drop in salary.

'It is my intention, sir, to go into show business.'

'Much the same thing,' I agreed.

'You may remember I starred in *Private Lives* opposite Miss Osgood from the Old Bailey list office . . .'

'Bit of a hit, weren't you?'

'A rave notice, that's all, in the *Bexley Heath Advertiser*. Well, Dianne . . . Her cousin runs the Commonwealth Inn over in the Dandenongs. She's going as receptionist and I shall be placed in charge of entertainments.'

'You're going to perform, Henry?' Was there no end to the man's desperation?

'From time to time, I might make a personal appearance. I'm working up a nostalgia number. Songs of the war-time years. As my old father used to sing them.'

Songs of the war-time years! Then, as I drank up and Jack asked if we hadn't got homes, those sad, happy evenings when I fought with the ground staff at R.A.F. Dungeness came back to me. 'Roll out the barrel,' I began to sing softly, 'we'll have a barrel of fun,' and Henry chimed in with 'You Are My Sunshine'. 'Tell you what, you dear old Worship the Lady Mayoress,' I told him, 'how about coming home for a night-cap? I'm leading a lonely bachelor existence now, in the Gloucester Road.'

'A bachelor existence, Mr Rumpole?' Henry was pleased to accept my invitation. 'You gentlemen get all the luck.'

As Henry and I let ourselves in my front door, with a plastic bag of bottles supplied by Jack, who had seemed, at the end, anxious to get rid of us, we were giving a spirited rendering of 'We're Going to Hang Out the Washing on the Siegfried Line'. By the time we had made it to the kitchen and I was finding glasses and plying the corkscrew, we had moved on to a tearful rendering of that moving number, so beautifully given by Dame Vera Lynn, 'There'll be Blue Birds Over the White Cliffs of Dover'.

In fact I was just singing 'Tomorrow when the world is free' and Henry was applying a strange descant to 'And Billy shall go to sleep in his own little bed again', when I noticed a tell-tale and sinister chink of light between the shutters of that hatch Hilda introduced to improve communication between the kitchen and the living-room. At once I scented danger. I moved to the hatch and threw it open. I had been right to feel afraid.

Sitting in the brightly lit living-room were my wife She Who Must Be Obeyed and her old school-friend Dodo Mackintosh. The gas fire was off and they were both looking at the kitchen hatch with the implacable expressions of old-time judges who would wish to know of any reason why sentence of death should not be passed immediately.

Hilda and Dodo Mackintosh went to some academy for young ladies where they had, as Hilda sometimes says, 'the nonsense knocked out of them'. (I always think people are a lot better off with some of the nonsense left in them.) My wife and Dodo were, it seems, the terror of the lacrosse field and they still, given the slightest opportunity, work as a team in the long-running match *She Who Must Be Obeyed* v. *Rumpole*. The manner of my return home had given them an ample opening for a goal. Breakfast the next morning was like a snack with a couple of basilisks and the situation was not made easier for me by the fact that I had a sledgehammer fixed up between the temples and a mouth coated in sawdust. When I asked Hilda, in the politest of tones, whether it was coffee that I saw before me she answered, testily,

I thought, 'Of course, it's coffee. What did you have for breakfast when I was away for a few days with my old friend Dodo? Red Biddy, I suppose.'

'I think Hilda came to stay with me' – Dodo came up fast on my left flank – 'to give you a little time to think things over.'

'And I come back and find you carousing with your clerk!' Hilda expressed considerable disgust.

'It rather seemed to me, Hilda, as if they were singing together.' Dodo turned the screw.

'Singing with your clerk! And Daddy wouldn't even take a cup of coffee with his old clerk, Albert. He said it wasn't the done thing.'

'Hilda says it is so terribly important at the Bar to do the done thing, Rumpole.'

'I suppose neither of you ladies has got an aspirin tablet?' I asked to break up the duet.

'I don't think you'll find drugs are the answer, Rumpole.' Hilda gave me one of her sorrowful looks. 'The answer is not to do it in the first place.'

'Yes. But if you've already done the thing. I mean . . .'

'It's so important *now*, isn't it, Hilda?' Dodo asked her friend, 'that Rumpole should only do the done thing. At this moment in his career!'

'Exactly, Dodo!'

'What do you mean, "Exactly, Dodo"?' I was mystified. 'What moment?'

'Now you've applied to the Lord Chancellor to make you a Queen's Counsel.' Dodo supplied the answer. 'I don't suppose it would look quite the thing to have Rumpole, Q.C., singing with his clerk, would it, Hilda?'

'But I haven't asked the Lord Chancellor to make me a Q.C.!'

'Oh, yes, you have, Rumpole.'

'I can remember last night perfectly clearly. I think. I haven't done anything of the sort.'

'No, Rumpole,' Hilda appalled me by saying. 'I made the application for you.'

'You did *what*?'

'I wrote to the Lord Chancellor. I didn't mince my words. *It's perfectly disgraceful* I told him, *that Rumpole should have been passed over when Samuel Ballard, a younger man, is in a silk gown. I hope,* I put in my letter, *that Rumpole will be called to take his seat in the front row without further delay.'*

'Hilda. You didn't?' I tried to say it hopefully, but all hope was gone.

'Someone has to take your career in hand, Rumpole,' She told me. 'Before it's too late.'

Later that morning, when the sledgehammer had reduced its activities to an occasional thump, the Queen's case against young Nigel Timson opened at the Old Bailey before his Honour, Judge Graves. Graves and my old sparring partner, Judge Bullingham, were as different in their ways as life and death. Where one was bright red with rage, the other had a ghastly pallor. Bullingham went in for the full-frontal glare; Graves preferred the averted eye of disapproval. The atmosphere in Bullingham's Court was often red-hot; in Graves's it seemed that the central-heating was permanently off. A fight with Bullingham could have some of the excitement of the Corrida, with Graves it was like doing battle with creeping paralysis. Not to put too fine a point on it, Judge Gerald Graves was a fellow with about as much of the milk of human kindness as a defunct halibut on a marble slab. As my opponent's opening speech wound on I saw the Judge favouring me with a look of ancient and fish-like contempt. Of course, I thought to myself, he *knows*. Hilda's ill-advised letter urging my claim to a silk gown was no doubt the prime topic of conversation among the Judiciary and the subject of their greatest mirth. 'Rumpole, Q.C.?' they were all saying. 'Of course it would never do.' At that moment a sinister expression crossed the Judge's face; he was, chillingly enough, smiling at the richness of the joke.

Avoiding the Judge's eye, I forced myself to listen to the silken tones of Hector Vellacott, a barrister who smelled of eau de cologne and no doubt owned large portfolios of highly profitable shares. He explained the mysterious offence of insider dealing and the old darlings in the jury box nodded sagely, as though they were the Governors of the Bank of England. 'What the Crown says,' he went on, 'is this. Having got hold of the secret information that Cornucopia Jams was about to be taken over by Worldwide Groceries, this young man, Nigel Timson bought no less than sixty-eight thousand pounds' worth of Cornucopia shares. When the takeover was complete, those shares doubled their value. I say *he* bought them, Members of the Jury. He may be going to tell you that he bought them for a client, a Miss Mabel Gloag. Who is Miss Mabel Gloag, you may well ask? It appears that she had an address, a Post Office box number in Harrogate, to which a cheque was eventually sent. No one has been able to obtain any further informaton about Miss Gloag.'

Had they not? Before I went into Court that morning I had been accosted by Fred Timson who had appointed himself, as leader of the Timson clan, head of the Find Mabel Gloag Organization. He had with him his cousin Dennis Timson, the ageing villain who had made such a remarkable cock-up of the Penny-Wise Bank robbery, to which I have referred in my previous reminiscences.* Dennis, it seemed, had called at the Old Yorkshire Grey in Harrogate where a mate of his was on friendly terms with the landlord.

'Did you find Mabel Gloag?' I had asked.

'Well, to be quite frank with you, Mr Rumpole, no,' Dennis admitted. But as I moved away, disappointed, he added a titbit of information which I had found of some interest. 'I didn't find her, sir. But this guvnor of the Yorkshire Grey said there was an old girl there who was always talking about the stocks and shares she was buying. She came in in the mornings for a Guinness or two and she used the phone to her stockbroker. A Mrs Prescott.'

'Prescott? That's not much help. Anything else known about her?'

'Not really. Respectable old trout, apparently. She'd been a nursemaid to some smart City family. Seems that's where she got her taste for the high finance.'

'Nanny Prescott. Is she still about?'

'Hadn't seen her in the last three months, the guvnor said.'

I remembered this conversation as I sat listening to my learned friend Hector Vellacott cast some understandable doubt on the

* See 'Rumpole's Last Case' in *Rumpole's Last Case*, Penguin Books, 1987.

very existence of Nigel Timson's client. My instructing solicitor
was sitting in front of me, and next to him Rosie Japhet had
placed herself as a very interested spectator. In the short talk I
had had with her I was impressed by her good sense and obvious
affection for my client. She was a pretty and intelligent girl who
smiled occasional encouragement at her lover in the dock. He
looked back at her with all the confidence he could muster. They
were both, I thought, very much in love, and they might eventually marry and form a new, even more upwardly mobile, branch
of the Timson family, but this happy result might depend on the
shadowy figure of Miss Mabel Gloag. With these considera-
tions in mind I leant forward and muttered to Bernard, 'Nanny
Prescott. I suppose it's not possible . . .' At the mention of the
name, Rosie Japhet turned towards me and whispered eagerly,
'Did you say "Nanny Prescott"?'

'*You* don't know her?' I couldn't believe my luck.

'Well. That was the name of *our* nanny. When we were kids.
Mrs Prescott.'

'Mrs? Did she have a Christian name, by any chance?'

'"May Bee". That's what we used to call her.'

'Maybee? Possibly Mabel? You wouldn't have a photograph
of this Queen of the Nursery, would you?'

I was rudely interrupted by the Judge telling me that it was
customary for Counsel to discuss their cases with their clients and
solicitors before coming into Court and not during the opening
speech for the Prosecution. 'Thank you, my Lord.' I rose
obediently. 'Is my learned friend still opening? Fascinating stuff,
of course. I shall be all attention.' I sat, cupped my hand round
my ear, and listened eagerly. I didn't particularly like what I
heard.

'The sum of twenty thousand pounds was paid into the defendant Timson's bank account after this transaction was completed,'
Vellacott was saying. 'Can you doubt, Members of the Jury, that
this was the defendant's first dip into his ill-gotten gains, no
doubt spent on champagne and his Porsche motor car . . .'

Of course I had to rise then and interrupt. 'My Lord. What
this young man chooses to drink . . . Ooch!' – the sledgehammer
got in a final blow to the head – 'is entirely irrelevant.'

'Mr Vellacott, will there be evidence as to the defendant's earnings?' the Judge asked, ignoring my existence.

'In a good year, with bonuses, about seventy thousand. That will be Sir Christopher Japhet's evidence.'

'Good heavens.' The Judge looked severely shaken. 'That's more than . . .'

'More than an Old Bailey judge, your Lordship was about to say,' I suggested and was rewarded with a little ripple of laughter from the Jury, a call for silence from the Usher and a few cold words from the Judge.

'It's a considerable sum of money,' he said. 'Particularly if it's added to by the proceeds of illegal dealing.'

The first witness for the Prosecution was Nigel's fellow toiler among the computers, Hugo Shillingford. Hugo was about the same age as the accused, an affable young man who had been taught on the playing fields of Harrow to regard the world, and in particular the small world of stockbroking, as his oyster. He was led gently by Vellacott through his evidence. He was, he said, a friend, but not a close friend, of Nigel Timson, the accused. They worked at nearby desks on the dealing floor of the well-known firm of Japhet Jarroway. Yes, Hugo remembered an evening when he'd gone to the wine bar opposite the office with Timson and some other friends. It was just after the Cornucopia takeover by Worldwide Groceries.

'What did Timson say?' Vellacott prepared to play his trump.

'He said he'd just made a big killing in Cornucopia shares. That's all.'

'He'd just made a big killing,' Judge Graves repeated in sepulchral but satisfied tones as he noted down the damning evidence and underlined it with his red pencil.

'Mr Shillingford. You said you weren't a close friend of Nigel Timson's?' I started my cross-examination in the most silken of Rumpole tones.

'Well, I mean, we never went to school together.'

'Ah, yes. My client received his education at a comprehensive and Shepherd's Bush market. He got his financial expertise by fixing the price of Cox's Orange Pippins.' My tones became noticeably less silken. 'Isn't that what you gentlemen on the Stock Exchange sometimes call a "barrow boy"? As distinct from a Harrow boy, of course.' The Jury looked at Nigel with some sympathy and interest. The Judge looked at him with increased distaste.

'Honestly, I didn't know all that about Nigel.' Hugo Shillingford seemed painfully surprised.

'But you knew he hadn't been to a public school?'

'Yes. I knew that.'

'Thank you. Now then, when you heard Nigel say he'd made a killing on Cornucopia shares, did he not add the words "For some little old lady in Harrogate"?'

'I didn't hear that.'

'You didn't hear him say that.' Judge Graves continued to note down evidence adverse to the accused with obvious satisfaction.

'What were you celebrating in the wine bar? Was it *your* birthday on that occasion?' I asked the witness.

'Well, yes. Now I come to think of it.'

'And were you busy juggling?'

'Busy doing what, Mr Rumpole?'

'Juggling, my Lord. With a couple of glasses and a bottle of Dom Perignon.'

'Juggling with Dom Perignon!' His gloomy Honour made it sound as though he had caught Shillingford playing roulette on an altar cloth.

'Well, yes. As a matter of fact I was. I rather think I dropped it.'

'So, at that tragic moment, he might have mentioned the lady in Harrogate?' I suggested. 'When you weren't listening?'

'I suppose he might,' the witness conceded.

'Thank you. Oh, one other matter. There had been rumours of previous insider deals, had there not, around your firm of Japhet Jarroway?'

'My Lord. This can't be relevant.' Vellacott eased himself to his feet and the Judge looked at me as though I were an incompetent white-wig, who still hadn't learnt his trade.

'Whether it's relevant or not, it can't possibly help your client, Mr Rumpole!'

'We have seen Detective Inspector Arbuthnot's statement about reports of other suspect deals.' I reminded Graves of the depositions in the case and Vellacott looked particularly saintly as he said, 'I had no intention of putting in that evidence, in fairness to the accused.'

'In fairness to the accused I would like an answer to my question,' I insisted. 'What is it, Mr Hugo Shillingford?'

'There was a lot of talk, yes.' And after a considerable pause I got the answer I wanted. 'There were rumours that someone had been using information from the Corporate Finance department to buy shares.'

'*Someone* was using information.' Judge Graves made another of his notes, underlined it with his red pencil and looked at the young man in the dock, no doubt turning over the appropriate sentence in his mind.

After Hugo Shillingford, we had the Manager of the Cheapside branch of the National Wessex, who said that on the fourteenth of January last, a banker's draft for twenty thousand pounds had been paid into Nigel Timson's account. After further probing by Rumpole it appeared that the draft was on a bank called Transworld Archipelago, trading in the Cayman Islands, and it came as no surprise to discover that the Prosecution had been quite unable to trace the source of the money. 'I suppose, Mr Vellacott,' the Judge suggested, 'you will be asking the Jury to draw certain inferences?' To which dark hint my learned friend agreed, oozing charm and bowing from the waist.

Whilst these stirring events were taking place in Court, Rosie Japhet had gone back to her flat and found an old album of childhood photographs. In it she discovered a snap of her six-year-old self on a bucket and spade holiday in Cornwall. A comfortable-looking Nanny was helping her build a sand-castle. Anxious to help her lover, Rosie detached the photograph and brought it back to Court with no idea of what the consequences would be.

While Rosie Japhet was engaged in collecting evidence, her father Sir Christopher, had entered the witness-box. There he was received with the nearest thing to a smile of welcome that existed in Judge Graves's armoury of expressions, and some un-testing questions from my learned friend. He agreed that the Cornucopia takeover bid had been planned behind a Chinese wall in the Corporate Finance department of Japhet Jarroway. Nigel Timson, as a dealer in stocks and shares, had no right to know anything about it, but he had clearly found out somehow because he bought a large number of Cornucopia shares for 'his rather shadowy customer. Miss . . . What was her name?'

'Gloag. Miss Mabel Gloag,' I helped him out with a growl from my seat.

'And then, of course, a large sum was paid into Nigel Timson's bank account,' Sir Christopher went on, without so much as a glance in my direction.

'That twenty thousand pounds' – Vellacott was tightening the screws on his case – 'wasn't part of Timson's wages or a bonus from your firm, was it?'

'Quite definitely not. I have checked that most carefully, of course.'

In the ensuing atmosphere of quiet satisfaction which enveloped the Prosecution and the Bench, I rose to cross-examine. My first shot across the bows, delivered without any preliminary courtes-ies, was, 'You don't like barrow boys, do you, Sir Christopher?'

'I don't suppose the witness understands that question any more than I do, Mr Rumpole.' His Lordship was at his iciest.

'The witness understands it perfectly well,' I corrected him. 'Didn't you give an interview on the television programme "City Doings"?'

'Yes, I did.'

'And didn't you say that the crime wave in the City was due to the young barrow boys who've got into the Stock Exchange?'

'I said that the old tradition of a gentleman's word being his bond had died out. And I regret it.'

'I'm sure we all regret, Sir Christopher, that the standard of gentlemanly behaviour is declining.' The Judge looked at me in an unfriendly fashion. 'Even in the legal profession. Yes, Mr Rumpole.'

'Young Nigel Timson came to you as an office boy, didn't he?' I returned to the business in hand.

'I believe that is so.'

'And achieved his present position by honest hard work?'

'I believe he was honest.' But Nigel's possible future father-in-law couldn't resist adding, 'To start with.'

'He got to know your daughter extremely well?'

'I think they became quite friendly. Yes.'

'Don't let's mince matters, Sir Christopher. They're living together, aren't they, at a fashionable address in the Isle of Dogs?'

'Mr Rumpole!' Judge Graves's unfriendliness had turned to disgust. 'Has your client instructed you to attack the honour of this gentleman's daughter?'

'My client's honour has been attacked. He's been called dishonest.'

'But what on earth can his relations with Miss Japhet possibly have to do with it?'

'My Lord. May I make a suggestion?' Desperate measures were called for to stem the constant flow of cold water from the Bench. 'May I suggest that your Lordship sits quietly and allows me to develop my defence. Whether I succeed in doing so will be entirely a matter for the Jury!'

God knows what might have happened then had Sir Christopher not switched on his charm to full beam and said, 'Perhaps I can help? My daughter and Nigel Timson are living together, yes.'

'Thank you, Sir Christopher.' The Judge looked at the witness as though he were a good deed in a naughty world. 'That's the frankness I would expect from you, sir. Now perhaps we can pass to something relevant.'

'Certainly.' As ever I was anxious to oblige. 'Have you found out much about Nigel Timson's family?'

'I have made certain inquiries, yes.'

'And have you discovered that many members of the Timson clan have had more criminal convictions than we've had hot dinners?' This received a little laughter from the Jury, and the Usher called for silence. 'And has that led you to regard young Nigel Timson with disfavour?'

It was at this point that Rosie Japhet, her mission accomplished, came back into Court and resumed her seat beside Mr Bernard. She looked up at her father in the box as he said, 'I only want my daughter to be happy, Mr Rumpole.' Rosie opened her handbag then and gave the photograph she had discovered to my instructing solicitor. The cross-examination entered a rougher stage.

'But you don't want her married to a barrow boy, do you?'

There was a pause while Rosie's father thought of the nicest possible way of putting the matter. 'I should prefer my daughter not to marry into the Timson family. If I have to be honest.'

'Oh, yes, Sir Christopher. You have to be honest. So is that why you're giving evidence against him on this vague charge of insider dealing?'

'I have given my evidence because it's the truth,' the witness protested, a little too emphatically. The Judge obediently wrote down 'it's the truth' and underlined it, then he said wearily, 'Any other questions, Mr Rumpole?' Hoping, no doubt, to spare the great Sir Christopher Japhet further embarrassment.

'Just a few, my Lord.' It was then I whispered some quick orders to Bernard. The gist was that he was to send a clerk hot-footing it down to Somerset House to trace any relevant information about a Mrs Mabel Prescott, née Gloag. Before the learned judge got restive, I turned back to the witness. 'Sir Christopher. There had been a suspicion of a considerable amount of insider dealing in your firm before the Cornucopia takeover?'

'Unfortunately, yes.'

'And whoever was responsible might have wanted to pin the blame on this young barrow boy, Nigel Timson?'

'I suppose' – he shrugged off the suggestion – 'anything's possible.'

'And it's possible that this "someone" instructed Miss Gloag to buy Cornucopia shares through young Timson. Assuming that this "someone" knew the shares were going to rise?'

'As I said, it's possible.'

'And in order to make things look even worse for Nigel Timson, this "someone" might have paid twenty thousand pounds anonymously into his bank account?'

'He must have been a very generous "someone" indeed.' This won the witness a little laughter from the Jury and a wintry smile from his Lordship.

'Do you really think so? Out of a profit of sixty-eight thousand pounds?'

'You are suggesting' – Sir Christopher frowned as though seriously trying to follow my drift – 'that this person was responsible for the previous insider deals?'

The opening formalities were over and the time had come to let him have the case for Nigel Timson with both barrels. 'Oh, yes, Sir Christopher. That is precisely what I am suggesting. Have you got a bank account in the Cayman Islands?' And when he looked at the Judge, as though asking for permission not to answer, I fired another volley. 'What's the matter? Have you forgotten how many bank accounts you've collected? Before you commit yourself, may I remind you that we have a law of perjury, which applies even to the evidence of gentlemen.'

Only then did Judge Graves come to the rescue of the City gent. 'I don't need to remind you, Sir Christopher, that you are not bound to answer incriminating questions. That doesn't arise in your case, I'm sure.'

Sir Christopher could see the faces of the Jury. For the first time they were looking at him with a certain amount of doubt and suspicion, and not to have answered then would have been to destroy all his credibility, so he said, as casually as possible, 'Of course, I'm prepared to deal with your question. I have a small account in the Cayman Islands. Yes.'

'At the Transworld Archipelago?'

'I believe that's what the bank's called.' I gave the Jury one of my meaningful looks and changed the subject. 'Your daughter Rosie is a nicely brought up girl, no doubt.'

Rosie looked up at me puzzled, and her father smiled down at her.

'Yes, I hope so.'

'And her formative years were presided over by a devoted nursemaid?'

'We had a nanny.'

'Nanny Prescott?' Sir Christopher stood silent. I pressed on with 'Do you believe that was her name?'

'It was her name, yes.'

'Is that a photograph of Nanny Mabel Prescott?' When the Usher handed him the snap from his daughter's album Sir Christopher had to admit it.

'Can you tell us where Mrs Prescott is now?'

'I have absolutely no idea. I know she had a son in Australia. She may have gone out there.'

'How very convenient. Was there a Mr Prescott?'

'I think she was a widow when she came to us. I really can't remember.'

'We heard that she had a Post Office box number in Harrogate. Did you know she lived there?'

'I seem to remember something about a family in Harrogate.' The witness frowned and then Judge Graves stirred as though rising from the dead. 'Mr Rumpole, may I ask where these questions are leading?'

'I hope, my Lord, to the truth.'

'Which is?'

'That you, Sir Christopher,' I turned on the witness, 'got your old servant, using another name, to place the share order with young Nigel Timson. That you paid the twenty thousand pounds into his bank account. And you did all that because you wanted to cover up your own insider trading. Such a brilliant idea, wasn't it? To blame it all on one of those unspeakable barrow boys, who've let down the honourable traditions of you old City gents.' There followed one of those prolonged courtroom silences which can happen at the turning point of a case, when anyone who has a pin about them might drop it with a resounding crash. At long last, Sir Christopher spoke. 'That is an absolutely outrageous suggestion!' he said.

The day, I think you will agree, had not gone badly for the Defence. What I needed was a little hard evidence to back up my outrageous suggestions. Accordingly I asked the Judge for an adjournment 'out of consideration for the witness', who looked, I thought, drained as a result of our encounter. The old darling on the Bench went up a degree above freezing-point, found my suggestion excellent, and knocked off work until the following morning.

*

As I came out of Court, not a little flown with triumph, my spirits were somewhat dashed by my clerk, Henry. There had been a call to Chambers from Sir Robert Keith, the Lord Chancellor's chief adviser and right-hand man. Old Keith, Henry told me, wondered if I would care to join him for a drink at the Sheridan Club at six o'clock that evening. It was, it seemed, a matter of some urgency.

Perhaps, at this point, I should fill you in with a rough idea of the way in which humble junior barristers rise to become one of Her Majesty's Counsel, learned in the law. After at least ten years of practice, the aspirant applies to the Lord Chancellor of England for admission to the select band of Q.C.s. He, and occasionally she, must show great respectability, high earnings, and should have a few letters of commendation from friendly judges who are prepared to say he keeps his flies done up and doesn't quarrel overtly with the Judiciary or treat evidence of alleged admissions to the police with unseemly levity. The Lord Chancellor, with Sir Robert Keith at his elbow, goes through the list of applicants and rewards the chosen few with permission to wear a silk gown, long wigs and knee breeches on special occasions, and the right to charge higher fees, do 'bigger' cases, be called 'leading Counsel' and be serviced in Court by a 'junior' barrister, who is often the Q.C.'s senior in age and experience. Many juniors of the old school, Rumpole among them, prefer to hack on in gowns of more plebeian material and not deny themselves the daily bread and butter of petty thefts and indecent exposures. In this way I have been able to carve out a career which, as I hope you may agree, has had its splendour as well as its miseries. It will also be remembered that I achieved my greatest triumph, victory in the Penge Bungalow Murders, as a junior Counsel, alone and without a leader.

My date with Sir Robert Keith, a prospect which caused me to mutter 'Oh, my ears and whiskers' in a distracted manner as I walked up the Strand towards the Sheridan Club, had no doubt been caused by the highly embarrassing fact that She Who Must Be Obeyed, with no prompting at all from my learned self, had written to the Lord Chancellor urging my claim to a silken gown. After a critical looking-over by the hall porter, I was admitted to the Sheridan bar and into the company of a well-nourished, white-haired man with a florid complexion who now treated me to a large club claret and a look of amused sympathy.

'I thought a drink at my club, Rumpole, might be the best way to get over this rather tricky situation.'

'Yes. Well.' I lifted my glass to him. 'Here's mud in your eye.'

'Thank you.' Then he got down to business. 'As you may know, the Lord Chancellor has received an extremely awkward letter from Mrs Rumpole.'

'And Mrs Rumpole can be awkward.'

'She actually suggested we should give you silk! The Lord Chancellor was deeply embarrassed by it.'

'Made him squirm a bit on the woolsack, did it?'

'It's not unprecedented.'

'Oh, I'm glad of that.'

'The wife of a clerk to the Nuneaton magistrates kept writing insisting that her husband should be made Lord Chief Justice of England. Until they certified her.'

He laughed heartily at this. I didn't join him. I had noticed, among a little group of members at the bar, that unlikely club man, Soapy Sam Ballard, Q.C., and I didn't want the Head of our Chambers to overhear any part of my meeting with the Lord Chancellor's right-hand man. Then Keith looked at me seriously. 'Rumpole,' he said, 'you don't want to be a Q.C., do you?'

'Well. Of course it would be an honour.' There had been a moment, coming up the stairs, when I had considered if I might not accept a silk gown if it were to be thrust upon me, so I added, 'And when I look at the learned friends who've got it, I honestly don't see why . . .'

'Why you should bother to join them?' Keith said hopefully.

'I was going to say, why I'm not at least as good as they are.'

'Some men are natural juniors, Rumpole.' Keith adopted the man-to-man tones which might have gone down a treat in the Mess. 'You are one of the good old non-commissioned officers of the Bailey. Strong in battle. Loud-voiced on the parade ground. But absolutely no criticism of you, of course, never quite officer material. It'll be a relief to the Lord Chancellor to know that you don't really want it, Rumpole.' 'I didn't say that exactly,' I said, but failed to stop his flow. 'Because of course at your age, you know, and given your ... your type of practice silk is really out of the question. Rumpole, Q.C.? It just can't be done.'

'I see.'

'So you'll break it to your good lady? I know she'll be disappointed. Her father never got silk either. Old Wystan never quite made it.'

There was half a minute's silence whilst we paid tribute to Hilda's father, a perfectly hopeless barrister who almost fainted at the mere mention of bloodstains and was crassly ignorant of the subtler implications of rigor mortis. Then Keith said cheerfully, 'Battling down the Bailey now, are you?'

'Yes, a City fraud. Bit of insider dealing.' I hoped it sounded impressive.

'Jolly good show! You'll want to get along home now. Try and persuade your wife to stop writing letters. Scares the Lord Chancellor to get them. Nice to have had this little chat. Carry on, "Sergeant" Rumpole.'

Taking this as an order to dismiss I rose and made for the door only to be stopped by my Head of Chambers by the bar. 'Rumpole,' he said, in tones of awe and wonder, 'wasn't that Sir Robert Keith from the Lord Chancellor's office?'

'That was old Keith. Yes.' Deeply impressed, Ballard asked permission to buy me another large club claret, and I let him have his way. When it came, he pulled out a wallet and ferreted in it for a five pound note.

'Did Keith mention me at all?'

'You want to know what he said about you?'

'Well, it is interesting to know how one is regarded by the powers that be.' Ballard's search through his wallet had dislodged a pink slip of paper which fluttered to the ground. 'He said absolutely nothing at all about you, Ballard. And what's that you've dropped?'

I stooped with some difficulty and retrieved what turned out, happily as I thought for Henry, to be a cheque for fifty pounds from Snaresbrook & Higgs, Solicitors, in favour of Samuel Ballard.

'That wouldn't be the cheque you're accusing Henry of nicking?' I asked as I handed it back.

Ballard looked at it, gulped and giggled nervously. 'Stupid of me. I must ... Well, I must've just put it in the back of my wallet and forgotten all about it. Of course I'll tell Henry at once. No doubt he'll be extremely relieved.'

'Making false accusations against your faithful clerk.' I wasn't going to let the man off lightly. 'What's the Sheridan Club committee going to think of that?' I raised my glass to the light, admired the colour and then took a long and fruity swig. 'Take my advice, old darling. Don't ask anyone to blackball poor old Erskine-Brown.'

'No, no, of course not,' Ballard assured me hastily. 'I've always thought Claude would make a pretty good member here.'

'He might brighten the place up.' I looked around me. 'Bring on the dancing girls, for instance.'

Mrs Mabel Jane Prescott. Married Arthur Charlton Prescott, Harrogate, the 3rd April 1940. Born the 4th of June 1918, Mabel Jane Gloag.' I was robed and ready, standing outside the Court next morning and reading the results of Bernard's clerk's researches. The landlord of the Yorkshire Grey in Harrogate had, it seemed, identified the photograph, and would be coming to Court later that day. There couldn't, I thought, be a Q.C. in the business who would have taken the risk of cross-examining Sir Christopher as I had done and then been proved right.

'I knew it, Mr Rumpole.' Fred Timson was triumphant. 'I knew as you'd never let the Timsons down.'

'In this case,' I told him, 'I think the Timsons have been saved entirely by their own efforts.'

And now my learned friend Mr Vellacott, for the Prosecution, came padding up to ask, 'Might I have a word in your shell-like, old boy?' As we wandered away together, he gave me the word with some embarrassment. 'The truth of the matter is, we can't find Sir Christopher Japhet.'

'Oh, you do astonish me!' I feigned amazement. 'Have you looked in the Grand Cayman? Perhaps he's turned himself into an offshore island.'

'Well, Inspector Arbuthnot does seem to think he's done a bunk out of the country. Too quick for us, I'm afraid. We can't go on against Timson. The Judge isn't going to like it.'

'Don't worry, old darling. The shock may bring him back to life.'

I left him then to rejoin my client and tell him the news. Rosie Japhet was standing on her own and, while I was talking to Nigel, she began to move away towards the lifts. He left me to say, 'Rosie, I'm sorry. About your father . . .'

She looked at him for a moment and then said, 'I know. He's gone. You did it to him, didn't you? You and your barrister, and all your family out of various jails!'

She moved away quickly and he called her back. She stopped only for a moment to favour him with a look of complete contempt. 'Oh, for God's sake! Leave me alone,' she said and added, in a voice loud enough for us all to hear, 'Barrow boy!'

My business is saving people from the nick. It is no part of my duty to help them to happy marriages or ensure that the course of true love runs smoothly for them. But I knew then that, by the way I had had to win his case, I had done something for which my client might never forgive me. I went into Court then to hear the Prosecution offer no further evidence and a verdict of not guilty was returned, which Judge Graves swallowed like a cup of cold hemlock. Another case was over.

If I had failed to win the unqualified gratitude of Nigel Timson, my efforts on behalf of Henry were greeted with positive resentment. I went back to our Chambers to be greeted by a clerk bubbling over with resentment. 'You've done it now, haven't you, Mr Rumpole!' he said by way of a greeting.

'Oh, yes, Henry. It was a famous victory.' I tried to strike a cheerful note. 'The chief witness against me made a dash for the nearest airport in the middle of my cross-examination and the Prosecution was left in an embarrassing position without a paddle.'

'No. I mean you've only ruined my life, that's all.'

'Hasn't Mr Ballard told you, Henry? He's found the cheque. There's nothing but good news. Hasn't he apologized?'

'You found the cheque, as I understand it, Mr Rumpole, in

his wallet. You made him apologize. Where do you think that leaves me?'

'Leaves *you*. Where . . .?'

'Lady Mayoress. I've got no way out now.'

'Henry!'

'I'm not ruined any more. I won't have to leave the country. I can't take up a new life in show business in the Dandenong Mountains. Dianne and I won't be travelling to the Southern Hemisphere now, Mr Rumpole. I'm stuck for the rest of my life in Bexley Heath, married to a Chair.'

'Henry, I'm sorry.' It was sincerely meant. I had now got the man's drift.

'Perhaps you'd be so kind as to leave me, Mr Rumpole. I wish to be alone with my dreams. What little is left of them. Close the door quietly, would you, as you go out?'

As you see, it was not a time when Rumpole was leading in the popularity charts. And I had one further person to placate. She Who Must Be Obeyed must be told of my drink with old Keith. I waited for a friendly moment after dinner when I was sporting my old cardigan and bedroom slippers, smoking a small cigar and toasting my toes in front of the unlit gas fire.

'Oh, by the way, Hilda,' I broached the subject. 'I had a chat with old Keith from the Lord Chancellor's office. Matter of fact he asked me for a drink in his club.'

'He didn't.' I could see she was impressed.

'Oh, yes. We had a chat together in the Sheridan.'

'So what is it now? Rumpole, Q.C.?'

'Well, no Hilda.' I hated to disappoint her. 'It's not.'

'*Not?*' I could feel an east wind cutting my ankles and I started to invent hard. 'Old Keith was talking about your learned father, C. H. Wystan.'

'The man from the Lord Chancellor's office was talking about Daddy?' She was clearly gratified.

'Oh, at length. He said Wystan was such a brilliant lawyer they had decided to make *him* a Q.C. years ago.'

'Daddy, Q.C.?'

'Exactly. But your Daddy went off to a higher court, as old Keith puts it. The Great Appeal Court in the skies.'

'Daddy died,' Hilda had to admit.

'Sadly. So they felt that, as C. H. Wystan had missed it, they could hardly give it to his mere son-in-law. There's some sort of rule, I believe, about too many Q.C.s in the same family.' A silence fell between us and then Hilda looked at me.

'I do understand, Rumpole. After Daddy, it would be a bit of a come-down to give it to you.'

'But the Lord Chancellor sent you his love,' I hastened to assure her. 'From the woolsack. Oh, and he said don't bother to write again.'

'How very charming of him. Such a nice man. And very good legs, I always think, in breeches.' Hilda thought the matter over and then said, with considerable satisfaction, 'C. H. Wystan, Q.C! One of Her Majesty's Counsel, learned in the law.'

My duty was done. I closed my eyes and once again sought to knit up the ravelled sleeve of care with a little sleep. Hilda awoke me then with an extraordinary suggestion. 'If you're feeling chilly,' she said, 'we might have the gas fire on. Full on, shall we?' After that there was a warm silence and I was after a little of the balm of hurt minds when she switched on 'City Doings' at full blast on the television. She was, it seemed, thinking of buying British Airways.

Oh, well, Hilda had murdered sleep, and therefore Rumpole should sleep no more.

Rumpole and the Age of Miracles

The age of miracles is not past. I bring these glad tidings to my fellow hacks who trudge the treadmill between the Old Bailey and the Uxbridge Magistrates Court, seeming, at bleak moments, to lose cases by eloquent speeches to the Jury and greatly increase their clients' sentences by their impassioned pleas in mitigation. Life at the Bar may, more often than not, flicker palely between the hum and the drum. A man who has, let us say, won that great classic, the Penge Bungalow Murders, may find himself dealing with some petty matter such as turning back the mileage meters of clapped-out Ford Cortinas or receiving stolen fish. And then, perhaps, you hear a roll of distant thunder, a strange and alluring music is heard about Equity Court, a new star rises over Ludgate Circus, and an unusual and amusing brief drops into your lap. Such a miracle occurred to my good self when I found my services retained for the defence of the Reverend Timothy Donkin, Canon of Lawnchester Cathedral. Although the case did have an element of comedy, it was a deadly serious matter for the good canon. What was at stake for him was, if not his neck, at least his frock.

The matters which arose in the Donkin case were of an ecclesiastical nature, a strange territory to Horace Rumpole whose concerns have been, over a long life-time, largely secular. It is true that my old father was a cleric, so I was, to that extent, a child of the manse; but his increasing doubts about the Thirty-nine Articles were only just balanced by his certainty that he was unequipped to earn a living in any other profession. So he clung on to his draughty vicarage in East Anglia as a man might to a small raft in stormy seas.

It is also true that, in due course of time, I went up to Keble College, Oxford, where a number of future bishops were educated; but a future bishop makes a somewhat crude companion for a criminal student of tender years and I tended to avoid their brash and beery company. Having scraped a legal fourth (I have always found a knowledge of the law to be a positive disadvantage in a barrister's life), having, as I say, satisfied the examiners (it's libellous to suggest that I did so with the assistance of the names of any of the leading cases on constructive felony scribbled on my cuff), I went into a world where men of the cloth only appear occasionally to protest that the young mugger in the dock is a keen member of the ping-pong team in the Lads' Club, evidence which is always looked on with a sceptical and fish-like eye by his Honour Judge Roger Bullingham. And so it was for the next half a century until the unlikely figure of Canon Donkin swam into my ken and I was introduced into a world of magic and mystery where miracles were found to be very much alive and kicking.

The dim religious light first made its presence felt when I arrived at my Chambers in Equity Court one morning and was greeted on the stairs by the figure of our clerk, Henry, carrying a clipboard and ticking off names on a list. When I asked him the meaning of this extraordinary behaviour his explanation, given in tones which I thought not nearly apologetic enough, was that he was acting on the instructions of Samuel Ballard, Q.C., our Head of Chambers, who wanted our arrivals and departures noted, presumably so he could calculate precisely how much electric light, soap and lavatory paper we were each using. Ballard is the sort of Head of Chambers who spends a great deal of his time counting the paper clips and adding up the coffee money.

'Soapy Sam Ballard wants us clocked in, does he?' And I asked Henry, 'Where's he gone to earth this morning?'

It seemed that Ballard, Q.C., President of the Lawyers As Christians society (L.A.C.), was in his room and did not wish to be disturbed. When I duly did so, I was surprised to find him on his knees beside his desk, muttering some reverent phrases about having been chosen, unworthy as he was, to do the will of God and promote the true interests of the Church. I was dimly aware that he was not addressing me but some unseen presence and, barging into this conversation with the Almighty, I gave the man a substantial piece of my mind. 'What do you think you're running in Equity Court,' I asked him, 'a Chambers of ladies and gentlemen learned in the law or a maximum-security nick? And if you've just dropped your collar stud, don't expect me to crawl under the desk to help you look for it.'

'Ah, Rumpole.' Ballard climbed to his feet, smiling at me in a pious and soapy manner. 'You interrupted me. I was giving thanks for the honour that's been done to me. Quite undeserved, of course.'

'Of course. What honour?'

'I believe it's the first time in our long history that these chambers have contained a Chancellor.'

'A Chancellor!' I thought that if she had appointed Ballard to the woolsack the Prime Minister must have completely lost her marbles, and I said as much.

It turned out that Ballard's act of thanksgiving was due to a rather lesser distinction. He had been made Chancellor of Lawnchester, a judge of the Ecclesiastical Court in a diocese which contains an unusually beautiful cathedral and, as I was to discover later, an extremely unusual canon.

'You've been made a Grand Inquisitor? If I were you I'd have nothing whatever to do with it,' I warned the man, and he should have heeded my warning.

'It's a post only open to communicating members of the Church of England. It's hardly likely to be offered to someone like you, Rumpole. Oh thou of little faith.' Ballard looked at me in a sad and infuriating sort of way.

'I have a great deal of faith,' I protested.

'Oh, yes?' Now Ballard sounded sceptical. 'In what precisely?'

'The health-giving powers of claret.' I recited my creed. 'The presumption of innocence and not having to clock in in the mornings. Chancellor of the Diocese, eh?' I looked at him with a flicker of interest. 'Are you planning to burn anyone at the stake?'

'Try not to be frivolous, Rumpole. Nowadays the Ecclesiastical Courts deal mainly with ritual and matters of church furnishings.'

'Smells and bells?' I got his drift. 'How many eagles can perch on a lectern? All that sort of paraphernalia. Don't you get a decent chance to unfrock a priest occasionally?'

Ballard looked deeply serious. 'That painful duty,' he intoned, 'has not been asked of the Diocese, as I understand it, for at least twenty-five years.'

'Go to it, Bollard,' I encouraged the fellow as I left him. 'You never know your luck. Tear the frocks off the clergy and leave God-fearing barristers alone.' I seem to have been blessed at that moment, in addition to my many talents, with the gift of prophecy.

Returning after the day's work was done, having paid a brief visit to Pommeroy's Wine Bar, the claret level in my veins having sunk to a dangerous low, I returned *à côté de chez* Rumpole, the alleged mansion flat in the Gloucester Road. My wife, Hilda, known to me only as She Who Must Be Obeyed, greeted me in the hall, and as I hung up the Rumpole hat I told her briefly of the dark days of the Bollard inquisition. 'Odd,' I said, 'how the more they preach Christianity the less Christian people become.'

'Rumpole!' she whispered in a warning fashion. 'Do be careful. A priest would find that extremely upsetting.'

'Hilda' – I was puzzled – 'have you taken Holy Orders?'

'I'm just trying to tell you we have a visitor.' And she threw open the sitting-room door with something of a flourish. 'It's cousin Esmé's boy, Timmy. He wants to meet you very much indeed.'

Now the ramifications of Hilda's family are complex, and I have gone through life in constant fear of speaking to strangers in case they should turn out to be Hilda's long-lost cousin who would report to her on my behaviour. The relative now revealed to me was hitherto unknown; he was a small, tubby fellow in his forties with an eager expression and a quiff of hair which seemed to stand upright in an inquisitive sort of way, despite all efforts of the comb and brush to keep it in order. He wore that kind of understated dog-collar which consists of a discreet slip of white in place of a tie. 'Uncle Horace' – his voice was high and excitable but now slightly anxious, like a schoolboy who's lost his chewing-gum and fears he may have stuck it, absent-mindedly, on the Headmaster's desk – 'I'm so delighted to see you. It's a relief to me, a considerable relief.'

'Timmy's been made a canon of Lawnchester Cathedral,' Hilda said, and then broke a world record by adding, 'He's quite a big shot now. Aren't you, Timmy?'

'Hilda.' I was lost in wonder. 'Was that a funny?'

The joke, if such it had been, was over and She proposed to get tea for our clerical visitor. Looking at him again I was sure he hadn't simply dropped in to drink Darjeeling and eat digestives with his distant relatives. He had the distinct look, half-apologetic, half-challenging, of a client.

'You're in trouble!' I said as I caught a welcome whiff of business in a lean time. 'What is it? Fiddling the organ fund? Pawning the candlesticks? Choirboys?'

'Rumpole!' Hilda paused on her way to the door to rebuke me. 'Don't be ridiculous!'

'Nothing like that Uncle Horace, I promise you,' the Canon said, doing his best to smile. 'I suppose it's best described as old-fashioned adultery.' Hilda left us then with a resonant click of her tongue which indicated that Cousin Timmy had sunk in her estimation to something not much better than Rumpole.

When we were alone, Timothy Donkin told me his story. He was not the most popular preacher in his diocese; his views on miracles were, he explained, a little advanced for the good burghers of Lawnchester. It was not that he didn't believe that God could perform miracles. Multiplying loaves and fishes and turning water into wine were the sort of tricks the Almighty could manage in his sleep, but miracles, he felt, were just not in the Deity's style. There was a certain vulgarity, the Canon thought, about miracles; they brought an unwelcome touch of a magic show to God's true work which was to convert the estate agents, bank managers and hard-headed businessmen of Lawnchester to a more compassionate viewpoint. Jesus was, it seemed as he rambled on, best thought of as the Labour candidate for Lawnchester East, and Cousin Timothy had clearly given up assaulting the devil from the pulpit in favour of an all-out attack on the Poll Tax. All this, I ventured to suggest, was of the greatest interest, but hardly relevant to the charge of adultery.

'Well, you see, I'm a married man, Uncle Horace.'

'Makes it much easier to commit adultery.'

'I remember Mother saying that Auntie Hilda had married a barrister with a sense of humour.' Canon Donkin looked at me doubtfully.

'That has been the cross she has had to bear.'

'My wife, Gertrude, is an absolute saint, of course.' The Canon changed the subject.

'Of course.'

'But she's not the tidiest person in the world. And she quite fails to keep the children quiet.'

'You and Saint Gertrude are blessed with issue?'

'Two boys. Twelve and ten. Martin and Erasmus.' I detected a note of weariness and even a certain fear in the Canon's voice. 'It makes it difficult to get sufficient peace and quiet at home. So if I'm composing a difficult sermon . . .'

'You check in to the nearest monastery?' I suggested. Behind the kitchen hatch Hilda was rattling the tea cups with continued disapproval. 'I might join you sometime.'

'As a matter of fact I usually take a room at the Saint Edithna; it's our local Home-from-Home Hotel. I'm not a great one for monasteries and I like to be able to ring for a pot of tea and perhaps a round or two of hot buttered toast in the middle of the afternoon.'

'Pretty good screw you get, then, as a canon?' I was surprised by this account of high living among the clergy.

'The Saint Edithna doesn't charge very much, out of the tourist season,' Cousin Timmy explained. 'Of course I don't stay the night and I do have a little private money. No doubt it gave them the excuse they wanted.'

'Gave who?' I wasn't following the fellow's drift.

'My six accusers, the pillars of respectability, or, should I say, whited sepulchres of my congregation? They made a formal complaint against me to the Bishop.'

'For dropping into your local Home-from-Home?' I knew the chain of hotels from some unhappy nights on circuit. 'Unwise, perhaps, if you're allergic to frozen vegetables and cold claret but not, I should have thought, a criminal offence?'

'They say I had a woman in my room, Uncle Horace.'

This was more my line of country than a theological discussion, however fascinating, on the miraculous manifestations of the Almighty. This was a bit of human frailty I could get my teeth into. I settled in my chair, lit a small cigar and began my cross-examination. '*Who* says?'

'They've got witnesses. A maid says she saw me open the door to a woman.'

'And what do you say about that evidence?'

'I treat it with the contempt it deserves.' This was hardly the sort of answer which rings the bell and wins the prize in Court. I was about to tell the Canon to pull himself together and answer the question when he said something which gave promise of a miraculous change in the hum and the drum of my daily practice. 'Uncle Horace. Do you appear in Ecclesiastical Courts? They're going to charge me with conduct unbecoming a clerk in Holy Orders.'

'There is no Court in heaven or earth,' I told Timmy Donkin firmly, 'where Rumpole isn't ready and willing to appear. On the Day of Judgement, I can assure you, I shall be prepared to get up on my hind legs and put a few impertinent questions to the Prosecution. Why did you pick on me for this ecclesiastical *cause célèbre*? You've got the right man, of course,' I added hastily, before he had a chance to change his mind.

'I just didn't know any other barristers.'

'Oh, I see. Well, thank you very much.' It wasn't the most tactful answer in the world, and further discussion of the Ecclesiastical Trial was prevented by the return of Hilda with the tea. I saw, on the tray in her hands, a complete absence of biscuits. Chocolate-covered digestives, it seemed, were not be set out for clerics, however closely related, who were charged with conduct both unbecoming and adulterous.

That night, as we lay together in the matrimonial bed, separated by a couple of feet of mattress and the *Daily Telegraph* crossword puzzle, Hilda spoke up with deep feeling. 'It's absolutely disgusting!'

'A rude word' – I was surprised, I must confess – 'in the *Daily Telegraph* crossword?'

'Even the clergy at it!'

'It's *mainly* the clergy at it. From what you read in the *News of the World*.'

'From what *you* read in the *News of the World*, Rumpole. Only you take it.'

'A fellow has to keep up with the law reports, Hilda. As a matter of fact, I quite took to the Reverend Timothy.'

'Oh, I expect you did!' Hilda gave me the retort contemptuous. 'No doubt you're birds of a feather. I've always had my suspicions about that young pupil you go about with.'

She was referring, of course, to Mizz Liz Probert, the intense young barristerette, fruit of the loins of Red Ron Probert, the scourge of the South-East London Council. Mizz Liz is dedicated to a number of causes such as the welfare of one-parent gay and lesbian families in inner-city areas, but she clearly doesn't regard Rumpole as an object of romantic or even charitable interest. It seemed, however, that the alleged infidelities of Canon Donkin had made Hilda feel that all men are betrayers, and even fear that I might play an unaccustomed and unlooked-for role as the Casanova of Equity Court.

'Hilda. You can't be serious!' I made light of her suggestion, but Hilda's new-found jealousy had its part to play, as you will discover, in the miraculous events which surrounded the trial in Lawnchester Cathedral.

'I suppose she'll be helping you in Timothy's case?' Now She was cross-examining me.

'Well, if she's got nothing better to do.'

'Spending afternoons in hotel bedrooms, just for a bit of peace and quiet!' Hilda gave the Canon's defence a full blast of contempt. 'I never heard anything so ridiculous! And I suppose you're going to defend him. You'd never go near a cathedral unless someone had committed adultery; sometimes I think you'd go anywhere for a criminal.'

'The founder of Christianity was tried as a criminal, wasn't He?' I said piously enough to irritate Hilda. 'Sentenced too, from what I can remember.' A silence then fell between us until

She said, 'Anyway, there was always something peculiar about that family.'

'Jesus's family?' I was puzzled.

'Do try not to be blasphemous. The Donkin family. Bad blood. No doubt came from Arthur Donkin. Timmy's sister, Wendy, who no one ever mentions, went to gaol.'

'How do you know that, Hilda?'

'What?'

'I mean, how do you know that if no one ever mentions her?' It was a question Hilda didn't care to answer; instead she sighed heavily and turned out the light.

'Oh. Are we going to sleep now?' I asked politely in the darkness.

'If you can, Rumpole. With *your* conscience.' She Who Must Be Obeyed still had Mizz Probert firmly in her sights. I must say my conscience was perfectly clear. What kept me awake for the next ten minutes was the thought of Soapy Sam Ballard, the newly appointed Chancellor of Lawnchester, acting as the Grand Inquisitor and trying poor cousin Timmy for his frock.

> . . . high Heaven rejects the lore
> Of nicely calculated less or more;
> So deem'd the man who fashioned for the sense
> These lofty pillars, spread that branching roof
> Self-poised, and scooped into ten thousand cells,
> Where light and shade repose, where music dwells
> Lingering – and wandering on as loth to die;
> Like thoughts whose very sweetness yieldeth proof
> That they were born for immortality.

So wrote Wordsworth, sublime poet and old sheep of the Lake District, who, although born without a single joke in him, comforts my solitary hours. He was describing quite another building, but his lines will do very well for Lawnchester Cathedral. I arrived in the early afternoon of the day before Canon Timmy was due to stand before the Judgement Seat of Samuel Ballard, and found the Cathedral, grey and gold in the sunlight, quiet and dignified in a lake of green grass in the middle of the close.

It looked splendidly aloof, after centuries of war, thanksgiving and martyrdom, to the small matter of one of its clergy being guilty or not of conduct unbecoming his cloth.

I went in through the west entrance and wandered for a little under the stone branches of the ceiling, said hello to a few long-gone bishops and canons, sleeping in carved robes and mitres with their skeletons on the floor below them, and then I fell in with a small group, mainly of Americans, who were being shepherded round by a cathedral guide, an elderly man who, I thought, preserved his West Country accent carefully for the benefit of the tourists. As I joined them I heard him telling them that the original church had been built by some ecclesiastical developer called Bishop Sartorious in the year eight hundred and fifty-two, and was dedicated to Saint Edithna. 'Of course,' our guide fixed me with a beady and somewhat disapproving eye, 'you'll know our Saint Edithna, won't you, sir?'

'Not personally,' I assured him.

'She were a real Christian lady in the old Roman town of Lignum Castor, now known as Lawnchester. She were accused of . . . well, you know, naughty carryings-on. It were all lies. What they didn't like was her trying to convert them to Christianity. It were a trumped up charge but they brought in a guilty verdict against her, do you see?' The tourists nodded wisely, as though fully familiar with legal life in Roman Britain, and the guide continued with his rustic impersonation. 'So they stoned our Edithna to death on the site of what is now our Saint Edithna Hotel, part of the well-known Home-from-Home Hotels Limited chain in West Street. Some say that visitors to the hotel have seen the ghost of our saint, others say that she is only visible if you had a good dinner.' It wasn't a wonderful joke, but probably better than any Wordsworth could think of, and the tourists gave him a titter. 'Lady in a white gown, they sees. A wringing of her hands. Her martyrdom is shown in the stone carving in Bishop Sartorious's Chantry. If you would follow me, ladies and gents.'

The party moved off, but I didn't move with them. Instead I stood transfixed by a vision. In the middle of a sea of empty pews I had seen a familiar figure. He wasn't quite kneeling in

prayer but he had adopted that curious crouch with his bottom
stuck to the pew and one hand shielding his eyes which is typical
of members of the established church at their devotions. I approached quietly and intoned:

> 'When holy and devout religious men
> Are at their beads, 'tis much to draw them thence,
> So sweet is zealous contemplation.'

'Rumpole?' Claude Erskine-Brown, opera buff and hopeless
cross-examiner, old Wykehamist and husband of Phillida Trant
that was, the Portia of our Chambers, now Phillida Erskine-
Brown, Q.C., asked nervously and without removing the hand
from the eyes.

'Everyone in our Chambers seems to be at prayer nowadays.'

'What on earth,' Erskine-Brown now peered up at me, 'are
you doing here?'

'Oh, I drop in to West Country cathedrals from time to time,
just to charge up the spiritual batteries.' Well, I mean, ask a silly
question . . . 'As a matter of fact, I'm pursuing my career, in the
Ecclesiastical Courts.'

'You can't do that,' Claude hissed at me in an appalled
manner.

'Why ever not?' At this the fellow got up from the floor and
rose to his full height, which, as he is tall and willowy, is a good
deal higher than mine. 'You have to be a practising member of
the Church of England,' he said.

'I'm a member of the Church of England,' I told him, 'practising down the Old Bailey. How did you get in on the act?'

'Ballard was asked to suggest someone to prosecute a cleric on
behalf of the Bishop,' Claude explained. 'He happened to know I
was a practising member . . .'

'So here you are' – organ music was starting up somewhere in
the background – 'practising as hard as possible.'

'It's a case that's excited a great deal of attention in Lawnchester.' Claude sounded as though he just been briefed in the
trial of Joan of Arc.

'I know,' I told him, 'they're after my client's frock.'

*

'He hasn't got a hope in hell,' Claude told me.

'Hell, in this case, being a trial conducted by you before the Blessed Bollard?'

We were walking together away from the Cathedral through one of those ghastly and soulless areas known as a pedestrian shopping precinct. There were new shops and supermarkets built in livid red brick, somewhere to the east towered a huge concrete multi-storey car park, and a heavy smell of Kentucky fried chicken hung on the summer afternoon. It's a sad thought that, whereas our ancestors will be remembered for the cathedrals they built, we have nothing to offer history but our shopping precincts.

'By the way, Claude,' I wondered, 'don't you feel a little embarrassed at casting the first stone at the Reverend Timmy?'

'I don't understand what you mean.'

'Do you not? Invited any young ladies to the Opera lately, have you?' I was referring to a former occasion on which Claude had the temerity to invite Mizz Liz Probert to a passionate night of Wagner when Mrs Phillida Erskine-Brown was doing a murder in Cardiff.*

'Don't imagine I'm going to enjoy these proceedings,' he assured me in his defence. 'Anyway, Ballard's got to decide the case.'

'"And he took water and washed his hands before the multitude saying, 'I am innocent of the blood of this just person: see ye to it.'"' I reminded him of a previous Ecclesiastical Trial.

'I do hope you're not going to quote the Bible at me!'

'There is nothing I won't stoop to, Claude. In the ruthless defence of my client.'

We walked on together in thoughtful silence to the Saint Edithna Hotel. I suppose these premises had once housed an old-fashioned provincial inn, a place for Brown Windsor soup, coal fires and fading copies of *Country Life* in the sepulchral Residents Lounge. Home-from-Home Hotels Limited had done it up and given it all the joys of tinned muzak in the lifts, the

* See 'Rumpole and the Official Secret' in *Rumpole's Last Case*, Penguin Books, 1987.

Bishop Sartorious Coffee Shop, the Pride of the West Country Carvery and waitresses with black waistcoats, bow-ties and plastic name plates. Some of the original building, the façade and an imposing central staircase, remained. In front of the hotel a luridly painted sign showing the blessed Saint Edithna, a generously built lady in a white nightgown, acting as an easy target for a couple of Roman stone-throwers, reminded visitors that they were sleeping on a scene of ancient injustice.

When we arrived at the open-plan lounge and reception area Claude Erskine-Brown went off to join half a dozen worthy citizens, apparently his clients, seated round a tea table, whilst I did business with the girl at the desk, whose name, as appeared from her label, was Tracy. I had left my luggage with the porter whilst I visited the Cathedral and was now checking in, a process considerably delayed by the invention of the computer. Tracy, frowning but pretty, played repeated tunes on the keyboard of this instrument and then stared at it in complete bewilderment. While I was waiting for her machine to stop bleeping, a tall, studious-looking fellow inquired for me at the desk. He turned out to be Frank Marlin of Marlin, Marlin & Spikings, my instructing solicitors. I lost no time in asking him about the group treating Erskine-Brown to toasted tea cake on the other side of the lounge.

'Those are our six accusers. Of course, you know Ecclesiastical Law, Mr Rumpole.'

'Of course. My regular bedtime reading. Just remind me, will you?'

'A case of conduct unbecoming against a priest has to be brought by six of his parishioners. They have to put up the money for the trial, in the first instance.'

'Then they must be dead keen on unfrocking the Canon.'

'Oh, I think they are.'

Marlin then gave me a brief run-down on our accusers. There was a red-faced cove with snowy white hair and a walking-stick said to be Admiral Seal (Retired), a Mr Fox-Beasley, Manager of a local bank, and Mrs Elphick, Chairman of the Lawnchester Bench, who looked as though she were strongly in favour of the restoration of the death penalty for cases of non-renewed dog licences. There was also a Mr Grobley, chemist and lay preacher. Finally, Marlin pointed out a tall, well-fed and handsome couple, a man and a woman in tweed suits with a certain amount of gold jewellery, tanned as though from a recent encounter with a sun-ray lamp or a fortnight in their Marbella holiday home. These, it seemed, were Mr Peter Lambert, the most successful of the Lawnchester estate agents, and his lady wife, Cynthia Lambert. By the time I had learned the names and identities of the un-friendly six, the reluctant machine, urged by Tracy's flying fingers, had coughed up a room for me. I had my bags sent up to it and we set out to visit our client.

Our way led back past the Cathedral and almost on the edge of the green grass which surrounded it there was a line of small houses and a sign which read: THIS SITE SOLD BY LAMBERT & PALFREY TO CARNATION STORES. NEW PREMISES TO OPEN HERE SHORTLY. Our accuser, Lambert, it seemed, had conned the planners into allowing him to buy a plot of land within a stone's throw of the House of God and sell it for the erection of a giant Carnation supermarket. All this had happened in spite of a pained correspondence in the *Lawnchester Herald* and a Bach evening in the Cathedral to raise funds for the Stop Carnation Society.

Canon Donkin's house turned out to be a pleasant-looking Georgian rectory just outside the Cathedral precincts. The door was opened to us by a discontented woman in her forties, whom my instructing solicitor introduced as Tim Donkin's wife, Ger-trude. As she led us into the hall I could see why the Canon had had to flee, for peace and quiet, to the Saint Edithna Hotel. Up and down the stairs the two Donkin sons were practising guerrilla warfare, armed with plastic automatic rifles, uttering the realistic sounds of rapid fire and shouting orders. The dusty hall seemed to be a tip for old bicycles, supermarket baskets, broken um-brellas and cardboard boxes.

'I don't know why Tim thinks you'll save his bacon,' the daunting Gertrude said. 'Just because you're his Uncle Horace.'

'Charming house,' I murmured.

'I suppose they'll chuck us out of it as soon as the case is over.'

Gertrude didn't seem to give much for her husband's chances. 'I must say I can't wait. It's murder to keep clean.'

She pulled open a door to reveal Timmy trying to write letters in a living-room where every chair supported piles of mending, toy weapons and disintegrating exercise books. He looked desperate.

'It's your Uncle Horace.' Gertrude led us into the room. 'The one you're pinning your faith on.'

'My dear, perhaps our visitors would like some tea . . .?' The Canon did his best to sound hospitable, but his wife interrupted him.

'Well, you know where the kettle is, don't you?'

Marlin and I denied any desire for tea and we stood a moment, listening to the sounds of distant gunfire.

'My dear,' Timmy made so bold as to say, 'if you could keep the children a little quiet. It seems we have things to discuss.'

'Well, you wouldn't have things to discuss, would you? Not if you'd thought for a minute about me and the children.' On which friendly note Mrs Donkin left us, slamming the door behind her.

'I'm afraid Gertrude's tired.' Our client was apologetic.

'I understand,' I told him. 'And I understand why you take a hotel room to write your sermons.'

'Oh, yes. Please, Uncle Horace. Do take a seat. Frank . . .'

'May I remove the firearms?' When we were settled I asked Cousin Timmy for some further particulars of the family history.

'Odd things, families,' I started. 'We forget how many relatives we've got, knocking round the place. Let me see now, your mother Esme Donkin was my wife's cousin. And you had just one sister?'

'Oh. Yes . . .' He sounded only vaguely interested.

'What was her name again?'

'Wendy.'

'Younger sister?'

'I suppose she'd be about forty now. We don't keep up, you know.'

'Isn't that the way with families? Not in any trouble, is she?' I remembered a bedtime conversation with She Who Must Be Obeyed.

'Trouble? Why did you ask that?' Cousin Timmy was frowning.

'No particular reason. We can't have you both in a mess, can we? Well, to business . . . I think Mr Rumpole would like to discuss the evidence. What the maid actually saw.' Frank Marlin had his brief-case open, but I wanted to establish some first principles. 'For the moment,' I said, 'I'd rather discuss theology.'

'What?' The Canon seemed shocked at the suggestion.

'You know something about faith; blind, trusting belief. Are you capable of that?'

'I like to think so.'

'Putting yourself in someone else's hands entirely. Taking the great gamble.'

'Trusting God. Yes, I can manage that.'

'How about trusting me?' I suggested. 'No criticism of the Almighty, of course, but I wonder if He's had quite as much courtroom experience?'

'I trust you, of course.' But the Canon sounded as though I had not yet engaged his interest, let alone his faith. I stood up and stretched my legs round the untidy room. 'Then tell me, who was in the bedroom with you. Someone? No one?'

My client looked up with watery blue eyes. 'I think that's a matter I'd rather leave between the two of us.'

'You and the lady concerned?'

'I really meant between me and God.' He was smiling. 'My conscience is perfectly clear. He will be my judge, Uncle Horace.'

'Maybe eventually. But tomorrow your judge is going to be Soapy Sam Ballard who just can't wait to unfrock someone. So hadn't you better tell me?'

'I don't feel called upon to answer any questions on the subject.'

'Never?'

'Never!'

I was surprised by the Canon's determination.

'Not in the witness-box when you're on your oath?'

'I shall tell them I don't consider it any of their business.'

I lit a small cigar then, and looked at him through the smoke. 'You're making my job impossible.'

'I'm sure you'll do your best for me.' He paid me a compliment but put no trust in me.

'All I can do is cross-examine the witnesses against you.' I took a bundle of witness statements from Marlin's open brief-case and gave our client a taste of the unpleasant news to come. 'Evidence of Rita O'Keefe, chambermaid. After you left the hotel she found three filter-tip cigarette ends lightly stained with lip-stick in the ashtray on the dressing-table. Wear much make-up, do you, Timothy?' I chucked the script back to Marlin. 'Or is that another question you don't feel called upon to answer? Look, unless you give some sort of a reasonable explanation you're going to be out of a job and living with a wife who doesn't seem likely to forgive you. You'll be an unfrocked priest, a figure of fun for the rest of your life.'

'Perhaps that's what I've always been, to certain people.' With his schoolboy smile and the quiff of hair that wouldn't lie down Timmy seemed quite unperturbed by the idea.

'It's all very well for your God, Timothy,' I told him. 'According to you He doesn't feel called on to perform miracles. But I've got to pull off something a great deal trickier than the feeding of the five thousand, starting tomorrow morning!' That was about as far as I got with the Canon, a client who seemed to think that defending himself was in some way beneath his dignity. As we left, Gertrude Donkin came out from a dark and no doubt chaotic kitchen and asked with considerable satisfaction, 'Hopeless, isn't it?'

'Is that what you'd like, Mrs Donkin?' I hadn't taken to Gertrude.

'The sooner we get out of here the better. Those stuffed shirts have always hated us; they never even asked us to their beastly dinner parties.'

Later I discovered that the disapproval of the Lawnchester upper-crust to my client didn't stop at dinner parties. A sizeable contingent had got up and left during his cathedral sermon on Miracles. I did take one further step that day in my search for a defence for Cousin Timmy. I telephoned my old friend Inspector

Blackie at Criminal Records in Scotland Yard and asked him to undertake a little research on our behalf.

The wind got up that evening and there was heavy rain. The West Country Carvery was almost empty; the darkly clad figures of Rumpole, Erskine-Brown and Ballard, our judge, sat dotted about among the white tablecloths like penguins on an ice floe. I was attended to by a substantial waitress labelled 'Shirley'. I ordered the roast beef Edithna with the dewy-morning-picked mushrooms, the cottage-garden broccoli and the jumbo-sized Wessex spud with golden dairy butter. No doubt it had all been thawed from the freezer at dawn by peasants in smocks. When I had placed an order for this feast, to be washed down by a bottle of the Home-from-Home Ordinaire (red), I sent out a signal to the learned friends.

'How are you, Claude? Is that you, Bollard? What time did you check in?' I was calling all tables.

'Is that you, Rumpole?' Ballard affected surprise.

'Of course not. It's the Archbishop of Canterbury travelling incognito. Perhaps we three should get together for dinner?'

'With the case coming on tomorrow? That would be hardly appropriate.'

Erskine-Brown was a stickler for legal etiquette and Ballard agreed. 'I think it more seemly, Rumpole,' he said, 'if I dine alone.'

'But you'd have the Defence *and* the Prosecution with you. I mean, neither of us could nobble you,' I reasoned.

'I suppose, Judge . . .' Erskine-Brown began but Ballard was quick to correct him. '*Chancellor*, Erskine-Brown. It *is* an ecclesiastical title.'

'Of course,' Claude apologized, '*Chancellor*. I suppose I shouldn't have any rooted objection. If both the Defence and the Prosecution were represented at your table.'

'I should make sure of that, of course. I would make it my duty to see you were both represented.' Bollard spoke with authority.

'Very right and proper, if I may say so, Chancellor.'

'Thank you, Rumpole. Of course, it wouldn't be right for us to discuss the case.'

'Oh, good heavens, no.' I did my best to reassure him. 'For us to discuss the case would be quite improper! We can talk about anything else, though. Can't we?'

I must admit that my enthusiasm to share the Chancellor's table wasn't entirely due to the delights of Soapy Sam's company and conversation. I wanted, in my subtle way, to impress on him the serious nature of the task he was about to perform and point out the danger of stamping around in an ecclesiastical minefield where angels might well fear to tread. So, as the rain rattled against the windows and the Saint Edithna sign creaked in the wind, I took the opportunity of saying, when our dinner together drew to an end, 'A night like this makes you think of old injustices.'

'We mustn't discuss the case, Rumpole!' Ballard ruled firmly.

'Oh, no, Chancellor. Of course not. Not a word about the case. Could you unfrock the port, Erskine-Brown?'

'What's that?' Claude looked startled.

'I mean, could you pass the port, old darling?'

'Well. This is a bit of a new departure for us, isn't it?' Ballard said after the bottle had been circulated.

'Drinking port?'

'No. Ecclesiastical Law. I shall have to rely a good deal on you two fellows for the legal side.'

'I have spent the last couple of weeks boning up on the subject in Halsbury,' Claude boasted.

'It's not a question of law, is it?' I said.

'Oh, isn't it?' Claude looked disappointed, as though he'd been wasting his time.

'Like everything else in life it's a question of fact.' I ignored the Chancellor's warning 'Rumpole!' and soldiered on. 'Injustice is the same, isn't it, in a law court or a cathedral?'

'Rumpole! We really mustn't discuss . . .'

'Of course not!' I agreed, and in the following silence listened to the weather. 'Strange sound the wind's making tonight. Can you hear it?'

'It's been a dreadful summer, certainly.' Erskine-Brown has no imagination.

'Do you think you can hear,' I asked then, 'the sound of a woman . . . crying out?'

'No.' Erskine-Brown was unhelpful.

'Clearly you chaps have no belief in miracles.'

'Miracles are certainly an essential part of Christian dogma.' The faithful Ballard helped me a little. 'I'm sure we all accept that.'

'So we accept the story of the Blessed Saint Edithna?' I asked, but Erskine-Brown was still in mocking mood. 'I thought she was a hotel.'

'A Christian woman in Roman times, Erskine-Brown,' I began to tell him sadly, 'was falsely accused of adultery because her beliefs irritated the establishment. They stoned her to death. On this very spot. And where she fell dead a small stream of pure cold water came trickling from the ground.'

'Must have been the one that came out of my bath tap.'

'Oh, very funny. Mock on, Erskine-Brown.'

'Just a moment, Claude.' Ballard, I was pleased to see, was shocked by the fellow's levity. 'I don't think it does to take these mysteries lightly.'

'I say, I'm frightfully sorry, Chancellor.' Claude saw that there was no sense in upsetting tomorrow's judge.

'There are more things in heaven and earth, aren't there, than are dreamed of in Erskine-Brown's philosophy?' I refilled my glass and looked extra thoughtful. 'An old inn was built on Saint Edithna's well in the Middle Ages. But it's said she keeps walking . . .'

'Like Felix the cat!' Erskine-Brown couldn't resist it, but at least Ballard was impressed and slightly nervous. 'Walking, Rumpole?'

'Whenever some great injustice is done,' I assured him.

'I thought we decided we wouldn't discuss the case.' My prosecutor could see his arguments drifting away into the realms of the supernatural.

'Really, Erskine-Brown,' I rebuked him. 'Are you suggesting that Chancellor Ballard would be responsible for any sort of injustice? In *our case*?'

'Yes, really, Erskine-Brown. I must say, I take considerable exception . . .'

'Oh, terribly sorry, Chancellor. I do apologize!'

'This has got nothing whatever to do with Canon Donkin's case,' I told them clearly. 'This is a matter of history! She walks.'

'And when do they say she walked last, Rumpole?' Ballard's finger seemed anxious to loosen his collar; this was a man who took spooks seriously.

'They say, if my recollection serves me, when a Chancellor in Bloody Mary's time had a couple of extremely decent Church of England canons burnt to a cinder on the Cathedral Green' – I was inventing rapidly – 'Saint Edithna appeared on the staircase of the old inn, wringing her hands and crying out against injustice.'

'She was probably wondering what had happened to her breakfast.'

'Oh thou, Erskine-Brown' – I looked at him sadly – 'of little faith!'

'There is nothing in the teaching of our Church to suggest that miracles are no longer possible,' Ballard reminded us.

'Only too true, Chancellor. And injustice continues, from Roman times to today. We can only hope that the poor lady can rest in peace after this.'

'After this *what*, Rumpole?' Ballard seemed to think I was discussing his future judgment, but I reassured him.

'After this dinner, Chancellor. You can hear the wind, though, can't you? There seems to be a definite hint of sobbing.'

As I have said, the old central staircase had been preserved in the hotel. It was built in a well so that you could look down, let us say, from a bedroom door on the third floor to the doorways on the second. Erskine-Brown was berthed on the first floor, but as Ballard and I climbed on upwards, he asked, with increasing unease, 'Was it this staircase, Rumpole? Was this where the Blessed Saint walked?'

'This very spot. Probably undergone a few repairs since those days; the muzak is new, and the abstract prints.'

'Poor woman. Poor, unfortunate woman.'

'She probably hit on a bad judge,' I told him as we parted.

Later I emerged from my room to hang a breakfast order on my door. Looking down the staircase well I could see Ballard doing the same. I moved back into the shadows and uttered a

low but penetrating moan. It was the nearest I could get to the
sound of a woman in distress.

From my vantage point I could see the pale face of Chancellor
Ballard peering upward. It was, it seemed, the attitude of a man
in terror.

The trial of Canon Timothy Donkin took place in the Chapter
House of the Cathedral. For a man used to such down-market
venues as Snaresbrook and the Uxbridge Magistrates, it seemed
that justice, in such an environment, must be on a higher, purer
level. Under the carved flowers and branches on the stone ceiling,
in front of a stained-glass window depicting the expulsion from
the garden of Eden surmounted by the arms of the Earls of
Lawnchester, Ballard sat, robed and wigged, and on a tall chair
carved for a medieval bishop. Only by remembering the strict
limitations of Soapy Sam's intellectual powers could I prevent a
weak feeling that the Chancellor of the Diocese must be the
fountain of all wisdom. Ranged around him was the Jury of four
assessors, two clerics, one dark-suited elderly man, who might
have been the senior partner in a firm of undertakers, and a brisk
headmistress-like person, who, I thought, was regarding Cousin
Timmy with particular distaste. A solicitor dressed as a barrister
sat below Ballard as Clerk of the Court and another ecclesiastical
hanger-on was cast as the Usher. My learned friend, Claude
Erskine-Brown, was there with his cohort of official complainers,
and I sat on a somewhat unyielding chair as the sole protector of
the Canon. The stage was set for a trial of heresy, or at least of a
little illicit love in the local Home-from-Home Hotel.

Claude opened his case at some length. It is hard for me, with
advancing years, to keep fully awake during the speeches of the
learned friends, and I must have dozed off, temporarily over-
powered by the warmth and the smell of sunlight on stone and
dusty hassocks. When I awoke the Prosecution was dealing with
Timmy's reason for booking a hotel bedroom for the afternoon.

'Canon Donkin has said that he used this bedroom in the Saint
Edithna Hotel to write his sermons.' Claude spoke with contempt.
'This improbable excuse becomes incredible when the Court
hears that he frequently worked in the Cathedral library.'

'Did you?' I turned in my seat to whisper to my client.

'For my history of Lawnchester Cathedral,' Timmy whispered back. 'All the deeds and documents are there.'

'Then why not write your sermons in the library?' It seemed an obvious question.

'The old librarian's always chattering.'

So Cousin Tim was writing a history of Lawnchester Cathedral; the information seemed of no immediate interest so I tucked it away for possible future reference. And then Ballard, whose mind has always worked somewhat slowly, interrupted Claude's flow to say, 'Mr Erskine-Brown, what I really cannot understand is why a priest of the Church of England needs a hotel bedroom to write his sermons?'

It is never too early for a Defence Counsel to make his presence felt in a trial, so I rose slowly, but I hope impressively, to my feet. 'May I, with very great respect, your Worship, remind you of a point of legal procedure. It is customary to pass judgment at the end of a case and not at the beginning, and, sitting as your Worship does in this Cathedral, you must be particularly anxious that a great historical injustice may not be repeated!'

Ballard looked puzzled at this, but Claude kindly provided him with a clue. 'I imagine,' he said, 'my learned friend is referring to Saint Edithna.'

'Wrongly convicted of adultery,' I added.

'So far as I have read the history' – Erskine-Brown tried the approach sarcastic – 'I don't think that the Blessed Saint Edithna checked into a hotel bedroom for the purpose of writing her sermons.'

'My learned friend should not be quick to make such assumption,' I batted back.

'Mr Rumpole. Mr Erskine-Brown. Gentlemen! Shall we get on and hear the evidence?' Ballard now realized he would have done better to keep his mouth shut.

'The very course I was hoping your Worship might take!' I said, genuflecting a little. 'I'm so very much obliged.'

Claude's first witness was a Mr Thomas Campion, Manager of the Saint Edithna Hotel, a pin-striped young man with a small moustache and hair neatly combed over his ears. He produced a registration slip which showed that Canon Donkin occupied room thirty-nine on the 17th of March of that year, a double room with twin beds and a bathroom attached.

'Mr Campion, Canon Donkin had taken this room on many previous occasions?' I rose to start my cross-examination.

'He had taken similar rooms,' the witness admitted.

'You say number thirty-nine is a *double* room?'

'With twin beds, Mr Rumpole, which could be pulled *together*, no doubt, if occasion demanded it.' Ballard was clearly becoming over-excited by the evidence.

'Perhaps they could by any couple prepared to risk falling down the gap in the middle.' I was rewarded for this by a small ripple of laughter from the spectators, a call for silence from the Usher and a disapproving look from the Chancellor. I passed rapidly on to my next question. 'There is no reason, is there, why that room, number thirty-nine, shouldn't be used for occupation by a single person?'

'No reason. No.'

'And it frequently is?'

'Yes.'

'Do you, in fact, have any single rooms in your hotel?'

'No. Since our recent conversion all the rooms are either twin-bedded or have a king-sized double bed.'

'And the Canon made no particular request for a king-sized double bed?'

'Not as far as I remember,' the Manager had to admit. 'No.'

'So it doesn't look, does it, as though he came to your hotel for any sort of hanky-panky?'

'Mr Rumpole!' Chancellor Ballard was apparently outraged. 'We are within church precincts.'

'I was forgetting,' I said as innocently as possible, 'I thought we were in Court.'

'So perhaps the expression hanky . . . The expression you used was not entirely appropriate!' Ballard was not appeased.

'Oh, really? What expression would you like me to use, within the Cathedral precincts?'

'The charge is conduct unbecoming.' Erskine-Brown rose, no

doubt intending to ingratiate himself with the tribunal. I turned
to the witness and asked quickly, to avoid further interruption
from the Chancellor, 'The fact that he didn't order a king-sized
bed would indicate to you that he hadn't come for any sort of
conduct unbecoming a clerk in Holy Orders?'

'I didn't know why he had come.' The Manager was defensive.

'Did you not? He came to your hotel quite regularly, didn't
he? Once or twice a month?'

'Yes.'

'And each time he told you he came to work on a sermon.'

'He said that. Yes.'

'Did you believe him?'

'Your Worship, I object.' Erskine-Brown rose with rare courage. 'What this witness believed is totally irrelevant!'

'Oh, do sit down, Erskine-Brown.' I got in my question while
he was lost for words. 'You let him the room at a cheap rate,
didn't you?'

'Yes,' the witness answered, and Erskine-Brown, having apparently lost his bottle, subsided.

'Because he was only there for the afternoon and because he
was a canon of Lawnchester?'

'We like to do what we can to help the Cathedral authorities.'
The Manager looked as pious as he could manage.

'Well, you wouldn't be helping them very much, would you,
by assisting one of their clergy to commit hanky . . . to commit
conduct unbecoming?'

'I suppose not.'

'I mean, are we to believe that you and Home-from-Home
Hotels Limited are engaged in running some sort of church
knocking-shop?'

'In *what*, Mr Rumpole?' I had lit the blue touch-paper and
Ballard was about to explode again.

'I beg your Worship's pardon. I mean some sort of ecclesiastical house of ill-repute.'

'My Lord, I object. That's a perfectly monstrous suggestion!'
Erskine-Brown had recovered his bottle.

'No more monstrous than the slur of gross immorality that is

cast on the good name of Canon Donkin,' I answered the charge
against me.

'Mr Rumpole. I rule against the admissibility of that question.'
Ballard was now treating my cross-examination as though it were
a rude limerick uttered during matins.

'Very well,' I told him, 'if this trial is to be conducted with all
the ruthlessness of tea on the vicarage lawn, I have absolutely no
more to say.'

'Mr Rumpole. Mr Erskine-Brown.' Chancellor Ballard sighed
heavily. 'Perhaps this would be a convenient moment to rise for
luncheon?'

It was a convenient moment indeed and I was soon back in the
Carvery of the Saint Edithna Hotel toying with the Abbot's cold
English platter and freshly gathered side-salad in the presence of
a client who seemed unable to fancy his food. 'That judge of
yours,' he said with some justice, 'doesn't seem to be able to tell
the Church from Christianity.'

'I was going to ask you,' I said, more to take his mind off the
present painful proceedings than for any other good reason,
'about your history of Lawnchester Cathedral.'

'Oh, yes!' Cousin Timmy suddenly returned to life and his
pale eyes sparkled with excitement. 'I think I'm on the track of
something interesting.'

'Orgies in the organ loft?'

'Far more interesting than that. There seems to have been a
gift of land to the Cathedral from the Crown in 1672.'

'Sensational stuff! That ought to get you to the top of the best-
seller list.'

'I don't want to bore you . . .'

'No, please, Timothy. Tell me about it.'

He began to tell me. I listened, at first out of politeness and
then with increasing interest as he unfolded a tale which might,
just possibly and if handled correctly, strengthen the Canon's
precarious hold on his frock.

The afternoon witness was the chambermaid, Rita O'Keefe.
She stood in the witness-box, a woman with untidy hair and

bitten fingernails, who must once have been beautiful but who now looked overworked and anxious. Claude Erskine-Brown established that she had worked at the hotel for the past four years and that she was unmarried and lived on the premises. He then brought her gently to the afternoon of March the 17th and asked her to tell the Court exactly what she saw.

'I was standing at the end of the corridor,' Miss O'Keefe told us.

'That is, the third-floor corridor?'

'Yes. Well, I was standing there and the door from the emergency staircase opened and I saw a woman.'

'Can you describe her?' Claude asked.

'Not too well. The light was behind her. She was thin. I think she was dressed in a sort of grey suit. Reddish hair, from what I remember.'

'Was she an elderly lady?'

'No, I'd say, sir, about my age.'

'Then certainly not elderly.' Soapy Sam was indulging the well-known judicial habit of buttering up a prosecution witness.

'What happened then?' Claude got us back to business.

'She walked quickly, like, to the door of number thirty-nine.'

'We know that was Canon Donkin's room,' the Chancellor reminded us, unnecessarily I thought.

'She knocked at the door and I saw him open it to her.'

'By him, you mean Canon Donkin?' Claude was dotting all the 'i's.

'Yes, sir.'

'And then?'

'He let her into the room and shut the door on the both of them, sir.' At this the accusers indulged in a few sad sighs and the assessors looked more beadily than ever at the accused.

'And after that?' Claude spoke very solemnly, as though a service were in progress.

'I stayed watching for some time, but they didn't come out.'

'How long did you stand in the corridor?'

'About three quarters of an hour.' I found that answer somewhat astonishing and made a note of it.

'And then what did you do?'

'I went downstairs to the reception area. At about six o'clock I saw that gentleman.' She turned her still beautiful eyes sadly on the Canon. 'I saw him leave the hotel. Then I went up to number thirty-nine.'

'Did you notice anything about the room?'

'The beds were made up, like. But there were cigarettes with lipstick on them, in the ashtray beside the bed.'

As you can see, there seemed little enough to be said on Canon Timmy's behalf by the time Miss O'Keefe had finished her account. I began with a smile, calculated to lure the witness into a sense of false security, and asked very gently, 'Miss O'Keefe. What did you do with the lipstick-stained cigarette ends. Did you keep them?'

'I chucked them away.' The chambermaid gave a slight toss of her head, remembered from her more flirtatious years. 'In the rubbish bin.'

'And I suggest you might have done the same with the rest of your worthless evidence.' I was still being charming but Ballard gave me a warning 'Mr Rumpole!'

'Oh, very well, let's try to take it seriously. You say that after the Canon had left the beds were still made?'

'They could have been made *after* use, Mr Rumpole.' Ballard had clearly cast himself as leading Counsel for the Prosecution.

'If they were singularly domesticated lovers, yes,' I agreed with the Chancellor and then gave my full attention to the witness. 'Miss O'Keefe. You told us you stood watching in the corridor for about three quarters of an hour after you saw a woman was admitted.'

'Yes, sir.'

'You stood there, neglecting your other duties?'

'I didn't have any other duties.'

'It was three o'clock in the afternoon, Mr Rumpole,' Erskine-Brown reminded us all unnecessarily. I told him I was perfectly capable of cross-examining a witness without his assistance and then gave my full attention to Rita. 'Am I to understand that you had no duties on the third floor that afternoon?'

'That's right. It was my afternoon off.'

'Your afternoon off?' I looked round the Court as though astonished. 'So what on earth were you doing spying on Canon Donkin?'

'Mr Rumpole. She has told us she happened to be watching . . .' Ballard began another protest, but I cut him short now with '*Spying*, my Lord. There is no other word for it, even though we are in a cathedral.'

'The gentleman had asked me to keep an eye on the Reverend. When he came to the hotel, like,' Rita told us.

'So you did that, on your afternoon off?'

'Well, yes. To oblige the gentleman.'

'How much did the gentleman pay you? Thirty pieces of silver?'

'I do object!' Claude objected.

'Yes, Mr Rumpole!' Ballard sounded, as ever, pained. 'I think we should try to keep the Bible out of it.'

'Am I to understand,' I asked as innocently as I could manage, 'that the Gospels do not apply in the Ecclesiastical Court?'

'No, no. Of course not. Certainly not!' Ballard escaped my question by turning to the witness. 'Miss O'Keefe. I want to understand your evidence. Did some gentleman pay you to keep some sort of watch on the Reverend Timothy Donkin?'

'Ten pounds he gave me. For the afternoon.'

'And who was this generous gentleman?' I asked. 'This open-minded spy-master?'

'I assume it was the Manager.' Claude rose to make the uncalled-for assumption.

'Sit down, Mr Erskine-Brown! It wasn't Mr Campion, the hotel manager, was it?'

'No.'

There was a long silence and Miss Rita O'Keefe looked round the Court, seeming to be asking permission to answer the question. 'Who was it, Miss O'Keefe?' I repeated.

'It was . . . that gentleman.' She was pointing past Claude at one of our six accusers, straight at the suntanned face of the leading estate agent and property developer of Lawnchester and the man responsible for selling to Carnation supermarkets a prime site within a prayer's whisper of the Cathedral.

'You're pointing to Mr Peter Lambert?'

'Yes, sir.'

The evidence of Miss Rita O'Keefe threw the Prosecution ranks into some considerable confusion. Claude Erskine-Brown asked for a brief adjournment in order that he could consider 'an unexpected development'. Chancellor Ballard immediately retired, I suppose to some hallowed spot in which he might pray for guidance. I took a turn around the Cathedral close, smoked a small cigar, and wondered if my old friend Inspector Blackie at Criminal Records had managed to turn up the information I wanted. It had not been an unsuccessful afternoon in Court and I had the encouraging feeling that the Almighty, unlike his representative Ballard, had accepted a watching brief on behalf of the Defence.

Back in Court I had five minutes with my client to check the details of a subject he had broached at lunchtime, his research into the grant of certain Crown lands to the Cathedral by Charles II. Then Soapy Sam returned to the Seat of Judgment and Claude called Mr Peter Lambert to explain his employment of a hotel chambermaid to spy on a clerk in Holy Orders. 'I certainly paid Miss O'Keefe to keep watch on Canon Donkin,' Peter Lambert smiled, showing a lot of white teeth and the appearance of candour which must have helped him through a thousand dubious property deals. 'I had every reason to suspect that he was indulging in immoral behaviour and I thought he should be exposed. Miss O'Keefe's observation proved me absolutely right.' After this, Claude sat down as though the whole matter had now been settled quite satisfactorily, an illusion which I did my best to dispel when I rose to cross-examine.

'Mr Lambert.' Again I started politely. 'I think you're anxious to develop a site very near to the Cathedral Green as a new Carnation shopping market?'

'My Lord. I really don't know what this can have to do with this case.' Claude tried to give the witness time to think by his interruption, and I had to speak sharply to my learned friend. 'Sit still and listen, and you may find out. What's the answer?'

'Yes,' Lambert agreed, as he had to.

'In order that the view of the Cathedral may be spoiled and the citizens of Lawnchester may wander round a concrete super-store filling little wire wheelbarrows with things they never wanted in the first place.' I felt the assessors were warming to me for the first time, but Lambert flashed his teeth at them and said, 'We do hope to develop the site, yes.'

'And you knew that my client, Canon Donkin, has been delving into the history of the Cathedral?'

'When he was not otherwise engaged in his amorous affairs, yes.' Lambert couldn't resist the gibe, which I ignored.

'Did you not get wind of the fact, no doubt from the talkative librarian, that he was hoping to be in a position to prove that the very piece of land you want to develop as a supermarket was granted to the Cathedral by King Charles II in the year 1672 and has been Cathedral property ever since?'

There was a silence which lasted a little too long for Mr Lambert's credibility, and then he tried to sound unconcerned. 'I heard he had some wild idea about that. Yes.'

'If you have no title to that site whatsoever, bang goes your idea of making a packet out of a new, unwanted supermarket?'

'It seems that's what he was trying to prove. Yes.'

'So that's why you and your cronies, the Bank Manager and the Admiral and the Chairman of the Bench' – I looked round at our six accusers – 'that motley crew of self-interested guardians of public morality who have invested in the Carnation stores site, all want to get rid of the Reverend Timothy Donkin?' Now the silence produced no answer. 'Is that the truth and the whole truth about this case, Mr Lambert?'

'We honestly believe he's guilty of immorality, sir.' Lambert avoided the question as blatantly as any politician on television, and supplied a smile of sickening sincerity for good measure.

'Oh, really! How very convenient for you!'

'Mr Rumpole.' Ballard looked worried and as though he had completely underestimated the worldliness of the Ecclesiastical Court. 'Even if Mr Lambert and his friends have some financial interest in this case . . .'

'*Even* if, my Lord?' I raised the Rumpole eyebrows.

'I still have to consider Miss O'Keefe's evidence about the

woman who came to the Canon's room.' He looked around anxiously as though eager for a sign; when none was forthcoming he decided to knock off. 'Very well, gentlemen. Shall we say ten thirty tomorrow morning?'

When I got back to the Saint Edithna Hotel I shut myself in the telephone booth in the hall and got through to Inspector Blackie at the Yard who gave me some information which I knew might be to the considerable advantage of Canon Donkin if only he had the wit to make use of it. Then I walked into the lounge area and saw a sight which proved, if proof were ever needed, that God moves in a mysterious way his wonders to perform. For there sat She Who Must Be Obeyed, wearing a hat and consuming tea and scones with the air of a woman on a mission.

'Do I come as a bit of a shock to you, Rumpole?' Hilda asked as I sat down to await her explanation. I answered her as cheerfully as I could. 'Of course not. Come to see all the fun of the Ecclesiastical Court, have you?'

'I would hardly call adultery by a priest in Holy Orders fun, Rumpole.'

'No. I suppose you wouldn't. All the same, they may have quite enjoyed it at the time . . .'

'That seems to me a remark in extremely poor taste!'

Shirley, the waitress, flitted heavily by and I ordered a large claret. 'What's yours to be?' I tried to include Hilda in any little conviviality going, but She was clearly not in a party mood. 'I didn't come all this way to drink with you, Rumpole.'

'Then why did you come? Sightseeing? A tour of English cathedral cities? Salisbury next?'

'The sight I have come to see is you, Rumpole.'

'I might be known as an ancient monument in some quarters, but . . .'

'Far too ancient to stay in hotels with girls about you.'

I began to understand the reason for Hilda's visit. Delinquent clerics, hotel bedrooms and Mizz Liz Probert had weighed on her mind to produce a green-eyed monster which had driven her to take British Rail to the West Country. It was, I supposed, a sign of affection not often apparent in her day-to-day treatment of a husband with little time and almost no inclination for philandering. After a hard day in Court and a bottle or two of the ordinary red, my favoured pastime is sleep; I should hate to be kept awake by the pillow talk of such as Mizz Liz Probert.

I reassured her. 'Girls? Not one girl, Hilda. Until you arrived, of course.'

'Well. Where is she?'

'Where's who?'

'You know perfectly well who I mean. Upstairs, I suppose. Helping you with your work. You men are all exactly the same. Birds of a feather, you and Cousin Timmy. Miss Probert. That's who I'm talking about. And don't try to look innocent.'

'Mizz Liz! You came all this way to see *her*?' I asked and Hilda gave me the full explanation: '"Will she be coming with you?" I asked. "Oh yes," you said, "if she's got nothing better to do." I'm sure she had nothing better to do! I expect she's been looking forward to the away-days. Bought a new outfit, quite likely. And now she's getting ready for a little bit of dinner. Well, all I can say is, you'd better make it a table for three.'

'Two,' I told her firmly.

'You and that Probert person?'

'You and I. We shall be having dinner *à deux*, Hilda. Mizz Liz Probert's doing a spot of indecency at Snaresbrook. She's getting work of her own nowadays.'

There was a silence between us then, while Hilda tried not to look like someone who's come bravely downstairs to catch a burglar and found nothing but the cat knocking over the milk bottles.

'She's not here?'

'I'm so sorry, Hilda. Are you very disappointed?'

'Oh. Well. She's not here, then. I wanted to take another look at Lawnchester, anyway.' Say what you like about She Who Must Be Obeyed, She manages never to feel foolish for long. Hilda looked at her watch and announced, 'It's too late for me to go back home tonight.'

'I'm afraid it is. We'll find a restaurant. The food here is rather like my jokes.'

'Whatever do you mean?'

'Not always, old girl, in the very best of taste.'

The events that followed may be cited as proof that the Almighty has revised his thoughts on miracles and no longer feels them to be beneath his dignity. Mind you the miraculous events which took place that night in the Saint Edithna Hotel would not have had their effect on the trial of Canon Donkin without a little worldly assistance from Rumpole. Miraculous fish may be provided, but some human hand still has to cook them and add the lemon wedge and the sprig of parsley. But enough of this theological discussion, let me briefly describe the events which occurred after Hilda and I returned to my room, filled with a rapidly evaporating dinner taken in the Swinging Bamboo, Lawnchester.

The miraculous events of that night had begun with a cloud no bigger than a man's hand. The loo wasn't working. The plumbing in the Saint Edithna appeared temperamental and I had to complain of the flushing system in my *en suite* facility. Accordingly we returned to find a note taped to the seat of the lavatory informing us that it was temporarily out of order and would we please use the toilet situated at the end of the corridor. Hilda, who had already put on her nightdress and covered it with a long white dressing-gown, was considerably irked by the situation. 'These things happen, Hilda,' I told her. 'Even in the best regulated hotels.' A plan was already stirring in my mind, whether by divine inspiration or not I leave my reader to decide. Suffice it to say that our broken loo changed the course of history, at least the history of Canon Donkin.

When Hilda was safely installed along the corridor I emerged from our room. The lights were already dimmed sufficiently for my purpose. It was the work of a few moments to run, as lightly and as swiftly as I could manage, which was not all that lightly and swiftly to be honest, to Ballard's bedroom. As soon as I heard the sound of rushing water from above I knocked on the Chancellor's door and then stood back against the wall so I should be hidden from his view when he opened it.

Fate, if that is what you wish to call it, was on our side that night. Ballard in pyjamas opened the door and peered out into the gloaming. What he saw, on the landing above, must have filled him with terror and foreboding. A tallish woman, clothed all in white, was passing in a terrible and unearthly silence, her hands clasped together. Struck, I have no doubt, by the awful significance of this miracle, Soapy Sam uttered a strangled cry and bolted back into his bedroom, there to contemplate the dreadful results of human error in the Courts of Law.

Hilda rose early the next day and, declaring that She could stay no longer in a hotel with such primitive sanitary arrangements, took a taxi back to the station. Her mission, although She didn't know it, had been a triumphant success. Before the Court sat, I walked my client round the Cathedral Close and gave him the information I had got from Criminal Records, facts which I knew would come as no surprise to him.

'Miss Wendy Donkin,' I reminded him. 'Convicted two years ago for fraud and false pretences. Released on licence. Wanted for twenty other offences concerning cheques and stolen credit cards. So far she's avoided re-arrest. If they catch her, your sister'll be sent back to do the rest of her sentence, as well as any further bird she gets.'

'Poor Wendy.' The Canon shook his head sadly.

'Exactly.' I told my client what he already knew, what had happened on the afternoon of March the 17th. 'She telephoned you and you arranged to meet her in the hotel bedroom where you are eccentric enough to compose your sermons. Neither of you bargained for Mr Lambert or his spy. No doubt you gave your sister money.'

'I gave her a promise.'

'What?'

'Not to tell anyone that I'd seen her.'

'Well, it's a promise you'll have to break. I'm going to put you in the witness-box and you can tell Soapy Sam all about it.'

'No.'

'What?' We had reached the door of the Chapter House. The Canon faced me with a look of gentle obstinacy. 'No, Uncle Horace, I gave my word. I'm not bringing Wendy into it.'

'Look. Tim. Reverend Tim. Are you totally insane?'

'I don't think so, but I'm quite determined.'

'For God's sake, resist the temptation to be a martyr.'

'It's not that. I'm not going to go back on my word because of Peter Lambert.' He gave me, then, a look of infuriating sympathy. 'I'm sorry to disappoint you, Uncle Horace.'

'I must say, it adds a new terror to my job,' I told him, with ill-concealed irritation, 'having some sort of saint for a client.'

Further argument between us was avoided by the temporary, part-time Ecclesiastical Usher emerging from the shadows to tell us that Mr Chancellor Ballard would like to see both Counsel in private before the Court sat that morning.

The Chancellor, when Claude and I joined him in some sanctum behind the Chapter House, looked pale and weary as a man who had spent a rough night on the road to Damascus. However, he spoke like a man who had wrestled with his soul and reached some inner certainty.

'Come along in, Claude. Sit you down, Rumpole. Make yourselves comfortable, both you chaps.' His welcome was almost embarrassing. 'I must tell you both, I have given this case most anxious consideration.'

'I shouldn't have thought there was much doubt about it' – Claude Erskine-Brown tried to sound confident – 'on the facts.'

'Facts?' Ballard looked at him somewhat sadly. 'Facts are not everything. This isn't an ordinary Court and we are here exercising a very special jurisdiction. We must be particularly careful that we don't commit an injustice against a person who may very well be entirely innocent. We have, of course, the memory of a certain martyr very much in our minds.'

'Oh, very much, Chancellor. It's in my mind constantly,' I assured him.

'We must also be grateful for any sort of guidance this holy city of Lawnchester can give us.'

'Guidance, Chancellor?' Claude was puzzled.

'Guidance comes to us, Erskine-Brown, from many unexpected sources.'

'I think what his Worship means, Claude,' I translated for the benefit of the heathen, 'is that there are more things in heaven and earth than are dreamt of in your philosophy.'

'Exactly, Rumpole! Very well put, if I may say so.' The Chancellor moved me up to the top of the class. 'I have thought anxiously about this case, and I am not ashamed to say that I have prayed.'

'Haven't we all? You've prayed too, haven't you, Claude?' I put on my most pious expression.

'Well. Well, yes, but . . .'

'And I've come to a clear decision,' Ballard pronounced. 'Having regard to the evidence about the financial interests involved, and the possibility that Miss O'Keefe might have been tempted to, shall we say, invent for money . . .'

'All too possible, I'm afraid, Chancellor,' I agreed. 'Such a lot of original sin about nowadays.'

'. . . I have come to the conclusion that it would not be safe to proceed any further against Canon Donkin on this evidence. I propose to direct the Assessors to acquit. Of course, I'll hear argument if you want to address me.'

This last remark was directed at Claude Erskine-Brown who did seem about to open his mouth. In a penetrating aside, I gave him my best legal advice. 'Give up gracefully, Claude,' I warned the fellow, 'God's against you.'

When the Canon and his frock were both safe and clear of the Courtroom, I received the somewhat distracted thanks of Cousin Timmy and he went off, with well-justified apprehension, to break the good news to Gertrude. I lunched at leisure and took the train back to London, returning to the matrimonial home in Froxbury Mansions on the Gloucester Road in the early evening. I opened the front door to be greeted by Hilda's usual cry of 'Who's that?' from the kitchen. 'Fear not,' I told her. 'It is I Saint Rumpole and all angels.'

'I'm sorry your little holiday to the West Country was so short,' I told her later as we were sitting over our chops and two veg in the kitchen.

'I don't know why I came down in the first place.'

'Oh, it was enormously kind of you, Hilda. You were a power for good.'

'It's not because I'm jealous, Rumpole,' she hastened to assure me. 'Don't flatter yourself about that.' I was smiling, I must confess, as I poured myself another glass of Pommeroy's Very Ordinary, and this led Hilda to add, 'And don't look so pleased with yourself, just because you won a case.'

'A total victory,' I agreed. 'The Age of Miracles is not past.' And I said, as I raised my glass, 'Let us drink to the Blessed Saint Edithna. Also known,' I added, but not aloud, 'as She Who Must Be Obeyed.'

Rumpole and the Tap End

There are many reasons why I could never become one of Her Majesty's judges. I am unable to look at my customer in the dock without feeling 'There but for the Grace of God goes Horace Rumpole.' I should find it almost impossible to order any fellow citizen to be locked up in a Victorian slum with a couple of psychopaths and three chamber-pots, and I cannot imagine a worse way of passing your life than having to actually listen to the speeches of the learned friends. It also has to be admitted that no sane Lord Chancellor would ever dream of the appointment of Mr Justice Rumpole. There is another danger inherent in the judicial office: a judge, any judge, is always liable to say, in a moment of boredom or impatience, something downright silly. He is then denounced in the public prints, his resignation is called for, he is stigmatized as malicious or at least mad and his Bench becomes a bed of nails and his ermine a hair-shirt. There is, perhaps, no judge more likely to open his mouth and put his foot in it than that, on the whole well meaning, old darling, Mr Justice Featherstone, once Guthrie Featherstone, Q.C., M.P., a Member of Parliament so uninterested in politics that he joined the Social Democrats and who, during many eventful years of my life, was Head of our Chambers in Equity Court. Now, as a judge, Guthrie Featherstone had swum somewhat out of our ken; but he hadn't lost his old talent for giving voice to the odd uncalled-for and disastrous phrase. He, I'm sure, will never forget the furore that arose when, in passing sentence in a case of attempted murder in which I was engaged for the Defence, his Lordship made an unwise reference to the 'tap end' of a matrimonial bath-tub. At least the account which follows may serve as a terrible warning to anyone contemplating a career as a judge.

I have spoken elsewhere, and on frequent occasions, of my
patrons the Timsons, that extended family of South London
villains for whom, over the years, I have acted as Attorney-
General. Some of you may remember Tony Timson, a fairly
mild-mannered receiver of stolen video-recorders, hi-fi sets and
microwave ovens, married to that April Timson who once so
offended her husband's male chauvinist prejudices by driving a
getaway car at a somewhat unsuccessful bank robbery.* Tony
and April lived in a semi on a large housing estate with their
offspring, Vincent Timson, now aged eight, who I hoped would
grow up in the family business and thus ensure a steady flow of
briefs for Rumpole's future. Their house was brightly, not to say
garishly, furnished with mock tiger-skin rugs, Italian-tile-style
linoleum and wallpaper which simulated oak panelling. (I knew
this from a large number of police photographs in various cases.)
It was also equipped with almost every labour-saving device
which ever dropped off the back of a lorry. On the day when my
story starts this desirable home was rent with screams from the
bathroom and a stream of soapy water flowing out from under
the door. In the screaming, the word 'murderer' was often
repeated at a volume which was not only audible to young Vincent, busy pushing a blue-flashing toy police car round the hallway, but to the occupants of the adjoining house and those of the
neighbours who were hanging out their washing. Someone, it
was not clear who it was at the time, telephoned the local cop
shop for assistance.

In a surprisingly short while a real, flashing police car arrived
and the front door was flung open by a wet and desperate
April Timson, her leopard-skin-style towelling bath-robe
clutched about her. As Detective Inspector Brush, an officer
who had fought a running battle with the Timson family for
years, came up the path to meet her she sobbed out, at the top of
her voice, a considerable voice for so petite a redhead, 'Thank
God, you've come! He was only trying to bloody murder me.'
Tony Timson emerged from the bathroom a few seconds later,
water dripping from his ear-lobe-length hair and his gaucho

* See 'Rumpole and the Female of the Species' in *Rumpole and the
Golden Thread*, Penguin Books, 1983.

moustache. In spite of the word RAMBO emblazoned across his bath-robe, he was by no means a man of formidable physique. Looking down the stairs, he saw his wife in hysterics and his domestic hearth invaded by the Old Bill. No sooner had he reached the hallway than he was arrested and charged with attempted murder of his wife, the particulars being, that, while sharing a bath with her preparatory to going to a neighbour's party, he had tried to cause her death by drowning.

In course of time I was happy to accept a brief for the defence of Tony Timson and we had a conference in Brixton prison where the alleged wife-drowner was being held in custody. I was attended, on that occasion, by Mr Bernard, the Timsons' regular solicitor, and that up-and-coming young radical barrister, Mizz Liz Probert, who had been briefed to take a note and generally assist me in the *cause célèbre*.

'Attempted murderer, Tony Timson?' I opened the proceedings on a somewhat incredulous note. 'Isn't that rather out of your league?'

'April told me,' he began his explanation, 'she was planning on wearing her skin-tight leatherette trousers with the revealing halter-neck satin top. That's what she was planning on wearing, Mr Rumpole!'

'A somewhat tasteless outfit, and not entirely *haute couture*,' I admitted. 'But it hardly entitles you to drown your wife, Tony.'

'We was both invited to a party round her friend Chrissie's. And that was the outfit she was keen on wearing . . .'

'She says you pulled her legs and so she became submerged.' Bernard, like a good solicitor, was reading the evidence.

'"The Brides in the Bath"!' My mind went at once to one of the classic murders of all times. 'The very method! And you hit on it with no legal training. How did you come to be in the same bath, anyway?'

'We always shared, since we was courting.' Tony looked surprised that I had asked. 'Don't all married couples?'

'Speaking for myself and She Who Must Be Obeyed the answer is, thankfully, no. I can't speak for Mr Bernard.'

'Out of the question.' Bernard shook his head sadly. 'My wife has a hip.'

'Sorry, Mr Bernard. I'm really sorry.' Tony Timson was clearly an attempted murderer with a soft heart.

'Quite all right, Mr Timson,' Bernard assured him. 'We're down for a replacement.'

'April likes me to sit up by the taps.' Tony gave us further particulars of the Timson bathing habits. 'So I can rinse off her hair after a shampoo. Anyway, she finds her end that much more comfortable.'

'She makes you sit at the tap end, Tony?' I began to feel for the fellow.

'Oh, I never made no objection,' my client assured me. 'Although you can get your back a bit scalded. And those old taps does dig into you sometimes.'

'So were you on friendly terms when you both entered the water?' My instructing solicitor was quick on the deductions. 'She was all right then. We was both, well, affectionate. Looking forward to the party, like.'

'She didn't object to what you planned on wearing?' I wanted to cover all the possibilities.

'My non-structured silk-style suiting from Toy Boy Limited!' Tony protested. 'How could she object to that, Mr Rumpole? No. She washed her hair as per usual. And I rinsed it off for her. Then she told me who was going to be at the party, like.'

'Mr Peter Molloy,' Bernard reminded me. 'It's in the brief, Mr Rumpole.' Now I make it a rule to postpone reading my brief until the last possible moment so that it's fresh in my mind when I go into Court, so I said, somewhat testily, 'Of course I know that, but I thought I'd like to get the story from the client. Peanuts Molloy! Mizz Probert, we have a defence. Tony Timson's wife was taking him to a party attended by Peanuts Molloy.'

The full implications of this piece of evidence won't be apparent to those who haven't made a close study of my previous handling of the Timson affairs. Suffice it to say the Molloys are to the Timsons as the Montagues were to the Capulets or the Guelphs to the Ghibellines, and their feud goes back to the days when the whole of South London was laid down to pasture, and they were quarrelling about stolen sheep. The latest outbreak of hostilities occurred when certain Molloys, robbing a couple of elderly Timsons as *they* were robbing a bank, almost succeeded in getting Tony's relatives convicted for an offence they had not committed.* Peter, better known as 'Peanuts', Molloy was the young hopeful of the clan Molloy and it was small wonder that Tony Timson took great exception to his wife putting on her leatherette trousers for the purpose of meeting the family enemy.

Liz Probert, however, a white-wig at the Bar who knew nothing of such old legal traditions as the Molloy–Timson hostility, said, 'Why should Mrs Timson's meeting Molloy make it all right to drown her?' I have to remind you that Mizz Liz was a pillar of the North Islington women's movement.

'It wasn't just that she was meeting him, Mr Rumpole,' Tony explained. 'It was the words she used.'

'What did she say?'

'I'd rather not tell you if you don't mind. It was humiliating to my pride.'

'Oh, for heaven's sake, Tony. Let's hear the worst.' I had never known a Timson behave so coyly.

'She made a comparison like, between me and Peanuts.'

'What comparison?'

Tony looked at Liz and his voice sank to a whisper. 'Ladies present,' he said.

'Tony,' I had to tell him, 'Mizz Liz Probert has not only practised in the criminal courts, but in the family division. She is active on behalf of gay and lesbian rights in her native Islington. She marches, quite often, in aid of abortion on demand. She is a regular reader of the woman's page of the *Guardian*. You and I, Tony, need have no secrets from Mizz Probert. Now, what was this comparison your wife made between you and Peanuts Molloy?'

'On the topic of virility. I'm sorry, Miss.'

'That's quite all right.' Liz Probert was unshocked and un-amused.

* See 'Rumpole's Last Case' in *Rumpole's Last Case*, Penguin Books, 1987.

'What we need, I don't know if you would agree, Mr Rumpole,' Mr Bernard suggested, 'is a predominance of *men* on the Jury.'

'Underendowed males would condone the attempted murder of a woman, you mean?' The Probert hackles were up.

'Please. Mizz Probert.' I tried to call the meeting to order. 'Let us face this problem in a spirit of detachment. What we need is a sympathetic judge who doesn't want to waste his time on a long case. Have we got a fixed date for this, Mr Bernard?'

'We have, sir. Before the Red Judge.' Mr Bernard meant that Tony Timson was to be tried before the High Court judge visiting the Old Bailey.

'They're pulling out all the stops.' I was impressed.

'It *is* attempted murder, Mr Rumpole. So we're fixed before Mr Justice Featherstone.'

'Guthrie Featherstone.' I thought about it. 'Our one-time Head of Chambers. Now, I just wonder . . .'

We were in luck. Sir Guthrie Featherstone was in no mood to try a long case, so he summoned me and Counsel for the Prosecution to his room before the start of the proceedings. He sat robed but with his wig on the desk in front of him, a tall, elegant figure who almost always wore the slightly hunted expression of a man who's not entirely sure what he's up to – an unfortunate state of mind for a fellow who has to spend his waking hours coming to firm and just decisions. For all his indecision, however, he knew for certain that he didn't want to spend the whole day trying a ticklish attempted murder.

'Is this a long case?' the Judge asked. 'I am bidden to take tea in the neighbourhood of Victoria. Can you fellows guess where?'

'Sorry, Judge. I give up.' Charles Hearthstoke, our serious-minded young prosecutor, seemed in no mood for party games.

'The station buffet?' I hazarded a guess.

'The station buffet!' Guthrie enjoyed the joke. 'Isn't that you all over, Horace? You will have your joke. Not far off, though.' The joke was over and he went on impressively. 'Buck House. Her Majesty has invited me – no, correction – "commanded" me to a Royal Garden Party.'

'God Save The Queen!' I murmured loyally.

'Not only Her Majesty,' Guthrie told us, 'more seriously one's lady wife, would be extremely put out if one didn't parade in grey top-hat order!'

'He's blaming it on his wife!' Liz Probert, who had followed me into the presence, said in a penetrating aside.

'So naturally one would have to be free by lunch-time. Hearth-stoke, is this a long case from the prosecution point of view?' the Judge asked.

'It is an extremely serious case, Judge.' Our prosecutor spoke like a man of twice his years. 'Attempted murder. We've put it down for a week.' I have always thought young Charlie Hearth-stoke a mega-sized pill ever since he joined our Chambers for a blessedly brief period and tried to get everything run by a computer.*

'I'm astonished,' I gave Guthrie a little comfort, 'that my learned friend Mr Hearthrug should think it could possibly last so long.'

'Hearth*stoke*,' young Charlie corrected me.

'Have it your own way. With a bit of common sense we could finish this in half an hour.'

'Thereby saving public time and money.' Hope sprang eternal in the Judge's breast.

'Exactly!' I cheered him up. 'As you know, it is an article of my religion never to plead guilty. But, bearing in mind all the facts in this case, I'm prepared to advise Timson to put his hands up to common assault. He'll agree to be bound over to keep the peace.'

'Common assault?' Hearthstoke was furious. 'Binding over? Hold on a minute. He tried to drown her!'

'Judge.' I put the record straight. 'He was seated at the tap end of the bath. His wife, lying back comfortably in the depths, passed an extremely wounding remark about my client's virility.'

It was then I saw Mr Justice Featherstone looking at me,

---

* See 'Rumpole and the Judge's Elbow' in *Rumpole's Last Case*, Penguin Books, 1987.

apparently shaken to the core. 'The *tap end*,' he gasped. 'Did you say he was seated at the *tap end*, Horace?'

'I'm afraid so, Judge.' I confirmed the information sorrowfully.

'This troubles me.' Indeed the Judge looked extremely troubled. 'How does it come about that he was seated at the tap end?'

'His wife insisted on it.' I had to tell him the full horror of the situation.

'This woman insisted that her husband sat with his back squashed up against the taps?' The Judge's voice rose in incredulous outrage.

'She made him sit in that position so he could rinse off her hair.'

'At the *tap end*?' Guthrie still couldn't quite believe it.

'Exactly so.'

'You're sure?'

'There can be no doubt about it.'

'Hearthrug . . . I mean, *stoke*. Is this one of the facts agreed by the Prosecution?'

'I can't see that it makes the slightest difference.' The Prosecution was not pleased with the course its case was taking.

'You can't see! Horace, was this conduct in any way typical of this woman's attitude to her husband?'

'I regret to say, entirely typical.'

'Rumpole . . .' Liz Probert, appalled by the chauvinist chatter around her, seemed about to burst, and I calmed her with a quiet 'Shut up, Mizz.'

'So you are telling me that this husband deeply resented the position in which he found himself.' Guthrie was spelling out the implications exactly as I had hoped he would.

'What married man wouldn't, Judge?' I asked mournfully.

'And his natural resentment led to a purely domestic dispute?'

'Such as might occur, Judge, in the best bathrooms.'

'And you are content to be bound over to keep the peace?' His Lordship looked at me with awful solemnity.

'Reluctantly, Judge,' I said after a suitable pause for contemplation, 'I would agree to that restriction on my client's liberty.'

'Liberty to drown his wife!' Mizz Probert had to be 'shushed' again.

'Hearth*stoke*.' The Judge spoke with great authority. 'My compliments to those instructing you and in my opinion it would be a gross waste of public funds to continue with this charge of attempted murder. We should be finished by half past eleven.' He looked at his watch with the deep satisfaction of a man who was sure that he would be among those present at the Royal Garden Party, after the ritual visit to Moss Bros to hire the grey topper and all the trimmings. As we left the sanctum, I stood aside to let Mizz Probert out of the door. 'Oh, no, Rumpole, you're a man,' she whispered with her fury barely contained. 'Men always go first, don't they?'

So we all went into Court to polish off *R. v. Timson* and to make sure that Her Majesty had the pleasure of Guthrie's presence over the tea and strawberries. I made a token speech in mitigation, something of a formality as I knew that I was pushing at an open door. Whilst I was speaking, I was aware of the fact that the Judge wasn't giving me his full attention. That was reserved for a new young shorthand writer, later to become known to me as a Miss (not, I'm sure in her case, a Mizz) Lorraine Frinton. Lorraine was what I believe used to be known as a 'bit of an eyeful', being young, doe-eyed and clearly surrounded by her own special fragrance. When I sat down, Guthrie thanked me absent-mindedly and reluctantly gave up the careful perusal of Miss Frinton's beauty. He then proceeded to pass sentence on Tony Timson in a number of peculiarly ill-chosen words.

'Timson,' his Lordship began harmlessly enough. 'I have heard about you and your wife's habit of taking a bath together. It is not for this Court to say that communal bathing, in time of peace when it is not in the national interest to save water, is appropriate conduct in married life. *Chacun à son goût*, as a wise Frenchman once said.' Miss Frinton, the shorthand writer, looked hopelessly confused by the words of the wise Frenchman. 'What throws a flood of light on this case,' the Judge went on, 'is that you, Timson, habitually sat at the tap end of the bath. It seems you had a great deal to put up with. And your wife, she, it appears from the evidence, washed her hair in the more placid waters of the other end. I accept that this was a purely domestic dispute. For the common assault to which you have pleaded guilty you will be bound over to keep the peace ...' And the Judge added the terrible words, '... in the sum of fifty pounds.'

So Tony Timson was at liberty, the case was over and a furious Mizz Liz Probert banged out of Court before Guthrie was half way out of the door. Catching up with her, I rebuked my learned Junior. 'It's not in the best traditions of the Bar to slam out before the Judge in any circumstances. When we've just had a famous victory it's quite ridiculous.'

'A famous victory.' She laughed in a cynical fashion. 'For men!'

'Man, woman or child, it doesn't matter who the client is. We did our best and won.'

'Because he was a man! Why shouldn't he sit at the tap end? I've got to do something about it!' She moved away purposefully. I called after her. 'Mizz Probert! Where're you going?'

'To my branch of the women's movement. The protest's got to be organized on a national level. I'm sorry, Rumpole. The time for talking's over.'

And she was gone. I had no idea, then, of the full extent of the tide which was about to overwhelm poor old Guthrie Feather-stone, but I had a shrewd suspicion that his Lordship was in serious trouble.

The Featherstones' two children were away at university, and Guthrie and Marigold occupied a flat which Lady Featherstone found handy for Harrods, her favourite shopping centre, and a country cottage near Newbury. Marigold Featherstone was a handsome woman who greatly enjoyed life as a judge's wife and was full of that strength of character and quickness of decision his Lordship so conspicuously lacked. They went to the Garden Party together with three or four hundred other pillars of the establishment: admirals, captains of industry, hospital matrons and drivers of the Royal Train. Picture them, if you will, safely back home with Marigold kicking off her shoes on the sofa and Guthrie going out to the hall to fetch that afternoon's copy of the *Evening Sentinel*, which had just been delivered. You must, of course, understand that I was not present at the scene or other similar scenes which are necessary to this narrative. I can only do my best to reconstruct it from what I know of subsequent events and what the participants told me afterwards. Any gaps I have been able to fill in are thanks to the talent for fiction which I have acquired during a long career acting for the Defence in criminal cases.

'There might just be a picture of us arriving at the Palace.' Guthrie brought back the *Sentinel* and then stood in horror, rooted to the spot by what he saw on the front page.

'Well, then. Bring it in here.' Marigold, no doubt, called from her reclining position.

'Oh, there's absolutely nothing to read in it. The usual non-sense. Nothing of the slightest interest. Well, I think I'll go and have a bath and get changed.' And he attempted to sidle out of the room, holding the newspaper close to his body in a manner which made the contents invisible to his wife.

'Why're you trying to hide that *Evening Sentinel*, Guthrie?'

'Hide it? Of course I'm not trying to hide it. I just thought I'd take it to read in the bath.'

'And make it all soggy? Let me have it, Guthrie.'

'I told you . . .'

'Guthrie. I want to see what's in the paper.' Marigold spoke in an authoritative manner and her husband had no alternative but to hand it over, murmuring the while, 'It's completely inaccurate, of course.'

And so Lady Featherstone came to read, under a large photograph of his Lordship in a full-bottomed wig, the story which was being enjoyed by every member of the legal profession in the Greater London area. CARRY ON DROWNING screamed the banner headline. TAP END JUDGE'S AMAZING DECISION. And then came the full denunciation:

Wives who share baths with their husbands will have to be careful where they sit in the future. Because 29-year-old April Timson of Bexley Heath made her husband Tony sit at the tap end the Judge dismissed a charge of attempted murder against him. 'It seems you had a good deal to put up with,' 55-year-old Mr Justice Feather-stone told Timson, a 36-year-old window cleaner. 'This is male

*chauvinism gone mad,' said a spokesperson of the Islington Women's
Organization. 'There will be protests up and down the country and
questions asked in Parliament. No woman can sit safely in her bath
while this Judge continues on the bench.'*

'It's a travesty of what I said, Marigold. You know exactly
what these Court reporters are. Head over heels in Guinness
after lunch.' Guthrie no doubt told his wife.

'This must have been in the morning. We went to the Palace
after lunch.'

'Well, anyway. It's a travesty.'

'What do you mean, Guthrie? Didn't you say all that about the
tap end?'

'Well, I may just have mentioned the tap end. Casually. In
passing. Horace told me it was part of the evidence.'

'Horace?'

'Rumpole.'

'I suppose he was defending.'

'Well, yes . . .'

'You're clay in the hands of that little fellow, Guthrie. You're
a Red Judge and he's only a Junior, but he can twist you round
his little finger,' I rather hope she told him.

'You think Horace Rumpole led me up the garden?'

'Of course he did! He got his chap off and he encouraged you
to say something monumentally stupid about tap ends. Not, I
suppose, that you needed much encouragement.'

'This gives an entirely false impression. I'll put it right, Marigold. I promise you. I'll see it's put right.'

'I think you'd better, Guthrie.' The Judge's wife, I knew, was
not a woman to mince her words. 'And for heaven's sake try not
to put your foot in it again.'

So Guthrie went off to soothe his troubles up to the neck in
bath water and Marigold lay brooding on the sofa until, so she
told Hilda later, she was telephoned by the Tom Creevey Diary
Column on the *Sentinel* with an inquiry as to which end of the
bath she occupied when she and her husband were at their ablu-
tions. Famous couples all over London, she was assured, were
being asked the same question. Marigold put down the instru-

ment without supplying any information, merely murmuring to herself, 'Guthrie! What have you done to us now?'

Marigold Featherstone wasn't the only wife appalled by the Judge's indiscretions. As I let myself in to our mansion flat in the Gloucester Road, Hilda, as was her wont, called to me from the living-room, 'Who's that?'

'I am thy father's spirit,' I told her in sepulchral tones.

> 'Doomed for a certain term to walk the night,
> And for the day confined to fast in fires,
> Till the foul crimes done in my days of nature
> Are burnt and purged away.'

'I suppose you think it's perfectly all right.' She was, I noticed, reading the *Evening Sentinel*.

'What's perfectly all right?'

'Drowning wives!' She said in the unfriendliest of tones. 'Like puppies. I suppose you think that's all perfectly understandable. Well, Rumpole, all I can say is, you'd better not try anything like that with me!'

'Hilda! It's never crossed my mind. Anyway, Tony Timson didn't drown her. He didn't come anywhere near drowning her. It was just a matrimonial tiff in the bathroom.'

'Why should *she* have to sit at the tap end?'

'Why indeed?' I made for the sideboard and a new bottle of Pommeroy's plonk. 'If she had, and if she'd tried to drown him because of it, I'd have defended her with equal skill and success. There you are, you see. Absolutely no prejudice when it comes to accepting a brief.'

'You think men and women are entirely equal?'

'Everyone is equal in the dock.'

'And in the home?'

'Well, yes, Hilda. Of course. Naturally. Although I suppose some are born to command.' I smiled at her in what I hoped was a soothing manner, well designed to unruffle her feathers, and took my glass of claret to my habitual seat by the gas fire. 'Trust me, Hilda,' I told her. 'I shall always be a staunch defender of Women's Rights.'

'I'm glad to hear that.'

'I'm glad you're glad.'

'That means you can do the weekly shop for us at Safeways.'

'Well, I'd really love that, Hilda,' I said eagerly. 'I should regard that as the most tremendous fun. Unfortunately I have to earn the boring stuff that pays for our weekly shop. I have to be at the service of my masters.'

'Husbands who try to drown their wives?' she asked unpleasantly.

'And vice versa.'

'They have late-night shopping on Thursdays, Rumpole. It won't cut into your work-time at all. Only into your drinking time in Pommeroy's Wine Bar. Besides which I shall be far too busy for shopping from now on.'

'Why, Hilda? What on earth are you planning to do?' I asked innocently. And when the answer came I knew the sexual revolution had hit Froxbury Mansions at last.

'Someone has to stand up for Women's Rights,' Hilda told me, 'against the likes of you and Guthrie Featherstone. I shall read for the Bar.'

Such was the impact of the decision in *R. v. Timson* on life in the Rumpole home. When Tony Timson was sprung from custody he was not taken lovingly back into the bosom of his family. April took her baths alone and frequently left the house tricked out in her skin-tight, wet-look trousers and the exotic halterneck. When Tony made so bold as to ask where she was going, she told him to mind his own business. Vincent, the young hopeful, also treated his father with scant respect and, when asked where he was off to on his frequent departures from the front door, also told his father to mind his own business.

When she was off on the spree, April Timson, it later transpired, called round to an off licence in neighbouring Morrison Avenue. There she met the notorious Peanuts Molloy, also dressed in alluring leather, who was stocking up from Ruby, the large black lady who ran the 'offey', with raspberry crush, Champanella, crème de cacao and three-star cognac as his contribution to some party or other. He and April would embrace openly and then go off partying together. On occasion Peanuts would ask her how 'that wally of a husband' was getting on, and express his outrage at the lightness of the sentence inflicted on him. 'Someone ought to give that Tony of yours a bit of justice,' was what he was heard to say.

Peanuts Molloy wasn't alone in feeling that being bound over in the sum of fifty pounds wasn't an adequate punishment for the attempted drowning of a wife. This view was held by most of the newspapers, a large section of the public, and all the members of the North Islington Women's Movement (Chair, Mizz Liz Probert). When Guthrie arrived for business at the Judge's entrance of the Old Bailey, he was met by a vociferous posse of women, bearing banners with the following legend: WOMEN OF ENGLAND, KEEP YOUR HEADS ABOVE WATER. GET JUSTICE FEATHERSTONE SACKED. As the friendly police officers kept these angry ladies at bay, Guthrie took what comfort he might from the thought that a High Court judge can only be dismissed by a Bill passed through both Houses of Parliament.

Something, he decided, would have to be done to answer his many critics. So Guthrie called Miss Lorraine Frinton, the doe-eyed shorthand writer, into his room and did his best to correct the record of his ill-considered judgment. Miss Frinton, breathtakingly decorative as ever, sat with her long legs neatly crossed in the Judge's armchair and tried to grasp his intentions with regard to her shorthand note. I reconstruct this conversation thanks to Miss Frinton's later recollection. She was, she admits, very nervous at the time because she thought that the Judge had sent for her because she had, in some way, failed in her duties. 'I've been living in dread of someone pulling me up about my shorthand,' she confessed. 'It's not my strongest suit, quite honestly.'

'Don't worry, Miss Frinton,' Guthrie did his best to reassure her. 'You're in no sort of trouble at all. But you are a shorthand writer, of course you are, and if we could just get to the point when I passed sentence. Could you read it out?'

The beautiful Lorraine looked despairingly at her notebook and spelled out, with great difficulty, 'Mr Hearthstoke has quite wisely . . .'

'A bit further on.'

'Jackie a saw goo . . . a wise Frenchman . . .' Miss Frinton was decoding.

'*Chacun à son goût!*'

'I'm sorry, my Lord. I didn't quite get the name.'

'*Ça ne fait rien.*'

'How are you spelling that?' She was now lost.

'Never mind.' The Judge was at his most patient. 'A little further on, Miss Frinton. Lorraine. I'm sure you and I can come to an agreement. About a full stop.'

After much hard work, his Lordship had his way with Miss Frinton's shorthand note, and Counsel and solicitors engaged in the case were assembled in Court to hear, in the presence of the gentlemen of the Press, his latest version of his unfortunate judgment.

'I have had my attention drawn to the report of the case in *The Times*,' he started with some confidence, 'in which I am quoted as saying to Timson, "It seems you had a great deal to put up with. And your wife, she, it appears from the evidence, washed her hair in the more placid waters" etc. It's the full stop that has been misplaced. I have checked this carefully with the learned shorthand writer and she agrees with me. I see her nodding her head.' He looked down at Lorraine who nodded energetically, and the Judge smiled at her. 'Very well, yes. The sentence in my judgment in fact read "It seems you had a great deal to put up with, and your wife." Full stop! What I intended to convey, and I should like the Press to take note of this, was that both Mr and Mrs Timson had a good deal to put up with. At different ends of the bath, of course. Six of one and half a dozen of the other. I hope that's clear?' It was, as I whispered to Mizz Probert sitting beside me, as clear as mud.

The Judge continued. 'I certainly never said that I regarded being seated at the tap end as legal provocation to attempted murder. I would have said it was one of the facts that the Jury might have taken into consideration. It might have thrown some light on this wife's attitude to her husband.'

'What's he trying to do?' *sotto voce* Hearthstoke asked me.

'Trying to get himself out of hot water,' I suggested.

'But the attempted murder charge was dropped,' Guthrie went on.

'He twisted my arm to drop it,' Hearthstoke was muttering.

'And the entire tap end question was really academic,' Guthrie told us, 'as Timson pleaded guilty to common assault. Do you agree, Mr Rumpole?'

'Certainly, my Lord.' I rose in my most servile manner. 'You gave him a very stiff binding over.'

'Have you anything to add, Mr Hearthstoke?'

'No, my Lord.' Hearthstoke couldn't very well say anything else, but when the Judge had left us he warned me that Tony Timson had better watch his step in future as Detective Inspector Brush was quite ready to throw the book at him.

Guthrie Featherstone left Court well pleased with himself and instructed his aged and extremely disloyal clerk, Wilfred, to send a bunch of flowers, or, even better, a handsome pot plant to Miss Lorraine Frinton in recognition of her loyal services. So Wilfred told me he went off to telephone Interflora and Guthrie passed his day happily trying a perfectly straightforward robbery. On rising he retired to his room for a cup of weak Lapsang and a glance at the *Evening Sentinel*. This glance was enough to show him that he had achieved very little more, by his statement in open Court, than inserting his foot into the mud to an even greater depth.

BATHTUB JUDGE SAYS IT AGAIN screamed the headline. *Putting her husband at the tap end may be a factor to excuse the attempted murder of a wife.* 'Did I say that?' the appalled Guthrie asked old Wilfred who was busy pouring out the tea.

'To the best of my recollection, my Lord. Yes.'

There was no comfort for Guthrie when the telephone rang. It was old Keith from the Chancellor's office saying that the Lord Chancellor, as Head of the Judiciary, would like to see Mr Justice Featherstone at the earliest available opportunity.

'A Bill through the Houses of Parliament.' A stricken Guthrie put down the telephone. 'Would they do it to me, Wilfred?' he asked, but answer came there none.

'You do look, my clerk, in a moved sort, as if you were dismayed.' In fact, Henry, when I encountered him in the clerk's room, seemed distinctly rattled. 'Too right, sir. I am dismayed. I've just had Mrs Rumpole on the telephone.'

'Ah. She Who Must wanted to speak to me?'

'No, Mr Rumpole. She wanted to speak to me. She said I'd be clerking for her in the fullness of time.'

'Henry,' I tried to reassure the man, 'there's no immediate cause for concern.'

'She said as she was reading for the Bar, Mr Rumpole, to make sure women get a bit of justice in the future.'

'Your missus coming into Chambers, Rumpole?' Uncle Tom, our oldest and quite briefless inhabitant, was pursuing his usual hobby of making approach shots to the waste-paper basket with an old putter.

'Don't worry, Uncle Tom.' I sounded as confident as I could. 'Not in the foreseeable future.'

'My motto as a barrister's clerk, sir, is anything for a quiet life,' Henry outlined his philosophy. 'I have to say that my definition of a quiet life does not include clerking for Mrs Hilda Rumpole.'

'Old Sneaky MacFarlane in Crown Office Row had a missus who came into his Chambers.' Uncle Tom was off down Memory Lane. 'She didn't come in to practice, you understand. She came in to watch Sneaky. She used to sit in the corner of his room and knit during all his conferences. It seems she was dead scared he was going to get off with one of his female divorce petitioners.'

'Mrs Rumpole, Henry, has only just written off for a legal course in the Open University. She can't yet tell provocation from self defence or define manslaughter.' I went off to collect things from my tray and Uncle Tom missed a putt and went on with his story. 'And you know what? In the end Mrs MacFarlane went off with a co-respondent she'd met at one of these conferences. Some awful fellow, apparently, in black and white shoes! Left poor old Sneaky high and dry. So, you see, it doesn't do to have wives in Chambers.'

'Oh, I meant to ask you, Henry. Have you seen my Ackerman on *The Causes of Death*?' One of my best-loved books had gone missing.

'I think Mr Ballard's borrowed it, sir.' And then Henry asked, still anxious, 'How long do they take then, those courses at the Open University?'

'Years, Henry,' I told him. 'It's unlikely to finish during our lifetime.'

When I went up to Ballard's room to look for my beloved Ackerman, the door had been left a little open. Standing in the corridor I could hear the voices of those arch-conspirators, Claude Erskine-Brown and Soapy Sam Ballard, Q.C. I have to confess that I lingered to catch a little of the dialogue.

'Keith from the Lord Chancellor's office sounded *you* out about Guthrie Featherstone?' Erskine-Brown was asking.

'As the fellow who took over his Chambers. He thought I might have a view.'

'And have you? A view, I mean.'

'I told Keith that Guthrie was a perfectly charming chap, of course.' Soapy Sam was about to damn Guthrie with the faintest of praise.

'Oh, perfectly charming. No doubt about that,' Claude agreed.

'But as a judge, perhaps, he lacks judgment.'

'Which is a pretty important quality in a judge,' Claude thought.

'Exactly. And perhaps there is some lack of . . .'

'Gravitas?'

'The very word I used, Claude.'

'There was a bit of lack of gravitas in Chambers, too,' Claude remembered, 'when Guthrie took a shine to a temporary typist . . .'

'So the upshot of my talk with Keith was . . .'

'What was the upshot?'

'I think we may be seeing a vacancy on the High Court Bench.' Ballard passed on the sad news with great satisfaction. 'And old Keith was kind enough to drop a rather interesting hint.'

'Tell me, Sam?'

'He said they might be looking for a replacement from the same stable.'

'Meaning these Chambers in Equity Court?'

'How could it mean anything else?'

'Sam, if you go on the Bench, we should need another silk in Chambers!' Claude was no doubt licking his lips as he considered the possibilities.

'I don't see how they could refuse you.' These two were clearly hand in glove.

'There's no doubt Guthrie'll have to go.' Claude pronounced the death sentence on our absent friend.

'He comes out with such injudicious remarks.' Soapy Sam put in another drop of poison. 'He was just like that at Marlborough.'

'Did you tell old Keith that?' Claude asked and then sat open-mouthed as I burst from my hiding-place with 'I bet you did!'

'Rumpole!' Ballard also looked put out. 'What on earth have you been doing?'

'I've been listening to the Grand Conspiracy.'

'You must admit, Featherstone J. has made the most tremendous boo-boo.' Claude smiled as though he had never made a boo-boo in his life.

'In the official view,' Soapy Sam told me, 'he's been remarkably stupid.'

'He wasn't stupid.' I briefed myself for Guthrie's defence. 'As a matter of fact he understood the case extremely well. He came to a wise decision. He might have phrased his judgment more elegantly, if he hadn't been to Marlborough. And let me tell you something, Ballard. My wife, Hilda, is about to start a law course at the Open University. She is a woman, as I know to my cost, of grit and determination. I expect to see her Lord Chief Justice of England before you get your bottom within a mile of the High Court Bench!'

'Of course you're entitled to your opinion.' Ballard looked tolerant. 'And you got your fellow off. All I know for certain is that the Lord Chancellor has summoned Guthrie Featherstone to appear before him.'

The Lord Chancellor of England was a small, fat, untidy man with steel-rimmed spectacles which gave him the schoolboy look which led to his nickname 'The Owl of the Remove'. He was given to fits of teasing when he would laugh aloud at his own jokes and unpredictable bouts of biting sarcasm during which he would stare at his victims with cold hostility. He had been, for many years, the Captain of the House of Lords croquet team, a game in which his ruthless cunning found full scope. He received Guthrie in his large, comfortably furnished room overlooking the Thames at Westminster, where his long wig was waiting on its stand and his gold-embroidered purse and gown were ready for his procession to the woolsack. Two years after this confrontation, I found myself standing with Guthrie at a Christmas party given in our Chambers to members past and present, and he was so far gone in *Brut* (not to say Brutal) Pommeroy's *Méthode Champenoise* as to give me the bare bones of this historic encounter. I have fleshed them out from my knowledge of both characters and their peculiar habits of speech.

'Judgeitis, Featherstone,' I hear the Lord Chancellor saying. 'It goes with piles as one of the occupational hazards of the judicial profession. Its symptoms are pomposity and self-regard. It shows itself by unnecessary interruptions during the proceedings or giving utterance to private thoughts far, far better left unspoken.'

'I did correct the press report, Lord Chancellor, with reference to the shorthand writer.' Guthrie tried to sound convincing.

'Oh, I read that.' The Chancellor was unimpressed. 'Far better to have left the thing alone. Never give the newspapers a second chance. That's my advice to you.'

'What's the cure for judgeitis?' Guthrie asked anxiously.

'Banishment to a golf club where the sufferer may bore the other members to death with recollections of his old triumphs on the Western Circuit.'

'You mean, a Bill through two Houses of Parliament?' The Judge stared into the future, dismayed.

'Oh, that's quite unnecessary!' The Chancellor laughed mirthlessly. 'I just get a Judge in this room and say, "Look here, old fellow. You've got it badly. Judgeitis. The Press is after your blood and quite frankly you're a profound embarrassment to us all. Go out to Esher, old boy," I say, "and improve your handicap. I'll give it out that you're retiring early for reasons of health." And then I'll make a speech defending the independence of the Judiciary against scurrilous and unjustified attacks by the Press.'

Guthrie thought about this for what seemed a silent eternity and then said, 'I'm not awfully keen on golf.'

'Why not take up croquet?' The Chancellor seemed anxious to be helpful. 'It's a top-hole retirement game. The women of England are against you. I hear they've been demonstrating outside the Old Bailey.'

'They were only a few extremists.'

'Featherstone, all women are extremists. You must know that, as a married man.'

'I suppose you're right, Lord Chancellor.' Guthrie now felt his position to be hopeless. 'Retirement! I don't know how Marigold's going to take it.'

The Lord Chancellor still looked like a hanging judge, but he stood up and said in businesslike tones, 'Perhaps it can be postponed in your case. I've talked it over with old Keith.'

'Your right-hand man?' Guthrie felt a faint hope rising.

'Exactly.' The Lord Chancellor seemed to be smiling at some private joke. 'You may have an opportunity some time in the future, in the not-too-distant future, let us hope, to make your peace with the women of England. You may be able to put right what they regard as an injustice to one of their number.'

'You mean, Lord Chancellor, my retirement is off?' Guthrie could scarcely believe it.

'Perhaps adjourned. *Sine die.*'

'Indefinitely?'

'Oh, I'm so glad you keep up with your Latin.' The Chancellor patted Guthrie on the shoulder. It was an order to dismiss. 'So many fellows don't.'

So Guthrie had a reprieve and, in the life of Tony Timson also, dramatic events were taking place. April's friend Chrissie was once married to Shaun Molloy, a well-known safe breaker, but their divorce seemed to have severed her connections with the Molloy clan and Tony Timson had agreed to receive and visit her. It was Chrissie who lived on their estate and had given the party before which April and Tony had struggled in the bath together; but it was at Chrissie's house, it seemed, that Peanuts Molloy was to be a visitor. So Tony's friendly feelings had somewhat abated, and when Chrissie rang the chimes on his front door one afternoon when April was out, he received her with a brusque 'What you want?'

'I thought you ought to know, Tony. It's not right.'

'What's not right?'

'Your April and Peanuts. It's not right.'

'You're one to talk, aren't you, Chrissie? April was going round yours to meet Peanuts at a party.'

'He just keeps on coming to mine. I don't invite him. Got no time for Peanuts, quite honestly. But him and your April. They're going out on dates. It's not right. I thought you ought to know.'

'What you mean, dates?' As I have said, Tony's life had not been a bed of roses since his return home, but now he was more than usually troubled.

'He takes her out partying. They're meeting tonight round the offey in Morrison Avenue. Nine thirty time, she told me. Just thought you might like to know, that's all,' the kindly Chrissie added.

So it happened that at nine thirty that night, when Ruby was presiding over an empty off licence in Morrison Avenue, Tony Timson entered it and stood apparently surveying the tempting bottles on display but really waiting to confront the errant April and Peanuts Molloy. He heard a door bang in some private area behind Ruby's counter and then the strip lights stopped humming and the off licence was plunged into darkness. It was not a silent darkness, however; it was filled with the sound of footsteps, scuffling and heavy blows.

Not long afterwards a police car with a wailing siren was screaming towards Morrison Avenue; it was wonderful with what rapidity the Old Bill was summoned whenever Tony Timson was in trouble. When Detective Inspector Brush and his sergeant got into the off licence, their torches illuminated a scene of violence. Two bodies were on the floor. Ruby was lying by the counter, unconscious, and Tony was lying beside some shelves, nearer to the door, with a wound in his forehead. The Sergeant's torch beam showed a heavy cosh lying by his right hand and pound notes scattered around him. 'Can't you leave the women alone, boy?' the Detective Inspector said as Tony Timson slowly opened his eyes.

So another Timson brief came to Rumpole, and Mr Justice Featherstone got a chance to redeem himself in the eyes of the Lord Chancellor and the women of Islington.

Like two knights of old approaching each other for combat, briefs at the ready, helmeted with wigs and armoured with gowns, the young black-haired Sir Hearthrug and the cunning old Sir Horace, with his faithful page Mizz Liz in attendance, met outside Number One Court at the Old Bailey and threw down their challenges.

'Nemesis,' said Hearthrug.

'What's that meant to mean?' I asked him.

'Timson's for it now.'

'Let's hope justice will be done,' I said piously.

'Guthrie's not going to make the same mistake twice.'

'Mr Justice Featherstone's a wise and upright judge,' I told him, 'even if his foot does get into his mouth occasionally.'

'He's a judge with the Lord Chancellor's beady eye upon him, Rumpole.'

'I wasn't aware that this case was going to be decided by the Lord Chancellor.'

'By him and the women of England.' Hearthstoke smiled at Mizz Probert in what I hoped she found a revolting manner. 'Ask your learned Junior.'

'Save your breath for Court, Hearthrug. You may need it.' So we moved on, but as we went my learned Junior disappointed me by saying, 'I don't think Tony Timson should get away with it again.' 'Happily, that's not for you to decide,' I told her. 'We can leave that to the good sense of the Jury.'

However, the Jury, when we saw them assembled, were not a particularly cheering lot. For a start, the women outnumbered the men by eight to four and the women in question looked large and severe. I was at once reminded of the mothers' meetings that once gathered round the guillotine and I seemed to hear, as

Hearthstoke opened the prosecution case, the ghostly click of knitting needles.

His opening speech was delivered with a good deal of ferocity and he paused now and again to flash a white-toothed smile at Miss Lorraine Frinton, who sat once more, looking puzzled, in front of her shorthand notebook.

'Members of the Jury,' Hearthrug intoned with great solemnity. 'Even in these days, when we are constantly sickened by crimes of violence, this is a particularly horrible and distressing event. An attack with this dangerous weapon' – here he picked up the cosh, Exhibit One, and waved it at the Jury – 'upon a weak and defenceless woman.'

'Did you say a *woman*, Mr Hearthstoke?' Up spoke the anxious figure of the Red Judge upon the Bench. I cannot believe that pure chance had selected Guthrie Featherstone to preside over Tony Timson's second trial.

Our Judge clearly meant to redeem himself and appear, from the outset, as the dedicated protector of that sex which is sometimes called the weaker by those who have not the good fortune to be married to She Who Must Be Obeyed.

'I'm afraid so, my Lord,' Hearthstoke said, more in anger than in sorrow.

'This man Timson attacked a *woman*!' Guthrie gave the Jury the benefit of his full outrage. I had to put some sort of a stop to this so I rose to say, 'That, my Lord, is something the Jury has to decide.'

'Mr Rumpole,' Guthrie told me, 'I am fully aware of that. All I can say about this case is that should the Jury convict, I take an extremely serious view of any sort of attack on a woman.'

'If they were bathing it wouldn't matter,' I muttered to Liz as I subsided.

'I didn't hear that, Mr Rumpole.'

'Not a laughing matter, my Lord,' I corrected myself rapidly.

'Certainly not. Please proceed, Mr Hearth*stoke*.' And here his Lordship whispered to his clerk, Wilfred, 'I'm not having old Rumpole twist me round his little finger in *this* case.'

'Very wise, if I may say so, my Lord,' Wilfred whispered back as he sat beside the Judge, sharpening his pencils.

'Members of the Jury,' an encouraged Hearthstoke proceeded.
'Mrs Ruby Churchill, the innocent victim, works in an off licence
near the man Timson's home. Later we shall look at a plan of the
premises. The Prosecution does not allege that Timson carried
out this robbery alone. He no doubt had an accomplice who
entered by an open window at the back of the shop and turned
out the lights. Then, we say, under cover of darkness, Timson
coshed the unfortunate Mrs Churchill, whose evidence you will
hear. The accomplice escaped with most of the money from the
till. Timson, happily for justice, slipped and struck his head on
the corner of the shelves. He was found in a half-stunned condition, with the cosh and some of the money. When arrested by
Detective Inspector Brush he said, "You got me this time, then".
You may think that a clear admission of guilt.' And now Hearthstoke was into his peroration. 'Too long, Members of the Jury,'
he said, 'have women suffered in our Courts. Too long have men
seemed licensed to attack them. Your verdict in this case will be
awaited eagerly and hopefully by the women of England.'

I looked at Mizz Liz Probert and I was grieved to note that
she was receiving this hypocritical balderdash with starry-eyed
attention. During the mercifully short period when the egregious
Hearthrug had been a member of our Chambers in Equity Court, I
remembered, Mizz Liz had developed an inexplicably soft spot for
the fellow. I was pained to see that the spot remained as soft as ever.

Even as we sat in Number One Court, the Islington women
were on duty in the street outside bearing placards with the
legend JUSTICE FOR WOMEN. Claude Erskine-Brown and
Soapy Sam Ballard passed these demonstrators and smiled with
some satisfaction. 'Guthrie's in the soup again, Ballard,' Claude
told his new friend. 'They're taking to the streets!'

Ruby Churchill, large, motherly, and clearly anxious to tell
the truth, was the sort of witness it's almost impossible to cross-
examine effectively. When she had told her story to Hearthstoke,
I rose and felt the silent hostility of both Judge and Jury.

'Before you saw him in your shop on the night of this attack,'
I asked her, 'did you know my client, Mr Timson?'

'I knew him. He lives round the corner.'

'And you knew his wife, April Timson?'

'I know her. Yes.'

'She's been in your shop?'

'Oh, yes, sir.'

'With her husband?'

'Sometimes with him. Sometimes without.'

'Sometimes without? How interesting.'

'Mr Rumpole. Have you many more questions for this unfortunate lady?' Guthrie seemed to have been converted to the view that female witnesses shouldn't be subjected to cross-examination.

'Just a few, my Lord.'

'Please. Mrs Churchill,' his Lordship gushed at Ruby. 'Do take a seat. Make yourself comfortable. I'm sure we all admire the plucky way in which you are giving your evidence. *As a woman.*'

'And as a woman,' I made bold to ask, after Ruby had been offered all the comforts of the witness-box, 'did you know that Tony Timson had been accused of trying to drown his wife in the bath? And that he was tried and bound over?'

'My Lord. How can that possibly be relevant?' Hearthrug arose, considerably narked.

'I was about to ask the same question.' Guthrie sided with the Prosecution. 'I have no idea what Mr Rumpole is driving at!'

'Oh, I thought your Lordship might remember the case,' I said casually. 'There was some newspaper comment about it at the time.'

'Was there really?' Guthrie affected ignorance. 'Of course, in a busy life one can't hope to read every little paragraph about one's cases that finds its way into the newspapers.'

'This found its way slap across the front page, my Lord.'

'Did it really? Do you remember that, Mr Hearthstoke?'

'I think I remember some rather ill-informed comment, my Lord.' Hearthstoke was not above buttering up the Bench.

'Ill-informed. Yes. No doubt it was. One has so many cases before one . . .' As Guthrie tried to forget the past, I hastily drew the witness back into the proceedings. 'Perhaps your memory is better than his Lordship's?' I suggested to Ruby. 'You remember the case, don't you, Mrs Churchill?'

'Oh, yes. I remember it.' Ruby had no doubt.

'Mr Hearthstoke. Are you objecting to this?' Guthrie was looking puzzled.

'If Mr Rumpole wishes to place his client's previous convictions before the Jury, my Lord, why should I object?' Hearthstoke looked at me complacently, as though I were playing into his hands, and Guthrie whispered to Wilfred, 'Bright chap, this prosecutor.'

'And can you remember what you thought about it at the time?' I went on plugging away at Ruby.

'I thought Mr Timson had got away with murder!'

The Jury looked severely at Tony, and Guthrie appeared to think I had kicked a sensational own goal. 'I suppose that was hardly the answer you wanted, Mr Rumpole,' he said.

'On the contrary, my Lord. It was exactly the answer I wanted! And having got away with it then, did it occur to you that someone . . . some avenging angel, perhaps, might wish to frame Tony Timson on this occasion?'

'My lord. That is pure speculation!' Hearthstoke arose, furious, and I agreed with him. 'Of course it is. But it's a speculation I wish to put in the mind of the Jury at the earliest possible opportunity.' So I sat down, conscious that I had at least chipped away at the Jury's certainty. They knew that I should return to the possibility of Tony having been framed and were prepared to look at the evidence with more caution.

That morning two events of great pith and moment occurred in the case of the Queen against Tony Timson. April went shopping in Morrison Avenue and saw something which considerably changed her attitude. Peanuts Molloy and her friend Chrissie were coming out of the off licence with a plastic bag full of assorted bottles. As Peanuts held his car door open for Chrissie they engaged in a passionate and public embrace, unaware that they were doing so in the full view of Mrs April Timson, who uttered the single word 'Bastard!' in the hearing of the young hopeful Vincent who, being on his school holidays, was accompanying his mother. The other important matter was that Guthrie, apparently in a generous mood as he saw a chance of reestablishing his judicial reputation, sent a note to me and Hearth-stoke asking if we would be so kind as to join him, and the other judges sitting at the Old Bailey, for luncheon.

Guthrie's invitation came as Hearthstoke was examining Miss Sweating, the schoolmistress-like scientific officer, who was giving evidence as to the bloodstains found about the off licence on the night of the crime. As this evidence was of some import-ance I should record that blood of Tony Timson's group was traced on the floor and on the corner of the shelf by which he had fallen. Blood of the same group as that which flowed in Mrs Ruby Churchill's veins was to be found on the floor where she lay and on the cosh by Tony's hand. Talk of blood groups, as you will know, acts on me like the smell of greasepaint to an old actor, or the cry of hounds to John Peel. I was pawing the ground and snuffling a little at the nostrils as I rose to cross-examine.

'Miss Sweating,' I began. 'You say there was blood of Tim-son's group on the corner of the shelf?'

'There was. Yes.'

'And from that you assumed that he had hit his head against the shelf?'

'That seemed the natural assumption. He had been stunned by hitting his head.'

'Or by someone else hitting his head?'

'But the Detective Inspector told me . . .' the witness began, but I interrupted her with 'Listen to me and don't bother about what the Detective Inspector told you!'

'Mr Rumpole!' That grave protector of the female sex on the Bench looked pained. 'Is that the tone to adopt? The witness is a woman!'

'The witness is a scientific officer, my Lord,' I pointed out, 'who pretends to know something about bloodstains. Looking at the photograph of the stains on the corner of the shelf, Miss Sweating, might not they be splashes of blood which fell when the accused was struck in that part of the room?'

Miss Sweating examined the photograph in question through her formidable horn-rims and we were granted two minutes' silence which I broke into at last with 'Would you favour us with an answer, Miss Sweating? Or do you want to exercise a woman's privilege and not make up your mind?'

'Mr Rumpole!' The newly converted feminist judge was outraged. But the witness admitted, 'I suppose they might have got there like that. Yes.'

'They are consistent with his having been struck by an assailant. Perhaps with another weapon similar to this cosh?'

'Yes,' Miss Sweating agreed, reluctantly.

'Thank you. "Trip no further, pretty sweeting" . . .' I whispered as I sat down, thereby shocking the shockable Mizz Probert.

'Miss Sweating' – Guthrie tried to undo my good work – 'you have also said that the bloodstains on the shelf are consistent with Timson having slipped when he was running out of the shop and striking his head against it?'

'Oh, yes,' Miss Sweating agreed eagerly. 'They are consistent with that, my Lord.'

'Very well.' His Lordship smiled ingratiatingly at the women of the Jury. 'Perhaps the ladies of the Jury would like to take a little light luncheon now?' And he added, more brusquely, 'The gentlemen too, of course. Back at five past two, Members of the Jury.'

When we got out of Court, I saw my learned friend Charles Hearthstoke standing in the corridor in close conversation with the beautiful shorthand writer. He was, I noticed, holding her lightly and unobtrusively by the hand. Mizz Probert, who also noticed this, walked away in considerable disgust.

A large variety of judges sit at the Old Bailey. These include the Old Bailey regulars, permanent fixtures such as the Mad Bull Bullingham and the sepulchral Graves, judges of the lower echelon who wear black gowns. They also include a judge called the Common Sergeant, who is neither common nor a sergeant, and the Recorder who wears red and is the senior Old Bailey judge – a man who has to face, apart from the usual diet of murder, robbery and rape, a daunting number of City dinners. These are joined by the two visiting High Court judges, the Red Judges of the Queen's Bench, of whom Guthrie was one, unless

and until the Lord Chancellor decided to put him permanently
out to grass. All these judicial figures trough together at a single
long table in a back room of the Bailey. They do it, and the sight
comes as something of a shock to the occasional visitor, wearing
their wigs. The sight of Judge Bullingham's angry and purple
face ingesting stew and surmounted with horse-hair is only for
the strongest stomachs. They are joined by various City aldermen
and officials wearing lace jabots and tailed coats and other guests
from the Bar or from the world of business.

Before the serious business of luncheon begins, the company
is served sherry, also taken whilst wearing wigs, and I was ensconced in a corner where I could overhear a somewhat strange
preliminary conversation between our judge and Counsel for the
Prosecution.

'Ah, Hearth*stoke*,' Guthrie greeted him. 'I thought I'd invite
both Counsel to break bread with me. Just want to make sure
neither of you had anything to object to about the trial.'

'Of course not, Judge!' Hearthstoke was smiling. 'It's been a
very pleasant morning. Made even more pleasant by the appearance of the shorthand writer.'

'The . . .? Oh, yes! Pretty girl, is she? I hadn't noticed,' Guthrie
fibbed.

'Hadn't you? Lorraine said you'd been extraordinarily kind to
her. She so much appreciated the beautiful pot plant you sent
her.'

'Pot plant?' Guthrie looked distinctly guilty, but Hearthstoke
pressed on with 'Something rather gorgeous she told me. With
pink blooms. Didn't she help you straighten out the shorthand
note in the last Timson case?'

'She corrected her mistake,' Guthrie said carefully.

'*Her* mistake, was it?' Hearthstoke was looking at the Judge.
'She said it'd been yours.'

'Perhaps we should all sit down now.' Guthrie was keen to end
this embarrassing scene. 'Oh and, Hearthstoke, no need to mention that business of the pot plant around the Bailey. Otherwise
they'll all be wanting one.' He gave a singularly unconvincing
laugh. 'I can't give pink blooms to everyone, including Rumpole!'

'Of course, Judge.' Hearthstoke was understanding. 'No need to mention it at all *now*.'

'*Now?*'

'Now,' the Prosecutor said firmly, 'justice is going to be done to Timson. At last.'

Guthrie seemed thankful to move away and find his place at the table, until he discovered that I had been put next to him. He made the best of it, pushed one of the decanters in my direction and hoped I was quite satisfied with the fairness of the proceedings.

'Are *you* content with the fairness of the proceedings?' I asked him.

'Yes, of course. I'm the Judge, aren't I?'

'Are you sure?'

'What on earth's that meant to mean?'

'Haven't you asked yourself why you, a High Court judge, a Red Judge, have been given a paltry little robbery with violence?' I refreshed myself with a generous gulp of the City of London's claret.

'I suppose it's the luck of the draw.'

'Luck of the draw, my eye! I detect the subtle hand of old Keith from the Lord Chancellor's office.'

'Keith?' His Lordship looked around him nervously.

'Oh, yes. "Give Guthrie *Timson*," he said. "Give him a chance to redeem himself by potting the fellow and sending him down for ten years. The women of England will give three hearty cheers and Featherstone will be the Lord Chancellor's blue-eyed boy again." Don't fall for it! You can be better than that, if you put your mind to it. Sum up according to the evidence and the hell with the Lord Chancellor's office!'

'Horace! I don't think I've heard anything you've been saying.'

'It's up to you, old darling. Are you a man or a rubber stamp for the Civil Service?'

Guthrie looked round desperately for a new subject of conversation and his eye fell on our prosecutor who was being conspicuously bored by an elderly alderman. 'That young Hearthstoke seems a pretty able sort of fellow,' he said.

'Totally ruthless,' I told him. 'He'd stop at nothing to win a case.'

'Nothing?'

'Absolutely nothing.'

Guthrie took the decanter and started to pour wine into his own glass. His hand was trembling slightly and he was staring at Hearthstoke in a haunted way.

'Horace,' he started confidentially, 'you've been practising at the Old Bailey for a considerable number of years.'

'Almost since the dawn of time.'

'And you can see nothing wrong with a judge, impressed by the hard work of a court official, say a shorthand writer, for instance, sending that official some little token of gratitude?'

'What sort of token are you speaking óf, Judge?'

'Something like' – he gulped down wine – 'a pot plant.'

'A plant?'

'In a pot. With pink blossoms.'

'Pink blossoms, eh?' I thought it over. 'That sounds quite appropriate.'

'You can see nothing in any way improper in such a gift, Horace?' The Judge was deeply grateful.

'Nothing improper at all. A "Busy Lizzie"?'

'I think her name's Lorraine.'

'Nothing wrong with that.'

'You reassure me, Horace. You comfort me very much.' He took another swig of the claret and looked fearfully at Hearthstoke. Poor old Guthrie Featherstone, he spent most of his judicial life painfully perched between the horns of various dilemmas.

'In the car after we arrested him, driving away from the off licence, Tony Timson said, "You got me this time, then,"' This was the evidence of that hammer of the Timsons, Detective Inspector Brush. When he had given it, Hearthstoke looked hard at the Jury to emphasize the point, thanked the officer profusely and I rose to cross-examine.

'Detective Inspector. Do you know a near neighbour of the Timsons named Peter, better known as "Peanuts", Molloy?'

'Mr Peter Molloy is known to the police, yes,' the Inspector answered cautiously.

'He and his brother Greg are leading lights of the Molloy firm? Fairly violent criminals?'

'Yes, my Lord,' Brush told the Judge.

'Have you known both Peanuts and his brother to use coshes like this one in the course of crime?'

'Well. Yes, possibly . . .'

'My Lord, I really must object!' Hearthstoke was on his feet and Guthrie said, 'Mr Rumpole. Your client's own character . . .'

'He is a petty thief, my Lord.' I was quick to put Tony's character before the Jury. 'Tape-recorders and freezer-packs. No violence in his record, is there, Inspector?'

'Not up to now, my Lord,' Brush agreed reluctantly.

'Very well. Did you think he had been guilty of that attempted murder charge, after he and his wife quarrelled in the bathroom?'

'I thought so, yes.'

'You were called to the scene very quickly when the quarrel began.'

'A neighbour called us.'

'Was that neighbour a member of the Molloy family?'

'Mr Rumpole, I prefer not to answer that question.'

'I won't press it.' I left the Jury to speculate. 'But you think he got off lightly at his first trial?' I was reading the note Tony Timson had scribbled in the dock while listening to the evidence as D.I. Brush answered, 'I thought so, yes.'

'What he actually said in the car was "I suppose you think you got me this time, then?" '

'No.' Brush looked at his notebook. 'He just said, "You got me this time, then." '

'You left out the words "I suppose you think" because you don't want him to get off lightly this time?'

'Now would I do a thing like that, sir?' Brush gave us his most honestly pained expression.

'That, Inspector Brush, is a matter for this Jury to decide.' And the Jury looked, by now, as though they were prepared to consider all the possibilities.

*

Lord Justice MacWhitty's wife, it seems, met Marigold Featherstone in Harrods, and told her she was sorry that Guthrie had such a terrible attitude to women. There was one old judge, apparently, who made his wife walk behind him when he went on circuit, carrying the luggage, and Lady MacWhitty said she felt that poor Marigold was married to just such a tyrant. When we finally discussed the whole history of the Tony Timson case at the Chambers party, Guthrie told me that Marigold had said that she was sick and tired of women coming up to her and feeling sorry for her in Harrods.

'You see,' Guthrie had said to his wife, 'if Timson gets off, the Lord Chancellor and all the women of England will be down on me like a ton of bricks. But the evidence isn't entirely satisfactory. It's just possible he's innocent. It's hard to tell where a fellow's duty lies.'

'Your duty, Guthrie, lies in keeping your nose clean!' Marigold had no doubt about it.

'My nose?'

'Clean. For the sake of your family. And if this Timson has to go inside for a few years, well, I've no doubt he richly deserves it.'

'Nothing but decisions!'

'I really don't know what else you expected when you became a judge.' Marigold poured herself a drink. Seeking some comfort after a hard day, the Judge went off to soak in a hot bath. In doing so, I believe Lady Featherstone made it clear to him, he was entirely on his own.

Things were no easier in the Rumpole household. I was awakened at some unearthly hour by the wireless booming in the living-room and I climbed out of bed to see Hilda, clad in a dressing-gown and hairnet, listening to the device with her pencil and notebook poised whilst it greeted her brightly with 'Good morning, students. This is first-year Criminal Law on the Open University. I am Richard Snellgrove, law teacher at Hollowfield Polytechnic, to help you on this issue. . . . Can a wife give evidence against her husband?'

'Good God!' I asked her, 'what time does the Open University open?'

'For many years a wife could not give evidence against her

husband,' Snellgrove told us. 'See *R. v. Boucher* 1952. Now, since the Police and Criminal Evidence Act 1984, a wife can be called to give such evidence.'

'You see, Rumpole.' Hilda took a note. 'You'd better watch out!' I found and lit the first small cigar of the day and coughed gratefully. Snellgrove continued to teach me law. 'But she can't be compelled to. She has been a competent witness for the defence of her husband since the Criminal Evidence Act 1898. But a judgment in the House of Lords suggests she's not compellable . . .'

'What's that mean, Rumpole?' She asked me.

'Well, we could ask April Timson to give evidence for Tony. But we couldn't make her,' I began to explain, and then, perhaps because I was in a state of shock from being awoken so early, I had an idea of more than usual brilliance. 'April Timson!' I told Hilda, 'she won't know she's not compellable. I don't suppose she tunes into the "Open at Dawn University". Now I wonder . . .'

'What, Rumpole. What do you wonder?'

'Quarter to six.' I looked at the clock on the mantelpiece. 'High time to wake up Bernard.' I went to the phone and started to dial my instructing solicitor's number.

'You see how useful I'll be to you' – Hilda looked extremely pleased with herself – 'when I come to work in your Chambers.'

'Oh, Bernard,' I said to the telephone, 'wake you up, did I? Well, it's time to get moving. The Open University's been open for hours. Look, an idea has just crossed my mind . . .'

'It crossed *my* mind, Rumpole,' Hilda corrected me. 'And I was kind enough to hand it on to you.'

When Mr Bernard called on April Timson an hour later, there was no need for him to go into the nice legal question of whether she was a compellable witness or not. Since she had seen Peanuts and her friend Chrissie come out of the 'offey' she was, she made it clear, ready and willing to come to Court and tell her whole story.

'Mrs April Timson,' I asked Tony's wife when, to the surprise of most people in Court including my client, she entered the witness-box, as a witness for the defence, 'some while ago you had a quarrel with your husband in a bathtub. What was that quarrel about?'

'Peanuts Molloy.'

'About a man called Peter "Peanuts" Molloy. What did you tell your husband about Peanuts?'

'About him as a man, like. . . .?'

'Did you compare the virility of these two gentlemen?'

'Yes, I did.' April was able to cope with this part of the evidence without embarrassment.

'And who got the better of the comparison?'

'Peanuts.' Tony, lowering his head, got his first look of sympathy from the Jury.

'Was there a scuffle in your bath then?'

'Yes.'

'Mrs April Timson, did your husband ever try to drown you?'

'No. He never.' Her answer caused a buzz in Court. Guthrie stared at her, incredulous.

'Why did you suggest he did?' I asked. 'My Lord. I object. What possible relevance?' Hearthrug tried to interrupt but I and everyone else ignored him. 'Why did you suggest he tried to murder you?' I repeated.

'I was angry with him, I reckon,' April told us calmly, and the Prosecutor lost heart and subsided. The Judge, however, pursued the matter with a pained expression. 'Do I understand,' he asked, 'you made an entirely false accusation against your husband?'

'Yes.' April didn't seem to think it an unusual thing to do.

'Don't you realize, madam,' the Judge said, 'the suffering that accusation has brought to innocent people?' 'Such as you, old cock,' I muttered to Mizz Liz.

'What was that, Rumpole?' the Judge asked me. 'Such as the man in the dock, my Lord,' I repeated.

'And other innocent, innocent people.' His Lordship shook his head sadly and made a note.

'After your husband's trial did you continue to see Mr Peanuts Molloy?' I went on with my questions to the uncompellable witness.

'We went out together. Yes.'

'Where did you meet?'

'We met round the offey in Morrison Avenue. Then we went out in his car.'

'Did you meet him at the off licence on the night this robbery took place?'

'I never.' April was sure of it.

'Your husband says that your neighbour Chrissie came round and told him that you and Peanuts Molloy were going to meet at the off licence at nine thirty that evening. So he went up there to put a stop to your affair.'

'Well, Chrissie was well in with Peanuts by then, wasn't she?' April smiled cynically. 'I reckon he sent her to tell Tony that.'

'Why do you reckon he sent her?'

Hearthstoke rose again, determined. 'My Lord, I must object,' he said. 'What this witness "reckons" is entirely inadmissible.' When he had finished, I asked the Judge if I might have a word with my learned friend in order to save time. I then moved along our row and whispered to him vehemently, 'One more peep out of you, Hearthrug, and I lay a formal complaint on your conduct!'

'What conduct?' he whispered back.

'Trying to blackmail a learned judge on the matter of a pot plant sent to a shorthand writer.' I looked across at Lorraine. 'Not in the best traditions of the Bar, that!' I left him thinking hard and went back to my place. After due consideration he said, 'My Lord. On second thoughts, I withdraw my objection.'

Hearthstoke resumed his seat. I smiled at him cheerfully and continued with April's evidence. 'So why do you think Peanuts wanted to get your husband up to the off licence that evening?'

'Pretty obvious, innit?'

'Explain it to us.'

'So he could put him in the frame. Make it look like Tony done Ruby up, like.'

'So he could put him in the frame. An innocent man!' I looked at the Jury. 'Had Peanuts said anything to make you think he might do such a thing?'

'After the first trial.'

'After Mr Timson was bound over?'

'Yes. Peanuts said he reckoned Tony needed a bit of justice, like. He said he was going to see he got put inside. 'Course, Peanuts didn't mind making a bit hisself, out of robbing the offey.'

'One more thing, Mrs Timson. Have you ever seen a weapon like that before?'

I held up the cosh. The Usher came and took it to the witness.

'I saw that one. I think I did.'

'Where?'

'In Peanuts' car. That's where he kept it.'

'Did your husband ever own anything like that?'

'What, Tony?' April weighed the cosh in her hand and clearly found the idea ridiculous. 'Not him. He wouldn't have known what to do with it.'

When the evidence was complete and we had made our speeches, Guthrie had to sum up the case of *R.* v. *Timson* to the Jury. As he turned his chair towards them, and they prepared to give him their full attention, a distinguished visitor slipped unobtrusively into the back of the Court. He was none other than old Keith from the Lord Chancellor's office. The Judge must have seen him, but he made no apology for his previous lenient treatment of Tony Timson.

'Members of the Jury,' he began. 'You have heard of the false accusation of attempted murder that Mrs Timson made against an innocent man. Can you imagine, Members of the Jury, what misery that poor man has been made to suffer? Devoted to ladies as he may be, he has been called a heartless "male chauvinist". Gentle and harmless by nature, he has been thought to connive at crimes of violence. Perhaps it was even suggested that he was the sort of fellow who would make his wife carry heavy luggage! He may well have been shunned in the streets, hooted at from the pavements, and the wife he truly loves has perhaps been unwilling to enter a warm, domestic bath with him. And then, consider,' Guthrie went on, 'if the unhappy Timson may not have also been falsely accused in relation to the robbery with violence of his local "offey". Justice must be done, Members of the Jury. We must do justice even if it means we do nothing else for the rest of our lives but compete in croquet competitions.' The Judge was looking straight at Keith from the Lord Chancellor's office as he said this. I relaxed, lay back and closed my eyes. I knew, after all his troubles, how his Lordship would feel about a man falsely accused, and I had no further worries about the fate of Tony Timson.

When I got home, Hilda was reading the result of the trial in the *Evening Sentinel*. 'I suppose you're cock-a-hoop, Rumpole,' she said.

'Hearthrug routed!' I told her. 'The women of England back on our side and old Keith from the Lord Chancellor's office looking extremely foolish. And a miraculous change came over Guthrie.'

'What?'

'He suddenly found courage. It's something you can't do without, not if you concern yourself with justice.'

'That April Timson!' Hilda looked down at her evening paper. 'Making it all up about being drowned in the bathwater.'

'When lovely woman stoops to folly' – I went to the sideboard and poured a celebratory glass of Château Thames Embankment – 'And finds too late that men betray,/What charm can soothe her melancholy . . .'

'I'm not going to the Bar to protect people like her, Rumpole.' Hilda announced her decision. 'She's put me to a great deal of trouble. Getting up at a quarter to six every morning for the Open University.'

' "What art can wash her guilt away?" *What* did you say, Hilda?'

'I'm not going to all that trouble, learning Real Property and Company Law and eating dinners and buying a wig, not for the likes of April Timson.'

'Oh, Hilda! Everyone in Chambers will be extremely disappointed.'

'Well, I'm sorry.' She had clearly made up her mind. 'They'll just have to do without me. I've really got better things to do, Rumpole, than come home cock-a-hoop just because April Timson changes her mind and decides to tell the truth.'

'Of course you have, Hilda.' I drank gratefully. 'What sort of better things?'

'Keeping you in order for one, Rumpole. Seeing you wash up properly.' And then she spoke with considerable feeling. 'It's disgusting!'

'The washing up?'

'No. People having baths together.'

'Married people?' I reminded her.

'I don't see that makes it any better. Don't you ever ask me to do that, Rumpole.'

'Never, Hilda. I promise faithfully.' To hear, of course, was to obey.

That night's *Sentinel* contained a leading article which appeared under the encouraging headline BATHTUB JUDGE PROVED RIGHT. *Mrs April Timson, it read, has admitted that her husband never tried to drown her and the Jury have acquitted Tony Timson on a second trumped-up charge. It took a Judge of Mr Justice Featherstone's perception and experience to see through this woman's inventions and exaggerations and to uphold the law without fear or favour. Now and again the British legal system produces a Judge of exceptional wisdom and integrity who refuses to yield to pressure groups and does justice though the heavens fall. Such a one is Sir Guthrie Featherstone.*

Sir Guthrie told me later that he read these comforting words whilst lying in a warm bath in his flat near Harrods. I have no doubt at all that Lady Featherstone was with him on that occasion, seated at the tap end.

Rumpole and the Chambers Party

Christmas comes but once a year. Once a year I receive a gift of socks from She Who Must Be Obeyed; each year I add to her cellar of bottles of lavender water, which she now seems to use mainly for the purpose of 'laying down' in the bedroom cupboard (I suspect she has only just started on the 1980 vintage).

Tinselled cards and sprigs of holly appear at the entrance to the cells under the Old Bailey and a constantly repeated tape of 'God Rest Ye Merry Gentlemen' adds little zest to my two eggs, bacon and sausage on a fried slice in the Taste-Ee-Bite, Fleet Street; and once a year the Great Debate takes place at our December meeting. Should we invite solicitors to our Chambers party?

'No doubt at the season of our Saviour's birth we should offer hospitality to all sorts and conditions of men . . .' 'Soapy' Sam Ballard, Q.C., our devout Head of Chambers, opened the proceedings in his usual manner, that of a somewhat backward bishop addressing Synod on the wisdom of offering the rites of baptism to non-practising, gay Anglican converts of riper years.

'All conditions of men and *women*.' Phillida Erskine-Brown, Q.C., née Trant, the Portia of our Chambers, was looking particularly fetching in a well-fitting black jacket and an only slightly flippant version of a male collar and tie. As she looked doe-eyed at him, Ballard, who hides a ridiculously susceptible heart beneath his monkish exterior, conceded her point. 'The question before us is, does all sorts and conditions of men, and women too, of course, include members of the junior branch of the legal profession?'

'I'm against it!' Claude Erskine-Brown had remained an ageing junior whilst his wife Phillida fluttered into silk, and he was never in favour of radical change. 'The party is very much a family thing for the chaps in Chambers, and the clerk's room, of course. If we ask solicitors it looks very much as though we're touting for briefs.'

'I'm very much in favour of touting for briefs.' Up spake the somewhat grey barrister, Hoskins. 'Speaking as a man with four daughters to educate. For heaven's sake, let's ask as many solicitors as we know, which, in my case, I'm afraid, is not many.'

'Do you have a view, Rumpole?' Ballard felt bound to ask me, just as a formality.

'Well, yes, nothing wrong with a bit of touting, I agree with Hoskins. But I'm in favour of asking the people who really provide us with work.'

'You mean solicitors?'

'I mean the criminals of England. Fine conservative fellows who should appeal to you, Ballard. Greatly in favour of free enterprise and against the closed shop. I propose we invite a few of the better-class crooks who have no previous engagements as guests of Her Majesty, and show our gratitude.'

A somewhat glazed look came over the assembly at this suggestion and then Mrs Erskine-Brown broke the silence with 'Claude's really being awfully stuffy and old-fashioned about this. I propose we invite a smattering of solicitors, from the better-class firms.'

Our Portia's proposal was carried *nem con*, such was the disarming nature of her sudden smile on everyone, including her husband, who may have had some reason to fear it. Rumpole's suggestion, to nobody's surprise, received no support whatsoever.

Our clerk, Henry, invariably arranged the Chambers party for the night on which his wife put on the Nativity play in the Bexley Heath Comprehensive at which she was a teacher. This gave him more scope for kissing Dianne, our plucky but somewhat hit-and-miss typist, beneath the mistletoe which swung from the dim, religious light in the entrance hall of number three, Equity Court.

Paper streamers dangled from the bookcase full of All England Law Reports in Ballard's room and were hooked up to his views of the major English cathedrals. Barristers' wives were invited,

and Mrs Hilda Rumpole, known to me only as She Who Must
Be Obeyed, was downing sherry and telling Soapy Sam all about
the golden days when her Daddy, C. H. Wystan, ran Chambers.
There were also six or seven solicitors among those present.

One, however, seemed superior to all the rest, a solicitor of the
class we seldom see around Equity Court. He had come in with
one hand outstretched to Ballard, saying, 'Daintry Naismith,
Happy Christmas. Awfully kind of you fellows to invite one of
the junior branch.' Now he stood propped up against the mantelpiece, warming his undoubtedly Savile Row trousers at Ballard's
gas fire and receiving the homage of barristers in urgent need of
briefs.

He appeared to be in his well-preserved fifties, with grey wings
of hair above his ears and a clean-shaven, pink and still single
chin poised above what I took to be an old Etonian tie. Whatever
he might have on offer it wouldn't, I was sure, be a charge of
nicking a frozen chicken from Safeways. Even his murders, I
thought, as he sized us up from over the top of his gold-rimmed
half glasses, would take place among the landed gentry.

He accepted a measure of Pommeroy's very ordinary white
plonk from Portia and drank it bravely, as though he hadn't been
used to sipping Chassagne-Montrachet all his adult life.

'Mrs Erskine-Brown,' he purred at her, 'I'm looking for a
hard-hitting silk to brief in the Family Division. I suppose you're
tremendously booked up.'

'The pressure of my work,' Phillida said modestly, 'is enormous.'

'I've got the Geoffrey Twyford divorce coming. Pretty hairy
bit of in-fighting over the estate and the custody of young Lord
Shiplake. I thought you'd be just right for it.'

'Is that the Duke of Twyford?' Claude Erskine-Brown looked
suitably awestruck. In spite of his other affectations Erskine-
Brown's snobbery is completely genuine.

'Well, if you have a word with Henry, my clerk' – Mrs
Erskine-Brown gave the solicitor a look of cool availability – 'he
might find a few spare dates.'

'Well, that is good of you. And you, Mr Erskine-Brown,
mainly civil work now, I suppose?'

'Oh, yes. Mainly civil.' Erskine-Brown lied cheerfully; he's not above taking on the odd indecent assault when tort gets a little thin on the ground. 'I do find crime so sordid.'

'Oh, I agree. Look here. I'm stumped for a man to take on our insurance business, but I suppose you'd be far too busy.'

'Oh, no. I've got plenty of time.' Erskine-Brown lacked his wife's laid-back approach to solicitors. 'That is to say, I'm sure I could make time. One gets used to extremely long hours, you know.' I thought that the longest hours Erskine-Brown put in were when he sat, in grim earnest, through the *Ring* at Covent Garden, being a man who submits himself to Wagner rather as others enjoy walking from Land's End to John O'Groats.

And then I saw Naismith staring at me and waited for him to announce that the Marquess of Something or Other had stabbed his butler in the library and could I possibly make myself available for the trial. Instead he muttered, 'Frightfully good party,' and wandered off in the general direction of Soapy Sam Ballard.

'What's the matter with you, Rumpole?' She Who Must Be Obeyed was at my elbow and not sounding best pleased. 'Why didn't you push yourself forward?' Erskine-Brown had also moved off by this time to join the throng.

'I don't care for divorce,' I told her. 'It's too bloodthirsty for me. Now if he'd offered me a nice gentle murder . . .'

'Go after him, Rumpole,' she urged me, 'and make yourself known. I'll go and ask Phillida what her plans are for the Harrods sale.' Perhaps it was the mention of the sales which spurred me towards that undoubted source of income, Mr Daintry Naismith. I found him talking to Ballard in a way which showed, in my view, a gross over-estimation of that old darling's forensic powers. 'Of course the client would have to understand that the golden tongu of Samuel Ballard, Q.C., can't be hired on the cheap,' Naismith was saying. I thought that to refer to our Head of Chambers, whose voice in Court could best be compared to a rusty saw, as 'golden-tongued' was a bit of an exaggeration.

'I'll have to think it over.' Ballard was flattered but cautious. 'One does have certain principles about' – he gulped, rather in the manner of a fish struggling with its conscience – 'encouraging the publication of explicitly sexual material.'

'Think it over, Mr Ballard. I'll be in touch with your clerk.' And then, as Naismith saw me approach, he said, 'Perhaps I'll have a word with him now.' So this legal Santa Claus moved away in the general direction of Henry and once more Rumpole was left with nothing in his stocking.

'By the way,' I asked Ballard. 'Did you invite that extremely smooth solicitor?'

'No, I think Henry did.' Our Head of Chambers spoke as a man whose thoughts are on knottier problems. 'Charming chap, though, isn't he?'

Later in the course of the party I found myself next to Henry. 'Good work inviting Mr Daintry Naismith,' I said to our clerk. 'He seems set on providing briefs for everyone except me.'

'I don't really know the gentleman,' Henry admitted. 'I think he must be a friend of Mr Ballard's. Of course we hope to see a lot of him in the future.'

Much later, in search of a small cigar, I remembered the box, still in its special Christmas reindeer-patterned wrapping, that I had left in my brief tray. I opened the door of the clerk's room and found the lights off and Henry's desk palely lit by the old gas lamp outside in Equity Court.

There was a dark-suited figure standing beside the desk who seemed to be trying the locked drawers rather in the casual way that suspicious-looking youths test car handles. I switched on the light and found myself staring at our star solicitor guest. And as I looked at him, the years rolled away and I was in Court defending a bent house agent. Beside him in the dock had been an equally curved solicitor's clerk who had joined my client as a guest of Her Majesty.

'Derek Newton,' I said. 'Inner London Sessions. Raising mortgages on deserted houses that you didn't own. Two years.'

'I knew you'd recognize me, Mr Rumpole. Sooner or later.'

'What the hell do you think you are doing?'

'I'm afraid . . . well, barristers' chambers are about the only place where you can find a bit of petty cash lying about at Christmas.' The man seemed resolved to have no secrets from Rumpole.

'You admit it?'

'Things aren't too easy when you're knocking sixty, and the business world's full of wide boys up to all the tricks. You can't get far on one good suit and the Old Etonian tie nowadays. You always defend, don't you, Rumpole? That's what I've heard. Well, I can only appeal to you for leniency.'

'But coming to our party,' I said, staggered by this most confident of tricksters, 'promising briefs to all the learned friends . . .'

'I always wanted to be admitted as a solicitor.' He smiled a little wistfully. 'I usually walk through the Temple at Christmas time. Sometimes I drop in to the parties. And I always make a point of offering work. It's a pleasure to see so many grateful faces. This is, after all, Mr Rumpole, the season of giving.'

What could I do? All he had got out of us, after all, was a couple of glasses of Pommeroy's Fleet Street white; that and the five pound note he 'borrowed' from me for his cab fare home. I went back to the party and explained to Ballard that Mr Daintry Naismith had made a phone call and had to leave on urgent business.

'He's offered me a highly remunerative brief, Rumpole, defending a publisher of dubious books. It's against my principles, but even the greatest sinner has a right to have his case put before the Court . . .'

'And put by your golden tongue, old darling,' I flattered him. 'If you take my advice you'll go for it.'

It was, after all, the season of goodwill, and I couldn't find it in my heart to spoil Soapy Sam Ballard's Christmas.

Rumpole and Portia

This is a story of family life, of parents and children, and, like many such stories, it began with a quarrel. There was I, ensconced one evening in a quiet corner of Pommeroy's Wine Bar consuming a lonely glass of Château Thames Embankment at the end of a day's labours, when the voices of a couple in dispute came drifting over from the other side of one of Jack Pommeroy's high-backed pews which give such an ecclesiastical air to his distinguished legal watering-hole. The voices I heard were well known to me, being those of my learned friend, Claude Erskine-Brown, and of his spouse, Mrs Phillida Erskine-Brown, née Trant, the Portia of our Chambers, whom I befriended and advised when she was a white-wig, and who, no doubt taking advantage of that advice, rose to take silk and become a Queen's Counsel when Claude was denied that honour, and thus had his nose put seriously out of joint. The union of Claude and Phillida has been blessed with a girl and a boy named, because of Claude's almost masochistic addiction to the lengthier operas of Richard Wagner (and an opera isn't by Richard Wagner if it's not lengthy), Tristan and Isolde. It was the subject of young Tristan which was causing dissension between his parents that evening.

'Tristan was still in bed at quarter to eight this morning,' Claude was complaining. 'He won't be able to do that when he goes away to Bogstead.'

'Please, Claude' – Phillida sounded terminally bored – 'don't go on about it.'

'You know when I was at Bogstead' – no Englishman can possibly resist talking about his boarding-school – 'we used to be woken up at half past six for early class, and we had to break the ice in the dormy wash-basins.'

'You have told me that, Claude, quite often.'

'We had to run three times round Tug's Patch before early church on saints' days.'

'Did you enjoy that?'

'Of course not! I absolutely hated it.' Claude was looking back, apparently on golden memories.

'Why do you imagine Tristan would enjoy it then?'

'You don't *enjoy* Bogstead,' Claude was pointing out patiently. 'You're not meant to enjoy it. But if I hadn't gone there I wouldn't have got into Winchester and if I hadn't got into Winchester I'd never have been to New College. And I'll tell you something, Philly. If I hadn't been to Bogstead, Winchester and New College, I'd never be what I am.'

'Which might be just as well.' Our Portia sounded cynical.

'Whatever do you mean by that?' Claude was nettled. I strained my ears to listen; things were obviously getting nasty.

'It might be just as well if you weren't the man you are,' Claude's wife told him. 'If you hadn't been at Bogstead you might not make such a terrible fuss about losing that gross indecency today. I mean, the way you carried on about that, you must still be in the fourth form at Boggers. I notice you don't talk about sending Isolde to that dump.'

'Bogstead is not a dump,' Claude said proudly. 'And you may not have noticed this, Philly, but Isolde is a girl. They don't *have* girls there.'

'Oh, I see. It's a boy's world, is it?'

'I didn't say that.'

'Poor old Isolde. She's going to miss all the fun of breaking the ice at six thirty in the morning and running three times round Tug's Patch on saints' days. Poor deprived child. She might even grow up to be a Queen's Counsel.'

'Come on, Philly. Isn't that a bit . . .?'

'A bit what?' I had taught Phillida to be dead sharp on her cross-examination.

'Well, not quite the thing to say. Of course I'm terrifically glad you've been made a Q.C. I think you've done jolly well.'

'For a woman!' A short, somewhat bitter laugh from Mrs Erskine-Brown emphasized her point.

'But it's just not "the thing" to crow about it.' Erskine-Brown spoke with the full moral authority of his prep school and Winchester.

'Sorry, Claude! I don't know what "the thing" is. Such a pity I never went to Boggers. Anyway, I don't see the point of having children if you're going to send them away to boarding-school.'

At that point, and much to my regret, the somewhat grey and tedious barrister named Hoskins of our Chambers, a man weighed down with the responsibility of four daughters, sat down at my table in order to complain about the extortionate price of coffee in our clerk's room, and I lost the rest of the Erskine-Brown family dispute. However, I have given you enough of it to show the nature of their disagreement and Phillida's reluctance to part with her young hopeful. These were matters which were to assume great importance in the defence of Stanley Culp on a charge of illicit arms dealing, for Stanley was a father who would have found our Portia's views entirely sympathetic.

In most other respects, the home life of the Culps and the Erskine-Browns was as different as chalk and cheese. Stanley Culp was a plump, remorselessly cheerful, disorganized dealer in second-hand furniture – bits of junk and dubious antiques – in a jumbled shop near Notting Hill Gate. Unlike the Erskine-Browns, the Culps were a one-parent family, for Stanley was in sole charge of his son, Matthew, a scholarly, bespectacled little boy of about Tristan's age. Some three and a half years before, Mrs Culp, so Stanley informed me when we met in Brixton prison, had told her husband that he had 'nothing romantic in his nature whatever'. 'So she took off with the Manager of Tesco's, twenty years older than me if he was a day. Can you understand that, Mr Rumpole?'

I have long given up trying to understand the inscrutable ways of women in love, but I did come to understand Stanley Culp's attachment to his son. My son Nicky and I enjoyed a similar rapport when we used to walk in the park together and I would tell him the Sherlock Holmes stories in the days before he took up the mysterious study of sociology and went to teach in Florida. It was for young Matthew's sake, Stanley Culp told me, that he preferred to work at home in his antique business. 'We are good companions, Mr Rumpole. And I have to be there when he comes home from school. I don't approve of these latch-key children, left alone to do their homework until Mum and Dad come back from the office.'

The events which drew me and Stanley Culp together took place early one morning, not long before I heard the Erskine-Browns arguing in Pommeroy's. Young Matthew, a better cook and housekeeper than his father, was making the breakfast in the kitchen upstairs whilst Stanley was engaged in some business with an early caller in the shop below. Matthew put bread in the antique electric toaster, heard a car door slam, and then looked out of the window. What he saw was an unmarked car which in fact contained three officers of the Special Branch in plain clothes. A fourth man, wearing slightly tinted gold-rimmed glasses, who will have some importance in this account, was walking away from the car and paused to look up at the shop. Then the toast popped up and Matthew transferred it to a tarnished 'Georgian' rack and went to the top of the staircase which led down to the shop to call his father up for breakfast.

From his viewpoint at the top of the stairs Matthew saw the familiar jumble of piled tables, chairs and other furniture, and he saw Stanley talking to a thick-set, ginger-haired man who was carrying a brief-case. Matthew said, 'Breakfast, Dad!', at which moment the shop door was kicked open and two of the men from the car, Superintendent Rodney and Detective Inspector Blake, were among the junk and informing Stanley that they were officers of the Special Branch who had come to arrest him. As they said this, the thick-set ginger-haired man, whose name turned out to be MacRobert, made a bolt for the back door and was out in the untidy patch of walled garden behind the building. He was there pursued by a third officer from the car, Detective Sergeant Trump, and shot dead in what Trump took to be the act of pulling out a gun. MacRobert, it transpired at the trial, was an important figure in a Protestant paramilitary group dedicated to open warfare in Northern Ireland.

Stanley was removed in the car and a subsequent search revealed, in a large storeroom behind his shop, a number of packing-cases filled with repeating rifles of a forbidden category.

Matthew didn't go to school that day, but a woman police constable and a social worker arrived for him and he was taken into the care of the local council. His fate was that which Phillida feared for young Tristan; he was sent away from home to be brought up by strangers.

Unhappiness, you see, was getting in everywhere, not only *à côté de chez* Erskine-Brown, but also among the Culps. And things had also taken an unfortunate turn in the Rumpole household. I came back one evening to the mansion flat in the Gloucester Road, and, as I unlocked the front door, I heard the usual cry of 'Is that you, Rumpole?'

'Good heavens, no!' I called back. 'It's the Lord High Chancellor of England just dropped in to read the meter. What're you talking about, Hilda?'

'Ssh, Rumpole,' Hilda said mysteriously. 'It's Boxey!'

'Is it? Just a little fresh, I noticed, coming out of the Underground.'

'No. It's Boxey Horne. You must have heard me speak of my second cousin. Cousin Nancy's youngest.' We had spent many hours discussing the complexities of Hilda's family tree, but I couldn't immediately recollect the name. 'We were so close when we were youngsters but Boxey felt the call of Africa. He rang up this afternoon from Paddington Station.'

A masculine voice called through the open sitting-room door, 'Is that old Horace, back from the treadmill?'

'Boxey?' I was perplexed. 'Yes, of course.' And Hilda warned me, 'You will try and behave yourself, won't you, Rumpole?'

With that she led me into our sitting-room where a skinny, elderly and, I thought, cunning-looking cove was sitting in my chair nursing a glass of my Château Fleet Street and smiling at me in the slightly lopsided manner which I was to know as characteristic of Mr Boxey Horne. He wore a travel-stained tropical suiting, scuffed suede shoes and an M.C.C. tie which had seen better days. When Hilda introduced me, he rose and gripped me quite painfully by the hand. 'Good old Horace,' he said. 'Back from the office same time every evening. I bet you can set your watch by the old fellow, can't you, Hilda?'

'Well. Not exactly,' Hilda told him.

'Your wife gave me some of this plonk of yours, Horace.' Boxey raised his glass to me. 'We'd have been glad of this back on the farm in Kenya. We might have run a couple of tractors on it!'

'Get Boxey a whisky, Rumpole,' Hilda instructed me. 'I expect you'd like a nice strong one, wouldn't you? Boxey couldn't get into the Travellers' Club.'

'Blackballed?' I asked on my way to the sideboard.

'Full up.' Boxey grinned cheerfully. 'Hilda was good enough to say I might camp here for a couple of weeks.' It seemed an infinity. I poured a very small whisky, hoping the bottle would last him out, and drowned it in soda.

'I've been knocking around the world, Horace,' Boxey told me. 'While you were off on your nine to five in a lawyers' office.'

'Not office,' I corrected him as I handed him his pale drink, 'Chambers.'

'That sort of life would never have suited old Boxey,' he told me, and I wondered if his name might be short for anything. 'Oh no,' Hilda laughed at my ignorance. 'We called him that because of the beautiful brass-bound box he had when he set off to Darkest Africa.'

'Always been a rover, Horace.' Boxey was in a reminiscing mood. 'All my worldly goods were in that old box. Tropical kit. Mosquito net. Dinner-jacket to impress the natives. Family photographs, including one of cousin Hilda looking young and alluring.' He drank and looked suitably disappointed, but Hilda, clearly entranced, said, 'You took me to Kenya? In your box?'

'Many a time I've sat alone,' he assured her, 'listening to the strange sounds of an African night and gazing at your photograph. You have been looking after Cousin Hilda, haven't you, Horace?'

'Looking after her?' I poured myself a bracing Pommeroy's plonk and confessed myself puzzled. 'Hilda's in charge.'

'A sweet, sweet girl, cousin Hilda. I always thought she needed looking after but I suppose I had itchy feet and couldn't resist the call of Africa.' He propelled himself to the sideboard then, and with his back towards us, poured himself a straight whisky and then made a slight hissing noise imitating a siphon.

'What were you doing in Africa?' I asked him. 'Something like discovering the source of the Zambesi?'

'Well, not exactly. I was in coffee.'

'All your life?'

'Most of it.' Boxey returned to my chair to enjoy his drink.

'Working for the same firm?'

'Well, one has certain loyalties. You've never seen dawn over Kilimanjaro, Horry? Pink light on the snow. Zebra stampeding.'

'What time did you start work?' I was pursuing my own line of cross-examination.

'Well,' Boxey remembered, 'after my boy had got my bacon and eggs, coffee and Oxford marmalade . . . then I'd ride round the plantation.'

'Starting at nine o'clock?'

'About then, I suppose.'

'And knocking off?'

'Around sundown. Get a chair on the verandah and shout for a whisky.'

'At about five o'clock?'

'Why do you ask?'

'The old routine!' I muttered and the Defence rested.

'What was that?'

'What a rover you've been,' I said without envy.

'Well, I had itchy feet.' Boxey slapped my knee. 'But thank God for chaps like you who're prepared to slog it out in the old country, and look after girls like Hilda.' Then he leant back in his chair, took a sizeable swig and prepared to give us another chapter of his memories. 'Ever been tiger-shooting, Horace?'

'Not unless you could call my frequent appearances before Judge Bullingham tiger-shooting,' I assured him.

'Best sport in the world! Tie an old goat to a tree and lie doggo. Your loader says, 'Bwana. Tiger coming.' There she is, eyes glittering through the undergrowth. She starts to eat the goat and . . .' – he raised an imaginary rifle – 'aim just above the shoulder. Pow!'

'What do you think of that, Rumpole?' Hilda was starry-eyed.

'I think it sounds bad luck on the goat.' We had a short silence while Boxey renewed his whisky. Then he said, 'I suppose it's another long day in Court for you tomorrow.'

'Oh, yes,' I agreed, 'dusty old law.'

'I don't know how you put up with it!'

'Tedious case about an Ulster terrorist shot by the police in Notting Hill,' I told him – by then I had received the brief for the defence in *R. v. Culp* – 'an inefficient gun-runner who acts as mother and father to his twelve-year-old son, and the curious activities of the Special Branch. Not nearly so exciting as nine to five on the old coffee plantation.'

That night, Hilda lay for a long time with the light on, when I was in dire need of sleep, staring into space. She was also in a reminiscing mood. 'I remember when we used to go to dances at Uncle Jacko's,' she said. 'Boxey was quite young, then. He brought his dancing pumps along in a paper bag. He was simply marvellous at the valeta.'

'It's a wonder he didn't join the Royal Ballet.'

'Rumpole. You *are* jealous!'

'I just thought he might've found *Casse Noisette* a good deal more interesting than coffee.'

'In those days I got the feeling that Boxey had taken a bit of a shine to me.' It wasn't, I thought, much to boast about, but Hilda seemed delighted. 'A definite shine! How different my life might have been if I'd married Boxey and gone to Africa!'

'My life would have been a bit different too,' I told her. 'With no one to make sure I didn't linger too long in Pommeroy's after work. No one to make sure I didn't take a second helping of mashed potatoes. And,' I added, *sotto voce*, 'magical!'

'What did you say, Rumpole?'

'Tragical, of course. Is there any chance of turning out the light?'

Mr Bernard, my favourite instructing solicitor, had briefed me in the Culp case, and we went together to Brixton, where, in the cheerfully painted interview room with its pot plants and reasonably tolerant screws, I made the acquaintance of Stanley. His first request was to get him out of confinement so that he could be with his son, to which I made not very encouraging noises, reminding him that he'd been charged with delivering automatic rifles to a known Irish terrorist and that my name was Rumpole and not Houdini.

The story he told me went roughly as follows. He dealt, he said, in bric à brac, *objets d'art*, old furniture – anything he could make a few bob out of. Asked where this property came from, he said we'd find it wise not to ask too many questions (Well, I sometimes feel the same about my practice at the Bar.) He had a certain amount of space at the back of his shop and he put an advertisement in the local newsagent's window offering to store people's furniture for a modest fee. Some months previously a man had telephoned Stanley saying he was a Mr Banks, from the Loyalist League of Welfare and Succour for Victims of Terrorist Attack, and he wanted storage space for a number of packing-cases which contained medical supplies for his organization in Northern Ireland. As a result, he received a visit from Mr Banks who paid him three months' rent in advance, a sum of money which Stanley found extremely welcome. Asked to describe this mysterious Banks he could only remember a man of average age and height, wearing a dark business suit and a white shirt. His sole distinguishing mark was apparently a large pair of gold-rimmed, slightly tinted spectacles. Stanley never saw Mr Banks again, but in due course a lorry arrived with the packing-cases which it took a couple of blokes to lift. When I put the point to him he said they did seem heavy for sticking plaster and bandages.

Later Mr Banks telephoned and said that a man called Mac-Robert, a name which Stanley assured me meant nothing to him, would be calling to arrange the collection of the cases. MacRobert called whilst Matthew was preparing the breakfast and had wanted to see the goods inside, but before he could do so their conversation was interrupted by the Special Branch in the way I have described. Stanley was arrested and, while trying to escape across the garden wall, MacRobert was shot, so he was not in a position to tell us anything about the mysterious Mr Banks.

When he had finished his account Stanley looked at me beseechingly. 'You've got to get me out, Mr Rumpole,' he said. 'It's where they've put my Matthew.'

'Don't worry,' Bernard tried to console the client. 'He's being well looked after, Mr Culp. He's been put into care.'

'Me too. We're both in care.' Stanley managed a smile. 'That's it, isn't it? And it won't suit either of us. As I say, we've always been used to looking after each other.'

I looked at him, wondering what sort of a client I'd got hold of. If Stanley wasn't innocent, he was a tender-hearted gun-runner, so keen to be at home with Master Matthew that he flogged automatic rifles to political terrorists to fire off at other people's sons. It didn't make sense, but then not very much did in crime or politics.

Whilst I exercised my legal skills on a bit of gun-running in Notting Hill Gate, Portia's practice went on among the jet-setters. Cy Stratton, it seems – I have to confess his name was unknown to me – was an international film star for whom Hilda, who pays more attention to the television set than I can manage, has a soft spot. He had been detected, as well-known film stars too often are, carrying exotic smoking materials through the customs at London Airport. In the consequent proceedings he hired, at a suitable fee, Mrs Phillida Erskine-Brown to make his apologies for him. She was ably assisted in this task by Mizz Liz Probert, to whom I am grateful for an account of the proceedings. Picture then the West Middlesex Magistrates Court, unusually filled with reporters and spectators. On the bench sat three seri-ous-minded amateurs: a grey-haired schoolmaster chairman, a forbidding-looking woman in a hat, and a stout party with a toothbrush moustache and a Trades Union badge. In the dock, Mr Cy Stratton, a carefully suntanned specimen, whose curls were now greying, sat wearing a contrite expression and a suit and tie in place of his usual open-necked shirt and gold chain. On his behalf, our Portia, sincere and irresistible, spoke words which, when Liz Probert reported them to me, seemed to come straight out of Rumpole's first lesson on getting round to the soft side of the West Middlesex Magistrates as taught by me to Mrs Erskine-Brown in her white-wigged years.

'Cy Stratton is, of course,' she ended, 'a household name, known throughout the world from a string of successful films.'

The star in the dock looked gratified. 'The Bench won't, I'm sure, punish him for his fame. He is entitled to be treated as anyone else found at London Airport with a small amount of cannabis for his own personal use. At the time he was under considerable personal strain, having just completed a new film, *Galaxy Wives.*' The Trades Union official, clearly a fan, nodded wisely. 'And, may I say this, Mr Stratton is absolutely opposed to hard drugs. He is a prominent member of the Presidential "Say No to Coke" Committee of Los Angeles. In these circumstances, I do most earnestly appeal to you, sir, and to your colleagues. You will do justice to Cy Stratton.' And here Portia used a gambit which even I have long since rejected as being over-ripe ham. 'But let it be justice tempered with that mercy which is the hallmark of the West Middlesex Magistrates Court!'

Well, sometimes the old ones work best. Much moved, Cy Stratton looked as though he were about to applaud; even the lady in the hat seemed mollified. The Chairman smiled his thanks at Phillida and, after a short retirement and a warning to Cy to set a good example to his huge army of fans, imposed a fine of three hundred pounds.

'And I had that,' said Cy to his learned Counsel and Liz outside the Court, 'in my pants pocket.'

'They might have given you two months,' Phillida told him, 'and you wouldn't have had *that* in your pants pocket.'

On that occasion Cy told Phillida he had a proposition to put to her and invited her to share a celebratory bottle of Dom Perignon with him in some private place. However, she declined politely, gathered her legal team about her, and saying, 'We do have to work, you know, at the Bar,' drove back to the Temple, doing so, Liz thought, in a sort of reverie brought on by an impulsive kiss from her grateful client.

I was in our clerk's room a few days later, with Claude and Phillida, sorting out our business affairs when a messenger arrived with a huge cellophane-wrapped bouquet and called out, 'Flowers for Erskine-Brown!' I asked Claude if he had an admirer, but they appeared to be for his wife and he asked, somewhat nervously, I thought, as she read the card attached, if they were from anyone in particular.

'Oh, no. Flowers just drop on me by accident, from the sky.'
Phillida sounded testy. 'Do try not to be silly, Claude.'

'Perhaps they're from a satisfied client,' I suggested.

'Yes, they are!'

'Really, Portia? Who was that?'

'Oh, someone I kept out of prison. Nothing tremendously
important.' She sounded casual, and Uncle Tom, our oldest
inhabitant, who was as usual practising approach shots at the
waste-paper basket, began to reminisce. 'I've never had a present
from a satisfied client,' he told us. 'Not that I've had many
clients at all, come to that, satisfied or not. I suppose it's better
to have no clients than those that aren't satisfied. Damn! I seem
to be in a bunker.' His golf ball had taken refuge behind Dianne's
desk.

'What've I got this afternoon, Henry?' Phillida asked. And
when he told her she had a three-thirty conference she supposed,
after some thought, that she could be back in time. Meanwhile
Uncle Tom was off down Memory Lane in pursuit of presents
from satisfied clients. 'Old Dickie Duckworth once had a satisfied
client,' he told us. 'Some sort of a Middle-Eastern Prince who
was supposed to have got a Nippy from Lyons Corner House in
pod and Dickie turned up at Bow Street and got him off. So you
know what this fellow sent as a token of his appreciation? An
Arab stallion! Well, Dickie Duckworth only had a small flat in
Lincoln's Inn. No one ever sent me an Arab stallion. Chip shot
out of the bunker!'

At that moment, Superintendent Rodney of the Special
Branch, together with an official from the prosecution service,
entered our clerk's room. Soapy Sam Ballard, Q.C., the Head of
our Chambers, had been briefed to prosecute Stanley Culp and
they were to see him in conference. Unfortunately Uncle Tom's
chip shot was rather too successful; his golf ball rose into the air
and struck the Superintendent smartly on the knee-cap, producing a cry of pain and dire consequences for Uncle Tom.

The note on Phillida's bouquet was a pressing invitation to
meet Cy Stratton for lunch at the Savoy Hotel. I suppose the
suntanned and ageing Adonis had figured too largely in her
thoughts since the trial for her to pass up the invitation, and

when they met he surprised her by suggesting that they share a bottle of champagne and a surprise packet from the delicatessen on a bench in the Embankment Gardens. So Phillida found herself eating pastrami on rye and drinking Dom Perignon out of a plastic cup, both excited by the adventure and nervous at the amount of public exposure she was receiving. I learnt, long after the event, and when certain decisions had been made, the gist of Cy's conversation on that occasion from my confiding ex-pupil. It seems that after complimenting her on looking great – 'Great hair, great shape. Classy nose. Great legal mind' – Cy informed her that their 'vibes' were good and that they should spend more time together. He had, he said, 'A proposition to put'.

'Perhaps you shouldn't.' Phillida was flattered but nervous.

'What?'

'You shouldn't put a proposition to me.'

'Can't a guy ask?'

'It might be a great deal better if a guy didn't.'

'I need you, Phillida.' The actor was at his most intense, and he moved himself and the sandwiches closer to her.

'You may think you do.'

'I know I do. Desperately.'

'Don't exaggerate.' There has always been a strong streak of common sense in our Portia.

'I swear to you. I can't find anyone to do what I'd expect of you.'

'You can't?'

'Not a soul. They haven't the versatility.'

'What would you expect of me exactly?' Phillida was still nervous, but interested. His answer, she confessed, came as something of a surprise. 'Only, to take over the entire legal side of Cy Stratton Enterprises. Real estate. Audio-visual exploitations. Cable promotions. I want your cool head, Phillida, and your legal know-how.'

'Oh, is that what you want?' She tried not to sound in the least disappointed.

'Come to the sunshine. I'll find you a house on the beach.'

'I *have* got two children,' she told him.

'The kids'll love it.'

'And a husband,' she admitted. 'He's a lawyer too.'

'Maybe we could use him, as your assistant?'

'You don't send children away from home in California?' The idea was beginning to appeal to Portia.

'Summer camps, maybe. Think about it, Phillida. Our vibes are such we should spend more time together.'

'I'll think about it. Can I have another sandwich?' She put out her hand and Cy held it and looked into her eyes. And then Liz Probert, walking through the Gardens, stopped in front of them as Cy was saying, 'Find our own space together. That's all it takes!'

'Good afternoon. Having a picnic?' Liz's greeting was somewhat cold. Phillida quickly released her hand. 'Oh, Probert,' she greeted her colleague formally. 'You remember Cy Stratton?'

'Of course. Illegal possession.' Liz looked at Phillida. 'A satisfied client?'

The Erskine-Browns' private life was, you see, not exactly private – either they were spied on by Liz Probert or overheard by Rumpole. A few evenings later I was at my corner table in Pommeroy's trying to raise my alcohol level from the dangerous low to which it had sunk, when I heard their raised voices once again from the pew behind me. 'Haven't we been getting into a bit of a rut lately, Claude?' was the far from original remark which collared my attention.

'It's hardly fair to say that.' Claude sounded pained. 'When I got us tickets for *Tannhäuser*.'

'It's like Tristan's education. You want him to go to Bogstead and Winchester and New College. Because you went to Winchester and New College and your father went to Winchester . . .'

'And Balliol. There was an unconventional streak in Daddy.'

'Claude. Don't you ever long to go to work in an open-necked shirt and cotton trousers?'

'Of course not, Philly.' The man was shocked. 'In an open-necked shirt and cotton trousers, the Judges at the Old Bailey can't even hear you. You'd be quite inaudible and sent up to the public gallery.'

'Oh, I don't mean that, Claude. Don't you ever long for the sun?'

'You want me to book up for Viareggio again?' Claude clearly thought he'd solved it, but his wife disillusioned him.

'Not just a holiday, Claude. I mean a change in our lives. It's only fair I should tell you this. There's someone I might want to spend time with in, well, a different sort of life. It's not that I'm in love in the least. Nothing to do with that. I just want a complete change. I sometimes feel I never want to go back to Chambers.'

This fascinating dialogue was interrupted again by the arrival of Ballard at their table. He had come to report the disgraceful occurrence of a superintendent of the Special Branch smitten by a golf ball, a blow from which, it seemed, he didn't think Chambers would ever recover. I didn't know then how the differences of the Erskine-Browns were to be resolved, but Phillida did come into Chambers the next morning, and there found an official-looking letter from the Lord Chancellor which was to have some considerable effect on the case of *R*. v. *Culp*.

In due course, Miss Sturt, his social worker, brought young Matthew Culp to visit his father in Brixton prison. A special room was set aside for visits by prisoners' children, and the two Culps sat together trying to cheer each other up, Matthew being, by all accounts, the more decisive of the two. He told his father that he was determined to help him and that he meant to see to it that they were soon able to renew their contented domestic life together. He also asked Stanley to pass on certain information to me, his brief, as a consequence of which Mr Bernard made another appointment for me to visit the alleged gun-runner.

'My Matthew saw him, Mr Rumpole,' Stanley told me as soon as we were ensconced in the interview room. 'He says he saw that Mr Banks you were so interested in.'

'He did?'

'Oh, yes. Once when he came about leaving the packing-cases, what he said were medical supplies for his charitable organization. Matthew can tell them all about it. And that last morning, my Matthew'll say, he saw the same man in gold-rimmed glasses get out of the police car.'

'So that's the trap you walked into?' If Stanley were a criminal, he was clearly incompetent.

'Trap?' He looked at me, puzzled.

'Oh, yes. Isn't that the way they shoot tigers? Tie a goat to a tree, wait for the tiger to come hunting and then shoot. In this case, Mr Culp, you were the bait. Possibly innocent. The only question is . . .' I looked thoughtfully at Stanley. 'How much did the goat know?'

'I didn't know anything, Mr Rumpole,' he protested. 'Medical supplies they were, as far I was concerned. But Matthew will tell you all about it.'

'Your boy's prepared to give evidence?' Mr Bernard looked encouraged.

'Ready and willing. He wants to help all he can.'

'And you want me to put him in the witness-box? How old is he? Twelve?'

'But such an old head on his shoulders, Mr Rumpole. I told you how he masters his geometry.'

'He may be a demon on equilateral triangles, but he's a bit young for a starring role, down the Old Bailey.'

'Please, Mr Rumpole,' my client begged me. 'He'd never forgive me if we didn't let him have his say. We make it a rule, you see, to look after each other.'

The man was so eager, and obviously proud of the son he trusted to save him. But I was still not convinced of the wisdom of calling young Matthew to give evidence in the daunting atmosphere of the Central Criminal Court.

When Phillida had opened her official-looking envelope she spread the news it contained around Chambers. Ballard then called a meeting, and opened the agenda in his usual ponderous, not to say, pompous, fashion.

'The first business today,' he began, 'is to congratulate Phillida Erskine-Brown, who has received gratifying news from the Lord Chancellor's office. She has been made a Recorder and so will sit in as a criminal judge from time to time, in the intervals of her busy practice.'

'A Daniel come to justice!' I saluted her.

'How do you feel about having your wife sit in judgment, Claude?' Hoskins asked.

'I'd say, used to it by now,' Claude gave him the reply jocular.

'Thank you very much.' Phillida looked becomingly modest. 'Quite honestly, it's come as a bit of a shock.'

'Of course, we all know that the Lord Chancellor is anxious to promote women, so perhaps, Phillida, you've found the way to the Bench a little easier than it's been for some of us.' Ballard was never of a generous nature and he found congratulating other learned friends very hard.

'I suppose we'd see you Lord Chancellor by now, Bollard, if only you'd been born Samantha and not Sam,' was my comment.

'My second duty is a less pleasant one.' Soapy Sam ignored me. 'Which is why I have asked Uncle Tom not to join this meeting. Something quite inexcusable in a respectable barristers' Chambers has occurred. An officer of the Special Branch arrived to see me in conference. Rather a big matter. Gun-running to Ulster. You may have read about *R. v. Culp* in the newspapers? Terrorist got shot in Notting Hill Gate . . . Well, you can see it's an extremely heavy case.'

'Oh, I'm in that,' I told him casually. 'Storm in a teacup, I think you'll find.'

'Superintendent Rodney came here for a consultation with myself,' Ballard continued with great seriousness. 'He walked into the clerk's room and was struck on the knee by a golf ball! I need hardly say who was responsible.'

'Uncle Tom!' Hoskins guessed the answer.

'He's been playing golf in there as long as I can remember.' Erskine-Brown was querulous.

'It wasn't Uncle Tom's fault,' I told them. 'I clearly heard him shouting, "Fore!"'

'He shouldn't have been shouting "fore" or anything else.' Ballard showed a very judicial irritation. 'A clerk's room is for collecting briefs, and discussing a chap's availability with Henry. A clerk's room isn't for shouting "fore" and driving off into superintendants' knee-caps!'

'He wasn't driving off,' I insisted.

'Oh. What was he doing then, Rumpole?'

'He was getting out of a bunker.'

'Sometimes you defeat me! I have no idea what you're talking about; there are no bunkers in our clerk's room!' Ballard seemed to think that decided the matter.

'It was an imaginary bunker.'

'I don't understand.'

'That's because you have no imagination.'

'Perhaps I haven't. In any event I can't see why Uncle Tom has to play golf in our clerk's room. It's quite unnecessary.'

'Of course it is,' I agreed.

'I'm glad you admit it, Rumpole.'

'Just as poetry is unnecessary,' I pointed out. 'You can't eat it. It doesn't make you money. I suppose people like you, Bollard, can get through life without Wordsworth's sonnet "Upon Westminster Bridge". What we are discussing is the quality of life. Uncle Tom adds an imaginative touch to what would otherwise be a fairly dreary, dusty little clerk's room, littered with biscuits, briefs and barristers.'

'Personally I don't understand why Uncle Tom comes into Chambers every day; he never gets any work.' Now Erskine-Brown showed his lack of imagination. If he lived with Uncle Tom's sister he'd come into Chambers every day whether there was any work for him there or not. Not that there was anything wrong with Uncle Tom's sister, she'd just worked her way through the entire medical directory without having had a day's illness in her life. Uncle Tom also, strange as it may have seemed, enjoyed our company.

Ballard now proceeded to judgment. 'Uncle Tom and his golf balls are,' he said, 'in my considered opinion, a quite unnecessary health hazard in Chambers. I intend to ask him to make his room available to us.'

'You're going to ask him to leave?' I wanted to get the situation perfectly clear.

'Exactly that.' Ballard made it perfectly clear, so I stood up.

'If Uncle Tom goes, I go,' I told him.

'That would seem to make the departure of Uncle Tom even more desirable,' Soapy Sam was saying with a faint smile as I left the room.

*

So that was how I decided, after so many years enduring the splendours and miseries of an Old Bailey hack, to leave our Chambers in Equity Court and perhaps quit the Bar for ever. The decision was one which I couldn't wait to tell that lately re-united couple of lovebirds, She Who Must Be Obeyed and Boxey Horne. As I entered the mansion flat that evening I was singing 'You take the High Road and I'll take the Low Road, and I'll be in Zimbabwe before you!' I entered our sitting-room and I spotted Hilda pouring Boxey a generous whisky. 'I have news for you both,' I told them. 'My feet itch!'

'What do you mean by that, Rumpole?' My wife seemed puzzled.

'I can smell the hot wind of Africa,' I told them. 'I hear the cry of the parrot in the jungle and the chatter of monkeys. I wish to see the elephant and the gazelle troop shyly up to the waterhole at night. You have inspired me, Boxey, my old darling. I'm leaving the Bar.'

'Don't talk nonsense!' Hilda was somewhat rattled.

'I have handed in my resignation.'

'You've *what*?'

'I have informed our learned Head of Chambers, Soapy Sam Ballard, Queen's Counsel, that I no longer wish to be part of an organization which can't tolerate golf in the clerk's room.'

'Uncle Tom!' Hilda got my drift.

'Of course.'

'I've never understood why he had to play golf in the clerk's room.'

'Because no one sends him any briefs,' I enlightened her. 'Do you think he wants to be seen doing nothing? Anyway. I've handed in my resignation. One more case – I intend to defeat Soapy Sam over a spot of illicit arms dealing – and then travels Rumpole East away!'

'You're not serious?' Boxey also looked alarmed.

'Farewell to dusty old law! No more nine to five in the office. Ask for me in the Nairobi Club in five years' time and the fellows might have news of me. Up country.'

'He's joking,' Hilda told her childhood sweetheart. 'Definitely joking.' But then she sounded uncertain. 'Aren't you, Rumpole?'

'I wish I could come back with you,' Boxey told me. 'But . . .'

'Oh, you can't do that, Boxey. Of course not. Somebody's got to stay here and look after Hilda.' I was gratified to see that they looked at each other with a wild surmise. They wanted to talk further, but I refused to discuss the matter until my Swan Song, the Queen against Stanley Culp, was safely over and, I hoped, won.

Some days later I invited Phillida for a drink in Pommeroy's. When we were safely seated with glasses in our hands, she asked me if I were really thinking of leaving Chambers. I told her that my future depended on Ballard, and Hilda's long-lost cousin, who rejoiced in the name of Boxey Horne. She Who Must Be Obeyed, I explained, said she might have married Boxey.

'And I might not have married Claude.' Our Portia stared thoughtfully into her vodka and tonic. As Shelley would probably have said, in the circumstances, 'We look before and after; We pine for what is not.' 'I might,' she added, 'have had a husband full of energy, and jokes, with a taste for adventure. Someone unconventional. A rebel who hadn't been to Bogstead and Winchester.'

'Portia. You're flattering me.' I smiled modestly.

'What do you mean?'

'But mightn't I have been a little old for you?'

'Why did you ask me for this drink?' Portia looked at me and asked sharply. It was time for me to put my master plan into practice. I began, I hope, as tactfully as possible with: 'There's a bit of an east wind blowing between you and Claude on the subject of young Tristan's education . . .'

'I don't see why the family has to be split up.' She was quite clear on the subject.

'Exactly. A boy needs his father.'

'And his mother, don't forget.'

'Worst thing that can happen,' I argued profoundly, 'for families is to be separated, torn apart by society's unnatural laws and customs.'

'You understand that?' She looked at me with more than usual sympathy.

'Handing a small boy over for other people to bring up has to be avoided at all costs.'

'You ought to tell Claude that.'

'Oh, I certainly shall,' I promised her as I raised my glass. 'Family togetherness. Here's to it, Portia, and I hope you support it, whenever you sit in judgment.'

Mizz Liz Probert had her own, somewhat uncomfortable, standards of honesty, which were usually calculated to cause trouble to others. It will be recalled that when Claude had incautiously invited her to a night à deux at the Opera, she immediately told Phillida of the invitation, thus causing prolonged domestic disharmony.* It was therefore predictable that she should tell Claude that she had seen Phillida on a bench in the Embankment Gardens, drinking champagne and holding hands with a famous film star. My learned friend, Mr Erskine-Brown, gave me an account of this conversation at a later date. It seems that Mizz Probert had her own explanation for this event, one hard to understand by anyone not intimately connected with the North Islington Women's Movement. 'You drove her to it, Claude,' Liz said. 'If a woman does that sort of thing, it's always the man's fault, isn't it?'

'And if a man does that sort of thing?'

'Well, it's always his fault. Don't you understand? Phillida's just rebelling against your enormous power and sexual domination.'

'Oh?' Claude tried to reason with Mizz Probert. 'Phillida is a Queen's Counsel. She wears a silk gown. She's about to sit as a Recorder. In judgment at the Old Bailey. I'm still a junior barrister. With a rough old gown made of some inferior material. How can I possibly dominate her?'

'Because you're a man, Claude,' Liz told him. 'You were born for domination!'

'Oh, really? Do you honestly think so?' At the time, Claude was not entirely displeased by this view. Later, in the privacy of his home, Phillida told me, he apologized to his wife for his terrible habit of domination. 'I suppose I can't help it; it's

* See 'Rumpole and the Official Secret' in *Rumpole's Last Case*, Penguin, 1987.

a bit of a curse really. Men just don't know their own strength.'

'Claude' – Phillida tried to keep a straight face – 'I have to decide on the shirts you want to buy. When we went out to dinner with the Arthurian Daybells you asked me to remind you whether you like smoked mackerel!'

'Do I?' her husband asked seriously.

'Not very much.'

'Ah. That's right.'

'You seem to suffer from terminal exhaustion directly your head hits the pillow. Can you please tell me exactly how you are exercising this terrible power over me? Could you give me one single instance of your ruthless domination?'

'I suppose it's just the male role. I'll try not to play it, Philly. I honestly will.'

'Oh, Claude!' Portia could no longer contain her laughter. 'Do you think I ought to stay here and look after you?'

'Well, you'll have to stay here now, won't you, anyway?' Claude told his wife.

'Because you tell me to?' She was still laughing.

'No. Because you're a Recorder.'

Portia had become a part-time judge and Portia was devoted to the idea of keeping children within the family circle. There was only one element of my equation left to supply, and to do so I entered our clerk's room with the intention of having a confidential chat with Henry. As good luck would have it, I found him patiently addressing Dianne, who sat with a book on her typewriter. '"I knew that suddenly, when we were dancing,"' Henry told her, '"an enchantment swept over me. An enchantment that I've never known before and shall never know again. My heart's bumping. I'm trembling like a fool."'

'"Thumping",' Dianne insisted.

'What's that?'

'"My heart's thumping." Otherwise very good.'

'The late Sir Noël Coward, Henry?' I guessed.

'Oh, yes, Mr Rumpole. The Bexley Thespians. We're putting on *Tonight at 8.30*, sir. We likes his stuff. I do happen to have the starring role.'

'With your usual co-star?' Fate was giving me unusual help with *R.* v. *Stanley Culp*.

'I shall be playing opposite Miss Osgood from the Old Bailey List Office. As per always.'

'Miss Osgood, who fixes the hearings and the Judges. A talented actress, of course?'

'Sarah Osgood has a certain magic on stage, Mr Rumpole.'

'And considerable powers in the List Office also, Henry. Remind me to send her a large bouquet on the first night. And for our Portia's début on the Old Bailey Bench, I thought it would be nice if Miss Osgood gave her something worthy of her talents.'

'No doubt you had something in mind, sir?' Our clerk wasn't born yesterday.

'*R.* v. *Culp*.' I told him what I had in mind. 'A drama of gun-dealing in Notting Hill Gate. Likely to run and run. It might be Portia's way to stardom. Mention it to your fellow Thespian during a break in rehearsals, why don't you?' My hint dropped, I moved out of the room past our ever-putting oldest inhabitant. 'Still golfing, Uncle Tom?'

'Ballard wants to see me,' he said, almost proudly.

'Oh, yes. When?'

'Any time at my convenience before the end of the month. Do you think he's fixed me up with a junior brief?'

'Would you like that?'

'I'm not sure. I haven't kept my hand in at the law.'

'Never mind, Uncle Tom. Your putting's coming on splendidly!' And I left him to it.

And so it came about that fate spun its wheel and, with a little help from my good self and Miss Osgood at the List Office, the Queen against Culp was selected as the case to be tried by Mrs Recorder Erskine-Brown when she made her first appearance on the Old Bailey Bench. She sat there, severely attractive, a large pair of horn-rimmed glasses balanced on that delicate nose which has sent the fantasies whirling in the heads of many barristers, distinguished and otherwise. I thought how I had advised and trained her up, from white-wig to judge's wig, to lean to the Defence, particularly when the defendant has a twelve-year-old son who is the apple of his eye. I also thought that there was no judge in England better suited to try the case against Stanley Culp.

As I rose to cross-examine the Special Branch superintendent, Portia selected a freshly sharpened pencil and prepared to make a note. This was in great contrast to such as Judge Bullingham who merely yawns, examines his nails or explores his ear with a little finger during cross-examination by the Defence, that is, if he's not actively heckling.

'Superintendent Rodney,' I began. 'Have you, as a Special Branch officer, ever heard of the Loyalist League of Welfare and Succour for Victims of Terrorist Attack?'

'Not till your client told us they sent him those packing-cases.'

'Or of a Mr Banks, who apparently runs that philanthropic organization?'

'Not till your client told us his story.'

'A story you believed?'

'If I had we wouldn't be here, would we, Mr Rumpole?' Rodney smiled as though he'd won a point, but the Judge interrupted for the first time.

'Mr Rumpole. What does it matter what this officer believes? It's what the Jury believes that matters, isn't it?'

'Your ladyship is, of course, perfectly right. A Daniel come to judgment,' I whispered to Mizz Probert. 'Yea, a Daniel!' I then asked, 'Did my client Mr Culp give you a description of Banks, the man who had asked him to store the packing-cases for him?'

'Superintendent,' her Ladyship said quite properly, 'you may refresh your memory from your notes, if you wish to.'

'Thank you, my Lady.' He turned a page or two in his notebook. 'Yes. Culp said, "Mr Banks called on me and asked me to store some ... medical supplies. He was a man of average height, he had gold-rimmed glasses with ...".'

'Slightly tinted lenses?' I suggested.

'Tinted lenses. Yes.'

'Well. You know perfectly well who that is, don't you?' I asked, looking at the Jury.

'Excuse me, Mr Rumpole' – the superintendent rather over-acted complete bewilderment – 'I have absolutely no idea.'

'Really?' And I asked, 'Have the Special Branch made any effort whatsoever to find this elusive Banks? Have you sought him here, Superintendent? Have you sought him there?'

'My Lady' – Soapy Sam arose with awful solemnity – 'it is my duty to object to this line of questioning.'

'*Your duty*, Mr Bollard?' I thought his duty was to sit still and let me get on with it.

'My patriotic duty!' The fellow seemed about to salute and run up a small Union Jack. 'My Lady. This is a case in which the security of the realm is involved. The activities of the Special Branch necessarily take place in secret. The inquiries they have made cannot be questioned by Mr Rumpole.'

'What do you say, Mr Rumpole?' Portia was ever anxious to know both sides of the question.

'What do I say?' I came to the defence of the legal system against the Secret Police. 'I say quite simply that contrary to what Mr Ballard seems to believe, this trial is not taking place behind the Iron Curtain. We are in England, my Lady, breathing English air. The Special Branch is not the K.G.B. They are merely a widely travelled department of our dear Old Bill.' This got me a little refreshing laughter from the jury box. 'I should be much obliged for an answer to my question.'

'Is the whereabouts of this man Banks vital to your defence?' Portia asked judicially.

'My lady, they are.'

'And you wish me to make a ruling on this matter?'

'The first, I'm sure, of many wise judgments your Ladyship will make in many cases.'

'Then in my judgment . . .' I whispered to Liz to keep her fingers crossed, but happily justice triumphed and her Ladyship ruled, '. . . Mr Rumpole may ask his question.' A wise and up-right judge, a Daniel come to judgment, but Superintendent Rodney stonewalled our efforts by saying, 'We have not been able to trace Mr Banks or the Loyalist League of Welfare.'

'Much good did that do you!' Ballard muttered to me, and I muttered back, 'Wait for it. I'm not finished yet, Comrade Bollardski!' I said to the witness, 'Superintendent. You arrived at breakfast time on the 4th of May outside the shop in Notting Hill Gate to arrest my client. Who was in the car with you?'

'Detective Inspector Blake and Detective Sergeant Trump, my Lady.'

'And who had told you that a transaction in arms was likely to take place in Mr Culp's shop that morning?'

'My Lady . . .' the Superintendent appealed to the Judge, who ruled with a smile I found quite charming, 'I don't think the officer can be compelled to give the name of his informer, Mr Rumpole.' I accepted her decision gratefully and asked, 'Was your informer, let's call him Mr X, in the car with you and the other officers when you arrived at the shop?'

'My Lady.' Ballard rose again to maintain secrecy. 'The Court no doubt understands that any information about a police informer on terrorist activities would place the man's life in immediate danger.'

'Very well.' Portia saw the point. 'I don't think you can take the matter further, can you, Mr Rumpole?'

I could and did with my next question. 'Let me just ask this, with your Ladyship's permission. Did a man wearing gold-rimmed spectacles and tinted lenses get out of the police car in front of the shop that morning and walk away before the arrest took place?'

'I'm not prepared to answer that, my Lady,' the Superintendent stonewalled again.

'And was that man "Mr Banks"?' I pressed on.

'I have already told you, sir. We don't know Mr Banks.'

'But you do know whoever it was, an officer of your Special Branch, perhaps, who stored the packing-cases in Mr Culp's shop, who told Mr Culp they were medical supplies, and arranged for this man MacRobert, who wanted to buy arms for his Ulster terrorists, to walk into your trap?'

'All I can tell you is that the cases of arms were in the shop and MacRobert called for them.' The Superintendent sighed, as though my defence were no more than a waste of his precious time.

'Had MacRobert met Mr Banks?'

'I can't say.'

'And the Jury will never know because MacRobert has been silenced forever.'

'Detective Inspector Blake saw him in the act of pulling out a weapon. He fired in self defence.'

'No doubt he did. But it leaves us, doesn't it, a little short of evidence?'

We weren't entirely bereft of evidence, of course. All through my cross-examination I had been aware of a small, solemn, spectacled boy sitting outside the Court with his social worker, longing to help his father. I had hoped to get enough out of the Superintendent to avoid having to put young Matthew through the rigours of the witness-box, but I hadn't succeeded. Now, Bernard whispered to me, 'The little lad's just longing to go in. Are you going to call him?' The business of being a barrister involves the hard task of making decisions, instantly and on your feet. You may make the right decision, you may often get it wrong. The one luxury not open to you is that of not making up your mind. I stood silent as long as I dared and then committed myself.

'Fortunately,' I told the Superintendent, 'I am in a position to call a witness who might be able to tell us a little more about the damned elusive Banks.'

'Oh, please, Mr Rumpole' – Sam Ballard's whispered disapproval echoed through the court – 'don't swear, particularly in front of a lady Judge.'

Dressed in his best brown suit, a white shirt and a red bow-tie, in the dock Stanley somehow looked more crumpled and less impressive than ever. He sat slumped like a sack of potatoes; the Court seemed too hot for him and he frequently dabbed his forehead with a folded handkerchief. However, when his son, a more alert figure, stepped into the witness-box and had the nature of the oath gently explained to him by Portia, Stanley pulled himself together. He sat up straight, his eyes shone with pride and he looked like a devoted parent whose son has just stood up to collect the best all-rounder prize at the school Speech Day. His pride only seemed to increase as I led young Matthew through his examination-in-chief.

'Matthew. Do you remember a man coming to ask your father to store some boxes?'

'I was in the shop.'

'You were in the shop when he arrived?'

'Yes. He said he was Mr Banks and I went and fetched Dad from the back. He was mending something.' The boy answered clearly, without hesitation.

The Jury seemed to like him and I felt encouraged to ask for further details.

'Can you remember what Mr Banks looked like?'

'He had these gold-rimmed glasses. And they were coloured.'

'What was coloured?'

'The glass in them.'

'Did your father talk to Mr Banks?'

'Yes. I went upstairs. To finish my homework.' Portia was listening carefully and noting down the evidence. Matthew was doing well and his ordeal, I hoped, was almost over. I asked him, 'Did you see Mr Banks again?'

'Oh, yes.'

'When?'

'When the policemen arrived for Dad. Mr Banks got out of the police car.'

I looked at the Jury and repeated slowly, 'Mr Banks got out of the police car. What did he do then?'

'He walked away.' I smiled at Matthew, who didn't smile back, but remained standing seriously at attention. 'Yes. Thank you, Matthew. Oh, just wait there a minute, will you?' I had to sit down then, and leave him to the mercy of Ballard. I had no particular fear, for Soapy Sam had never been a great cross-examiner. His first question, however, was not badly chosen. 'Matthew. Are you very fond of your father?'

'We look after each other.' For the first time Matthew looked, unsmiling, at the dock. His father beamed back at him.

'Oh, yes. I'm sure you do.' Ballard tried the approach cynical. 'And you want to help him, don't you? You want to look after him in this case?'

'I'd like him to come home.' I was pleased to see Portia give Matthew a small smile before busying herself with her notes.

'I'm sure you would. And have you and your father discussed
this business of Mr Banks getting out of the police car?' Ballard
asked an apparently innocent question.

'I told Dad what I saw.'

'And did he tell you it was going to be his story that the police
had set up this deal, through Mr Banks?'

'He said something like that. Yes.' It wasn't exactly the best
answer we could have expected.

'So does it come to this? You'd say anything to help your
father's defence?'

'My Lady. That was a completely uncalled for –' I rose with not
entirely simulated rage, anxious to give the boy a little respite.

'Yes, Mr Rumpole,' Portia agreed and then turned to the
young witness. 'Matthew. Are you sure you saw a man with
glasses get out of the police car?'

I subsided. My interruption had been a mistake. I had changed
a poor and unsympathetic cross-examiner for a humane and
understanding one who might put our case in far more damage.
'Yes, I am. Quite sure.'

'Apart from the fact that he had gold-rimmed glasses with
tinted lenses, can you be sure it was the same man who came to
your father's shop and said he was Mr Banks?' Portia probed
gently and Ballard got on the band-wagon with a sharp 'You
can't be *sure*, can you?'

'Please, Mr Ballard.' Unhappily, Phillida didn't let Soapy Sam
show himself at his worst. 'Just think, Matthew,' she said.
'There's absolutely no hurry.'

There was a long silence then. Matthew was frowning and worried.

'I *think* it was the same man,' he said, and my heart sank.

'You think it was.' The Judge made a perfectly fair note and
Ballard's voice rose triumphantly as he repeated. 'You *think* it
was! But you can't be sure.'

'Well . . . Well, he looked the same. He *was* the same!' And
then Matthew turned from a carefully controlled, grown-up witness to a child again. He called across to his father in the dock,
'He was, Dad? Wasn't he?'

And Stanley looked at him helplessly, unable to speak. The

Jury looked embarrassed, fiddled with their papers or stared at their feet. The blushing, confused child in the witness-box stood beyond the reach of all of us until the Judge mercifully released him. 'I don't think we should keep Matthew here a moment longer,' she said. 'Have either of you gentlemen any further questions?'

Ballard had done his worst and there was no way in which I could repair the damage. Phillida said, 'Thank you, Matthew. You can go now.' And the boy walked down from the witness-box and towards the door of the Court. His social worker rose to follow him. As he got to the dock he looked at his father and said quietly, 'Did I let you down, Dad?'

I could hear him, but Stanley couldn't. All the same his father raised his thumb in a hopeful, encouraging signal as Matthew left us to be taken back into care.

Henry told me that, whilst we were on our way back from Court, the world-famous film star called at our clerk's room in search of Phillida. When he was told that she had been sitting as a judge down at the Old Bailey, he looked somewhat daunted.

'Isn't she too pretty to be a judge?'

'I don't think the Lord Chancellor considered that, sir' – Henry was at his most dignified – 'when he made Mrs Erskine-Brown a Recorder.'

'A judge, ugh!' Cy seemed to think this new position of Phillida's was something of a bar to romance. 'Anyway. Tell her I called by, will you? I'm getting the red-eye back to the Coast tonight. Say, that's a great gimmick!' This came as a direct result of seeing Uncle Tom putting in the corner of the room. 'What a great selling-point for your legal business.'

On his way downstairs, Cy met Soapy Sam Ballard and engaged him in some conversation which our Head of Chambers later reported to me. It seems that Cy had asked Ballard if he worked with Phillida and, on being told that Sam was Head of our Chambers, said, 'You run the shop! What a great gimmick you got, having an old guy playing golf in reception.' When Ballard explained he meant to put an end to it, Cy said, 'Are you crazy? Wait till I let them know on the Coast. There's a British lawyers' office, I'll tell them, where they keep an old guy to play golf in reception. Kind of traditional. I tell you. You'll get so much business from American lawyers! They'll all want to come in here and they won't *believe* it!'

'You think Uncle Tom'll bring us business?' Ballard was puzzled.

'You wait till I spread the word. You won't be able to handle it.'

In due course we made our final speeches and I sat back, my duty done, to hear her Ladyship sum up. 'Members of the Jury,' she concluded, 'the defence case is that this arms sale was staged by the police to trap the man, MacRobert. Mr Rumpole has said that the arms were deposited in the shop by a Mr Banks, who was a police officer in plain clothes, and that Mr Culp was simply told they were medical supplies. He was a quite innocent man, used as bait to trap the terrorist MacRobert. Are you sure that Mr Culp knew what was in those packing cases? They must have been extremely heavy for medical supplies. Do you accept young Matthew's identification of Mr Banks as the man in the police car? He *thinks* it was Banks but, you remember, he couldn't be sure. Members of the Jury, the decision on the facts is entirely for you. If there's a doubt, Mr Culp is entitled to the benefit of that doubt. Now, please, take all the time you need and, when you're quite ready, come back and tell me what you have decided. Thank you.'

So the Usher swore to conduct the Jury to their room and not to communicate with them until they had reached a verdict. As I said to my learned friend Mizz Liz Probert, it had been an utterly fair summing up by a completely unbiased judge – always a terrible danger to the Defence.

The Jury were out for almost three hours and then returned with a unanimous verdict of guilty. Of course, an Old Bailey hack should take such results as part of the fair wear and tear of legal life. 'Win a few, lose a few', should be the attitude. I have never managed to do this, but I still hoped, by an argument which I thought might be extremely sympathetic to our particular judge, to keep Stanley out of prison.

Accordingly, when the time came for my speech in mitigation,

I aimed straight for our Portia's maternal instincts. 'Whoever may be guilty in this case,' I ended, 'one person is entirely innocent. Young Matthew Culp has broken no laws, committed no offence. He is a hard-working, decent little boy and his only fault may be that he loves his father and wanted to help him. But if you sentence his father to prison, you send Matthew also. You sentence him to years in council care. You sentence him to years as an orphan, because his mother has long gone out of his life. You sentence him to being cut off from his only family, from the father he needs and who needs him. You sentence this small boy to a lonely life in a crowd of strangers. I ask your Ladyship to consider that and on behalf of Matthew Culp I ask you to say . . . no prison for this foolish father!'

Phillida looked somewhat moved. She said quietly, 'Yes. Thank you, Mr Rumpole. Thank you for all your help.'

'If your Ladyship pleases.' I sat and then Stanley Culp was told to stand for sentence. The fact that the Judge was an extremely pretty woman in no way softened the awesome nature of the occasion. 'Culp,' she began, 'I have listened most carefully to all your learned Counsel has said, and said most eloquently, on your behalf.' So far so good. 'Unhappily, all the crimes we commit, all the mistakes we make, affect our innocent children. I am very conscious of the effect any prison sentence would have on your son, to whom I accept that you are devoted.' So far so hopeful, but this wasn't the end. 'However, I have to protect society. And I have to remember that you were prepared to deal in murderous weapons which might have left orphans in Northern Ireland.' This was not encouraging, and Portia then concluded, 'The most lenient sentence I can impose on you is one of four years' imprisonment. Take him down.'

Stanley Culp was looking hopelessly round the Court as though searching for his son Matthew before the Dock Officer touched his arm and removed him from our sight.

Pommeroy's was the place to attempt to drown the memory of my failure, and Stanley's four years. I sat alone at my corner table and there my old pupil, her day of judging done, sought me out. 'I'm sorry about Culp,' Portia said.

'Never plead guilty,' I advised her.

'I was only . . .'

'Doing your job?'

'Well, yes.'

'It is your job, isn't it, Portia?' I told her. 'Deciding what's going to happen to people. Judging them. Condemning them. Sending them downstairs. Not a very nice job, perhaps. Not as agreeable as cleaning out the drains or holding down a responsible position as a pox doctor's clerk. Every day I thank heaven I don't have to do it.'

'Shouldn't I have become a Recorder? Is that what you're saying?'

'Oh, no. No. Of course you should. Someone's got to do it. I just thank God it's not me.'

'You're lucky.' She looked at me and I think she meant it.

'I enjoy the luxury of defending people, protecting them where I can, keeping them out of chokey by the skin of my teeth. I've said a good many hard words in my time but "take him down" is an expression I've never used.'

'Rumpole!' She was hurt. 'Do you imagine I enjoyed it?'

'No, Portia. No, of course not. I never imagined that. You had to do your job and you did it so bloody fairly that my fellow got convicted. He was caught in a trap. Like the rest of us.'

'Cheer up, Rumpole.' Then she smiled. 'I'll buy you a large Pommeroy's plonk.'

'I am greatly obliged to your Ladyship.' I drank up. 'And what about young Tristan? Is he to pay his debt to society?'

'I don't know what you mean. He's going to Bogstead.' She announced another verdict.

'Your Ladyship passed judgment in favour of my learned friend Mr Claude Erskine-Brown?' I couldn't believe it.

'Well. Not exactly. As a matter of fact Tristan passed judgment on himself.'

What had happened, it seemed, was that, saying good-night to her son, Phillida had been amazed to hear him say that he was eagerly looking forward to Bogstead. 'But don't you want to stay with us?' his mother asked, and Tristan confessed that being in the bosom of his family all the time was a bit of a strain on his nerves as his father was forever listening to operas and his mother always had her nose inside some brief or other. It was difficult to talk to either of them.

'I told him I'd talk to him whenever he wanted, that I'd tell him what I'd been doing, being a judge, and all that sort of thing.'

'And what did young Tristan say to that?' I asked her.

'He thought he'd find more to talk about with the chaps at Boggers,' Phillida said more than a little sadly.

I went back to Chambers to collect a brief for the next day, and there I met Sam Ballard, who was still unusually excited by his conversation with Cy Stratton, and had decided not to fire Uncle Tom, which made it unnecessary for me to set out for darkest Africa. I bought some flowers for Hilda at the Temple underground station, and when I got home and presented them to her I noticed our so-called 'mansion' flat was strangely silent.

'Boxey's gone.' Hilda spoke in a businesslike tone, concealing whatever emotion she may have felt. 'And what are *they* for?'

'Oh, to stick in a vase somewhere.' I restrained myself, with difficulty, from dancing with joy.

'He must have gone when I was out buying chops for our supper and he didn't even say goodbye. Why would Boxey do a thing like that?'

'Certainly not running away from the prospect of looking after you, Hilda. Never mind.' We went into the sitting-room and I poured her a large gin and tonic and myself a celebratory Pommeroy's. 'He was always such *fun* as a young man was Boxey,' Hilda said.

> 'We look before and after;
> We pine for what is not;
> Our sincerest laughter
> With some pain is fraught,'

I told her.

'Quite honestly, Rumpole' – Hilda was becoming daring – 'did you think Boxey had become a bit of a bore in his old age?'

'"Our sweetest songs are those that tell of saddest thought." I'm not going to Africa, Hilda.'

'I didn't think you were.'

'I shall never see the elephant and gazelle gathering at the waterhole. I shall never see zebra stampeding in the dawn. I shall get no nearer Africa than Boxey did.'

'What on earth do you mean, Rumpole?'

'All that talk about evening-dress to impress the natives. I bet he got that straight out of H. Rider Haggard. And didn't it occur to you, Hilda? There are absolutely no tigers in Kenya!'

There was a long silence, and then Hilda said with a rueful smile, 'Boxey asked me for a thousand pounds to start a small-holding, with battery hens.'

'I don't believe he's been further East than Bognor. You didn't give him anything?'

'Out of the overdraft? Don't be foolish, Rumpole. So you're staying here.'

'Soapy Sam Ballard told Uncle Tom to carry on golfing; he thinks it'll bring us a great deal of business with American law-yers.' I poured myself another comforting glass. 'You know, I lost the case against Ballard.'

'I thought so. You're not so unbearable when you lose.' She thought the situation over and then said, 'So we'll have to get along without Boxey.'

'How on earth shall we manage?'

'As we always do, I suppose. Just you and I together.'

'Nothing changes, does it, Hilda?' The day had given me an appetite and I was looking forward to Boxey's chops. 'Nothing changes very much at all.'

Rumpole and the Quality of Life

It's impossible to hack away for getting on for half a century in the Criminal Courts, rising to your feet, bending low to say 'If Your Lordship pleases' to ignorant white-wigs, or stooping to lick the boots of the Uxbridge Magistrates, without feeling a little out of sorts, occasionally. The truth of the matter is that I was suffering an attack of Bullinghamitis, a condition of which the symptoms are exhaustion and bouts of nervous depression and nausea brought about by frequent appearances before Judge Bullingham down the Bailey. 'You're feeling seedy, Rumpole. You'd better go to Dr MacClintock for a check-up.' She Who Must Be Obeyed said this not once, but three or four times a day, over a period of months. It was as effective as the Chinese water torture and it was to escape the merciless persistence of Hilda's advice that I was driven to an appointment with our friendly neighbourhood quack. 'And whatever Hector Mac-Clintock tells you to do,' were Hilda's orders, 'you do it.'

Dr MacClintock was a small, lightweight, puritanical Scot who looked as though he existed on a glass of cold water and a handful of Quaker Oats a day. Once in his power, he had me stripped to the waist, braces hanging useless in the breeze, as he plied his stethoscope and asked me about my daily intake of calories. 'For instance,' he murmured as though receiving my confession, 'tell me about breakfast.'

'Taken at the Taste-Ee-Bite in Fleet Street if I'm busy. A fairly light affair.'

'Good.' He nodded approval.

'Couple of eggs on a fried slice.'

'Fried slice?' I might have admitted a taste for hard drugs with my morning tea; the good Doctor was clearly shaken.

'Three or four rashers ...'

'That's all, I hope?'

'Apart from the sausages. Rounds of toast. Marmalade.'

The Doctor put away his stethoscope nervously and said, 'Let's have you up on the scales, then. And for luncheon?'

'We only get an hour. It's a bit of a snack as it so happens.' I stood on the fatally revealing platform.

'A salad, perhaps?' MacClintock tried to sound hopeful as he arranged the weights.

'Who am I to take food from the mouths of starving rabbits?' I denied salad. 'A quick steak and kidney pud in the pub opposite the Bailey. A few boiled potatoes. Serving of cabbage. I find a pint of draught Guinness keeps the strength up at lunch-time.' The Doctor forced himself to look at the scales, and sighed heavily. 'Then I take nothing at all until dinner.'

'Nothing? Well, I'm glad of that at least. Oh, do put your shirt back on.' He sat at his desk and started to write voluminous notes.

'Unless you count a small crumpet at tea-time.' I had to be honest.

'There have been times,' the Doctor said mournfully, 'when I have known indulgence in a small crumpet at tea-time to make the difference between life and death. Dinner?'

'Hilda usually grills a few chops with two veg, and I confess to a weakness for a touch of jam roly-poly.' I was restoring the shirt.

'Drink?'

'Oh, thank you very much.' Dr MacClintock was getting out the blood-pressure apparatus.

'No. *Do* you drink? Apart from non-alcoholic beverages.'

'Oh, I hardly touch them.'

'Very good. Just roll up the sleeve.'

'I hardly touch non-alcoholic beverages. Pommeroy's Very Ordinary claret, in my medical experience, keeps you astonishingly regular. Of course, I'm extremely modest in my consumption.'

'Modest?' The Doctor was pumping. 'Good.'

'Château Thames Embankment. About all I can afford nowadays.'

'And how much? Shall we say a bottle?'

'Oh, a couple. Maybe a little more when I'm before Judge Bullingham or Graves.'

'Two bottles a week?' He looked at the blood-pressure gauge and sighed again.

'A day. I haven't signed the pledge,' I told him.

'Smoke. A lot?'

'Do you, really?' I was glad to hear the man had some weak-nesses, and getting out a packet of small cigars, I offered one to the Doctor.

'Let's face the fact' – he shook his head – 'there is a great deal too much of you, Mr Rumpole.'

'Oh, I don't know.' I tried to sound modest. 'If a fellow's a decent barrister, knows a thing or two about bloodstains, sharp cross-examiner, makes an effective final speech, how can there possibly be too much of a good thing?'

'The question is,' the Doctor asked with great seriousness, 'do you want to drop dead?'

It was an interesting question, and I gave it due attention. When I'm doing a hopeless rape, say, under the icy stare of Judge Gerald Graves, I might. On the other hand, when I've got the Jury on my side I feel I could live forever. As it happened, I had just received the brief in *R. v. Derwent*, one of the most fascinating cases of homicide I have encountered since the great days of the Penge Bungalow Murders. So I told the Doctor, quite frankly, 'No. I don't think I'd like to do that.'

'Then you must go on the diet I'm giving you at once. No wine. No meat. No fish, eggs, bread, butter, milk . . .'

'Ugh. Milk!' I agreed.

'Bread or pastry of any sort.'

'How do I manage without food?'

'Thin-O-Vite.' Dr MacClintock produced a name I was to learn to dread. 'Mix it with water and eat as much of it as you like. Make a pig of yourself. I hope to see less of you in about a month's time.'

'Meanwhile, "I eat the air, promise-crammed. You cannot feed capons so."'

'Who said that?'

'Hamlet. A Dane who'd no doubt have been a great deal less gloomy with a square meal inside him. Good day, Doctor.'

Is not being dead really enough, even if you have to keep alive on Thin-O-Vite? Battery hens aren't dead. Chained-up fattening pigs aren't dead. Even Judge Graves down the Bailey appears to be still breathing, if you watch him very closely. Life is not enough, in my opinion, *per se*. It's the quality of life that matters, and a fellow has to have something to live *for*. Some fine, ennobling, enriching experience. And that essential was supplied for me, in the absence of steak and kidney pud, by my engagement to defend in the case of *R*. v. *Derwent*. So, I was induced by that, and the insistence of She Who Must Be Obeyed, to follow the Doctor's Spartan regime. And now I must tell you something of that strange and, in many ways, pathetic case which had tempted me to go on living.

Sir Daniel Derwent, C.H., R.A., was a painter of the old school. He had a head like an elderly, bearded lion; he was given to wearing capes, wide-brimmed hats or the occasional beret. His portraits of important men and beautiful women were always competent, often charming, but never stunning. It might be said that Sir Daniel looked too much like a great artist to be one entirely. All the same, his work was greatly admired by many people including himself. He had, in his life, two great loves, painting and beautiful women.

Perdita, Derwent's wife at the time he died, was extremely beautiful and less than half his age. She had been a student at St Matthew's School of Art, where her husband was the Professor of Painting. He took her to live with him in his Chelsea house and subsequently married her. His household there consisted of his old mother, Barbara, always known as Bunty, Derwent, and Helen, his daughter by a previous marriage, who had run his life and continued to do so and make his new young wife extremely unwelcome.

The story begins on an evening which was described in detail in the evidence given at the Old Bailey. In the old-fashioned studio which was a feature of the house, Lady Derwent was seated on a model's throne, wearing a long skirt and no top. Sir Daniel was painting a three-quarter-length portrait of his wife. Bunty Derwent, a large, spreading and cheerful woman, was knitting by the stove, and Helen Derwent was making trouble because her new step-mother had forgotten to order the fish for supper.

'I'm terribly sorry, Helen.' Perdita opened her blue eyes wide, in a sort of panic. 'Did I really forget?'

'Don't move,' Daniel growled from behind his canvas.

'It's too bad of you!' Helen was unforgiving. 'You know how Daddy looks forward to his fish pie. It's really not much to ask of anyone, just to ring up and order the fish.'

'Don't make such a fuss about it, Helen.' Bunty was always the peacemaker. 'It's really not important. We'll have eggs.'

Perdita gave a small, grateful smile, being very careful not to move. And then, so the evidence told us, Daniel's brush-bearing hand started to tremble as it approached the canvas, misfired and made a long smear across Perdita's portrait. He threw down his brush in a fury and clasped his hand to his forehead.

'Hell and *death*!' he was heard to say.

That night Miss Helen Derwent couldn't sleep. She got up at about four o'clock and, going downstairs to make herself a cup of tea, she saw a light under the studio door. She opened it and found her father lying, fully dressed, on the studio couch. His eyes were open but she closed them. He was quite dead.

Later that morning, the youngish, spectacled and earnest Doctor Harman, who had been treating Sir Daniel, returned to the Chelsea house and was closeted with his late patient's wife and mother. He had been surprised by the sudden onset of death, and he had established that Nurse Gregson, who helped care for the painter, had been called and visited at tea-time on the previous afternoon to give an injection. I must here deal with the medication given to relieve the pain caused by the cancer from which Sir Daniel was suffering. He regularly took morphine in the form of syrup, but, to cope with the 'breakthrough' of severe pain, he received booster injections of diamorphine which were administered by the visiting nurse. She gave him the usual supplementary dose when she called the previous afternoon, and then she went off duty. On checking her medical bag the next morning, Nurse Gregson found that a number of additional

ampoules, containing what would have been a fatal dose of diamorphine, had been removed. She remembered leaving the bag,
for a while, unwatched in the hall of the Derwent household.

'You're sure he didn't take anything after the nurse left?' the
Doctor asked the young widow.

'I don't think so.' Because of his illness, the Derwents had
been occupying separate bedrooms, each one with a bathroom
attached. As Perdita gave this answer, her step-daughter Helen
came into the room, holding, almost triumphantly, some articles
which later became important exhibits in the case.

'Don't you think you ought to tell Doctor Harman about these,
Perdita? I found them in your bedroom.' What she had found
was a number of empty ampoules which had once contained
diamorphine, a hypodermic syringe and a pamphlet which I was
to get to know almost by heart, advocating euthanasia for those
suffering from terminal illness.

This discovery led to investigations by the police, instigated
by Doctor Harman. It was not until another breakfast-time,
about three weeks later, that I was telephoned by my old friend
and instructing solicitor, Mr Bernard. He told me that Lady
Derwent had been taken to Chelsea police station and charged
with the murder of her husband, by poison. 'Haven't had a
poison case through my hands, oh, since the Bride of Orpington
in 1958. That was chocolates, if you recollect. And this is? An
overdose of what? We'll go into that when we meet in Holloway.'

'Poison, Hilda,' I said as I put down the telephone. 'Something
to live for at last.'

'If you want to live,' she told me, 'you'd better go straight
round and see Hector MacClintock.' So I did, with what results
you already know.

The conference at Holloway was fixed for a week after my
visit to the Doctor, and before it took place an event occurred
which removed most of the gilt from the gingerbread of my most
recent murder case. I was leaving the Temple underground
station on my way to Chambers, a little weakened by the sole
intake of Thin-O-Vite, when I heard a familiar voice issue some
kind of military command behind me.

'Pick 'em up, Rumpole!'

'Pick what up?'

Soapy Sam Ballard, Q.C., his umbrella shouldered and his brief-case swinging, marched up beside me. 'Pick up your feet. One . . . two . . . One . . . two . . .' he intoned. 'I have just walked the entire way from Liverpool Street station, along the river. Chin up, now. Swing the arms!'

'What's the matter with you, Bollard? The war's over.'

'The war may be over, Rumpole, but the battle for fitness goes on. I mean to introduce a new scheme of health education in Chambers. You know what I've got in this brief-case?'

'Astonish me.'

'I have a device in here for expanding the chest,' he said proudly. 'I intend to use it, during the odd free moment. Keep the chest open! Keep the lungs free! It's my duty as your Head of Chambers to prolong my life, as much as possible.'

'Why should you want to do that?'

'Can't let you fellows down.'

'We wouldn't want to put you to any trouble,' I assured him.

'Anyway, I can't let *you* down, Rumpole, now that I'm leading you.'

'You're doing *what*?' I felt a cold thrill of horror. Was my precious poisoning case to be taken out of my hands?

'Haven't you heard? Terrible business. Murder of Sir Daniel Derwent, R.A. Well-known painter, so they tell me. I know nothing of these things. Oh, yes. I'm leading you.'

'I hope you'll be able to keep up with me!' was all I could say, extremely ungraciously. But Ballard only quickened his pace and marched away. 'One . . . two! One . . . two!' he called as he went.

'I shall be leading you from behind,' I threatened him.

'It's you that's going to have to keep up, Rumpole,' he said as the distance between us grew. 'I just hope you're fit enough for it!' I'm afraid I was no longer audible as I said, 'Don't bother about prolonging your life, old darling. Not on my account.'

When I arrived in our clerk's room, things were much as usual. Dianne was making coffee, Henry was telephoning, Uncle Tom was trying to get his putts into the waste-paper basket and

Mizz Liz Probert, looking slightly better groomed than usual, was getting a brief from her tray. My learned friend, Claude Erskine-Brown, arrived out of breath. 'Terrible traffic jam in Islington today, and you know what caused it?' He laughed mirthlessly. 'A procession of gay and lesbian demonstrators, demanding more services off the rates.'

'Why's that funny?' Mizz Probert pricked up her ears.

'I say!' Erskine-Brown looked at her with sudden admiration. 'Is that a new hairdo?'

'I don't see that it's at all funny. And what's my hair got to do with it?'

'It looks jolly nice, actually.' Claude became somewhat inarticulate. 'Much softer and . . . well, more feminine. Congratulations!'

'Oh, for God's sake, Claude!' Liz was losing patience with the man. 'Give us a break. And why shouldn't the Islington Council provide gay and lesbian counselling? Think of what they save you on education and . . .'

'Radiant!' Claude continued to stare. 'Quite honestly, you're looking radiant.'

'Of course, I'd expect *you* to be against it. I'd expect discrimination from you, Claude.'

'Discrimination?' He looked hurt.

'Oh, yes. How many gay and lesbian members have we got in these Chambers?'

'None, I hope. I mean, none, I think. No, I'm sure . . .'

'There you are, then! Discrimination.'

'Perhaps it's just because we don't get many gay and lesbian applications.' Claude was trying to be reasonable.

'Well, I'd like to see what'd happen if you got one. Just one! I can imagine your middle-class, middle-aged, male attitudes bristling.'

'Middle-aged, Liz? Did you say middle-aged?' He was clearly wounded.

'Sexual discrimination comes in a packet, Claude. With middle-aged spread.'

'Radiant!' He avoided the subject of the Erskine-Brown figure. 'You look absolutely radiant. Come for a coffee later? I'll let you pay for yourself,' he promised.

'Improve your attitudes, Claude. That's all you need.' Liz removed herself and her brief in a rapid and businesslike fashion, and Erskine-Brown was left staring after her. 'Miss Probert's got a new hairdo, Henry,' he said, entranced.

'Really, sir? I can't say I noticed. Got the ginger biscuits there, have you, Dianne?' Dianne put a number of biscuits on a plate by Henry's coffee, thus presenting the staring Rumpole with a terrible temptation. I protested to Henry about Bernard's insanity in taking in Soapy Sam to lead me, and he started on a long story about how Bernard got the case from Jones, the Derwent family solicitor, who didn't do crime, and Ballard had done a bit of insurance work for Jones's firm and they had been greatly impressed.

'This is poisoning, Henry,' I told him. 'Not fooling around with some piffling insurance.'

So I left him and heard, as I made it to the door, Henry's pained cry, 'You're not going to believe this, Dianne! Mr Rumpole's just nicked two of my biscuits.'

So, in due course, I rolled up at Holloway prison to play an ill-tempered second fiddle to Ballard, Q.C., and act as his far older and wiser 'Junior' in our first conference with Lady Derwent. Mr Bernard, who was no longer in my good books, was also of the party. Ballard started off in the voice of a most hostile prosecutor and said to the beautiful young woman we were meant to be defending, 'Lady Derwent. The extremely serious allegation in this case is that you deliberately administered a massive overdose of diamorphine to your husband, who had recently made a will in your favour. It is further suggested that you took the morphine ampoules from the bag of a Nurse Gregson who had called at the house that afternoon. Now the question is, did you administer that fatal dose, Lady Derwent?'

'Be careful,' I muttered a warning to my learned leader, but Ballard paid no attention and continued to attack our client.

'I'd advise you to be perfectly frank with your legal advisers, madam,' he said. 'Well, did you?'

'Just a minute, Ballard,' I interrupted before Perdita had a chance to answer. 'If I may make so bold. As your mere Junior.'

'Well, what is it, Rumpole?'

'A word, if I may, over here.' I got up and went to a corner of the room. Ballard followed me reluctantly. 'Don't ask her that!' I whispered.

'What?'

'Don't ask if she pumped her husband full of morphine so she could get her fingers on a bit of ready cash. Of all the tactless questions!'

'But isn't that what this case is all about?'

'Of course it's what it's all about. That's why you don't ask.'

'Why not?'

'In case she says "yes",' I hissed.

Bernard and Lady Derwent sat at the table, no doubt curious about the *sotto voce* dialogue taking place in the corner of the room. 'Then we'd know, for certain.' Ballard seemed to think that would be no bad thing.

'Exactly. And I'd be sitting in Chambers unemployed, having fantasies about steak and kidney pudding, and you'd be back to motor insurance. First lesson in murder, old darling. Never ask the customer if she did it. She might tell you.'

'Really, Rumpole!' Ballard seemed shocked. 'What do you suggest I ask her?'

'Ask her about the weather. Ask her if she's seen any good films lately. Murder conferences aren't for asking awkward questions, Bollard. Save those for the Prosecution. All we need now is to give the client a little confidence.'

'Confidence, Rumpole . . .?' It seemed a quality Ballard didn't know how to impart. 'Watch carefully,' I said, 'and you might learn something.' I led him back to the table, sat, smiled at Perdita and began to conduct the conference in my own way, starting with an entirely harmless question. 'Lady Derwent. You met your husband when he was a professor at St Matthew's?'

'Yes. I was a student.'

'And he fell in love with you? Quite understandably.'

'I don't know about that.' She rewarded me with a faint smile. 'I fell in love with him.'

'Then he got a divorce and married you. I think you were twenty-four at the time.'

'Twenty-three.'

'And his daughter Helen continued to live with you. She was about fifteen years older?'

'I'm afraid Helen always resented me. She thought I'd taken Daniel away from her mother. It wasn't like that at all.'

'Of course not.' I looked understanding. 'They'd separated before you met, hadn't they?'

'They used to separate and come together. It was never happy. But when it finally ended, well, Daniel's wife was very bitter.'

'Helen was bitter too?' I could imagine the jealousy an older daughter felt towards the younger beauty who she thought had ensnared her father.

'I think she worshipped Daniel. She didn't make it particularly easy for me.' Then Ballard couldn't resist what he clearly considered an awkward question for Perdita. 'So did you resent your husband having his daughter to live with you? Were there quarrels about that? Were there, Lady Derwent?'

'Daniel hated quarrels. I did my best not to have them,' she said, and I believed her. In my role as the nice policeman I asked gently, 'I suppose Helen wanted to go on running the house. Just as her mother had for so many years?'

'You understand!' She looked at me gratefully.

'I'd better understand Helen Derwent,' I told her, 'if I'm going to cross-examine her.' Bernard cleared his throat in an embarrassed manner and Ballard protested, 'I imagine *I* will be cross-examining Miss Helen Derwent, Rumpole. It will fall to *me*, as *leading* Counsel for the Defence.'

'But if you happen to be feeling tired. When we get to that stage,' I suggested hopefully.

'I don't anticipate feeling in the least tired, Rumpole. At any stage.'

'Don't let's look on the black side.'

And then, desperate to make peace between his barristers, Mr Bernard was ill-advised enough to say, 'Mr Rumpole. Mr Ballard is briefed as leading Counsel in this case. On our client's previous solicitor's instructions.'

'Mr Bernard!' I interrupted him with some force. 'Perhaps I should remind you. There is a trial which has gone down to history as the Penge Bungalow Murders. If you happen to consult the relevant volume of Notable British Trials you will find that I brought home victory in that case alone *and without a leader*. That is my last word to you on the subject. Now, Lady Derwent.' I smiled at Perdita and took over control of the conference again. 'You also lived with your mother-in-law, Mrs Barbara Derwent. How did you get on with her?'

'I've always loved Bunty,' Perdita told us. 'She never criticized me, or made me feel a fool about the house or anything. And she was so pleased when Daniel and I got married. She said Imogen . . .'

'That's the first Lady Derwent,' Mr Bernard explained to Soapy Sam, who was looking a little lost.

'Yes. Bunty said Imogen was the most terrible snob. Bunty wasn't a snob at all. She'd been a dancer when she was young. In the chorus. Of course, you'd never guess that now. She's got so fat. Funny, isn't it?'

'We all change, Lady Derwent, over the ears, and we can't all get many laughs out of it. I suppose you don't have a biscuit about you, by any chance? No? Of course not.' I had been stopped in my tracks by pangs of hunger and Ballard, seizing his chance, took over again with 'Lady Derwent. We've had the *post mortem* results on your husband.'

'The medical evidence.' I put it more attractively.

'He was clearly suffering from an illness which gave him only a short time to live.'

'It doesn't make any sense,' I said thoughtfully, and Perdita, with whom I had set up a certain rapport, nodded. 'I've been trying to work it out. Danny loved life so much. Everything about it. He loved his work. I think he loved me.'

'What doesn't make sense,' I suggested, 'is the idea of anyone killing Sir Daniel for his money when he was going to die anyway. No doubt that's a point that's even occurred to you, Ballard.'

Ballard, however, was busy getting out of his papers a copy of a pamphlet to which he obviously attached great importance. 'We also have seen,' he told our client, 'copies of this booklet found among the clothes in your bedroom, Lady Derwent. It's a work entitled "Helping the Loved One Across the River".'

'I honestly don't know how it got there. I'd never seen it before.' Perdita looked at us anxiously.

'It seems to advocate euthanasia . . .'

'Ballard!' It was my duty to warn him.

'*The troubled soul in a state of acute pain or terminal illness . . .*' Soapy Sam started to read, and there was nothing else for it. I rose to my feet. 'Well, now, Lady Derwent,' I said. 'It's been most useful for us to have this little chat with you.'

But Ballard went on reading remorselessly from the work in his hand: '*Relatives or dear friends may provide a loved one with a bridge or at least a little raft on which to float gently away to a happier land. All that is needed is a rudimentary knowledge of medical science and the effects of various drugs on the unnecessary prolongation of life. Join Across the River, 19A Goshawk Street, Kentish Town for full details . . .*'

'Must be getting along now.' I managed a realistic stagger and grasped the back of my chair. 'The truth of the matter is, I'm not feeling absolutely up to snuff.'

'Rumpole! You look decidedly unfit, sir.' Mr Bernard was easily persuaded. 'What is it?'

'The prolongation of life, Bernard! It usually proves fatal in the end.'

'Mr Rumpole . . .?' Perdita was touchingly concerned. 'I shall be all right, Lady Derwent,' I reassured her. 'You and I will probably be all right. Mr Bernard, how about running us back to the Temple in your sturdy little motor?' At that moment I would have dropped dead rather than let Ballard ask the idiotic question he had in mind.

Some time later I was having breakfast in the Taste-Ee-Bite tearoom in Fleet Street, loading my tray with nothing but a cup of black coffee, a glass of orange juice and *The Times*, when I saw Mizz Probert in front of me in the queue. She looked at my iron rations and I explained that some dotty doctor wanted to keep me alive, although I supposed she held the view that when men get to a certain age they should be bagged up and put out with the dustbins. She didn't deny the charge but went off to breakfast with a pleasant-looking young man who I judged to be an embryo barrister. When she had gone I weakened and added a sugar bun to my purchases; this I secreted in my pocket for use only in an emergency. Then I went to a table near Mizz Probert and hid behind my *Times*. From this point of vantage I was able to hear Liz making what I thought was a rather rash promise to her companion.

'I'll get you into our Chambers I promise you, Dave. It just needs a little organization. There's a man called Claude Erskine-Brown in charge of admission. To be honest, he reckons he fancies me.'

'Liz' – the young man was clearly of a pure and moral disposition – 'you don't mean to say you'd use sexual manipulation?'

'It's all in a good cause, Dave.' She put out her hand and held his across the table. 'We can work together on the rent inquiry in Tower Hamlets. You wouldn't mind going for an interview with Claude, would you?'

'For you, Liz,' young Dave spoke with a certain amount of passion, 'I'd go for an interview with the Lord Chancellor.'

'Oh, don't worry. Claude's not a bit like the Lord Chancellor. For one thing he can't seem to keep his mind off sex.'

After this meeting, Mizz Probert went to her admirer Claude Erskine-Brown and again accused him of discrimination against gay and lesbian persons. When he hotly denied all such prejudices she challenged him with 'I bet you don't let Dave Inchcape into Chambers. He's coming to see you next week.' From this, Erskine-Brown made certain deductions about young Inchcape. His subsequent interview with the new applicant took, as he told me much later, a somewhat unusual course.

'Inchcape?' Claude asked nervously when the young man entered his room.

'Yes. Dave Inchcape.'

'Dave. Of course.' Claude raised a hand. 'Hi! Why don't you sit down?' He pointed to a distant chair. 'Over there.' He sat himself safely behind his desk and seemed to have difficulty in starting the conversation. 'Well . . . Dave. Fact is, Liz Probert's had a long talk to me about you. Great girl, Liz. She's tremendously keen that we shouldn't have any kind of . . . discrimination

in Chambers. I mean, we shouldn't be against you simply because
you are what you are.'

'What am I?'

'Well. What you are. Entirely through no fault of your own.'
Claude was unable to make himself completely clear.

'You mean, young?' Inchcape was puzzled.

'Well. Yes. Young, I suppose. And . . . well, these things are
no doubt decided for us at a very early age.'

'You mean, wanting to be a barrister?' The young man was
doing his best to follow Claude's drift.

'Well, that. And . . . I mean, it's a matter of the sort of genes
you get born with. Biologically speaking.'

'You think I got born with a barrister's genes?' Inchcape asked
seriously.

'Oh, very good that!' Claude laughed appreciatively. 'Very
funny. Of course, you lot always have a marvellous sense of
humour and, we always noticed at Winchester, a great aptitude
for the violin.'

'I can't do it,' Inchcape said after a thoughtful silence.

'What?'

'Play the violin.'

'Well, you can rest assured, Dave,' Claude said generously,
'we're not going to hold that against you.'

'well, thanks.' And after another somewhat embarrassed pause
Inchcape added, 'I expect you want to know about my experience.'

'Good heavens, no!' quick as a flash, Claude answered.

'You don't?'

'I take the view, Dave, that your experiences are entirely a
matter between you and . . . well, whoever you've had the experiences with.'

'Tomkins. In Testament Buildings.' Inchcape mentioned the
name of the elderly barrister whose pupil he'd been.

'Please. Don't tell me! It's absolutely none of my business!'
Claude was incredulous, but couldn't help asking, 'You mean
Tommy Tomkins?'

'Yes. I was with him for about a year.'

'But I thought Tommy was married to a lady magistrate?'
Claude was shocked.

'So he is. Does that make any difference?'

'Well. Not nowadays, I suppose.' Liz, Claude thought, would condemn his attitude as ridiculously old-fashioned. 'The way I look at it is this, Dave. My attitude is . . . There's no real difference between us!'

'Except you've had a great deal more experience than I have,' Inchcape suggested.

'I wouldn't say that,' Claude denied hastily. 'But of course I do have the children. Young Tristan and Isolde. A perpetual joy. Named after Wagner's star-crossed lovers, of course. You don't know what it's like having little ones around you.'

'No, I'm sorry,' the young bachelor apologized, but Claude reassured him, 'No one's going to blame you. And think what you save us on the rates.'

'What do you mean?' Now Inchcape was completely lost.

'By not having children. In my view you're absolutely entitled to counselling services.' Claude stood up, conscious of a duty well done. 'I'll be reporting to Ballard. I'm sure we'll be able to squeeze you in.'

'I don't mind sharing a room . . .' Inchcape stood and advanced on Claude Erskine-Brown who backed away, saying, 'Not with me, I'm afraid. That would hardly do, would it? Perhaps we can put you in with Liz Probert. Then you wouldn't have any . . . distractions!'

'Well, thank you, Claude. Thanks very much.' Inchcape seemed to like the idea.

'Not at all. That way out, Dave.'

It was about the noon
Of a glorious day in June
When our General rode along us
For to form us for to fight . . .

The battle was an exciting and exhilarating occasion, the trial of Lady Derwent on a charge of poisoning her husband. It was the General who let the side down, for I had been landed with a commanding officer with about as much talent for Old Bailey warfare as a sheep in Holy Orders. He was interested in body-building, which wouldn't do a thing except unnecessarily prolong the life of Ballard, but courage-building was what he needed – the talent to draw the sabre and charge into the gunfire of Judge Gerald Graves. Into the mouth of hell! I couldn't see Ballard doing it. Cannon to right of him, cannon to left of him, and Ballard would sneak off home and exercise with his chest-expander. However, there was little I could do about it.

'Mine not to reason why, Mine but to do or die,' I murmured to myself as I arrived short of breath, but fully wigged and gowned for the fight ahead, in front of Judge Graves's Court. 'Mine though I damn well know Bernard has blundered ... Briefing Bollard to lead *me*!' And then a resonant contralto voice interrupted my thoughts with 'Your big case today, isn't it? I just saw Sam Ballard going up to the robing-room.'

'That must have been a treat for you, Matron,' I said, for the speaker was none other than the Old Bailey medical supremo, Mrs Marguerite Plumstead, a powerfully built, still handsome woman who could deal in a swift and determined manner with fainting jurors or malingering criminals.

'I suppose it's a case of follow my leader for you today, isn't it, Mr Rumpole?' I winced. 'And our Sam was looking wonderfully well.' She gave me a quick look over and put me in the C.3 category. 'Aren't we letting that naughty tummy of ours get a little out of hand?'

'I'm melting into thin air, thank you, Matron.' I went on about my business and she called after me, 'That's all right my dear. I like to keep an eye on all my barristers.'

The Court was full and the press benches crowded for the Derwent murder. That cold fish, Judge Gerald Graves, promoted above his station to try the case, decorated the Bench like something lifeless on a marble slab. Perdita was looking beautiful in the dock, but as though her thoughts were far away. Bunty was sitting largely in the public seats; she smiled at Perdita, who smiled faintly back. Marcus Griffin, the Senior Treasury Counsel, was prosecuting. Griffin is a perfectly nice, rather fair prosecutor, whom I like to treat as though he were some particularly ruthless Grand Inquisitor. His Junior, Arthurian Daybell, was seated behind him, and I, God save the mark, was seated behind Soapy Sam Ballard, Q.C. Such was the scene in which Marcus Griffin rose to his feet to open his case to the Jury.

'Members of the Jury,' prosecuting Counsel began. 'This case concerns the death, from a massive overdose of diamorphine, of Sir Daniel Derwent, R.A., the well-known portrait painter. He had made a will leaving his entire estate, a considerable sum of money, Members of the Jury – something well over two million pounds – to his wife Perdita, the defendant in this case. He made no provision for his mother, Mrs Barbara Derwent, or his daughter by a previous marriage, Helen, although the two ladies lived with him at number one, Ruskin Street, Chelsea, as members of his family.'

'He settled money on them during his lifetime,' I whispered urgently to the back of my not-so-learned leader. 'It's quite unfair to suggest that our client scooped the pool.'

'Horace, I do know.' He tried to quieten me. 'It *is* my brief.'

'The Jury haven't read your brief! Get up and tell them.'

'Horace.' He only wanted to be left in peace.

'Don't "Horace" me! Get up on your hind legs, why don't you? Make your presence felt.'

'Mr Ballard.' The Judge sounded his most sepulchral note. 'I think your Junior is trying to tell you something.'

'I'm extremely sorry, my Lord.' Ballard rose sycophantically. 'I must apologize most sincerely for any interruption.'

'No need to apologize. Sit down, Bollard.' I couldn't resist rising to address the Court. 'I was trying to communicate vital information to the Jury, my Lord. Sir Daniel Derwent made a generous financial settlement on his mother and daughter during his life-time.'

'My Lord. That would appear to be correct,' Griffin conceded after a brief word with his Junior.

'Of course it's correct!' I continued somewhat to my leader's chagrin. 'It would also be correct if the Prosecution were to present the facts in a full and unbiased way to the Jury at this stage, and not try to colour the evidence by a one-sided account.'

'My Lord. I assure the Court that any mistake I may have made was quite unintentional,' Griffin protested. I had got him on the defensive and followed on with 'Provided it's agreed that this Prosecution is capable of mistakes.'

'Mr Rumpole!' I had succeeded in provoking a sort of frozen fury in his Lordship. 'My understanding is that you appear here as Junior Counsel to your learned and very experienced leader, Mr Samuel Ballard.'

'Strange things happen down the Old Bailey,' I muttered to no one in particular and my leader chimed in with 'My Lord. That is perfectly correct.'

'Thank you, Mr Ballard. I'm grateful for your assistance.' When the Judge said that, Ballard bowed humbly and sat down. I was left standing on my own. 'Then, no doubt, Mr Rumpole,' Graves continued, 'you can safely leave any further objections and interruptions in the skilful hands of Mr Samuel Ballard.'

'You must be joking,' I muttered again.

'I find difficulty in hearing you, Mr Rumpole.'

'You can rest assured I shall only interrupt again when the interests of justice demand it, my Lord.' I said it very loudly and then sat down to give way to Griffin, who outlined the facts of Sir Daniel's death and showed the Jury the incriminating articles – the used ampoules, the pamphlet and the hypodermic – he undertook to prove were found in our client's bedroom. Then he told them, 'It will be our case that Lady Derwent, knowing exactly what she was doing because she had read this pamphlet, administered that massive overdose to her husband. She may have deluded herself into thinking that she was helping him to a peaceful and painless death, but of course that would be no defence to a charge of murder. Her true motive, the Prosecution will suggest, is money. The freehold of the Chelsea house and Sir Daniel's considerable investments would be hers on his death. Members of the Jury. You will hear evidence about the matrimonial relationship of this couple. I have told you that they occupied separate bedrooms . . .'

'Because he couldn't *sleep*.' I tried to stir my leader into some sort of activity.

'Do you wish to interrupt *again*, Mr Rumpole?' the judge was asking.

'No, my Lord.' I rose as impressively as I could manage to my feet and stared at the Jury. 'I am quite content to let my learned friend Mr Griffin continue with his inaccuracies. Our time will come!'

*

An early prosecution witness was Nurse Gregson, a thin, wiry, grey-haired lady who ministered to the sick and dying around Chelsea and took, I imagined, no nonsense from them. In answer to Marcus Griffin, she remembered calling at the house about four p.m. on the day Sir Daniel died to give him his injection. Miss Helen and Mrs Barbara Derwent, the deceased's mother, were there, and, of course, Lady Derwent. Nurse Gregson glanced disapprovingly at the dock and said, 'I couldn't help noticing her.'

'Why not?' Griffin asked innocently.

'She was sitting on a chair, my Lord, stripped to the waist.'

'Am I to understand that this young lady was sitting among the family with her bosoms unclothed?' His Lordship sounded incredulous.

'That is right, my Lord.'

'Is that a criminal offence?' I whispered to my leader, loudly enough for the Jury to hear. 'Mr Rumpole?' the Judge inquired, and I rose to address him. 'I only ask for a legal direction, my Lord. At the moment this evidence seems utterly irrelevant.'

At which point I sat down and the Judge spoke despairingly to my leader. 'Mr Ballard. Is there any way in which you can discourage further interruptions by your learned Junior?'

'I can only say I will do my best, my Lord.' Soapy Sam rose humbly.

'Thank *you*, Mr Ballard.' The Judge was very much obliged and Marcus Griffin went back to work. 'And you saw Sir Daniel Derwent?'

'Oh, yes. He was there. He was painting his wife's portrait.'

'Painting unclothed bosoms,' I whispered again for the benefit of the Jury. 'An unfortunate habit of artists throughout the centuries!'

'Mr Ballard, I think Mr Rumpole spoke again.' The Judge was on to it, quick as a shot. Ballard rose sadly to admit. 'That may very well be so, my Lord.'

'See to it, Mr Ballard.' Those were his Lordship's orders. So Ballard said, 'Ssh, Horace!' and I told him to keep quiet because I was trying to listen to the evidence, which now reached a vital point. Nurse Gregson described giving Sir Daniel the injection of diamorphine. 'I understand,' Griffin said, 'this was a top-up injection, as he was in considerable pain?'

'Yes, it was. They always got me to give the injections. They had acquired a hypodermic but none of the family could use it, so I always did the job for them.'

'*This* was the hypodermic they kept but didn't normally use?' My learned friend lifted the exhibit he said was found in Perdita's bedroom.

'I imagine so.'

'Was the diamorphine you injected in ampoules?'

'Yes.'

'Did you have other ampoules of morphine in your medical bag?'

'Yes, I did. I had other patients, of course.' Nurse Gregson went on to give evidence of the number of missing ampoules and the milligrammes they contained. Griffin said, 'We have heard such a dose might prove fatal.' He had called an expert who had testified to that; it was evidence that Ballard had not felt able to challenge. 'Did you use any of the other ampoules when you gave Sir Daniel Derwent his injection?'

'No.'

'Were the ampoules and their wrappings similar to these?' Griffin held up more of the treasure trove found in Perdita's bedroom.

'Yes, they were.'

'After you had given the injection, what did you do?'

'I went out into the hall, with my bag, and I was putting on my coat when Mrs Derwent . . .'

'The deceased's mother?'

'Yes. She asked if I'd like to stay for a cup of tea. I said I would and I went back into the studio. I left my bag in the hall.'

'Unattended?'

'Yes. Mrs Derwent went out to make the tea and Lady Derwent was given a break from sitting. She put on some kind of a wrap and went out to help her mother-in-law.'

'What about you?'

'Oh, I stayed in the studio.'

'Did Sir Daniel leave the studio at all, while you were there?'

'I couldn't be certain. If he did, it was only for a few minutes.'

'Did Miss Helen Derwent leave it?'

'No. I'm sure she didn't.'

'Why do you say that?'

'We were talking about the garden she looked after. We're both keen gardeners.'

'And how did your visit end?'

'We all had tea and I collected my bag and left. I went off duty then and didn't check the contents of my bag until next morning. I discovered that a large number of diamorphine ampoules were missing from my bag. These were to be used in the treatment of other patients, my Lord. I also heard on the radio that Sir Daniel had died during the night. I immediately telephoned the Derwent household. Dr Harman was there and I told him the whole thing.'

'Nurse Gregson,' Griffin ended, 'are you quite sure that you didn't administer a massive overdose of diamorphine on that afternoon to your patient, Sir Daniel Derwent?'

'I am a state registered nurse with twenty-five years' experience, my Lord. I am quite certain that I did not.'

'"I am quite certain that I did not."' Graves was delighted to make that note. Griffin sat and Ballard rose slowly; it was, as I whispered to him, his great moment. He stood in silence for a while and then turned to whisper for my help. 'Is there any particular question?'

'Couldn't Sir Daniel have administered the overdose to himself? If he had the diamorphine and a hypodermic syringe.' I loaded him with my best ammunition.

'Ah, yes.' Ballard tried to look as though he'd thought of it himself. 'If Sir Daniel had been in possession of that syringe, and a large number of diamorphine ampoules, could he not have administered an overdose to himself?'

'I suppose it's possible,' Nurse Gregson answered reluctantly.

'And might he not have left the studio when your bag was unattended in the hall?' I filled Ballard with another round. He turned to the witness, appeared to think the matter over carefully and said, 'And let me ask you this. Sir Daniel might have left the studio when tea was being prepared. And your bag was in the hall and he might have taken the diamorphine from it?'

'I have said he might have gone out for a few minutes. That's all.'

Our work was done, but still Ballard lingered on his feet. I whispered some words of command. 'Sit down and shut up. Don't spoil it now.'

'And you admit that Sir Daniel *could* have injected himself?' Soapy Sam couldn't take orders.

'He *could* have. But I don't think he did,' the witness told him.

'Leave it alone, Bollard!' The situation was desperate, but my leader went on, delighted with himself. 'Tell the Members of the Jury, Nurse Gregson. *Why* don't you think so?' It was, of course, the one question that shouldn't have been asked, and the witness was delighted to answer it.

'Sir Daniel had a horror of hypodermic needles,' she told the Jury. 'I'm quite sure he could not have done such a thing on his own.'

My learned leader had scored an own goal, and it was four o'clock, crumpet-time, although I wasn't allowed crumpets. Marcus Griffin said he thought it was too late to embark on the evidence of Miss Helen Derwent, which might take a little time, and the Judge told the Members of the Jury that they would meet again at ten thirty the next morning when 'we shall hope to proceed without further interruptions from Mr Rumpole'.

When the Court rose, Ballard retired to the Q.C.s' robing-room on the top floor of the Old Bailey. He was delighted to find the room empty, as he had some sort of work-out in mind. He removed his wig and gown, tailed Court coat and waistcoat, and then opened his brief-case and removed his much-loved chest-expander. This particular instrument of torture had two wooden handles, which Ballard gripped, and he proceeded to haul away at the steel spring, expanding his chest and shouting orders to himself, 'One . . . two! One . . . two!' This is what he was doing when I opened the door and put my head round it, having had a few ideas on the cross-examination of Miss Helen Derwent.

'One . . . two! In . . . out!' chanted my leader, who didn't seem to have heard me. He had the chest-expander pulled out to its fullest possible extent when I called out sharply, 'Bollard!'

At that, he turned suddenly, loosing his grip on one of the handles, which flew inwards, propelled by the spring, and having struck him smartly on the side of the head felled him to the ground. I was left standing, looking down at an unconscious leader. I suppose I should have warned him that exercise is likely to prove fatal. I crossed to the telephone and asked the operator to put out an urgent call for Matron on the Tannoy.

Soon the great Palais de Justice was ringing with the call of 'Matron to the Q.C.s' robing-room at once, please!' They heard it in the canteen, in the Judge's corridors and in the cells. In no time at all, Mrs Marguerite Plumstead was kneeling beside the fallen figure who had been stunned by his own chest-expander. Ballard opened his eyes, focused on the concerned face peering down at him, and whispered, 'Matey!'

'*You* are to carry on, Mr Rumpole?' Judge Graves looked at me in some horror as I rose in Court the next morning to announce the unfortunate indisposition of my learned leader. I had met Matron in the corridor and she had told me that Ballard was suffering from the after-effects of concussion, a back muscle was strained and he had been severely shocked. The Doctor, it seemed, had ordered him to take two days' complete rest. 'He's being so wonderfully brave about it.' Matron looked a little misty-eyed. 'Never a thought of "self". Well, isn't that our lovely Sam all over? Almost his last words as we got him into the ambulance were "Of course Rumpole will ask for an adjournment."'

'Delirious, no doubt,' I said, and went into Court to announce that I was prepared to act without the inestimable advantage of Mr Ballard's inspired leadership. 'My client,' I assured Judge Graves 'is most anxious there should be no further delays. She has waited too long to be cleared of these monstrous allegations.' He sighed heavily, but came to the conclusion that he had no choice but to continue with the case if I weren't asking for an adjournment until the recovery of Ballard. 'I hope your client realizes the risk she is taking,' he said in a voice of terrible warning, 'in depriving herself of her leading Counsel's wisdom and *moderation*.'

I bowed and resumed my seat. Happily, the time for moderation was over and I meant to launch an immoderate attack on the principal witness against us. Whilst Griffin was taking Miss Helen Derwent gently through her evidence-in-chief, I whispered a few vital instructions to Bernard. I wanted him to issue a subpoena on the organization Across the River or use any other means at his disposal to get a list of their members. Then I leaned back to look at my client's step-daughter.

Helen was dark and Perdita fair. Helen was intense, serious and capable, I thought, of bearing long grudges. Perdita was gentle, smiled easily and was, I judged, forgiving. No doubt, Helen was like her mother, Derwent's first wife, and if that were so, I could imagine with what relief he embraced his second marriage. He would have been like a man enjoying a late summer holiday. As I watched her, Helen told the Jury, in quiet, unemotional tones, that she had found the empty ampoules and the pamphlet in Perdita's chest-of-drawers and the hypodermic in her bedroom cupboard, although it was usually kept in the cupboard in her late father's bathroom.

This was the witness I rose to cross-examine in the welcome absence of my learned leader. I decided to go right to the heart of her evidence and waste no time on polite persiflage. 'Miss Derwent. You didn't approve of your father's second wife?'

'She was very young and feckless. I suppose he was besotted with her, in a way.' She looked at Perdita in the dock, and the young woman lowered her eyes, avoiding a confrontation.

'I suppose some men enjoy being besotted?' I suggested.

'Perhaps.'

'By "feckless" you mean incompetent?'

'Totally incompetent! On the very night my father died, for instance, she had forgotten to order the fish.'

'How terrible!' I looked at the Jury.

'It may not sound much but Daddy looked forward to his fish pie on a Friday night. Of course, Perdita had forgotten to order it so we had to have omelettes.'

'Did Lady Derwent cook them?'

'Perdita?' The witness smiled scornfully. 'Of course not. She was just about up to boiling water. I think Granny cooked them.'

'Just omelettes for dinner?'

'I think we had some mulligatawny soup Granny had made the day before. Oh, and treacle tart. Is that what you wanted to know?'

It wasn't really. I just couldn't keep off the subject of food. I forced myself to another topic. 'His painting meant a great deal to your father?'

'It was his whole life.'

'His increasing illness meant that a time was coming when he would no longer be able to paint. That night he'd spoiled a picture, didn't he?'

'I remember that.'

'That was a terrible prospect for an artist who loved his work?'

'Yes.'

'So might he not have felt he had nothing left to live for and taken his own life? Have you considered that possibility?' I turned and asked the Jury to consider it, but Helen said quickly, 'Daddy never mentioned suicide!'

'Never mentioned it to you, perhaps.'

'Or to anyone, as far as I know. Besides, he still had a lot to live for.'

'You mean he had his happiness with a beautiful young wife?'

'No.' She looked at me with intense dislike. 'I didn't mean that.'

'Miss Derwent.' I leant forward and kept my eyes on her face. We were coming to the vital part of her testimony. 'You found your father dead in his studio?'

'I couldn't sleep so I went downstairs. I found him then. On the couch ...' She put her hand over her face and trembled a little, but I don't think she was crying.

'Please' – Judge Graves looked almost human – 'don't distress yourself, Miss Derwent.'

'Then you telephoned Doctor Harman. He called and arranged for the removal of your father's body. He called again later, and spoke to your mother and your step-mother. While he was doing that, do you say you searched Lady Derwent's bedroom?'

'I took a look round in there. Yes.'

'You took a look round? In the hope of finding something that would incriminate your step-mother?'

'No . . .'

'Then *why*?'

Helen was silent then, thinking. At last she said, 'I never thought Perdita would be able to face looking after Daddy through his final illness. She was just too young and . . .'

' "Feckless". Is that the word you'd use?'

'Exactly! So it often occurred to me that she might try and well . . . help Daddy out of this world. And,' she added coldly, 'especially if it would be so much to her financial advantage.'

'Did Daddy tell you he was leaving all his money to his young wife?'

'He said that. Yes.'

'Having previously settled comfortable incomes on you and his mother.'

'That's been agreed by the Prosecution,' the Judge thought fit to remind me. 'We needn't waste time on that.'

'Your Lordship is always helpful.' I smiled sweetly at the old darling and asked the witness, 'You know something, I expect, about the law of wills?'

'I know a little.'

'Do you know that if Lady Derwent is found guilty of her husband's murder she will inherit nothing?'

'We all know *that*, Mr Rumpole.' The Judge's patience, never in lavish supply, was running out.

'Oh, I'm sorry, my Lord,' I apologized. 'I'd forgotten that the Members of the Jury had all passed their Bar exams.' I got a little laughter from the Jury, quickly silenced by an angry 'Mr Rumpole!' from the Judge. I turned hurriedly back to the witness. 'Very well, Miss Derwent. Did you know that or didn't you?'

'I suppose I may have had some idea that that was the law. It would only be fair.'

'So that this two-million-pound estate would then be divided between you and your grandmother.'

'Yes, I suppose it would.'

'An extremely satisfactory result so far as you're concerned?'

For the first time the Jury looked at Helen Derwent with suspicion, so the Judge thought it time to interrupt my flow. 'Mr

Rumpole,' he asked, 'are you suggesting that these exhibits, the used ampoules, the syringe and the pamphlet, were never in your client's bedroom at all?'

'Your Lordship sees the point so quickly.' I gave him the retort courteous, and then turned on the witness. 'You found these used ampoules didn't you, near your father's body. Probably the syringe was there too. And the pamphlet, was that his?'

Helen Derwent no longer disliked me, she hated me. But her voice was still controlled as she asked, 'What are you accusing me of?'

'Mr Rumpole.' The Judge came to her rescue. 'May I remind you of the evidence Nurse Gregson gave. This witness remained in the studio with the nurse during the whole time the medical bag was left unattended. She had no chance at all of removing the diamorphine ampoules.'

'Oh, I agree with that, my Lord.' I was Rumpole respectful. 'I'm not suggesting for a moment that Miss Helen Derwent killed her father.'

'Well, what are you suggesting, may I ask?'

'That she put those exhibits in my client's bedroom in the hope that some gullible jury might convict her of murder, my Lord.'

'Oh, really!' Helen was still fighting. 'And how do you say my father died?'

'I say what the Jury is going to say, when they have considered all the evidence,' I answered her with all the confidence I could muster. 'He killed himself when his painter's hand would no longer obey his orders.'

That night, as I was ingesting Thin-O-Vite, Mr Bernard telephoned and told me he had managed to get a membership list of the Across the River society at last. So I learned something that I should, perhaps, have thought of before. Now I had learnt it too late. My defence had been firmly planted in the minds of the Jury and it would be dangerous to change horses in midstream, particularly as the other horse was so dark and so uncertain a runner. I lay awake thinking of my final speech to the Jury, my last opportunity to convince them of the possibility of Daniel Derwent's suicide.

By morning I had decided not to put Perdita in the witness-box. More customers sink themselves by their own evidence than ever get scuppered by the prosecution witnesses. I saw no point in calling my client so that Marcus Griffin could try to squeeze some admission out of her to boost his tottering case. I had all the facts I wanted; now was the time for some gentle persuasion. I thought of another cogent argument for going straight to final speeches and not calling Perdita. If I did so, there was a decent chance of getting the case over before Ballard got back to ruin it all.

'No accused person can be forced into the witness-box,' I told the Jury. 'Lady Derwent has been accused of the abominable crime of murdering the husband she loved. She is fully entitled, as you or I would be, were we accused, to say to this blundering Prosecution "All right. Prove it. Don't expect any help in your unsavoury work from me." And at the end of the day, to say to you now that nothing, nothing at all, has been proved beyond reasonable doubt. A successful painter, who loves his art, finds that, through illness, he can paint no longer. Can you not understand, can't we all understand, his deciding to end his life? Nurse Gregson leaves her bag in the hall. Sir Daniel Derwent leaves the studio for just long enough, perhaps only a few minutes, to take those diamorphine ampoules. Later that night he injects himself with a massive overdose. Nurse Gregson tells us he didn't like needles; not many of us do, Members of the Jury, but if we are desperate enough we can all use them. The desperate addict forces himself to use them when longing for his fix. The desperately ill artist was also forced to inject himself when longing for death. So what remains of this pathetic prosecution? Merely Helen Derwent's evidence of what she says she found after her father's death. Why did she, cold and calculating as she is, go up to her step-mother's bedroom on that terrible morning after she had found her father dead, when any normal woman would be too overcome with grief to do anything? Was it to find evidence? Or to *plant* evidence? Of course, these things were in the house, her father had used them. Did she lie and say she had found them in Perdita's bedroom to feed her spite and to satisfy her greed for money? Members of the Jury . . . I suggest that you wouldn't convict in a case of non-renewed dog licence on the evidence of Miss Helen Derwent!'

One of the happier moments in a barrister's life is when he sits down at the end of his final speech. A huge weight seems to have been lifted from his shoulders. He has done all he can and his work is over. The Jury has to decide the case, and in that decision he can take no further part.

Judge Graves summed up in a manner as hostile to the Defence as he could manage, without giving a free run to the Court of Appeal. His delivery, however, was so lugubrious and monotone that even the eagerest juror could be seen closing his eyes occasionally and I doubted if the subtle insertions of his boot would have much effect.

When the Jury had gone, my anxiety returned. I have never paced a Court corridor smoking too many cigars, or sat in the canteen drinking too many cups of coffee, waiting for a verdict, without a dry mouth and sweaty palms, as though it was Rumpole and not his client who stood in danger of the nick. The stakes were perhaps higher in this case, as I had taken the great gamble of not calling my client. If she were convicted I would never be sure I had made the right decision. And had I fought the whole case on a false assumption? Now I knew the truth, or thought I did, should I have taken the desperate step of trying to start again? I lit another small cigar and told myself that the game was over, the judicial croupier had called 'rien n'va plus!' and there was nothing to do except wait for the roulette wheel to stop spinning.

As these thoughts were going through my mind I saw a spreading figure in a black dress sitting alone on a distant bench. As I sat down beside Bunty Derwent, she looked at me and asked, 'She'll get off, won't she?' Although she was a fat old woman she had, I thought, the calm and trusting face of a child.

'I suppose you think anyone should get off,' I told her. 'I mean, anyone who killed him, speaking as a member of the Across the River Society. You are a member, aren't you? It was *your* pamphlet?'

There was a silence and then she said, 'He couldn't paint any more. He wouldn't want to live if he couldn't paint.'

'Are you sure?' That had been my defence, but I was an advocate; I wasn't necessarily convinced by it.

'Oh, yes. Perfectly sure. It was for the best.'

'Individual omelettes?' I asked her. 'And the soup, served out in the kitchen, was it? Mulligatawny. I suppose that would hide the taste of the diamorphine.'

'What are you trying to say, Mr Rumpole?' She was like a child, I thought again, and determined not to understand difficult questions.

'Nothing very complicated,' I assured her. 'Only that you pinched the ampoules from the nurse's bag. You knew exactly what they looked like. You got the contents of those ampoules into your son's food somehow. I suppose you left them somewhere in the kitchen where Helen found them and used them to put all the blame on the step-mother she hated. What I'd like to know is this . . .'

'There's something you want to know? I thought you had *all* the answers!' The old woman was almost laughing at me.

'Did you discuss this sudden decision to end his life with your son at all? What were his views on the subject?'

'Oh, there was no need for a discussion,' she explained carefully, as though I were the child. 'A mother knows, Mr Rumpole. A mother always knows.'

'And you let Perdita go through this trial . . .' It was hard to forgive her.

'Oh, you'll get her off.' I found her confidence in my powers a little chilling. 'I've got absolutely no doubt about that. She's quite innocent.'

'I wish I had your simple faith in British justice,' I told her, but then the Usher came out of the door of the Court and called to us. The Jury was coming back and Perdita's fate had been decided.

The formalities, as always, seemed to take for ever. The Jury had to answer to their names; the foreman had to be asked to stand, and then to be asked if they had reached a verdict upon which they were all agreed. When that had been done, the Court door opened and Ballard was suddenly among us like a wounded soldier, unexpectedly back from the wars, his head bandaged under his wig and walking with the aid of a stick and Matron. He settled into the row in front of me just as the final question was asked. 'Do you find the defendant Perdita Derwent guilty or not guilty of murder?'

The answer, as always, seemed to take for ever, and I held my breath until it came.

'Not guilty, my Lord.'

I saw Perdita in the dock, her eyes filled with tears of sorrow and relief, which, now that it was over, she was finding it hard to control. I saw Bunty, the mother who knew best, smiling as though there had never been any doubt about the verdict. Then Ballard had the nerve to stand and ask if our client could be released, just as though he'd done all the work.

'Lady Derwent,' Ballard said to Perdita when they sprang her from the dock. 'I'm so very glad we were able to pull it off for you.'

'It's a wonderful victory for Sam, isn't it?' Matron was looking as pleased as Punch. 'Considering he was away so much of the time.'

'Matron was a ministering angel, Rumpole,' Ballard confided in me. 'She practically camped out in the hospital. She wouldn't let me come back until she was quite sure I was out of danger.'

'Well, I suppose we should all be grateful for that,' I said, and then took my leave of Perdita. 'Mr Rumpole,' she said as Ballard looked on, 'how can I thank you?'

'Oh, I don't know. Just go on living,' I suggested. 'You've got a great deal of it left to do.' We parted then, and I hoped she'd find another husband and never set her foot in a Law Court again.

Not long after his self-proclaimed triumph in the Derwent murder case, Ballard called a Chambers meeting. There were two items on the agenda, the admission of a new tenant and what our Head had advertised as a 'big surprise' – the exact nature of which he didn't propose to tell us until we met. Claude Erskine-Brown proposed a new member for our gallant band of legal hacks in Equity Court. 'I just think it'd be jolly bad if this Chambers got the reputation for any sort of discrimination,' he told us.

'I'm with you there, Claude.' Ballard nodded wisely. 'Entirely with you.'

'Which is why I'm particularly keen on the admission of young David, "Dave".' Claude looked serious. 'He prefers the style "Dave" Inchcape.'

'Is Inchcape black?' Uncle Tom muttered.

'No, Uncle Tom,' Claude told him. 'Dave is not black.'

'Pity.' Uncle Tom searched for a precedent. 'They had a little black chap in old Batty Jackson's Chambers. Let him in after a great deal of soul-searching. And then this little chap went off and became Prime Minister of Limpopoland or whatever, and he made old Batty Lord Chief Justice. Other fellows in Chambers got Attorney-General and all sorts of rich pickings. Would you like to go off to Limpopoland, Rumpole?'

'Anywhere where they don't have Chambers meetings.'

'It seems that Liz Probert and Dave are prepared to share a room, so there should be no problems accommodation-wise.' Claude then moved to a subject which caused him only minor embarrassment. 'As I say, I have met Dave and he has been extremely frank with me. "Out of the closet", as we would say.'

'Out of what closet?' Uncle Tom was puzzled. 'Are they going to put this black fellow in the closet?'

It seemed that Ballard wanted to get on to the next item on the agenda. He dealt with the matter shortly. 'So, if no one has any objections to Inchcape . . . Rumpole?'

'Is he keen on exercise?' I wanted to know.

'I don't think people like Dave usually are, are they?' Claude smiled tolerantly.

'Then I don't mind him in the least.'

'Good. That's settled then.' Here Ballard took a deep breath and looked around us with a certain pride. It was the moment to divulge his great secret. 'Now I have an announcement to make of a purely personal and private nature,' he began. 'You will all know Mrs Marguerite Plumstead, the Matron down at the Old Bailey. She is respected and, may I say, loved by so many barristers.'

'A formidable lady!' I agreed.

'During my recent indisposition,' he went on undeterred,

"Matey", as I shall always think of her, was a ministering angel to me. She was at my bedside in hospital. She saw me through my convalescence. We have been thrown together as a result of my accident. I am now happy to tell you that I shall no longer be living a bachelor existence in Waltham Cross. Mrs Plumstead has consented to become my wife!'

If I didn't know what a stunned silence was like, I discovered then. We had all imagined that Soapy Sam Ballard was settled in his ways and resigned to solitude, and if he had been smitten by a final irresistible passion, the masterful figure of the Old Bailey Matron seemed an unlikely love object. However, it was useless to speculate on the mysterious chemistry which had drawn these two together and I only had one question for our Head of Chambers.

'Have you consulted *Mr* Plumstead at all?'

'Mr Plumstead, after long service in the Department of the Environment, has, I regret to say, passed over.'

'Oh, I see. Across the river!'

'Of course, you will all be invited to attend the celebrations, with your wives.'

'And in the case of Dave Inchcape, no doubt' – Claude widened the invitation in the interests of tolerance – 'live-in companions.'

Ballard was as good as his word and in due course we all hired toppers and tailed coats from Moss Bros and were invited to guzzle and sluice in a handsome marquee erected for the purpose, after the unlikely union had been celebrated in the Temple Church. There was a large cake on which the tiny figures of a gowned and wigged Ballard and a uniformed Matron stood over a scrawled message in pink icing which read BEST OF LUCK TO SAM AND MARGUERITE. Matron cut the cake to general applause and then approached Hilda with a minute segment on a plate. I watched the scene moodily, eating a few peanuts, whilst the barristers around me were stuck into the salmon and champagne. 'Won't you have a wee slice of cake, Mrs Rumpole,' Matron asked, 'as it's *such* a special occasion?' 'Of course I will. Why ever not?' Hilda found the offering with some difficulty.

'I thought you might be watching that naughty tummy. Like your husband.'

'Rumpole and I are both perfectly fit, thank you, Matron.' No one can say 'Thank you' with such bitter irony as She Who Must Be Obeyed.

'Oh, I know. Sam says your husband was such a help to him in the big murder. I'm so glad old Rumpole can still lend a hand as a *junior* barrister.'

'Old Rumpole, as you call him, seems to have done the big murder largely on his own.' Hilda was displeased. 'As he did the Penge Bungalow Murders. You must have heard of that case.'

'I'm not sure I have . . .'

'I really envy you, Matron' – Hilda smiled sweetly – 'having so much to learn about the law.'

I wandered off then to have a look at more food I couldn't participate in and found Henry depressed. 'It's happened, Mr Rumpole,' he told me. 'My wife's turn has come. She is no longer a Chair.'

'What now?'

'My year has started. I am now Mayoress of Bexley Heath.'

'Henry! My heart bleeds for you.'

'Dianne is being extremely brave about it.'

I had hardly had time to give our clerk my full sympathy when Hoskins, the grey barrister much concerned with the education of his daughters, came up with some more extraordinary news. 'Rumpole! Terribly sad, isn't it?'

'Oh, I don't know. I suppose if you want to prolong your life you've got no alternative but to marry "Matey".'

'No. Sad about Hector MacClintock. He was your doctor too, wasn't he?'

'What's happened?'

'Dropped dead. And he must have been considerably younger than you.'

'Oh, dear! I *am* sorry. Poor Dr MacClintock. I'm very sorry. And he took all those precautions . . .' It was of course a blow, but one fact stood out a mile. Unlike the careful doctor, I was still alive. I took a large dinner plate and began to fill it methodically, decorating cold beef, a chicken drumstick and fish with a generous dollop of potato salad. Looking up from this work for a moment I saw a young couple, clearly in love, embracing behind a palm in a corner of the tent. They were Mizz Liz Probert and our new entrant David or 'Dave' Inchcape, and watching them like a man who has been totally deceived and is feeling particularly bitter about it was my learned friend, Claude Erskine-Brown.

'Look at that, Rumpole.' The man was clearly outraged. 'The ice-cold cheek of it. The fellow's a raving heterosexual!'

'That Inchcape.' Uncle Tom joined us, apparently puzzled. 'Remarkably fair skin for an African prime minister. Do you think we've been led up the garden?'

I took my plate over to where Hilda was sitting and told her why I now felt free to scoff at will, filling our glasses with Ballard's bubbly. She might have had a few words to say on the subject, but Claude had gone to the centre of the tent and embarked on a speech.

'A big welcome to you all,' he said. 'Ladies and gentlemen. Fellow members of Chambers. As Sam Ballard's best man, and as his learned leader in the field of matrimony' – there was a smidgin of laughter at this and Phillida sighed – 'it's my pleasure to wish the happy couple health . . .'

'Not too much health . . .' I was refilling my champagne glass. 'Just enough health to stand up in Court and lift a glass to your lips. It's the quality of life that matters, isn't it? The quality of life. And the hell with Thin-O-Vite.'

Rumpole
à la Carte

To Ann Mallalieu and Tim Cassell

Rumpole à la Carte

I suppose, when I have time to think about it, which is not often during the long day's trudge round the Bailey and more down-market venues such as the Uxbridge Magistrates Court, the law represents some attempt, however fumbling, to impose order on a chaotic universe. Chaos, in the form of human waywardness and uncontrollable passion, is ever bubbling away just beneath the surface and its sporadic outbreaks are what provide me with my daily crust, and even a glass or two of Pommeroy's plonk to go with it. I have often noticed, in the accounts of the many crimes with which I have been concerned, that some small sign of disorder – an unusual number of milk bottles on a doorstep, a car parked on a double yellow line by a normally law-abiding citizen, even, in the Penge Bungalow Murders, someone else's mackintosh taken from an office peg – has been the first indication of anarchy taking over. The clue that such dark forces were at work in La Maison Jean-Pierre, one of the few London eateries to have achieved three Michelin stars and to charge more for a bite of dinner for two than I get for a legal aid theft, was very small indeed.

Now my wife, Hilda, is a good, plain cook. In saying that, I'm not referring to She Who Must Be Obeyed's moral values or passing any judgment on her personal appearance. What I can tell you is that she cooks without flights of fancy. She is not, in any way, a woman who lacks imagination. Indeed some of the things she imagines Rumpole gets up to when out of her sight are colourful in the extreme, but she doesn't apply such gifts to a chop or a potato, being quite content to grill the one and boil the other. She can also boil a cabbage into submission and fry fish. The nearest her cooking comes to the poetic is, perhaps, in her baked jam roll, which I have always found to be an emotion best recollected in tranquillity. From all this, you will gather that Hilda's honest cooking is sufficient but not exotic, and that happily the terrible curse of *nouvelle cuisine* has not infected Froxbury Mansions in the Gloucester Road.

So it is not often that I am confronted with the sort of fare photographed in the Sunday supplements. I scarcely ever sit down to an octagonal plate on which a sliver of monkfish is arranged in a composition of pastel shades, which also features a brush stroke of pink sauce, a single peeled prawn and a sprig of dill. Such gluttony is, happily, beyond my means. It wasn't, however, beyond the means of Hilda's cousin Everard, who was visiting us from Canada, where he carried on a thriving trade as a company lawyer. He told us that he felt we stood in dire need of what he called 'a taste of gracious living' and booked a table for three at La Maison Jean-Pierre.

So we found ourselves in an elegantly appointed room with subdued lighting and even more subdued conversation, where the waiters padded around like priests and the customers behaved as though they were in church. The climax of the ritual came when the dishes were set on the table under silvery domes, which were lifted to the whispered command of *'Un, deux, trois!'* to reveal the somewhat mingy portions on offer. Cousin Everard was a grey-haired man in a pale grey suiting who talked about his legal experiences in greyish tones. He entertained us with a long account of a takeover bid for the Winnipeg Soap Company which had cleared four million dollars for his clients, the Great Elk Bank of Canada. Hearing this, Hilda said accusingly, 'You've never cleared four million dollars for a client, have you, Rumpole? You should be a company lawyer like Everard.'

'Oh, I think I'll stick to crime,' I told them. 'At least it's a more honest type of robbery.'

'Nonsense. Robbery has never got us a dinner at La Maison Jean-Pierre. We'd never be here if Cousin Everard hadn't come all the way from Saskatchewan to visit us.'

'Yes, indeed. From the town of Saskatoon, Hilda.' Everard gave her a greyish smile.

'You see, Hilda. Saskatoon as in *spittoon*.'

'Crime doesn't pay, Horace,' the man from the land of the igloos told me. 'You should know that by now. Of course, we have several fine-dining restaurants in Saskatoon these days, but nothing to touch this.' He continued his inspection of the menu. 'Hilda, may I make so bold as to ask, what is your pleasure?'

During the ensuing discussion my attention strayed. Staring idly round the consecrated area I was startled to see, in the gloaming, a distinct sign of human passion in revolt against the forces of law and order. At a table for two I recognized Claude Erskine-Brown, opera buff, hopeless cross-examiner and long-time member of our Chambers in Equity Court. But was he dining tête-à-tête with his wife, the handsome and successful Q.C., Mrs Phillida Erskine-Brown, the Portia of our group, as law and order demanded? The answer to that was no. He was entertaining a young and decorative lady solicitor named Patricia (known to herself as Tricia) Benbow. Her long golden hair (which often provoked whistles from the cruder junior clerks round the Old Bailey) hung over her slim and suntanned shoulders and one generously ringed hand rested on Claude's as she gazed, in her usual appealing way, up into his eyes. She couldn't gaze into them for long as Claude, no doubt becoming uneasily aware of the unexpected presence of a couple of Rumpoles in the room, hid his face behind a hefty wine list.

At that moment an extremely superior brand of French head waiter manifested himself beside our table, announced his presence with a discreet cough, and led off with, '*Madame, messieurs*. Tonight Jean-Pierre recommends, for the main course, *la poésie de la poitrine du canard aux céleris et épinards crus*.'

'*Poésie* . . .' Hilda sounded delighted and kindly explained, 'That's poetry, Rumpole. Tastes a good deal better than that old Wordsworth of yours, I shouldn't be surprised.'

'Tell us about it, Georges.' Everard smiled at the waiter. 'Whet our appetites.'

'This is just a few wafer-thin slices of breast of duck, marin-

ated in a drop or two of Armagnac, delicately grilled and
served with a celery remoulade and some leaves of spinach
lightly steamed . . .'

'And mash . . .?' I interrupted the man to ask.

'*Excusez-moi?*' The fellow seemed unable to believe his ears.

'Mashed spuds come with it, do they?'

'Ssh, Rumpole!' Hilda was displeased with me, but turned
all her charms on Georges. 'I will have the *poésie*. It sounds delicious.'

'A culinary experience, Hilda. Yes. *Poésie* for me too, please.'
Everard fell into line.

'I would like a *poésie* of steak and kidney *pudding*, not pie,
with mashed potatoes and a big scoop of boiled cabbage.
English mustard, if you have it.' It seemed a reasonable enough
request.

'Rumpole!' Hilda's whisper was menacing. 'Behave yourself!'

'This . . . "pudding"' – Georges was puzzled – 'is not on
our menu.'

'"Your pleasure is our delight". It says that on your menu.
Couldn't you ask Cookie if she could delight me? Along those
lines.'

'"Cookie"? I do not know who M'sieur means by "Cookie".
Our *maître de cuisine* is Jean-Pierre O'Higgins himself. He is
in the kitchen now.'

'How very convenient. Have a word in his shell-like, why
don't you?'

For a tense moment it seemed as though the looming,
priestly figure of Georges was about to excommunicate me,
drive me out of the Temple, or at least curse me by bell, book
and candle. However, after muttering, '*Si vous le voulez.
Excusez-moi,*' he went off in search of higher authority. Hilda
apologized for my behaviour and told Cousin Everard that she
supposed I thought I was being funny. I assured her that there
was nothing particularly funny about a steak and kidney pudding.

Then I was aware of a huge presence at my elbow. A tall,
fat, red-faced man in a chef's costume was standing with his

hands on his hips and asking, 'Is there someone here wants to lodge a complaint?'

Jean-Pierre O'Higgins, I was later to discover, was the product of an Irish father and a French mother. He spoke in the tones of those Irishmen who come up in a menacing manner and stand far too close to you in pubs. He was well known, I had already heard it rumoured, for dominating both his kitchen and his customers; his phenomenal rudeness to his guests seemed to be regarded as one of the attractions of his establishment. The gourmets of London didn't feel that their dinners had been entirely satisfactory unless they were served up, by way of a savoury, with a couple of insults from Jean-Pierre O'Higgins.

'Well, yes,' I said. 'There is someone.'

'Oh, yes?' O'Higgins had clearly never heard of the old adage about the customer always being right. 'And are you the joker that requested mash?'

'Am I to understand you to be saying,' I inquired as politely as I knew how, 'that there are to be no mashed spuds for my delight?'

'Look here, my friend. I don't know who you are . . .' Jean-Pierre went on in an unfriendly fashion and Everard did his best to introduce me. 'Oh, this is Horace Rumpole, Jean-Pierre. The *criminal* lawyer.'

'*Criminal* lawyer, eh?' Jean-Pierre was unappeased. 'Well, don't commit your crimes in my restaurant. If you want "mashed spuds", I suggest you move down to the working-men's caff at the end of the street.'

'That's a very helpful suggestion.' I was, as you see, trying to be as pleasant as possible.

'You might get a few bangers while you're about it. And a bottle of OK sauce. That suit your delicate palate, would it?'

'Very well indeed! I'm not a great one for wafer-thin slices of anything.'

'You don't look it. Now, let's get this straight. People who come into my restaurant damn well eat as I tell them to!'

'And I'm sure you win them all over with your irresistible charm.' I gave him the retort courteous. As the chef seemed about to explode, Hilda weighed in with a well-meaning 'I'm sure my husband doesn't mean to be rude. It's just, well, we don't dine out very often. And this is such a delightful room, isn't it?'

'Your husband?' Jean-Pierre looked at She Who Must Be Obeyed with deep pity. 'You have all my sympathy, you unfortunate woman. Let me tell you, Mr Rumpole, this is La Maison Jean-Pierre. I have three stars in the Michelin. I have thrown out an Arabian king because he ordered filet mignon well cooked. I have sent film stars away in tears because they dared to mention Thousand Island dressing. I am Jean-Pierre O'Higgins, the greatest culinary genius now working in England!'

I must confess that during this speech from the patron I found my attention straying. The other diners, as is the way with the English at the trough, were clearly straining their ears to catch every detail of the row whilst ostentatiously concentrating on their plates. The pale, bespectacled girl making up the bills behind the desk in the corner seemed to have no such inhibitions. She was staring across the room and looking at me, I thought, as though I had thoroughly deserved the O'Higgins rebuke. And then I saw two waiters approach Erskine-Brown's table with domed dishes, which they laid on the table with due solemnity.

'And let me tell you,' Jean-Pierre's oration continued, 'I started my career with salads at La Grande Bouffe in Lyons under the great Ducasse. I was rôtisseur in Le Crillon, Boston. I have run this restaurant for twenty years and I have never, let me tell you, in my whole career, served up a mashed spud!'

The climax of his speech was dramatic but not nearly as startling as the events which took place at Erskine-Brown's table. To the count of 'Un, deux, trois!' the waiters removed the silver covers and from under the one in front of Tricia Benbow sprang a small, alarmed brown mouse, perfectly visible by the light of a table candle, which had presumably been nibbling at the *poésie*. At this, the elegant lady solicitor uttered a piercing scream and leapt on to her chair. There she stood, with her skirt held down to as near her knees as possible, screaming in an ever-rising scale towards some ultimate crescendo. Meanwhile the stricken Claude looked just as a man who'd planned to have a quiet dinner with a lady and wanted to attract no one's attention would look under such circumstances. 'Please, Tricia,' I could hear his plaintive whisper, 'don't scream! People are noticing us.'

'I say, old darling,' I couldn't help saying to that three-star man O'Higgins, 'they had a mouse on that table. Is it the *spécialité de la maison?*'

A few days later, at breakfast in the mansion flat, glancing through the post (mainly bills and begging letters from Her Majesty, who seemed to be pushed for a couple of quid and would be greatly obliged if I'd let her have a little tax money on account), I saw a glossy brochure for a hotel in the Lake District. Although in the homeland of my favourite poet, Le Château Duddon, 'Lakeland's Paradise of Gracious Living', didn't sound like old Wordsworth's cup of tea, despite the 'king-sized four-poster in the Samuel Taylor Coleridge suite'.

'Cousin Everard wants to take me up there for a break.' Hilda, who was clearing away, removed a half-drunk cup of tea from my hand.

'A break from what?' I was mystified.

'From you, Rumpole. Don't you think I need it? After that disastrous evening at La Maison?'

'Was it a disaster? I quite enjoyed it. England's greatest chef laboured and gave birth to a ridiculous mouse. People'd pay good money to see a trick like that.'

'*You* were the disaster, Rumpole,' she said, as she consigned my last piece of toast to the tidy-bin. 'You were unforgivable. Mashed spuds! Why ever did you use such a vulgar expression?'

'Hilda,' I protested, I thought, reasonably, 'I have heard some fairly fruity language round the Courts in the course of a long life of crime. But I've never heard it suggested that the words "mashed spuds" would bring a blush to the cheek of the tenderest virgin.'

'Don't try to be funny, Rumpole. You upset that brilliant chef, Mr O'Higgins. You deeply upset Cousin Everard!'

'Well' – I had to put the case for the Defence – 'Everard kept on suggesting I didn't make enough to feed you properly. Typical commercial lawyer. Criminal law is about life, liberty and the pursuit of happiness. Commercial law is about money. That's what I think, anyway.'

Hilda looked at me, weighed up the evidence and summed up, not entirely in my favour. 'I don't think you made that terrible fuss because of what you thought about the commercial law,' she said. 'You did it because you have to be a "character", don't you? Wherever you go. Well, I don't know if I'm going to be able to put up with your "character" much longer.'

I don't know why but what she said made me feel, quite suddenly and in a most unusual way, uncertain of myself. What was Hilda talking about exactly? I asked for further and better particulars.

'You have to be one all the time, don't you?' She was clearly getting into her stride. 'With your cigar ash and steak and kidney and Pommeroy's Ordinary Red and your arguments. Always arguments! Why do you have to go on arguing, Rumpole?'

'Arguing? It's been my life, Hilda,' I tried to explain.

'Well, it's not mine! Not any more. Cousin Everard doesn't argue in public. He is quiet and polite.'

'If you like that sort of thing.' The subject of Cousin Everard was starting to pall on me.

'Yes, Rumpole. Yes, I do. That's why I agreed to go on this trip.'

'Trip?'

'Everard and I are going to tour all the restaurants in England with stars. We're going to Bath and York and Devizes. And you can stay here and eat all the mashed spuds you want.'

'What?' I hadn't up till then taken Le Château Duddon entirely seriously. 'You really mean it?'

'Oh, yes. I think so. The living is hardly gracious here, is it?'

On the way to my place of work I spent an uncomfortable quarter of an hour thinking over what She Who Must Be Obeyed had said about me having to be a 'character'. It seemed

an unfair charge. I drink Château Thames Embankment because it's all I can afford. It keeps me regular and blots out
certain painful memories, such as a bad day in Court in front
of Judge Graves, an old darling who undoubtedly passes iced
water every time he goes to the Gents. I enjoy the fragrance of
a small cigar. I relish an argument. This is the way of life I
have chosen. I don't have to do any of these things in order to
be a character. Do I?

I was jerked out of this unaccustomed introspection on my
arrival in the clerk's room at Chambers. Henry, our clerk, was
striking bargains with solicitors over the telephone whilst
Dianne sat in front of her typewriter, her head bowed over a
lengthy and elaborate manicure. Uncle Tom, our oldest inhabitant, who hasn't had a brief in Court since anyone can remember, was working hard at improving his putting skills
with an old mashie niblick and a clutch of golf balls, the hole
being represented by the waste-paper basket laid on its side.
Almost as soon as I got into this familiar environment I was
comforted by the sight of a man who seemed to be in far
deeper trouble than I was. Claude Erskine-Brown came up to
me in a manner that I can only describe as furtive.

'Rumpole,' he said, 'as you may know, Philly is away in
Cardiff doing a long fraud.'

'Your wife,' I congratulated the man, 'goes from strength to
strength.'

'What I mean is, Rumpole' – Claude's voice sank below the
level of Henry's telephone calls – 'you may have noticed me
the other night. In La Maison Jean-Pierre.'

'Noticed you, Claude? Of course not! You were only in the
company of a lady who stood on a chair and screamed like a
banshee with toothache. No one could have possibly noticed
you.' I did my best to comfort the man.

'It was purely a business arrangement,' he reassured me.

'Pretty rum way of conducting business.'

'The lady was Miss Tricia Benbow. My instructing solicitor
in the V.A.T. case,' he told me, as though that explained everything.

'Claude, I have had some experience of the law and it's a

good plan, when entertaining solicitors in order to tout for briefs, *not* to introduce mice into their *plats du jour*.'

The telephone by Dianne's typewriter rang. She blew on her nail lacquer and answered it, as Claude's voice rose in anguished protest. 'Good heavens. You don't think I did *that*, do you, Rumpole? The whole thing was a disaster! An absolute tragedy! Which may have appalling consequences . . .' 'Your wife on the phone, Mr Erskine-Brown,' Dianne interrupted him and Claude went to answer the call with all the eager cheerfulness of a French aristocrat who is told the tumbril is at the door. As he was telling his wife he hoped things were going splendidly in Cardiff, and that he rarely went out in the evenings, in fact usually settled down to a scrambled egg in front of the telly, there was a sound of rushing water without and our Head of Chambers joined us.

'Something extremely serious has happened.' Sam Ballard, Q.C. made the announcement as though war had broken out. He is a pallid sort of person who usually looks as though he has just bitten into a sour apple. His hair, I have to tell you, seems to be slicked down with some kind of pomade.

'Someone nicked the nail-brush in the Chambers loo?' I suggested helpfully.

'How did you guess?' He turned on me, amazed, as though I had the gift of second sight.

'It corresponds to your idea of something serious. Also I notice such things.'

'Odd that you should know immediately what I was talking about, Rumpole.' By now Ballard's amazement had turned to deep suspicion.

'Not guilty, my Lord,' I assured him. 'Didn't you have a meeting of your God-bothering society here last week?'

'The Lawyers As Christians committee. We met here. What of it?'

'"Cleanliness is next to godliness." Isn't that their motto? The devout are notable nail-brush nickers.' As I said this, I watched Erskine-Brown lay the telephone to rest and leave the room with the air of a man who has merely postponed the evil hour. Ballard was still on the subject of serious crime in the facilities. 'It's of vital importance in any place of work, Henry,' he batted on, 'that the highest standards of hygiene are maintained! Now I've been instructed by the City Health Authority in an important case, it would be extremely embarrassing to me personally if my Chambers were found wanting in the matter of a nail-brush.'

'Well, don't look at me, Mr Ballard.' Henry was not taking this lecture well.

'I am accusing nobody.' Ballard sounded unconvincing. 'But look to it, Henry. Please, look to it.'

Then our Head of Chambers left us. Feeling my usual reluctance to start work, I asked Uncle Tom, as something of an expert in these matters, if it would be fair to call me a 'character'.

'A what, Rumpole?'

'A "character", Uncle Tom.'

'Oh, they had one of those in old Sniffy Greengrass's Chambers in Lamb Court,' Uncle Tom remembered. 'Fellow called Dalrymple. Lived in an absolutely filthy flat over a chemist's shop in Chancery Lane and used to lead a cat round the Temple on a long piece of pink tape. "Old Dalrymple's a character," they used to say, and the other fellows in Chambers were rather proud of him.'

'I don't do anything like that, do I?' I asked for reassurance.

'I hope not,' Uncle Tom was kind enough to say. 'This Dalrymple finally went across the road to do an undefended divorce. In his pyjamas! I believe they had to lock him up. I wouldn't say you were a "character", Rumpole. Not yet, anyway.'

'Thank you, Uncle Tom. Perhaps you could mention that to She Who Must?'

And then the day took a distinct turn for the better. Henry put down his phone after yet another call and my heart leapt up when I heard that Mr Bernard, my favourite instructing solicitor (because he keeps quiet, does what he's told and hardly ever tells me about his bad back), was coming over and was anxious to instruct me in a new case which was 'not on the legal aid'. As I left the room to go about this business, I had one final question for Uncle Tom. 'That fellow Dalrymple. He didn't play golf in the clerk's room did he?'

'Good heavens, no.' Uncle Tom seemed amused at my ignorance of the world. 'He was a character, do you see? He'd hardly do anything normal.'

Mr Bernard, balding, pin-striped, with a greying moustache and a kindly eye, through all our triumphs and disasters remained imperturbable. No confession made by any client, however bizarre, seemed to surprise him, nor had any revelation of evil shocked him. He lived through our days of murder, mayhem and fraud as though he were listening to 'Gardeners' Question Time'. He was interested in growing roses and in his daughter's nursing career. He spent his holidays in remote spots like Bangkok and the Seychelles. He always went away, he told me, 'on a package' and returned with considerable relief. I was always pleased to see Mr Bernard, but that day he seemed to have brought me something far from my usual line of country.

'My client, Mr Rumpole, first consulted me because his marriage was on the rocks, not to put too fine a point on it.'

'It happens, Mr Bernard. Many marriages are seldom off them.'

'Particularly so if, as in this case, the wife's of foreign extraction. It's long been my experience, Mr Rumpole, that you can't beat foreign wives for being vengeful. In this case, extremely vengeful.'

'Hell hath no fury, Mr Bernard?' I suggested.

'Exactly, Mr Rumpole. You've put your finger on the nub of the case. As you would say yourself.'

'I haven't done a matrimonial for years. My divorce may be a little rusty,' I told him modestly.

'Oh, we're not asking you to do the divorce. We're sending that to Mr Tite-Smith in Crown Office Row.'

Oh, well, I thought, with only a slight pang of disappointment, good luck to little Tite-Smith.

'The matrimonial is not my client's only problem,' Mr Bernard told me.

' "When sorrows come," Mr Bernard, "they come not single spies, But in battalions!" Your chap got something else on his plate, has he?'

'On his plate!' The phrase seemed to cause my solicitor some amusement. 'That's very apt, that is. And apter than you know, Mr Rumpole.'

'Don't keep me in suspense! Who is this mysterious client?'

'I wasn't to divulge the name, Mr Rumpole, in case you should refuse to act for him. He thought you might've taken against him, so he's coming to appeal to you in person. I asked Henry if he'd show him up as soon as he arrived.'

And, dead on cue, Dianne knocked on my door, threw it open and announced, 'Mr O'Higgins.' The large man, dressed now in a deafening checked tweed jacket and a green turtle-necked sweater, looking less like a chef than an Irish horse coper, advanced on me with a broad grin and his hand extended in a greeting, which was in strong contrast to our last encounter.

'I rely on you to save me, Mr Rumpole,' he boomed. 'You're the man to do it, sir. The great criminal defender!'

'Oh? I thought *I* was the criminal in your restaurant,' I reminded him.

'I have to tell you, Mr Rumpole, your courage took my breath away! Do you know what he did, Mr Bernard? Do you know what this little fellow here had the pluck to do?' He seemed determined to impress my solicitor with an account of my daring in the face of adversity. 'He only ordered mashed spuds in La Maison Jean-Pierre. A risk no one else has taken in all the time I've been *maître de cuisine*.'

'It didn't seem to be particularly heroic,' I told Bernard, but O'Higgins would have none of that. 'I tell you, Mr Bernard' – he moved very close to my solicitor and towered over him – 'a man who could do that to Jean-Pierre couldn't be intimidated by all the judges of the Queen's Bench. What do you say then, Mr Horace Rumpole? Will you take me on?'

I didn't answer him immediately but sat at my desk, lit a small cigar and looked at him critically. 'I don't know yet.'

'Is it my personality that puts you off?' My prospective

client folded himself into my armchair, with one leg draped
over an arm. He grinned even more broadly, displaying a
judiciously placed gold tooth. 'Do you find me objectionable?'

'Mr O'Higgins.' I decided to give judgment at length. 'I
think your restaurant pretentious and your portions skimpy.
Your customers eat in a dim, religious atmosphere which
seems to be more like Evensong than a good night out. You
appear to be a self-opinionated and self-satisfied bully. I have
known many murderers who could teach you a lesson in courtesy. However, Mr Bernard tells me that you are prepared to
pay my fee and, in accordance with the great traditions of the
Bar, I am on hire to even the most unattractive customer.'

There was a silence and I wondered if the inflammable
restaurateur were about to rise and hit me. But he turned to
Bernard with even greater enthusiasm. 'Just listen to that!
How's that for eloquence? We picked the right one here, Mr
Bernard!'

'Well, now. I gather you're in some sort of trouble. Apart
from your marriage, that is.' I unscrewed my pen and prepared
to take a note.

'This has nothing to do with my marriage.' But then he
frowned unhappily. 'Anyway, I don't think it has.'

'You haven't done away with this vengeful wife of yours?'
Was I to be presented with a murder?

'I should have, long ago,' Jean-Pierre admitted. 'But no.
Simone is still alive and suing. Isn't that right, Mr Bernard?'

'It is, Mr O'Higgins,' Bernard assured him gloomily. 'It is
indeed. But this is something quite different. My client, Mr
Rumpole, is being charged under the Food and Hygiene
Regulations 1970 for offences relating to dirty and dangerous
practices at La Maison. I have received a telephone call from
the Environmental Health Officer.'

It was then, I'm afraid, that I started to laugh. I named the
guilty party. 'The mouse!'

'Got it in one.' Jean-Pierre didn't seem inclined to join in
the joke.

'The "wee, sleekit, cow'rin, tim'rous beastie",' I quoted at
him. 'How delightful! We'll elect for trial before a jury. If we

can't get you off, Mr O'Higgins, at least we'll give them a little harmless entertainment.'

Of course it wasn't really funny. A mouse in the wrong place, like too many milk bottles on a doorstep, might be a sign of passions stretched beyond control.

I have always found it useful, before forming a view about a case, to inspect the scene of the crime. Accordingly I visited La Maison Jean-Pierre one evening to study the ritual serving of dinner.

Mr Bernard and I stood in a corner of the kitchen at La Maison Jean-Pierre with our client. We were interested in the two waiters who had attended table eight, the site of the Erskine-Brown assignation. The senior of the two was Gaston, the station waiter, who had four tables under his command. 'Gaston Leblanc,' Jean-Pierre told us, as he identified the small, fat, cheerful, middle-aged man who trotted between the tables. 'Been with me for ever. Works all the hours God gave to keep a sick wife and their kid at university. Does all sorts of other jobs in the day-time. I don't inquire too closely. Georges Pitou, the head waiter, takes the orders, of course, and leaves a copy of the note on the table.'

We saw Georges move, in a stately fashion, into the kitchen and hand the order for table eight to a young cook in a white hat, who stuck it up on the kitchen wall with a magnet. This was Ian, the sous chef. Jean-Pierre had 'discovered' him in a Scottish hotel and wanted to encourage his talent. That night the bustle in the kitchen was muted, and as I looked through the circular window into the dining-room I saw that most of the white-clothed tables were standing empty, like small icebergs in a desolate polar region. When the Prosecution had been announced, there had been a headline in the *Evening Standard* which read GUESS WHO'S COMING TO DINNER? MOUSE SERVED IN TOP LONDON RESTAURANT and since then attendances at La Maison had dropped off sharply.

The runner between Gaston's station and the kitchen was the commis waiter, Alphonse Pascal, a painfully thin, dark-eyed young man with a falling lock of hair who looked like the hero of some nineteenth-century French novel, interesting and doomed. 'As a matter of fact,' Jean-Pierre told us, 'Alphonse is full of ambition. He's starting at the bottom and wants to work his way up to running a hotel. Been with me for about a year.'

We watched as Ian put the two orders for table eight on the serving-table. In due course Alphonse came into the kitchen and called out, 'Number Eight!' 'Ready, frog face,' Ian told him politely, and Alphonse came back with, '*Merci*, idiot.'

'Are they friends?' I asked my client.

'Not really. They're both much too fond of Mary.'

'Mary?'

'Mary Skelton. The English girl who makes up the bills in the restaurant.'

I looked again through the circular window and saw the unmemorable girl, her head bent over her calculator. She seemed an unlikely subject for such rivalry. I saw Alphonse pass her with a tray, carrying two domed dishes and, although he looked in her direction, she didn't glance up from her work. Alphonse then took the dishes to the serving-table at Gaston's station. Gaston looked under one dome to check its contents and then the plates were put on the table. Gaston mouthed an inaudible '*Un, deux, trois!*', the domes were lifted before the diners and not a mouse stirred.

'On the night in question,' Bernard reminded me, 'Gaston says in his statement that he looked under the dome on the gentleman's plate.'

'And saw no side order of mouse,' I remembered.

'Exactly! So he gave the other to Alphonse, who took it to the lady.'

'And then . . . Hysterics!'

'And then the reputation of England's greatest *maître de cuisine* crumbled to dust!' Jean-Pierre spoke as though announcing a national disaster.

'Nonsense!' I did my best to cheer him up. 'You're forgetting the reputation of Horace Rumpole.'

'You think we've got a defence?' my client asked eagerly. 'I mean, now that you've looked at the kitchen?'

'Can't think of one for the moment,' I admitted, 'but I expect we'll cook up something in the end.'

Unencouraged, Jean-Pierre looked out into the dining-room, muttered, 'I'd better go and keep those lonely people company,' and left us. I watched him pass the desk, where Mary looked up and smiled and I thought, however brutal he was with his customers, at least Jean-Pierre's staff seemed to find him a tolerable employer. And then, to my surprise, I saw him approach the couple at table eight, grinning in a most ingratiating manner, and stand chatting and bowing as though they could have ordered doner kebab and chips and that would have been perfectly all right by him.

'You know,' I said to Mr Bernard, 'it's quite extraordinary, the power that can be wielded by one of the smaller rodents.'

'You mean it's wrecked his business?'

'No. More amazing than that. It's forced Jean-Pierre O'Higgins to be polite to his clientele.'

After my second visit to La Maison events began to unfold at breakneck speed. First our Head of Chambers, Soapy Sam Ballard, made it known to me that the brief he had accepted on behalf of the Health Authority, and of which he had boasted so flagrantly during the nail-brush incident, was in fact the prosecution of J.-P. O'Higgins for the serious crime of being in charge of a rodent-infested restaurant. Then She Who Must Be Obeyed, true to her word, packed her grip and went off on a gastronomic tour with the man from Saskatoon. I was left to enjoy a lonely high-calorie breakfast, with no fear of criticism over the matter of a fourth sausage, in the Taste-Ee-Bite café, Fleet Street. Seated there one morning, enjoying the company of *The Times* crossword, I happened to overhear Mizz Liz Probert, the dedicated young radical barrister in our Chambers, talking to her close friend, David Inchcape, whom she had persuaded us to take on in a somewhat devious manner – a barrister as young but, I think, at heart, a touch less radical than Mizz Liz herself.*

* See 'Rumpole and the Quality of Life' in *Rumpole and the Age of Miracles*, Penguin Books, 1988.

'You don't really *care*, do you, Dave?' she was saying.

'Of course, I care. I care about you, Liz. Deeply.' He reached out over their plates of muesli and cups of decaff to grasp her fingers.

'That's just physical.'

'Well. Not just physical. I don't suppose it's *just*. Mainly physical, perhaps.'

'No one cares about old people.'

'But you're not old people, Liz. Thank God!'

'You see. You don't care about them. My Dad was saying there's old people dying in tower blocks every day. Nobody knows about it for weeks, until they decompose!' And I saw Dave release her hand and say, 'Please, Liz. I *am* having my breakfast.'

'You see! You don't want to know. It's just something you don't want to hear about. It's the same with battery hens.'

'What's the same about battery hens?'

'No one wants to know. That's all.'

'But surely, Liz. Battery hens don't get lonely.'

'Perhaps they do. There's an awful lot of loneliness about.' She looked in my direction. 'Get off to Court then, if you have to. But do *think* about it, Dave.' Then she got up, crossed to my table, and asked what I was doing. I was having my breakfast, I assured her, and not doing my yoga meditation.

'Do you always have breakfast alone, Rumpole?' She spoke, in the tones of a deeply supportive social worker, as she sat down opposite me.

'It's not always possible. Much easier now, of course.'

'Now. Why *now*, exactly?' She looked seriously concerned.

'Well. Now my wife's left me,' I told her cheerfully.

'Hilda!' Mizz Probert was shocked, being a conventional girl at heart.

'As you would say, Mizz Liz, she is no longer sharing a one-on-one relationship with me. In any meaningful way.'

'Where does that leave you, Rumpole?'

'Alone. To enjoy my breakfast and contemplate the crossword puzzle.'

'Where's Hilda gone?'

'Oh, in search of gracious living with her cousin Everard from Saskatoon. A fellow with about as many jokes in him as the Dow Jones Average.'

'You mean, she's gone off with another man?' Liz seemed unable to believe that infidelity was not confined to the young.

'That's about the size of it.'

'But, Rumpole. *Why*?'

'Because he's rich enough to afford very small portions of food.'

'So you're living by yourself? You must be terribly lonely.'

'"Society is all but rude,"' I assured her, '"To this delicious solitude."'

There was a pause and then Liz took a deep breath and offered her assistance. 'You know, Rumpole. Dave and I have founded the Y.R.L. Young Radical Lawyers. We don't only mean to reform the legal system, although that's part of it, of course. We're going to take on social work as well. We could always get someone to call and take a look at your flat every morning.'

'To make sure it's still there?'

'Well, no, Rumpole. As a matter of fact, to make sure you are.'

Those who are alone have great opportunities for eavesdropping, and Liz and Dave weren't the only members of our Chambers I heard engaged in a heart-to-heart that day. Before I took the journey back to the She-less flat, I dropped into Pommeroy's and was enjoying the ham roll and bottle of Château Thames Embankment which would constitute my dinner, seated in one of the high-backed, pew-like stalls Jack Pommeroy has installed, presumably to give the joint a vaguely medieval appearance and attract the tourists. From behind my back I heard the voices of our Head of Chambers and Claude Erskine-Brown, who was saying, in his most ingratiating tones, 'Ballard. I want to have a word with you about the case you've got against La Maison Jean-Pierre.'

To this, Ballard, in thoughtful tones, replied unexpectedly, 'A strong chain! It's the only answer.' Which didn't seem to follow.

'It was just my terrible luck, of course,' Erskine-Brown complained, 'that it should happen at my table. I mean, I'm a pretty well-known member of the Bar. Naturally I don't want my name connected with, well, a rather ridiculous incident.'

'Fellows in Chambers aren't going to like it.' Ballard was not yet with him. 'They'll say it's a restriction on their liberty. Rumpole, no doubt, will have a great deal to say about Magna Carta. But the only answer is to get a new nail-brush and chain it up. Can I have your support in taking strong measures?'

'Of course, you can, Ballard. I'll be right behind you on this one.' The creeping Claude seemed only too anxious to please. 'And in this case you're doing, I don't suppose you'll have to call the couple who actually *got* the mouse?'

'The couple?' There was a pause while Ballard searched his memory. 'The mouse was served – appalling lack of hygiene in the workplace – to a table booked by a Mr Claude Erskine-Brown and guest. Of course he'll be a vital witness.' And then the penny dropped. He stared at Claude and said firmly, '*You'll* be a vital witness.'

'But if I'm a witness of any sort, my name'll get into the papers and Philly will know I was having dinner.'

'Why on earth *shouldn't* she know you were having dinner?' Ballard was reasoning with the man. 'Most people have dinner. Nothing to be ashamed of. Get a grip on yourself, Erskine-Brown.'

'Ballard. Sam.' Claude was trying the appeal to friendship. 'You're a married man. You should understand.'

'Of course I'm married. And Marguerite and I have dinner. On a regular basis.'

'But I wasn't having dinner with Philly.' Claude explained the matter carefully. 'I was having dinner with an instructing solicitor.'

'That was your guest?'

'Yes.'

'A solicitor?'

'Of course.'

Ballard seemed to have thought the matter over carefully, but he was still puzzled when he replied, remembering his instructions. 'He apparently leapt on to a chair, held down his skirt and screamed three times!'

'Ballard! The solicitor was Tricia Benbow. You don't imagine I'd spend a hundred and something quid on feeding the face of Mr Bernard, do you?'

There was another longish pause, during which I imagined Claude in considerable suspense, and then our Head of Chambers spoke again. 'Tricia Benbow?' he asked.

'Yes.'

'Is that the one with the long blonde hair and rings?'

'That's the one.'

'And your wife knew nothing of this?'

'And must never know!' For some reason not clear to me, Claude seemed to think he'd won his case, for he now sounded grateful. 'Thank you, Ballard. Thanks awfully, Sam. I can count on you to keep my name out of this. I'll do the same for you, old boy. Any day of the week.'

'That won't be necessary.' Ballard's tone was not encouraging, although Claude said, 'No? Well, thanks, anyway.'

'It *will* be necessary, however, for you to give evidence for the Prosecution.' Soapy Sam Ballard pronounced sentence and Claude yelped, 'Have a heart, Sam!'

'Don't you "Sam" me.' Ballard was clearly in a mood to notice the decline of civilization as we know it. 'It's all part of the same thing, isn't it? Sharp practice over the nail-brush. Failure to assist the authorities in an important prosecution. You'd better prepare yourself for Court, Erskine-Brown. And to be cross-examined by Rumpole for the Defence. Do your duty! And take the consequences.'

A moment later I saw Ballard leaving for home and his wife, Marguerite, who, you will remember, once held the position of matron at the Old Bailey.* No doubt he would chatter to her of nail-brushes and barristers unwilling to tell the whole truth. I carried my bottle of plonk round to Claude's stall in order to console the fellow.

* See 'Rumpole and the Quality of Life' in *Rumpole and the Age of Miracles*, Penguin Books, 1988.

'So,' I said, 'you lost your case.'

'What a bastard!' I have never seen Claude so pale.

'You made a big mistake, old darling. It's no good appealing to the warm humanity of a fellow who believes in chaining up nail-brushes.'

So the intrusive mouse continued to play havoc with the passions of a number of people, and I prepared myself for its day in Court. I told Mr Bernard to instruct Ferdinand Isaac Gerald Newton, known in the trade as Fig Newton, a lugubrious scarecrow of a man who is, without doubt, our most effective private investigator, to keep a watchful eye on the staff of La Maison. And then I decided to call in at the establishment on my way home one evening, not only to get a few more facts from my client but because I was becoming bored with Pommeroy's ham sandwiches.

Before I left Chambers an event occurred which caused me deep satisfaction. I made for the downstairs lavatory, and although the door was open, I found it occupied by Uncle Tom who was busily engaged at the basin washing his collection of golf balls and scrubbing each one to a gleaming whiteness with a nail-brush. He had been putting each one, when cleaned, into a biscuit tin and as I entered he dropped the nail-brush in also.

'Uncle Tom!' – I recognized the article at once – 'that's the Chambers nail-brush! Soapy Sam's having kittens about it.'

'Oh, dear. Is it, really? I must have taken it without remembering. I'll leave it on the basin.'

But I persuaded him to let me have it for safe-keeping, saying I longed to see Ballard's little face light up with joy when it was restored to him.

When I arrived at La Maison the disputes seemed to have become a great deal more dramatic than even in Equity Court. The place was not yet open for dinner, but I was let in as the restaurant's legal adviser and I heard raised voices and sounds of a struggle from the kitchen. Pushing the door open, I found Jean-Pierre in the act of forcibly removing a knife from the hands of Ian, the sous chef, at whom an excited Alphonse

Pascal, his lock of black hair falling into his eyes, was shouting abuse in French. My arrival created a diversion in which both men calmed down and Jean-Pierre passed judgment on them. 'Bloody lunatics!' he said. 'Haven't they done this place enough harm already? They have to start slaughtering each other. Behave yourselves. *Soyez sages!* And what can I do for *you*, Mr Rumpole?'

'Perhaps we could have a little chat,' I suggested as the tumult died down. 'I thought I'd call in. My wife's away, you see, and I haven't done much about dinner.'

'Then what would you like?'

'Oh, anything. Just a snack.'

'Some pâté, perhaps? And a bottle of champagne?' I thought he'd never ask.

When we were seated at a table in a corner of the empty restaurant, the patron told me more about the quarrel. 'They were fighting again over Mary Skelton.'

I looked across at the desk, where the unmemorable girl was getting out her calculator and preparing for her evening's work. 'She doesn't look the type, exactly,' I suggested.

'Perhaps,' Jean-Pierre speculated, 'she has a warm heart? My wife Simone looks the type, but she's got a heart like an ice-cube.'

'Your wife. The vengeful woman?' I remembered what Mr Bernard had told me.

'Why should she be vengeful to me, Mr Rumpole? When I'm a particularly tolerant and easy-going type of individual?'

At which point a couple of middle-aged Americans, who had strayed in off the street, appeared at the door of the restaurant and asked Jean-Pierre if he were serving dinner. 'At six thirty? No! And we don't do teas, either.' He shouted across at them, in a momentary return to his old ways, 'Cret-ins!'

'Of course,' I told him, 'you're a very parfait, gentle cook.'

'A great artist needs admiration. He needs almost incessant praise.'

'And with Simone,' I suggested, 'the admiration flowed like cement?'

'You've got it. Had some experience of wives, have you?'

'You might say, a lifetime's experience. Do you mind?' I poured myself another glass of unwonted champagne.

'No, no, of course. And your wife doesn't understand you?'

'Oh, I'm afraid she does. That's the worrying thing about it. She blames me for being a "character".'

'They'd blame you for anything. Come to divorce, has it?'

'Not quite reached your stage, Mr O'Higgins.' I looked round the restaurant. 'So, I suppose you have to keep these tables full to pay Simone her alimony.'

'Not exactly. You see she'll own half La Maison.' That hadn't been entirely clear to me and I asked him to explain.

'When we started off, I was a young man. All I wanted to do was to get up early, go to Smithfield and Billingsgate, feel the lobsters and smell the fresh scallops, create new dishes, and dream of sauces. Simone was the one with the business sense. Well, she's French, so she insisted on us getting married in France.'

'Was that wrong?'

'Oh, no. It was absolutely right, for Simone. Because they have a damned thing there called "community of property". I had to agree to give her half of everything if we ever broke up. You know about the law, of course.'

'Well, not everything about it.' Community of property, I must confess, came as news to me. 'I always found knowing the law a bit of a handicap for a barrister.'

'Simone knew all about it. She had her beady eye on the future.' He emptied his glass and then looked at me pleadingly. 'You're going to get us out of this little trouble, aren't you, Mr Rumpole? This affair of the mouse?'

'Oh, the mouse!' I did my best to reassure him. 'The mouse seems to be the least of your worries.'

Soon Jean-Pierre had to go back to his kitchen. On his way, he stopped at the cash desk and said something to the girl, Mary. She looked up at him with, I thought, unqualified adoration. He patted her arm and went back to his sauces, having reassured her, I suppose, about the quarrel that had been going on in her honour.

I did justice to the rest of the champagne and pâté de foie and started off for home. In the restaurant entrance hall I saw the lady who minded the cloaks take a suitcase from Gaston Leblanc, who had just arrived out of breath and wearing a mackintosh. Although large, the suitcase seemed very light and he asked her to look after it.

Several evenings later I was lying on my couch in the living-room of the mansion flat, a small cigar between my fingers and a glass of Château Fleet Street on the floor beside me. I was in vacant or in pensive mood as I heard a ring at the front-door bell. I started up, afraid that the delights of *haute cuisine* had palled for Hilda, and then I remembered that She would undoubtedly have come armed with a latchkey. I approached the front door, puzzled at the sound of young and excited voices without, combined with loud music. I got the door open and found myself face to face with Liz Probert, Dave Inchcape and five or six other junior hacks, all wearing sweat-shirts with a picture of a wig and YOUNG RADICAL LAWYERS written on them. Dianne was also there in trousers and a glittery top, escorted by my clerk, Henry, wearing jeans and doing his best to appear young and swinging. The party was carrying various bottles and an article we know well down the Bailey (because it so often appears in lists of stolen prop-erty) as a ghetto blaster. It was from this contraption that the loud music emerged.

'It's a surprise party!' Mizz Liz Probert announced with considerable pride. 'We've come to cheer you up in your great loneliness.'

Nothing I could say would stem the well-meaning invasion. Within minutes the staid precincts of Froxbury Mansions were transformed into the sort of disco which is patronized by under-thirties on a package to the Costa del Sol. Bizarre drinks, such as rum and blackcurrant juice or advocaat and lemonade, were being mixed in what remained of our tumblers, sup-plemented by toothmugs from the bathroom. Scarves dimmed the lights, the ghetto blaster blasted ceaselessly and dancers gyrated in a self-absorbed manner, apparently oblivious of each other. Only Henry and Dianne, practising a more old-fashioned ritual, clung together, almost motionless, and carried on a lively conversation with me as I stood on the outskirts of the revelry, drinking the best of the wine they had brought and trying to look tolerantly convivial.

'We heard as how Mrs Rumpole has done a bunk, sir.' Dianne looked sympathetic, to which Henry added sourly, 'Some people have all the luck!'

'Why? Where's your wife tonight, Henry?' I asked my clerk. The cross he has to bear is that his spouse has pursued an ambitious career in local government so that, whereas she is now the Mayor of Bexleyheath, he is officially her Mayoress.

'My wife's at a dinner of South London mayors in the Mansion House, Mr Rumpole. No consorts allowed, thank God!' Henry told me.

'Which is why we're both on the loose tonight. Makes you feel young again, doesn't it, Mr Rumpole?' Dianne asked me as she danced minimally.

'Well, not particularly young, as a matter of fact.' The music yawned between me and my guests as an unbridgeable generation gap. And then one of the more intense of the young lady radicals approached me, as a senior member of the Bar, to ask what the hell the Lord Chief Justice knew about being pregnant and on probation at the moment your boyfriend's arrested for dope. 'Very little, I should imagine,' I had to tell her, and then, as the telephone was bleating pathetically beneath the din, I excused myself and moved to answer it. As I went, a Y.R.L. sweatshirt whirled past me; Liz, dancing energetically, had pulled it off and was gyrating in what appeared to be an ancient string-vest and a pair of jeans.

'Rumpole!' the voice of She Who Must Be Obeyed called to me, no doubt from the banks of Duddon. 'What on earth's going on there?'

'Oh, Hilda. Is it you?'

'Of course it's me.'

'Having a good time, are you? And did Cousin Everard enjoy his sliver of whatever it was?'

'Rumpole. What's that incredible noise?'

'Noise? Is there a noise? Oh, yes. I think I do hear music. Well . . .' Here I improvised, as I thought brilliantly. 'It's a play, that's what it is, a play on television. It's all about young people, hopping about in a curious fashion.'

'Don't talk rubbish!' Hilda, as you may guess, sounded far from convinced. 'You know you never watch plays on television.'

'Not usually, I grant you,' I admitted. 'But what else have I got to do when my wife has left me?'

Much later, it seemed a lifetime later, when the party was over, I settled down to read the latest addition to my brief in the O'Higgins case. It was a report from Fig Newton, who had been keeping observation on the workers at La Maison. One afternoon he followed Gaston Leblanc, who left his home in Ruislip with a large suitcase, with which he travelled to a smart address at Egerton Crescent in Knightsbridge. This house, which had a bunch of brightly coloured balloons tied to its front door, Fig kept under surveillance for some time. A number of small children arrived, escorted by nannies, and were let in by a manservant. Later, when all the children had been received, Fig, wrapped in his Burberry with his collar turned up against the rain, was able to move so he got a clear view into the sitting-room.

What he saw interested me greatly. The children were seated on the floor watching breathlessly as Gaston Leblanc, station waiter and part-time conjuror, dressed in a black robe ornamented with stars, entertained them by slowly extricating a live and kicking rabbit from a top hat.

For the trial of Jean-Pierre O'Higgins we drew the short straw in the shape of an Old Bailey judge aptly named Gerald Graves. Judge Graves and I have never exactly hit it off. He is a pale, long-faced, unsmiling fellow who probably lives on a diet of organic bran and carrot juice. He heard Ballard open the proceedings against La Maison with a pained expression, and looked at me over his half-glasses as though I were a saucepan that hadn't been washed up properly. He was the last person in the world to laugh a case out of Court and I would have to manage that trick without him.

Soapy Sam Ballard began by describing the minor blemishes in the restaurant's kitchen. 'In this highly expensive, allegedly three-star establishment, the Environmental Health Officer discovered cracked tiles, open waste-bins and gravy stains on the ceiling.'

'The ceiling, Mr Ballard?' the Judge repeated in sepulchral tones.

'Alas, yes, my Lord. The ceiling.'

'Probably rather a tall cook,' I suggested, and was rewarded with a freezing look from the Bench.

'And there was a complete absence of nail-brushes in the kitchen handbasins.' Ballard touched on a subject dear to his heart. 'But wait, Members of the Jury, until you get to the –'

'Main course?' I suggested in another ill-received whisper and Ballard surged on '– the very heart of this most serious case. On the night of May the 18th, a common house mouse was served up at a customer's dinner table.'

'We are no doubt dealing here, Mr Ballard,' the Judge intoned solemnly, 'with a defunct mouse?'

'Again, alas, no, my lord. The mouse in question was alive.'

'And kicking,' I muttered. Staring vaguely round the Court, my eye lit on the public gallery where I saw Mary Skelton, the quiet restaurant clerk, watching the proceedings attentively.

'Members of the Jury' – Ballard had reached his peroration – 'need one ask if a kitchen is in breach of the Food and Hygiene Regulations if it serves up a living mouse? As proprietor of the restaurant, Mr O'Higgins is, say the Prosecution, absolutely responsible. Whomsoever in his employ he seeks to blame, Members of the Jury, he must take the consequences. I will now call my first witness.'

'Who's that pompous imbecile?' Jean-Pierre O'Higgins was adding his two pennyworth, but I told him he wasn't in his restaurant now and to leave the insults to me. I was watching a fearful and embarrassed Claude Erskine-Brown climb into the witness-box and take the oath as though it were the last rites. When asked to give his full names he appealed to the Judge.

'My Lord. May I write them down? There may be some

publicity about this case.' He looked nervously at the assembled reporters.

'Aren't you a Member of the Bar?' Judge Graves squinted at
the witness over his half-glasses.

'Well, yes, my Lord,' Claude admitted reluctantly.

'That's nothing to be ashamed of – in most cases.' At which
the Judge aimed a look of distaste in my direction and then
turned back to the witness. 'I think you'd better tell the Jury
who you are, in the usual way.'

'Claude . . .' The unfortunate fellow tried a husky whisper,
only to get a testy 'Oh, do speak up!' from his Lordship.
Whereupon, turning up the volume a couple of notches, the
witness answered, 'Claude Leonard Erskine-Brown.' I hadn't
know about the Leonard.

'On May the 18th were you dining at La Maison Jean-
Pierre?' Ballard began his examination.

'Well, yes. Yes. I did just drop in.'

'For dinner?'

'Yes,' Claude had to admit.

'In the company of a young lady named Patricia Benbow?'

'Well. That is . . . Er . . . er.'

'Mr Erskine-Brown' – Judge Graves had no sympathy with
this sudden speech impediment – 'it seems a fairly simple
question to answer, even for a Member of the Bar.'

'I was in Miss Benbow's company, my Lord,' Claude
answered in despair.

'And when the main course was served were the plates
covered?'

'Yes. They were.'

'And when the covers were lifted what happened?'

Into the expectant silence, Erskine-Brown said in a still,
small voice, 'A mouse ran out.'

'Oh, do speak up!' Graves was running out of patience with
the witness, who almost shouted back, 'A mouse ran out, my
Lord!'

At this point Ballard said, 'Thank you, Mr Erskine-Brown,'
and sat down, no doubt confident that the case was in the bag –
or perhaps the trap. Then I rose to cross-examine.

'Mr Claude Leonard Erskine-Brown,' I weighed in, 'is Miss
Benbow a solicitor?'

'Well. Yes . . .' Claude looked at me sadly, as though wanting
to say, *Et tu*, Rumpole?

'And is your wife a well-known and highly regarded Queen's
Counsel?'

Graves's face lit up at the mention of our delightful Portia.
'Mrs Erskine-Brown has sat here as a Recorder, Members of
the Jury.' He smiled sickeningly at the twelve honest citizens.

'I'm obliged to your Lordship.' I bowed slightly and turned
back to the witness. 'And is Miss Benbow instructed in an
important forthcoming case, that is the Balham Mini-Cab
Murder, in which she is intending to brief Mrs Erskine-Brown,
Q.C.?'

'Is – is she?' Never quick off the mark, Claude didn't yet
realize that help was at hand.

'And were you taking her out to dinner so you might discuss
the Defence in that case, your wife being unfortunately
detained in Cardiff?' I hoped that made my good intentions
clear, even to a barrister.

'Was I?' Erskine-Brown was still not with me.

'Well, weren't you?' I was losing patience with the fellow.

'Oh, yes.' At last the penny dropped. 'Of course I was! I do
remember now. Naturally. And I did it all to help Philly. To
help my wife. Is that what you mean?' He ended up looking at
me anxiously.

'Exactly.'

'Thank you, Mr Rumpole. Thank you very much.' Erskine-
Brown's gratitude was pathetic. But the Judge couldn't wait to
get on to the exciting bits. 'Mr Rumpole,' he boomed mournfully, 'when are we coming to the mouse?'

'Oh, yes. I'm grateful to your Lordship for reminding me.
Well. What sort of animal was it?'

'Oh, a very small mouse indeed.' Claude was now desperately anxious to help me. 'Hardly noticeable.'

'A very small mouse and hardly noticeable,' Graves repeated
as he wrote it down and then raised his eyebrows, as though,
when it came to mice, smallness was no excuse.

'And the first you saw of it was when it emerged from under a silver dish-cover? You couldn't swear it got there in the kitchen?'

'No, I couldn't.' Erskine-Brown was still eager to cooperate.

'Or if it was inserted in the dining-room by someone with access to the serving-table?'

'Oh, no, Mr Rumpole. You're perfectly right. Of course it might have been!' The witness's cooperation was almost embarrassing, so the Judge chipped in with 'I take it you're not suggesting that this creature appeared from a dish of duck breasts by some sort of miracle, are you, Mr Rumpole?'

'Not a miracle, my Lord. Perhaps a trick.'

'Isn't Mr Ballard perfectly right?' Graves, as was his wont, had joined the prosecution team. 'For the purposes of this offence it doesn't matter *how* it got there. A properly run restaurant should not serve up a mouse for dinner! The thing speaks for itself.'

'A talking mouse, my Lord? What an interesting conception!' I got a loud laugh from my client and even the Jury joined in with a few friendly titters. I also got, of course, a stern rebuke from the Bench. 'Mr Rumpole!' – his Lordship's seriousness was particularly deadly – 'this is not a place of entertainment! You would do well to remember that this is a most serious case from your client's point of view. And I'm sure the Jury will wish to give it the most weighty consideration. We will continue with it after luncheon. Shall we say, five past two, Members of the Jury?'

Mr Bernard and I went down to the pub, and after a light snack of shepherd's pie, washed down with a pint or two of Guinness, we hurried back into the Palais de Justice and there I found what I had hoped for. Mary Skelton was sitting quietly outside the Court, waiting for the proceedings to resume. I lit a small cigar and took a seat with my instructing solicitor not far away from the girl. I raised my voice a little and said, 'You know what's always struck me about this case, Mr Bernard? There's no evidence of droppings or signs of mice in the kitchen. So someone put the mouse under the cover deliberately. Someone who wanted to ruin La Maison's business.'

'Mrs O'Higgins?' Bernard suggested.

'Certainly not! She'd want the place to be as prosperous as possible because she owned half of it. The guilty party is someone who wanted Simone to get nothing but half a failed eatery with a ruined reputation. So what did this someone do?'

'You tell me, Mr Rumpole.' Mr Bernard was an excellent straight man.

'Oh, broke a lot of little rules. Took away the nail-brushes and the lids of the tidy-bins. But a sensation was needed, something that'd hit the headlines. Luckily this someone knew a waiter who had a talent for sleight of hand and a spare-time job producing livestock out of hats.'

'Gaston Leblanc?' Bernard was with me.

'Exactly! He got the animal under the lid and gave it to Alphonse to present to the unfortunate Miss Tricia Benbow. Consequence: ruin for the restaurant and a rotten investment for the vengeful Simone. No doubt someone paid Gaston well to do it.'

I was silent then. I didn't look at the waiting girl, but I was sure she was looking at me. And then Bernard asked, 'Just who are we talking about, Mr Rumpole?'

'Well, now. Who had the best possible reason for hating Simone, and wanting her to get away with as little as possible?'

'Who?'

'Who but our client?' I told him. 'The great *maître de cuisine*, Jean-Pierre O'Higgins himself.'

'No!' I had never heard Mary Skelton speaking before. Her voice was clear and determined, with a slight North Country accent. 'Excuse me.' I turned to look at her as she stood up and came over to us. 'No, it's not true. Jean-Pierre knew nothing about it. It was my idea entirely. Why did *she* deserve to get anything out of us?'

I stood up, looked at my watch, and put on the wig that had been resting on the seat beside me. 'Well, back to Court. Mr Bernard, take a statement from the lady, why don't you? We'll call her as a witness.'

*

Whilst these events were going on down the Bailey, another
kind of drama was being enacted in Froxbury Mansions. She
Who Must Be Obeyed had returned from her trip with cousin
Everard, put on the kettle and surveyed the general disorder
left by my surprise party with deep disapproval. In the sitting-
room she fanned away the bar-room smell, drew the curtains,
opened the windows and clicked her tongue at the sight of
half-empty glasses and lipstick-stained fag ends. Then she
noticed something white nestling under the sofa, pulled it out
and saw that it was a Young Radical Lawyers sweatshirt,
redolent of Mizz Liz Probert's understated yet feminine perfume.

Later in the day, when I was still on my hind legs performing
before Mr Justice Graves and the Jury, Liz Probert called at
the mansion flat to collect the missing garment. Hilda had met
Liz at occasional Chambers parties but when she opened the
door she was, I'm sure, stony-faced, and remained so as she
led Mizz Probert into the sitting-room and restored to her the
sweatshirt which the Young Radical Lawyer admitted she had
taken off and left behind the night before. I have done my best
to reconstruct the following dialogue, from the accounts given
to me by the principal performers. I can't vouch for its total
accuracy, but this is the gist, the meat you understand. It
began when Liz explained she had taken the sweatshirt off
because she was dancing and it was quite hot.

'You were *dancing* with Rumpole?' Hilda was outraged. 'I
knew he was up to something. As soon as my back was turned.
I heard all that going on when I telephoned. Rocking and
rolling all over the place. At his age!'

'Mrs Rumpole. Hilda . . .' Liz began to protest but only
provoked a brisk 'Oh, please. Don't you Hilda me! Young
Radical Lawyers, I suppose that means you're free and easy
with other people's husbands!' At which point I regret to
report that Liz Probert could scarcely contain her laughter and
asked, 'You don't think I fancy Rumpole, do you?'

'I don't know why not.' Hilda has her moments of loyalty.
'Rumpole's a "character". Some people like that sort of thing.'

'Hilda. Look, please listen,' and Liz began to explain. 'Dave

Inchcape and I and a whole lot of us came to give Rumpole a party. To cheer him up. Because he was lonely. He was missing you so terribly.'

'He was *what*?' She Who Must could scarcely believe her ears, Liz told me. 'Missing you,' the young radical repeated. 'I saw him at breakfast. He looked so sad. "She's left me," he said, "and gone off with her cousin Everard."'

'Rumpole said that?' Hilda no longer sounded displeased.

'And he seemed absolutely broken-hearted. He saw nothing ahead, I'm sure, but a lonely old age stretching out in front of him. Anyone could tell how much he cared about you. Dave noticed it as well. Please can I have my shirt back now?'

'Of course.' Hilda was now treating the girl as though she were the prodigal grandchild or some such thing. 'But, Liz . . .'

'What, Hilda?'

'Wouldn't you like me to put it through the wash for you before you take it home?'

Back in the Ludgate Circus verdict factory, Mary Skelton gave evidence along the lines I have already indicated and the time came for me to make my final speech. As I reached the last stretch I felt I was making some progress. No one in the jury-box was asleep, or suffering from terminal bronchitis, and a few of them looked distinctly sympathetic. The same couldn't be said, however, of the scorpion on the Bench.

'Ladies and gentlemen of the Jury.' I gave it to them straight. 'Miss Mary Skelton, the cashier, was in love. She was in love with her boss, that larger-than-life cook and "character", Jean-Pierre O'Higgins. People do many strange things for love. They commit suicide or leave home or pine away sometimes. It was for love that Miss Mary Skelton caused a mouse to be served up in La Maison Jean-Pierre, after she had paid the station waiter liberally for performing the trick. She it was who wanted to ruin the business, so that my client's vengeful wife should get absolutely nothing out of it.'

'Mr Rumpole!' His Lordship was unable to contain his fury.

'And my client knew nothing whatever of this dire plot. He was entirely innocent.' I didn't want to let Graves interrupt my flow, but he came in at increased volume, 'Mr Rumpole! If a restaurant serves unhygienic food, the proprietor is guilty. In law it doesn't matter in the least how it got there. Ignorance by your client is no excuse. I presume you have some rudimentary knowledge of the law, Mr Rumpole?'

I wasn't going to tangle with Graves on legal matters. Instead I confined my remarks to the more reasonable Jury, ignoring the Judge. 'You're not concerned with the law, Members of the Jury,' I told them, 'you are concerned with justice!'

'That is a quite outrageous thing to say! On the admitted facts of this case, Mr O'Higgins is clearly guilty!' His Honour Judge Graves had decided but the honest twelve would have to return the verdict and I spoke to them. 'A British judge has no power to direct a British jury to find a defendant guilty! I know that much at least.'

'I shall tell the Jury that he is guilty in law, I warn you.' Graves's warning was in vain. I carried on regardless.

'His Lordship may tell you that to his heart's content. As a great Lord Chief Justice of England, a judge superior in rank to any in this Court, once said, "It is the duty of the Judge to tell you as a jury what to do, but you have the power to do exactly as you like." And what you do, Members of the Jury, is a matter entirely between God and your own consciences. Can you really find it in your consciences to condemn a man to ruin for a crime he didn't commit?' I looked straight at them. 'Can any of you? Can you?' I gripped the desk in front of me, apparently exhausted. 'You are the only judges of the facts in this case, Members of the Jury. My task is done. The future career of Jean-Pierre O'Higgins is in your hands, and in your hands alone.' And then I sat down, clearly deeply moved.

At last it was over. As we came out of the doors of the Court, Jean-Pierre O'Higgins embraced me in a bear hug and was, I greatly feared, about to kiss me on both cheeks. Ballard gave me a look of pale disapproval. Clearly he thought I had broken all the rules by asking the Jury to ignore the Judge. Then a cheerful and rejuvenated Claude came bouncing up bleating, 'Rumpole, you were brilliant!'

'Oh yes,' I told him. 'I've still got a win or two in me yet.'

'Brilliant to get me off. All that nonsense about a brief for Philly.'

'Not nonsense, Leonard. I mean, Claude. I telephoned the fair Tricia and she's sending your wife the Balham Mini-Cab Murder. Are you suggesting that Rumpole would deceive the Court?'

'Oh' – he was interested to know – 'am I getting a brief too?'

'She said nothing of that.'

'All the same, Rumpole' – he concealed his disappointment – 'thank you very much for getting me out of a scrape.'

'Say no more. My life is devoted to helping the criminal classes.'

As I left him and went upstairs to slip out of the fancy dress, I had one more task to perform. I walked past my locker and went on into the silks' dressing-room, where a very old Q.C. was seated in the shadows snoozing over the *Daily Telegraph*. I had seen Ballard downstairs, discussing the hopelessness of an appeal with his solicitor, and it was the work of a minute to find his locker, feel in his jacket pocket and haul a large purse out of it. Making sure that the sleeping silk hadn't spotted me, I opened the purse, slipped in the nail-brush I had rescued from Uncle Tom's tin of golf balls, restored it to the pocket and made my escape undetected.

I was ambling back up Fleet Street when I heard the brisk step of Ballard behind me. He drew up alongside and returned to his favourite topic. 'There's nothing for it, Rumpole,' he said, 'I shall chain the next one up.'

'The next what?'

'The next nail-brush.'

'Isn't that a bit extreme?'

'If fellows, and ladies, in Chambers can't be trusted,' Ballard said severely, 'I am left with absolutely no alternative. I hate to have to do it, but Henry is being sent out for a chain tomorrow.'

We had reached the newspaper stand at the entrance to the Temple and I loitered there. 'Lend us 20p for the *Evening Standard*, Bollard. There might be another restaurant in trouble.'

'Why are you never provided with money?' Ballard thought it typical of my fecklessness. 'Oh, all right.' And then he put his hand in his pocket and pulled out the purse. Opening it, he was amazed to find his ten pees nestling under an ancient nail-brush. 'Our old nail-brush!' The reunion was quaintly moving. 'I'd recognize it anywhere. How on earth did it get in there?'

'Evidence gets in everywhere, old darling,' I told him. 'Just like mice.'

When I got home and unlocked the front door, I was greeted with the familiar cry of 'Is that you, Rumpole?'

'No,' I shouted back, 'it's not me. I'll be along later.'

'Come into the sitting-room and stop talking rubbish.'

I did as I was told and found the room swept and polished and that She, who was looking unnaturally cheerful, had bought flowers.

'Cousin Everard around, is he?' I felt, apprehensively, that the floral tributes were probably for him.

'He had to go back to Saskatoon. One of his clients got charged with fraud, apparently.' And then Hilda asked, unexpectedly, 'You knew I'd be back, didn't you, Rumpole?'

'Well, I *had* hoped . . .' I assured her.

'It seems you almost gave up hoping. You couldn't get along without me, could you?'

'Well, I had a bit of a stab at it,' I said in all honesty.

'No need for you to be brave any more. I'm back now. That nice Miss Liz Probert was saying you missed me terribly.'

'Oh, of course. Yes. Yes, I missed you.' And I added as quietly as possible, 'Life without a boss . . .'

'What did you say?'

'You were a great loss.'

'And Liz says you were dreadfully lonely. I was glad to hear that, Rumpole. You don't usually say much about your feelings.'

'Words don't come easily to me, Hilda,' I told her with transparent dishonesty.

'Now you're so happy to see me back, Rumpole, why don't you take me out for a little celebration? I seem to have got used to dining *à la carte*.'

Of course I agreed. I knew somewhere where we could get it on the house. So we ended up at a table for two in La Maison and discussed Hilda's absent relative as Alphonse made his way towards us with two covered dishes.

'The trouble with Cousin Everard,' Hilda confided in me, 'is he's not a "character".'

'Bit on the bland side?' I inquired politely.

'It seems that unless you're with a "character", life can get a little tedious at times,' Hilda admitted.

The silver domes were put in front of us, Alphonse called out, '*Un, deux, trois!*' and they were lifted to reveal what I had no difficulty in ordering that night: steak and kidney pud. Mashed spuds were brought to us on the side.

'Perhaps that's why I need you, Rumpole.' She Who Must Be Obeyed was in a philosophic mood that night. 'Because you're a "character". And you need me to tell you off for being one.'

Distinctly odd, I thought, are the reasons why people need each other. I looked towards the cashier's desk, where Jean-Pierre had his arm round the girl I had found so unmemorable. I raised a glass of the champagne he had brought us and drank to their very good health.

Rumpole and the
Summer of Discontent

Change and decay in all around I see. Our present masters seem to have an irresistible urge, whenever they find something that works moderately well, to tinker with it, tear it apart and construct something worse, usually on the grounds that it may offer more 'consumer choice'. Now, many things may be said of the British legal system, but it seems odd to me that it should be run as a supermarket, round which you trundle a wire wheelbarrow and pick up a frozen packet of the burden of proof or a jumbo-sized prison sentence, with 10p off for good behaviour. By and large, I have always thought there is little wrong with the system and all the criticism should be levelled at the somewhat strange human beings who get to run it, such as the mad Judge Bullingham, the sepulchral Judge Graves or Soapy Sam Ballard, Q.C., the less than brilliant advocate whom an incalculable fate has placed in charge of our Chambers. However, in the summer of which I speak, all sorts of plans were afoot, in Equity Court as well as in Parliament, to streamline the system, to give solicitors the doubtful privilege of appearing before Judge Graves, to abolish all distinctions between barristers and solicitors and to elevate solicitors to the Bench. So the Old Bailey hack, skilled in the art of advocacy, which is his daily bread, would be in danger of extinction. Well, the best that can be said of such plans is that they do something to reconcile you to death.

In that same summer, strikes seemed to spread like the measles. One day the tubes didn't run, on another the postman didn't deliver (to my great relief, as I was denied the pleasure of those sinister brown envelopes from Her Majesty). In due course the infection spread to the legal profession and even into the matrimonial home; but I mustn't anticipate the events which began with that more or less simple case of manslaughter, which I think of as the Luxie-Chara killing, and which turned out to be one of my more interesting and dramatic encounters with homicide.

The scene of the crime was a large garage, yard and adjacent office premises in South London. A huge notice over the open gateway read: ERNIE ELVER'S LUXIE-CHARAS. TOILETS. DOUBLE-GLAZING. VIDEOS. HOSTESS-SERVED SNACKS. SCHOOLS, FAN CLUBS AND SENIOR CITIZENS' OUTINGS SPECIALLY CATERED FOR. At the window of an upstairs office Ernie Elver, the owner of the business, a large, soft-eyed man with a moustache, a silk suit and a heavy gold ring, was squinting down the sights of a video-camera, recording, for posterity and for ultimate use in the Old Bailey, what had become a common scene that summer in England.

A small crowd of about twenty pickets was guarding the gates. It consisted mainly of middle-aged coach drivers, but there were a number of young men among them, and a particular youth in a red anorak was joining vociferously in the protest. The object of the picket was to stop the coaches, driven by non-union men, from leaving the garage. The officer in command of the posse was a tall, gaunt fellow, named Ben, but known affectionately as 'Basher', Baker, a prominent shop steward of the National Union of Charabanc Drivers and Operators (N.U.C.D.O.). The incident began when a coach was driven out of the garage and towards the gateway to be met with cries from the pickets of 'Bash the blacklegs!', 'Kill the cowboy bastards!', 'Scrag the scabs!' and suchlike terms of endearment.

As the coach reached the gateway, Ben Baker stood in front of it with an arm upraised, saying, 'Halt, brother. I wish to reason politely with you as to why you should not cross this picket line in an officially recognized dispute.' This invitation to a debate had no effect whatsoever on the driver. The coach surged forward. Ben stood his ground until the Luxie-Vehicle was almost upon him, then he stepped aside with the unexpected agility of a bull-fighter and was seen to stoop suddenly, perhaps as though picking something up from the ground. Seconds later, the windscreen of the coach was shattered by a hard object, flung with considerable force. The driver was seen twisting the wheel and he then crashed into the gatepost, where the coach came to a full stop. When the door was pulled open, the driver was found to have been cut on the head and neck by flying glass. An artery had been severed and within minutes he was dead.

The police car arrived in a surprisingly short time. Although, when it stopped by the crashed coach, the band of pickets had diminished and the younger men had scarpered. As the dead coach driver was removed by the ambulance men, who had come on the scene, Basher Baker was standing near the body, singing 'The Red Flag':

> 'Then raise the scarlet standard high!
> Within its shade we'll live or die.
> Tho' cowards flinch and traitors sneer,
> We'll keep the red flag flying here.'

He was immediately arrested and later charged with the manslaughter of the coach driver. In due course, and thanks to our old legal system still being in operation, Basher was able to obtain the services of the most wily and experienced member of the Criminal Bar.

Dramatic events were also taking place in our Chambers in Equity Court. Work was a touch thin on the ground at that time and I used to drop into Chambers to do the crossword and as a temporary refuge from domestic bliss. I arrived a little late one morning to be told by Henry, our clerk, that a Chambers meeting was taking place and that they were waiting for me. Accordingly, I went up to Soapy Sam Ballard's room to find that some sort of boardroom table had been installed. Our Head of Chambers was seated at the top of it with Claude Erskine-Brown, now apparently restored to favour, at his elbow. Among those present were Uncle Tom, our oldest inhabitant; Mizz Liz Probert, the well-known young radical barristerette; her friend Dave Inchcape; the greyish practitioner Hoskins

and one or two others. 'Not another Chambers meeting?' I
asked with some displeasure as I joined the group.

'In the new age of efficiency at the Bar,' Ballard told me, 'it
might be more appropriate to call it a "board meeting".'

'Quite right.' I took a seat next to Uncle Tom. 'I must say, I
feel bored to tears already.'

'I'm afraid yours is a voice making jokes in the wilderness.'
Claude, back at the top, was at his most pompous. 'We at
Equity Court decided, while you were away doing your stint of
minor crime in the North of England . . .'

'It was gross indecency. In Leeds.' It was also my last
serious case and it seemed a long time ago.

'We have decided to put our full weight behind the Government's plans to drag the English Bar into the twentieth
century.' Erskine-Brown spoke as though he were making a
statement in the House, and was almost overcome by the
gravity of the occasion.

'There was a man called Whympering in Chambers in Fountain Court,' Uncle Tom reminded us. '*He* told them he was
going to drag the Bar into the twentieth century. So he bought
a new automatic coffee machine instead of the old kettle they
used in the briefs cupboard . . .'

'Please, Uncle Tom!' Ballard's mind was clearly on higher
things than electric kettles. 'We have decided that, to give the
consumer a real service, we are going to run Equity Court on
strictly business lines. You may look on me as Chairman of the
Board. Claude Erskine-Brown is Managing Director. He will
be speaking to our new ideas on possible partnership with solicitors.'

'And how will your new ideas be answering him back?' I
inquired. 'Rudely, I hope!'

'The Office Italiano.' Uncle Tom was still remembering
things past. 'That was what the machine was called. It was
meant to brew up the sort of inky black stuff you used to get at
foreign railway stations.'

'We're going to start by working proper business hours.'
Erskine-Brown began to outline a bleak future. 'Nine to six and
no more than an hour for luncheon! And there'll be a simple

form for you to fill in each week. So we can monitor each member's productivity.'

'How do we monitor your productivity, Claude?' I asked, purely for information. 'By the number of years in chokey you manage to achieve for your unfortunate clients?'

'The up-to-date Office Italiano machine exploded, destroying a number of original documents, including three wills!' Uncle Tom was determined we should hear the end of his story. 'There was a most terrible stink about it. Poor old Whympering was sued for negligence.'

'We're aiming for a more streamlined, slimmed-down operation here at Equity Court.' Claude ignored the interruption and then tried, unsuccessfully, to be witty. 'Do you think *you* could manage a slimmed-down operation, Rumpole?'

'Very amusing, Claude. But do try to remember, *I* tell the jokes at Chambers meetings.'

'I hope, in the future, we can get through our business in an atmosphere of quiet efficiency,' Soapy Sam Ballard rebuked us, 'without too many jokes.'

'No jokes at all, if you have anything to do with it, Bollard.' I wasn't to be put down, but then neither was Uncle Tom. 'He had to leave the Bar,' he told us, 'and take up chicken farming in Norfolk.'

'Who had to leave the Bar?' Hoskins, as usual, was a few lengths behind.

'This fellow Whympering who introduced the new coffee machine. They went back to the old kettle on the gas ring. Far more satisfactory.'

'I think I went into the law because I wanted to be a barrister.' This was from young Inchcape, who earned my immediate approval. 'I don't want an office job, quite honestly.'

'Times change, Inchcape,' Ballard told him. 'We've got to change with them. Now, to get back to Claude's paper.'

Hoskins, however, was troubled. 'I'm not sure we want solicitors joining us,' he said. 'Do we need the competition? I speak as a man who has four daughters to bring up and jolly well needs every brief he can get hold of.'

'I suppose, Hoskins, it's just possible that some solicitors have got daughters too.' It was one of Ballard's better lines but Mizz Liz Probert, who had been frowning thoughtfully, piped up, 'If we're making these changes . . .'

'Oh, we are, Probert,' Ballard told her firmly. 'The Lord Chancellor expects it of us. Very definitely.'

'Carry on, Elizabeth. We'd like to hear your contribution. Don't be shy.' Claude smiled at her in the sickly and yearning manner he reserves for young ladies.

'Then why don't we become a really *radical* Chambers?' Liz suggested, and this triggered off more memories from Uncle Tom. 'This fellow Whympering was a bit of a radical. Wore coloured socks, from what I can remember.'

'I mean, why don't we concentrate on civil liberties?' Liz's intervention was clearly going down like a lead balloon at the board meeting. 'Stop the Government using the Courts for another spot of union-bashing. My Dad knows a union leader who's been arrested. That's just the sort of case . . .'

'Defending trades unions?' Ballard looked pained. 'I don't think that's quite the sort of image we want to give Equity Court.'

'I'm afraid I agree.' Claude was soaping up to Sam Ballard. 'Arguing cases for the Amalgamated Sausage-Skin Operatives, or whatever they are. Not quite the name of the game at this particular moment in history.'

'Oh, really, Claude! You're a barrister, aren't you? You belong to the oldest trade union of the lot,' Liz gave it to him straight, 'cram full of restrictive practices.'

'Well, really, Elizabeth! Isn't that just a little bit hard on a fellow?' Erskine-Brown smiled at the young radical with all his charm, but I applauded her aim. 'Got you there, old darling!' I told him. 'Mizz Liz Probert has scored a direct hit. Below the water-line!'

That evening, when I made my duty call at Pommeroy's Wine Bar for a glass of Château Fleet Street, my alcohol level having sunk to a dangerous low, I came upon our clerk sitting alone at the bar and looking extremely doleful. 'Why so pale and wan, fond Henry?' I asked politely, and I must say his answer surprised me. 'To be quite honest with you, Mr Rumpole, I am seriously considering industrial action.' At which point I advised him to consider another drink instead and instructed Jack Pommeroy to put a mammoth-sized Dubonnet and bitter lemon, Henry's favourite refreshment, on my slate. At this, my clerk paid me an unusual tribute, 'You're a generous man, Mr Rumpole.'

'Think nothing of it, Henry.'

'If only there were other gentlemen in Chambers as generous as you, Mr R.'

'Meaning, Henry?'

'Meaning Mr Erskine-Brown.'

'To name but a few?'

'Ah, there, Mr Rumpole. You've put your finger on it. As is your way, sir. As is your invariable way.' I was quite overcome by my clerk's tribute and I tended to agree with his general conclusions, 'Old Claude was behind the door when they handed out generosity.'

'It's not that, sir. It's his business plan. To slim down Chambers, Mr Rumpole.' At which, my unhappy clerk lowered his nose towards the large Dubonnet.

'Never trust anyone who wants to slim down anything, Henry.' I raised my glass in a general salutation. 'God rot all slimmers!'

'He's suggesting taking me off my percentage, sir. And putting me on wages! He says a clerk should be a constant figure on their new balance sheets. Should I withdraw my labour?'

'Industrial action by barristers' clerks?' I was doubtful. 'It sounds a bit like a strike by poets or pavement artists. Hardly going to bring the country to its knees.'

'Too true, Mr Rumpole. Too very true. So I'd be grateful of your opinion.'

'My opinion, Henry, is this. You and I are the last of the freelancers.' I came out with a speech I had been polishing for some time. 'We're the knight errants of the law, old darling. We rode the world with our swords rusty and our armour

squeaking. We did battle with the fire-breathing dragons on
the Bench and rescued a few none too innocent damsels in
distress. We don't fit anyone's business plan or keep office
hours or meet productivity targets. We can't offer the consumer any choice but freedom or chokey. It may well be,
Henry, that our day is over.'

'Over, Mr Rumpole?'

'"From too much love of living."' I gave him a choice bit of
Swinburne at his most melodious:

> 'From hope and fear set free,
> We thank with brief thanksgiving
> Whatever gods may be
> That no man lives forever,
> That dead men rise up never;
> That even the weariest river
> Winds somewhere safe to sea . . .'

'There now, does that cheer you up, Henry?'

'Not very much, sir. If I have to be extremely honest.'

He had, however, perked up considerably about three hours,
and numerous large reds and Dubonnets, later, when we
filtered out into Fleet Street. I was still in a moderately melancholy mood, however, and lamenting life passing, as I gave my
clerk, and the rest of the bus queue, my version of Walter
Savage Landor, which went, so far as I can remember, as follows:

> 'I strove with everybody that was worth my strife;
> I loved the Bailey and the Uxbridge Court;
> I warmed both hands before the fire of life;
> It sinks, and you and I are off, old sport.'

As the bus crawled towards Gloucester Road, I was conscious
that it was somewhat later than usual. Accordingly, as soon as
I let myself into the mansion flat, I called out, as cheerfully as
possible, 'Hilda! Hilda!' I repeated the cry as I searched
through the sitting-room, the bedroom and finally entered the
kitchen. This room was in an orderly condition and showed no
signs of anyone being about to prepare anything like dinner.

As I surveyed this discouraging scene, I heard the front door open and my wife joined me. Something in her manner suggested that the welcome was unlikely to be warm. She asked me what I was doing and I said I was looking for the note.

'Which note?'

'The one that says "Your stew's in the oven".'

'There isn't one.'

'Why not?'

'Because there isn't any stew in the oven.'

'Chops, then. Actually, I'd prefer chops.'

'There aren't any chops in the oven either.'

At this point I opened the oven door and found that it was, as she had predicted, empty. All the same I was determined not to make trouble. 'Well, if you'd like to run something up, I don't really mind what it is,' I told her. Her answer, I have to confess, astonished me. 'Rumpole, I'm not going to run anything up. I waited for you until eight o'clock. Then I went out for a bridge lesson with Marigold Featherstone.'

'I'm sorry. There was a problem in Chambers,' I explained. 'I had to commiserate with Henry.'

'Oh, I expect you did.' I'm afraid I detected a note of cynicism in Hilda's voice. 'And I suppose that meant carousing with him too.'

'I had to carouse a bit,' I explained, 'in order to commiserate.'

'Daddy would have drawn the line at carousing with his clerk.'

'Your Daddy wasn't much of one for carousing with anyone, was he?'

'Let's hope you drew the line at singing. This time.'*

'No, of course we didn't sing. Things have got past singing. Although I did recite a bit of poetry. Look, Hilda. You don't feel like turning your hand to a little cookery?'

'No, Rumpole. I'm finished with cooking for you, when you don't come home until all hours. I'm sorry, this is the end of the line.'

* See 'Rumpole and the Barrow Boy' in *Rumpole and the Age of Miracles*, Penguin Books, 1988.

'You're not leaving home?' I did my best to exclude any
note of eager anticipation from my voice.

'No, Rumpole. I am not leaving home. I am taking industrial
action. Withdrawing my labour!'

'Hilda! Not you too?' I looked at her in astonishment. I had
not yet seen She Who Must Be Obeyed in the role of a shop
steward.

'It's not what you know, but who you know that matters', as
my learned friend Claude Erskine-Brown is fond of saying,
although the fact that he was so well acquainted with Miss
Tricia Benbow, the fair instructing solicitor, got him into quite
a bit of trouble lately. I knew Mizz Liz Probert pretty well, and
she knew her father, Red Ron Probert, the much-feared and
derided Labour Councillor, even better. Red Ron had lots of
lines out to members of the trades union movement, including
that well-known libertarian Ben Basher Baker of N.U.C.D.O.,
and this chain of friendship landed me and Liz Probert briefs
for the Defence in the Luxie-Chara case. Accordingly, we
made a tryst with the client and met in the interview room at
Brixton, where Liz, Mr Bernard, our solicitor, and I sat around
the Basher hoping to hear something to our, and his, advantage.
Our client was the sort of man who always seems to be suffering
from a deep sense of injustice. His beaky nose and tuft of
unbrushed, receding hair, combined with a paunch and long,
thin legs, gave him the appearance of a discontented heron.
'Brother Rumpole, Sister Probert, the brother from the solicitors' office.' He started off, as though he were addressing the
strike committee, 'Comrades and brothers.'

'You make it sound like a case in the Family Division,' I told
him.

'Brother Rumpole' – Ben looked at me suspiciously – 'I was
assured you was taking on this case as an expression of your
solidarity with the workers' struggle and the right to withdraw
labour.'

'Let's say I'm doing it as an expression of *my* right to do
cases that don't bore me to extinction,' I told him. 'And above
all, of course, to irritate Brother Bollard.'

'Who's Bollard?'

'No one of the slightest importance. Don't worry your pretty head about him, my old darling.' And then I started to cross-examine the client quite energetically. 'Now let me put the case against you, Mr Baker. Manslaughter!'

'Me kill someone? That's a joke, that is.' The Basher gave us a hollow laugh.

'"Manslaughter in jest; no offence i' the world?" There's evidence that as the unfortunate coach driver, now deceased, was being carried to the ambulance, you were heard intoning some ditty about the people's flag being deepest red.'

'"The Internationale", Brother,' the client instructed me. 'We sings it at social events. It's just like "Auld Lang Syne".'

'Or "Somewhere over the Rainbow"?' I suggested, and then went back to the attack. 'At one stage of the negotiations you told your employer, one Ernest Elver . . .'

'Ernie the Eel, we call him. He's that slippery.' Ben Baker's intervention was not encouraging.

'You told Elver that if your demands were not met, it might well lead to death?'

'The patience of my executive committee was exhausted.' His answer sounded like a statement on the six o'clock news. 'Elver was employing non-union cowboys to drive kids on outings. They didn't know the road and they didn't know the vehicles. There was going to be an accident sooner or later.'

'Is that what you meant?' I wasn't convinced.

'I swear to God!'

'Are you a religious man, Mr Baker?'

'No. Of course, no. Load of codswallop.'

This fellow was clearly going to be a walkover for prosecuting counsel, so I warned him, 'Then try and be careful how you give your evidence. In this industrial dispute, I suggest you behaved with total disregard for the law.'

'We never!'

'You were on a picket line with more than six people.'

'That's not a law. That's a code of practice.'

A little knowledge of the law is a dangerous thing, especially for clients. I warned him again, 'Please, Mr Basher . . . Mr

Baker. Let's leave such niceties to Mizz Probert. She has the legal textbooks. Neither you nor I have got time to read them. Do you deny you were with more than six people?'

'Some other brothers turned up. To give us extra support, yes.'

'Brothers from your place of work?'

'Not necessarily.'

'Or brothers you'd never seen in your life before?'

'Some of them was. Yes. We needs all the help we can get.'

'Even illegal help?'

'I . . . I suppose so.'

'Even the help of a brick chucked through the window of a moving charabanc?' I was doing it better than anyone we were likely to have prosecuting us, but Basher came back at me with 'I never did that. I swear it.'

'A witness named Jebb was on the picket line. He says he saw you throw it.'

'Then he's a bloody liar.'

'Not a brother, eh? Possibly a more distant relation.' I sifted through my brief and found the forensic evidence. 'Down at the local nick you were examined forensically . . .'

'They took a liberty!' I had clearly touched the button marked 'civil rights', but I went on regardless, 'Distinct traces of brick dust were found on your shirt, your trousers and hands.'

'I'd been doing building in my back garden, hadn't I? A man's got to do something when he's out of work.' It wasn't the greatest explanation in the world, and I made so bold as to give him the retort cynical. 'So you indulged in a little brick-laying?' I said. 'How extremely convenient.'

Not much later, when Mizz Liz Probert, Mr Bernard and I were making our way towards the gatehouse of the nick, crossing that wasteland where screws stood about with Alsatians, and a few trusties planted pansies in the black earth, my radical junior said, 'So you think he's guilty?'

'Not at all, Sister Liz,' I told her. 'I know he's innocent.'

'Innocent?'

'No criminal's going to stand around singing "The Red

Flag" over his victim's dead body,' I explained. 'Not in the presence of the Old Bill, anyway. You wouldn't get the Timsons behaving like that, would you?'

'If he's innocent we might get him off at the committal.' Mr Bernard was on the verge of a dangerous train of thought.

'Our only chance of getting him off is before a jury, Brother Bernard. We say as little as possible at the committal.'

'All the same, I'd like you there, Mr Rumpole.' I didn't at once follow our instructing solicitor's drift and I said, as jovially as possible, 'Would you, Brother? Always ready to oblige.'

'You see, I might need a few tips,' Mr Bernard said, and I must confess I was puzzled, so I asked, 'Tips, Brother Bernard?'

And then the man revealed all. 'I thought I'd do the advocacy in the preliminary hearing,' he said. 'Bit of a dummy run for the Lord Chancellor's changes, when we solicitors can appear in the highest Courts of the land. So if you'll sit behind me, Mr Rumpole.'

'Behind you, Brother?' I could only give a sigh of resignation and quote Swinburne again: ' "That even the weariest river/ Winds somewhere safe to sea".'

Change, as I have said, and also decay, in all around I see. True to the Lord Chancellor's fearless and totally misguided shake-up of the Bar, Mr Bernard was encouraged to represent Ben Baker before the South London stipendiary magistrate, a small, pinkish, self-important, failed barrister of mediocre intelligence. The Prosecution was in the hands of a deeply confused young man from the Crown Prosecution Service who kept losing documents. Detective Inspector Walcroft, the officer in charge of the case, sat listening and taking notes, clearly pained by the poor performances on offer. And, if you can believe it, Horace Rumpole, star of the Penge Bungalow Murders and leading actor in so many dramas down the Bailey, sat mum and junior to his instructing solicitor. After enough evidence had been given to send a canonized saint for trial, Mr Bernard, against all my advice, arose in order to argue that the case should be thrown out. 'And so far as the brick dust on our client's trousers goes,' I heard him saying, 'we have a complete answer!'

'Don't tell the Old Bill what it is.' I whispered a terrible warning, as I saw D. I. Walcroft preparing to note down our defence. 'The truth of the matter is perfectly simple,' Bernard banged on regardless, 'my client was building a wall in his back garden.' I saw the D. I. write this down with a smile of cynical amusement, and the Beak suggested that where the brick dust came from was surely a matter for the Jury. But Bernard had the bit between his teeth and said there was no evidence to commit the Basher to trial.

'But, Mr Bernard' – at least the perky little magistrate knew the rudiments of his job – 'we have the statement of a Mr Gerald Jebb who actually saw your client hurl the brick.'

'Clearly an unreliable witness.' Bernard was enjoying himself. 'If you recall, he couldn't even remember how many pickets there were between him and my client. Or how they were dressed, or . . .'

'The time of high tide at Dungeness?' I suggested in a whisper and the Bench weighed in with 'Whether or not Mr Jebb is a reliable witness is also a matter for the Jury.'

'But, sir! What about the presumption of innocence?' Bernard had a stab at pained outrage.

'Very well, Mr Bernard. What about it?' The Beak was clearly bored, and my solicitor chose this inopportune moment to attempt a Rumpolesque peroration, complete with gestures. After all, he's seen me do it often enough.'With the evidence in doubt, my client is entitled to be acquitted!' he boomed majestically. 'That is the golden thread which runs through British justice. We are all of us innocent until you can be certain sure we *must* be guilty. And I put it to you, sir. In my humble submission. My contention is. You couldn't find my client guilty on a charge of non-renewed dog licence on the vague and unsatisfactory evidence of this fellow Jebb!'

'Not now, old darling,' I whispered to the fellow on his feet. 'We don't do that bit now. We save it for the Jury.' And the Magistrate clearly agreed. 'Mr Bernard,' he said through a prodigious yawn, 'your client will be committed for trial in the Central Criminal Court. Before a jury and a judge.'

'As you please, sir.' And Bernard hissed under his breath, 'And I very much hope he's a judge with no prejudice against trades unions.'

The moving finger wrote on the history of *The Queen* v. *'Basher' Baker* and spelled out the name of Mr Justice Guthrie Featherstone. Those familiar with these records will know that, many years ago, the Head of our Chambers was Hilda's father, C. H. Wystan. When old Wystan dropped off the twig I had hoped to have become Head, but a far younger man named Guthrie Featherstone, Q.C., M.P., 'popp'd in between the election and my hopes' and came to rule our roost at Equity Court. Guthrie was either a left-wing member of a right-wing party, or a right-wing member of a left-wing party – for the life of me, I can't now recall which. Whichever it was, I don't remember him ever coming out strongly in favour of the brothers on the shop floor. Guthrie was married to the formidable Marigold Featherstone, a handsome woman who managed to speak like a ventriloquist – you couldn't see her lips move. The Featherstones lived in Knightsbridge, which Marigold found convenient for Harrods, and had two perfectly acceptable children called Simon and Sarah. My wife, Hilda, greatly admires Marigold, takes bridge lessons with her and often complains to her about Rumpole.

For some reason the then Lord Chancellor took it into his head to make Guthrie, who suffered from a total inability to make up his mind about anything, a red judge. Clad in scarlet and ermine, Mr Justice Featherstone presided over his cases in a ferment of doubt, desperately anxious to do the right thing, fearful of the Court of Appeal, and frequently tempted to make the most reckless pronouncements which got him into trouble with the newspapers. Despite all these glaring character defects, there was something quite decent about old Guthrie. He often tried, in his nervous and confused fashion, to do justice, and he was, in every way, a better egg than Soapy Sam Ballard, Q.C., who succeeded him as Head of Chambers at Equity Court.

Having given the old darling the benefit of every conceivable
doubt, I have to report that he was pretty shocked when the
Prosecution opened a case of homicide on the picket line. He
had an ancient and reptilian clerk named Wilfred who frequently fell asleep in Court. One morning, early in the trial,
Wilfred was helping his master into fancy dress for the day's
performance and they had something like the following conversation – the gist of which I owe to Wilfred's recollection,
prompted by a pint or two of draft Guinness. 'We've got to
watch the trades unions,' Mr Justice Featherstone started off.
'They're getting too much power again. Trying to run the
country.'

'Getting too big for their boots, my Lord?' Wilfred suggested. To which Guthrie replied, laughing, 'And their boots
are probably big enough in all conscience! Remember the
Winter of Discontent, do you?' Here he referred to a strike of
many trades, including that of grave-diggers, some years ago
under another government. 'You couldn't even get buried
then!'

'Terrible thing, my Lord,' Wilfred clucked with disapproval.

'Oh, yes, Wilfred. A terrible thing. Not that I want to get
buried. Not yet awhile, anyway. I don't particularly want to go
on a chara. But people do. And they should be given the
opportunity.'

'Very good, some of these charas, I believe, my Lord,'
Wilfred pointed out. 'They have toilets.'

'Yes. Oh, yes, I dare say they do. Not that I suppose I'll ever
find out. I can't quite picture Lady Featherstone aboard a chara!'

'No, my Lord. I can't picture it myself,' said Wilfred,
joining in the judicial mirth.

'Think they're above the law, these union bosses do.' Guthrie became serious again. 'What's the country coming to,
Wilfred? The Summer of Discontent, that's what I call it.'

'What it brings to mind, my Lord,' Wilfred suggested, 'is
the French Revolution.'

'Does it, Wilfred? Well, yes. I suppose it does. Well, let me
tell you this. Rumpole's not getting away with it again.'

'With the French Revolution, my Lord?' Ideas were flowing a little too fast for Wilfred.

'Don't be silly! With manslaughter! You know there's a sort of legend grown up round the Bailey. Old Rumpole gets away with it every time. Even my wife, even Lady Featherstone, thinks Rumpole can twist me round his little finger!'

'Very astute lady, if I may say so, my Lord.' Wilfred had a healthy respect for Marigold.

'That's as may be, Wilfred. But old Rumpole is not getting away with this one. I tell you, I've taken a good look at Union Boss Baker. And I don't like what I see. I intend to pot him good and proper' – at this, his Lordship imitated a man playing billiards – 'in off the red! At least he won't be able to go on strike in prison!'

It was at this point that, after a brief knock, another judge, considerably senior in years and experience to Guthrie, named Sir Simon Parsloe, blew into the room to discuss what he called the 'dotty schemes the Lord Chancellor's got to reform the Bar'. Stowing away Guthrie's mufti jacket and hat, Wilfred was privy to a plan for a few top judges to rise early and meet in Mr Justice Parsloe's room in the Law Courts to discuss the best way of foiling the lunatic scheme which would have solicitors appearing in the top Courts, solicitors sitting on the Bench, 'solicitors in the House of Lords, if we're not bloody careful, overturning our judgments' – to adopt the vivid language of Sir Simon Parsloe – 'and,' he added, 'we judges have got to take some sort of action.' 'You don't mean' – poor old Featherstone was aghast – 'our jobs are at risk?'

'Well, who knows? Anything can happen. Can you make yourself free, Guthrie?'

'They'd better try and stop me!' Our judge was uncharacteristically decisive. 'Sound fellow!' Parsloe departed with a vague salute and Guthrie turned to confide in his clerk. 'Jobs at risk!' He seemed close to tears. 'Can you believe it, Wilfred? The Summer of Discontent, I tell you. That's what I call it.'

The Prosecution of Ben Baker was in the hands of Soapy Sam

Ballard, Q.C., with Claude Erskine-Brown as his learned junior.
It seemed that this pair were quite ready to do trades union
cases, so long as they weren't on the side of the workers. That
morning, Ballard called Gerald Jebb, who was Basher Baker's
contemporary and a fellow member of N.U.C.D.O. Mr Jebb
was a small, cheerful man with a turned-up nose who looked
like a grey-haired schoolboy. I feared that he was the most
dangerous of all adversaries, an honest witness. Ballard took
him through the events of the fatal day, until he reached the
point when my client got hurriedly out of the way of an
advancing Luxie-Coach. Then he asked Mr Jebb, 'From your
position on the picket line, did you see the defendant Baker
stoop down?'

'My Lord' – I rose slowly to my hind legs – 'I didn't know
that leading questions were allowed. Even in cases against
trades union officials.'

'Leading questions are not allowed in any case, Mr Rumpole,' my Lord said. 'As you know perfectly well. Yes, carry
on, Mr Ballard.' I subsided, clear in the knowledge of which
side Guthrie was on.

'I'm obliged to your Lordship.' Ballard was in a particularly
servile mood. 'Yes. What did you see Baker do?'

'He stooped down and picked up a brick, my Lord. Then he
hurled it at the coach driver.' Jebb gave us the facts with
effective reluctance.

'Did he hurl it hard?' And although I rumbled a warning
'Don't lead, Mr Ballard!' the witness supplied the answer. 'He
hurled it with full force, my Lord.'

'He hurled it with full force at the driver,' Guthrie repeated
with great satisfaction as he noted the evidence down. Ballard
subsided, well satisfied, and I rose to cross-examine, with no
very clear plan of campaign. 'Mr Jebb. You said you saw my
client stoop to the ground.' I began quietly as the Jury clearly
liked Mr Jebb and would have hated to see him bullied.

'Yes, I did.'

'Hadn't he just jumped out of the path of a charabanc
travelling at speed?'

'He had got out of its way. Yes.'

'Wasn't the driver doing his best to kill *him*?'

'I'm not sure what he was doing,' Jebb answered perfectly fairly. It was a slim chance but I jumped on it. 'Just as you're not sure what my client was doing when he stumbled and stooped to the ground?'

'He has given evidence that he saw your client pick up a brick and hurl it, Mr Rumpole.' Guthrie was quick to the witness's aid in a time of not very great trouble.

'I'm sure my learned friend Mr Ballard is most grateful to your Lordship for that intervention,' I said to Guthrie with an irony that I was afraid might be lost on him. And then I turned to the witness. 'Oh, one more thing, Mr Jebb. When the police arrived on the scene you said nothing about seeing Mr Baker throw the brick. You made your first statement' – I picked it up and looked at it – 'some three weeks afterwards. Why was that?'

'I didn't want to get Basher into no trouble.'

'Well, you've got him into trouble now, haven't you? Why did you change your mind?'

'Because I thought I should tell the truth.'

Judge and jury loved that answer and it was clear I was getting absolutely nowhere with Brother Jebb. Accordingly I asked to postpone the rest of my cross-examination to the next day. I said I was waiting for some further inquiries to be made, when what I meant was that I was waiting for a touch of inspiration. Rather to my surprise, both Guthrie and Soapy Sam agreed to have Mr Jebb back at the end of the prosecution case, but before he was released his Lordship got one in below the defence belt. 'Just a moment before you go, Mr Jebb. You just referred to the defendant as "Basher". The Jury might like to know how he got that nickname?' And although I naturally objected, I was rapidly overruled and the witness answered the Judge's question to devastating effect. 'Because he was always talking about bashing people what took the boss's side, my Lord.'

'Thank you, Mr Jebb. That was extremely helpful.' His Lordship was effusive, but the answer had been about as helpful to me as a cup of cold poison. And then Guthrie made the announcement which, like a stone thrown into a lake, would make waves in an ever-expanding circle.

'Mr Ballard. Mr Rumpole. I shan't be able to sit this afternoon.'

'Oh. May we ask why, my Lord?'

'No.'

'No?'

'I mean, well, yes. Yes, of course. It's an urgent matter. A matter of public duty. I will rise now.' And he was off like a rabbit out of a trap. Mizz Liz Probert was gone almost as quickly, saying she couldn't chat about the case as she had a lunch fixed with young Dave Inchcape. Then my learned opponent Claude Erskine-Brown appeared beside me, staring after Liz with a look of sickly yearning on his face. 'It's the contrast, isn't it,' he babbled, 'between the strict white wig and the impish little face? No disrespect to your cross-examination, Rumpole, but I couldn't take my eyes off her.'

'How's your wife, Erskine-Brown?' I tried to bring the great lover back to reality with a bump.

'Philly?' He seemed to have difficulty remembering the name. 'Doing a rather grand corruption in Hong Kong. We see so little of each other nowadays.'

'So you want to invite Mizz Liz Probert to the Opera again?' I had, of course, got it in one.

'She'd never come,' Claude answered dolefully. 'She doesn't really like me very much, does she? I mean, the way she told me off at the Chambers meeting! Look. I don't want you to get the wrong idea, Rumpole. What I have in mind is merely a social event, entirely innocent. You believe that, don't you?'

'Oh, yes. Everyone's innocent until they're proven guilty.' And then an idea occurred to me, which had in it more than my usual high per cent of brilliance. If it could only be made to work, it might solve a number of problems. 'I have, perhaps,' I told him, 'a little influence with my former pupil, Mizz Liz Probert. She sometimes takes my advice.'

'Do you think you could advise her, Horace?'

'Of course, I couldn't connive at anything but a purely musical evening.' I sounded as pious as Soapy Sam Ballard.

'Purely musical, I promise you. Scout's honour.'

'I'll do my best.' I gave him a boy scout's salute. 'And do a good deed for somebody every day.' And then I scuttered off in the direction of lunch, satisfied with a good deal of ground well prepared.

Women, it seemed to me, make a great mystery about such simple tasks as cooking the dinner. After Hilda withdrew her labour, there I was in the kitchen, peeling the potatoes, with a saucepan of water bubbling, ready to receive them. (There is, after all, no very great skill required in the boiling of water.) The chops were warmly ensconced under the grill and cooking well. Another saucepan was steaming for the inundation of the frozen peas. I took these out of the fridge and it would be a matter of moments, I thought, before I had them open and swimming. Then I ran up against a problem in what, up to then, had seemed the simple art of cooking. Those selling frozen peas clearly regard them as being as precious as jewels or krugerrands; enormous precautions are taken to prevent a break-in and the packet is covered with tough, seamless and apparently impregnable cellophane. I tried to rip off this covering. I tore at it with my teeth, I worried it as a dog worries a bone, but all in vain. Finally I stabbed it with a sharp knife, causing a fusillade of frozen green bullets to ricochet off the cooker and adjacent walls. One of them hit the overhead light with a most melodious twang. At last I got a reasonable proportion of the elusive vegetables into hot water, but I was distracted by a 'whoosh' and a sheet of flame which shot out at me from under the grill. Naturally I had covered the chops with fat to ensure a sound cooking and, it seemed, this substance was dangerously inflammable. I had never invested in a fire extinguisher, but, with great presence of mind, I remembered the siphon on the sitting-room sideboard. It was a matter of moments to search for it, and, returning, to direct a powerful stream at the blaze.

Strangely enough the soda water also appeared to be

inflammable, because it strengthened rather than diminished
the blaze. Then it occurred to me to turn off the grill, and I
was beating the dying conflagration with a wet dishcloth when
Hilda, who had been out when I started cooking, arrived upon
the scene, coughing at the cloud of smoke in what I thought
was an exaggerated manner and asking if she should call the
fire brigade.

'No longer necessary,' I assured her, 'I'm just cooking the
dinner.'

'Oh, really?' She was examining the charred chops critically.
'I thought you were arranging your interesting collection of
fossils.'

'Hilda,' I protested, 'I've had absolutely no training in this
line of work.'

'Perhaps you should have thought of that before you decided
to stay out all hours.'

'Be reasonable. Couldn't we refer the matter to the conciliation service, A.C.A.S.? Or at least discuss it over beer and
sandwiches, like they used to in the good old days?'

Then the front-door bell rang and Hilda went to answer it,
after advising me that if I put the potatoes on immediately, I
could have them for pudding. She was back in short order,
with a figure familiar to me, but not to her. 'Can you believe
it?' Fred Timson said. 'Mrs Rumpole and I have never had the
pleasure, not after all these years you've been working for the
Timsons.' Fred was the undoubted chief of the Timsons, that
large clan of South London villains who, by their selfless
application to petty crime, had managed to keep the Rumpoles
in such basic necessities of life as sliced bread, Vim, Château
Fleet Street and the odd small cigar. Luxuries might depend
on an occasional well-paid dangerous driving or a long-lasting
homicide, but the Timsons, in their humble way, gave us solid
support. They were the sort to breed from.

'Fred!' I greeted him. 'Good of you to drop in.'

'Well, I happened to be in the vicinity. Not getting up to
any naughtiness, Mrs Rumpole,' he assured Hilda. 'I wasn't
doing over the downstairs or nothing. And I come on the off
chance you and your old ball and chain might be sat in front of

the telly. Also I have a bit of info which may be of interest in that job what you're doing at the Bailey, Mr R.'

Fred has a far from villainous appearance. He is cheerful, a grandfather, and wears the sort of tweed jackets and cavalry twill trousers a bank manager might sport in the pub at weekends. None of the Timsons is first class at their jobs, but in his day Fred was a fair to average safe-blower. Despite his look of respectability, She Who Must Be Obeyed was eyeing one of our best customers with deep suspicion. When I invited Fred to stay for a bite of supper, she announced that she was off for a bridge evening at Lady Featherstone's, where, no doubt, she could keep going on the cheesy bits provided. 'I think it's a little much,' she said as I saw her out of the front door, 'having the criminal classes calling here at all hours!' And although I told her there was absolutely no violence in Fred's record and he was an old sweetie, she didn't seem in the least mollified.

I returned to the kitchen and poured out a hospitable Pommeroy's Ordinary for each of us. 'I looked for you at your place of business, Mr Rumpole, but your boy Henry said as you were out shopping for groceries. I said I found that hard to believe.'

'Difficult times, Fred. What's called the Summer of Discontent. Got yourself into a bit of trouble, have you?'

'No. Not at the moment. Cor! This wine!' He made a disapproving face. 'Bit rough, isn't it?'

'Liquid sandpaper,' I agreed. 'But you get used to it.' I was worried by his apparent idleness. 'What's the matter? *You're* not on strike, are you?'

'Course not. Matter of fact, I thought I might help you for a change, Mr Rumpole.'

'Oh, yes?'

'Thought I might tell you about our holiday. In Marbella.' He sat at the table and I felt a pang of boredom at the prospect before me. 'Oh, really? Want to show me the snaps?'

'To be quite honest, I brought one along. You see, our enjoyment was just that little bit ruined by the arrival of this shower.'

And then he carefully removed a photograph from his wallet and showed it to me. I saw a coach by a white wall in sunshine, with a number of people, including a familiar, scowling young man in a red anorak, grouped about it. 'Good heavens! Isn't that the clan Molloy? Your rival firm in South-East London?'

'Not rival, Mr Rumpole. The Timsons wouldn't stoop to their way of doing business. But it's the Molloys all right, including young Peanuts. That case you is on, as is reported in the paper, it's manslaughter, isn't it? I thought you might just be interested in the Molloys' vehicle.'

I examined the picture more closely and the words painted on the coach. I could make out: ERNIE ELVER'S LUXIE-CHARAS. COMPLETE WITH TOILETS AND DOUBLE-GLAZING. And, then, I was delighted to see young Peanuts Molloy. 'Bless you, old darling!' I thanked Fred.

'They said as they got lent the chara for a free holiday by the firm concerned. And you'll notice the grey-haired old party with his arm round Peanuts' Aunty Dolly.'

'My God, I notice him!' It was none other than the honest witness in person. Whoever is in charge of the universe clearly felt that it was time to do old Rumpole a favour.

'Gerry Jebb,' Fred confirmed it. 'What used to drive get-aways for Peanuts' father. Know what I mean?'

'Fred, you're a treasure. Please. Stay for supper.'

'I don't think so, Mr R.' Fred glanced at the chops on offer. 'Look, why don't we attack a Chink?' He stood, ready to be off.

'What *are* you talking about?'

'Go for a Chinese.' It was simple and offensive, like all the Timsons' jokes.

'You want a radical Chambers, Mizz Liz? Only way we'll get it is to persuade Claude Erskine-Brown to stop trying to be a whizz kid and go back to the old ways. Then Equity Court'll be a place fit for freelancers to live in again. We can ride forth like the knights of old and rescue the brothers in distress.'

I was walking with Mizz Liz down to the Old Bailey the next morning and putting into operation stage one of my master plan to prevent Chambers slipping off into the twenty-first century.

'Who's going to persuade Claude?' Liz asked reasonably.

'The person who has the greatest influence on him. The Member of the Bar he'd do anything to impress.'

'You mean, you?'

'No, you! Tell him you liked him better when he was an old-fashioned sort of barrister, keeping up the best traditions of the Bar and taking snuff. Tell him he was much sexier like that. It'd sound better, coming from you.'

'Rumpole!' Mizz Probert was shocked. 'Are you suggesting I exploit my femininity?'

'In a good cause, old thing! And can you think of a better? Also you might put up with a little Wagner, in the interests of justice.'

So we proceeded on towards the workplace. And that was not the only useful conversation I had that morning, for when I had got robed and come downstairs I found Wilfred, Guthrie's old clerk, hovering about the door of the Court. I asked him if the Judge was honouring us with his presence, after having taken yesterday afternoon off. 'Bless you, yes, Mr Rumpole.' Wilfred looked at me with sleepy, crocodile eyes. 'We're not going on strike yet.'

'On strike?' I pricked up my ears.

'We think it might come to it,' Wilfred told me. 'That's what our judge was saying. If the Lord Chancellor wants to put up solicitors over our heads. We may have to take action, Mr Rumpole.'

'Quite right, Wilfred, I'm sure.' I sounded deeply understanding. 'So yesterday afternoon . . .?'

'Just a taster, Mr Rumpole. Just to show the public we're not to be pushed around. Of course, there *was* a meeting.'

'A union meeting?'

'A meeting of judges, Mr Rumpole. Some very senior men was there,' Wilfred couldn't help boasting, 'including us.'

'Of course! The brothers. Have you ever thought of that, Wilfred? Judges and trades unionists always call themselves "brothers". It doesn't mean they like each other any more.'

'I must be off, Mr Rumpole.' Wilfred clearly didn't care for this line of thought. 'I must go and get us on the Bench.'

'Must be quite a heave for you. Some mornings.'

'And, Mr Rumpole. You will try not to twist us round your little finger, won't you? Because we're determined to pot you on this one. I thought we ought to warn you.'

'Very charming of you, Wilfred,' I said as the man went about his business. 'Very charming indeed!'

In Court that day we were treated to an entertainment. The place was plunged into darkness and television sets were placed among us on which Ernie Elver's home video played. We saw the pickets shouting at the gates, as the coach driven by the working driver approached them. I sat watching with the photograph Fred Timson had given me in my hand, and, at a vital moment, I reared to my hind legs and called 'Stop!' An officer in charge of the telly pressed a button and the picture froze.

'My Lord. I call on my learned friend, Mr Bollard . . .'

'Ballard!' Soapy Sam was not in the best of tempers that morning.

'Makes no difference. I call on him to make the following admission. That the young dark-haired man wearing the red jacket on that picket line is otherwise known as Peter "Peanuts" Molloy.'

'I don't suppose your learned friend has any idea.' Guthrie was unhelpful.

'Then let him ask the Detective Inspector in charge of the case. He'll very soon find out.'

Ballard had a whispered conversation with D. I. Walcroft and then emerged and admitted grudgingly, 'That would seem to be correct, my Lord.' It was a good moment for the Basher, but as he sat frowning in the dock it seemed that, like most clients, he had very little idea of what was going on.

After his movie show, Ernie Elver was called to give evidence, and, as a hard-pressed boss more sinned against than sinning, he clearly had the sympathy of his Lordship. As we got towards the end of his questioning, Ballard asked, 'Mr Elver. Throughout this industrial dispute was there any doubt in your mind who the leader was?'

'The man in the dock, my Lord.' Ernie had no doubt.

'Baker?'

'Yes, my Lord.'

'Did he say anything you remember during the negotiations?'

'Yes, my Lord. He said someone was going to get killed if it wasn't settled.'

'Someone was going to get killed.' Guthrie was taking another note with great satisfaction.

'Mr Elver. What was the man Baker's reputation, in industrial disputes?' Ballard's question caused me to rise with the outrage turned up to full volume. 'This is monstrous! If my learned friend's going to practise at the Bar, he ought to do a bit of practising at home. He can't ask questions about reputation!'

'I think we might leave it there, Mr Ballard.' His Lordship poured a little oil on troubled Rumpole. 'After all, the Jury have heard this man's nickname.'

Ballard sat down looking displeased and I rose to smile charmingly at the witness I hoped to devour.

'Mr Elver. This dispute at your charabanc garage was about your employing non-union untrained drivers?'

'That's what they said it was.' The big man in the shiny suit grinned at the Jury as though to say, Pull the other one, it's got bells on it.

'And my client took the view, rightly or wrongly, that if you employed these cowboys there might be an accident. Someone might get killed?'

'I wanted to offer the public a wider choice.' Ernie Elver sounded like a party political broadcast and old Claude chimed in with a penetrating whisper, 'Consumer choice. That's the name of the game nowadays.'

'Oh, mind your own business, Mr Erskine-Brown!' I gave him a sharp whisper back. Then I turned to the witness with 'So you wanted to offer the public a choice between good drivers and bad ones who might not know the routes.'

'If you want to put it that way.' Ernie clearly didn't.

'Oh, I do,' I assured him. 'And I suggest that even the most gentle, mild-mannered man might take industrial action in that situation. Take his Lordship . . .'

'Mr Rumpole?' Guthrie woke up with a start the moment his name was mentioned.

'As you probably know,' I confided in Mr Ernie Elver, 'the powers that be have suggested that solicitors can get jobs as High Court judges. Appeal judges! Lords of Appeal!'

'Mr Rumpole!' His Lordship was about to draw the line. 'These questions are quite irrelevant!'

'Is your Lordship stopping my cross-examination?' Then I said to Mizz Liz in a deafening mutter, 'It's not a particularly long walk to the Court of Appeal.' At the mention of these dreaded words, his Lordship could be heard going into reverse. 'No. No, of course, I'm not stopping you,' he said hurriedly. 'But I fail to understand . . .'

'Then might I suggest you sit quietly, my Lord. All will become clear.' I was beginning to lose patience with his Lordship, and he came back with a rather sour 'Mr Rumpole. Don't get the idea that you can twist this Court round your little finger!'

'My little finger, my Lord?' I played the retort courteous. 'What an idea!' Then I resumed my conversation with Ernie. 'Solicitors who haven't spent a lifetime arguing in Courts might not be up to the job. That's the suggestion,' I told him.

'I didn't know.' Ernie looked as though he might have thought that solicitors were ladies of the street who probably were unsuited to the work in the Court of Appeal.

'Well, you know now, Mr Elver. And that suggestion caused even such a reasonable, sensible, moderate man as his Lordship to go on strike.'

'On strike, Mr Rumpole?' His poor old Lordship could contain himself no longer. 'What can you be talking about?'

'Yesterday afternoon, my Lord' – I tried to keep as calm as possible – 'I seem to remember not very much work was done. Was not your Lordship on strike?'

'No, I was not on strike!' The Judge gave his desk a moderate, middle-of-the-road sort of thump. 'Simply withdrawing your labour?' I smiled sweetly.

'As I told the Court, I had to go to an important meeting' – Guthrie was making the mistake of defending the charge – 'with a very senior judge and brother judges from the Chancery and the Family Division.'

'Of course. The shop stewards. And what was the discussion about?'

'Mr Rumpole!' the Judge asked with deep suspicion, 'are you cross-examining me?'

'Cross-examining your Lordship? Perish the thought!' Of course I was, and on I went. 'I can understand that if the Judges are in dispute with their employers it may be a delicate matter. Better kept secret.'

'I don't think it's any secret that certain changes have been proposed in the legal system.' As a witness, his Lordship was proving almost too easy to handle.

'Cowboys on the Bench, my Lord?' I suggested.

'No, but perhaps' – he searched for a tactful way of putting it – 'persons whose training may not entirely fit them for the Bench.'

'And if they get there? *Can we expect further industrial action?* Down the Old Bailey?' Poor old Guthrie was now really in deep water. 'It's a possibility,' he said. 'We hope wiser counsels will prevail.' And then he tried to swim for the shore. 'Mr Rumpole, we have had quite enough of this. High Court judges are not, and never have been, members of a trades union.'

'Is that a legal proposition, my Lord,' I asked, 'or a subject of debate?'

'Will you please return to the question we have to try? Did your client commit manslaughter?'

That was not one I felt like answering just yet, so I turned back to the witness. 'Mr Elver. I was just venturing to point out that reasonable people may withdraw their labour when their jobs are threatened. I'm sure his Lordship would agree.'

Elver didn't care to answer that, but Guthrie couldn't resist it. He leant towards the witness and said, 'Surely that's a reasonable proposition, Mr Elver?'

'I suppose so.' Ernie was disconcerted by a judge who was suddenly talking like one of the brothers.

'And you wanted to make it look as *unreasonable* as possible?' I asked him.

'Why would I want to do that?'

'Childishly simple, Mr Elver,' I told him. 'Because if you could prove there were more than six pickets you could get an injunction. If you could prove there was violence and intimidation you could get the union fined large sums of money. You could get rid of that thorn in your flesh, Mr "Basher" Baker, and employ all the cheap cowboy labour you wanted.'

'But there *was* violence on the picket line,' Ernie protested.

'Of course there was! Because you put it there. Usher, give that to the witness.' What I passed up was the photograph Fred Timson had given me of the Molloys on holiday. 'You know the Molloy family, don't you?' I asked as Ernie looked at it with some reluctance. 'I'm not sure,' he said, after a considerable silence.

'Come on, Mr Elver,' I encouraged him. 'You employ Gerry Jebb. He's one of the clan. They're a pretty hard firm of criminals, the Molloys. Well known to the Inspector in this case. You hired the Molloys, didn't you, no doubt through Jebb, to swell the picket line and create as much violence as possible? Then, when you'd arranged the performance, you went and filmed it all from your office window.'

'Baker was in charge of the picket line,' Ernie insisted.

'In charge of the peaceful pickets, yes. He didn't know the new arrivals, those he took for sympathetic workers from other firms. They were your gang of hired troublemakers. Weren't they?'

'Mr Rumpole. Are you suggesting this witness planned the death of the driver?' Guthrie, as usual, looked puzzled.

'Oh, no, my Lord.' I explained, careful to allow for the slow pace of the judicial mind, 'No doubt he was as surprised as anyone when young Peanuts Molloy, who probably threw the brick, went too far. But it was a blessed opportunity to get the awkward Mr Baker into real trouble.' Then I asked the witness, 'How much did it cost you to get Jebb to give that perjured evidence?'

'My Lord, I object.' Ballard rose plaintively. 'There's no basis whatever for that suggestion!'

'Or did you get the whole package for a free holiday in Marbella?' Ballard's interruption was worth ignoring. 'Just take a look at that photograph. Is that one of your Luxie-Charas in Spain?'

'It seems to be,' Ernie had to admit.

'Do you see Mr Jebb there?'

'Yes.'

'I have asked the Prosecution to admit that the man in the red jacket is Peanuts Molloy. Was that a free holiday? A present from your firm?'

'I don't think so.' Ernie saw the dangers ahead, and I snapped at him, 'Can you produce evidence that your coach was paid for by the Molloys?'

'Maybe not.'

'Why not?'

'Gerry Jebb had been with the firm a long time. I wanted to do him a favour.'

'So he did you a favour in return?'

'Mr Rumpole' – Guthrie was restive again – 'none of these serious suggestions was put to the witness, Jebb.'

'Your Lordship is perfectly right,' I agreed, now that I had plenty of questions to put to Jebb. 'That is why I have asked the Prosecution to have him back here tomorrow.'

'Very well.' Guthrie looked wistfully at the clock. 'I see it's a little early. But I will rise now.'

'Public duty, my Lord?' I wanted to help the old darling.

'Yes, Mr Rumpole. Public duty. You may put your case to Mr Jebb in the morning.'

'I'm very much obliged to your Lordship.' I bowed low and added, under my breath, 'Keep the red flag flying here!'

'Did you say something, Mr Rumpole?'

'I said what an interesting case we're trying here.'

For a full understanding of *The Queen* v. *Basher Baker*, we must now follow his Lordship into private life. My source for what follows is the account Lady Marigold Featherstone gave

to She Who Must Be Obeyed. Further details were supplied
by Wilfred, the faithful clerk, in whom Guthrie often
confided. It's clear from all the evidence available that the
'public duty' for which he had risen 'a little early' was going
back to the Knightsbridge flat for the purpose of resting up
on the sofa with a cup of tea. While he was so engaged, his
wife Marigold returned home with a full Harrods bag and a
copy of the *Evening Standard*. I have done my best to reconstruct their dialogue from the information I have
received, and my knowledge of the characters of the two
Featherstones. Marigold's opening salvo did not augur well
for his Lordship's continued repose. 'Working hard, Guthrie?' I think she may well have said, 'or are you taking industrial action?'

'Oh, Marigold' – Guthrie had no doubt awoken with a start
– 'there you are! Well, hard day in Court. What's that you say
about industrial action?' And I imagine that he slid somewhat
guiltily off the sofa as Marigold announced, in awesome tones,
'I have been reading the paper.'

'Oh. Yes, of course. Got a bit about my case in it, has it?
Interesting discussion about union law. But let me tell you
this, Marigold. I'm going to pot the shop steward. Old Rumpole's not going to twist me round his little finger this time!'

'Aren't you fit to be let off the lead, Guthrie? Ought I to be
up there on the Bench beside you all the time, telling you
when to keep your mouth shut?'

'Why? They must have got it wrong. Let me see. What am I
supposed to have said?'

Marigold didn't hand over the paper but read him the best
bits: '"Industrial action is a possibility, says Mr Justice
Featherstone, 53, if jobs on the Bench are open to solicitors".'
Did you say *that*, Guthrie dear?' She must have smiled with
misleading sweetness.

'Well, something like it, I suppose. Something quite like it.'
The Judge was beginning to wilt under cross-examination and
Marigold read on without mercy: '"The Judge agreed with
Mr Horace Rumpole, counsel for Baker, that he had been
'withdrawing his labour' yesterday afternoon when he closed

down his Court to attend a protest meeting of senior judges whom he called 'shop stewards'.'"

'That's a libel! Rumpole called them that!' Guthrie felt he had a genuine grievance.

'Sounds a pretty accurate description, if you ask me. There's a leading article on page six.' And as she turned the pages, Guthrie said, in stricken tones, 'A leading article!'

'"Judges add to nation's misery",' his wife read out, and his protest rose to a quavering wail, 'Marigold. It's simply not *fair!*'

'"Train drivers, air-traffic controllers, local government workers, prison officers and drain-clearance operatives"' – Marigold carried on reading. 'What charming company you keep, Guthrie! – "have all managed to put the public through the hell of a Summer of Discontent. Now, if you go mad and strangle a porter when you've been waiting three days for a train at Waterloo, you won't even be tried for it, according to Mr Justice Featherstone, who also went on strike yesterday afternoon. Come off it, your Lordship! Drop the old Spanish practices and offer the public a decent service".'

'Marigold' – Guthrie felt he knew who to blame – 'it's entirely the fault of Rumpole.'

'Of course it is,' his wife agreed. 'Why can't you twist him round *your* little finger for a change? You're bigger than he is!'

'I shall deny it all! In Court.' His Lordship was adopting what might be called the Timson defence.

'Oh, do' – Lady Featherstone was cynical – 'then everyone will believe it. I had to read this paper at lunch in Harrods. In the Silver Grill! I was deeply humiliated.'

'Marigold. I'm sorry, but . . .'

'I bought you a present.' At this sign of affection I'm sure our judge was considerably relieved. 'Oh, darling,' he said, 'I knew you'd understand.'

'Oh, yes. I understand perfectly.' At which she opened her Harrods bag, took out a decisively checked cloth cap and plonked it on her husband's head. 'It's your flat 'at, Guthrie. Now you can go down the working-men's club and play darts over a pint of wallop with the charge hands. I'm going to my bridge class with Hilda Rumpole. Her husband may have his drawbacks, but at least she's not married to a shop steward.'

At this, Hilda told me, Marigold said she left the unhappy man alone. I see him looking at himself in the mirror, seeing the cloth cap, symbol of the working-class struggle, on his head, and uttering something really desperate like 'Oh, brother!'

Another direct result of Rumpole's advocacy was taking place in the crush bar of Covent Garden during a welcome interval in some opera by Richard Wagner whose music, as the late Mark Twain once said, is not as bad as it sounds. My learned friend Claude Erskine-Brown and the radical lawyer Mizz Liz Probert were crushed up against the bust of Sir Thomas Beecham. Claude was doing his best to pour her a glass of champagne without moving his arms and looking at her with the Erskine-Brown version of smouldering passion, and Liz was gamely twinkling back, noticing his bow-tie, watch-chain and conservatively tailored gents three-piece suiting. I do my best to reconstruct their conversation from the detailed account of Mizz Probert who, acting on the instructions of my good self, kicked off with, 'This is how I like you, Claude.'

'You do like me a little then, Elizabeth?' The dear old ass was suitably gratified.

'When you're the old English barrister.'

'Did you say, "old"?' Claude sounded miffed. 'I mean, I'm not "old" exactly.'

'Old-fashioned. That's what I mean.'

'Oh, I see. You like that, do you? I should've thought you wouldn't.'

'Oh, yes,' she assured him. 'It's the old-fashioned elegance I admire. The bow-tie and all that. It's rather sweet.'

'Actually it's an old Wykehamist bow-tie,' Claude said modestly.

'Is it, really?' Liz was less than impressed.

'I wouldn't wear it in the day-time. But it goes rather well with a great evening out like this!'

'You're charming when you look like a good old traditional barrister,' Liz told him. 'You know. The sort who takes snuff!'

'Snuff?' Claude was doubtful.

'Yes. Snuff.'

'You think I ought to take it?'

'As a simple working-class girl, Claude, I do find that sort of thing a wild turn-on.'

'Oh, do you, really? Snuff, eh? Well. I suppose I might give it a whirl.' Claude was ready for anything in the pursuit of love.

'Out of a little silver box, I'd find that irresistible. Oh, and stop trying to be a whizz-kid. Talking about slimming down and productivity targets. Sounds like some naff little middle manager in a suit. Horribly unsexy.'

'Elizabeth. Is that why you went off me?' The penny was dropping fast.

'And "consumer choice". Consumer choice is absolutely yuk! You know what I've always loved about you, Claude?'

'Loved?' The poor fellow seemed to have run out of breath. 'Please, Elizabeth. Tell me!'

'You being so square. And vague. And beautifully un-businesslike. And sort of dusty.'

'Dusty?' He frowned.

'In the nicest possible way. Dreamy, with all sorts of ideals. You do believe in freelance barristers, don't you, Claude?'

'I believe in them passionately, Elizabeth. Radical ones too, of course.' Men in love will say anything.

'Then would you mind saying so at the next Chambers meeting?' Liz got straight down to business. 'That is, if you're not too much in awe of Ballard.'

'In awe of Ballard! I'll show you if I'm in awe of Ballard. Elizabeth' – he tried to hold her hand – 'do you think we'll ever sing the love duet together?'

'Not now, Claude.' She released her hand.

'When?'

'Perhaps after the next Chambers meeting.' And then the bells rang and Wagner called them both to another, sterner duty.

Whilst these historic events were taking place, I slept the

peaceful sleep of the just and went off to the Bailey with a light
step, ready to fire off my considerable ammunition at Mr
Gerry Jebb, who was to be recalled as the last prosecution
witness. But when a somewhat shaken Guthrie resumed his
seat on the Bench, he was faced with nothing but a flustered
and apologetic Soapy Sam Ballard. 'My Lord,' the dis-
comforted Prosecutor started. 'I gave the Court an undertaking
that the witness Gerald Jebb would return today. He was
warned that he must be available. But I regret to inform the
Court that Jebb has vanished.'

'Not unexpectedly,' I whispered for all the world to hear.

'Vanished, Mr Ballard?' The Judge clearly didn't believe in
miracles.

'The Inspector thinks he has probably left the country.'

'Try Marbella,' I suggested.

'My Lord, the flight of this witness, for it must be described
as a flight, must cast considerable doubt on his evidence,'
Ballard admitted, and then threw in, 'if it can be described as
evidence. Our inquiries have also disclosed that the defendant
was in fact laying bricks in his garden, which could account for
the brick dust on his clothing.' And Ballard concluded, 'I
therefore feel that it would not be right for the Prosecution to
persist with these charges.'

'Mr Rumpole?' His Lordship asked my view of the matter,
so I rose politely. 'I'm sure we are all grateful to my learned
friend. It's a wise decision. And I have no doubt your Lordship
has other matters to attend to?'

'Oh, yes, indeed. I have an important meeting,' and Guthrie
added, with some apprehension, 'with the Lord Chancellor.'

So Basher Baker was set at liberty and walked out, after a
gruff 'Thanks, Brother Rumpole', to the world of pay claims
and union meetings, and Mr Justice Featherstone prepared to
face a higher tribunal.

Henry Fairmile had been a rather dusty, tall, scarecrow of a
Q.C. and M.P., with a voice like dead twigs snapping in the
wind. He had been an ultra-loyal member of his party and had
been promoted, by way of such dull jobs as Solicitor-General

and Attorney-General, to the woolsack and the splendour of
the Lord Chancellor's office. Now in command of the Judiciary, Lord Fairmile developed a quirky and ironic sense of
humour and he enjoyed teasing the Judges who had not taken
much notice of him at the Bar. He also enjoyed discovering
character weaknesses – drink, women or holidays in the Greek
islands with young men in advertising – which would debar
ambitious advocates from the Bench. He constantly lectured
his colleagues on 'judgeitis', which he defined as pomposity
and self-regard, whilst congratulating himself on his peculiar
modesty for one who has, in his keeping, the great seal of the
Realm. When the Government he served decided to reform
the Bar, in the interests of consumer choice and the free
market economy, he welcomed such plans as giving him ample
scope to irritate the other judges. When the papers came out
with news of Guthrie's industrial action, the Lord Chancellor
sent for his striking Lordship, who naturally turned up in the
office in the House of Lords in fear and trembling, fully
expecting to be asked to hand in his resignation, as an alternative to being dismissed by a special act of Parliament. It was
not, after all, the first time, that Featherstone J. had been
hauled up before the Chancellor.*

When he arrived in the big room and saw the lanky old man
sitting in his white bands and tailed coat, his gold-encrusted
robe and purse and the long full-bottomed wig on stands ready
for his appearance at the woolsack, he was surprised by the
warmth of the Chancellor's welcome. 'Come along in, my dear
old fellow. Drink? Beer and sandwiches.' The long-abandoned
symbols of conciliation stood on a side table.

'That's very kind, but not at the moment. Look, Lord
Chancellor' – Guthrie embarked on his long-prepared explanation – 'all that business about striking . . .'

'That's why I wanted to see you, Guthrie.' Lord Fairmile
abandoned his usual pastime of fitting a large number of
paper clips into a sort of daisy-chain and stood up, whether

* See 'Rumpole and the Tap End' in *Rumpole and the Age of
Miracles*, Penguin Books, 1988.

Featherstone wanted it or not, to open a bottle of beer. 'I mean, we just fined the drain-clearance operatives a quarter of a million for not taking a ballot. Do you have that sort of money in your trousers? Do change your mind and take a small light ale?'

The Chancellor smiled and his ready hospitality gave Guthrie courage. 'Well,' he said and took the proffered glass, 'I think the Judges pretty well agree, Lord Chancellor, that if it *came* to a ballot, they might well take action.'

'Oh, dear. Oh, my ears and whiskers. I don't think the Cabinet's going to like that. The idea of all the Judges on a picket line with the local elections coming up. I don't think the Cabinet's going to be attracted by that. Got a cloth cap, have you?' Lord Fairmile gave himself a light ale.

'Well, Lord Chancellor, as a matter of fact I have,' Guthrie admitted.

'A little something to eat?'

'Beer and sandwiches? The way they settled disputes in the Labour Government.' Guthrie smiled as he took a sandwich which he found to be filled with Civil Service Class C hospitality fish-paste.

'Sometimes the old-fashioned ways are the best,' the Lord Chancellor admitted. 'Look here. I have no wish to quarrel with you fellows. And I don't really know why these solicitor chaps want to be judges anyway.'

'Quite agree.' Guthrie was further encouraged. 'They can make much more money sitting in their offices selling houses.'

'Or whatever it is they do.' The Lord Chancellor's voice was slightly muffled by a sandwich.

'Well, exactly!'

'In fact I don't know why anyone wants to be a judge. Unless their practice is a bit rocky. That your trouble, was it?'

'Certainly not!' Guthrie was hurt. 'I felt a call for public duty.'

'Well, I suppose your wife likes it. But no more talk about going on strike, eh? What do you say we leave the whole question of solicitors joining the Judges as one for the Judges to decide?'

'Absolutely super!' Mr Justice Featherstone's reaction was enthusiastic.

'I'm thinking along those lines,' the Head of the Judiciary told him. 'Good to talk to you, Guthrie.'

'Thank you, Lord Chancellor. It's been a most successful negotiation. May I tell my committee . . . I mean, my brother judges?'

'Of course! We'll probably put something rather vague through Parliament. Ought to keep everybody quiet. Now, then. Why don't you try the cheese and tomato?'

'It's all ended happily.' Guthrie was smiling with joy as he took the penultimate sandwich. 'I can't wait to tell Marigold!'

Not long afterwards we legal hacks in Equity Court met again round Ballard's boardroom table. Erskine-Brown, who was toying with a small, silver snuff-box which he tapped occasionally, interrupted Ballard's tedious speech about streamlining our Chambers business-wise, to increase productivity and market share, with the following, unexpected contribution. 'With all due respect to you, Ballard,' he said, 'aren't we in danger of throwing the baby out with the bathwater? We mustn't lose our freedom. Our eccentricity.' He looked at Liz. 'That's what makes us, us barristers' – he smiled modestly – 'so attractive. Ever since the Middle Ages we have been the great freelancers! The independent radicals! The champions of freedom and against tyranny and oppression wheresoe'er it might be! We must preserve, at all costs, the great, old British tradition!'

'Erskine-Brown' – Soapy Sam looked as though he had just sat down on a favourite armchair which had gone missing – 'am I to understand I can no longer count on your support, in getting Chambers efficient, business-wise?'

'No, Ballard,' Claude told him frankly. 'I'm afraid you no longer have my support on this one.'

'Does that mean we're not getting a new coffee machine?' Uncle Tom asked hopefully.

'Yes, Uncle Tom. I rather think it does,' I told him.

'Oh, good!'

'Let's stop trying to be a lot of whizz-kids,' Claude addressed the meeting. 'Talking about "slimming down" and "productivity targets". It makes us sound like awful little middle managers in suits. Yuk!' At this point he took a large pinch of snuff and broke down in hopeless, helpless sneezing, waving a large silk handkerchief.

'I say, you've got the most terrible cold!' Uncle Tom seemed deeply concerned.

I was looking at Liz, who was holding hands with Dave Inchcape under the table, something poor old Claude didn't see. Not for the first time I felt a distinct pang of sympathy for the chap.

That night I went home with a plastic bag, on which was written THEODORAKIS TAKEAWAY KEBABS, which contained what I feared was going to be my dinner. But in the hallway I smelt a magic perfume, a distinct whiff of roast beef and Yorkshire pudding. When I pushed open the kitchen door, there was Hilda preparing these delicacies, together with cabbage, baked potatoes, an apple tart with cream. The whole was to be washed down, I was delighted to see, with a bottle of Pommeroy's Extraordinary Troisième Cru.

'Has peace,' I asked, 'broken out?'

'Well, poor Marigold Featherstone! She was so upset when Guthrie went on strike. Do you know what she bought him? A cloth cap! Rather funny, really. But there are certain people at the top who just shouldn't strike. In the public interest. Judges and generals and well, and . . .'

'Decision-makers of all kinds?' I looked respectfully at Hilda.

'Well, I felt that going on strike was really not on.'

'Distinctly orf?'

'It's just not a thing that people like me and Guthrie should do.' She looked at me, I thought nervously. 'You wouldn't buy me a cloth cap, would you, Rumpole?'

'Perish the thought!'

'So, I thought to myself, it's a long time since you had Yorkshire pudding.'

'Thank you, Hilda.' I was truly grateful. 'Thank you very much.'

'You don't want it to get cold, do you? After I've been to all this trouble. Sit down, Rumpole, and have your dinner.' What could I do then but obey?

Rumpole and the Right to Silence

What distresses me most about our times is the cheerful manner in which we seem prepared to chuck away those blessed freedoms we have fought for, bled for and got banged up in chokey for down the centuries. We went to all that trouble with King John to get trial by our peers, and now a lot of lawyers with the minds of business consultants want to abolish juries. We struggled to get the presumption of innocence, that golden thread that runs through British justice, and no one seems to give a toss for it any more. What must we do, I wonder. Go back to Runnymede every so often to get another Magna Carta and cut off King Charles's head at regular intervals to ensure our constitutional rights? Speaking entirely for myself, and at my time of life, I really don't feel like going through all that again.

The hard-won privilege most under attack at the moment is a suspect's right to silence. Those upon whom the Old Bill looks with disfavour are, it is suggested, duty-bound to entertain the nick with a flood of reminiscence, which will make the job of convicting them of serious crimes a push-over. Now if I were to be arrested – a thought which lurks constantly in the back of my mind – and found myself, an innocent Old Bailey hack, confronted by Detective Chief Inspector Brush and his merry men, I should say nothing, saving my eloquence for a jury of common-sense citizens. And those accused of malpractices may have other reasons for silence apart from a natural shyness in the presence of the law. On the other hand, of course, they may be guilty as charged. These were the questions which confronted me during the Gunster murder case, when a pall of silence hung not only over my client but over some of those dearest, or at least nearest, to me.

Gunster University stands in a somewhat grim Northern landscape, far from the dreaming spires of Oxford or the leafy Cambridge backs. It seems to have been built in the worst age of concrete brutalism and looked, as Hilda and I approached it in a taxi from the station, like an industrial estate or an exceptionally uninviting airport. We had gone there to see young Audrey Wystan graduate in English. Readers of these reminiscences will know that, when it comes to breeding, the Wystans are up there with the rabbits and She Who Must Be Obeyed has relatives scattered all over the world. Were I to be shipwrecked and cast upon some Pacific island, I should not be in the least surprised to find that the fellow in charge of banana production was one of her long-lost cousins. 'Audrey is Dickie's daughter,' She had told me, and, when I looked blank, had explained, 'Dickie was Daddy's brother Maurice's oldest. Her mother was inclined to be flighty, but Audrey was always a clever girl. She has Daddy's blood, you see. And now she's got first-class honours in English. You never got first-class honours in anything, did you, Rumpole?' From all this you will gather that Hilda has a strong sense of family loyalty, and when she heard of young Audrey's success she felt she had to be in at the prizegiving, and, as crime appeared to be a little thin on the ground at that time of the year, I was brought along to swell the applause.

So far as entertainment value went, the degree ceremony at Gunster University ranked a little below a boy scout jamboree in the Albert Hall and a notch or two above a Methodist service in a civic centre. Its main fault was a certain monotony. When you have watched one young person doff a mortar board, shake hands and accept a scroll you have seen them all and you still have about a thousand more to get through. When it was the turn of the English students to file across the platform, their names were called by Professor Clive Clympton, tall, more powerfully built than your usual academic, with gingery hair, an aggressive beard and a resonant voice. When called, the students presented themselves in front of the Chancellor, Sir Dennis Tolson, Chairman of the Tolson's Tasty Foods chain, and the University's main source of finance in these days of decreasing government support. Sir Dennis was a small, plump, round-shouldered man with drooping eyes and a turned-down mouth who looked like a frog in some children's story-book who'd got dressed up in a mortar board and a black-and-gold embroidered velvet gown. Standing next to him, and dressed in similar academic robes, was Hayden Charles, Vice-Chancellor. Charles, apparently a distinguished economist, was slight, grey-haired and good-looking in a dapper sort of way. His smile seemed somewhat patronizing, as though the idea that these honours would help their recipients land a decent job in a merchant bank was really rather quaint.

When the ceremony was over young Audrey told us we were invited to the Vice-Chancellor's house, a handsome Georgian mansion, which stood on the edge of the campus like a good deed in a concrete world. Tea and sandwiches were being served in the big, marble-paved entrance hall, from which a staircase with a wooden balustrade curled up to the higher floors and a painted dome. Nibbling and sipping academics and their families packed out the place, and the party was being ably supervised by a grey-haired, competent-looking woman whom I later discovered to be Mrs O'Leary, the Vice-Chancellor's housekeeper.

'They're destroying the universities! The Government's condemning us to death by a thousand cuts.' Clive Clympton, the English Professor, was haranguing our group which consisted of my good self, Hilda, Audrey and a vaguely anxious-looking person with a purple gown continually slipping off his shoulders. He had introduced himself as Martin Wayfield, Head of Classics.

'You should see what they're doing to the law, Professor,' I said to Clympton, adding my pennyworth of gloom to the party.

'We're going to have nothing but computer courses and business studies. Our masters don't want literature,' the Professor told us.

'Or jury trials. Or freelance barristers. Or the right to silence.' I joined in the litany and earned a rebuke from Hilda, 'Ssh, Rumpole. You're not down the Old Bailey now.'

'The right to what?' The Professor seemed puzzled, so I explained. 'Silence. If you're accused, you can keep quiet and make the Prosecution prove its case. That's what they want to abolish. Bang goes freedom! Nowadays the law's supposed to work with business efficiency like a bank!'

'Most of the people reading English are going into banks.' Audrey, who seemed a bright and reasonably attractive young lady, despite her Wystan ancestry, joined in. And Professor Clympton's mouth curved in a mirthless sort of way over his beard as he said, 'What can you expect, Audrey, with a Vice-Chancellor like Hayden Charles who writes books about money?' He was looking across the hall to Charles, who was talking to Sir Dennis Tolson. Beside him was a well-turned-out, well-groomed female, who looked as though she might have featured on the cover of *Vogue* ten or fifteen years before. Audrey had told us that this was Mercy Charles, the Vice-Chancellor's wife.

'You know Sir Dennis, our Chancellor, is head of that great cultural institution, Tolson's Tasty Foods? And poor old Hayden has to spend most of his time licking the Chancellor's boots.' As Clympton said this, the housekeeper had drawn up beside him and was offering him a plate of what, I deduced from pursed lips, she might have hoped were cyanide sandwiches.

'But Professor Clympton' – Hilda was fair-minded as always – 'they do quite good frozen curries at Tolson's in the Gloucester Road.'

'Don't remind me!' I shuddered at the memory of an occasional evening when Hilda hadn't felt like cooking, and the gangling Martin Wayfield came into the conversation with a fluting protest. 'Perhaps they do, Mrs Rumpole. But they don't do Latin. Nothing's been said yet but I may be the last Professor of Classics the University of Gunster will have.'

'*Amo, amas, amat*. Wordsworth. The right to silence.' I joined in the lament. 'The bloom is gone, and with the bloom go I!'

'"*Eheu fugaces, Postume, Postume*",' Wayfield quoted.

'*Onus probandi, in flagrante delicto,*' I told him.

'What did you say?' The classical scholar seemed puzzled by my Classics.

'Sorry. That's about all the Latin I know,' I explained. 'But I do know Wordsworth.' And I recited, in what I thought was a very moving manner, some lines from the old sheep of the Lake District:

> 'Waters on a starry night
> Are beautiful and fair;
> The sunshine is a glorious birth:
> But yet I know, where'er I go,
> That there hath passed away a glory from the earth'

Far from being touched by this, Clympton looked at me as though I had made a joke in poorish taste. 'Wordsworth,' he barked with disapproval, 'ended up a Tory!'

'Perhaps,' I told him, 'but he can still bring tears to the old eyes.'

'The purpose of literature' – Clympton seemed to be conducting a seminar – 'is not to produce tears, but social change. Your precious Wordsworth betrayed the French Revolution.' Then he stopped lecturing me and sought other company. Mercy Charles was now standing alone, a still beautiful woman with long, soft hair and a smart dark-blue suit with golden buttons. The English Professor excused himself and went over to her, and Audrey said, 'Clive Clympton's a wonderful teacher. What do you think of him, Uncle Horace?' At which point I claimed the right to silence.

Later we were introduced to Hayden Charles, who spoke highly of Audrey's attainments and talked about the fellowship she was being offered. Hilda pointed out that she came from the sort of family to which brains had been handed out with the greatest generosity. I was also introduced to the head of Tolson's Tasty Foods, who held out his hand to me in a somewhat curious manner, with the first two fingers extended and the others tucked into his palm. I paid little attention to this at the time as I was watching Professor Clympton, all

aggression drained away, talking to Mrs Charles in a gentle
voice and with smiling eyes.

'Mercy Charles is pretty, don't you think?' Audrey said as
we were leaving. 'Did you know she used to be quite a famous
model?' Hilda frowned at me when I asked if that meant she
was a model wife, or merely a model model.

Such were the characters in the drama which was played out
on the evening of the graduation ceremony, in the Vice-
Chancellor's home. After dinner, Mrs O'Leary was in the
kitchen, engaged in polishing some of Charles's silver, the care
of which was her particular pride. The kitchen door was a little
open and it gave on to the paved entrance hall, which had been
the scene of our tea party, so she was able to hear the sound
of upraised male voices from the doorway of the Vice-
Chancellor's study on the first floor. She distinguished the
words 'licking the Chancellor's boots' and she was afterwards
able to swear that they were shouted in Professor Clympton's
voice. Then she heard Charles shout, 'You've gone mad!
Totally mad!' and footsteps on the staircase, followed by the
words she couldn't altogether make out in Clympton's voice.
However, she was sure she heard an 'oh!' and then 'temporary'
and finally 'more is'. This was followed by further incomprehensible shouting, a noise like wood breaking and a crash.
There were then footsteps running across the marble, and the
sound of the front door opening and banging shut.

When she got out into the hall, she first noticed that part of
the wooden banister of the staircase was broken. And then
beneath it she saw the slight, elegant figure of Hayden Charles
lying on the blood-stained floor. She knelt beside him, held his
wrist and called his name but he was past hearing her.

The next day, after the police had been called and made
their preliminary inquiries, Detective Inspector Wallace and
Detective Sergeant Rose, both of the local force, called on
Professor Clive Clympton and asked him to account for his
movements at around ten o'clock the previous evening. The
Professor, who must have remembered what I had told him
about the right to silence, said he had no intention of answering

their questions. From then on, in all matters of importance concerning the Gunster case, he shut up like an oyster.

It wasn't only among those accused of crime that silence appeared to be golden. Shortly after the news of Hayden Charles's death had appeared in the papers, I was in my room in Chambers, preparing for an extremely tedious Post Office fraud due in the next day, when Soapy Sam Ballard, Q.C., the sanctimonious leader of our group of legal hacks in Equity Court, put his head round my door and said, 'You're working late.'

'Oh, no,' I told him. 'I'm just arranging my large collection of foreign postage stamps.' 'Are you, really?' 'No, of course not!' The fellow does ask the most idiotic questions. Undeterred by the coolness of my welcome, he made his way into the room, carrying, I couldn't help noticing, a moderate-sized zipper-bag covered in some tartan, and no doubt plastic, material.

'I just called in to put this away in my room,' Ballard said, as though it explained everything.

'This what?'

'This bag.'

'Oh, that.'

Ballard clearly had more in mind than introducing me to his bag, for he sat in my client's chair and prepared to unburden himself.

'I wanted to talk to you some time. I mean, Rumpole, how do you find marriage?'

'In my experience, you usually don't. It finds you. It comes creeping up unexpectedly and grabs you by the collar. How's Matey?' I was referring, of course, to Mrs Ballard for whom Soapy Sam had fallen whilst she was the Old Bailey matron, administering first aid to both sides of the law. 'You mean my wife, I assume?' Ballard guessed right. 'You remember the wonderful work she did at the Central Criminal Court?'

'She was a dab hand with the Elastoplast from what I can remember,' I assured him.

'Much loved, wasn't she, by all you fellows?'

'Well, let's say, highly respected.'

'Highly respected! Yes!'

When we had reached this accord, Ballard seemed stumped for words. He straightened his tie, crossed and recrossed his legs, pulled at his fingers until he seemed in danger of wrenching them off, and finally came out with, 'Rumpole, what's your opinion of secrets? In married life?'

'Absolutely essential.' I had no doubt about it.

'Is one entitled to keep things from one's spouse, for instance?' He asked the question after a good deal of finger pulling and, out of consideration for his joints, I was able to reassure him, 'As many things as possible. Everything you tell the other side just gives them material for cross-examination. That's the first lesson in advocacy, Bollard.'

'I wanted your opinion because of the slight, well, difference, that has arisen between Marguerite and myself.'

'Who the hell's Marguerite?' I was no longer following the fellow's drift.

'Marguerite, Rumpole, is my wife. The person you call Matey.'

'Oh, yes, of course.' My memory was now jogged. 'Why didn't you say so?' But here Ballard drew a deep breath and took me into his confidence. 'She called into Chambers, having been at her refresher course in sprains and fractures. She doesn't work now, of course, but she likes to keep her hand in. And Henry told her I'd already left. At five o'clock. And he thoughtlessly added that he imagined I'd gone home because I was carrying my "tartan bag". He meant this very bag, Rumpole. This one!' And to remove all doubt, he slapped the small item of luggage on the floor beside him. 'It's most unfortunate that Henry should have mentioned this bag at all,' he went on mysteriously, 'because I never take it home!'

'Oh, naturally not.' I had no idea what the fellow was talking about.

'And Marguerite keeps on asking where I was going with this particular bag,' he told me. 'I think, quite honestly, she's curious to know about what's inside it.'

'I'll look up some of the defences to a charge of carrying

house-breaking instruments.' I tried to comfort him with a helpful suggestion. 'Let's say you're doing evening-classes in locksmithery?'

'I've told her that there are certain things, even in married life, which a man is entitled to keep to himself.' He ignored my attempt to treat him like one of my more villainous clients and asked, 'Am I within my rights, Rumpole?'

'Your right to silence,' I reminded him, I hope, correctly, 'it's been yours since Magna Carta!'

'I'm glad you said that.' Soapy Sam seemed enormously relieved. 'I'm very glad to hear you say that, as a married man.'

'Of course, you can't stop the other side thinking the worst,' I warned him.

'Just at the moment,' Ballard admitted, 'that's exactly what she thinks. Really she needs something to take her mind off it. It would make a great deal of difference to Marguerite's happiness if she saw more of you fellows in Chambers.'

'She can see us at any time,' I told him. 'Not that we're much to look at.'

'No. I mean, I think it might be a terrific help if you and Hilda invited her to dinner at your place.'

'Is that what she'd like?' I was greatly taken aback.

'Well. Yes.'

'You're telling me in confidence that Matey would like to be asked to dinner in Froxbury Mansions?' I was still incredulous.

'Well, yes. She would.'

'Don't worry,' I promised him, 'I won't breathe a word to Hilda about it.'

'Rumpole!' Ballard gave a plaintive sort of bleat.

'Oh, well. Come if you want to!' I decided to humour the man. 'Dinner with She Who Must? Your Matey's got a curious idea of fun.' And then I could restrain my curiosity no longer and had to ask, 'What on earth *have* you got in that bag?'

'I think, Rumpole' – Ballard was standing firmly on his rights – 'that's a question I prefer not to answer.'

When I got back to the mansion flat I broke the news to Hilda.

'Ballard's invited himself and Matey to dinner,' I said. 'I fear for the man's sanity. He's carrying round a sort of tartan hold-all, the contents of which he refuses to divulge. It makes him look like a Scottish pox-doctor.' But She Who Must Be Obeyed had other news to impart. 'Do stop prattling, Rumpole,' she said. 'Just come along in and listen to what she's got to say.'

'Who's got to say?'

'Audrey, of course. She's got nobody but us to turn to.'

I found Audrey Wystan in the living-room. She was one of the apple-cheeked, dark-haired girls with the bright-eyed, enthusiastic appearance of those Russian dolls which come in various sizes. If you can imagine an apple-cheeked Russian doll on the verge of tears, that's how Audrey looked as I joined her. 'Thank God you've come, Uncle Horace,' she said in a shaky voice to me. 'They've arrested Clive.'

'Clive?'

'Professor Clympton. You remember?'

'Of course. The academic revolutionary.'

'He wants you to appear at his trial.'

At that moment I had only read about Hayden Charles's death in the paper and knew nothing of the questioning of the English Professor or of his possible involvement in the matter. So I said he had made a wise choice and asked, 'What sort of trial? Driving whilst tiddly?'

'They say it's murder. He thinks you'll understand.'

'About murder? Well, yes. A little . . .'

'No!' Audrey said with particular emphasis, as though delivering a message. 'He says you'll understand about keeping silent.'

So, accompanied by Mizz Liz Probert, as note-taker and general amanuensis, and Mr Beazley, a small, puzzled Gunster solicitor, who had probably up till then spent a blameless life conveying houses and drafting wills, I turned up in the interview room at Brixton prison to take instructions from the captive Professor. I was surprised by his presence there, as the crime had taken place in the North, but the trial was fixed at the Old Bailey. However, we started by discussing what seemed to be Clympton's principal concern. 'The right to silence,' he said, 'they haven't abolished it yet?'

'Not here, old darling,' I reassured him. 'Only in Northern Ireland, where we've handed the forces of evil a famous victory by allowing them to rob us of one of our priceless freedoms. Sorry, I'll save that for the Jury. You can still keep your mouth shut, if that's what we think you ought to do. Silence can't be evidence of guilt.'

'Audrey Wystan says you've won a lot of cases,' Clympton began doubtfully.

'I've won more murders than you've had degrees, Professor.'

'And you've got people off who refused to answer questions?' he asked, anxiously.

'When I thought it was right for them to do so. Yes.'

'It's right now.' His mouth closed firmly, his beard jutted. He seemed to have made up his mind.

'I'll consider that,' I told him, 'when I know a little more about your case.'

'I've decided already.'

In the ensuing quiet I pulled out my watch, lit a small cigar and told him that he had an hour of my time and if he wouldn't discuss the case perhaps he'd rather we talked about Wordsworth.

'If you like.' He shrugged his broad shoulders and looked sullen. I wondered why young Audrey, and perhaps Mrs Charles, found him so attractive, but men never know that about other men. Then I had second thoughts about the topic for the day. 'No, we shan't agree about Wordsworth. Let's discuss your Vice-Chancellor, Hayden Charles. A slightly built man who crashed through some worm-eaten banisters to his death on a marble floor. Pushed, no doubt, by a stronger opponent. You didn't like him?'

'I didn't like his money-mad politics, or his way of running the University.'

'And Mrs Charles?'

'She was a good friend.' The Professor sounded cautious. 'As a matter of fact, she reads a lot of poetry.'

'Read it together, do you?' I made so bold as to ask.

'Sometimes. Mercy's very bright, for an ex-model.'

'And I'm very bright for an Old Bailey hack. I can see a motive rearing its ugly head.'

'I don't understand.' I think he understood perfectly well, but I spelled it out all the same. 'Husband finds out about his beautiful wife's infidelity. Has it out with the lover in his study on the first floor of his house. A row develops and continues on the stairs. It becomes violent. The lover's bigger than the husband. He takes him by the throat, that's where there were bruises, finger marks but no finger-prints. The lover pushes the husband into the banisters. They're not built of reinforced concrete like the rest of Gunster University and they collapse. End of outraged husband. The lover runs out into the night. And that, my Lord, is the case of the Prosecution.' I ground out the remains of my small cigar in the top of the cocoa tin provided as an ashtray.

'The Prosecution can believe that if they want to,' the Professor said at last, with an unconvincing sort of defiance.

'And if the Jury believes it?'

'They won't have any evidence!' He was making the mistake of quarrelling with his defender, so I decided to confront him with the reality of the matter. 'I'll ask my learned junior to read us the statement of Mrs O'Leary, the housekeeper,' I said. Mizz Probert was quick to find the document in her bundle of papers and recited, 'Statement of Mrs Kathleen O'Leary. "I have been housekeeper at the Vice-Chancellor's house for ten years, and before that I worked for Mr and Mrs Charles in Oxford." Blah, blah, blah. "I have observed an intimate friendship develop between Mrs Charles and Professor Clympton." Blah, blah. "I heard quarrelling on the stairs shortly before 10 p.m. I heard Mr Charles's voice and another man's. All I heard the other man say clearly was something about 'licking the Chancellor's boots'. I am quite sure I recognized Professor Clympton's voice."'

'Do *you* think I said that, then?' the Professor challenged me and again I let him have the uncomfortable truth. 'It seems probable. That's exactly what I heard you say in the hearing of half a dozen other people that afternoon over tea and sandwiches. Don't worry, old darling. I'm not going to give evidence for the Prosecution. Someone else might, though.'

'Who?'

'Young Audrey Wystan, for one.'

'She won't.'

'You're very sure of her.'

'Oh, yes. Quite sure.' The Professor, I decided, was behind the door when modesty was handed out.

'The Professor of Classics?'

'Martin Wayfield's an old friend . . .' he began but I interrupted him.

'You were seen earlier by a young man called – What was his name? Peters?'

'Perkins. He'd just got a degree –' Mizz Probert found the statement with her customary efficiency and Clympton told us, with a good deal of contempt '– in business studies. He was one of Hayden Charles's favourites.'

'Christopher Perkins saw Professor Clympton at about 9.15 p.m. He seemed to be in a hurry,' Liz reminded us and I reminded the Professor, 'Mrs O'Leary heard the front-door bell ring at twenty to ten. Charles called out that he was going to answer it, so she didn't see whoever arrived. Was it you?'

'No,' Clympton said after a long silence.

'Then you have to tell us exactly where you went and what you did between nine thirty and just after ten, when Mrs O'Leary found the Vice-Chancellor dead.' But there was no answer. 'Say something to us, Professor,' I begged him. 'Even if it's only goodbye.'

After another long silence the Professor took refuge in literature. 'The sentimental approach to nature in Wordsworth's early poetry,' he told me, 'is his excuse for ignoring the conditions of the urban poor.'

'Say something sensible,' I warned him. 'Because if you don't, the Jury are going to find their own reasons for your silence, however much the Judge warns them not to.'

'Compare and contrast the deeper social message in George Eliot,' was all that Clympton had to say.

'Where were you that night, Professor?' I tried for the last time, and as he still didn't answer, I stood up to go. 'All right, then. Keep quiet. You're entitled to. But there's one line of

Wordsworth it might pay you to remember, "All silent and all damn'd!"'

I can't help experiencing a strong feeling of relief when I walk out of the gates of Brixton prison. It's a case of 'There, but for the Grace of God, stay I.' As we emerged that morning Mizz Probert said, 'What's he got to hide, do you reckon? Guilt?'

'Or he was tucked up somewhere with that ex-model girl you were talking about and he doesn't want to give her away,' Mr Beazley suggested.

'You soliciting gentlemen have got incurably romantic natures,' I told him. 'But there is one thing I can't understand about this case.'

'The silence of the Professor?'

'Not just that. The crime, if it were a crime, occurred up in Gunster, in the wilds of the North, your neck of the woods, Mr Beazley. All the witnesses are up there. But the Prosecution get him committed here in London and sent for trial at the Old Bailey. What's their exquisite reason for that?'

'Search me, Mr Rumpole.' My instructing solicitor was of no assistance.

'Shall we ever know, my Bonny Beazley?' I wondered. 'Shall we ever know?'

It was a time when everyone in Chambers seemed to be coming to me for advice, so that I felt I ought to start charging them for it. I was busily engaged in trying to think out some reasonable line of defence in the Gunster murder when my learned friend, Claude Erskine-Brown, put his head round the door to announce that his wife, Phillida, the Portia of our Chambers, was back from doing a corrupt policeman in Hong Kong.

'Then she can buy us a bottle of Pommeroy's bubbly on the oriental constabulary,' I suggested. 'We can celebrate!'

'Absolutely nothing to celebrate. In view of what she found when she got back.' Claude sat disconsolately in my client's chair and told me his troubles, as a non-fee-paying client. 'I'm afraid I had carelessly left two programmes for *Tristan and Isolde* at Covent Garden on the kitchen table.'

'Pretty scurrilous reading.' I understood the problem at once. 'Was our Portia shocked?'

'She asked whom I'd taken to the Opera.'

'Your wife can always get to the heart of a case, however complicated. She can put her finger on the nub!'

'Of course, I'd been with Liz Probert, as you remember,' Erskine-Brown confessed. 'We had a talk about the future of Chambers in the crush bar at Covent Garden.'

'And I'm sure that when your wife heard that, Claude, she decided not to press charges.'

'That's exactly the trouble, Rumpole. She didn't hear that. In fact, to be perfectly honest with you, I didn't tell her that. I told her I'd taken Uncle Tom.'

'You what?'

'I said I took Uncle Tom with me to the Opera.'

'Uncle Tom?' I couldn't believe my ears.

'Exactly.'

'To five hours of unmitigated Wagner?' It was incredible.

'I'm afraid so.'

'You must have eaten on the insane root,' I told the chap, 'That takes the reason prisoner.'

'Well, this is the point, Rumpole.' Claude suddenly became voluble in his own defence. 'I knew Phillida wouldn't have taken well to the idea of Lizzie and me drinking champagne in the crush bar. Although absolutely nothing happened. I mean, Liz bolted off down the underground almost as soon as the curtain fell. She even left me with her programme, which is why I had two. But on our way from Chambers earlier, we'd met Uncle Tom and he said it was his birthday, so he was off to buy himself a chop at Simpson's in the Strand, and Lizzie said what a pity we didn't have a spare ticket, so we could take him to the Opera as a treat. Of course we hadn't. But when Phillida asked me for an explanation . . . Well, Uncle Tom sprang to mind.'

'Erskine-Brown' – sometimes I despaired of the man ever becoming a proper, grown-up barrister – 'have you learnt nothing from your long years at the Criminal Bar? If you're going to invent a defence at least make it credible.'

'The point is' – he looked desperate – 'I'm terrified Philly's going to ask him.'

'Ask who?'

'Uncle Tom!'

'To another opera?' I was, frankly, puzzled.

'No, of course not. Ask him if he went with me. And if she does *that* . . .'

'You'll be in the soup. Up to the ears.' The situation was now crystal clear to me.

'Exactly. Unless he says he did.'

'You're not going to ask Uncle Tom to commit perjury?'

'I've got no influence over Uncle Tom,' Claude admitted, 'but *you* have, Rumpole. You've known the old boy forever. You can put it to him, as a matter of life and death. He's got to help a fellow member of the Bar.'

'No, Erskine-Brown.' I was shocked by the suggestion. 'Absolutely and definitely no! I will not enter into conspiracy with an elderly and briefless barrister to pervert the course of justice.'

'Is that your last word on the subject?' Claude was deeply disappointed.

'Absolutely my last word,' I assured him.

'You expect me to plead guilty?' He seemed to have reached the end of the road.

'Throw yourself on the mercy of the Court,' I advised him in as friendly a manner as possible.

'Rumpole, I know you call her Portia, but my wife's forgotten all about the Quality of Mercy. I came to you for advice.'

'You came too late. The moment was when she asked you about those two programmes.'

'What should I have done?'

'Claimed the right not to answer any questions,' I told him. 'Everyone else is doing it!'

At last the day arrived, awaited with a certain amount of grim foreboding, when Mr and Mrs Soapy Sam Ballard, on pleasure bent, arrived to dine with the Rumpoles in the Gloucester Road. Marguerite Ballard, the former Old Bailey matron, is a

substantial woman who seems to move with a crackle of starch
and a rattle of cuffs, and it's still hard to picture her without a
watch pinned to her ample bosom. Her hair, done up in what I
believe is known as a 'beehive' coiffure, looks as though it were
made of something brittle, like candy-floss. So far as weight
and stamina are concerned, she is one of the few ladies who
might be expected to go ten rounds with She Who Must Be
Obeyed. 'The wonderful thing about marriage, Hilda,' the ex-
Matey said as we reached the pudding without any major
disaster, 'I'm sure you'd agree, is telling each other *everything*.
I bet when old Horace climbs into bed with you at night . . .'

'You don't care for baked jam roll, Mrs Ballard?' Hilda
discouraged further inquiry into the secrets of the Rumpole
marriage bed. 'Baked jam roll is on my naughty list, I'm
afraid.' Matron pouted with disappointment. 'We've all got to
watch our tummies, haven't we?'

'Marguerite is very keen on keeping fit,' Ballard explained.
'And I'm with her one hundred per cent. I've lost a good deal
of weight, you know. You should see my trousers. They hang
quite loose. Look!' At which point, he stood up and jerked his
waistband in a distasteful demonstration.

'I was saying to Hilda, Sam,' Mrs Ballard banged on regardless, 'I bet when Horace climbs into bed with her, he tells her
all the events of the day. And about all the little cases he gets as
a *junior* barrister.'

'The little murders in provincial universities,' I agreed.

'I expect you'll be taking in a leader on the Gunster murder,
won't you, Horace?' Ballard sounded hopeful.

'I expect not. The client seems to think I'm the world's
greatest expert on the right to silence.' I looked at Soapy Sam.
'You're keen on that, aren't you? Silence?'

'When I was on duty down at the Old Bailey –' Marguerite
was off again – 'everyone used to confide in me. All the way
from the Recorder of London to the lads down in the cells. I
think they found me wonderfully easy to talk to. "Matey," the
old Recorder said more times than I care to remember, "you're
the only person I feel I can really take into my confidence on
the subject of my feet." Everyone seems to be able to confide

in me except my husband.' And she repeated, at increased volume to Ballard, the refrain, 'I said everyone seems able to confide in me except you, Sam.'

'So good of you to have us to dinner, Hilda.' Ballard was clearly anxious to change the subject. 'It's really a fun evening. We'll have to fix up a time to return your hospitality.'

'Oh, please, don't put yourself out,' I begged him, but my voice was drowned in Marguerite's continued harangue. 'Sam's a new boy, of course. But we're old hands at marriage, aren't we, Hilda? When I was married to poor Henry Plumstead, who passed away, we told each other every little thing. We just knew all there was to know about each other. I'm sure old Horace would agree with that.'

'Old Horace isn't so sure.' And I gave them an example of the blessings of silence. 'You remember George Frobisher? Hopeless at cross-examination so they made him a circus judge. Before your time, Bollard. Anyway he wanted to marry this Mrs Tempest. Frightfully struck with her, George was. I happened to recognize her as an old client with a tendency to burn down hotels for the sake of the insurance money.'*

'The women he's known! Old Horace has been around, hasn't he?' Marguerite joked and was rewarded with a freezing look from Hilda.

'I took it on myself to let old George know about Mrs Tempest's past,' I told them. 'He never forgave me. I don't think I've ever forgiven myself. They'd probably have been quite happily married, provided he didn't leave the matches lying around. When it comes to a nearest and dearest, a profound ignorance is usually best.'

I could tell by the way Hilda stood up and cleared away the plates that she wasn't best pleased by my conclusion. She then retired into the kitchen to wash up and Matey insisted on coming with her to dry. I was left with our Head of Chambers who, no doubt still hoping for a brief, re-opened the subject of Gunster. 'Funnily enough, I had an old uncle who lived there.'

* See 'Rumpole and the Man of God' in *The Trials of Rumpole*, Penguin Books, 1979.

I didn't find the fact especially amusing, but he went on, 'Used to be an estate agent, but he had to give it up. He said you couldn't get anywhere in Gunster unless you were an Ostler. They practically run the show.'

'A what?'

'Ancient Order of Ostlers. Rather like the Freemasons, only more so. My uncle didn't hold with it, so they squeezed him out.'

'Did he say what they did, these Ostlers, or whatever they called themselves?' I felt a faint stirring of interest. 'Oh, all sorts of secret ceremonies, I believe,' Ballard told me. 'Mumbo-jumbo, Uncle Marcus said. And they had a peculiar handshake.'

'Like that?' I asked. I remembered something and extended my hand with two fingers stretched out and the others bent back.

'Yes, I rather think it was. Look, wouldn't you like my assistance as a leader in that case?'

'No, thanks,' I hastened to assure him. 'You've been a great help to me already. Ah, Hilda. Is that the coffee?'

She Who Must Be Obeyed had come back with Marguerite and a tray. Her face was set grimly, with the look of a jury returning with a guilty verdict, as she ignored me totally and merely asked Marguerite if she took sugar.

'I'm going up to Gunster tomorrow,' I told my wife, and, when she still ignored me, I repeated the news. 'Gunster, dear. It's in the North of England. I'll probably be taking my junior, Mizz Probert, with me. You won't mind that, will you, Hilda?' In the normal course of events this information would have set off an avalanche of protest from Hilda. Now she simply handed Ballard coffee and asked him, 'Are you still keeping busy in Daddy's old Chambers?'

'So I'll probably be away tomorrow night,' I intruded firmly into the conversation. 'You won't be lonely, will you?' My wife looked at me but said nothing at all. So far as Rumpole was concerned the rest was silence.

It was not until long afterwards that I discovered what had transpired in the kitchen. 'Sam is up to tricks,' Mrs Ballard

had confided in Hilda, 'and your Horace is encouraging him.'
When asked for further and better particulars, Matey referred
to the mysterious zipper-bag which Sam left in his Chambers
and was apparently ashamed to bring home. When asked
about its contents by his wife he had replied, 'Old Rumpole
takes the view that married people are entitled to a little
privacy. Rumpole says we all have the right to silence, even in
married life.' 'So you see,' Marguerite summed the situation
up, 'it seems your Horace takes sides with husbands who get
up to tricks.' This information was, of course, more than
enough to cause She Who Must Be Obeyed to sever diplomatic
relations with my good self.

Once again I was at Gunster and in the Vice-Chancellor's
house. I stood on the stairway, by the broken banister, and
shouted at the top of my voice, 'You spend your life licking the
Chancellor's boots!' Then the kitchen door opened and Liz
Probert came out, followed shortly by Mr Beazley. We had
been able to make this experiment by kind permission of the
local force and Hayden Charles's widow. 'You heard that?' I
asked Liz.

'Clearly!'

'You could tell it was me?'

'Oh, it was you, all right. Just the sort of thing you would
say!'

'Let's try it again. This time I'll come down the stairs after
I've shouted and run across the hall.'

'Did you say "run", Rumpole?' Liz was incredulous.

'Well, move fairly rapidly.'

They went off to the kitchen again and I was left alone to
repeat my performance and cross the hall. Then the front door
was opened and Mercy Charles came into the house. 'You
were kind enough,' I thanked her, 'to say we could inspect the
scene of the crime.'

'It's rather a long inspection.' She still looked beautiful but
the creases at the corners of her eyes, which had looked like the
signs of laughter, now seemed the marks of tiredness or age. 'I
know,' I sympathized with her, 'crimes take such a short time

to commit and so terribly long to investigate. Do you think
Professor Clympton killed your husband?'

She looked at me and, instead of answering, asked another
question. 'Do you think you'll get him off?'

'The Professor won't tell me where he was on the night in
question,' I told her. 'He's not being much help to me at the
moment, imitating the oyster.'

'What do you want me to do about it?'

'He might just be keeping quiet to protect a lady's reputation,' I suggested. 'Rather an old-fashioned idea, I suppose.
But it's possible, isn't it?'

'That Clive was in bed with me and he doesn't want to tell
anyone? Is that what you'd like me to say? Then of course I
will, if it'll be a help.'

'Is it true?' I had to ask her.

'What's it matter to you if it's true or not? You're a lawyer,
aren't you? It's your job to get Clive off.'

She was looking at me, smiling, when Liz and Mr Beazley
came out of the kitchen to join us. I asked then if they'd heard
my footsteps going to the door and they said they had. 'You
know Mrs Charles, of course?' And I instructed our solicitor,
'Please, Beazley. On no account take a statement from her.'
We left the house then and Mercy was still standing in the
hall, looking lonely and mystified – a woman who, as far as I
was concerned, had just disqualified herself from giving
evidence.

'What was all that about Mrs Charles and her statement?'
Liz asked me as we crossed the Gunster University quadrangle,
an area which looked like a barrack square for some bleak army
of the future.

'It wouldn't have been the slightest use to us,' I told her.
'She'd have been torn apart in cross-examination. Silence may
not always be golden, but it's worth more than lies. Lots of
people need to learn that lesson including Claude Erskine-
Brown.'

'Claude? What's he done?'

'Sssh! Don't say a word. I suppose it was my fault, really. I

got him into it.* Here we are at the library. At least books have
to give up their secrets.'

The library was another concrete block. We went up in a lift
to a floor which hummed with word processors and computers and even had shelves of books available. The presiding
librarian was seated at his desk, a small, worried man, who
seemed nervous of the machinery which surrounded him and
was likely to take over his job.

'Sir,' I addressed him with due formality, 'I am engaged on
a history of the fair city of Gunster. I wonder if you have
anything on the Ancient Order of Ostlers?'

'Order of what?' The librarian frowned as though he didn't
understand me.

'Ostlers. Men who look after horses, although I don't think
there's many grooms among them now. I would say there are
more chairmen of committees, planners, property developers,
chief constables, even, dare it be said, heads of universities.
Important people in the long history of Gunster.'

'I'm quite sure we haven't got anything like that.' The man
was almost too positive. I managed to sound amazed. 'Your
library is silent on this important subject?'

'Nothing about it at all. In fact I've never heard of these
grooms or whatever it is you're talking about.'

'Mr Rumpole?' I heard a gentle voice beside us. 'You're
asking about the Ostlers?' I turned to see Martin Wayfield,
the Classics Professor, who had stolen up on us, his fingers
still keeping his place in some dusty volume of textual criticism.
'It's all a lot of nonsense but I can tell you a bit about them.
I was once coming out of the gents in the Gunster Arms
hotel . . .'

'Professor Wayfield! Silence, please!' the Librarian interrupted him in a panic-stricken whisper. 'You know the rules of
the library.'

'Oh, all right. Come over to my room. We don't want to
wake up the students, do we?'

Wayfield's room, a bleak modern office mercifully buried in

* See 'Rumpole and the Summer of Discontent'.

books, piles of papers, files, reproductions of busts from the
British Museum, fading photographs of other antiquities and
posters for cruises round Greece and Turkey, seemed a haven
of civilization in the grim Gunster desert. When we had settled
there, he encouraged Mizz Probert to boil a kettle and make
tea, filled an old pipe, lit it and said, 'What were we talking
about?'

'Something that interested me strangely,' I reminded him.
'You were just coming out of the Gunster Arms gents . . .'

'Ah, yes.' He took up his story again. 'And there was one of
these fellows, wearing a leather apron and gauntlets, with a
bloody great gilded horseshoe hung round his neck, just about
to slink into the private dining-room to swear some terrible
oath of secrecy and offer to have his throat cut if he ever let on
what they were up to. They do that, apparently. Well, I
recognized him as a chap who used to be' – here he started to
laugh – 'the University Registrar. So I called out, "Hullo,
Simkins! Your old lady cast a shoe, has she?" And he bolted
like a rabbit!'

I laughed with him and then became serious. 'Hayden
Charles, the late Vice-Chancellor,' I asked, 'was he one of the
brotherhood?'

'Hayden always laughed about them. No. I'm sure he wasn't.
You know, he got appointed because he was well in with the
Ministry at that time. It almost seemed a condition of our
grant to have Hayden. Some of the dedicated Ostlers were
furious about it.' Then he became serious also. 'So you're
defending Clive Clympton. Think you'll get him off?'

'Everyone's asking that. I don't know. Do you think he
pushed the Vice-Chancellor over the staircase?'

'Who can tell what anyone'll do? When they're in a temper.'
Wayfield was opening a battered carton of milk to add to
our tea. It looked sour, so I said I'd have mine black and then I
asked if my client was popular around the University.

'The leftie students love him and there are plenty of those,'
Wayfield told us.

'And the old dons must hate him?' Liz Probert suggested.

'Not really. He's pretty universally respected. Even by Sir

Dennis Tolson, although they're chalk and cheese, politically.' He relit his pipe which never kept going for very long. 'You've probably heard stories about his private life?'

'You think they're true?' I knew what he was talking about, of course.

'Why not? Mercy Charles is a very attractive woman.'

'Everyone says that. And she finds the Professor a very attractive man?'

'"*Sed mulier cupido quod dicit amanti. In vento et rapida scribere oportet aqua*",' Wayfield replied unhelpfully. 'Not everyone says that.' And I had to ask him, 'What does it mean?'

'"But a woman's sayings to her lusting lover should be written in wind and running water." It's all there. In the Latin. But it's going to be forgotten when they abolish the Classics. I ought to get back to my Catullus.' He looked longingly at the book he had brought with him from the library. So I stood up and thanked him, rather glad to be dismissed before we had experienced his tea. Then I held out my hand, two fingers extended, the rest folded into my palm. Wayfield looked sympathetic. 'You've hurt your hand?' he asked.

'Not at all.' I opened my hand. 'Nothing wrong with it at all.' And the head of the Classics Department gave me a firm, strong, but quite normal, handshake.

Back in London, Uncle Tom was, as usual, practising putts with an old mashie niblick into the clerk's room waste-paper basket, when Claude Erskine-Brown approached him in a conspiratorial fashion. My account of the conversation that follows is derived from Uncle Tom's memory of it, so I cannot vouch for its total accuracy. However, it went somewhat along these lines. Claude opened the bowling by saying, 'Uncle Tom, I've got something very important to tell you. I'd be glad of your full attention.'

'Not offering me a brief, are you?' Uncle Tom asked nervously. 'I'm not sure I remember what to do with a brief.'

'No, Uncle Tom. I want you to understand this perfectly clearly. You see, I wanted to take you to the Opera.'

'No, you didn't!' The old golfer was clear about that. 'I did,'

Claude assured him, 'on your birthday. I met you in the street and I wanted to ask you.'

'And if you had, I wouldn't have gone! I don't care for opera. Now if it'd been a musical comedy, it might have been different.'

'Well, this was a sort of musical comedy' – Claude smiled as though to a child – 'called *Tristan and Isolde*.'

'I remember old Sneaky Purbright used to be in these Chambers . . .' Uncle Tom helped out a difficult conversation with a reminiscence. 'Before your time. Sneaky had tickets for a musical comedy. They were reviving *The Bing Boys*. It was a most delightful evening.' And here he broke into song, '"If you were the only girl in the world, And I was the only boy . . ."'

'Well, I wanted to give you a most delightful evening,' Claude assured him. 'But I couldn't because I was taking someone else.'

'Sneaky wanted to take someone else too, but his wife wouldn't have liked it. So he took me. To *The Bing Boys*.'

'Well, that's just it! I wanted to take someone else to Covent Garden and I did. But my wife wouldn't have liked it. So I told her I took you.'

Uncle Tom thought this over carefully and came out with 'Funny thing to say. When you didn't.'

'Well, I know. But, please, Uncle Tom. If anyone asks you – particularly if anyone called Phillida Erskine-Brown asks you – if you went to the Opera House with me, I beg you to say yes.'

'Oh, I see.' Somewhere deep within Uncle Tom a penny dropped. 'I see exactly what's going on!'

'Thank God for that!' Claude seemed greatly relieved.

'Oh, yes I wasn't born yesterday, you know! Sneaky Purbright was having hanky-panky with old Mat Mattingley's secretary in King's Bench Walk. That meant he was out of Chambers a lot, so whenever Sneaky's wife rang up we had to say, "He's gone over to the library to read Phipson on Evidence."'

'But this time it's the Opera,' Claude was anxious to explain, 'and absolutely nothing occurred.'

'So. In the fulness of time' – Uncle Tom ignored the interruption – 'our phrase for hanky-panky in Chambers became "reading Phipson on Evidence". That was our expression for hanky-panky. I mean, "reading Phipson" meant you know what.'

'Please, Uncle Tom, I'd be very grateful. It's really quite innocent.'

'If you ask me, I'm to say I went to the Opera with you.' Uncle Tom was keen to cooperate.

'No,' Claude was still patient, 'if *my wife* asks you.'

'Absolutely,' Uncle Tom agreed. 'I'll tell Mrs Erskine-Brown it was a most delightful evening.' He started to play golf again, singing the while, ' "Nothing else would matter in the world today,/We would go on loving in the same old way./ If you were the only girl in the world . . ." '

'I don't know how to thank you, Uncle Tom,' Claude said, but the old man was busy completing the ditty. ' ". . . and I was the only boy." '

Mr Justice Oliphant, known, not particularly affectionately, to the legal profession as 'Ollie' Oliphant, hailed from somewhere near Gunster and had done his practice in the deep North. He was a pallid, shapeless, rubbery sort of man, and every movement he made seemed to cost him considerable effort. As he made a note he would purse his lips, frown, suck in his breath, concentrate visibly, and then, when he read through what he had written, he would rub his eyes with his fist and gasp with surprise. He was fond of treating us like a lot of Southern layabouts, full of far-fetched fantasies, who eat grapes to the sound of guitars and take siestas. He was always telling us about his down-to-earth, North Country common sense and he was proud of calling a spade a spade, usually long before anyone had proved it was a toothpick. Perhaps because he knew the area, he was chosen to preside over the Gunster murder trial at the Old Bailey. The Prosecution was represented by Mordaunt Bissett, Q.C., a large, florid man with a plummy voice, who hunted every weekend in the season and was said to be extremely 'clubbable'. (There were many occasions in Court when I could have clubbed the fellow, if a suitable blunt instrument were handy. He had a talent for jumping over the rules of evidence as though they were low hedges in the Bicester country.) He was assisted by a junior whose name I now forget and whose only task seemed to be fetching coffee for his learned leader when we retired to the Bar mess. The Defence was in the more than capable hands of Mr Horace Rumpole and Mizz Liz Probert.

The trial was well attended by members of the press and, in the public gallery, I spotted a number of interested academics, including Martin Wayfield, the Professor of Classics. Let me begin my account of the proceedings at the point when Mrs O'Leary, the late Hayden Charles's housekeeper, was in the witness-box and Mordaunt Bissett, examining her in chief, began a question, 'Now tell us, when you were in the kitchen on the night of the murder . . .'

'My Lord, I object!' I was on my feet with the agility that constantly surprises my opponents. 'No one's proved it was a murder! It might be anything from manslaughter to accident.'

'Oh, come, come, Mr Rumpole.' The voice of the North Country comedian on the Bench tried to stifle my protests. 'The Jury and I will use our common sense. Mr Mordaunt Bissett is just using the word in the indictment your client faces.'

'To use that word before it's been proved isn't common sense. It is uncommon nonsense,' I insisted, at which Ollie became testy. 'If the Defence is going nit-picking, Mr Rumpole, we'll call it an "incident". Will that satisfy you?'

'It's not me that has to be satisfied, my Lord,' I answered grandly, 'it's the interests of justice!'

I sat down then and the Judge said, in his best down-to-earth manner, 'come along, Mr Mordaunt Bissett. Let's get back to work, shall we, now Mr Rumpole's had his say.' At which the mighty hunter smiled in an ingratiating sort of way and said to the witness, 'During the "incident" you could distinguish some of the words the man on the stairs was shouting. You told us you heard him say something about "licking the Chancellor's boots"?'

'I heard that. Yes,' Mrs O'Leary agreed.

'Could you recognize the man's voice?'

'I was sure I could.'

'Whose was it?' Mrs O'Leary looked at the tall, red-bearded man in the dock as though she regretted the abolition of the death penalty. 'It was *his* voice,' she said.

'You mean it was the voice of Professor Clympton?' Bissett was one for hammering home the message, and Mrs O'Leary obliged again with 'I'm sure it was.'

At this point Bissett sat and closed his eyes, as though the verdict was no longer in doubt. Ollie Oliphant made a note of the witness's last answer, pursed his lips, gasped for air like a porpoise and underlined the words heavily with a red pencil in a way the Jury couldn't help noticing. Then he asked me if I had any questions for Mrs O'Leary in a way which meant 'Do have a go, if you think it will do you the slightest good, young fellow, my lad!'

'Mrs O'Leary' – I rose to my feet, more slowly this time – 'Did you hear any other words you could distinguish, from Mr Charles's attacker?'

'Only a few, my Lord.'

'What were they?'

'I didn't think they were important. I couldn't make sense of them, anyway.'

'Let's see if we can.'

'I heard him say "oh!" loudly.'

'Oh, and then what?'

'Well, it sounded like "temporary". And then another "oh!" And then, I think I heard, "more is" . . .'

'Does all this make sense to you, Mr Rumpole?' his Lordship asked.

'Not at the moment, my Lord,' I admitted.

'So this evidence is merely brought out to puzzle the Jury?'

'Or perhaps, my Lord,' I suggested, 'to test their powers of deduction.' And then I turned my attention to the witness again. 'You say you heard the man shout something about licking the Chancellor's boots?'

'She's told us that!' The good old North Country patience was running out fast.

'Yes, but let me suggest *when* you heard it, Mrs O'Leary.

You heard it at tea-time, did you not? When you were helping serve sandwiches to the graduates and their families. Professor Clympton said the Vice-Chancellor licked the Chancellor's boots. It was said quite clearly.'

'Mr Rumpole! How do you know it was said clearly? You weren't there, were you?' Ollie Oliphant grinned at the Jury, clearly feeling he was on to a good thing. I hated to disappoint him. 'As a matter of fact I was,' I told the Court. 'But I'm not here to give evidence. This lady is. You heard that at tea-time, didn't you, Mrs O'Leary?'

'Yes, I did. And I thought it was a disgusting thing to say about Mr Charles.'

'So when you heard those words again from the hallway at about 10 p.m., you naturally thought it was Professor Clympton shouting them?'

'I thought so. Yes.' The answer was only a shade less confident.

'Because that was something you'd *already heard him* say?'

'I had. Yes.'

'And if someone *else* had used the same words at night time, a man you never saw perhaps, you'd be likely to assume it was Professor Clympton?'

There was a long pause. The Jury looked interested, Mordaunt Bissett, Q.C. still feigned sleep and the Judge didn't risk my wrath by putting in his two penn'orth.

'I suppose so,' the witness said at last.

'Even though you couldn't really recognize his voice?' I asked her. There was another long pause, and then she said, with even less certainty, 'I *think* I recognized it.'

'You *think* you recognized it.' I gave the Jury a look which was more triumphant than I felt. 'Thank you very much, Mrs O'Leary.' I sat down, having done all that was possible in the circumstances. Whereupon Mr Justice Oliphant set about trying to undo all the good I had done the Professor.

'Mrs O'Leary,' the Judge began in his most down-to-earth manner, 'let's use our common sense about this. You told Mr Mordaunt Bissett you were sure it was Professor Clympton's voice?'

'Yes.'

'And you told Mr Rumpole you *think* it was.'

'That's right.'

'So does it come to this, you *think* you're sure?'

'Yes. I suppose so,' the witness agreed reluctantly and the Judge looked pleased with himself. 'Common sense, Members of the Jury,' he said, with great satisfaction, 'it always does it.'

The next witness was young Christopher Perkins, the student who had just graduated when the 'incident' took place, and while he was being summoned and sworn, I took the opportunity of speaking to the beefy Prosecutor. 'Mordaunt, old darling,' I whispered, 'a word in your shell-like. Why did the Prosecution start this case in London?'

'We've got you a North Country judge,' he answered, as though that were some kind of compensation.

'Thank you very much but the Defence sometimes asks for cases to be moved because of local prejudice against the accused. Did you think some of the Jury might be prejudiced in favour of the Professor if he'd been tried in Gunster?'

Mordaunt Bissett gave me a smiling 'no comment' and rose to examine the young man in the neat blue suit, with slicked-down hair, rimless glasses and a minute moustache, who had sworn to tell nothing but the truth. 'Are you Christopher Perkins?'

'Yes, sir.'

'Did you graduate with first-class honours in Business Studies last July?'

'Yes, I did.'

'On the night of the incident, were you crossing the quadrangle past Tolson buildings?'

'Yes, I was.'

'Did you see Professor Clympton?'

'Don't lead,' I growled and Bissett smiled tolerantly and changed the question to 'What did you see?'

'I'd looked at my watch as I was due to meet a friend in the J.C.R. It was just nine fifteen. Then I saw Professor Clympton coming out of his rooms. He seemed to be in a hurry. He was carrying a bag, I remember.'

'Thank you, Mr Perkins.' Bissett sat down satisfied and I climbed to my feet with a new interest in the evidence. 'We haven't heard about the bag,' and I asked, 'Can you describe it?'

'Just an ordinary zipper holdall. I thought he was on his way to play squash or something.'

'On his way to play squash at that time of evening?'

'Well, I didn't know where he was going, did I?'

'Of course not.' The Judge was, as always, reluctant to exercise his right to silence.

'Well, I hope no one's suggesting he was carrying special equipment for pushing people downstairs,' I said, and couldn't resist adding, 'After all, we've got to use our common sense about this, haven't we, Members of the Jury?'

It was a time when everyone seemed to be carrying mysterious luggage. When I got back to Chambers I telephoned young Audrey Wystan, who was still in residence in Gunster, working at some thesis on the importance of cosmetics in metaphysical poetry, or something of the sort, by which she hoped to further her academic career. I asked her if she wanted to help the Professor and, when I got an enthusiastic and breathless 'yes', I gave her certain instructions about getting into his rooms on some pretext and conducting a search.

When I left Equity Court I saw a familiar figure hurrying through the gloaming. It was Soapy Sam Ballard, and in his hand was his tartan zipper-bag, the piece of luggage which had been the subject of so much speculation. I must confess that my curiosity overcame me and, instead of heading straight for Pommeroy's Wine Bar as I had intended, I set out, like that irreplaceable sleuth Fig Newton, to tail Ballard. I wanted to know where he was going and what he did with the mysterious holdall.

Keeping a discreet distance between us, I followed him across Fleet Street, down Fetter Lane and through some of the narrow and dingier lanes behind Holborn. At last we came to an anonymous and gloomy building, which might have been a converted warehouse. Windows on the first floor were lit up, and the regular pulse of loud disco music was audible in the street below. Moving quickly and, I thought, furtively, Ballard sneaked in through the swing-doors of this establishment. I loitered in the street and lit a small cigar.

After a decent interval I followed our Head of Chambers' footsteps in at the door and climbed a stone staircase to the first floor and the source of the music which was, by now, almost deafening. There was another pair of doors on the landing, over which a notice was fixed which read alliteratively ANNIE ANDERSON'S AEROBOTICS ATELIER. SESSIONS TWICE NIGHTLY. I approached the doors with a good deal of natural hesitation and found that they had small, circular windows in them. Peering through, I was able to discern a hefty blonde, no doubt Annie herself, clad in a yellow track-suit, leaping up and down and shouting commands in time to the music. The corybants she commanded were mainly young, but among them I spotted a breathless Ballard, pale and eager, leaping as best he could, clad in a bright purple track-suit and elaborately constructed plimsolls that had no doubt been the secret contents of his much discussed holdall. If I was laughing, my laughter was happily drowned by the dreadful sound of the musical accompaniment.

At about the same time as I was watching Ballard trip the heavy and fantastic toe at Annie Anderson's Aerobotics Atelier, young Audrey Wystan had entered Professor Clympton's rooms in Gunster. He had left a key with the porter and Audrey had borrowed it, saying that Clympton needed some things urgently for his trial. She was so anxious to help him that she practised this small deception on my express instructions. She went through his study without finding what I had sent her to look for, but at last she opened a big built-in cupboard in the bedroom. There was a zipper-bag on the floor, beneath the hanging suits and academic gowns, and when she opened it she found it to contain, to her bewilderment, a gilded horseshoe on a chain and a leather apron. She telephoned me and I got on to the indrustious Beazley to tell him to get out a witness summons for the man we should have to call the next day, with the permission of the Judge.

*

So, much to his obvious irritation, a reluctant witness, looking, at that moment, like an extremely displeased frog, was called to the witness-box and I asked him, as soothingly as possible, whether he were Sir Dennis Tolson.

'I am.'

This simple question an answer produced an outcry from the dock, where my client, foregoing his right to silence at last, began to utter fruitless cries of 'No! I forbid it!', 'I'm not having it!' and 'Stop it, Rumpole! What the hell do you think you're doing?' What I was hoping to do was to get the Professor off, despite all his efforts to land himself in the slammer for life. Fortunately Ollie Oliphant did something useful at last. 'Mr Rumpole,' he said, showing a rare grasp of the facts of the case, 'your client is creating a disturbance!'

'Is he really, my Lord?' I tried to keep calm in spite of the Professor. 'It's these literary chaps, you know. Very excitable natures.'

'Well, he's not getting excitable in my Court. Do you hear that, Clympton? Any more of this nonsense and you'll be taken down to the cells. Now' – here the Judge smiled winsomely at the witness – 'did you say, *Sir* Dennis Tolson?'

'Yes, my Lord.'

'Some of us do our weekly shop at Tolson's Tasty Foods. Don't we, Members of the Jury?' A few of the more sycophantic jury members nodded and Ollie started to exchange reminiscences with the fat little fellow in the witness-box. 'Sir Dennis, it may interest you to know, I come from your part of England.'

'Is that so, my Lord?' Tolson sounded as though he had received more fascinating information.

'I used to practise often at the old Gunster Assizes,' the Judge went on. 'Never dreamt I'd find myself sitting down here, at the Old Bailey.' I refrained from telling the old darling that it came as a bit of a shock to us too, and asked Sir Dennis if he attended by summons.

'It was served on me last night,' he told us. 'It was most inconvenient.'

'I'm sorry, but it would be most inconvenient for my client

to have to go to prison for a crime he didn't commit. Are you an Ostler?'

'A what, Mr Rumpole?' Ollie was clearly having difficulty keeping up.

'A member of the Ancient Order of Ostlers,' I explained. 'An organization with considerable power and influence in the City of Gunster.'

At which point the witness raised his arm in what looked like a mixture between a benediction and a Fascist salute and intoned, 'By the Great Blacksmith and Forger of the Universe . . .'

'That means you are?' I assumed.

'He doesn't permit me to answer that question.' Sir Dennis was also having a go at the right to silence.

'Don't bother about the Great Blacksmith for a moment,' I told him. 'His Lordship is in control here and he will direct you to answer my questions.'

'Provided they're relevant!' Ollie snapped like a terrier at my heels. 'What've you got to say, Mr Mordaunt Bissett?'

'I think the Defence should be allowed to put its case, my Lord.' The not very learned Prosecutor showed some unusual common sense. 'We have to consider the Court of Appeal.' Now, if there's anything which makes Ollie wake up in a cold sweat in the middle of the night it's the fear of being criticized by that august assembly. 'The Court of Appeal? Yes,' he agreed hastily. 'You're quite right. Get on with it then, Mr Rumpole. The Jury don't want to be kept here all night, you know.'

'Are most of the important people in Gunster members of the Ostlers?' I asked the witness.

'We are sworn to secrecy.'

'Are they members?' I was prepared to go on asking the question all day if I didn't get an answer.

'Our Ostlers are men of talent and ambition. Yes.' I got a sort of an answer.

'And is membership a path to promotion in local government, for instance, and in the University?'

'An Ostler will do his best to help another Ostler, yes. All things being equal.'

'And all things being equal, an ambitious English Professor might do well to join you, if he had his eyes on becoming Vice-Chancellor. In the fulness of time?'

There was a long silence then. I saw my client sit with his arms crossed, his eyes on the ground. He only lifted his head to look at the witness with an unspoken protest when he answered, 'Professor Clympton was one of our members. Yes. If that's what you're getting at.'

'Thank you, Sir Dennis.' I was genuinely grateful. 'That's exactly what I was getting at. Now did you, by any chance, have a meeting on the night Hayden Charles met his death?'

'As a matter of fact we did.'

'What time did that meeting begin?'

'Our normal time. Nine thirty.'

'Where was it?'

'The usual place.'

'The Gunster Arms hotel?' I remembered Wayfield's story.

'Yes.'

'And when did Professor Clympton arrive?'

'About ten minutes before the meeting was due to begin.'

'That's nine twenty. When Hayden Charles was still alive. When did he leave?'

'We broke up around midnight. We had a few drinks when the meeting was over.'

'And by eleven o'clock the police had found Hayden Charles dead. And Professor Clympton was with you all the time? From nine thirty to midnight?'

'Yes. He initiated a couple of candidates and . . .'

'Thank you, Sir Dennis' – I was prepared to spare the witness further embarrassment – 'you can keep the rest of your secrets intact.'

I sat down and Mordaunt Bissett got up to start a quite ineffective attempt to repair the fatal damage done to his case. While this was going on, Mizz Probert asked me in a whisper what on earth a decent left-wing professor thought he was doing with a lot of old businessmen in aprons.

'He was ambitious,' I told her. 'But he'd rather be suspected of murder than let it be known just how ambitious. Perhaps that's why he'll never thank me. He's lost the young.' And looking behind me at the man in the dock, I saw his face back in his hands, his shoulders bowed and felt some pity for him, but more for young Audrey Wystan who had so admired his outspoken independence of the University establishment.

The case of Claude Erskine-Brown was not going so happily. He and Uncle Tom were both in our clerk's room when Dianne announced that Mrs Erskine-Brown was on the phone and wanted to speak to the aged golfer in the corner. I was just back from a day's work at the Bailey and I saw Uncle Tom take the call, and was a witness to the agony of Erskine-Brown as he heard how it was going.

'Oh, Mrs Erskine-Brown. Where are you? Winchester Crown Court. Just checking up? Oh.' And then Uncle Tom obliged Claude by saying, 'When you were in Hong Kong, your husband did take me to a show. It was very kind of him indeed. It was my birthday. What was the show called? Just a moment . . .' Here he put his hand over the instrument and whispered to Claude, 'What was it called?' And received the answer, '*Tristan and Isolde.*'

'Oh, yes.' Uncle Tom was back in contact with our Portia. '*Tristan* and somebody else. No. Claude's not here at the moment. I think he's over in the library. Reading Phipson on Evidence. Yes. It was a most delightful show. *Tristan*, yes. I'm very fond of a musical, d'you see?'

'Uncle Tom!' Claude, in spite of himself, cried out, fearing what was coming. 'The tunes are unforgettable, aren't they?' Uncle Tom blundered on. 'I was singing to myself all the way home.' And here he burst into song with 'Nothing else would matter in the world today,/We would go on loving in the same old way,/If you were the only girl in the world . . .'

This is not, of course, the best-known number from Wagner's *Tristan.* Uncle Tom's voice faded as the phone was put down at the other end, and he turned to Claude and asked, amazed that his deception hadn't met with more success, 'Did I say something wrong?'

All over the place the truth was emerging despite the

conspiracy of silence. Walking to the bus stop, I caught up with Ballard, and greeted him with a cry of 'Hop, skip and jump!'

'What?' Our leader look startled.

'Or can't you do it without the purple jump-suit?' I asked politely. 'I bet that garment skips of its own accord.'

'Rumpole!' Ballard looked stricken. 'You know everything!'

'Pretty well.'

'Marguerite was so insistent that I should get what she calls my "naughty tummy" down,' he began to explain his extra-ordinary behaviour, 'she practically talked of nothing else.'

'I know.' I understood.

'At last I could stand it no more. I saw an advertisement for this "studio". It seemed so jolly. Music and . . .'

'. . . Young ladies?'

'That's why I kept it from Marguerite. I thought she might not appreciate . . .'

'You skipping about with young ladies? I think she'd admire your heroism, Bollard. Tell her you made the supreme sacrifice and got into a purple jump-suit, just for her. And you've lost weight?'

'A few inches.' He sounded modestly pleased. 'As I told you, my trousers hang loose.'

'Superb! Tell her, Bollard. Boast of it to her.'

'That's really your advice to me, Rumpole?'

'Why not? Bring it all out into the open, old darling. The time for secrets is over.'

'Although steps may be taken soon to bring the law into line with good, old-fashioned common sense, Members of the Jury' – Ollie Oliphant's summing up was drawing to a close – 'Pro-fessor Clympton has chosen not to enter the witness-box and give evidence. But you have had the testimony of Sir Dennis Tolson.' He said this as though the Holy Ghost had given tongue in Number One Court at the Old Bailey. 'Sir Dennis and I come from the same part of England. We have a rule up there in the North, Members of the Jury, Use your common sense. Sir Dennis isn't a stranger to us, is he? I expect some of you brought your sandwiches in Tolson's bags, didn't you? And Sir Dennis is quite sure the Professor was at the meeting when the deceased man fell from the stairs. Has he any reason for inventing? Use your common sense, Members of the Jury! Now. Take all the time you need to consider your verdict.'

With these words ringing in their ears, the Jury retired and I went out into the corridor to light a small cigar, walk up and down and hope for victory. As I was so engaged I met the Professor of Classics wandering vaguely, and I offered to buy him a coffee in the Old Bailey canteen. This fluid now comes from a machine which also emits tea, cocoa and soup, these beverages being indistinguishable. We sat at a table in a corner of the big room, among the witnesses, families, barristers and police officers engaged in other cases, and I said, 'You're taking a lot of interest in these proceedings?'

'Why not?' Wayfield filled his pipe but didn't get around to lighting it. 'Clive Clympton's a valued colleague.'

'Hayden Charles wasn't such a valued colleague, was he?'

'What do you mean?' Wayfield frowned, as though over a particularly obscure Latin text.

'I've been thinking about those odd words Mrs O'Leary heard. "Oh, temporary", she said, if you remember. "Oh, more is" . . . As I told you. I don't know much Latin, but didn't Cicero express his disgust with the age he lived in? Didn't he say, *"O tempora, O mores!"*? Oh, our horrible times and our dreadful customs! – or words to that effect?'

'Cicero said that. Yes.'

Wayfield seemed surprised I knew such things, and I wouldn't have done had I not spent a good ten minutes with *The Oxford Dictionary of Quotations.*

'And did a Classics Professor,' I asked him then, 'shout it on the staircase, furious with the man who was going to stop its study at Gunster University?'

'I don't understand what you're saying, Mr Rumpole.' For once in his life, I thought, Martin Wayfield wasn't telling the truth. He lied without any talent.

'Don't you, Professor Wayfield? "Licking the boots of the Chancellor" and turning Gunster into a training-ground for bankers and accountants? You heard Clympton say that and you thought it was a pretty good description of Charles's activities. So good, in fact, that it was worth shouting at him again on the stairs.'

'Mr Rumpole, you argued Clive's case very well, but . . .' Wayfield tried an unconvincing bluster which also didn't suit him.

'But the Vice-Chancellor was seized by the throat with a strong grasp. I've felt your handshake, Professor. He was thrown against the banister by someone who thought all he believed in, his whole life, was threatened. Isn't that possible?'

'Just who is suggesting that?'

'Oh, no one but me. If anyone else does, I'll make them prove it. There's really no evidence, except for a rough translation from the Latin.'

Wayfield said nothing to that, but he took out his diary, tore a scrap of paper out of it and wrote something down. 'Look, if you're ever in Gunster again,' he said, 'do ring me. We could have dinner. I'll give you my number.'

'Thank you, Professor. I think I'll give Gunster a wide berth from now on.'

'Here's the number, anyway.' And he handed me the scrap of paper, just as Mizz Liz Probert, whom I had left downstairs to await events, came to tell us that the Jury were back with a verdict.

'I suppose I'm expected to thank you.' Clive Clympton parted from me with a singular lack of grace.

'No need. I get people off murder charges every day of the week. It's just part of the Rumpole service.'

'Couldn't you have done it without Tolson?'

'Probably not. Silence may be golden but it can also be extremely dangerous. It tends to give people ideas.'

So Professor Clympton went back to Gunster. Whether or not he ended up with Mercy Charles I don't know, but young Audrey Wystan took up a teaching job in America and we didn't see her again. In due course Martin Wayfield retired to Devon to write a new life of Cicero, but died before the task could be completed. Claude Erskine-Brown's difficulties were solved more easily. He told me that Phillida and he were on excellent terms again. 'How did you manage that?' I asked him. 'Did you teach Uncle Tom to sing the love duet?'

'Oh, no. I told her the truth. I said you'd persuaded me to take Liz Probert secretly to the Opera to settle a problem in Chambers. I made it perfectly clear that the whole wretched business was entirely your fault.' It is the touching loyalty of my fellow hacks that's such a feature of the great camaraderie of the Bar.

On the day I won *R. v. Clympton*, the Gunster murder, I returned home to the mansion flat, went into the kitchen, poured myself a sustaining glass of Château Fleet Street, and hoped to enjoy a post-mortem on my triumph with She Who Must Be Obeyed as she prepared supper for the hero of Court Number One.

'You know what first gave me the idea?' I told her. 'When the Prosecution moved the case to London. It wasn't for the Professor's benefit; they were afraid of Ostlers on the Jury who might let their fellow Ostler off. You see the point, don't you, old thing?' Hilda answered with a stunning silence.

'Secrets! It's extraordinary, Hilda. The secrets people think important. Take my Professor, now. He'd rather risk prison than break his oath of secrecy to a lot of middle-aged businessmen tricked out in fancy dress in a hotel dining-room. You follow me?' But once again, answer came there none. 'Of course, he wanted it all ways. He wanted to be the hero of the young. And he wanted the secret help of the Ancient Order of Ostlers. Do you see the point?' I sent out words like soldiers to battle and they never returned. 'Oh, thanks,' I said, 'always glad of your opinion, Hilda. So he resorted to silence. It's what everyone does when life gets too difficult. Take cover in silence. Wrap silence round your ears like a blanket. If you say nothing, you can't come to any harm. But no one can keep silent forever. You get lonely. You have to say something some time. Unless you're struck dumb by some unfortunate disease. Is that your problem, Hilda?' But my wife, peeling potatoes, seemed unaware of my existence.

'And what about the other Professor? The Latin scholar. He didn't say much, but I could see he found it difficult to keep quiet, extremely difficult. Look at this.' I showed her Wayfield's diary page and got no reaction. 'He gave me his number and wrote something on it. A Latin quotation. Of course. *Atque inter silvas Academi quaerere verum*. I might find my old school dictionary.' I went and found a Latin dictionary on a shelf in the living-room. It still smelled of ink and gob-stoppers. When I returned to the kitchen, the telephone on the wall was ringing. Hilda held it to her ear and said, 'Yes. Oh, hello, Marguerite.'

'A miracle,' I muttered, as I looked up the Latin words, 'she speaks!' In fact Hilda was talking quite jovially to the telephone. 'Rumpole told Sam to confess it all to you, *he* did that?' There was a further miracle. She Who Must Be Obeyed was smiling. 'Gymnastics? Lost four inches . . .? Plimsolls in the bag? Well, that is a relief, dear, isn't it?'

I had made sure that *silva* was a wood, and *quaerere* meant to seek, when Hilda put down the telephone and said, 'I hear you told Sam Ballard you didn't believe in secrets between married people.'

'Secrets between married people? Perish the thought!' I protested and went back to the dictionary. '*Verum* . . . Well, that's obvious.'

'Sam's trousers hang loose.' Hilda had got on to a sensitive subject. 'Your trousers don't hang loose, do they, Rumpole? Take up gymnastics. Lose four inches round the waist like Sam Ballard!'

'You want me to hop around in a bright purple jump-suit? To the sound of disco music. Perish the thought!' I repeated. And then I tried a rough translation of Wayfield's message: '"And seek for truth in the groves of Academe . . ." You see? Even the Professor of Classics couldn't keep things to himself.'

Rumpole at Sea

Mr Justice Graves. What a contradiction in terms! Mr 'Injustice' Graves, Mr 'Penal' Graves, Mr 'Prejudice' Graves, Mr 'Get into Bed with the Prosecution' Graves – all these titles might be appropriate. But Mr 'Justice' Graves, so far as I'm concerned, can produce nothing but a hollow laugh. From all this you may deduce that the old darling is not my favourite member of the Judiciary. Now he has been promoted, on some sort of puckish whim of the Lord Chancellor's from Old Bailey Judge to a scarlet and ermine Justice of the Queen's Bench, his power to do harm has been considerably increased. Those who have followed my legal career will remember the awesome spectacle of the mad Judge Bullingham, with lowered head and bloodshot eyes, charging into the ring in the hope of impaling Rumpole upon a horn. But now we have lost him, I actually miss the old Bull. There was a sort of excitement in the corridas we lived through together and I often emerged with a couple of ears and a tail. A session before Judge Graves has all the excitement and colour of a Wesleyan funeral on a wet day in Wigan. His pale Lordship presides sitting bolt upright as though he had a poker up his backside, his voice is dirge-like and his eyes close in pain if he is treated with anything less than an obsequious grovel.

This story, which ends with mysterious happenings on the high seas, began in the old Gravestones' Chambers in the Law Courts, where I was making an application one Monday morning.

'Mr Rumpole' – his Lordship looked pained when I had outlined my request – 'do I understand that you are applying to me for bail?' 'Yes, my Lord.' I don't know if he thought I'd just dropped in for a cosy chat.

'Bail having been refused,' he went on in sepulchral tones, 'in the Magistrates Court and by my brother judge, Mr Justice Entwhistle. Is this a frivolous application?'

'Only if it's frivolous to keep the innocent at liberty, my Lord.' I liked the phrase myself, but the Judge reminded me that he was not a jury (worse luck, I thought) and that emotional appeals would carry very little weight with him. He then looked down at his papers and said, 'When you use the word "innocent", I assume you are referring to your client?'

'I am referring to all of us, my Lord.' I couldn't resist a speech. 'We are all innocent until found guilty by a jury of our peers. Or has that golden thread of British justice become a little tarnished of late?'

'Mr Rumpole' – the Judge was clearly unmoved – 'I see your client's name is Timson.'

'So it is, my Lord. But I should use precisely the same argument were it Horace Rumpole. Or even Mr Justice Graves.' At which his Lordship protested, 'Mr Rumpole, this is intolerable!'

'Absolutely intolerable, my Lord,' I agreed. 'Conditions for prisoners on remand are far worse now than they were a hundred years ago.'

'I mean, Mr Rumpole,' the Graveyard explained, with a superhuman effort at patience, as though to a half-wit, 'it's intolerable that you should address me in such a manner. I cannot imagine any circumstances in which I should need your so-called eloquence to be exercised on my behalf.' You never know, I thought, you never know, old darling. But the mournful voice of judicial authority carried on. 'No doubt the Prosecution opposes bail. Do you oppose bail, Mr Harvey Wimple?'

Thus addressed, the eager, sandy-haired youth from the Crown Prosecution Service, who spoke very fast, as though he wanted to get the whole painful ordeal over as quickly as possible, jabbered, 'Oppose it? Oh, yes, my Lord. Absolutely. Utterly and entirely opposed. Utterly.' He looked startled when the Judge asked, 'On what precise grounds do you oppose bail, Mr Wimple?' But he managed the quick-fire answer, 'Grounds that, if left at liberty, another offence might be committed. Or other offences. By the defendant Timson, my Lord. By him, you see?'

'Do you hear that, Mr Rumpole?' The Judge re-orchestrated the piece for more solemn music. 'If he is set at liberty, your client might commit another offence or, quite possibly, offences.'

And then, losing my patience, I said what I had been longing to say on some similar bail application for years. 'Of course, he might,' I began. 'Every man, woman and child in England might commit an offence. Is your Lordship suggesting we keep them all permanently banged up on the off-chance? It's just not on, that's all.'

'Mr Rumpole. What is not "on", as you so curiously put it?' The Judge spoke with controlled fury. It was a good speech, but I had picked the wrong audience. 'Banging up the innocent, my Lord.' I let him have the full might of the Rumpole eloquent outrage. 'With a couple of psychopaths and their own chamber-pots. For an indefinite period while the wheels of justice grind to a halt in a traffic jam of cases.'

'Do try to control yourself, Mr Rumpole. Conditions in prisons are a matter for the Home Office.'

'Oh, my Lord, I'm so sorry. I forgot they're of no interest to judges who refuse bail and have never spent a single night locked up without the benefit of a water closet.'

At which point, Graves decided to terminate the proceedings and, to no one's surprise, he announced that bail was refused and that the unfortunate Tony Timson, who had never committed a violent crime, should languish in Brixton until his trial. I was making for the fresh air and a small and soothing cigar when the Judge called me back with 'Just one moment, Mr Rumpole. I think I should add that I find the way that this matter has been argued before me quite lamentable, and very far from being in the best traditions of the Bar. I may have to report the personal and improper nature of your argument to proper authorities.' At which point he smiled in a nauseating manner at the young man from the Crown Prosecution Service and said, 'Thank you for *your* able assistance, Mr Harvey Wimple.'

★

'Had a good day, Rumpole?' She Who Must Be Obeyed asked me on my return to the mansion flat.

'Thank God, Hilda,' I told her as I poured a glass of Pommeroy's Very Ordinary, 'for your wonderful sense of humour!'

'Rumpole, look at your face!' She appeared to be smiling brightly at my distress.

'I prefer not to. I have no doubt it is marked with tragedy.' I raised a glass and tried to drown at least a few of my sorrows.

'Whatever's happened?' She Who Must Be Obeyed was unusually sympathetic, from which I should have guessed that she had formulated some master plan. I refilled my glass and told her:

> 'I could a tale unfold', Hilda, 'whose lightest word
> Would harrow up thy soul, freeze thy young blood,
> Make thy two eyes, like stars, start from their spheres,
> Thy knotted and combined locks to part,
> And each particular hair to stand on end,
> Like quills upon the fretful porpentine: . . .'

'Oh come on, I bet it wouldn't.' My wife was sceptical. 'What you need, Rumpole, is a change!'

'I need a change from Mr Justice Graves.' And then I played into her hands, for she looked exceptionally pleased when I added, 'For two pins I'd get on a banana boat and sail away into the sunset.'

'Oh, Rumpole! I'm so glad that's what you'd do. For two pins. You know what I've been thinking? We need a second honeymoon.'

'The first one was bad enough.' You see I was still gloomy.

'It wouldn't've been, Rumpole, if you hadn't thought we could manage two weeks in the South of France on your fees from one short robbery.'

'It was all I had about me at the time,' I reminded her. 'Anyway, you shouldn't've ordered lobster.'

'What's the point of a honeymoon,' Hilda asked, 'if you can't order lobster?'

'Of course, you can *order* it. Nothing to stop you ordering,' I conceded. 'You just shouldn't complain when we have to leave three days early and sit up all night in the train from Marseilles. With a couple of soldiers asleep on top of us.'

'On our second honeymoon I shall order lobster.' And then she added the fatal words, 'When we're on the cruise.'

'On the *what?*' I hoped that I couldn't believe my ears.

'The cruise! There's still a bit of Aunt Tedda's money left.' As I have pointed out, Hilda's relations are constantly interfering in our married lives. 'I've booked up for it.'

'No, Hilda. Absolutely not!' I was firm as only I know how to be. 'I know exactly what it'd be like. Bingo on the boat deck!'

'We need to get away, Rumpole. To look at ourselves.'

'Do you honestly think that's wise?' It seemed a rash project.

'Moonlight on the Med.' She Who Must became lyrical. 'The sound of music across the water. Stars. You and I by the rail. *Finding* each other, after a long time.'

'But you can find me quite easily,' I pointed out. 'You just shout "Rumpole!" and there I am.'

'You said you'd sail away into the sunset. For two pins,' she reminded me.

'A figure of speech, Hilda. A pure figure of speech! Let me make this perfectly clear. There is no power on this earth that's going to get me on a cruise.'

During the course of a long and memorable career at the Bar, I have fought many doughty opponents and won many famous victories; but I have never, when all the evidence has been heard and the arguments are over, secured a verdict against She Who Must Be Obeyed. It's true that I have, from time to time, been able to mitigate her stricter sentences. I have argued successfully for alternatives to custody or time to pay. But I have never had an outright win against her and, from the moment she suggested we sail away, until the time when I found myself in our cabin on the fairly good ship S.S. *Boadicea*, steaming out from Southampton, I knew, with a sickening certainty, that I was on to a loser. Hilda reviewed her application for a cruise every hour of the days that we were together, and at most hours of the night, until I finally threw in the towel on the grounds that the sooner we put out to sea the sooner we should be back on dry land.

The *Boadicea* was part of a small cruise line and, instead of flying its passengers to some southern port, it sailed from England to Gibraltar and thence to several Mediterranean destinations before returning home. The result was that some of the first days were to be spent sailing through grey and troubled waters. Picture us then in our cabin as we left harbour. I was looking out of a porthole at a small area of open deck which terminated in a rail and the sea. Hilda, tricked out in white ducks, took a yachting cap out of her hat box and tried it on in front of the mirror. 'What on earth did you bring that for?' I asked her. 'Are you expecting to steer the thing?'

'I expect to enter into the spirit of life on shipboard, Rumpole,' she told me briskly. 'And you'd be well advised to do the same. I'm sure we'll make heaps of friends. Such nice people go on cruises. Haven't you been watching them?'

'Yes.' And I turned, not very cheerfully, back to the porthole. As I did so, a terrible vision met my eyes. The stretch of deck was no longer empty. A grey-haired man in a blue blazer was standing by the rail and, as I watched, Mr Justice Graves turned in my direction and all doubts about our fellow passengers, and all hopes for a carefree cruise, were laid to rest.

'"Angels and ministers of grace defend us!" It can't be. But it *is*!'

'What is, Rumpole? Do pull yourself together.'

'If you knew what I'd seen, you wouldn't babble of pulling myself together, Hilda. It's *him*! The ghastly old Gravestone in person.' At which I dragged out my suitcase and started to throw my possessions back into it. 'He's come on the cruise with us!'

'Courage, Rumpole' – Hilda watched me with a certain contempt – 'I remember you telling me, is the first essential in an advocate.'

'Courage, yes, but not total lunacy. Not self-destruction.

Life at the Bar may have its risks, but no legal duty compels me to spend two weeks shut up in a floating hotel with Mr Justice Deathshead.'

'I don't know what you think you're going to do about it.' She was calmly hanging up her clothes whilst I repacked mine. 'It's perfectly simple, Hilda,' I told her, 'I shall abandon ship!'

When I got up on the deck, there was, fortunately, no further sign of Graves, but a ship's officer, whom I later discovered to be the Purser, was standing by the rail and I approached him, doing my best to control my panic.

'I've just discovered,' I told him, 'I'm allergic to graves. I mean, I'm allergic to boats. It would be quite unsafe for me to travel. A dose of sea-sickness could prove fatal!'

'But, sir,' the purser protested. 'We're only just out of port.'

'I know. So you could let me off, couldn't you? I've just had terrible news.'

'You're welcome to telephone, sir.'

'No, I'm afraid that wouldn't help.'

'And if it's really serious we could fly you back from our next stop.' And he added the terrible words, 'We'll be at Gibraltar in three days.'

Gibraltar in three days! Three days banged up on shipboard with the most unappetizing High Court judge since Jeffreys hung up his wig! I lay on my bed in our cabin as the land slid away from us and Hilda read out the treats on offer: ' "Daily sweepstake on the ship's position. Constant video entertainment and films twice nightly. Steam-bath, massage and beauty treatment. Exercise rooms and fully equipped gymnasium" – I think I'll have a steam-bath, Rumpole – "First fancy-dress ball immediately before landfall at Gib. Live it up in an evening of ocean fantasy. Lecture by Howard Swainton, world-famous, best-selling mystery novelist, on 'How I Think Up My Plots'." '

'Could he think up one on how to drown a judge?'

'Oh, do cheer up, Rumpole. Don't be so morbid. At five thirty this evening it's Captain Orde's Welcome Aboard Folks cocktail party, followed by a dinner dance at eight forty-five. I can wear my little black dress.'

'The Captain's cocktail party?' I was by no means cheered up. 'To exchange small talk and Twiglets with Mr Justice Deathshead. No, thank you very much. I shall lie doggo in the cabin until Gibraltar.'

'You can't possibly do that,' She told me. 'What am I going to tell everyone?'

'Tell them I've gone down with a nasty infection. No, the Judge might take it into his head to visit the sick. He might want to come and gloat over me with grapes. Tell them I'm dead. Or say a last-minute case kept me in England.'

'Rumpole, aren't you being just the tiniest bit silly about this?'

But I stuck desperately to my guns. 'Remember, Hilda,' I begged her, 'if anyone asks, say you're here entirely on your own.' I had not forgotten that Graves and She had met at the Sam Ballard–Marguerite Plumstead wedding, and if the Judge caught sight of her, he might suspect that where Hilda was could Rumpole be far behind? I was prepared to take every precaution against discovery.

During many of the ensuing events I was, as I have said, lying doggo. I therefore have to rely on Mrs Rumpole's account of many of the matters that transpired on board the good ship *Boadicea*, and I have reconstructed the following pages from her evidence which was, as always, completely reliable. (I wish, sometimes, that She Who Must Be Obeyed would indulge in something as friendly as a lie. As, for instance, 'I do think you're marvellous, Rumpole,' or 'Please don't lose any weight, I like you so much as you are!') Proceedings opened at the Captain's cocktail party when Hilda found herself part of a group consisting of the world-famed mystery writer, Howard Swainton, whom she described vividly as 'a rather bouncy and yappy little Yorkshire terrier of a man'; a willowy American named Linda Milsom, whom he modestly referred to as his secretary; a tall, balding, fresh-complexioned, owlish-looking cleric wearing gold-rimmed glasses, a dog-collar and an old tweed suit, who introduced himself as Bill Britwell; and his wife, Mavis, a rotund grey-haired lady with a face which

might once have been pretty and was now friendly and cheerful. These people were in the act of getting to know each other
when the Reverend Bill made the serious mistake of asking
Howard Swainton what he did for a living.

'You mean you don't know what Howard does?' Linda, the
secretary, said, as her boss was recovering from shock. 'You
ought to walk into the gift shop. The shelves are just groaning
with his best-sellers. Rows and rows of them, aren't there,
Howard?'

'They seem to know what goes with the public,' Swainton
agreed. 'My motto is keep 'em guessing and give 'em a bit of
sex and a spot of mayhem every half-dozen pages. I'm here to
research a new story about a mysterious disappearance on a
cruise. I call it *Absence of Body*. Rather a neat title that, don't
you think?'

'Howard's won two Golden Daggers,' Linda explained. 'And
Time magazine called him "The Genius of Evil".'

'Let's say, I'm a writer with a taste for a mystery.' Swainton
was ostentatiously modest.

'I suppose' – Bill Britwell beamed round at the company –
'that since I've been concerned with the greatest mystery of
all, I've lost interest in detective stories. I do apologize.'

'Oh, really?' Swainton asked. 'And what's the greatest mystery?'

'I think Bill means,' his wife explained, 'since he's gone into
the Church.'

'What I've always wanted,' the Reverend Bill told them,
'after a lifetime in insurance.'

'So you've joined the awkward squad, have you?' Swainton
was a fervent supporter of the Conservative Party on television
chat shows, and as such regarded the Church of England as a
kind of Communist cell.

'I'm sorry?' Bill blinked, looking genuinely puzzled.

'The Archbishop's army of Reverend Pinkos' – Swainton
warmed to his subject – 'always preaching morality to the
Government. I can't think why you chaps can't mind your
own business.'

'Morality *is* my business now, isn't it?' Bill was still looking irrepressibly cheerful. 'Of course, it used to be insurance. I came to all the best things late in life. The Church and Mavis.' At which he put an arm round his wife's comfortable shoulder.

'We're on our honeymoon.' Hilda told me that the elderly Mrs Britwell sounded quite girlish as she said this.

'Pleasure combined with business,' her husband explained. 'We're only going as far as Malta, where I've landed a job as padre to the Anglican community.'

And then Hilda, intoxicated by a glass of champagne and the prospect of foreign travel, confessed that she was also on a honeymoon, although it was a second one in her case.

'Oh, really?' Swainton asked with a smile which Hilda found patronizing. 'And which is your husband, Mrs –?'

'Rumpole. Hilda Rumpole. My husband is an extremely well-known barrister. You may have read his name in the papers?'

'I don't spend much time reading,' Swainton told her. 'I'm really too busy writing. And where is your Mr Rumbold?'

'Oh, well,' Hilda had to confess, 'he's not here.'

'You mean?' – Swainton was smiling and inviting the group to enjoy the joke – 'you're having a second honeymoon with a husband who isn't here?'

'No. Well. You see something rather unexpected came up.'

'So, now' – and Swainton could barely conceal his mirth – 'you're having a second honeymoon on your own?'

But Hilda had to excuse herself and hurry away, as she had seen, through the window of the saloon in which the Captain's cocktail party was taking place, stationed on a small patch of windy and rain-beaten deck, Rumpole signalling urgently for supplies.

What had happened was that, being greatly in need of sustenance and a nerve-cooling drink in my Ducal Class dug-out (second only to the real luxury of Sovereign Class), I had rung repeatedly for a steward with absolutely no result. When I telephoned, I was told there would be a considerable delay as the staff were very busy with the Captain's cocktail party. 'The Captain's cock up, you mean,' I said harshly, and made my way to the outskirts of the port (or perhaps the starboard)

deck, where it took me considerable time to attract Hilda's
attention through the window. 'Make your mind up, Rumpole,' She said when she came out. 'Are you in hiding or aren't
you?' and 'Why don't you come in and meet a famous author?'

'Are you mad? *He's* in there.' I could see the skeletal figure
of Graves in the privileged party around Captain Orde. He
was no doubt entertaining them with an account of the Rumpole clientele he had kept under lock and key.

'Really,' Hilda protested, 'this is no way to spend a honeymoon. Mr Swainton looked as though he thought I'd done you
in or something. Apparently he's doing research on a new
book called *Absence of Body*. He says it's all about someone
who disappears during a cruise.'

'Hilda,' I said, 'couldn't you do a bit of research on a glass
or two of champagne? And on what they've got on those little
bits of toast?'

So She Who Must Be Obeyed, who has her tender moments,
went off in search of provisions. I watched her go back into the
saloon and make for the table where the guzzle and sluice were
laid out. As she did so, she passed Mr Justice Graves. I saw
him turn his head to look at her in a stricken fashion, then he
muttered some apology to the Captain and was off out of the
room with the sudden energy of a young gazelle.

It was then I realized that not only was Rumpole fleeing the
Judge, the Judge was fleeing Rumpole.

Back in the cabin, Hilda put on her dress for the dinner dance
and added the finishing touches to her *maquillage*, whilst I,
wearing bedroom slippers and smoking a small cigar, paced
my confinement like a caged tiger. 'And you'll really like the
Britwells,' she was saying. 'He's going to be a parson in
Malta. They're quite elderly, but so much in love. Do come up
to dinner, Rumpole. Then we could dance together.'

'We did that on our first honeymoon!' I reminded her. 'And
it wasn't an astonishing success, so far as I can remember.
Anyway, do you think I want Gravestone to catch me dancing?'

'I don't know why you're so frightened of him, quite

honestly. You don't exactly cower in front of him in Court
from all you tell me.'

'Of course I don't cower!' I explained. 'I can treat the old
Deathshead with lofty disdain in front of a jury! I can thunder
my disapproval at him on a bail application. I have no fear of
the man in the exercise of my profession. It's his friendship I
dread.'

'His friendship?'

'Oh, yes. That is why, Hilda, I have fled Judge Graves
down the nights and down the days.' And here I gave my wife
a heady draught of Francis Thompson:

> 'I fled Him, down the arches of the years;
> I fled Him, down the labyrinthine ways
> Of my own mind; and in the mist of tears
> I hid from Him, and under running laughter.'

'Well, there's not much running laughter for me' – Hilda
was displeased – 'going on a second honeymoon without a husband.'

When Hilda was made-up, powdered and surrounded with
an appropriate fragrance, she left me just as the Britwells were
emerging from the cabin opposite. They were also in evening-
dress and were apparently so delighted to see my wife that
they cordially invited her to inspect the amenities which they
enjoyed. As the Britwell berth seemed in every way a carbon
copy of that provided for the Rumpoles, Hilda found it a little
difficult to keep up an interesting commentary or show any
genuine surprise at the beauty and convenience of their quarters. At a loss for conversation she looked at their dressing-
table where, she told me, two large photographs in heavy
silver frames had been set up. The first was a recent wedding
portrait of the Reverend and Mrs Britwell standing proudly
together, arm-in-arm, outside a village church. The bride was
not in white, which would have been surprising at her age, but
she wore what Hilda called a 'rather ordinary little suit and a
hat with a veil'. The other was a studio portrait of a pretty,
smiling young girl in a sequined evening-gown. She asked if
that were Bill's daughter, to which he laughed and said, 'Not

exactly.' Before she could inquire further I whistled to Hilda from our door across the corridor as I had an urgent piece of advice for her.

'For God's sake, if you see the Judge,' I warned her through a chink in our doorway, 'don't encourage the blighter. Please, don't dream of dancing with him!'

I was not in the least reassured when She answered, 'You never know what I might dream of, Rumpole.'

Hilda didn't dance with the Judge that night. Indeed Mr Injustice Graves didn't even put in an appearance at the function and was busily engaged in lying as low as Rumpole himself.

Most of the dancing was done by the Britwells, who whirled and twirled and chasséed around the place with the expertise of a couple of ballroom champions. 'Aren't they good?' Hilda was playing an enthusiastic gooseberry to Swainton and his secretary, Linda. 'Don't you think he dances rather *too* well?' Swainton sat with his head on one side and looked suspiciously at the glittering scene.

'I don't know exactly what you mean.' Hilda was puzzled, but Linda told her, 'Howard looks below the surface of life. That's his great talent!'

When the husband and wife team came off the floor, perspiring gently after the tango, Howard Swainton repeated, 'We were saying you dance unusually well, Britwell, for a vicar.'

'Don't forget I wasn't always a vicar. I spent most of my life in insurance.'

'Oh, yes. I remember now. You told us that.' Howard Swainton seemed to be making a mental note.

Hilda said, 'Do men in insurance dance well?'

'Better than vicars!' Mrs Britwell was laughing. The elderly newly-weds did seem an ideally happy couple.

'I was in insurance and Mavis ran a secretarial agency.' Bill was telling the story of his life. 'Of course, I married her for her money.' He raised his glass of wine to his wife and drank her health.

'And I married him for his dancing!' Mavis was still

laughing. 'Why don't you let Bill give you a slow foxtrot, Mrs Rumpole?'

'Oh, that would be very nice' – Hilda had not had a great deal of practice at the foxtrot – 'but not this evening, perhaps.' She was looking anxiously about the room, a fact which the sleuth Swainton immediately noticed. 'Are you looking for someone?' he asked.

'Oh. Oh, well. A judge, actually. I happen to have met him before. I'm sure he was at the Captain's cocktail party but I don't seem to see him here.'

'A judge?' Swainton was interested.

'Oh, yes. He used to be just down the Bailey, you know,' Hilda told them. 'But now he's been put up to the High Court. Scarlet and ermine. A red judge. Sir Gerald Graves.'

'Graves?' Howard Swainton was smiling. 'That's a rather mournful name.' But the Reverend Bill didn't join in the laughter. He made a sudden movement and knocked over his glass of red wine. It spread across the tablecloth, Hilda told me, in words I was to remember, like blood.

> Swiftly, swiftly flew the ship,
> Yet she sailed softly too:
> Sweetly, sweetly blew the breeze –
> On me alone it blew.

It blew on me alone because I was taking a solitary stroll in the early morning before the waking hour of the most energetic judge. The good ship *Boadicea* clove the grey waters, seagulls chattered and soared in the sky behind us, hoping for scraps, and I trod carefully in the shadows of boats and deck buildings.

> Like one, who on a lonesome road
> Doth walk in fear and dread,
> And having once turned round walks on,
> And turns no more his head;
> Because he knows, a frightful judge
> Doth close behind him tread.

Coleridge's memorable lines were sounding in my ears as I

looked fearfully around me and then, almost too late, spotted an energetic old party in a blue blazer out for a constitutional. I ducked into the doorway of the Ladies Health and Beauty Salon, while Graves stopped and peered furtively into the window of the room where breakfast was being served to the Ducal passengers.

I know that he did this from the account that Hilda gave me later. She was at a table with Swainton and Linda Milsom, getting stuck into the coffee and eggs and bacon, when she saw the judicial features peering in at her. She only had time to say, 'Ah. There he is!' before the old darling vanished, and she said, 'He's gone!' Bill Britwell joined them with a plate of cornflakes he'd been fetching from a central table. 'Who's gone?' he asked.

'Mr Justice Graves. He must be an early bird.' The Reverend Bill sat and ate his breakfast and Swainton asked how Mavis, who was noticeably absent, was that morning.

'Well, not too good, I'm afraid. Mavis isn't quite the ticket.'

'The what?' Linda Milsom seemed to be listening to a foreign language.

'Not quite up to snuff.' Bill did his best to explain his meaning.

'He means she's sick,' Howard Swainton translated for Linda's benefit and his secretary looked deeply sympathetic. 'What, on her honeymoon?'

'Do tell her we're all so sorry for her.' Swainton was also solicitous, and then he turned his attention to Hilda and asked her, with obvious scepticism, 'And how's *your* husband, Mrs Rumpole? Have you heard from him lately?'

'Oh, yes, I have,' Hilda told him.

'Still busy, is he?'

'Well, he's on the move all the time.'

'Gee, I hope your wife gets better,' Linda was saying to Bill Britwell in a caring sort of way. 'I've got these great homoeopathic capsules. I could drop them into your cabin.'

'That's very kind of you but,' Bill told her firmly, 'I think she'd like to be left alone for the moment.'

'Such a terrible shame!' Hilda was also sympathetic. 'And she seemed so full of life last night.'

'Yes, that's exactly what I thought.' Howard Swainton was looking at the Reverend Bill as though he were an interesting piece of research and he repeated Hilda's words, 'So full of life!'

After funking a meeting with Hilda in the breakfast room, it seemed that Mr Injustice settled himself down in a deck-chair, with a rug over his knees, in a kind of passage on the upper deck between the side of the gymnasium and a suspended boat into which his Lordship, in time of trouble, ought, I suspected, to be ready to jump ahead of the women and children. There he sat, immersed in *Murder Most Foul*, the latest Howard Swainton, when, glancing up after the discovery of the fourth corpse, he saw Hilda standing at the end of the passage. His immediate reaction was to raise the alleged work of literature over his face, but he was too late. My wife gave a glad cry of 'Mr Justice Graves!' And, advancing towards him with indescribable foolhardiness, added, 'It is Sir Gerald Graves, isn't it? Hilda Rumpole. We met at Sam Ballard's wedding. You remember he got spliced to the ex-matron of the Old Bailey and astonished us all.' Whereupon she sat down in one of the empty chairs beside him and seemed prepared for a long chat.

'Mrs Rumpole' – Hilda, who is always a reliable witness, alleges that the old Deathshead here 'smiled quite charmingly' – 'of course, I remember. I had no idea you were on the boat.' And he added nervously, 'Are you here on your own?'

'Well, yes. On my own. In a sort of way.'

'Oh, I see. Oh, good!' His Lordship was enormously relieved, but then, Hilda told me, a sort of hunted look came into his eyes as he inquired anxiously, 'Your husband isn't about?'

'Not about? No. Well. Definitely not about. Of course, Horace's got a very busy practice,' Hilda explained. 'I believe you had him before you quite recently. I don't know if you remember?'

'Your husband's appearances before me, Mrs Rumpole,' Graves assured her, 'are quite unforgettable.'

'How sweet of you to say so.' She was gratified.

'In fact, we judges are all agreed,' Mr Justice added, 'there's simply no advocate at the Criminal Bar in the least like Horace Rumpole.'

'A "one off". Is that what you'd say about him?'

'Without doubt, a "one off". We're all agreed about that.'

'I'm sure you're right. That may be why I married him. He's a bit of a "one off" as a husband.' Hilda began, strangely enough, to treat the old Gravestone as a confidant.

'Forgive me, Mrs Rumpole' – Graves clearly didn't want to be let into the secrets of the Rumpole marriage – 'I have absolutely no idea what Rumpole is like as a husband.'

'No. Silly of me!' And here I believe that She laid a friendly hand on the old party's arm. 'Of course, you don't know what it's like to go on one honeymoon with him, let alone two.'

'No idea at all, I'm delighted to say.'

'But I'll tell him all the nice things you've said about him. About him being "unforgettable" and a "one off" and so on.'

'You'll tell him?' His Lordship's hunted expression returned.

'When I next see him.'

'Oh, yes, of course.' And he suggested hopefully, 'Back in England?'

'Or wherever. It may encourage him to break cover.'

'To do *what*, Mrs Rumpole?' There was a distinct note of panic in the judicial question.

'Well, to come out into the open a little more. Would it surprise you to know, Rumpole's really a very shy and retiring sort of person?'

By this time the shy and retiring Rumpole had outstayed his welcome in the entrance hall of the Ladies Health and Beauty Salon and I began to make my way back to the safety of our cabin, taking cover, from time to time, in such places as the children's play area (where I might have been spotted peering anxiously out from behind a giant cut-out clown) and the deck quoits' storage cupboard. Then, getting near to home, I glanced down a passage between a building and a boat and saw Hilda seated on a deck-chair, her knees covered with a rug. The back of the hanging boat prevented me seeing her companion, until it was far too late. 'Hilda!' I called. 'Yes, Rumpole. Here I am,' came the answer. And then, as I moved towards her, the sight I dreaded most hoved into view. We were forced together and there was no way in which a meeting between old enemies could be avoided. What was remarkable was that the Deathshead greeted me with apparent *bonhomie*.

'Rumpole!' He didn't rise from his seat but otherwise he was cordial. 'My dear fellow! This *is* a surprise. Your good lady told me that you weren't about.'

'Well,' I admitted, 'I haven't been about. Up to now.'

'What's up, old chap? Not got your sea legs yet? I always thought of you as a bit of a landlubber, I must say. Come along, then. Sit yourself down.'

I did so with a good deal of trepidation on the seaward side of She Who Must Be Obeyed.

'The Judge has been sweet enough to tell me that your appearances before him were "unforgettable",' Hilda said.

'Oh, yes? How terribly sweet of him,' I agreed.

'And like no one else.'

'And I honestly meant it, my dear old fellow,' Graves assured me. 'You are absolutely *sui generis*.'

'To name but a few?'

'Even if you have so very little Latin. What was the last case you did before me?'

'It was an application for bail.' And I added, with heavy irony, 'With the greatest respect, my Lord.'

'Of course it was!' Graves seemed to recall the incident with delight. 'You should have been there, Mrs Rumpole. We had great fun over that, didn't we, old fellow?'

'Oh, yes,' I assured him. 'It was a riot. Tony Timson's been laughing so much he could hardly slop out in Brixton.'

'He will have his joke, won't he, Mrs Rumpole?' The Judge's cheerfulness was undiminished. 'Your Horace is a great one for his little joke. Well, now I've met you both, there's no reason why we shouldn't have a drink together. After dinner in the Old Salts' bar at, shall we say, five minutes past nine exactly?'

At which point, the Gravestone took up his copy of *Murder*

Most Foul and left us to the sound of my, I hope derisory, 'If your Lordship pleases.' When he had withdrawn, I turned a tragic face to Hilda. 'The Old Salts' bar,' I repeated. 'At five past nine. *Now* look what you've done!'

'I had to flush you out somehow, Rumpole,' She said, unreasonably I felt. 'I had to get you to take part in your own honeymoon.'

But my mind was on grimmer business. 'I told you, it's the awful threat of his friendship. That's what I dread!'

That evening, in the privacy of our cabin, Hilda read out an account of the delights of the Old Salts' bar from the ship's brochure: '"Tonight and every night after dinner,"' she told me, '"Gloria de la Haye sings her golden oldies. Trip down Memory Lane and sing along with Gloria, or hear her inimitable way of rendering your special requests."'

'And that's not the only drawback of the Old Salts' bar,' I added. 'What about "Stiff sentences I have passed", the long-playing record by Mr Justice Gravestone?'

'Oh, do cheer up, Rumpole. We've got each other.'

'Next time you decide to go on a honeymoon, old thing,' I warned her, 'would you mind leaving him behind?'

'Poor Mavis Britwell getting sick like that!' Hilda's mind flitted to another subject. 'She'll be missing all the fun.'

'Tonight,' I told her, having regard to the rendezvous ahead, 'the sick are the lucky ones.'

When we left the cabin on our way to dinner, Hilda's mind was still on the misfortunes of Mavis, and she knocked on the door of the cabin opposite with the idea of visiting the invalid. After some delay, the Reverend Bill called from behind the door that he wouldn't be a minute. Then the little man I was to discover to be Howard Swainton, the famous author, came bouncing down the corridor, carrying a bunch of red roses and a glossy paperback of his own writing. 'Visiting the sick, are we?' he said. 'We all seem to have the same idea.'

'Well, yes. This is my husband.' Hilda introduced me and Swainton raised his eyebrows higher than I would have believed possible.

'Is it, really?' he said. 'I *am* surprised.'

'And this is Mr Howard Swainton,' Hilda went on, undeterred, '*the* Howard Swainton.'

'How do you do. I'm *the* Horace Rumpole,' I told him.

'Your wife says you're a barrister.' Swainton seemed to find the notion somewhat absurd, as though I were a conjuror or an undertaker's mute. 'I am an Old Bailey hack,' I admitted.

'And we've all been wondering when you'd turn up.' Swainton was still smiling, and I asked him, 'Why? Are you in some sort of trouble?'

Before matters could further deteriorate, the vicar opened his cabin door and Hilda once again performed the introductions. 'I'm afraid Mavis is still feeling a little groggy,' Bill Britwell told us. 'She just wants to rest quietly.' Hilda said she understood perfectly, but Howard Swainton, saying, 'I come bearing gifts!' and calling out 'Mavis!', invaded the room remorselessly, although Bill protested again, 'I'm not sure she feels like visitors.'

We followed, somewhat helplessly, in Howard's wake as he forged ahead. The woman whom I took to be Mavis Britwell was lying in the bed furthest from the door. The clothes were pulled up around her and only the top of her head was visible from where we stood. Howard Swainton continued his advance, saying, 'Flowers for the poor invalid and my latest in paperback!' I saw him put his gifts down on the narrow table between the two beds, and, in doing so, he knocked over a glass of water which spilled on to Mavis's bed. She put out an arm automatically to protect herself and I couldn't help seeing what Swainton must also have noticed: the sick Mrs Britwell had apparently retired to bed fully dressed.

'Oh, dear. How terribly clumsy of me!' Swainton was dabbing at the wet bed with his handkerchief. But Mavis had drawn the covers around her again and still lay with her face turned away from us. 'Perhaps you could go now?' her husband said with admirable patience. 'Mavis does want to be perfectly quiet.' 'Yes, of course.' Swainton was apologetic. 'I *do* understand. Come along, the Rumpoles.'

We left the cabin then and Swainton soon parted from us to collect his secretary for dinner.

'She was dressed,' Hilda said when we were left alone. 'She was wearing her blouse and cardie.'

'Perhaps the Reverend Bill fancies her in bed in a cardie.'

'Don't be disgusting, Rumpole!' And then Hilda told me something else she had noticed. The two heavy silver-framed photographs, which had stood on the dressing-table when she first visited the Britwells' cabin, had disappeared. She Who Must Be Obeyed has a dead eye for detail and would have risen to great heights in the Criminal Investigation Department.

The Old Salts' bar was liberally decorated with lifebelts, lobster nets, ships in bottles, charts, compasses and waitresses with sailor hats. There was a grand piano at which a small, pink-faced, bespectacled accompanist played as Miss Gloria de la Haye sang her way down Memory Lane. Gloria, a tall woman in a sequined dress, who made great play with a green chiffon handkerchief, must have been in her sixties, and her red curls no doubt owed little to nature. However, she had kept her figure and her long-nosed, wide-mouthed face, although probably never beautiful, was intelligent and humorous. She was singing 'Smoke Gets in Your Eyes' and, with dinner over, we were awaiting our assignation with Gravestone in the company of Bill Britwell, Linda Milsom and Howard Swainton – Mrs Mavis Britwell still being, her husband insisted, unwell and confined to her room. Hilda was giving an account of what she would have it thought of as a happy meeting with Sir Gerald Graves.

'Is he someone you've crossed swords with?' Swainton asked me. 'In the Courts?'

'Swords? Nothing so gentlemanly. Let's say, chemical weapons. The old darling's summing up is pure poison gas.'

'Oh, go on, Rumpole!' Hilda was having none of this. 'He was absolutely charming to you on the boat deck.'

'What's the matter with the claret, Hilda? Glued to the table? – That was just part of his diabolical cunning.'

'Rumpole, are you sure you haven't had enough?' She was reluctant to pass the bottle.

'Of course, I'm sure. Coping with his lethal Lordship without a drink inside you is like having an operation without an anaesthetic.'

At which, dead on time, Mr Injustice berthed himself at our table, saying, 'You're remarkably punctual, Rumpole.'

'Oh, Judge! Everyone' – Hilda introduced the old faceache as though she owned him – 'this is Sir Gerald Graves. Howard Swainton, *the* Howard Swainton, Linda, his personal assistant, and Bill Britwell, the Reverend Bill. Sir Gerald Graves.'

'Five past nine exactly.' The Judge had been studying his watch during these preliminaries and I weighed in with 'Silence! The Court's in session.'

'Well, now. Our second night at sea. I'm sure we're all enjoying it?' Graves's face contorted itself into an unusual and wintry smile.

'Best time we've had since the Luton Axe Killing, my Lord,' I told him.

'What was that you said, Rumpole?'

'It's absolutely thrilling, my Lord,' I translated, a little more loudly.

'I'm afraid' – the Reverend Bill got up – 'you'll have to excuse me.'

'Oh. So soon?'

'Can't you relax, Bill? Forget your troubles.' Swainton tried to detain him. 'Enjoy a drink with a real live judge.'

'I must get back to Mavis.'

'It's his wife, Judge. She hasn't been well,' Howard Swainton said with apparent concern. And as Gloria switched from 'Smoke Gets in Your Eyes' to 'Thanks for the Memory', Bill agreed, 'Well, not quite the ticket.'

'I'm sorry to hear it.' Graves was sympathetic. 'Well, I do hope she's able to join us tomorrow.'

'I'm sure she hopes so too.' Swainton was smiling as he said it. 'Give her all our best wishes. Tell her the Judge is thinking of her.'

'Yes. Yes, I will. That's very kind.' And Bill Britwell retreated from the Old Salts' bar saying, 'Please! Don't let me break up the party.' Whereupon Swainton came, like the terrier

Hilda had described, bounding and yapping into the conversation with 'I say, Judge. Horace Rumpole was just talking about your little scraps in Court.'

'Oh, yes? We do have a bit of fun from time to time. Don't we, Rumpole?' Graves smiled contentedly but Swainton started to stir the legal brew with obvious relish. 'That wasn't exactly how Rumpole put it,' he said. 'Of course, I do understand. Barristers are the natural enemies of judges. Judges and, well, my lot, detective-story writers. We want answers. We want to ferret out the truth. In the end we want to tell the world who's guilty!'

'Well put, if I may say so, Mr Swainton!' Graves had clearly found a kindred spirit. 'In your tales the mysteries are always solved and the criminal pays –'

'Enormous royalties!' I chipped in, 'I have no doubt.'

'His heavy debt to society!' Graves corrected me and then continued his love affair with the bouncy little novelist. 'You always find the answer, Swainton. That's what makes your books such a thumping good read.'

Gloria had stopped singing now and was refreshing herself at the bar. Her plump accompanist was going round the tables with a pad and pencil, asking for requests for the singer's next number.

'Thank you, Judge. Most kind of you.' Howard Swainton was clearly not above saluting the judicial backside. 'But the Horace Rumpoles of this world always want to raise a verbal smokescreen of "reasonable doubt". Tactics, you see. They do it so the guilty can slide away to safety.'

'*Touché*, Rumpole! Hasn't Mr Swainton rather got you there?' Graves was clearly delighted by the author's somewhat tormented prose.

'Not *touché* in the least!' I told him. 'Anyway, I've heard it so many times before from those who want to convict someone, anyone, and don't care very much who it is. There speaks the voice of the Old Bill.'

'But I don't understand. His name's Howard.' Miss Linda Milsom, however rapid her shorthand, was not exactly quick on the uptake.

'Detective Inspector Swainton' – I was now in full flood – 'distrusts defending counsel and wants all trials to take place in the friendly neighbourhood nick. He's so keen on getting at the truth that, if he can't find it, he'll invent it – like the end of a detective story.'

'Is this how he goes on in Court?' Swainton asked with a smile to the Judge, who assured him, 'Oh, all the time.'

'Then you have my heartfelt sympathy, Judge,' Swainton said, and I could scarcely withhold my tears for his poor old Lordship. 'Thank you,' Graves said. 'Tell me, Swainton, are you working on some wonderful new mystery to delight us?'

Then my attention was distracted by the little accompanist, who asked me if I'd care to write down a request for Gloria. I looked across at the tall, sequined woman, apparently downing a large port and lemon, and I was whisked back down the decades to my carefree bachelor days. I was leaving Equity Court, when the Chambers were then run by Hilda's Daddy, C. H. Wystan, for a chop and a pint of stout at the Cock tavern, and had decided to give myself a treat by dropping in to the Old Metropolitan music hall, long since defunct, in the Edgware Road. There I might see jugglers and adagio dancers and Max Miller, the 'Cheeky Chappie', and . . . At this point I scribbled a song title on the accompanist's pad. He looked at it, I thought, with some surprise, and carried it back to Gloria. And then, bringing me painfully back to the present, I heard Swainton tell us the plot of his latest masterpiece.

'In *Absence of Body*,' he said, 'I am now thinking along these lines. A woman, a middle-aged woman, perfectly ordinary, is on a cruise with her new husband. He's a fellow who has taken the precaution of insuring her life for a tidy sum. He tells everyone she's ill, but in fact she's lying in bed in their cabin' – here Swainton leant forward and put a hand on Graves's knee for emphasis – 'fully *dressed*.'

'I see!' Graves was delighted with the mystery. 'So the plot thickens.'

'It's the truth, you understand,' Swainton assured him. 'It's so much stranger than fiction. Rumpole was a witness to the fact that when we called on Mrs Mavis Britwell in her cabin, she was lying in bed with her clothes on! I don't know why it is, but I seem to have a talent for attracting mysteries.'

'You mean she wanted you to believe she was ill?' Graves asked.

'Or *someone* wanted us to believe she was ill,' Swainton told him. 'Of course, one doesn't want to make any rash accusations.'

'Doesn't one?' I asked. 'It sounds as though one was absolutely longing to.' But Mr Justice Graves was clearly having the time of his old life. 'Swainton,' he said, 'I'd very much like to know how your story ends.'

'Would you, Judge? I'm afraid we'll all just have to wait and see. No harm, of course, in keeping our eyes open in the meanwhile.'

At which moment, the accompanist pounded some rhythmic chords on the piano and Gloria burst into the ditty whose words I could still remember, along with long stretches of *The Oxford Book of English Verse*, better than most of the news I heard yesterday:

> 'Who's that kicking up a noise?
> My little sister!
> Whose that giggling with the boys?
> My little sister!
> Whose lemonade is laced with gin?
> Who taught the vicar how to sin?
> Knock on her door and she'll let you in!
> My little sister!
> Who's always been the teacher's pet?
> Who took our puppy to the vet?
> That was last night and she's not home yet!
> My little sister!'

'What an extraordinary song!' Hilda said when my request performance was over.

'Yes,' I told her. 'Takes you back, doesn't it? Takes *me* back, anyway.'

When the party in the Old Salts' bar was over, Hilda slipped her arm through mine and led me across the deck to the ship's rail. I feared some romantic demonstration and looked around for help, but the only person about seemed to be Bill Britwell, wrapped in a heavy raincoat, who was standing some way from us. It was somewhat draughty and a fine rain was falling, but there was a moon and the sound of a distant dance band. Hilda, apparently, drew the greatest encouragement from these facts.

'The sound of music across the water. Stars. You and I by the rail. Finding each other . . . Listen, Rumpole! What do you think the Med. is trying to say to us?'

'It probably wants to tell you it's the Bay of Biscay,' I suggested.

'Is there nothing you feel romantic about?'

'Of course there is.' I couldn't let that charge go unanswered.

'There you are, you see!' Hilda was clearly pleased. 'I always thought so. What exactly?'

'Steak and kidney pudding.' I gave her the list. 'The jury system, the presumption of innocence.'

'Anything else?'

'Oh. Of course. I almost forgot,' I reassured her.

'Yes?'

'Wordsworth.'

There was a thoughtful silence then and Hilda, like Gloria, went off down Memory Lane. 'It doesn't seem so very long ago,' she said, 'that I was a young girl, and you asked Daddy for my hand in marriage.'

'And he gave it to me!' I remembered it well.

'Daddy was always so generous. Tell me, Rumpole. Now we're alone' – Hilda started off. I'm not sure what sort of intimate subject she was about to broach because I had to warn her, 'But we're not alone. Look!'

She turned her head and we both saw Bill Britwell standing by the rail, staring down at the sea and apparently involved in his own thoughts. Then, oblivious to our existence, he opened his coat, under which he had concealed two silver-framed photographs, much like those Hilda had seen on the dressing-table on her first visit to his cabin. He looked at them for a moment and dropped them towards the blackness of the passing sea. He turned from the rail then and walked away, not noticing Hilda and me, or Howard Swainton, who had also come out of the Old Salts' bar a few minutes before and had been watching this mysterious episode with considerable fascination.

Time, on a cruise ship, tends to drag; watching water pass by you slowly is not the most exciting occupation in the world. Hilda spent her time having her hair done, or her face creamed, or taking steam-baths, or being pounded to some sort of pulp in the massage parlour. I slept a good deal or walked round the deck. I was engaged in this mild exercise when I came within earshot of that indefatigable pair, Graves and Swainton, the Judge and the detective writer, who were sitting on deck-chairs, drinking soup. I loitered behind a boat for a little, catching the drift of their conversation.

'Photographs?' The Judge was puzzled. 'In silver frames? and he threw them into the sea?'

'That's what it looked like.'

'But why would a man do such a thing?'

'Ask yourselves that, Members of the Jury.' I emerged and posed the question, 'Is the Court in secret session or can anyone join?'

'Ah, Rumpole. There you are.' Graves, given a case to try, seemed to be in excellent humour. 'Now then, I believe you were also a witness. Why would a man throw photographs into the sea? That is indeed the question we have to ask. And perhaps, with your long experience of the criminal classes, you can suggest a solution?'

'I'm on holiday. What Britwell did with his photographs seems entirely his own affair.' But Swainton clearly didn't think so. 'I can offer a solution.' He gave us one of his plots for nothing. 'Suppose the Reverend Bill isn't a Reverend at all. I believe a lot of con men go on these cruises.'

'That is an entirely unfounded suggestion by the Prosecution, my Lord.' I had the automatic reaction of the

life-long defender, at which moment the steward trundled the
soup trolley up to me and Graves, by now well in to presiding
over the upper-deck Court, said, 'Please, Mr Rumpole! Let Mr
Swainton complete his submission. Your turn will come later.'

'Oh, is that soup?' I turned my attention to the steward.
'Thank you very much.'

'Suppose Bill Britwell wanted to remove all trace of the
person in the photographs?' Swainton suggested.

'Two persons,' I corrected him. 'Hilda told me there were
two photographs. One was Bill Britwell and his wife. The
other was of a young girl. Are you suggesting he wanted to
remove all trace of two people? Is that the prosecution case?'

'Please, Mr Rumpole, it hasn't come to a prosecution yet,'
Graves said unconvincingly.

'His wife? This is *very* interesting!' Swainton yelped terrier-
like after the information. 'One picture was of his wife. Now,
why should he throw that into the sea?'

'God knows. Perhaps it didn't do her justice,' I suggested,
and Swainton looked thoughtful and said, in a deeply meaningful sort of way, 'Or was it a symbolic act?'

'A what?' I wasn't following his drift, if indeed he had one.
'He got rid of her photograph,' Swainton did his best to
explain, '*because he means to get rid of her.*'

'That is a most serious suggestion.' Graves greeted it with
obvious relish, whilst I, slurping my soup, said, 'Balderdash,
my Lord!'

'What?' The little novelist looked hurt.

'The product of a mind addled with detective stories,' I suggested.

'All right!' Swainton yapped at me impatiently. 'If you
know so much, tell us this. Where do you think Mrs Mavis
Britwell is? Still in bed with her clothes on?'

'Why don't you go and have a peep through the keyhole?' I
suggested.

'I wasn't thinking of that, exactly. But I was thinking . . .'

'Oh, do try not to,' I warned him. 'It overexcites his Lordship.'

'The steward does up the cabins along our corridor at about

this time,' Swainton remembered. 'If we happened to be passing, we might just see something extremely interesting.'

'You mean we might take a view?' The Judge was clearly
enthusiastic and I tried to calm him down by saying, '– Of the
scene of a crime that hasn't been committed?'

'It's clearly our duty to investigate any sort of irregularity.'
Graves was at his most self-important.

'And no doubt your delight,' I suggested.

'What did you say, Rumpole?' The Judge frowned.

'I said you're perfectly right, my Lord. And no doubt you
would wish the Defence to be represented at the scene of any
possible crime.'

'Have you briefed yourself, Rumpole?' Swainton gave me an
unfriendly smile. I took a final gulp of soup and told him, 'I
certainly have, as there's no one else to do it for me.'

When we got down to the corridor outside the cabins, the
trolley with clean towels and sheets was outside the Graves's
residence, where work was being carried out. We loitered
around, trying to look casual, and then Bill Britwell greatly
helped the Prosecution by emerging from his door, which he
shut carefully behind him. He looked at Graves in a startled
and troubled sort of way and said, 'Oh. It's you! Good morning, Judge.'

'My dear Britwell. And how's your wife this morning?' The
Judge smiled with patent insincerity, as though meaning, We
certainly don't hope she's well, as that would be far too boring.

'I'm afraid she's no better,' Britwell reassured them. 'No
better at all. In fact she's got to stay in bed very quietly. No
visitors, I'm afraid. Now, if you'll excuse me.' He made his
way quickly down the corridor and away from us on some
errand or other, and Hilda opened the door of our cabin
which, you will remember, was dead opposite the berth of the
Britwells. 'Ah, Mrs Rumpole.' His Lordship was delighted to
see her. 'Perhaps you'd allow us to be your guests, just for a
moment?' and, although I gave Hilda a warning about helping
the Prosecution, She eagerly invited the judicial team in, although she asked them to forgive 'the terrible mess'. 'Oh, we
can put up with any little inconvenience,' the Judge boomed in

his most lugubrious courtroom accent, 'in our quest for the truth!'

So the search party took refuge in our cabin until the steward pushed his trolley up to the Britwells' door, unlocked it with his pass key and went inside, leaving the door open. Graves waited for a decent interval to elapse and then he led Swainton and me across the corridor and through the door, while the steward was putting towels in the bathroom. There was no one in either of the twin beds, and only one of them seemed to have been slept in. There was no powder, make-up or perfume on the dressing-table and, so far as one quick look could discover, no sign of Mrs Mavis Britwell at all.

'Can I help you, gentlemen?' The steward came in from the bathroom, surprised by the invasion. 'Oh, I'm sorry!' Swainton apologized with total lack of conviction. 'We must have got the wrong cabin. They all look so alike. Particularly,' he added with deep meaning, 'those with only a *single* occupant.'

That night, in the Old Salts' bar, Graves and Swainton were seated at the counter, and Gloria was drawing towards the end of her act, when I intruded again on their discussion of the state of the evidence.

'Britwell told us a deliberate lie,' the Judge was saying.

'He distinctly said she was in the room,' Swainton agreed.

'In my view his evidence has to be accepted with extreme caution,' Graves ruled. 'On any subject.'

'I don't see why.' I put my oar in and Swainton gave a little yapping laugh and said, 'Here comes the perpetual defender.'

'We all tell the odd lie, don't we?' I suggested, and then I ordered a large glass of claret, which I had christened Château Bilgewater, from Alfred, the barman.

'Speak for yourself, Rumpole.' Graves looked at me as though I was probably as big a liar as the Reverend Bill. I wasn't going to let him get away with that without a spot of cross-examination, so I put this to his Lordship. 'When you met my wife on the deck the other morning, didn't you tell her that you had no idea she was on the boat?'

'I *may* have said that,' the Judge conceded.

'And I distinctly saw you at the Captain's cocktail party the night before. You caught sight of Mrs Hilda Rumpole and went beetling out of the room because you recognized her!'

'Rumpole! That is . . .' The Judge seemed unable to find words to describe my conduct so I supplied them for him. 'I know. A grossly improper argument. You may have to report it to the proper authorities.'

'Gentlemen!' Swainton was, unusually, acting as a peacemaker. 'We may all tell the odd white lie occasionally, but this is a far more serious matter. We have to face the fact that Mrs Britwell has apparently disappeared.'

'In the midst of the words she was trying to say,' I suggested:

> 'In the midst of her laughter and glee,
> She softly and suddenly vanished away
> For the Snark *was* a Boojum, you see.'

'The question is' – Swainton was in no mood for Lewis Carroll – 'what action should we take?'

'But who exactly *is* the Boojum – or the Snark, come to that?' This, I felt, was the important question.

'The circumstances are no doubt very suspicious.' Graves had his head on one side, his lips pursed, his brandy glass in his hand, and was doing his best to sound extremely judicial.

'Suspicious of what?' I had to put the question. 'Is the theory that Bill Britwell pushed his wife overboard for the sake of a little life insurance and then kept quiet about it? What's the point of that?'

'It's possible he may have got rid of her,' Swainton persisted, 'for whatever reason . . .'

'If you think that, stop the boat,' I told them. 'Send for helicopters. Organize a rescue operation.'

'I'm afraid it's a little late for that.' Swainton looked extremely serious. 'If he did anything, my feeling is, he did it last night. In some way, I think, the event may have been connected with the photographs that were thrown into the water.'

So they sat on their bar stools and thought it over, the Judge and the fiction writer, like an old eagle and a young sparrow on their perches, and then Graves rather lost his bottle. 'The circumstances are highly suspicious, of course,' he spoke carefully, 'but can we say they amount to a certainty?'

'Of course we can't,' I told them, and then launched my attack on the learned Judge. 'The trouble with the Judiciary is that you see crime in everything. It's the way an entomologist goes out for walks in the countryside and only notices the beetles.'

Graves thought this over in silence and then made a cautious pronouncement. 'If we were sure, of course, we could inform the police at Gibraltar. It might be a case for Interpol.' But Swainton had dreamed up another drama. 'I have a suggestion to make, Judge. If you agree. Tomorrow I'm giving my lecture, "How I Think Up My Plots". I presume you're all coming?' 'Don't bet on it!' I told him. But he went on, undeterred. 'I may add something to my text for Britwell's benefit. Keep your eyes on him when I say it.' 'You mean, observe his demeanour?' The Judge got the point.

Looking down the bar, I saw Gloria talking to Alfred, the barman, while beside me Swainton was babbling with delight at his ingenious plan. 'See if he looks guilty,' he said. 'Do you think that's an idea?'

'Not exactly original,' I told him. 'Shakespeare used it in *Hamlet*.'

'Did he, really?' The little author seemed surprised. 'It might be even better in my lecture.'

By now I had had about as much as I could take of the Judge and his side-kick, so I excused myself and moved to join Gloria, who was giving some final instructions to the barman. 'A bottle of my usual to take away, Alfred,' I heard her say. 'The old and tawny. Oh, and a couple of glasses, could you let us have? They keep getting broken.'

'Miss Gloria de la Haye?' I greeted her, and she gave me a smile of recognition. 'Aren't you the gentleman that requested my old song?'

'I haven't heard you sing it for years,' I told her. 'Music halls don't exist any more, do they?'

'Worse luck!' She pulled a sour face. 'It's a drag, this is,

having to do an act afloat. Turns your stomach when the sea
gets choppy, and there's not much life around here, is there?'
She looked along the bar. 'More like a floating old people's
home. I'm prepared to scream if anyone else requests "Smoke
Gets in Your Eyes". I want to say it soon will, in yours, dear,
in the crematorium!'

'I remember going to the Metropolitan in the Edgware
Road.'

'You went to the old Met.?' Gloria was smiling.

' "Who's that kicking up a noise?" ' I intoned the first line of
the song and she joined me in a way that made the Judge stare
at us with surprise and disapproval:

> 'Who's that giggling with the boys?
> My little sister!'

'That was my act, the long and short of it,' Gloria confirmed
my recollection. 'Betty Dee and Buttercup. I was Buttercup's
straight man.'

'Wasn't an alleged comic on the same bill?' I asked her.
'Happy Harry someone. A man who did a rather embarrassing
drunk act, if I remember.'

'Was there?' Gloria stopped smiling. 'I can't recall, exactly.'

'And about Buttercup?' I asked. 'Rather a pretty girl, wasn't
she? What's happened to her?'

'Can't tell you that, I'm afraid. We haven't kept in touch.'
And Gloria turned back to the barman. 'My old and tawny,
Alfred?' She picked up the bottle of port and the glasses the
barman had put in front of her and went out of the bar. I let
her get a start and then I decided to follow her. She went down
corridors between cabin doors and down a flight of stairs to a
lower deck where a notice on the wall read SECOND-CLASS
PASSENGERS. From the bottom of the stairs I watched as she
walked down a long corridor, a tall, sequined woman with a
muscular back. Then she opened a cabin door and went inside.

In the normal course of events, a lecture 'How I Think Up My
Plots' by Howard Swainton would have commanded my attention somewhat less than an address by Soapy Sam Bollard to

the Lawyers As Christians Society on the home-life of the Prophet Amos. However, Swainton's threatened re-enactment of the play scene from *Hamlet* seemed likely to add a certain bizarre interest to an otherwise tedious occasion, so I found myself duly seated in the ship's library alongside Hilda and Judge Graves.

Bill Britwell, whom Swainton had pressed to attend, was a few rows behind us. Dead on the appointed hour, the best-selling author bobbed up behind a podium and, after a polite smattering of applause, told us how difficult plots were to come by and how hard he had to work on their invention in order to feed his vast and eager public's appetite for a constant diet of Swainton. An author's work, he told us, was never done, and although he might seem to be enjoying himself, drinking soup on the deck and assisting at the evening's entertainment in the Old Salts' bar, he was, in fact, hard at work on his latest masterpiece, *Absence of Body*, the story of a mysterious disappearance at sea. This led him to dilate on the question of whether a conviction for murder is possible if the corpse fails to put in an appearance.

'The old idea of the *corpus delicti* as a defence has now been laid, like the presumably missing corpse, to rest.' Swainton was in full flow. 'The defence is dead and buried, if not the body. Some years ago a steward on an ocean-going liner was tried for the murder of a woman passenger. It was alleged that he'd made love to her, either with or without her consent, and then pushed her through a porthole out into the darkness of the sea. Her body was never recovered. The Defence relied heavily on the theory of the *corpus delicti*. Without a body, the ingenious barrister paid to defend the steward said, there could be no conviction.'

At this, Graves couldn't resist turning round in his seat to stare at Bill Britwell, who was in fact stirring restlessly. 'The Judge and the Jury would have none of this,' Swainton went on. 'The steward was condemned to death, although, luckily for him, the death sentence was then abolished. This case gave me the germ of an idea for the new tale which I am going to introduce to you tonight. Ladies and Gentlemen. You are privileged to be the first audience to whom I shall read chapter one of the brand-new Stainton mystery entitled *Absence of Body*.' He produced a wodge of typescript and Linda Milsom gazed up at him adoringly as he started to read: ' "When Joe Andrews suggested to his wife that they go on a cruise for their honeymoon, she was delighted. She might not have been so pleased if she had had an inkling of the plan that was already forming itself at the back of his mind . . ." ' At which point there was the sound of a gasp and a chair being scraped back behind us. Obediently playing the part of guilty King Claudius, Bill Britwell rose from his seat and fled from the room.

'You saw that, Rumpole,' the Judge whispered to me with great satisfaction. 'Isn't that evidence of guilt?'

'Either of guilt,' I told him, 'or terminal boredom.'

The ship's gift shop, as well as stocking a large selection of Howard Swainton, and others of those authors whose books are most frequently on show at airports, railway stations and supermarket checkouts, sold all sorts of sweets, tobacco, sun oil (not yet needed), ashtrays, table mats and T-shirts embellished with portraits of the late Queen Boadicea, giant pandas and teddy bears, cassettes and other articles of doubtful utility. On the day of the first fancy-dress ball, which was to take place on the evening before our arrival at Gibraltar, the gift shop put on display a selection of hats, false beards, noses, head-dresses and other accoutrements for those who lacked the skill or ingenuity to make their own costumes. In the afternoon the shop was full of passengers in search of disguises in which they could raise a laugh, cut a dash, or realize a childhood longing to be someone quite different from whoever they eventually turned out to be.

'Rumpole,' Hilda was kind enough to say, 'you look quite romantic.' I had put a black patch over one eye and sported a three-cornered hat with a skull and cross-bones on the front. Looking in the shop mirror, I saw Jolly Roger Rumpole or Black Cap'n Rumpole of the Bailey. And then She looked across the shop to where the Reverend Bill was picking over a selection of funny hats. 'You wouldn't think he'd have the nerve to dress up this evening, would you?' She said with a disapproving click of her tongue. I left her and joined Britwell. I spoke to him in confidential but, I hope, cheering tones. 'You must be getting tired of it,' I said sympathetically.

'Tired of what?'

'People asking "How's your wife?"'

'They're very kind.' If he were putting on an act, he was doing it well. 'Extremely considerate.'

'It must be spoiling your trip.'

'Mavis being ill?' He beamed at me vaguely through his spectacles. 'Yes, it is rather.'

'Mr Justice Graves,' I began and he looked suddenly nervous and said, 'The Judge?' 'Yes, the Judge. He seems very worried about your wife.'

'Why's he worried?' Britwell asked anxiously.

'About her illness, I suppose. He wants to see her.'

'Why should he want that?'

'You know what judges are,' I told him. 'Always poking their noses into things that don't really concern them. Shall we see your wife tonight at the fancy-dress party?'

'Well. No. I'm afraid not. Mavis won't be up to it. Such a pity. It's the sort of thing she'd love so much, if she were only feeling herself.' And then Hilda joined us, looking, although I say it myself, superb. She was wearing a helmet and breastplate and carrying a golden trident and a shield emblazoned with the Union Jack. Staring at my wife with undisguised admiration, I could only express myself in song:

> 'Rule Britannia!
> Britannia rules the waves, (I warbled)
> Britain never, never, never shall be . . .'

'Is it going too far?' She asked nervously. But I shook my head and looked at Bill Britwell as I completed the verse:

> 'Marri–ed to a mermai–ed,
> At the bottom of the deep blue sea!'

There was a sound of considerable revelry by night and as that old terror of the Spanish Main, Pirate Cap'n Rumpole made his way in the company of assorted pierrots, slave girls, pashas, clowns, Neptunes and mermaids towards the big saloon from which the strains of dance music were sounding, I passed an office doorway from which a Chinese mandarin emerged in the company of Captain Orde, who was attending the festivities disguised as a ship's captain. As I passed them I heard Orde say, 'The police at Gib have the message, sir. So if he can't produce the lady . . .' 'Yes, yes, Captain.' The mandarin, who looked only a little less snooty and superior than Mr Justice Graves in his normal guise, did his best to shut the officer up as he saw this old sea-dog approaching from windward. 'Why there you are, Rumpole! Have you had some sort of an accident to your eye? Nothing serious, I hope.'

Hilda and I have not danced together since our first honeymoon. As I have already indicated, the exercise was not a startling success and that night, with all the other excitement going on, she seemed content not to repeat the experiment. We sat in front of a bottle of the Bilgewater red, to which I had grown quite attached in an appalling sort of way, and we watched the dancers. Howard Swainton, as an undersized Viking, was steering the lanky Linda Milsom, a slave girl, who towered over him. It might be an exaggeration to say his eye-level was that of the jewel in her navel, but not too much of one. Across the room we could see the Reverend Bill holding a glass and admiring the scene. He was wearing a turban, a scimitar and a lurid beard. 'Bluebeard!' Hilda said. 'How very appropriate.'

'Oh, for heaven's sake!' I told her, 'don't *you* start imagining things.' And then a familiarly icy voice cut into our conversation. 'Mrs Rumpole,' said the ridiculously boring mandarin, 'might I ask you to give me the honour of this dance?' She Who Must Be Obeyed, apparently delighted, said, 'Of course, Judge, what tremendous fun!' My worst fears were confirmed and they waltzed away together with incomprehensible zest.

In due course, Swainton and his houri came to sit at our table and, looking idly at the throng, we witnessed the entry of two schoolgirls in gym-slips and straw hats. One was tall and thin and clearly Gloria. The other, small and plump, wore a schoolgirl mask to which a pigtailed wig was attached. Swainton immediately guessed that this was Miss de la Haye's little accompanist in disguise. 'Betty Dee and Buttercup,' I said, only half aloud, as this strange couple crossed the room, and Linda Milsom, who was having trouble retaining the liverish-looking glass eye in her navel, said, 'Some people sure like to make themselves look ridiculous.' A little time passed and then Swainton said, 'Well, that beats everything!' 'What?' I asked, removing my nose from my glass and shifting the patch so that I had two eyes available.

'An alleged vicar dancing with a bar pianist in drag.' It was true. The Reverend Bill and the small schoolgirl were waltzing expertly. 'I think,' I said, 'I could be about to solve the mystery of the Absent Body.'

'I very much doubt it.' Swainton was not impressed with my deductive powers.

'Would you like me to try?' And, before he could answer, I asked Linda to cut in and invite Bill Britwell for a dance.

'Oh,' she appealed to her boss, 'do I have to?' 'Why not?' Swainton shrugged his shoulders. 'It might be entertaining to watch Counsel for the Defence barking up the wrong tree.'

When instructed by the best-selling author, Miss Milsom acted with decision and aplomb. I saw her cross the floor and speak to Bill Britwell. He looked at his partner, who surrendered more or less gracefully and was left alone on the floor. Before the small schoolgirl could regain the table where Gloria was waiting, Cap'n Rumpole had drawn up alongside.

'I'm afraid I'm no dancer,' I said. 'So shall we go out for a breath of air?' Without waiting for a reply, I took the schoolgirl's arm and steered her towards the doors which led out to the deck.

So there I was by the rail of the ship again, in the moonlight with music playing in the background, faced, not by Hilda, but by a small, round figure wearing a schoolgirl mask.

'Betty Dee and Buttercup,' I said. 'You were Buttercup, weren't you? The little sister, the young girl in the photograph

Bill Britwell threw into the sea? Not that there was any need for that. No one really remembered you.'

'What do you want?' A small voice spoke from behind the mask.

'To set your mind at rest,' I promised. 'No one knows you've been part of a music-hall act. No one's going to hold that against you. Bill can preach sermons to the Anglicans of Malta and no one's going to care a toss about Betty Dee and Buttercup. It's the other part you were worried about, wasn't it? The part you played down the Old Bailey. A long time ago. Such a long time. When we were all very young indeed. Oh, so very young. Before I did the Penge Bungalow Murders, which is no longer even recent history. All the same I was at the Bar when it happened. You know, you should've had me to defend you. You really should. It was a touching story. A young girl married to a drunk, a husband who beat her. Who was he? "Happy" Harry Harman? He even did a drunk act on the stage, didn't he? Drunk acts are never very funny. I read all about it in the *News of the World* because I wanted the brief. He beat you and you stabbed him in the throat with a pair of scissors. You should never have got five years for manslaughter. I'd've got you off with not a dry eye in the jury-box, even though the efficient young Counsel for the Prosecution was a cold fish called Gerald Graves. It's all right. He is not going to remember you.'

'Isn't he?' The small voice spoke again.

'Of course not. Lawyers and judges hardly ever remember the faces they've sent to prison.'

'Are you sure?'

I was conscious that we were no longer alone on the deck. Bill Britwell had come out of the doors behind us, followed by Graves and Howard Swainton, who must have suspected that the drama they had concocted was reaching a conclusion. 'Oh, yes,' I said, 'you can come out of hiding now.'

She must have believed me because she lifted her hands and carefully removed the mask. She was only a little nervous as she stood in the moonlight, smiling at her husband. And the Judge and the mystery writer, for once, had nothing to say.

'Such a pleasure, isn't it,' I asked them, 'to have Mrs Mavis Britwell back with us again?'

The Rock of Gibraltar looked much as expected, towering over the strange little community which can be looked at as the last outpost of a vanishing Empire or as a tiny section of the Wimbledon of fifty years ago, tacked improbably on to the bottom of Spain. The good ship *Boadicea* was safely docked the next morning and, as the passengers disembarked for a guided tour with a full English tea thrown in, I stood once more at the rail, this time in the company of Mr 'Miscarriage of Justice' Graves. I had just taken him for a guided tour round the facts of the Britwell case.

'So she decided to vanish?' he asked me.

'Not at all. She went to stay with her old friend, Miss Gloria de la Haye, for a few days.' And then I asked him, 'She didn't look familiar to you?'

'No. No, I can't say she did. Why?'

'"Old men forget"' – I wasn't about to explain – '"yet all shall be forgot."'

'What did you say?' His Lordship wasn't following my drift.

'I said, "What a load of trouble you've got."'

'Trouble? You're not making yourself clear, Rumpole.'

'You as good as accused the Reverend Bill of shoving his dear wife through the porthole.' I recited the charges. 'You reported the story to the ship's captain, who no doubt wired it to the Gibraltar police. That was clear publication and a pretty good basis for an action for defamation. Wouldn't you say?'

'Defamation?' The Judge repeated the dread word. 'Oh, yes,' I reminded him, 'and juries have been quite absurdly generous with damages lately. Remember my offer to defend you?' My mind went back to a distant bail application. 'Please call on my services at any time.'

'Rumpole' – the Judicial face peered at me anxiously – 'you don't honestly think they'd sue?'

'My dear Judge, I think you're innocent, of course, until you're proved guilty. That's such an important principle to keep in mind on all occasions.'

And then I heard a distant cry of 'Rumpole!' Hilda was kitted out and ready to call on the Barbary apes.

'Ah, that's my wife. I'd better go. We're on a honeymoon too, you see. Our second. And it may disappoint you to know, we're innocent of any crime whatsoever.'

Rumpole and the Quacks

There is, when you come to think about it, no relationship more important than that of a man with his quack – or 'regular medical attendant', as Soapy Sam Ballard would no doubt choose to call him. A legal hack relies on his quack to raise him to his feet, to keep him breathing, to enable him to cross-examine in a deadly manner and then, gentle as any sucking dove, move the Jury to tears. Without the occasional ministrations of his quack, the criminal defender would be but a memory, an empty seat in Chambers to be filled by some white-wig with a word processor, and a few unkind anecdotes in the Bar mess. There might be tears shed around Brixton and the Scrubs, but the Judiciary would greet my departure with considerable relief. In order to postpone the evil hour as long as possible, I am in need of the life-support of a reasonably competent quack.

Mind you, I do a great deal for my own health by what is known in the Sunday papers as a 'sensible life-style'. I am careful to take, however rough and painful the experience may be, a considerable quantity of Pommeroy's Very Ordinary, which I have always found keeps me astonishingly regular. I force myself to consume substantial luncheons of steak and kidney pud and mashed potatoes in the pub opposite the Old Bailey, and I do this in order to ward off infection and prevent weakness during the afternoon.

My customary exercise consists of a short stroll from the Temple tube station to Equity Court, and rising to object to impertinent questions put by prosecuting counsel. I avoid all such indulgences as jogging or squash – activities which I have known to put an early end to many a promising career at the Bar.

The quack By Appointment to the House of Rumpole used to be a certain Dr MacClintock, a Scot of the most puritanical variety, who put me on the scales and sentenced me to a spell on nothing more sustaining than a kind of chemical gruel called Thin-O-Vite. He did this with the avowed intent of causing a certain quantity of Rumpole to vanish into thin air and leave not a wrack behind. I never felt that this was a scheme likely to contribute to anyone's good health, and readers of these chronicles will recall that MacClintock kicked the bucket not long after prescribing it.* The poor old darling was your pessimistic brand of quack who foresees death following hard upon your next slap-up tea of crumpets and Dundee cake.

So you don't want a quack who is too gloomy and turns your mind to being carried downstairs in your box by sweating undertaker's men complaining of the weight. On the other hand, the quack who tells you there's absolutely nothing wrong with you and that you've got the liver of a five year old and you'll probably go on forever is also disconcerting. Does he protest too much? Is he just trying to keep up your spirits? And has he secretly informed She Who Must Be Obeyed that you have, at the best, two more weeks to live? On the whole, and to sum up, all you can say is that a man's relationship with his quack is a matter of mutual confidence and judicious balance.

When Dr MacClintock was translated to the great geriatric ward in the skies, the responsibility for the health and well-being of the Rumpoles eventually passed to Dr Ghulam Rahmat. Dr Rahmat had been highly spoken of by MacClintock, who had made him a partner in that small quackery which served the area around Froxbury Mansions. He was a short, thick-set man, perhaps in his late forties, with greying hair and large, melting brown eyes behind heavy spectacles. He was the most optimistic, indeed encouraging, quack I have ever known.

* See 'Rumpole and the Quality of Life' in *Rumpole and the Age of Miracles*, Penguin Books, 1988.

'How are you, Rumpole?'

'I am dying, Egypt, dying.' She Who Must Be Obeyed, whose title, as you will know, derives from the legendary and all-powerful Queen Cleopatra, answered me with a brisk 'Then we'd better call the Doctor.'

'Call nobody,' I warned her, wincing at the deafening sound of my own voice. 'I am returning to my bed. There's nothing on today except a Chambers meeting to consider the case of a Mrs Whittaker who wants to come in as a pupil to Erskine-Brown. That's something worth missing. If Henry telephones tell him that Rumpole's life is ebbing quietly away.'

'Stuff and nonsense, Rumpole. You drank too much, that's all.'

Was that all? My head felt as though I had just received a short back-and-sides from the mad axe-man of Luton and a number of small black fish seemed to be swimming before my eyes. No doubt it was all because the Lord Chancellor, in a moment of absent-mindedness, had decided to make Hoskins a circuit judge. Hoskins, the colourless and undistinguished member of our Chambers, mainly concerned with the heavy cost of educating his four daughters, had never found it easy to come by or do his briefs. Now, presumably on the basis that if you can't argue cases you'd be better off deciding them, Hoskins had been elevated to the Circus Bench. The net result was a party in Chambers, at which the large and hungry-looking Misses Hoskins appeared and giggled over their sherry. This soirée was followed by a longer and more serious session in Pommeroy's, which had ended once again, I regret to say, with Henry and me recalling the great hits of Dame Vera Lynn. So now I turned my face to the wall, closed my eyes and knew what it was like to stand loitering on the edge of eternity.

'And how is the great barrister-at-law feeling now?'

I was awoken from a troubled doze by a voice which sounded like that of an actor playing the part of an Indian doctor. His dialogue also had the sound of words invented to create a character. This was my first meeting with him, but in all our subsequent encounters I felt that there was something unreal, almost theatrical, about Ghulam Rahmat, and the way he pronounced the absurd title he always insisted on giving me, 'barrister-at-law'.

'I am,' I confessed to the smiling character at my bedside, 'feeling like death.'

'Temporary, sir. A purely temporary indisposition. No need to fly the flag over the Old Bailey at half-mast yet awhile. Tomorrow there will be rejoicing there. The crowds in the street will be cheering. Word will go round. The great barrister-at-law is returned to us, stronger than ever. I have told your good lady while you were sleeping, sir. From the look of him, your husband strikes me as strong as a horse.'

Now I had a lifetime's experience of the evil after-effects of over-indulgence in Pommeroy's plonk, but they had, up till now, not included the presence of an Asian quack doing Peter Sellers impressions at the Rumpole bedside. I appealed to Hilda, who had joined the party.

'Did you tell Doctor . . .'

'Rahmat, sir. Ghulam. Medical doctor, Bachelor of Arts of the University of Bombay. A professional like you, sir. But not with a title so imposing and universally feared as barrister-at-law.'

'Did you tell Dr Rahmat that I felt near to death?' I asked Hilda.

'We are all near to death.' The thought seemed to cause the Doctor a good deal of amusement. He began to laugh, but suppressed the sound as though it were somehow impolite, like a belch. 'But, no doubt, Mr Rumpole will survive us all. Sit up, please. Will you do me the honour to let me listen to your chest? What a lung you have there, sir! It's a pleasure to listen to your hearty breathing. No doubt about it. You will go on forever.'

'Really?' I must say the man had cheered me up considerably. 'So there's nothing seriously wrong?'

'Nothing at all. I diagnose a severe attack of the collywobbles brought on by food-poisoning, perhaps?'

'*Food*-poisoning?' She Who Must repeated with an unbelieving sigh.

'For which I prescribe two Alka-Seltzers in a glass of water,

strong black coffee, a quiet day in bed and even more than
the usual kindness and consideration from your lady wife.
And tomorrow we shall say the barrister-at-law is himself
again!'

When she had seen the medical man off the premises and
returned to the sick-room, I restrained myself from telling
Hilda that for her to treat me with more than her usual
kindness and consideration wouldn't greatly tax her ingenuity.
Instead, I gave her a weak smile and quaffed the Alka-Seltzer.
'What a very charming and sensible quack,' I said as I
effervesced quietly.

But events were soon to occur which placed considerable
doubt on the charm and good sense of Dr Ghulam Rahmat.

The following facts emerged during the subsequent proceedings. At 10.30 a.m. on the day in question, the waiting-room in
the local surgery was full of assorted bronchials, flus, eczemas,
rheumatics, carbuncles and suspected and feared anti-social
diseases. The receptionist, a Miss Dankwerts, was seated
behind her desk, in charge of the proceedings. The names of
the doctors were written upon an electric device on the wall
behind her, and beside each name a red light flashed if they
were engaged or a green if they were available. At the moment
with which we are concerned Dr Rahmat's light was red as he
was seeing a Miss Marietta Liptrott, who had been waiting to
be treated for a sore throat. She had previously been a patient
of Dr Cogger, but as he was busy she had asked specifically for
the Indian doctor. Miss Liptrott had been closeted with her
chosen quack for about ten minutes when a scream was heard
from behind Dr Rahmat's door. With her clothes somewhat
disarrayed, she flew past the assorted complaints and the
startled receptionist and, crying, 'The beast! The beast!',
rushed out of the building and into the wastelands around the
Gloucester Road. The doctors were accustomed to press their
buttons as soon as a patient left, but Dr Rahmat's light remained red for some time after Miss Liptrott ran out. When it
changed to green and his next patient, a Mrs Rodway, was
admitted she found the Doctor nervous, apparently unable to

concentrate on her urticaria and looking, so the witness was to testify, as though 'he'd had the fright of his life'.

Towards the end of the afternoon surgery on that day, that is to say shortly after six o'clock, I happened to call in to get a prescription for She Who Must Be Obeyed (whose blood pressure is inclined to rise, especially if I have overstayed my allotted time in Pommeroy's). The surgery was almost empty, but a youngish man in a blue suit was opening his brief-case on the receptionist's desk and I saw it contained a number of printed folders, pill bottles and a portable telephone. I took him to be the rep for a firm of manufacturing chemists and he was rattling on about the wonders of a miracle cure for something or other when Dr Cogger's light went green and he shot out of his door and recognized me.

'Hullo there, Mr Rumpole.' Tim Cogger had treated me on a couple of occasions for temporary voice loss, the occupational hazard of Old Bailey hacks and opera singers. He was considerably younger than old MacClintock, but he seemed to have inherited the leadership of the practice. Cogger was the hearty type of quack who once played rugby football for Barts and seemed to believe in the short, sharp shock treatment for most illnesses. He was continually complaining that his patients were 'typical National Health pill-scroungers' and, on my rare visits to him, he seemed to regard a head cold as the mark of a wimp. 'You're looking well!' he told me, as though daring me to complain of anything.

'I was looking for Dr Rahmat,' I said. 'He promised my wife a prescription.'

'Oh, I'm afraid Rahmat's gone home.' Dr Cogger seemed to know all about something extremely serious. 'He may not be back at work for a day or two. If it's for Mrs Rumpole, perhaps I could help?' Dr Cogger then got the receptionist to look up Hilda's records and scribbled a new prescription in the most obliging manner. I then knew nothing of the dramatic event of the morning, but by the evening it was certainly service with a smile down at the local quackery.

In due course Miss Marietta Liptrott sent in a complaint to

the General Medical Council, alleging approaches made to her
by Dr Rahmat far beyond the call of medical duty. With the
ponderous tread which characterizes all judicial proceedings,
that august body began to move towards the trial of my encouraging quack for serious professional misconduct. Meanwhile life in Equity Court continued as usual without any
earth-shaking changes. Uncle Tom perfected his putts in the
clerk's room, where Henry and Dianne did their best to control
their emotions and only allowed themselves a few covert
glances of mutual adoration as they unwrapped their sandwiches at lunchtime. Mizz Liz Probert tried to start a movement to turn Chambers into a cooperative dedicated to the
entirely fallacious principle that all barristers are created equal,
but whenever she brought up the subject, Claude Erskine-
Brown stuffed bits of his Walkman into his ears and she was
left listening to the distant twittering of *Die Walküre*. Phillida
Erskine-Brown, our Portia, continued to star in a number of
causes célèbres and enjoyed a success which Claude took with
manful resignation. Sam Ballard made out a list of do's and
don'ts for members of Chambers, which he pinned up on the
notice-board in the clerk's room. This included such precepts
as: DO NOT ALLOW SUCH ARTICLES AS SOLICITORS' LETTERS
OR WITNESS STATEMENTS TO BE DROPPED INTO THE UP-
STAIRS LAVATORY. Well, sometimes there seems to be no
other place for them. DO NOT BE SEEN DRINKING WITH A
LAY CLIENT IN A FLEET STREET WINE BAR. THIS SORT OF
THING BRINGS CHAMBERS INTO DISREPUTE. Well, it had
been the fortieth anniversary of Fred Timson's first Court
appearance under my auspices. Finally, to show that Ballard
was deeply concerned about the environment, DO REMEMBER
THE FORESTS. SAVE PAPER. To which I had added, on my
return from Pommeroy's after the glass or two with Fred,
AND DON'T WASTE IT ON BLOODY SILLY NOTICES IN THE
CLERK'S ROOM. After which the list vanished mysteriously,
no doubt to be re-cycled and re-emerge as a Green Party news-
letter.

'Rumpole. A word with you.' Sam Ballard accosted me one
morning. 'I wanted to let you know. Heather Whittaker has

joined us as Erskine-Brown's pupil.' He uttered this news with a good deal of awe and wonder, as though announcing that the Queen Mother had agreed to drop in afternoons to answer the telephone. 'I just wanted to explain this to you. She's not young. She's taking up the Bar in middle life. And she is a thoroughly nice type of person.'

'Oh, good,' I told him. 'We could do with a few of those around here.'

'I think you were away when we had the Chambers meeting and agreed to take her.'

'Yes,' I remembered, 'I was dying.'

'Oh, really?' I was afraid I detected, in Soapy Sam's eye, a glimmer of hope.

'Yes. But I changed my mind. I'm not dying any more. Sorry to disappoint you.'

'Well, I want to make this quite clear to you. Mrs Whittaker is, well, not the sort of person who would enjoy rough be-haviour in Chambers. Members coming in, perhaps from some wine bar, singing and so on.'

'You mean she doesn't like Dame Vera Lynn?'

'And I don't suppose she'd relish a working environment where people scribble obscenities on notices pinned up in the clerk's room.'

'Does it occur to you, Ballard, that the Whittaker woman may have joined the wrong profession?'

'She was at Girton' – this news seemed to me quite irrelevant – 'with my cousin Joyce.'

'Well, this isn't Girton. She'll be in daily contact with murder, grievous bodily harm and indecent exposure. She'll have to take in incest, adultery and dubious magazines with her tea and buns. You're not seriously suggesting she's going to scream with horror at a bit of graffiti on the notice-board? Anyway, it wasn't obscene.'

'I'm glad you admit you wrote it!' Ballard looked triumph-ant.

'I admit nothing,' I said. 'So what's this new pupil going to specialize in? The theft of knitting patterns? Excuse me, Bol-lard. I'm off to confer about a bit of gross indecency on the

National Health. Don't tell La Whittaker. She might have a fit of the vapours.'

In fact I had a conference in a type of litigation new to me. During a life spent earning my crusts before some pretty unlikely tribunals, I had never yet appeared before the General Medical Council. But Dr Rahmat had telephoned me and told me he was in trouble. I had fixed him up with the dependable Bernard as an instructing solicitor and he was even then waiting for me in my consulting room – an ailing medic who hoped that Rumpole would work the miracle cure.

'In all my troubles and tribulations I had one thought to comfort me. I know an absolutely wizard barrister-at-law!'

Dr Rahmat was no longer smiling. He sat in my client's armchair, looking somewhat thinner and older than when he had stood at my bedside. But he was still playing the Indian doctor in a way which he seemed to hope I would find entertaining. 'How could I be accused of such a dreadful thing? Me, Ghulam Rahmat? All my life I have been a peaceful fellow. I have been anxious to please and to make trouble for no one!'

Perhaps you were too anxious to do what you thought would please Miss Liptrott, I felt like saying. Instead, I asked him to tell me about himself. He told me about his training in Bombay, his coming to England and discovering there was a vacancy in old MacClintock's practice.

'Dr MacClintock was a man who showed no prejudices at all. I said, "Do you mind taking on an Indian doctor in your very British practice?" "Certainly not," he told me. "You can be as Indian as you damn well please."' I looked at the smiling client and had the strange idea that the exaggerated accent and vocabulary had been put on to oblige Dr MacClintock, who wanted to demonstrate his open-mindedness. 'And how are things,' I asked, 'since Dr Cogger's taken over?'

'Just the same.' The smile continued. 'Dr Tim Cogger is a thoroughly good man. A chap with a fine sense of humour. You know what they say of him at Barts? He was a great practical joker. Perhaps not a brilliant doctor but . . .'

'Are you?'

'What?'

'A brilliant doctor?'

'Most of us are not. Most of us are at a loss, more than we like to admit. But we try to be kind and cheerful and wait for the disease to go away. To be perfectly frank, that is how I treated the great barrister-at-law.'

'I'm afraid' – I had to break the news to him – 'Miss Marietta Liptrott doesn't seem likely to go away.'

'No, dash it all.' His cheerfulness, which had come back as he described his professional life so candidly, had drained away like bathwater, leaving him disconsolate again. 'What a pain in the neck. If I can be so jolly rude about a young lady.'

'Had you seen her before?'

'No. And if I have to be honest with you, I hope and pray I never see her again.'

'What did she look like?'

For an answer he took out his wallet and handed me a cutting from the *Daily Beacon*. 'First time,' he said ruefully, 'that I ever got my name in the paper.' INDIAN DOCTOR TRIED TO STRIP AND MAKE LOVE TO ME. NANNY TELLS OF SURGERY ANTICS blared the headline. The story went on:

Children's nurse, Marietta Liptrott, 27, who works for a wealthy Kensington family, only had a sore throat but Dr Rahmat had his own ideas about treatment. He made her lie down on a couch, she said in her complaint to the General Medical Council, and wanted her to pull down her knickers. Dr Ghulam Rahmat, 50, who only came to England 12 years ago said, 'I have the best barrister in the country and I shall fight this every inch of the way.'

I was looking at Miss Liptrott's photograph: a pale face with large, trusting eyes and an upper lip drawn over slightly protruding teeth. This gave her a breathless and eager look.

'I never took a shine to her, Mr Rumpole, to be perfectly frank with you.'

'What's your situation, Doctor? Have you a wife?'

'Had, Mr Rumpole. There is poor hygiene in some of our

hospitals and I lost her. My son is in Bombay, studying. He hopes, in his humble way, to be a barrister-at-law, third-class merely. Not in your league, I may say.' To my embarrassment I saw tears in the eyes behind his heavy spectacles. We hacks see clients at their most emotional moments, but remain oddly embarrassed when they start weeping.

'So. What's our defence?' I was anxious to get back to business.

'The same,' he announced with great satisfaction, 'as in E. M. Forster's fine work, *A Passage to India*.'

When I was up at Oxford, studying night and day for my record-breaking fourth in law, I remembered a chap called Perkins, who greatly admired this Forster. He told me that personal relationships were all important and if he had to choose between betraying his country or Rumpole, he hoped he'd choose his country. Happily, Perkins became a clergyman in Wales and didn't have to make this agonizing decision, but he did get me to read *A Passage to India*, the gist of which had, I was ashamed to say, now slipped my mind.

'Of course,' I said, 'just remind me of the plot.'

'This English lady accuses an Indian doctor of raping her in the Marabar caves,' the Doctor reminded me.

'Ah, yes, of course. It all comes back to me. And what was his defence exactly?'

'That it all went on in her fevered imagination.'

'I see.' I was a little doubtful. 'And how did it work out?'

'He was acquitted! You will enjoy a similar triumph, great barrister-at-law.'

'Well, let's hope so.' I was by no means convinced. 'We've got to remember that was a work of fiction.' I then brought the Doctor down to earth by trying to get his exact clinical reasons for asking a patient who had come in to complain of a sore throat to remove her knickers.

When Dr Rahmat had left me he was in a mood of unbridled optimism. I wandered out into the passage with my mind set on a little refreshment at Pommeroy's. The door of Erskine-Brown's room opened and out stepped a well-groomed, neatly dressed, grey-haired lady, who greeted me with a friendly smile and carefully controlled cry of 'Mr Rumpole, isn't it?'

'A piece of him,' I told her.

'I've been so longing to meet you. I'm Heather Whittaker, Erskine-Brown's pupil. I've taken to the Bar rather late in life I'm afraid.'

'It's probably a profession for the aged,' I consoled her. 'The young can't stand the pace.'

'You're a legend, Mr Rumpole. Of course you know that. I'm absolutely dying to hear you on your feet.'

'Well,' I said hospitably, 'why not pop along to the General Medical Council? I've got a doctor in trouble.'

'Oh, I'd love that.' She seemed genuinely enthusiastic. 'Of course, I've heard Erskine-Brown on his feet.'

'Oh, really? And did you manage to keep awake?'

'Just about.' She allowed herself a small but charming giggle. 'With you I'm sure I should be on the edge of my seat. What's your doctor been up to?'

'I'd better not tell you. Our Head of Chambers says you shock easily.'

'What nonsense!' Her smile widened. 'I want to know all the gory details.' I must say that Ballard was right about one thing. Our new pupil, Mrs Heather Whittaker, seemed a nice type of person.

My life at that time was bedevilled by women. Not only had a person of that persuasion got my unfortunate doctor in trouble, but a client of mine, similarly constituted, was becoming a pain in my neck.

'So. She's been ringing up again,' said She Who Must Be Obeyed in threatening tones as I got home that evening.

'She?' I asked with carefully simulated innocence. 'Who on earth's she?' Of course, I knew perfectly well. She was the worst driver who ever skidded her gleaming white Volkswagen off the Uxbridge Road, mounted the pavement, terrorized the passers-by, hit a municipal waste disposal bin and someone's mobile shopping-basket, and finally crashed into a lamp-post.

The driver's name was Mrs Bambi Etheridge. Only

Rumpole's skill, and the fact that the chief prosecution witness lectured the lady Chairman of the Bench on the hopeless incompetence of woman drivers, led to her triumphant acquittal on the grounds of poor road surface and fast oncoming traffic. Whatever might be said of her as a driver, Mrs Etheridge was a social menace. She was a generously built lady who, as she moved, clattered with what I believe is known as costume jewellery and gave off a deafening smell of what she was at pains to tell me was Deadly Sins by St Just. Her hair was unconvincingly blonde and her make-up strove to represent the effect of too much sunbathing in Florida. She spoke as though she were trying to attract the attention of a deaf and uncooperative waiter on the far side of a noisy dining-room.

'Mr Rumpole,' she bellowed, as we came out of Court 'you are an absolute sweetie. How can I reward you, Mr Rumpole, darling?' I told her that it was normal to do it with a cheque sent through her solicitors.

'But I mean something more personal. What about a naughty lunch? Just the two of us. Could you get a long afternoon off? And do you enjoy scrumptious desserts as much as I do? Oh, good. All men enjoy scrumptious desserts, don't they? That's settled then. I'll give you a tinkle. Are you in the book? I'm sure you are.'

'Lunch,' I said regretfully, for I'm particularly fond of lunch, 'no, I'm afraid that's impossible. The pressure of work, you see.'

'Oh, come on, Mr Rumpole. Give yourself a bit of fun, why don't you? Has anyone ever told you, you're a very cuddly sort of barrister?'

My blood ran cold. I saw Mr Bernard, our admirable instructing solicitor, avert his eyes in shame. And this woman was going in search of my telephone number. I fervently wished I had lost her case and she was even now being led off to the dungeons.

'Mrs Etheridge, please don't trouble yourself to telephone. I'm afraid I rarely lunch out nowadays. In fact I do nothing except work.'

'All work and no play makes Mr Rumpole a dull boy.' She

slapped my wrist lightly. 'And I'm sure you're not that, are you? Be seeing you!'

And with that she was gone, with a whiff of Deadly Sins, a carillon of costume jewellery and the relentless beat of her high heels on the entrance hall of the Uxbridge Magistrates Court. Three evenings later the telephone rang in Froxbury Mansions. Hilda answered it, frowned with extreme displeasure and handed me the instrument with a grim 'There's a woman asking for you who rejoices in the name of Bambi Etheridge.'

'Oh,' I said weakly, 'what does she want?'

'God knows what she wants with you, Rumpole. You'd better ask her.'

'Yes!' I barked into the instrument in a way which I hoped would put an end once and for all to the hideous notion that I am in the least cuddly. 'Rumpole speaking.'

'Oh, dear.' The Etheridge menace appeared to coo down the line. 'Is it a bad moment? Are you with your wife? Ought I to have pretended to be the Water Board or something?'

'No,' I said firmly, 'I don't think you can.'

'Can what, Mr Rumpole? What are you suggesting? I only rang to invite you to lunch.'

'I don't think you can get costs against the police. Yes. I know you won. But you did hit a lamp-post. It was quite a reasonable prosecution to bring. I'm sorry. That's my final legal opinion.'

'Oh, of course,' Bambi purred understandingly. 'You can't talk now, can you? I'll ring again.'

'Don't do it,' I said. 'You'll be throwing good money after bad by appealing.'

'What a thing to say! You're not bad money are you, Mr Rumpole? I said I'll ring again when you're not in the bosom of your family. By-ee.'

'Stupid woman!' I said when I put the phone down. 'She wants to appeal on costs.'

'Oh, yes?' Hilda looked at me with profound disbelief. 'Is that why she called you my lovely husband?'

'She didn't?'

'She did to me. I said, "Hilda Rumpole speaking," and she said, "Oh, yes. And is your lovely husband about by any chance?"'

'Look' – I felt called on to defend myself on a most serious charge of which I was undoubtedly innocent, having been put in the frame by the appalling Bambi – 'she's only a customer.'

'Well, that poor girl was only a customer of Dr Rahmat's, wasn't she? And look what happened to her!' And She Who Must Be Obeyed adjourned for supper, clearly having made up her mind without the need for further argument.

I did get taken out for an expensive lunch not long after that fatal phone call, and I was invited by a lady whose brains and beauty far exceeded the modest attainments in either of those departments by Bambi Etheridge. Mrs Phillida Erskine-Brown, Q.C., our Portia, knocked at my door in Chambers late one morning and said, 'Come on, you old devil. I'm taking you out to lunch.' Expecting a couple of sandwiches at Pommeroy's, I was surprised when she said, 'Savoy Grill suit you, would it?'

'Well,' I admitted, 'if we're really roughing it. But what's come over you, Portia? Are they putting you on the High Court Bench?'

'They're not putting me anywhere. The question is, where am I putting myself? I'm just about fed up, Rumpole. I've had it up to here. So we're going out to spend what's left of Claude's money and I hope he finds *that* boring!' With which enigmatic statement she set off along the Strand at a pace so brisk that I had to break into a trot to keep up with her.

It was not until we were seated on the plush and had our hands round a couple of cocktails that Phillida started to unburden herself. 'Rumpole,' she said, 'tell me honestly. Am I boring?'

'Whatever gave you that idea?'

'Am I a rut?'

'Scarcely.'

'Humdrum? Would you call me humdrum?'

I looked at our Portia. Her hair was reddish, inclined to

gold. Her face, that of one of the most intelligent Pre-Raphaelite models, had grown, I thought, finer in the years since I had known her. The formal white blouse and dark suit, combined with the horn rims she used to read the menu, merely added to that charm which had, in the past, completely turned the heads of such connoisseurs of feminine beauty as the Hon. Mr Justice Featherstone. As I looked at her, the only wonder was how, all those years ago, she had been put in the club and then married by a character as un-exotic as my learned friend, Claude Erskine-Brown.

'Run of the mill. Am I run of the mill?'

'You are certainly not.'

Apart from her beauty, Mrs Erskine-Brown has brains. Not for nothing had I named her Portia. When she spoke up for the Defence the general opinion in the jury-box was that if a nice girl like that was on his side, the villain in the dock couldn't be nearly as black as he was painted. When prosecuting, she could pot the prisoner with all the aplomb of the Avenging Angel on a good day.

'Men,' she now said, 'are all the same!'

'Are we? I'm not sure I'm exactly like Claude.'

'Perhaps not you, Rumpole. You're not really interested, are you?'

'Not interested in what?'

'In what everyone else who happens to be male seems to spend their time thinking about, sex.'

'Oh, that,' I said, and gave a small shudder of fear at the thought of returning home to be cooed at over the telephone by Bambi.

'They're all the same. Take that wretched doctor of yours.'

'Dr Rahmat?'

'A woman only has to wander into his surgery with a sore throat and he's trying to get into her knickers. Just like Claude.'

'Claude looks after people with sore throats?' I wasn't following her drift.

'I'll get him, though. I'll cross-examine the life out of him. He'll be struck off for ten years.'

'Claude?'

'No. Dr Rahmat.'

'What's Dr Rahmat got to do with it?'

'I'm prosecuting him before the General Medical Council.'

'First rate!' I tried to sound enthusiastic, but I saw the unhappy doctor's hopes fading rapidly. 'I'll have a foeman worthy of my steel. Foe-woman, I'm sorry. You have to be so careful when you talk to lady barristers nowadays.'

'I don't know how you could defend a person like that.'

'You know I have to defend a person like anyone.'

'But you couldn't defend a real snake.'

'Dr Rahmat?'

'No!' And she added in such a tone that I came to the conclusion that hell hath absolutely no fury like a Mrs Phillida Erskine-Brown, Q.C. scorned, 'Claude!'

'All right,' I said. 'What's Claude done now?'

As the waiter had set smoked salmon and Sancerre before us, it seemed a suitable moment to get on with putting the indictment. By way of answer, Mrs Erskine-Brown opened the slender black brief-case she had brought with her and produced a copy of a somewhat lurid magazine called *Casanova*. On the cover of this publication a bikini-clad young woman disported herself with a medicine ball, both articles looking as though they had been inflated with a bicycle pump.

'Let me read you this.' Phillida flicked through what were, no doubt, distressing pages of photographs and came to rest among the advertisements which, when I got a chance to examine them at my leisure, were mostly of the lonely hearts variety.

'"Barrister. Good-looking and young at heart,"' Phillida read in tones of such disgust that they almost put me off my lunch. '"In a rut. Bored with the humdrum of married life. Seeks a new partner for the occasional fling. Country walks, opera-going, three-star restaurant treats and all the other pleasures of life. Tall and slender preferred. Write with a photograph, if possible, to . . ."' And there's a box number. There you are! Read it for yourself if you want to.' She almost threw the exhibit at me, drained her wine glass at a gulp and ordered us both a refill from the waiter. I glanced at it as I asked, 'So how do you connect this with Claude?'

'It's obvious, isn't it? He's a barrister and "opera-going".'

'There are about four thousand barristers and some of them must go to the Opera. I don't think, Mrs Erskine-Brown, that your evidence is absolutely conclusive.'

'I found this in his room in Chambers, Rumpole,' Phillida said between gritted teeth. 'Now. What further proof do you want?'

'I see.' This last piece of testimony did seem to have landed the unfortunate Claude in the manure. 'Well,' I admitted, 'things are beginning to look rather black for the accused.' As I said this, I was glancing further down the page of *Casanova* and found boxes announcing the service of 'escorts' and ladies equipped to give massage treatment 'in the hotel or home'. These announcements were embellished with photographs and one struck me as familiar. It was under the heading NAUGHTY MARIETTA WILL KEEP YOU COMPANY AT DINNERS OUT OR BUSINESS FUNCTIONS. There was a snap of this companionable girl. Her hair had been done over more elaborately than when she appeared in the *Daily Beacon*, but there was no mistaking the wide eyes and small, even features and slightly protruding teeth of Miss Liptrott, the girl who was about to bring about the downfall of Doctor Rahmat.

During the beef and Beaujolais, our Portia rattled on about her husband's character defects and his pathetic failure even to be unfaithful without advertising for it in the public prints. Then, perhaps, feeling she had confided too much, she remembered a conference in Chambers, paid the bill and left me. She went so hurriedly, in fact, that I found myself still in possession of the copy of *Casanova*, and I finished the Brouilly, which would never have been seen dead in Pommeroy's, and again contemplated the features of the undoubted Miss Liptrott. Dr Rahmat's case seemed to follow me around that day, for, glancing across the restaurant, I spotted the large, muscular and jovial figure of Dr Tim Cogger, lunching profusely with someone I recognized as the fellow with the brief-case, who had apparently been trying to flog his pills and potions around the quackery. I raised what remained in my glass in salutations but Dr Rahmat's senior partner, although he glanced in my direction, seemed not to have noticed me at all.

When I got back to my room in Chambers, I propped *Casanova* up on my desk, got a line from Henry and started to dial. I heard a ringing tone and, as I was saying, 'Is that the Naughty Marietta escort service?', I was aware of the door opening and our Head of Chambers sidled into the room and stood agape as I heard the whispered reply, 'Yes. This is Marietta speaking.'

'Marietta Liptrott, I presume?'

'Who are you? Are you the newspapers?'

'No, I promise you. Just someone in need of an escort. I heard from a friend that you were a very companionable young lady.'

'Oh, well. Yes. I suppose that's all right.' There was a pause but no denial of the name. 'When's the function?'

'It's not for me, actually.' I raised my voice slightly and turned to smile at the intruder. 'It's for a friend of mine. He wants to take you along to add a little colour to a ladies' night at the Lawyers As Christians Society. Call you back with the details. Nice to talk to you, Miss Liptrott.' I put down the telephone.

'Rumpole! Is that your idea of a joke?'

'Well, you shouldn't have been standing there listening to a private conversation.'

'I couldn't help hearing that you were using Chambers telephone facilities to call up an escort agency.'

'Of course, you could help it. You could have beaten a hasty retreat.'

'Rumpole. You're a married man.'

'That has not escaped my attention.'

'I don't ask why you should feel the need to do that sort of thing . . .'

'Good. Nice to chat to you, Bollard. Now, if you don't mind closing the door on your way out . . .'

He moved towards the exit and then paused. 'Rumpole,' he said solemnly, 'don't you think you ought to make a clean breast of it to Hilda?'

'A clean breast of what?'

'The fact that you're troubled by those sort of, well, needs.'

'Ballard' – I looked at the man with pity – 'when you next feel the need to talk absolute balderdash, why don't you make a clean breast of it to Matey?'

He went then but was back in a twinkling, his head round the door. 'I forgot why I dropped in,' he confessed.

'On the chance of earwigging a salacious phone call?' I suggested.

'No, it wasn't that. Now I remember. I've had a word with Mrs Whittaker. It seems you've asked her to take a note for you in that G.M.C. case of yours. Are you sure it's not distasteful in any way?'

'I promise. She can resort to ear-plugs for the more sensational parts of the evidence.' When I was finally relieved of Bollard's company, I continued a close study of infectious mononucleosis in the *Principles and Practice of Medicine* I had got out of the library. Then I called on Mrs Erskine-Brown to return the incriminating magazine she had left with me in the restaurant.

'There you are,' I said, when I entered the comfortably appointed Q.C.'s room Phillida inhabited apart from her husband. I dropped the distasteful magazine on her desk. 'You left the vital evidence in the restaurant. What are you going to do to the unfortunate Claude? Confront him with it?'

'No good at all.' She came to a quick legal decision. 'He'd only say it wasn't him or something equally devious. No. I shall trap him with it. Leave him absolutely no way of escape.'

Traps were being set all around by Phillida, not only for Claude but for the unfortunate Dr Rahmat as well.

'There are some exquisite echoes in India; there is the whisper round the dome at Bijapur; there are the long, solid sentences that voyage through the air at Mandu, and return unbroken to their creator.' So wrote old E. M. Forster, whose work I had turned to, together with the *Principles and Practice of Medicine*, by way of preparation for the struggle ahead. The old literary darling might well have had something to say about the echoes

that the accusation against Dr Rahmat sent reverberating round
the small world of Rumpole, to be half heard, mainly mis-
understood and set up fresh rumours. One evening as we sat
over our chops in Froxbury Mansions, Hilda, who had apparently caught one such echo said, 'I've arranged for you to see
Dr Cogger.'

'Why on earth?'

'Well, you certainly can't see Dr Rahmat. I don't know why
on earth you're defending him.'

'I'm defending him because he's in trouble.'

'Anyway, that Marguerite Ballard rang up and said Sam was
worried about you and that you'd seemed rather strange lately.
What were you doing strange, Rumpole?'

'I suppose phoning up escorts,' I answered her through a
certain amount of chop and mashed potato.

'What did you say?'

'I said I suppose I was feeling out of sorts.' I had changed
my mind about taking Hilda into my confidence. It would
have taken too long and she might well not have accepted my
evidence.

'Well, if you're feeling out of sorts, stop complaining to *me*
about it. Go and see Dr Cogger tomorrow evening, on your
way home from Chambers. Do try and have a bit of sense, Rumpole.'

So evening surgery found me, ever obedient, waiting for the
green light to flash beside Dr Cogger's name. I sat among
people with varying degrees of illness, coughing and sneezing
their way through outdated copies of *Punch*, the *Sunday
Fortress* cooking supplement, *Good Housekeeping* and the
Illustrated London News. Pale children played with the broken-
down toys provided, an antique Chinaman clutched the handle
of his walking-stick and muttered ferociously to himself, a
very thin girl bit her lip and sat holding her boyfriend's
hand. The flats and bedsits around the Gloucester Road had
handed over their sick and dying. Then I put down the back
number of *Country Life* which hadn't been holding my attention and saw what surely must have been an unusual sight in a
doctor's waiting-room, the lurid cover of *Casanova*.

'Do you take this regularly?' I approached the receptionist with the dubious periodical in my hand.

'Not at all. It shouldn't have been left out there. Of course it'd upset the old people.'

From Miss Dankwerts's look of pity, I could see I was being taken for one of the easily upset old people. 'You mean' – my curiosity was aroused – '*Casanova* isn't normally available in the waiting-room?'

'Of course not. As a matter of fact,' she gave a small smile at the expense of the medical men from whom she obviously felt as aloof as she did from her patients, and whispered, 'the cleaning lady found it in one of the doctors' rooms. It should never have been put out.'

'Of course. The advertisements are rather interesting though. You might find a friend.' And, before she could deal with this outrageous suggestion, the green light flashed and I was admitted into Dr Cogger's presence with the folded *Casanova* swelling my jacket pocket.

'Well, Mr Rumpole. What seems to be the trouble?' The Doctor was as cheerful and hearty as ever.

'I don't know. Failing eyesight, perhaps. I thought I saw you having lunch in the Savoy Grill, but I must've been mistaken. You didn't seem to recognize me when I raised my glass to you.'

'The Savoy Grill?' He smiled at me, a big man with huge hands and a surprisingly gentle voice. 'That's a bit out of the class of a struggling G.P.'

'So it wasn't you then?'

'I hardly think so.' He shook his head. 'Now' – he was turning over my notes – 'it seems your wife made this appointment. What does she think is wrong with you?'

'Someone told her I was behaving rather strangely in my Chambers.'

'Behaving strangely?' He was adding these words to the log of Rumpole's weaknesses, where they would be immortalized together with my weight. 'What sort of strangeness?'

'Well, ringing up escort agencies.'

'Escort agencies? But, Mr Rumpole, why ever should you do that?'

'I suppose they thought I was looking for escorts.'

'You mean, young girls to take out to dinner? That sort of thing?'

'That sort of thing. Yes.'

'My dear Mr Rumpole' – he leant back in his chair and his smile was entirely kindly – 'I shouldn't let that worry you in the least. A lot of men, perfectly decent chaps, in my experience, feel the need of young, fresh – well, young company. It doesn't mean they're sick in any way. It's perfectly natural.'

'Is that what you think?'

'Oh, yes. I do, quite honestly.'

'I thought it might be.'

'Oh, did you?' His smile faded and he gave me a look, I thought, of some unease. Of course, that may have been because I was being such a terse and unforthcoming patient.

'Yes. When I saw that magazine *Casanova* in your waiting-room.'

'Oh, that!' He was smiling again, at full beam. 'I can't think how it got there.'

'It's full of advertisements for escorts, companions, people for nights out on the town. All that sort of thing.'

'Is it? I didn't look. It seems to have interested you.'

'Yes, it did. Your receptionist said it was found in one of the doctors' rooms.'

'Well, Mr Rumpole, my partners are big boys now. I really can't be expected to nanny them. Perhaps I should have, though. When I think of the trouble poor old Rahmat's got himself into – Now' – he looked at his watch and seemed to decide that his time was being wasted in idle chatter – 'what would you say your problem is, medically?'

'Medically,' I told him, 'I can't sleep. I seem to wake up around one o'clock in the morning and worry about poor old Rahmat, as you rightly call him.'

'My dear Mr Rumpole. Why should *you* worry?'

'I suppose, because I'm defending him.'

For the first time Dr Cogger looked startled and unsure of himself. 'You are?' He frowned. 'I hadn't realized that. Perhaps we shouldn't have been talking about it. I've been asked to give evidence.'

'For the Doctor? I didn't think we'd asked you.'

'No. Well, for the Council. I just told them what I knew. I certainly don't want to make things any more difficult for Rahmat. Look. I'll write you out some pills. Perfectly harmless. Just take one when you wake up in the middle of the night. At least that should stop you worrying.'

'About Dr Rahmat?'

'If you can manage it. I know. It's distressing for all of us when a doctor goes off the rails.'

'Rumpole, I'm terribly worried.'

'Oh, dear.'

'Worried and frankly mystified.' It didn't take much to mystify Erskine-Brown, and as we sat together in Pommeroy's, our day's work done, I waited to hear what detail of our life on earth was puzzling him at the moment.

'It's about Philly. She's taken to calling herself "The Rut".'

'The what?'

'The Rut! I come home and there'll be a note: GONE ROUND TO MARGOT'S, SO I DON'T BORE YOU TO DEATH. "THE RUT". Why do you think she calls herself "The Rut"?'

'I have no idea.'

'Do you think it has some amorous significance? I looked it up in *The Oxford English* in the Bar library. It refers, Rumpole, to periods of sexual excitement in certain animals.'

'Didn't you ask your wife what she meant?'

'Of course.'

'What did she say?'

'That I should know, if anyone did.'

'And you found that reply enigmatic?'

'I certainly did.'

I looked at the man. I wouldn't have thought Claude had any special talent for lying, but he spoke with apparent conviction and not an eyelid was batted.

'She's also begun to ask me about country walks.'

'Say again.'

'She says, "When are you going out for another country walk, Claude?" She knows that country walks are just not my scene.'

'I shouldn't have thought so.'

'They tire you out and you get your shoes dirty. Whatever gave her the idea I want to go tramping around the countryside?'

'Are you sure *you* didn't?'

For an answer he shook his head sadly and said, 'Do you know I really am worried about Philly. Do you think she ought to see a doctor?'

'I think,' I told him, 'that she's about to see about a dozen of them. In the General Medical Council. And I'm sure she'll do this case like she does all her cases – brilliantly.' And she'll have you stitched up too, Claude, I thought as I looked at the man who still seemed to be seeing his perilous situation through a glass darkly.

I left Pommeroy's and when I disembarked from the bus and was making my way towards the mansion flat, I saw Dr Rahmat hurrying along the street in front of me. I called out and he turned like a startled hare and then managed a smile of greeting. 'The barrister-at-law. And looking extremely fit, if I may say so.'

'I wanted to see you. There's a question that I should have asked. Mr Bernard was trying to get hold of you at the surgery.'

'Alas, I am seldom there now. The patients don't seem too dead keen on seeing me. But shall we walk along? I have an appointment.'

'All right. It's about Dr Cogger,' I said, when we were on the move. 'Did you and he ever quarrel about anything?' Dr Rahmat walked a few steps in silence and I prompted him, 'If I'm going to defend you, you'd better trust me.'

'Well,' he admitted, 'we had a few words once. About the drugs.'

'What about the drugs?'

'He was always wanting me to prescribe . . .' Here he mentioned a number of long, Latinized trade names which went, I have to confess, in at one of my ears and out at the other. 'They were very expensive drugs, most of them from March-main's, and I told him that my patients would be just as well off with a few kind words and a couple of aspirins.'

'How did he react to that?'

'Badly. He got in a most terrible bait. He went so far as to say that he didn't want partners who were so pig ignorant on the subject of new drugs. I'm sure it was said in the heat of the moment and he didn't mean it exactly.'

We had reached the Star of Hyderabad, our local Indian eatery, and Dr Rahmat stopped in front of its red and gold door. 'I am most reluctant to part from you, great barrister-at-law, but, alas, I have an appointment.'

'I'll come in with you for a moment. You can buy me a beer.'

'It would be a pleasure, but some other time, I'm afraid. This is an appointment of a private nature.' He then bolted into the Star of Hyderabad and, resisting all temptations to peer in and see who he was dating, I headed off to an empty house, for it was one of the nights when Hilda was at her bridge lesson with Marigold Featherstone.

At about nine o'clock the phone rang and a familiar voice said, 'Is Horace there? It's Bambi.' 'This is a recorded message,' I answered in a nasal and mechanical tone. 'I'm afraid we are not available at the moment, but if you will leave your name and telephone number, we will get back to you as soon as possible. Please speak after the tone. *Bleep.*' I then held the instrument at arm's length and, when it had finished twittering, laid it to rest. I woke up at one in the morning with Dr Rahmat's case going round and round in my head. I wondered about mononucleosis, Dr Cogger's strange reluctance to be recognized in the Savoy Grill and his practical jokes at Barts. What exactly had he done there? I imagined in those feverish hours a live lady, substi-tuted for a corpse on the dissecting table, who sat up suddenly and made several students faint. I imagined trying to connect an escort agency with a row about prescribing expensive drugs with long names – and sleep eluded me. At about two thirty I took one of Dr Cogger's pills, which had no effect on me at all.

*

The General Medical Council rules from an imposing headquarters in that mecca of doctors, the purlieus around Harley
Street. I crossed Portland Place, walked down Hallam Street,
and entered, wigless and without gown, the building in which
the top medics, playing, for a while, the parts of judges, decide
the fate of their fellow quacks.

Up the stairs I found an imposing square chamber, decorated
with the portraits and busts of solemn, whiskered old darlings
who, no doubt, bled their customers with leeches and passed
on the information to alarmed small boys that self-abuse leads
to blindness. A large stained-glass window bore the image of a
ministering angel and two balconies, decorated with Adam-
style plaster-work, held up the visiting public and a large body
of journalists from such scandalsheets as the *Daily Beacon*,
whose ears were pricked up for all the details of Dr Rahmat's
unusual medical treatment. At tables round three sides of a
rectangle sat the eleven judges, a few of whom were not doctors,
but lay brothers or sisters from allied worlds, such as nursing
or sociology. Presiding at the top table was a lean and elderly
Scot, the distinguished saw-bones, Sir Hector MacAuliffe,
who looked as though he would have found Calvin himself a
bit of a libertine.

I found myself seated at a small table, as in an American
courtroom, with Dr Rahmat in embarrassing proximity to me. I
have always found it a great advantage to sit as far away from
clients as possible, as their suggestions on how to conduct the
trial, if adopted, almost always prove fatal. On my other side,
Mrs Whittaker, grey-haired and clad in a decent black suit,
was ready to take a note – a task she was to perform with
admirable efficiency.

At a table opposite me sat our Portia and the prosecution
team. Between us, in the wide open spaces of the room, was
the solitary chair and small table at which the witnesses gave
evidence in some comfort. We were all provided with heavy-
duty microphones, so that our voices boomed and echoed as
though we were in a swimming-pool.

'Yes, Mrs Erskine-Brown.' Sir Hector gave a nod of encouragement to the opposition and Claude's Philly stood up

and, with an almighty swipe, drove straight down the fairway. 'This, sir, is a flagrant and distressing case of a doctor's violent and unprovoked sexual assault upon a young woman. When you have heard all the evidence, we have little doubt that you will find the charge of professional misconduct proved against Dr Rahmat beyond any shadow of reasonable doubt.' So Phillida went on to tell the story of this young children's nurse (making Naughty Marietta sound like some kind of junior Florence Nightingale) who called in to the surgery with a sore throat and was told to lie on the couch and, when her knickers were removed, Dr Rahmat 'thrust his hand between her legs, tried to kiss her and suggested that there was time for a quick one'.

'Meaning sexual intercourse?' Sir Hector was clearly not about to take the view that my client was offering his patient a small sherry.

'That is what we ask the committee to infer.' Phillida went on, 'Miss Liptrott screamed and had to struggle to free herself from the Doctor's embraces. She pulled her clothes back on and she was still screaming, "The beast! The beast!" as she ran into the reception area. There she was seen by the waiting patients and by a Miss Dankwerts. After the incident she suffered extreme bouts of nervous depression and was treated for that complaint by Dr Cogger, a senior member of the practice, whom I shall be calling as a witness.'

'Very fair. She puts the case most fairly. And old Tim Cogger. He will be fair to me also.' Dr Rahmat, since he arrived in Court, had seemed in a confident mood. Now his optimistic words were caught up by the microphone, causing a glare of disapproval from Sir Hector and an ironic smile from Phillida, which seemed to promise stormy weather to come.

I imposed a vow of silence on my client until he came to give his evidence, and then I heard Phillida ask if she might call Dr Cogger first as he was a busy man and had to get away to his practice. To this I readily agreed, as it would suit me very well to put the case I had worked out in the early hours to the senior doctor before I came to cross-examine the mysterious Marietta.

Dr Cogger was apparently well known to Sir Hector, and to

several members of the committee to whom he nodded in a
friendly fashion as he settled himself in the witness's chair.
Yes, he told Phillida, he had known Dr Rahmat since he joined
the practice and always found him a pleasant and hard-working
colleague 'within his limitations'. He had been shocked at the
complaint Miss Liptrott made when he treated her for nervous
depression, following the incident in the surgery. Finally, with
great seriousness, Mrs Erskine-Brown asked, 'And tell us, Dr
Cogger, if a young woman came to you with a sore throat, can
you think of any reason for asking her to lie on a couch and
remove her knickers?'

There was a certain amount of chortling from the Press
Gallery, at which an attendant in a commissionaire's uniform
shouted, 'Silence!' Sir Hector glared savagely upwards and Dr
Cogger shrugged his muscular shoulders and said, with apparent sorrow, 'I'm afraid I can't.'

'Dr Cogger. You are no doubt familiar with infectious mononucleosis, commonly known as glandular fever?' I began my
cross-examination.

'Of course.'

'Is it not so prevalent among young people that it is sometimes called the "kissing disease"?'

'I think you may take it, Mr Rumpole' – Sir Hector spoke
whilst still gazing up at the ceiling, apparently bored – 'that we
all know what glandular fever is.'

'Well, I should have thought so, sir.' I tried a charming
smile which he didn't notice. 'That's why I can't understand
why anyone should find Dr Rahmat's method of examination in
the least peculiar. Is not a symptom of glandular fever' – I
turned to the witness – 'a sore throat?'

'It can be,' Dr Cogger agreed reluctantly.

'In fact, the patient may complain of a sore throat only?'

'That may happen.'

'But if you suspect glandular fever you may look for the
other symptoms, such as swellings in the armpits and the
groin?'

'You might.'

'A competent doctor would do so?'

'If he suspected mononucleosis. Yes.'

'So when a young woman, who complained of a sore throat, came to a competent doctor, he might ask her to lie on the couch and remove her knickers so that he could examine her groin?'

'It's possible.'

'Dr Cogger. Are you trying to assist this committee by telling us the truth?'

'Yes. Of course.'

'Then why did you tell my learned friend, Mrs Erskine-Brown, that you could think of no reason why Dr Rahmat should examine this young lady in the way described?'

'Steady on, Mr Rumpole!' Dr Rahmat did his best to keep his whisper away from the microphone, but he was clearly agitated. 'You don't mean to attack Tim Cogger, do you? Such a decent fellow!'

'I mean to win this case for you, if you'll only shut up,' I whispered back, and wished my client would go for a walk in the park until it was all over. 'Well, what's the answer?'

'I suppose the complaint you're suggesting didn't occur to me.'

'You mean, you're a good doctor, like Dr Rahmat, within your limitations? One limitation being you forget the odd disease occasionally?'

Dr Cogger flushed and moved restlessly, looking as though he'd have liked to have got me out on the rugger field and done for me in the scrum. Rahmat whispered, 'Don't be so merciless, Rumpole,' and Sir Hector came to the witness's rescue with 'I hope you're not suggesting that a routine examination includes the doctor trying to kiss his patient and suggesting there might be "time for a quick one"?' The lugubrious Scot had, unhappily, put his finger on the weakness of our case.

Instead of arguing, I decided that the best form of defence was the attack which I had planned during the sleepless watches of the night and which, in daylight and under the cold eyes of the hostile medics, seemed even more perilous. And my client was probably going to hate it.

'Dr Cogger. You say you treated Miss Liptrott for nervous tension. What did you give her? A couple of aspirins?'

'No. I prescribed Phobomorin, so far as I can remember.'

'Is that an expensive drug?'

'I believe it's fairly expensive. I haven't looked up the price lately.'

'Is it supplied by the firm of manufacturing chemists whose representative buys you lunch at the Savoy Hotel?'

The question took the witness by surprise and he seemed to feel in danger. He had denied he'd ever been at such a lunch to me, but now, on his oath, he seemed to feel an unexpected compulsion to tell the truth. He did his best by smiling confidentially at Sir Hector and saying, 'Peter Kellaway of Marchmain's is a personal friend. We lunch together occasionally.'

'And when you last lunched together who paid?'

'I can't remember.'

'Try to think.'

'It may have been Peter.'

'Or may it have been his company, Marchmain's? The manufacturing chemist?'

'Mr Rumpole' – Sir Hector spoke as though I was a backward medical student who insisted on asking questions about housemaid's knee in the brain surgery class – 'we are here to decide if your client made a sexual assault on his patient. What on earth have Dr Cogger's lunches at the Savoy got to do with it?'

'I quite agree, sir. These questions can't possibly be relevant.' Counsel for the Prosecution arose in all her glory.

'One at a time, please, Portia.' I managed a resonant whisper across the room and then turned on the elder of the kirk. 'It is a well-known fact that in any trial questions which may seem irrelevant at first lead straight to the truth, however deeply it is buried. Therefore wise judges are extremely reluctant to interrupt a cross-examination by the Defence. Less experienced tribunals are, of course, frequently tempted to do so.'

I got a look from the presiding Scot which seemed to indicate a desire to sentence me to a long stretch in the Aberdeen Home for Incurables, but then he conferred with his legal assessor, a balding barrister in mufti, and decided to let me go on. 'Continue, Mr Rumpole, provided the next question shows some relevance to this case.'

'You said Dr Rahmat had his limitations?' I attacked the witness again. 'Did you mean that he was unwilling to agree to prescribe certain drugs?'

'We had some disagreements about drugs. Yes. I thought his treatment often old-fashioned.'

'You mean he wouldn't prescribe expensive drugs from Marchmain's?'

In the silence that followed, Sir Hector at last leant forward attentively and the other doctors appeared interested. I thought they'd known cases of drug companies offering sweeteners to medical practitioners.

'Some of the drugs I thought we should use came from Marchmain's, I suppose.'

'Yes, I suppose so. Tell me, did you only get expensive lunches out of it, or did a little cash change hands occasionally?'

'Hold on, Mr Rumpole! This is quite unnecessary.' My client was clearly upset.

'Oh, do shut up, Rahmat!' Hostile witnesses can be coped with, but mutinous clients are intolerable. Then I regained my composure and smiled quite winsomely at Dr Cogger. 'Well, Doctor. Would you care to answer the question?'

'Perhaps' – Phillida rose and smiled at the seat of judgment in a way which was far more winsome than anything I could have managed – 'the witness should be warned that he needn't answer questions which might, well' – she picked up and inserted the distasteful words as though with a delicate pair of forceps – 'incriminate him.'

This was a grave tactical error by the fair prosecutor because Sir Hector duly warned the witness and Dr Cogger came to the conclusion that it was a question which, with the best will in the world, he preferred not to answer. From then on, of course, his credibility content sank rapidly.

'Quite right!' Rhamat's behaviour was extraordinary. 'No need at all for Tim to answer such an impertinent question!'

'You can't make an omelette without breaking eggs,' I told him, and then turned to the witness. 'And because he refused to take part in your prescription racket' – Rahmat winced and sighed with disapproval again – 'you wanted to get him out of the practice?'

'It's very hard to get rid of a partner as you know, Mr Rumpole.' Dr Cogger may have thought his answer clever. In fact, it was unwise in the extreme.

'Very hard,' I agreed, 'unless you can get him found guilty of professional misconduct.'

'Mr Rumpole!' Dr Cogger leaned back in his witness's chair, all his self-confidence returned as he said with great good humour, 'You're not suggesting I went into Dr Rahmat's room and tempted him into seducing *me*, are you?'

'Don't ask me questions!' I tried the snub brutal and was pleased to see that the Judges around us had been less than amused by Dr Cogger's fantasy seduction. 'Just look at *this*, will you.'

This was a document unhappily familiar to the Prosecutor – another copy of that issue of *Casanova*, which had turned up both in Erskine-Brown's room and Dr Cogger's surgery. It was carried to the witness by one of the aged commissionaires, with a marker in the relevant page. 'Do you see an advertisement there, headed NAUGHTY MARIETTA?'

'What on earth has this got to do with the case we're trying?' Sir Hector had noticed the cover of *Casanova* and knew the devil's work when he saw it.

'If you listen,' I told him, 'you will soon discover the answer.' And I asked the witness if it didn't appear to be an advertisement for an escort service.

'It would seem so.'

'And do you see a photograph of the young lady who calls herself Naughty Marietta?'

'Yes, I do.'

'Is that Miss Marietta Liptrott? The lady you treated for a nervous disorder and the complainant in this case?'

There was a long silence. Sir Hector looked at the ceiling. Other doctors examined their finger-nails or sat with their pencils poised waiting to write down the answer. Portia looked at me with a half-smiling tribute to Rumpole's ability to pull something out of the hat in the most unlikely cases and Rahmat, of course, whispered, 'Stop the attack on poor Tim, Mr Rumpole. It is quite uncalled for.'

'It looks like her,' Dr Cogger admitted at last.

'It *is* her,' I said. After all, I had confirmed that fact on the telephone. 'This children's nurse we've heard about goes out to dinner for money. Rather like you, Dr Cogger.'

'Just what are you suggesting?'

'You know quite well, don't you? I'm suggesting you paid this girl to stage the scene in Dr Rahmat's consulting room. The scream, the rushing out into the waiting-room, the complaint and the nervous disorder. It was all an act. A put-up job. So you could get Dr Rahmat out of your practice. Because he wouldn't cooperate. Did you suggest she should complain of a sore throat, or was it just a bit of luck that Dr Rahmat suspected glandular fever?'

'That's absolutely ridiculous! I didn't know of the existence of Miss Liptrott until after the incident took place.'

'Did you not? This incident, we've heard, took place on March 13th of this year. Will you look at the cover of that *Casanova*? What is the date on it?'

Dr Cogger took the magazine with some reluctance and announced with even more hesitation, 'January of this year.'

'And you know where this magazine was found, don't you? We can ask Miss Dankwerts, if you don't wish to answer.'

'I know.'

'Will you tell the tribunal?'

'Apparently it was found in the waiting-room.'

'Of *your* surgery?'

'Yes.'

I sat down then next to a client, who, far from congratulating me on a cross-examination of even more than my usual brilliance, sat with his head in his hands, murmuring, 'Oh, Mr Rumpole. You shouldn't have put poor old Tim through the mill like that. There was no need, I told you that. No need whatsoever.'

'Nonsense, old darling. Pull yourself together. You can't make an omelette without breaking eggs, as I told you.' And then I had to leave him to stew because Miss Liptrott, who

had come into the room and was taking the oath, now
demanded my full attention.

The complainant was not, in any sense, beautiful, but she was
young, her eyes were bright, her jeans clean and well-ironed,
and she seemed, even in the circumstances in which she found
herself, unexpectedly cheerful. She admitted, in answer to
Portia's gentle questioning, that she was a children's nurse
who often went out in the evenings, as one of a number of
friends who had got together to form an escort agency, which
they had named – and this seemed to give her particular
pleasure – after her.

Looking at Miss Liptrott, I was discouraged to see what
appeared to be an honest witness. I had fired all my ammunition at Dr Cogger and, although severely holed below the
water-line, he had not quite sunk. He had not admitted the
conspiracy and I would need to get Marietta to crumble if Dr
Rahmat were to be back plying his stethoscope as usual. All
right, I guessed the more sensible doctors on the committee
were thinking to themselves, perhaps she is an escort, which
may mean she's a call girl. She's still entitled to have her sore
throat seen to without being molested.

Carefully, slowly, and with extreme tact my opponent took
the girl through her story. Now we were in the consulting
room and Dr Rahmat had asked her to lie on the couch.

'And what happened then?'

'He said he just wanted to see if I had any swellings and
asked if I'd mind him feeling.'

'Did he remove your knickers?'

'No. I think I may have pulled them down.'

'And then? What happened then?'

'I am not . . . quite sure.' The witness frowned slightly and
seemed to be doing her very best to remember. 'I think he
went to a basin in the corner of the room to wash his hands.'

'And what did you do?'

'Oh, I ran screaming out of the door.'

Marietta smiled at Sir Hector as though inviting him to join
her in laughing at the silliness of her behaviour.

'What made you do that?' Phillida was still admirably patient.

'I don't know, really. I'd been up late with a very boring gentleman who kept me up talking half the night about the mortgage rates. I was overtired, I think. My nerves were bad. I suppose I just lost control of myself.'

'Had Dr Rahmat tried to kiss you?'

'Don't lead,' I grumbled, but the protest was unnecessary. Whatever lead Phillida gave, the girl was clearly not going to follow it.

'I'm . . . I'm sure he hadn't.'

'Did he put his hand between your legs?'

'Oh, no!' Miss Liptrott looked shocked. 'I'm sure he didn't do that either.'

'You apparently ran out of the room shouting, "The beast! The beast!" Do you remember that?'

'Not really. If I did, I wasn't talking about Dr Rahmat. I'd met some other people who weren't very nice.'

'Miss Liptrott' – Sir Hector looked like an elder of the kirk who has just been reliably informed that there is no such thing as hell and that sin is now permissible – 'you made a statement to the General Medical Council to the effect that Dr Rahmat made improper advances to you.'

I looked round the Court in the pause that followed. Dr Cogger was now in the public gallery, leaning forward in his seat, looking as mystified as everyone except the witness, who seemed to find her behaviour perfectly natural.

'Well. I'd made such a fuss in the surgery. I felt I had to give some reason for it, otherwise you'd have thought me very silly, wouldn't you? But I always meant to tell the truth when I got here.'

'And what is the truth, Miss Liptrott?' Phillida's line sounded less like a question than a cry for help; but help for the prosecution case was not forthcoming.

'The truth' – Marietta now seemed to have no doubt about the matter – 'is that Dr Rahmat always behaved like a perfect gentleman.'

It was at this point that Phillida, after a whispered

consultation with her instructing solicitor, threw in the towel.
'In view of the evidence which has just been given, we do not
feel it would be right to continue with the case against Dr
Rahmat.' The battle was over and I had no idea how I had
come to gain such a decisive victory.

'Mr Rumpole' – Sir Hector was looking at me with slightly
less than his usual disgust – 'during the course of your cross-
examination you made certain serious allegations against Dr
Cogger. As I understand it, you suggested he joined with this
young lady in a conspiracy to "frame", if I may use a common
expression . . .'

'Oh, by all means, sir. "Frame" puts it very nicely.'

'Very well then. To "frame" Dr Rahmat. In view of the
evidence we have just heard, may we take it that all such
allegations are now withdrawn?'

I was about to open my mouth when Dr Rahmat was up beside
me, standing to attention and saying at the top of his voice,
'Unreservedly withdrawn, sir. Dr Tim Cogger is a fine man.
He leaves this Court without a stain on his character. My
barrister-at-law will confirm this without a moment's delay.'

'Do you agree, Mr Rumpole?'

'Oh, yes.' I may have sounded a little mournful as my
brilliant defence went out of the window, but I resigned gracefully. 'I agree. Not a stain on the Doctor's character.'

'*A Passage to India*' – I reminded Dr Rahmat when we went
for a celebratory bottle of plonk in a wine bar off the Maryle-
bone Road – 'ends with the girl, who's meant to have been
raped by the Indian doctor, withdrawing her whole story in
Court.'

'Such a brilliant writer, old E.M.F.,' Dr Rahmat agreed.
'Always so true to life.'

'Do you think the Naughty Marietta's read the book?'

'Well, sir, perhaps.'

There was a pause as I filled my mouth with the wine,
product, perhaps, of the same sun-starved vineyard which
grew the Château Thames Embankment grape. Then I said,
'Who do you think put her up to it?'

'Oh, Tim Cogger, undoubtedly.' Dr Rahmat smiled tolerantly. 'He wanted to get rid of me, you see. He thought I had tumbled to why he was wanting us all to use the Marchmain drugs.'

'You think he hired Marietta?' I looked at the man, amazed at his conversion to my view of the case.

'Oh, I'm sure he did so.'

'How are you sure?'

'She told me.'

I finished the glass. Soon I should finish the bottle.

'You've talked to her about it?'

'Oh, certainly. I have taken her out to dinner on a number of occasions. We go to the Star of Hyderabad. It was not something I thought you would wish to know.'

'Why?'

'I knew I had the most brilliant barrister-at-law. I knew you would win my case, but I didn't want to win by rubbishing poor old Tim Cogger. I want to keep my partnership, you know. I want to get on well with all the chaps in the surgery, Dr Tim included. So it seemed the best way out was to persuade Miss Liptrott to tell the truth, which is that nothing happened. It seemed to me such an easy way to win the case, but far too unsubtle, of course, for a brilliant barrister-at-law like yourself. But at least I managed, sir, to make an omelette without the breaking of a single egg!'

I looked at the chap with a sinking feeling. What if the infection spread and all clients got themselves off without any help from the learned friends? The future of the legal profession began to look bleak.

'There's one other thing you might tell me,' I asked, as I stared at the quack in amazement. 'How much did you give the lady to persuade her to tell the truth?'

'I gave her, as you might say, sir, all my worldly goods.'

'What are you talking about? Don't babble!'

'To be honest with you, Mr Rumpole, I do not babble. Miss Marietta Liptrott is as charming and honest as she is beautiful. She has done me the honour of agreeing to be my wife. The ceremony will be at the mosque in Regent's Park, with a reception to follow at the Star of Hyderabad in the Gloucester Road. You and your good lady are cordially invited.'

'And Dr Cogger, of course.' I began to get the picture.

'Oh, yes, indeed. All the surgery will come. And I hope that Tim Cogger will propose the toast to the happy couple. I shall certainly ask him.'

'And in all the circumstances,' I thought it fair to say, 'I don't see how he can refuse.'

'Rumpole. Something distinctly peculiar has happened.'

'You mean you lost "Rahmat", Portia? Not your fault, I assure you. That case took on a life of its own. We were both left with omelettes on our faces, in a manner of speaking.'

'No, it's not that exactly. Look. I'd better tell you and see if you can offer any sort of explanation. You know I was going to lay a trap for Claude?'

'You told me. And I trembled for the fellow.'

'Well. It didn't really come off.' Our Portia settled herself in the client's chair in my room. I lit a small cigar and prepared to listen to her account which went more or less as follows. She had written an answer to the advertisement in *Casanova* to the box number indicated, in the following terms:

Dear Barrister bored with married life, I am slim, intelligent and considered attractive. I am more than ready for the occasional fling, but I can think of better ways of spending an evening than going to the Opera. Sorry I haven't got a photograph, but I've had no complaints about my looks. Suggest we meet at a place convenient to you, in the Temple churchyard by Oliver Goldsmith's tomb, 5.30 next Thursday week. We'll both wear red carnations. I look forward eagerly to the ensuing fun and games. I'm also in a rut and bored to tears with married life!

She sent this missive, sure that it would trap the errant Claude and when he showed up, over-excited, with a flower in his button-hole, she would let him have it to some considerable effect. 'The odd thing is, Rumpole, I went to the churchyard with my red carnation and Claude never turned up. Do you think he'd got wind of what I was up to? You didn't say anything to him, did you?'

'Now, Portia. Would I?'

'I don't know. You men always stick together. I waited for about half an hour. In the drizzle. The churchyard was empty.'

'No one came?'

'Well, I didn't see a soul. Except that new pupil here. What's her name?'

'Mrs Whittaker.'

'Yes. She was hanging about, looking at the inscriptions on the tombs and, you know, it was rather a coincidence. She was wearing a red carnation.'

'Did you speak?'

'I think I said "hello" and she wandered off. Perhaps she'd been to a wedding or something.'

'Perhaps.' And then a vague memory struck me. I looked up Claude's alleged advertisement in the copy of *Casanova* I had brought back with my papers in the Rahmat case and read it through carefully. Then I read it through again.

'Portia,' I said, 'you're a brilliant advocate and your court-room manner is irresistible. But it's no good lightly skimming the written evidence. You haven't read every word, every letter. Just look at this again.' I handed her the document. 'Read it aloud, if you'd be so kind.'

'Barrister. Good-looking and young at heart. In a rut. Bored with the humdrum of married life . . .'

'Just look carefully after the word barrister. Isn't there a small letter in brackets?'

'Well, yes. It looks like an "f".'

'It is an "f". You were so sure you had Claude in the frame that you didn't notice it. "F" for female. It's a lady barrister in search of adventure. A lady barrister who shares Claude's room, which is why you found the magazine there. So it was a lady barrister who turned up wearing a carnation. I'm sorry, Portia. I'm afraid you disappointed her.'

'Mrs Whittaker?'

'The evidence seems conclusive. Poor old Mr Whittaker. He

must be of the humdrum persuasion. You know, perhaps we should take out a subscription to *Casanova*. We've learnt a good deal, haven't we, from a single issue?'

But Portia was off, smiling now, in search of her husband. She might even be going to buy him lunch at the Savoy. People only seek out Rumpole when they're in trouble.

There is little more to tell. Bambi rang once more to tell me that she had had another little mishap with the white Volkswagen and was being done for dangerous driving. 'Can't help, I'm afraid,' I told her. 'What you need for that is a brilliant Q.C. Only way to get off with your record. There's an absolutely scintillating silk called Sam Ballard. I might get him to take you on.'

'Oh, really? Is he cuddly?'

'Sam Ballard? Well known for it.' And I told her, 'He cuddles for England. And there's something else, he's in a rut. Bored to tears with married life.'

A week later I was in the clerk's room, talking to Uncle Tom, who, as usual, was practising putts into the waste-paper basket, when there was a tintinnabulation of costume jewellery, a clatter of high heels and Mrs Bambi Etheridge passed through on her way to Ballard's room. She flashed me a smile, but her mind was clearly on higher things, and she went up to her assignation leaving us with her lingering perfume.

'Odd sort of pong.' Uncle Tom was thoughtful. 'A bit reminiscent of the red light district of Port Said.'

'It's Deadly Sins,' I told him, 'by St Just.'

'Is it, really? Of course, I've never been to Port Said. I say, Rumpole. What a lot you know about women!'

'Not much,' I admitted. 'I am continually surprised.'

'I say' – Uncle Tom became so entranced by the thought that he failed to hole into the waste-paper basket in one – 'I wonder if Ballard'll make a play for her, and she'll come out screaming like the girl in your case! That'd liven things up a bit.'

'I'm afraid' – and I was already feeling a touch of pity for Soapy Sam – 'that Ballard'll be the one who comes out screaming.'

But all was silent from upstairs. I could only think I had brought two people together who needed, and deserved, each other.

Rumpole for the Prosecution

As anyone who has cast half an eye over these memoirs will know, the second of the Rumpole commandments consists of the simple injunction 'Thou shalt not prosecute.' Number one is 'Thou shalt not plead guilty.' Down the line, of course, there are other valuable precepts such as 'Never pay for the drink Jack Pommeroy is prepared to put on the slate', 'Never trust a vegetarian', 'If Sam Ballard thinks it, then it must be wrong', 'Never go shopping with She Who Must Be Obeyed', 'Don't ask a question unless you're damn sure you know the answer', 'If a judge makes a particularly absurd remark, rub his nose in it, i.e. repeat it to the Jury with raised eyebrows every hour on the hour' and 'Never ask an instructing solicitor if his leg's better'. This last is as fatal as asking a client if he happens to be guilty; you run a terrible danger of being told.

But the rule against prosecuting has been the lodestar of my legal career. I obey this precept for a number of reasons, all cogent. It seems to me that errant and misguided humanity has enough on its plate without running the daily risk of being driven, cajoled or hoodwinked into the nick by Rumpole in full flood, armed with an unparalleled knowledge of bloodstains and a remarkable talent for getting a jury to see things his way. As everyone – except a nun in a Trappist order and the Home Secretary – now knows, the prison system is bursting at the seams and it would be out of the question for even more captives to arrive at the gates thanks to my forensic skills.

Then again, prosecuting counsel tend to be fawned on by Mr Justice Graves and his like, characters whom I prefer to keep in a state of healthy hostility. Finally, I should point out that it is the task of prosecuting counsel to present the facts in a neutral manner and not try to score a victory. This duty (not always carried out, I may say, by those who habitually persecute down the Old Bailey) takes the fun out of the art of advocacy. There are many adjectives which might be used to describe Rumpole at work but 'neutral' is not among them. It is a sad but inescapable fact that as soon as I buckle on the wig and gown and march forth to war in the courtroom, the old adrenalin courses through my veins and all I want to do is win.

Bearing all this in mind, you may find it hard to understand how, in the case that came to be known as the 'Mews Murder', I took the brief in a private prosecution brought by the dead girl's father.

'All right, Mr Rumpole. You're out to protect the underdog, I understand that. I might say that I find it very sympathetic. You attack the establishment. Tease the judges. Give the police a hard time. Well, doesn't my daughter deserve defending as much as any of your clients?'

I looked down at the pile of press-cuttings on my desk and at the photograph of Veronica Fabian. She was a big, rather plain girl in her early twenties. I imagined that she had a loud laugh and an untidy bedroom. There was also, in spite of her smile, a look of disappointment and a lack of confidence about her, and I thought she might have been a girl who often fell unhappily in love. Whatever she had been like, she had died, beaten to death in an empty mews house in Notting Hill Gate. I didn't altogether understand what I could do in her defence, or how such an earthbound tribunal as a judge and jury down the Old Bailey could now pass judgment on her.

'You want me to defend your daughter?'

'Yes, Mr Rumpole. That's exactly what I want.'

Gregory Fabian, senior partner in the firm of Fabian & Winchelsea, purveyors of discreet homes to the rich and famous, dealers in stately homes and ambassadorial dwellings, had aged, I imagined, since the death of his daughter. There is something squalid about murder which brings a sense of shame to the victim's as well as the killer's family. In spite of this,

Fabian spoke moderately and without rancour. He was a
slim man, in his early sixties, short but handsome, clear-
featured, with creases at the sides of his eyes and the general
appearance of someone who laughed a good deal in happier
times.

'Isn't it a little late for that? To defend her, I mean?'

'There's no time limit on murder is there?' He smiled at me
gently as he said this, and I was prepared to accept that his
interest went beyond mere revenge.

'Justice! We haven't had much of that, sir. Not since they
decided not to charge Jago. We just wanted to know how much
that cost him. Whatever it was, he could probably afford it.'
Up spoke young Roger Fabian, the dead girl's brother and the
one who, being very close in appearance to his father, seemed
to have inherited all the good looks in the family and left little
for his sister. He looked what he probably had been, the most
popular boy in whatever uncomfortable and expensive public
school he had attended; but he bore his good fortune modestly,
and even managed to slander the fair name of the serious
crimes squad with a certain inoffensive charm. His habit of
calling me 'sir' made me feel uncomfortably respectable. I
wondered if all prosecuting counsel get called 'sir' at conferences.

'Why did the police let him go? That's what we want you to
find out.'

'You were recommended to us as a barrister who didn't
mind having a go at a man like Detective Chief Inspector
Brush.'

Brush? The very copper who, in his salad days, had been the
hammer of the Timsons and my constant sparring partner
down the Bailey, now promoted to giddy heights in charge of a
West London area, where he had brilliantly failed to solve the
'Mews Murder' and let Christopher Jago, the number one
suspect, out of his clutches.

'They say you'll never be a judge, so you're not afraid of
going for the police, Mr Rumpole.' Fabian senior managed to
make it sound like a compliment.

'They said we weren't to mind about the soup on the tie or

the cigar ash down the waistcoat.' Fabian junior was even more complimentary. 'And you don't care a toss for the establishment.'

'They said you'd do this job far better than the usual sort of polite and servile Q.C.' And when I asked George Fabian who they were, who spoke so highly of Rumpole, and he gave the name of Pyecraft & Wensleydale, our instructing solicitor and one of the poshest firms in the city, I could hardly forbear to preen myself visibly.

In answer to repeated inquiries from Pyecraft, Detective Chief Inspector Brush and his men had disclosed the gist of Christopher Jago's statement to them. He said he was a local estate agent, who had seen the For Sale notices outside 13A Gissing Mews, off Westbourne Grove, and wanted to view the property for a client of his own. He had rung Fabian & Winchelsea, and been put through to a young lady, believed to have been Veronica Fabian, who worked with her brother and father in the family business. He made an appointment to meet her at the house in question at eight thirty the following morning. The time was set by Jago, who was leaving that day to do a deal in some time-share apartments on the Costa del Sol. When Jago got to 13A Gissing Mews, the front door was open. He went in, expecting to meet Miss Fabian, whom he told the police he had never met before. The little mews house was still half-furnished and decorated, apparently, with African rugs and carvings. There were some spears fixed to the wall of the hallway, and a weighted knobkerrie, a three-foot black club, had been torn down and caused the fatal blow to the girl. Jago said he had knelt beside her body and tried to raise her head, during which operation his cuff had become smeared with blood.

Then there followed the events which might have made any family feel that they had good reason to suspect Christopher Jago. He said he panicked. There he was with a dead girl whose blood was on his clothing and he felt sure he would be accused of some sort of sex killing – one of the murders which had recently terrified the neighbourhood. He left the house, drove to the airport and went on his way to Spain. Two hours

later, the owner of the mews called to collect some of his
possessions, found the body and called the police. Veronica
Fabian had died from extensive wounds to her skull. The only
real clue was the name she had written against her eight thirty
appointment in her desk diary: Arthur Morrison. The police
spent a great deal of time trying to find or identify the man
Morrison but without success.

As luck would have it, Jago had parked his car on a resident's
parking place in the mews, and the irate resident had taken its
number. When he got back to England, Jago was questioned as
a possible witness. He immediately admitted that he had found
the dead girl, panicked and run away. However, after several
days when he was assisting the police with their inquiries (often
a euphemism for getting himself stitched up) Jago was released
to the surprise and fury of the surviving members of the
Fabian family.

'You'd've charged him at least, Mr Rumpole, wouldn't you?'
Fabian *père* sounded, as ever, reasonable.

'Perhaps. But I've grown up with the awkward habit of
believing everyone innocent until they're proved guilty.'

'But you'll take it on for us, won't you? At least let a jury
decide?'

'I'll have to think about it.' I lit a small cigar and blew out
smoke. If Fabian *fils* had come expecting ash down the waistcoat I might as well let him have it. It's a curious English
system, in my view, which allows private citizens to prosecute
each other for crimes with the aim of sending each other to
chokey, and I wasn't at all sure that it ought to be encouraged.
I mean, where would it end? I might be tempted to draft an
indictment against Sam Ballard, the Head of our Chambers,
on the grounds of public nuisance. I had caught this soapy
customer ostentatiously pinning up NO SMOKING notices in
the passage outside my door.

'But we've got to have justice, Mr Rumpole. Isn't that the
point?'

'Have we? "Use every man after his desert," as a well-
known Dane put it, "and who should escape whipping?"' I
puffed out another small cigar cloud, hoping it would eventu-

ally waft its way in the general direction of our Head of Chambers who would, no doubt, go off like a fire alarm. I was thinking of the difficulty of having a client I could never meet in this world, whom I could never ask what happened when she went to the mews house to meet this mysterious and vanished Morrison or, indeed, whether she wanted such secrets as she may have had to be dragged out in a trial which could no longer have any interest for her.

'The power of evil is everywhere, Rumpole. And I'm afraid everywhere includes our own Chambers at Equity Court. That is why I have sought you out, although one doesn't like to spend too much time in these places.'

'Does one not?' I consider any hour wasted which is not passed with a hand round a comforting glass of Château Thames Embankment in Pommeroy's haven of rest.

'Passive alcoholism, Rumpole.' Sam Ballard, who, I imagine, gets his hair-shirts from the Army & Navy Stores and whose belligerent puritanism makes Praise-God-Barebones look like Giovanni Casanova, had crept up on me at the bar and abandoned himself to a slimline tonic. 'You've heard of passive smoking, of course?'

'I've heard of it. Although, I have to say, I prefer the active variety.'

'Passive alcoholism's the same thing. Abstainees can absorb the fumes from neighbouring drinkers and become alcoholics. Quite easily.'

'Is that one of Matey's medical theories?' Sam Ballard, of course, had fallen for the formidable Mrs Marguerite Plumstead, the Old Bailey matron, and made her his bride, an act which lends considerable support to the theory that love is blind.

'Marguerite is, of course, extremely well informed on all health problems. So now, when we ask colleagues to dinner, we make it clear that our house is an alcohol-free zone.'

This colleague thought, with some gratitude, that the Bollard house in Waltham Cross would also be Rumpole-free in the future. 'But that wasn't why I wanted a word in confidence, Rumpole. I need to enlist your help, as a senior, in years anyway, a very senior member of Equity Court. A grave crime has been committed.'

'Oh my God!' I did my best to look stricken. 'Some bandit hasn't pinched the nail-brush again?'

'I'm afraid, Rumpole' – Bollard looked as though he were about to announce the outbreak of the Black Death, or at least the Hundred Years War – 'this goes beyond pilfering in the downstairs toilet.'

'Not nail-brush nicking this time, eh?'

'No, Rumpole. This time it would appear to be forgery, false pretence and obtaining briefs by fraud.' I lit another small cigar which had the desired effect of making Bollard tell his story as rapidly as possible, like a man with a vital message to get out before the poison gas rises above his head. It seemed that Miss Tricia Benbow – a somewhat ornate lady solicitor in whom Henry finds, when she enters his clerk's room with the light behind her, a distinct resemblance to the late Princess Grace of Monaco – had sent a brief in some distant and unappetizing County Court (Snaresbrook, Luton or Land's End, for all I can remember) to young David Inchcape whose legal career was in its tyro stages. Someone, as this precious brief was lying in the clerk's room, scratched out Inchcape's name and substituted that of Claude Erskine-Brown, who duly turned up at the far-flung Court to the surprise of Miss Benbow who had expected a younger man. An inquiry was instituted and, within hours, Sherlock Ballard, Q.C. was on the case. Henry denied all knowledge of the alteration, which seemed to have occurred before he entered the brief in his ledger, young Inchcape looked hard-done-by, and Claude Erskine-Brown, whose performances in Court were marked by a painstaking attention to the letter of the law, emerged as public enemy number one.

'That quality of evil is all pervasive.' The slimline tonic seemed to have gone to Ballard's head. He spoke in an impressive whisper and his eyes glittered with all the enthusiasm of a Grand Inquisitor preparing for the *auto-da-fé*. 'In my view it has entered into the character of Erskine-Brown.'

Not much can be said in criticism of that misguided, and

somewhat fatuous, old darling with whom I have shared Chambers at Equity Court for more years than we like to remember. Claude's taste for the headier works of Richard Wagner fills him with painful longings for young ladies connected with the legal profession, whom he no doubt sees as Rhine Maidens or mini-Valkyries in wig and gown. In Court his behaviour can vacillate between the ponderous and the panic-stricken, so those who think unkindly of him, among whom I do not number myself, might reasonably describe him as a pompous twit. All that having been said, the soul of Claude Erskine-Brown is about as remote from evil as Pommeroy's plonk is from Château Latour.

'Claude would be flattered to hear you say he was evil,' I told our Head of Chambers. 'He might feel he'd got a touch of the Nibelungens or something.'

'I noticed it from the time we did that case about the dirty restaurant. He wanted to conceal the fact that he'd been dining there with his female instructing solicitor. From what I remember, he wanted to mislead the Court about it.'*

'Well, that's true,' I conceded. 'Old Claude, so far as I can see, conducts his love life with the minimum of sexual satisfaction and the maximum amount of embarrassment to all concerned. If you want to call that evil . . .'

'A man who wishes to deceive his wife is quite capable of deceiving his Head of Chambers.' For a moment I caught in Ballard's voice an echo of that moral certainty which characterizes the judgments of She Who Must Be Obeyed.

'How do you know he'd deceive you? Have you asked him if he put his name on the brief?'

'I'm afraid Erskine-Brown has added perjury to his other offences.'

'You mean he denied it?'

'Hotly.'

'No one in the clerk's room did it?'

'Henry and Dianne say they didn't and I'm prepared to accept their evidence. Rumpole, when it comes to crime, you have considerably more experience than any of us.'

---

* See 'Rumpole à la Carte'.

'Thank you very much.'

'I want to undertake a thorough investigation of this matter. Examine the witnesses. And if Erskine-Brown's found
guilty . . .'

'What, then?'

'You know as well as I do, Rumpole. There is no place in
Equity Court for fellows who pinch other fellows' briefs.'

I gave Soapy Sam the chance of a little passive enjoyment of
the heady fumes of Château Fleet Street and thought the
matter over. Poor old Claude was probably guilty. The starring
role played by his wife, Phillida, now luxuriously wrapped in
the silk gown of Q.C., in so many long-running cases must
have made him despondent about his own practice, which
varied between the second-rate and the mediocre. The sight of
a brief delivered by a solicitor he fancied sufficiently to fill up
with priceless delicacies at La Maison Jean-Pierre to a white-
wig must have wounded him deeply.

Moreover, it had to be remembered that he had admitted
young Inchcape to our Chambers under the impression that he
was thereby proving his tolerance to those of the gay persuasion, only to discover that Inchcape was in fact a closet
heterosexual and his successful rival for the favours of Mizz
Liz Probert.* All these were mitigating factors which would
spring instantly to the mind of one who always acted for the
Defence. They were already outweighing any horror I might
have felt at the crime he had probably committed.

'I'm sorry, Bollard.' Our leader was still alongside me, his
nose pointedly aimed from the direction of the glass that
contained my ever-diminishing double red. 'I can't help you.
It's the second time today I've been asked; but prosecution
isn't my line of country. Rumpole always defends.'

Not long after that events occurred which persuaded me to
change my mind, with results which may have an incalculable
effect on whatever is left of my future.

*

* See 'Rumpole and the Quality of Life' in *Rumpole and the Age of
Miracles*, Penguin Books, 1988.

It was that grim season of the year, which now begins around the end of August and reaches its climax in the first week of December, known as the 'build-up to Christmas'. I have often thought that if the Son of Man had known what he was starting he would have chosen to be born on a quiet summer's day when everyone was off on holiday on what the Timson family always refers to as the Costa del Crime. As it was, crowds of desperate shoppers were elbowing their way to the bus stops in the driving rain. More crammed aboard as we crawled through the West End, where the ornamental lights had been switched on. I sat contemplating the tidings of great joy She Who Must Be Obeyed had brought to me a few weeks earlier. That very night her old school friend, Charmian Nichols, was to arrive to spend the festive season à côté de chez Rumpole in the Gloucester Road.

Readers of these chronicles will only have heard, up till now, of one of the old girls who sported with my wife, Hilda, on the fields of Bexhill Ladies College when the world was somewhat younger than it is today. You will recall the redoubtable Dodo Mackintosh, painter in watercolour and maker of 'cheesy bits' for our Chambers parties, who regards Rumpole with a beady, not to say suspicious, eye, whenever she comes to call. Dodo's place, on this particular Christmas, had been taken by Charmian Nichols. Charlie Nichols, no doubt exhausted by the wear and tear of marriage to a star, who had been not only a monitor and captain of hockey, but winner of the Leadership and Character trophy for two years in succession, had dropped off the twig quite early in the run up to Christmas and the widowed Charmian wrote to Hilda indicating that she had nothing pencilled in for the festive season and was inclined to grant us the favour of her company in the Gloucester Road. She added, in a brief postscript, that if Hilda had made a prior commitment to that 'dowdy little Dodo Mackintosh' she would quite understand. She Who Must Be Obeyed, in whose breast Mrs Nichols was able to awaken feelings of awe and wonder which had lain dormant during our married life, immediately bought a new eiderdown for the spare bedroom and broke the news to Dodo that there would be no room at the inn owing to family commitments. You see it took the winner of the Leadership and Character trophy to lure Hilda to perjury.

'Hilda, dear. Why ever can't you persuade Howard to buy a new Crock-a-Gleam? Absolutely no one plunges their hands into washing-up bowls any more. Of course, it is rather sweetly archaic of you both to still be doing it.'

The late Dean Swift, in one of those masterpieces of English literature which I shall never get around to reading, spoke of a country, I believe, ruled by horses, and there was a definite air of equine superiority about La Nichols. She stood, for a start, several hands higher than Rumpole. Her nostrils flared contemptuously, her eyes were yellowish and her greying mane was carefully combed and braided. She was, I had noticed, elegantly shod and you could have seen your face in her polished little hooves. She would, I devoutly hoped, be off with a thoroughbred turn of speed as soon as Christmas was over.

'You mean, get a dishwasher?' Hilda no longer trusted me to scour the plates to her satisfaction and Charmian had taken my place with the teacloth, dabbing a passable portrait of the Tower of London at our crockery and not knowing where to put it away. 'Oh, Rumpole and I are always talking about that, but we never seem to get around to buying one.' This was another example of the widow's fatal effect on She's regard for the truth; to the best of my recollection the word 'dishwasher' had never passed our lips.

'Well, surely, Harold,' Charmian whinnied at me over the glass she was polishing mercilessly, 'you're going to buy Hilda something white for Christmas?'

'You mean handkerchiefs? I hadn't thought of that. And the name is Horace, but as you're here for Christmas with the family you can call me Rumpole.'

'No, white! A machine to wash plates and things like that? Charlie had far too much respect for my hands to let them get into a state like poor Hilda's.' At this, she looked at my wife with deep sympathy and rattled on, 'Charlie insisted that I could only keep my looks if I was fully automated. Of course I just couldn't have lived the life I did without our Plan-ahead "archive" freezer, our jumbo-microwave and rôtisserie.' Something snapped beneath the teacloth at this point. 'Oh, Hilda. One of your glasses gone for a Burton! Was it terribly precious?'

'Not really. It was a Christmas present from Dodo. From what I can remember.'

'Oh, well then.' Charmian shot the shattered goblet, a reasonably satisfactory container for Pommeroy's Perfectly Ordinary, into the tidy-bin. 'But surely Hammond can afford to mechanize you, Hilda? He's always in Court from what you said in your letters.'

'Legal aid defences,' Hilda told her gloomily, 'don't pay for much machinery.'

'Legal aid!' Charmian pronounced the words as though they constituted a sort of standing joke, like kippers or mothers-in-law. 'Isn't that a sort of National Health? Charlie was always really sorry for our poor little doctor in Guildford who had to pig along on that!'

I wanted to say that I didn't suppose old Charlie had much use for legal aid in his stockbroking business, but I restrained myself. Nor did I explain that our budget was well off balance since our cruise,* which had taken a good deal more than Hilda's late aunt's money, that legal aid fees had been cut and were paid at the pace of a handicapped snail, and that whenever I succeeded in cashing a cheque at the Caring Bank I had to restrain myself from making a dash for the door before they remembered our overdraft. Instead, I have to admit, something about the condescending Charmian, as she looked with vague amusement around our primitive kitchen equipment, made me want to impress her on her own, unadmirable terms.

'As a matter of fact,' I said, casually filling one of Dodo's remaining glasses, 'I don't only do legal aid defences. I get offered quite a few private prosecutions. They can be extremely lucrative.'

'Really, Rumpole. Just how lucrative?' Hilda stood

* See 'Rumpole at Sea'.

transfixed, her rubber gloves poised above the bubbling Fairy
Liquid, waiting for the exact figures. The next morning, when
I arrived at my Chambers in Equity Court, Henry told me.

'Two thousand pounds, Mr Rumpole. And I've agreed
refreshers at five hundred a day. They've promised to send a
cheque down with the brief.'

'And it's a case likely to last a day or two?' I stood awestruck
at the price put upon my prosecution of Christopher Jago.

'We have got it down, Mr Rumpole, for two weeks.' I did
some not so swift calculations, mental arithmetic never having
been my strongest point, and then came to a firm decision.
'Henry,' I said, 'your lady wife, the Mayor of Bexleyheath . . .'

'No longer, Mr Rumpole. Her year of office being over, she
has returned to mere alderman.'

'So you, Henry' – I congratulated the man warmly – 'are no
longer Lady Mayoress?'

'Much to my relief, Mr Rumpole, I have handed in my chain.'

'Henry, you'll be able to tell me. Does the alderman ever
plunge her ex-mayorial hands into the Fairy Liquid?'

'Hardly, Mr Rumpole. We have had a Crock-a-Gleam for
years. You know, we're fully automated.'

Well, of course, I might have said, on a clerk's fees you
would be, wouldn't you? It's only penurious barristers who
are still slaving away with the dishcloth. Instead I made an
expansive gesture. 'Go out, Henry,' I bade him, 'into the
highways and byways of Oxford Street. Order up the biggest,
whitest, most melodiously purring Crock-a-Gleam that money
can buy and have it despatched to Mrs Rumpole at Froxbury
Mansions with the compliments of the season.'

'You're going to prosecute in Jago then, Mr Rumpole?'
Henry looked as surprised as if I had announced I meant to
spend Christmas in a temperance hotel.

'Well, yes, Henry. I just thought I'd try my hand at it. For a
change.'

Finally, my clerk declined a trip up Oxford Street but
Dianne, who was busily engaged in reading her horoscope in
Woman's Own and decorating her finger-nails for Christmas,

undertook to ring John Lewis on my behalf. At which moment my learned friend Claude Erskine-Brown entered the clerk's room looking about as happy as a man who has paid through the nose for tickets for *Die Meistersinger von Nürnberg* and found himself at an evening of 'Come Dancing'. He noted, lugubriously, that there were no briefs in his tray – even those with other people's names on them – and then drew me out into the passage for a heart to heart.

'It's a good thing you were in the clerk's room just then, Rumpole.'

'Oh, is it? Why exactly?'

'Well. Ballard says he doesn't want me to go in there unless some other member of Chambers is present. What's he think I'm going to do? Forge my fee notes or ravish Dianne?'

'Probably both.'

'It's unbelievable.'

'Perhaps. We've got to remember that Ballard specializes in believing the unbelievable. He also thinks you're sunk in sin. He's probably afraid of getting passive sinning by standing too close to you.'

'Rumpole. About that wretched brief in the Rickmansworth County Court . . .'

'Oh, was it Rickmansworth? I thought it was Luton.' I was trying to avoid the moment that barristers dread – when your client looks at you in a trusting and confidential manner and seems about to tell you that he's guilty of the charge on which you've been paid to defend him.

'Rumpole, I wanted to tell you . . .'

'Please, don't, old darling,' I spoke as soothingly as I knew to the deeply distressed Claude. 'We all know the feeling. Acute shortage of crime affecting one's balance of payments. Nothing in your tray, nothing in the diary. The bank manager and the taxman hammering on the door. The VAT man climbing in at the window. Then you wander into the clerk's room and all the briefs seem to be for other people. Well, heaven knows how many times I've been tempted.'

'But I didn't do it, Rumpole. I mean I'd've been mad to do it. It was bound to get found out in the end.'

Many crimes, in my experience, are committed by persons undergoing temporary fits of insanity, who are bound to be found out in the end but I didn't think it tactful to mention this. Instead I asked, 'What about the handwriting on the changed brief?'

'It's in block letters. Not like mine, or anyone else's either. All the same, Ballard seems to have appointed himself judge, jury and handwriting expert. Rumpole' – Claude's voice sank in horror – 'I think he wants me out of Chambers.'

'I wouldn't be surprised.'

'What on earth's Philly going to say?' The man lived in growing awe of Phillida Erskine-Brown, Q.C., the embarrassingly successful Portia of our Chambers. 'I should think she'd be very glad to have you at home to do the washing up,' I comforted him. 'That is, unless you have a Crock-a-Gleam like the rest of us.'

'Rumpole, please. This is no joking matter.'

'Everything, in my humble opinion, is a joking matter.'

'I want you to defend me.'

'Do you? Ballard's asked me to fill an entirely different role.'

'You!' The unfortunate Claude gave me a look of horror. 'But you don't ever prosecute, do you?'

'Well' – I did my level best to cheer the man up – 'hardly ever.'

I passed on up to my room, where I lit a small cigar and reopened the papers in the Jago case, which I read with a new interest since Henry had dealt with the little matter of my fee. I looked at the photograph of the big, plain victim and thought again how little she looked like her trim and elegant father and brother. I went through the account of Jago's statements, and decided that even the clumsiest cross-examiner could ridicule his unconvincing explanations. I turned the pages of a photostat of Veronica Fabian's diary and learnt, for the first time, that she had had six previous appointments with the man called Arthur Morrison, and I wondered why the name seemed to mean something to me. Then the door was flung open and an extremely wrathful Mizz Liz Probert came into my presence.

'Well,' she said, 'you've really deserted us for the enemy now, haven't you, Rumpole.'

'I haven't been listening to the news.' I tried to be gentle with her. 'Are we at war?'

'Don't pretend you don't know what I mean. Henry's told me all about it. In my opinion it's as contemptible as acting for a landlord who's trying to evict a one-parent family on supplementary benefit. You've gone over to the Prosecution.'

'Not gone over' – I did my best to reassure the inflamed daughter of Red Ron Probert, once the firebrand leader of the South-East London Labour Council – 'just there on a visit.'

'Just visiting the establishment, the powers that be, the Old Bill. Just there on a friendly call? How comfortable, Rumpole. How cosy. You know what I always admired about you?'

'Not exactly. Do remind me.'

'Oh, yes. No wonder you've forgotten, now you've taken up prosecution. Well, I admired the fact that you were always on the side of the underdog. You stopped the Judges sending everyone to the nick. You showed up the police. You stood up for the underprivileged.' Liz Probert was using almost the same words as the Fabians, but now she said, 'And you, of all people, are being paid by some posh family of ritzy estate agents to cook up a case against a bit of a naff member of their profession. They're narked he's been let free just because there isn't any evidence against him.'

'Let me enlighten you.' My tone, as always, was sweetly reasonable. 'There is plenty of evidence against him.'

'Like the fact that he never went to a "decent public school" like the Fabians?'

'And like the fact that he scooted out of the country when he found the body instead of telephoning the police.'

'Oh, I'm sure you'll find lots of effective points to make against him!' Hell hath no fury like an outraged radical lawyer, and Mizz Probert's outrage did for her what a large Pommeroy's plonk did for me – it made her extremely eloquent. 'You'll be able to argue him into a life sentence with a twenty-five-year recommendation. Probably you'll get the thanks of the Judge, an invitation to the serious crimes squad dinner dance and a weekend's shooting at the Fabians' place in Hampshire. I don't know why you did it – or, rather, I know only too well.'

'Why, do you think?'

'Henry told me.' Then she took, as I sometimes do, to poetry: '"Just for a handful of silver he left us." You're always quoting Wordsworth.'

'I do. Except that's by Browning. *About* Wordsworth.'

'About him, is it? "The Lost Leader"? Well. No wonder you like Wordsworth so much.'

All this was hardly complimentary to Rumpole or, indeed, to the Old Sheep of the Lake District whose job in the stamp office had earned him the fury of the young Robert Browning. I wasn't thinking of this, however, as Liz Probert continued her flow of denunciation. I was thinking of the unfortunate Claude Erskine-Brown and the way he had spoken to me in the passage. He had seemed angry, puzzled, depressed, but not, strangely enough, guilty.

It's rare for a criminal hack to be invited into his customer's home. We represent a part of their lives they would prefer to forget. Not only do they not ask us to dinner, but when catching sight of us at parties years after we have sprung them from detention they look studiously in the opposite direction and pretend we never met. No one, I suppose, wants the neighbours to spot the sturdy figure of Rumpole climbing their front steps. I may give rise to speculation as to whether it's murder, rape or merely a nice clean fraud that's going on in their family. The Fabians were different. Clearly they felt that they had, as representatives of law and order, nothing to be ashamed of, indeed much to be proud of in the way they were pursuing justice, in spite of the curious lassitude of the police and the Director of Public Prosecutions. Mrs Fabian, it seemed, suffered from arthritis and rarely left the house so my discreet and highly respected solicitor, Francis Pyecraft (of Pyecraft & Wensleydale), and my good self were invited there for drinks. The dead girl's mother wanted to look us over and grant us her good housekeeping seal of approval.

'It's not knowing, that's the worst thing, Mr Rumpole,' Mrs Fabian told me. 'I feel I could learn to live with it, if I knew just *how* Veronica died.'

'You mean who killed her?'

'Yes, of course, that's what I mean.'

I didn't like to tell her that a criminal trial, before a judge, who comes armed with his own prejudices, and a jury, whose attention frequently wanders, may be a pretty blunt instrument for prising out the truth. Instead, I looked at her and wondered if couples are attracted by physical likeness. Mrs Fabian was as small-boned, clear-featured and neat as her husband and son. And yet they had produced a big-boned and plain daughter, who had stumbled, no doubt, unwittingly, on death.

'Perhaps you could tell me a little more about Veronica. I mean about her life. Boyfriends?'

'No.' Mrs Fabian shook her head. 'That was really the trouble. She didn't seem to be able to find one. At least, not one that cared about her.' We sat in the high living-room of a house overlooking the canal in Little Venice. Tall bookshelves stretched to the ceiling, a pair of loud-speakers tinkled with appropriate baroque music. The white walls were hung with grey drawings which looked discreetly expensive. Young Roger moved among us, replenishing our glasses. The curtains hadn't been drawn and Mrs Fabian sat on a sofa looking out into the winter darkness, almost as though she was still expecting her daughter to come home early on yet another evening without a date. Veronica's mother, father and brother, I imagined, never found it difficult to find people who cared about them. Only their daughter had to get on without love.

'She worked in your firm. What were her other interests?'

'Oh, she read enormously. She had an idea she wanted to be a writer and she did some things for her school magazine, which were rather good, I thought,' Gregory told me.

'*Very* good.' Mrs Fabian gave the dead girl her full support.

'She never got much further than that, I'm afraid. I suggested she came and worked for us, and then she could write in her spare time. If she seemed to be going to make a success of it – the writing, I mean – of course, I'd've supported her.' 'Just do a little estate agency, darling, until you publish a best-seller.' I could imagine the charm with which Gregory Fabian had said it, and his daughter, unsure of her talent, had agreed.

A fatal arrangement; if she had stuck to literature, she would never have kept an appointment in a Notting Hill Gate mews.

'What did she read?'

'Oh, all sorts of things. Mainly nineteenth-century authors. She used to talk about becoming a novelist.'

'Her favourites were the Brontës,' Mrs Fabian remembered.

'Oh, yes. The Brontës. Charlotte, especially. She had a very romantic nature.' Veronica's father smiled, I thought, with understanding.

'This man Morrison,' I said, 'whoever he may be, keeps turning up in the desk diary. No one in the office's ever heard of him. He's never been a client of yours?'

'Not so far as I've been able to discover. There's no correspondence with him.'

'You don't know a friend of hers by that name?'

'We've asked, of course. No one's ever heard of him.'

I got up and crossed to the darkened window. Looking out, all I could see was myself reflected in the glass, a comfortably padded Old Bailey hack with a worried expression, engaged in the strange pursuit of prosecution.

'But in her diary she seems to have had six previous appointments with him.'

'Of course' – Mrs Fabian was smiling at me apologetically, as though she hardly liked to point out anything so obvious – 'we don't know everything about her. You never do, do you? Even about your own daughter.'

'All right, then. What do you know about Christopher Jago? You must have come across him in the way of business.'

'Not really.' Gregory Fabian stopped smiling. 'He has, well, a different type of business.'

'And does it in a different sort of way,' his son added.

'What does that mean?'

'Well, we've heard things. You do hear things . . .'

'What sort of things?'

'Undervaluing houses. Getting their owners to sell cheap to a chap who's really a friend of the agent. The friend sells on for the right price and he and the agent divide up the profits.'

'We've no evidence of that,' Gregory told me. 'It wouldn't

be right for you to assume that's what he was doing. Apparently he's rather a flashy type of operator, but that's really all we know about him.'

'He's a cowboy.' Roger was more positive. 'And he looks the part.'

They were silent then, it seemed, for a moment, fearful of the mystery that had disturbed their gentle family life. Roger crossed the room behind me and drew the curtains, shutting out the dark.

'She wasn't robbed. She hadn't been sexually assaulted. So far as we know she hadn't quarrelled with anyone and Jago didn't even know her. Why on earth should he want to kill her?' I asked the Fabians and they continued to sit in silence, puzzled and sad.

'The police couldn't answer that question either,' I said. 'Perhaps that's why they let him go.'

I left the house on my own, as Pyecraft was staying to discuss the effect of the girl's death on certain family trusts. Gregory came down to the hall and, as he helped me on with my coat, he said quietly, 'I don't know if Francis Pyecraft explained to you about Veronica.'

'No. What about her?'

'As a matter of fact she's not our daughter.'

'Not?'

'No. After Roger was born, we so wanted a girl. Evelyn couldn't have any more children, so we adopted. Of course, we loved her just as much as Roger. But now, well, it seems to make it even more important that she should be treated justly.' Again, I thought, he was talking as though Veronica were still alive and eagerly awaiting the result of the trial. Then he said, 'There's always one child that you feel needs special protection.'

Christmas came and we sat in the kitchen round the white coffin of the Crock-a-Gleam which flashed, sighed, belched a few times and delivered up our crockery. As I rescued the burning-hot plates from a cloud of steam, the widow Charmian said, 'At least I've made Howard cough up a dishwasher for you, Hilda. I've managed to do that.'

'It wasn't you' – I had long given up trying to persuade our
visitor to use my correct name – 'that made me buy it.' 'Oh?'
Charmian was miffed. 'Who was it, then?'

'I suppose whoever killed Veronica Fabian.' I don't know
why it was that Charmian gave me a distinct touch of the
Scrooges. Later, when we opened our presents in the sitting-
room, I bestowed on Hilda the gift of lavender water, which I
think she now uses for laying-down purposes, and I discovered that the three pairs of darkish socks, wrapped in holly-
patterned paper, were exactly what I wanted. Hilda opened a
small glass jar, which contained some white cream which
smelled faintly of hair oil and vaseline.

'Oh, how lovely.' She Who Must Be Obeyed was doing her
best not to sound underwhelmed. 'What is it, Charmian?'

'Special homoeopathic skin beautifier, Hilda dear.' Charmian was tearing open the wafer-thin china early-morning tea
set on which we had, I was quite convinced, spent far too
much. 'We've got to do something about those poor toil-worn
hands of yours, haven't we? And is this really for me?' She
looked at her present with more than faint amusement. 'What
funny little cups and saucers. And how very sweet of you to go
out and buy them. Or was it another old Christmas present
from Dodo Mackintosh?' It says a great deal for the awe in
which Hilda held her, and my own iron self-control, that
neither of us got up and beaned the woman with our Christmas
tree.

After a festive season of this nature, it may not surprise you to
know that I took an early opportunity to return to my place of
business in Equity Court, where I found not much business
going on. Such few barristers and clerks as were visible seemed
to be in a state of somnambulism. I made for Pommeroy's
Wine Bar, where even the holly seemed to be suffering from a
hangover and my learned friend Claude Erskine-Brown was
toying, in a melancholy and aloof fashion, with a half bottle of
Pommeroy's more upmarket St-Emilion-type red.

'You're wandering lonely as a Claude,' I told him. 'Did you
come up to work?'

'I came,' he said dolefully, 'because I couldn't stay at home.'

'Because of Christmas visitors?'

'No. Because of the shrink.'

I didn't catch the fellow's drift. Had his wits turned and did he imagine some strange diminution in size of his Islington home, so he could no longer crawl in at the front door?

'The what?'

'The shrink. Phillida knows all about the case of the altered brief. Ballard told her.'

'Ah, yes.' I knew my Soapy Sam. 'I bet he enjoyed that.'

'She was very understanding.'

'You said you were innocent, and she believed you?'

'No. She didn't believe me. She was just very understanding.'

'Ah.'

'She said it was the mid-life crisis. It happens to people in middle age. Mainly women who pinch things in Sainsbury's. But Philly thinks quite a lot of men go mad as well. So she said it was a sort of cry for help and she'd stand by me, provided I went to a shrink.'

'So?'

'It seemed easier to agree somehow.' Poor old Claude, the fizz had quite gone out of him and he had volunteered to join the great army of the maladjusted. 'She fixed me up with a Dr Gertrude Hauser who lives in Belsize Park.'

'Oh, yes. And what did Dr Gertrude have to say?'

'Well, first of all, she had this rather disgusting old sofa with a bit of Kleenex on the pillow. She made me lie down on that, so I felt a bit of a fool. Then she asked me about my childhood, so I told her. Then she said the whole trouble was that I wanted to sleep with my mother.'

'And did you?'

'What?'

'Want to sleep with your mother.'

'Of course not. Mummy would never have stood for it.'

'I suppose not.'

'Quite honestly, Rumpole. Mummy was an absolute sweetie in many ways, but – well, no offence to you, of course – she was *corpulent*. I didn't fancy her in the least.'

'Did you tell Gertrude that?'

'Yes. I said quite honestly I wouldn't have slept with Mummy if we'd been alone on a desert island.'

'What did the shrink say?'

'She said, "I shall write down 'fantasizes about being alone with his mother on a desert island'." Quite honestly, I can't go and see Dr Hauser again.'

'No. Probably not.'

'All that talk about Mummy. It's really too embarrassing. She'd have hated it so, if she'd been alive.'

'Yes, I do see. Excuse me a moment.' I tore myself away from the reluctant patient to a corner in which I had seen Mizz Liz Probert settling down to a glass of Pommeroy's newly advertised organic plonk (the old plonk, I strongly suspected, with a new bright-green label on the bottle). There was a certain matter about which I needed to ask her further and better particulars.

'Look here, Liz.' I pulled up a chair. 'How did you know all that about Christopher Jago?'

'You can't sit there,' she said. 'I'm expecting Dave Inchcape.'

'Just until he comes. How did you know that Jago didn't go to a public school, for instance?'

'He told me.'

'You met him?'

'Oh, yes. Dave and I got our flat through him. And I have to tell you, Rumpole, that he was absolutely honest, reliable and trustworthy throughout the whole transaction.' I had forgotten that Liz and Dave were now co-mortgagees and living happily ever after somewhere off Ladbroke Grove.

'What do you mean, he was honest and reliable?'

'Well. We got our place pretty cheaply, compared to the price Fabian & Winchelsea were asking for the other flats we saw. He never put up the price or let us be gazumped by other clients and he helped us fix up our mortgage. Oh, and he didn't conk me on the head with a Zulu knobkerrie.'

'Yes. I can see that. What else about him? Did he have a wife, girlfriend – anything like that?'

'Hundreds of girlfriends, I should think. He's rather attractive. Tall, fair and handsome. So you see, I shan't be giving
evidence for the Prosecution.'

'I imagine from what you said, you wouldn't come and take
a note for me? Act as my junior?'

'You must be joking!' Mizz Liz took a gulp of the alleged
organic brew and looked at me with contempt.

'I'll have to ask your co-habitee.'

'Save your breath. Tricia Benbow's already briefed Dave for
the Defence. He knows I'd never speak to him again if he took
part in a prosecution.'

'Christopher Jago's gone to La Belle Benbow?'

'Oh, yes. He asked me if I knew a brilliant solicitor and said
he preferred women in his life, so I sent him off to her.'

'But Dave Inchcape's not doing the case alone? I mean no
offence to him but he's still only a white-wig.'

'He's got a leader.'

'Who?' A foeman, I rather hoped, worthy of my steel. Liz
looked at me in silence for a moment, as though she was
relishing the news she had to impart.

'Our Head of Chambers,' she told me.

'Heavens above!' I nearly choked on my non-organic chemi-
cally produced Château Ordinaire. '"Thus the whirligig of
time brings in his revenges." Rumpole for the Prosecution and
Ballard for the Defence. He'd better sit close to me. He might
catch some passive advocacy.'

On my way out, I had a message for Claude Erskine-Brown,
who was still palely loitering. 'Come and help me in the
"Mews Murder",' I said. 'Be my hard-working junior. Take
your mind off your mother.'

'Rumpole!' The man looked pained and I hastened to comfort him. 'At least you'll find someone who's deeper in the
manure than you are, old darling,' I said.

Being in possession of two such contradictory views of Christopher Jago as those provided by the Fabians and Mizz Liz
Probert, I decided that a little investigative work was necessary.

I could hardly ask Francis Pyecraft to hang round such pubs and clubs as Jago might frequent, so I called in the services of my old friend and colleague, Ferdinand Isaac Gerald Newton, known as Fig Newton to the trade. You could pass through many bars and hardly notice the doleful, lantern-jawed figure, sitting in a quiet corner, nursing half a pint of Guinness and apparently engrossed in *The Times* crossword puzzle which he solves, I am ashamed to say, in almost less time than it takes me to spot the quotations. But he hoovers up every scrap of gossip and information dropped within a surprisingly wide radius. You can't make bricks without straw and Fig is straw-purveyor to the best Old Bailey defenders. Now he would have a chance, as I had, of seeing life from the prosecution side.

I met him a couple of weeks later in Pommeroy's. He was suffering, as usual, from a bad cold, having been up most of the night keeping watch on a block of flats in a matrimonial matter, but between some heavy work with the handkerchief he was able to tell me a good deal. Our quarry lived in a 1930s house near Shepherd's Bush Road, the ground floor of which served as his office. He drove an electric blue Alfa-Romeo, the car which had led to his arrest. He was well known in a number of pubs round Maida Vale and Notting Hill Gate, where many of the properties he dealt in were situated. He was unmarried but went out with a succession of girls, his taste running to young and pretty blonde secretaries and receptionists. None of them lasted very long and in the Benedict Arms, one of his favourite resorts near the Regent's Canal, the bar staff would lay bets on how soon any girl would go.

There was one notable exception, however, to the stage army of desirable young women. On half a dozen occasions, the suspect had come into the Benedict Arms with a big, awkward, pale and rather unattractive girl. They had sat in a corner, away from the crowd, and appeared to have had a lot to say to each other. When Fig told me that, the penny dropped. I smote the table in my excitement, rattling the glasses and attracting the stares of the legal hacks busy drinking around us. I had just remembered what I knew about Arthur Morrison.

On my way home I went to check the facts in the library, for Veronica Fabian had no doubt known a great deal more than I did about minor novelists in the last century. Arthur Morrison, a prolific author, was born in 1863 and lived on into the Second World War. His best-known book about life in the East End of London was published in 1896. It was called *A Child of the Jago*.

I put the *Companion to English Literature* back on the library shelf with a feeling of relief. God was in his heaven: the widow Charmian, despite a pressing invitation to stay from Hilda, had gone back to Guildford, and the first prosecution I had ever undertaken seemed likely to be a winner. As I have said, I find it very difficult to embark on any case without being dead set on victory.

'May it please you, my Lord, Members of the Jury. I appear in this case with my learned friend, Mr Claude Erskine-Brown, for the Prosecution. The Defence of Christopher Jago is in the hands of my learned friends, Mr Samuel Ballard and Mr David Inchcape.' As I uttered these unaccustomed words, I had the unusual experience of the scarlet Judge on the Bench welcoming me with the sort of ingratiating smile he usually reserved for visiting Supreme Court justices or extremely pretty lady plaintiffs entering the witness-box.

'Did you say you were here to *prosecute*?'

'That is so, my Lord.'

'Members of the Jury' – Mr Justice Oliphant, as was his wont, spoke to the ladies and gents in the jury-box as though they were a group of educationally subnormal children with hearing defects – 'Mr Rumpole is going to outline the story of this case to you. In perfectly simple terms. Isn't that right, Mr Rumpole?'

'I hope so, my Lord.'

'So my advice to you is to sit quietly and give him your full attention. The Defence will have its chance later.' This reference caused Soapy Sam Ballard to lift his posterior from the bench and smile winsomely, an overture which Mr Justice 'Ollie' Oliphant completely ignored. Ollie comes from the

northern circuit and prides himself on being a rough diamond
who uses his robust common sense. I hoped he wasn't going to
try to help me too much. Most acquittals occur when the
Judge sickens the Jury by over-egging the prosecution pudding.

So we went to work in Number One Court. The two neat
Fabians, father and son, sat in front of me. The man in the
dock couldn't have been a greater contrast to them. He was
tall, two or three inches over six feet, with a winter suntan that
must have been kept going with a lamp, as well as visits to
Marbella. His hair, clearly the victim of many hours' work
with a blow-drier, was bouffant at the front and, at the back,
swept almost down to his shoulders. His drooping moustache
and the broad bracelet of his watch were the colour of old gold
and his suit, like his car, might have been described as electric
blue. He looked less like the cowboy Roger Fabian had called
him than a professional footballer whose private and professional life is in a continual mess. He lounged between two
officers in the dock, with his long legs stuck out in front of
him, affecting alternate boredom and amusement. Underneath
it all, I thought, he was probably terrified.

So there I was, opening my case to the Jury in as neutral a
way as I knew how. I described the little mews house as I
remembered it when I went to inspect the scene of the crime:
the cramped rooms, the chill feeling of the home unused, the
African carvings and weapons on the wall. I asked the Jury to
picture the girl from the estate agents' office, who was waiting
in the hallway, with the front door left open, to greet the man
who had telephoned her.

Who was it? Was it Mr Morrison? Or was that a name she
used to hide the identity of someone she knew quite well? I
took the Jury through my theory that the literate Veronica had
picked the name of the author of a book with Jago in the title.
Then I waited for Ballard to shoot to his feet, as I would have
done had I been defending, and denounce this as a vague and
typical Rumpolean fantasy. I waited in vain. Ballard was inert,
indeed there was an unusually contented smile on his face as
he sat, perhaps deriving a little passive sensual satisfaction

from the close and perfumed presence of his instructing solicitor, Miss Tricia Benbow.

'The Defence will no doubt argue that there is a real Arthur Morrison who met Veronica Fabian in the mews and killed her before Jago arrived on the scene.'

Once again Ballard replied with a deafening silence as he stared appreciatively at the back of his solicitor's neck. My instincts as a defender got the better of me. Jago may have been a crooked estate agent with a lamentable private life and an appalling taste in suits, but he deserved to have the points in his favour put as soon as possible. 'That's what you're going to argue, Ballard, isn't it?' I said in a *sotto voce* growl.

'Oh, yes.' Ballard shot obediently to his feet. 'If your Lordship pleases. It will be my duty to submit to your Lordship, in the fulness of time and entirely at your Lordship's convenience, of course, that the Jury will have to consider Morrison's part in this case very seriously, very seriously indeed.'

'If there is a Morrison, Mr Ballard. We have to use our common sense about that, don't we?' His Lordship intervened.

'Yes, of course. If your Lordship pleases.' Ballard subsided without further struggle. The Judge's intervention had somewhat unnerved me. I felt like a tennis player, starting a friendly knock up, who suddenly sees the referee hurling bricks at his opponent.

'Of course, I can concede that we may be wrong about the reasons Veronica Fabian used that name when entering her eight thirty appointment.'

'Use your common sense, Mr Rumpole. Please.' His Lordship's tone became distinctly less friendly. 'Mr Ballard hasn't asked you to concede to anything. Your job is to present the prosecution case. Let's get on with it.'

The Fabians, father and son, were looking up at me, and it was their plea for justice, rather than the disapproval of Oliver Oliphant, which made me return to the attack. 'In any event, Members of the Jury, we intend to call evidence to prove that Jago was seeing the dead girl quite regularly, meeting her in a public house called the Benedict Arms and having long, intimate conversations with her. There will also be evidence that he told the police . . .'

'That he'd never seen her before in his life!' Mr Justice Oliphant was like the helpful wife who always supplies the punchline to the end of her husband's best stories.

'I was coming to that, my Lord.'

'Come to it then, Mr Rumpole. How long is this case expected to last?'

My reaction to that sort of remark was instinctive. 'It will last, my Lord, for as long as it takes the Jury to consider every point both for and against the accused, and to decide if they can be sure of his guilt or not.' I felt happier now, at home in my old position of arguing with the Judge. Ollie opened his mouth, no doubt to deliver himself of a little more robust common sense, but I went on before he could utter.

'The police decided not to charge Jago because there was no apparent motive for the crime. But if he knew Veronica Fabian, if they had some sort of relationship, they may have had to consider why he ran from that house, where Veronica was lying dead, and told no one what he had seen. Finally, Members of the Jury, it's for you to say why he lied to the police and said he never met her.' And then I repeated the sentence I had used so often from the other side of the Court. 'You won't convict him of anything unless you're certain sure that the only answer is he must be guilty. That's what we call the golden thread that runs through British justice.'

So we began to call the evidence, produce the photographs and listen to the monotonous tones of police officers refreshing their memories from their notebooks. When I was defending, such witnesses presented a challenge, each to be lured in a different way, with charm, authority or lofty disdain, to produce some fragment of evidence which might help the customer in the dock. Now all I had to do was let them rattle on and so prosecuting seemed a dull business. Then we got the scene of the crime officer, who produced the fatal knobkerrie, its end heavily rounded, still blood-stained and protected by cellophane, as was the three-foot black handle. Ballard, who had sat mum during this parade of prosecution evidence, showed no interest in examining this weapon and said he had no questions.

'What about the finger-prints?' I could no longer restrain myself from hissing at my so-called opponent, a foeman who, at the moment, was hardly being worthy of my attention, let alone my steel.

'What about them?' Ballard whispered back in a sudden panic. 'Jago's aren't there, are they?'

'Of course not!' By now my whisper had become entirely audible. 'There are no finger-prints at all.'

'Mr Rumpole,' the voice of robust common sense trumpeted from the Bench, 'I thought you told us you appeared for the *Prosecution*. If Mr Ballard wants to ask a question for the Defence no doubt he will get up on his hind legs and do so!' I rather doubted that but, in fact, Soapy Sam unwound himself, drew himself up to his full height and said, as though a brilliant idea had just occurred to him, 'Officer. Let me put this to you. There are absolutely no finger-prints of Christopher Jago's on the handle of that weapon, are there?'

'There are no finger-prints of any sort, my Lord.'

'I'm very much obliged. Thank you, officer.' Ballard bowed with great satisfaction and as he sat down I heard him tell his junior, Inchcape, 'I'm glad I managed to winkle that out of him.'

Later we got the officer who had been in charge of the investigation, Detective Chief Inspector Brush, and even though he was, for the first time, in recorded history, my witness, I couldn't resist teasing him a little.

'Tell me, Chief Inspector. After the body was found, you spent a good deal of time and trouble looking for Arthur Morrison.'

'We did, my Lord.'

'In fact Morrison was always your number one suspect.'

'He still is, my Lord.'

'You don't accept that Arthur Morrison and Jago were one and the same person?'

There was a pause and then 'I suppose that may be a possibility.'

'And that Arthur Morrison is nothing but a dead author.'

'I don't know much about dead authors, Mr Rumpole.' There, at least the Detective Chief Inspector was telling the truth.

'If you'd known that, whether or not Morrison existed, Jago had been meeting the dead girl regularly, would that have made any difference to the decision not to charge him?'

There was a long silence and then Brush admitted, 'Well, yes, my Lord. I think it might.'

'Let's use our common sense about this, shall we? Don't let's beat about the bush,' Ollie intervened. 'Jago told you he'd never met the girl. If you'd known he was lying, you'd've charged him.'

'Yes, my Lord.'

'Well, there we are, Members of the Jury. We've got that clear at last, thanks to a little bit of down-to-earth common sense.' Mr Justice Oliphant had joined me as leader of the Prosecution. And that might have been that, but there was one other question someone had to ask and I couldn't rely on Ballard.

'You first questioned Mr Jago because you had discovered that his car had been parked outside 13A Gissing Mews at the relevant time.'

'Yes.'

'You had no idea that he had been into the house and found the body?'

'At that time. No.'

'So he volunteered that information entirely of his own accord?'

'That's right.'

'Was that one of the reasons he wasn't charged?'

'That was one of the reasons we thought he was being honest with us, yes.'

I sat down, having made Ballard's best point for him. Of course he had to totter to his feet and ruin it.

'And, so far as that goes, Chief Inspector' – Ballard stood, pleased with himself, rocking slightly on the balls of his feet – 'do you still think he was being honest with you about the way he found the girl?'

'I'm not sure.' Brush paused and then gave it back to the poor old darling, right between the eyes. 'If he was lying to us about not knowing the girl, I can't be sure about any of his evidence, can I?' Mr Justice Oliphant wrote down that answer and underlined it with his red pencil. The Fabians looked as though they were slightly more pleased with the way Ballard was doing his case than with my performance, but no doubt they'd be too polite to say so.

At the end of our evidence we called my old friend, Professor Andrew Ackerman, Ackerman of the Morgue, with whom I have spent many fascinating hours discussing bloodstains and gun-shot wounds. He testified that Veronica Fabian had died from a heavy blow to the frontal bone of the skull, consistent with an attack by the knobkerrie, Exhibit P.1. I asked him if this must have been a blow straight down on her head, and he ruled out the possibility of it having been struck from either side. From the position of the wound it was clear to him that the club had been held by the end of the handle and swung in an upward trajectory. I felt that his evidence was important, but at the moment he gave it I didn't realize its full significance.

'So you're defending? I expect you have Mizz Liz Probert's full approval?' I was disarming in the robing-room, taking off the wig and gown and running a comb through what remains of my hair, when I found myself sharing a mirror with young Dave Inchcape.

'What do you mean?'

'Well, she thinks prosecuting's as bad as aiding merciless landlords evict their tenants.'

'I know she doesn't think you should be prosecuting.'

'And I rather think,' I told him as I got on the bow-tie and adjusted the silk handkerchief, 'that Mr Justice Ollie Oliphant would agree with her.'

'By the way, I think we're doing pretty well for Chris, don't you? He's promised us a great party if we get him off.' Dave Inchcape had fallen into the defender's habit of first-name familiarity with alleged criminals. I wondered if it were ever so and the robing-room once rang with cries of 'I think we're going to get Hawley off – Hawley Crippin, of course.'

I walked back to Chambers with the still despondent Erskine-Brown, who had just been cut dead by Ballard and La Belle Benbow as they were coming out of the Ludgate Circus Palais de Justice.

'By the way, Claude,' I said, 'what was that case you're meant to have pinched from Inchcape all about?'

'Please' – the man looked at a passing bus, as though tempted to dive under it – 'don't remind me of it.'

'But what was the subject matter? Just the gist, you understand.'

'Well, it was a landlord's action for possession. Nothing very exciting.'

'He wanted to turn out a one-parent family?'

'No. I think they were a couple of ladies in the Gay Rights movement. He said they were using the place to run a business. Why do you ask?'

'Because,' I tried to encourage him, 'the evidence you have just given may be of great importance.' But Claude didn't look in the slightest cheered up.

No two characters could have been more contrary than Christopher Jago and his defence counsel. Jago lounged in the witness-box, flashed occasional smiles at the Jury, whose female members looked embarrassed and the males stony-faced. He was a bad witness, truculent, defensive and flippant by turns, and Soapy Sam was finding it hard to conceal his deep disapproval of the blow-dried, shiny-suited giant he was defending.

As I had called several witnesses, who said they had seen him with Veronica in the Benedict Arms, Jago no longer troubled to deny it. He said he first saw her in the pub at lunchtime with another girl from Fabians' whom he knew slightly and he bought them both a drink. Some time after that he saw her eating her lunch in a corner, alone with a book, and he talked to her.

'What did you talk about?' I asked when I came to cross-examine.

'The house business. Prices and that around the area. I didn't chat her up, if that's what you're suggesting. She wasn't the sort of girl I could ever fancy, even if I weren't pretty well looked after in that direction.' He gave the Jury one of his least endearing grins.

'So why did you meet her so often?'

'I just happened to bump into her, that's all.'

'It's not all, is it? Your meetings were planned. She entered five or six appointments with Morrison in her diary.'

To my surprise he didn't answer with a blustering denial that he and Morrison were one and the same person. Had he forgotten his best line of defence, or was he overcome by that strange need to tell the truth, which sometimes seems to attack even the most unsatisfactory witnesses? 'All right then,' he admitted. 'She seemed to want to see me and we made a few dates to meet for a drink round the Benedict.'

'Why did she want to see you?'

'Perhaps she fancied me. It has been known.' He looked at the Jury, expecting a sympathetic giggle that never came. 'I don't know why she wanted us to meet. You tell me.'

'No, Mr Jago. You tell us.'

There was a silence then. Jago looked troubled and I thought that he was afraid of the evidence he would have to give.

'She was a bit scared to tell me about it. She said it would mean a lot of trouble if it got out.'

'What was it, Mr Jago?' I was breaking another of my rules and asking a question without knowing the answer. At that moment I was in search of the truth, a somewhat dangerous pursuit for a defence counsel, but then I wasn't defending Jago.

He answered my question then, quietly and reluctantly. 'She was worried about what was happening at Fabians'.'

I saw my clients, the father and son, listening, composed and expressionless. They didn't try to stop me and by now it was too late to turn back. 'What did she say was happening at Fabians'?'

'She said they gave the people who wanted to sell their houses very low valuations. Then they sold to some friend who looked independent, but who was really in business with them. The friend sold on at the proper price and they shared the difference. She reckoned they'd been doing that for years. On a pretty big scale, I imagine.'

Gregory Fabian was writing me a note quite impassively. His son was flushed and looked so angry that I was afraid he was going to shout. But his father put a hand on his son's arm before he passed me his message. I remembered that Roger had said Jago practised the same fraud the Fabians were now being accused of.

'Why do you think she told you that?' I read Gregory's note then: HE'S TRYING TO RUIN US BECAUSE WE KNOW HE KILLED VERONICA. STOP HIM DOING IT.

'She told me because she was worried. I was in the same business. She wanted my advice. Like I said, perhaps she fancied me, I don't know. She said she hadn't got anyone else, no real friends, she could tell about it.'

I thought of the lonely girl who was trapped in a business she couldn't trust, pinning her faith on this unlikely companion. Perhaps she thought her confidences would bring them together. At any rate they were an excuse to meet him.

'Mr Jago, when you called at Gissing Mews that morning . . .'

'Like I told you. I was interested in the place for a client. I phoned Veronica and . . .'

'And you kept the appointment and found her dead in the hallway.'

'Yes.'

'Why didn't you telephone the police?'

'Because I was afraid.'

'Afraid you'd be arrested for her murder?'

'No. Not afraid of that.'

'Of what then?'

There are moments in some trials when everyone in Court seems to hold their breath, waiting for an answer. This was such an occasion and the answer when it came was totally unexpected.

'I thought she'd been done over because she'd told me what

the Fabians were up to. I thought, that might be you, Christopher, if you get involved any more.'

'*You* killed her!' Roger Fabian couldn't restrain himself now. Ollie Oliphant uttered some soothing words about understanding the strength of the family feelings, but urged the young man to use his common sense and keep quiet. I did my best to pull myself together and behave like a prosecuting counsel. I asked Jago to take Exhibit P.1 in his hand, which he did without any apparent reluctance.

'I'm bound to put it to you,' I said, 'that you and Veronica Fabian quarrelled that morning when you met in the mews house. You lost your temper and took that knobkerrie off the wall. You swung it up over your head . . .'

'Like that, you mean?' He lifted the African club and as he did so all the odd pieces of the evidence came together and locked into one clear picture. Christopher Jago was innocent of the murder we had charged him with, and, from that moment, I was determined to get him off.

The case began and ended in the little house in Gissing Mews. I asked Ollie Oliphant to move the proceedings to the scene of the crime as I wished to demonstrate something to the Jury, having taken the precaution of telling my opponent that if he wanted to get his client off, he'd better support my application. So now the cold, gloomy mews house, with its primitive carvings and grinning African masks, was crammed to the gunwales with legal hacks, jury members, court officials and all the trimmings, including, of course, Jago and the Fabians. In one way or another, as many of us as possible got a view of the hall, where I stood by the telephone impersonating, with only a momentary fear that I might have got it entirely wrong, the victim of the crime. I got Jago to stand in front of me and swing the club, P.1, again in order to strike my head. I was not entirely surprised when neither Sam Ballard, Q.C. nor Mr Justice Oliphant tried to prevent my apparent suicide, although Claude Erskine-Brown did have the decency to mutter, 'Mind out, Rumpole. We don't want to lose you.'

Everyone was watching as the tall, flamboyant accused lifted the knobkerrie and tried to swing it above his head. He tried and failed. When I was cross-examining him, I remembered the cramped rooms and low ceilings of the mews cottage. Now as the club bumped harmlessly against the plaster, everyone present understood why Jago couldn't have struck the blow which killed Veronica Fabian. Whoever killed her must have been at least six inches shorter.

It was my first prosecution and I had managed, against all the odds, to secure an acquittal.

'You got him off?'

'Yes.'

A few days, it seemed a lifetime, later, I was alone with Gregory Fabian in his white, early Victorian house in Little Venice.

'Why?'

'Did you want an innocent man convicted? That's a stupid question. Of course you did.'

He said nothing and I went on, as I had to. 'You said there's always one child who needs protecting, but you weren't thinking of Veronica, were you? You were talking about your son.'

'What about Roger?'

'What about him? Odd, his habit of accusing other people of the things he did himself.'

'What did he do?' Gregory was quiet, unruffled, still carefully courteous, in spite of what I'd done to him.

'I think you know, don't you? The racket of undervaluing homes, so you could sell them to your secret nominees. He accused Jago of doing that, just as he accused him of Veronica's murder.'

The house was very quiet. Mrs Fabian was upstairs somewhere, resting. God knows where Roger was. Even the traffic sounded far away and muted in the darkness of an early evening in January.

'What are you trying to tell me?'

'What I think. That's all. I'm not setting out to prove anything beyond reasonable doubt.'

'Go on then.' He gave a small sigh, perhaps of resignation.

'Veronica discovered what was going on and didn't like it. She asked Jago's advice, and I expect he told her to keep him well-informed. No doubt so he could make something out of it when it suited him to do so. Then I think Roger found out what his sister was doing. Well, she wasn't his real sister, was she? She was the loved girl, who had arrived after he was born, the child he was always jealous of. I expect he found out she had a date to meet Jago at the mews house. He went after her to stop her. I don't think he meant to kill her.'

'Of course he didn't.' The father was still trying, I thought, to persuade himself.

'He lost his temper with her. They quarrelled. She tried to telephone for help and he ripped out the phone. Remember that's how they found it. Then he took the knobkerrie off the wall. He's short enough to have been able to swing it without hitting the ceiling. But you know all that, don't you?' Gregory Fabian didn't answer, relying, I suppose, on his right to silence.

'You wanted Roger to be safe. You wanted him to be protected, forever. And the best way of doing that was to get someone else found guilty. That's what you paid me to do. To be quite technical, Mr Fabian, you paid me to take part in your conspiracy to pervert the course of justice.'

'You said,' he sounded desperately hopeful, 'that you couldn't prove it . . .'

'It's not my business to prosecute. It never has been. And it's not my business to take part in crime. I told Henry to send your money back.'

He stood up then and moved between me and the door. I thought for a moment that the repressed violence of the Fabians might erupt and he would attack me. But all he said was 'Poor Roger.'

'No, Poor Veronica. You should never have stopped her becoming a novelist.'

I walked past him and out of the house. I heard him call after me 'Mr Rumpole!' But I didn't stop. I was glad to be out in the darkness, breathing in the mist from the canal, away from a house silenced by death and deception.

*

I decided to walk a while from the Fabian house, feeling I had, among other things, to think over what remained of my life. 'Mr Rumpole, although briefed for the Prosecution and under a duty to present the prosecution case to you, took it into his head, no doubt because of the habit of a lifetime, to act for the Defence. So, the basis of our fine adversarial system, which has long been our pride, has been undermined. Mr Rumpole will have to consider where his future, if any, is at the Bar. In the absence of a prosecutor, you and I, Members of the Jury, will just have to rely on good old British common sense.' These were the words with which Ollie sent the Jury out to consider its verdict, which turned out to be a resounding not guilty for everyone, except Rumpole whose conduct had been, according to his Lordship, in his final analysis, 'grossly unprofessional'.

It was while I was brooding on these judicial pronouncements that I heard the sound of revelry by night and noticed that I was passing a somewhat glitzy art nouveau pub, picked out in neon lights, called the Benedict Arms. I remembered that this was the night of Christopher Jago's celebration party, to which he had invited not only his defenders, but, and in all the circumstances of the case, this was understandable, the prosecution team as well. I had persuaded Claude not to sit moping at home and I'd promised to meet him there. Accordingly I called into the saloon of the Benedict and was immediately told that Chris's piss-up was on the first floor.

I climbed up to a celebration very unlike our Chambers parties in Equity Court. Music, which sounded to my untrained ear very like the sound produced by a pneumatic drill pounding a pavement, shook the windows. There were a number of metallically blonde girls in skirts the size of pocket handkerchiefs and tops kept up by some stretch of the imagination and a fair number of men with moustaches, whom I took for downmarket estate agents. Like dark islands in a colourful sea, the lawyers had clearly begun, with the exception of the doleful Erskine-Brown, to enjoy the party.

'Thanks for coming.' Jago stood before me. 'Do you always work for the other side? If you do, I'm bloody glad I didn't have you defending me.' It was the sort of joke I could do without and then, to my astonishment, I saw him put an arm around Mizz Liz Probert and say, 'You know this little legal lady, I'm sure, Mr Rumpole? I told her she can have my briefs any day of the week, quite honestly!' And I was even more astonished to see that Mizz Liz, far from kneeing this rampant chauvinist in the groin, smiled charmingly at the man she thought had been saved from a life sentence by the efforts of her co-mortgagee.

Wandering on into the throng of celebrators, I saw Bollard in close proximity to his grateful instructing solicitor, Tricia Benbow. It seemed to me that Soapy Sam had been the victim of much passive alcoholism, no doubt absorbed from the glass he held in his hand.

Then, under the sound of the pneumatic drill, I heard the shrilling of a telephone and I was hailed by Jago, who had answered it.

'Mr Rumpole. It's your clerk. He says it's urgent.'

'All right. For God's sake, turn off the music for five minutes.' I took the telephone from him. 'Henry!'

'I've got an awkward situation here, Mr Rumpole. The truth of the matter is Mrs Ballard is here.'

'Oh. Bad luck.'

'She happened to come out of her sprains and fractures refresher course and she wanted to meet up with her husband. She said –' Henry's voice sank to a conspiratorial murmur in which I could detect an almost irresistible tendency to laughter – 'he told her he was going to a Lawyers As Christians Society meeting tonight and might be late home. But she wants to know where the meeting's being held so she can join him, if at all possible.'

'Henry, you didn't tell her he was at a piss-up in the Benedict Arms, Maida Vale?'

'No, sir. I didn't think it would be well received.'

'Why involve me in this sordid web of intrigue?'

'Well, we don't want to land the Head of Chambers in it, do we, Mr Rumpole? Not in the first instance, anyway.' Our clerk was positively giggling.

'Where is the wife of Bollard now?'

'She's in the waiting-room, sir.'

'Put me through to her, Henry. Without delay.' And when Mrs Ballard came on the line, I greeted her warmly.

'Matey . . . I mean, Marguerite. This is Horace Rumpole speaking.'

'Horace! Whatever are you doing there? And where's Sam?'

'Oh, I'm afraid brother Ballard can't come to the phone. He's busy preparing to induct a new member.'

'A new member. Who?'

'Me.'

'You, Horace?' The ex-Matron sounded incredulous.

'Of course. I have decided to put away the sins of the world and lead a better, purer life in future.'

'But where are you meeting?'

'I'm afraid that can't be divulged over the telephone.'

'Why ever not?'

'For your own safety I think it's better for you not to know. We've had threatening calls from militant Methodists.'

'Horace. Are you sure Sam's all right? I can hear a lot of voices.'

'Oh, it's a very full house this evening. Hold on a minute.' I held the phone away from my ear for a while and then I told her, 'Sam really can't get away now. He says he'll see you back in Waltham Cross and don't wait up for him. He'll probably be exhausted.'

'Exhausted?' She sounded only a little suspicious. 'Why?'

'It's the spirit,' I said. 'You know how it tires him.'

'Is he filled with it?' Her suspicions seemed gone and her voice was full of admiration.

'Oh, yes,' I assured her, 'right up to the brim.'

I put down the phone and the blast of road-mending music was restored. I then approached our Head of Chambers, who was standing with Dave Inchcape – Tricia, the solicitor, having danced away with her liberated client.

'That was your wife on the phone,' I told him.

'Good heavens.' The man was still sober enough to panic. 'She's not coming here?'

'Oh, no. I gave you a perfect alibi. Tell you about it later. I'll also tell you my solution to the Case of the Altered Brief. I'm getting into the habit of solving mysteries.'

'I'd better go and find Liz.' Inchcape seemed anxious to get away.

'No, you stay here, David.' I spoke with some authority and the young man stood, looking anxious. 'We're all but toys in the hands of women and your particular commander-in-chief is Mizz Liz Probert. I know you come into the clerk's room early to see what's arrived in the post, all white-wigs do. To your horror you found you'd been engaged by a flinty-hearted landlord to kick two ladies, active in Gay Rights, out of house and home. How could you face your co-habitee, if you did a case like that? It was a matter of a moment, Members of the Jury,' I addressed an imaginary tribunal, 'for David Inchcape to scratch out his name and write Mr Claude Erskine-Brown in block capitals.'

'Is this true?' Ballard tried his best to look judicial, although he was somewhat unsteady on his pins.

David Inchcape's silence provided the answer.

I was rather late home that evening and climbed into bed beside Hilda's sleeping back. I had no professional duties the next day and wandered into the kitchen in my dressing-gown and with a head still throbbing from the pile-driving music at Jago's celebration. I found Hilda in a surprisingly benign mood, all things considered, but I also noticed something missing from our home.

'Where's the Crock-a-Gleam?' I said. 'You haven't pawned it? I know things aren't brilliant but . . .'

'I sent it back to John Lewis,' Hilda told me. 'We might get a little something for it.'

'Why?' I felt for a chair and lowered myself slowly into it. 'What's it done wrong?'

'Nothing, really. It just takes about twice as long to do the washing up as even you do, Rumpole. That's not it. It's *her*.'

'Her?'

'Charmian Nichols. She wrote to Dodo and said Christmas

with us was about as exciting as watching your finger-nails grow. And when I think of what we spent on her wretched tea set. "Charming Knickers", that was her nickname at school. We got her completely wrong. There wasn't anything charming about her.'

'How do you know what she wrote about Christmas?'

'Dodo sent me her letter, of course. Well, after that, I couldn't sit and look at the dishwasher you bought just to please her.'

Wonderfully loyal group, your old school friends, I thought of saying that but decided against it. Then Hilda changed the subject.

'Rumpole,' she said, 'are things very bad?'

'No one wants to employ me. Not since I changed sides in the middle of a case.'

'You did what you thought was right,' she said, surprisingly sympathetically. But then she added, 'Do be careful not to do what you think's right again. It does seem to have disastrous results.'

'I can't promise you that, Hilda.' I made my bid for independence. 'But I can promise you one thing.'

'What's that?'

'From now on, old thing, I promise you, Rumpole only defends.'

Rumpole
and the
Angel of Death

For Stephen Tumin
'So shines a good deed in a naughty world'

Rumpole and the Model Prisoner

Quintus Blake, O.B.E. and the staff cordially invite

Horace Rumpole Esq.

to a performance of *A Midsummer Night's Dream* by
William Shakespeare
15th September at 7 p.m. sharp.

Entry by invitation only. Proof of identity will be required.

RSVP
The Governor's Office
Worsfield Prison
Worsfield, Berks

I had been to Worsfield gaol regularly over the years and never
without breathing a sigh of relief, and gulping in all the fresh
air available, after the last screw had turned the last lock and
released me from custody. I never thought of going there to
explore the magical charm of a wood near Athens.

'Hilda,' I said, taking a swig of rapidly cooling coffee and
lining myself up for a quick dash to the Underground, 'can you
prove your identity?'

'Is that meant to be funny, Rumpole?' Hilda was deep in the
Daily Telegraph and unamused.

'I mean, if you can satisfy the authorities you're really She –
I mean (here I corrected myself hastily) that you're my wife,
I'll try for another ticket and we can go to the theatre together.'

'What's come over you, Rumpole? We haven't been to the
theatre together for three years – or whenever Claude last
dragged you to the opera.'

'Then it's about time,' I said, 'we went to the *Dream*.'

'Which dream?'

'The *Midsummer Night*'s one.'

'Where is it?' Hilda seemed prepared to put her toe in the water. 'The Royal Shakespeare?'

'Not exactly. It's in Her Majesty's Prison, Worsfield. Fifteenth September. Seven p.m. sharp.'

'You mean you want to take me to Shakespeare done by criminals?'

'Done, but not done in, I hope.'

'Anyway' – She Who Must Be Obeyed found a cast-iron alibi – 'that's my evening at the bridge school with Marigold Featherstone.'

Hilda, I thought, like most of the non-criminal classes, likes to think that those sentenced simply disappear off the face of the earth. Very few of us wonder about their wasted lives, or worry about the slums in which they are confined, or, indeed, remember them at all.

'You'll have to go on your own, Rumpole,' she said. 'I'm sure you'll have lots of friends there, and they'll all be delighted to see you.'

'Plenty of your mates in here, eh, Mr Rumpole? They'll all be glad to see you, I don't doubt.' I thought it remarkable that both She Who Must Be Obeyed and the screw who was slowly and carefully going over my body with some form of metal detector should have the same heavy-handed and not particularly diverting sense of humour.

'I have come for William Shakespeare,' I said with all the dignity I could muster. 'I don't believe he's an inmate here. Nor have I ever been called upon to defend him.'

Worsfield gaol was built in the 1850s for far fewer than the number of prisoners it now contains. What the Victorian forces of law and order required was a granite-faced castle of despair whose outer appearance was thought likely to deter the passers-by from any thoughts of evil-doing. Inside, five large cellular blocks formed the prison for men, with a smaller block set aside for the few women prisoners. In its early days all within was secrecy and silence, with prisoners, forbidden to speak to each other, plodding round the exercise yard and the treadmill – the cat o' nine tails and the rope for ever lurking in the shadows. When it was built it was on the outskirts of a small industrial town, a place to be pointed out as a warning to shuddering children being brought back home late on winter evenings from school. Now the town has spread over the green fields of the countryside and the prison is almost part of the city centre. This, I thought, as my taxi passed it on the way from the station, looked in itself, with its concrete office blocks, grim shopping malls and multi-storey carparks, as if it were built like the headquarters of a secret police force or a group of houses of correction.

Inside the prison there were some attempts at cheerfulness. Walls were painted lime green and buttercup yellow. There was a dusty rubber plant, and posters for seaside holidays, in the office by the gate where I filled in a visitor's form and did my best to establish my identity. But the scented disinfectant was fighting a losing battle with the prevailing smell of stale air, unemptied chamber-pots and greasy cooking.

The screw who escorted me down the blindingly lit passages, with his keys jangling at his hip, told me he'd been a school teacher but became a prison warder for the sake of more pay and free membership of the local golf club. He was a tall, ginger-haired man, running to fat, with that prison pallor which can best be described as halfway between sliced bread and underdone potato chips. On one of his pale cheeks I noticed a recent scar.

The ex-teacher led me across a yard, a dark concrete area lined with borders of black earth in which a few meagre plants didn't seem to be doing well. A small crowd of visitors from the outer world – youngish people whom I took to be social workers and probation officers with their partners, grey-haired governors of other prisons with their wives, enlightened magistrates and a well-known professor of criminology – was waiting. Their voices were muted, serious and respectful, as though, instead of having been invited to a comedy, they were expecting a cremation. They stood in front of the chapel, a gaunt Gothic building no doubt intended to put us all in mind of the terrible severity of the Last Judgement. There, convicted murderers had prayed while their few days of life ticked away towards the last breakfast. 'Puts the wretch that lies in woe / In remembrance of the shroud' – I remembered the lines at the end of the play we were about to see. Then the locked doors of the chapel opened and we were shepherded in to the entertainment.

'I have a device to make all well. Write me a prologue; and let the prologue seem to say, we will do no harm with our swords, and that Pyramus is not kill'd indeed; and for the more better assurance, tell them that I Pyramus, am not Pyramus but Bottom the weaver. This will put them out of fear!' The odd thing was – I had discovered by a glance at my programme before the chapel lights dimmed and the cold, marble-paved area in front of the altar was bathed in sunlight and became an enchanted forest – the prisoner playing Nick Bottom was called Bob Weaver. What he was in for I had no idea, but this weaver seemed to be less of a natural actor than a natural Bottom. There was no hint of an actor playing a part. The simple pomposity, the huge self-satisfaction, and the like-ability of the man were entirely real. When the audience laughed, and they laughed a good deal, the prisoner didn't seem pleased, as an actor would be, but as hurt, puzzled and resentful as bully Bottom mocked. And, when he came to the play scene, he acted Pyramus with intense seriousness which, of course, made it funnier than ever.

We were a segregated audience, divided by the aisle. On one side, like friends of the groom, sat the inmates in grey prison clothes and striped shirts – and trainers (which I used to call sand-shoes when I was a boy) were apparently allowed. On the other side, the friends of the bride were the great and the good, the professional carers and concerned operators of a curious and notoriously unsuccessful system. Of the two sides, it was the friends of the groom who coughed and fidgeted less, laughed more loudly and seemed more deeply involved in the magic that unfolded before them:

> 'But we are spirits of another sort.
> I with the morning's love have oft made sport,
> And like a forester the groves may tread
> Even till the eastern gate, all fiery red,
> Opening on Neptune with fair blessèd beams
> Turns into yellow gold his salt green streams.'

I hadn't realized how handsome Tony Timson would look without his glasses. His association, however peripheral, with an armed robbery (not the sort of thing the Timson family had any experience of, nor indeed talent for) had led him to be ruler of a fairy kingdom. Puck, small, energetic and Irish, I remembered from a far more serious case as a junior member of the clan Molloy. All too soon, for me anyway, he was alone on the stage, smiling a farewell:

> 'If we shadows have offended,
> Think but this, and all is mended:
> That you have but slumbered here,
> While these visions did appear . . .'

Then the house lights went up and I remembered that all the lovers, fairies and Rude Mechanicals (with the exception of the actresses) were robbers, housebreakers, manslaughterers and murderers, there because of their crimes and somebody's – perhaps my – unsuccessful defence.

'I think you'll all agree that that was a pretty good effort.' The Governor was on the stage, a man with a ramrod back, cropped grey hair and pink cheeks, who spoke like some commanding officer congratulating his men after a particularly dangerous foray into enemy territory. 'We owe a great deal to those splendid performers and all those who helped with the costumes. I suggest we might give a hand to our director who is mainly responsible for getting these awkward fellows acting.'

A small, middle-aged man with steel-rimmed spectacles rose up from the front row of the inmates and lifted a hand to acknowledge the applause. This the Governor silenced with a brisk mutter of words of command. 'Now will all those of you who live in, please go out. And those of you who live out, please stay in. You'll be escorted to the boardroom for drinks and light refreshments.'

The screws who had been waiting, stationed round the walls like sentries, reclaimed their charges. I saw the director who had been applauded walking towards them with his knees slightly bent, moving with a curious hopping motion, as though he were a puppet on a string. I hadn't seen his face clearly but something in the way he moved seemed familiar, although I couldn't remember where I'd met him before, or what crime he might, or might not, have committed.

'Never went much for Shakespeare when I was at school,' Quintus Blake, the Governor, told me. He was holding a flabby sausage-roll in one hand and, in the other, a glass of warmish white wine which, for sheer undrinkability, had Pommeroy's house blanc beaten by a short head. 'Thought the chap was a bit long-winded and couldn't make his meaning clear at times. But, by God, doesn't he come into his own in the prison service?'

'You mean, you use him as a form of punishment?'

'That's what I'd've thought when I was at school. That's what I'll tell Ken Fry if he complains we're giving the chaps too good a time. If they misbehave, I'll tell him we put them on Shakespeare for twenty-eight days.' Ken Fry is our new, abrasive, young Home Secretary who lives for the delighted cheers of the hangers and floggers at party conferences. Given time, he'll reintroduce the rack as a useful adjunct to police questioning.

'The truth of the matter' – Quintus bit bravely into the tepid flannel of his sausage-roll – 'is that none of the fellows on Shakespeare duty have committed a single offence since rehears-als began.'

'Is that really true?'

'Well, with one exception.' He took a swig at the alleged Entre Deux Mers, decided that one was enough and put his glass down on the boardroom table. 'Ken Fry says prison is such a brilliant idea because no one commits crimes here. Well, of course, they do. They bully each other and get up to sexual shenanigans which put me in mind of the spot behind the fives court at Coldsands. I don't know what it is about prison that always reminds me of my school-days. Anyway, as soon as they landed parts in the *Dream*, they were as good as gold, nearly all of them. And for that I've got to hand it to Gribble.'

'Gribble?'

'Matthew Gribble. Inmate in charge of Shakespeare. Just about due for release as he's got all the remission possible.'

'He produced the play?'

'And even got a performance out of that human bulldozer who played bully Bottom. One-time boxer who'd had his brains turned into mashed potatoes quite early in his career.'

'Gribble was the man who stood up at the end?'

'I thought I'd get this lot to give him a round of applause.' The Governor looked at the well-meaning elderly guests, the puzzled but hopeful social workers, who were taking their refreshments, as they took all the difficulties in their lives, with grim determination. It was then I remembered Matthew Gribble, an English teacher at a Berkshire polytechnic, who had killed his wife.

'I think,' I said, 'I defended him once.'

'I know you did!' The Governor smiled. 'And he wants you to do the trick again before the Board of Visitors. I said I'd try and arrange it because, so far as I'm concerned, he's an absolutely model prisoner.'

All this happened at a time when Claude Erskine-Brown (who had not yet become a Q.C. – I call them Queer Customers) took to himself a young lady pupil named Wendy Crump. Mizz Crump was a person with high legal qualifications but no oil painting – as Uncle Tom, of blessed memory, would have been likely to say. She had, I believe, been hand-picked by Claude's wife, the Portia of our Chambers, who had not yet got her shapely bottom on to the Bench and been elevated to the title of Mrs Justice Phillida Erskine-Brown, a puisne judge of the High Court.

'Your Mizz Crump,' I told Claude, when we met at breakfast time in the Tastee-Bite eatery a little to the west of our Chambers, 'seems a bit of an all-round asset.'

'All round, Rumpole. You've said it. Wendy Crump is very all round indeed.' He gave a mirthless laugh and spoke as a man who might have preferred a slimline pupil.

'Hope you don't mind,' I told him, 'but I asked her to look up the effect of self-induced drunkenness on crimes of violence. She came up with the answer in a couple of shakes, with reference to all the leading cases.'

'I'll agree she's a dab hand at the law.'

'Well, isn't that what you need a pupil for?' I knew it was a silly question as soon as I'd asked it. An ability to mug up cases on manslaughter was not at all what Claude required of a pupil. He wanted someone willing, husky-voiced and alluring. He wanted a heartshaped face and swooping eyelashes which could drive the poor fellow insane when they were topped by a wig. He wanted to fall in love and make elaborate plans for satisfying his cravings, which would be doomed to disaster. What the poor old darling wanted was yet another opportunity to make a complete ass of himself, and these longings were unlikely to be fulfilled by Wendy Crump.

'What a barrister needs, Rumpole, in a busy life with heavy responsibilities and a great deal of nervous tension is, well, a little warmth, a little adoration.'

'I shouldn't be in the least surprised if Mizz Crump didn't adore you, Claude.'

'Don't even suggest it!' The clever Crump's pupil master gave a shudder.

'Anyway, don't you get plenty of warmth and affection from Philly?'

'Philly's been on circuit for weeks.' Claude took a quick swig of the coffee from the Old Bailey machine and didn't seem to enjoy it. 'And when she's here she spends all her time criticizing me.'

'How extraordinary.' I simulated amazement.

'Yes, isn't it? Philly's away and I have to spend my days stuck here with Wendy Crump. But not my nights, Rumpole. Never, ever, my nights.'

I lost his attention as Nick Davenant from King's Bench Walk passed us, followed by his pupil Jenny Attienzer. She was tall, blonde, willowy and carrying his coffee. Poor old Claude looked as sick as a dog.

That afternoon I was seated at my desk, smoking a small cigar and gazing into space – the way I often spend my time when not engaged in Court – when there was a brisk knock at the door and Wendy Crump entered and asked if I had a set of Cox's Criminal Reports. 'Not in here,' I told her. 'Try upstairs. Cox's Reports are Soapy Sam Ballard's constant reading.' And then, because she looked disappointed at not finding these alluring volumes at once, I did my best to cheer her up.

'Claude thinks you're a wonderful pupil.' I exaggerated, of course. 'I told him you were a dab hand at the law. He's very lucky.'

It's rare nowadays that you see anyone blush, but Wendy's usually pale cheeks were glowing. 'I'm the lucky one,' she said, and added, to my amazement, 'to be doing my pupillage with Erskine-Brown. Everyone I know is green with envy.' Everyone she knew, I thought, must be strangely ignorant of life at the Bailey, where prosecution by Claude has come to be regarded as the key to the gaolhouse door.

Wendy ended her testimonial with 'I honestly do regard it as an enormous privilege.' I supposed the inmates of Worsfield would consider basketball or macramé a privilege if it got them out of solitary confinement. Looking at the enthusiastic Mizz Crump I thought that Claude had been unfair about her appearance. It was just that she had acquired the look of an intelligent and cheerful middle-aged person whilst still in her twenties. She was, I suppose, what would be called considerably overweight, but there was nothing wrong with that. With her wiry hair scraped back, her spectacles and her willing expression, she looked like the photographs of the late Dorothy L. Sayers, a perfectly pleasant sight.

'I just hope I can be a help to him.'

'I'm sure you can.' Although not, I thought, the sort of help the ever-hopeful Claude was after.

'I could never rise to be a barrister like that.'

'Perhaps it's just as well,' I encouraged her.

'I mean I could never stand up and speak with such command – and in such a beautiful voice too. Of course he's handsome, which means he can absolutely dominate a courtroom. You need to be handsome to do that, don't you?'

'Well,' I said, 'thank you very much.'

'Oh, I didn't mean that. Of course *you* dominate all sorts of courtrooms. And it doesn't matter what you look like.' She gave a little gasp to emphasize her point. 'It doesn't matter in the least!'

'The extraordinary thing is that his name is Weaver. He was on the same floor as me, a couple of cell doors away.' Matthew

Gribble spoke as if he were describing a neighbour in a country village. 'Bob Weaver. He used to laugh at me because I kept getting books from the library. He was sure I got all the ones with dirty bits in because I knew where to look for them. Of course, in those days, he couldn't tell the difference between soft porn and *Mansfield Park*. He was hardly literate.'

'You say he *was*.'

'Until I taught him to read, that is.'

'You taught him?'

'Oh, yes. I honestly don't know how I'd've got through the years here if I hadn't had that to do.' He gave a small, timid smile. 'As a matter of fact, I enjoyed the chance to teach again.'

'How did you manage it?'

'Oh, I read to him at first. I read all the stories I'd liked when I was a child. We started with *Winnie-the-Pooh* and got on to *Treasure Island* and *Kidnapped*. Then he began to want to read for himself.'

'So you decided to cast him?'

'If we ever did the *Dream*. He looked absolutely right. A huge mountain of a man with the outlook of a child. And kind, too. He *even* had the right name for it.'

'You mean, to play Nick, the weaver?'

'Exactly! I asked him to do it a long time ago. Two years at least. I asked him if he'd like to play Bottom.'

'And he agreed?'

'No.' The timid smile returned. 'He looked profoundly shocked. He thought I'd made some sort of obscene suggestion.'

We had been in the Worsfield interview room four and a bit years before, sitting on either side of the same table, with the bright blue paint and the solitary cactus, and the walls and door half glass so the screws could look in and see what we were up to. Then, we had been talking about his teaching, his production with the Cowshott drama group, the performances which he got out of secretaries and teachers and a particularly dramatic district nurse – and of his wife who apparently hated him and his amateur theatricals. When she flew at him and tore at his face with her fingernails during one of their nightly quarrels over the washing up, he had stabbed her through the heart. I thought I had done the case with my usual brilliance and got the jury to find provocation and reduce the crime to manslaughter, for which the Judge, taking the view that a kitchen knife is not the proper reply to an attack with finger-nails, had given him seven years. As the Governor told me, he was a model prisoner. With full remission he'd be out by the end of the month. That is, unless he was convicted on the charge I was now concerned with. If the Board of Visitors did him for dangerous assault on a prison warden, he'd forfeit a large chunk of his remission.

'The incident we have to talk about,' I said, 'happened in the carpenter's shop.'

'Yes,' he sighed, 'I suppose we have to talk about it.'

All subjects seemed to him, I guessed, flat, stale and unprofit-able after the miracle of getting an illiterate East End prize-fighter to enjoy acting Shakespeare. I remembered his account of the last quarrel with his wife. She had told him he was universally despised. She had mocked him for his pathetic sexual attainments while, at the same time, accusing him, quite without foundation, of abusing his child by a previous marriage. He had heard it all many, many times before. It was only when she told him that he had produced *Hamlet* as though it were a television situation comedy that their quarrel ended in violence.

'Yes, the carpenter's shop.' Matthew Gribble sighed. Then he cheered up slightly and said, 'We were building the set for the *Dream*.'

I had a note of the case given to me by the Governor. There were only four members of the cast working on the scenery, one civilian carpenter and a prison officer in overall charge. His name was Steve Barrington.

'Do you know' – my client's voice was full of wonder – 'Barrington gave up a job as a teacher to become a screw? Isn't that extraordinary?'

'Do you think he regrets it? He may not have got chisels thrown at him in class, with any luck.'

What was thrown was undoubtedly the tool which Matthew had been using. The screw was talking to one of the carpenters and didn't see the missile before it struck his cheek. The other cast members, except for one, said they were busy and didn't see who launched the attack.

'I put the chisel on the bench and I was just turning round to tack the false turf on to the mound we'd built. I didn't see who threw it. I only know that I didn't. I told you the truth in the other case. Why should I lie to you about this?'

Because you don't want to spend another unnecessary minute as a guest of Her Majesty, I thought of saying, but resisted the temptation. It was not for me to pass judgement, not at any stage of the proceedings. My problem was that there was a witness who said he'd seen Matthew Gribble throw the chisel. A witness who seemed to have no reason to tell lies about his friend and educator. It was Bob Weaver who had made the journey from illiteracy to Shakespeare, and been rewarded with the part of bully Bottom.

'Rumpole, a terrible thing has happened in Chambers!' Mizz Liz Probert sat on the edge of my client's chair, her face pale but determined, her hands locked as though in prayer, her voice low and doom-laden. It was as though she were announcing, to waiting relations on the quayside, the fact that the *Titanic* had struck an iceberg.

'Not the nailbrush disappeared again?'

'Rumpole, can't you ever be serious?'

'Hardly ever when it comes to things that have happened in Chambers.'

'Well, this time, perhaps your attitude will be more helpful.'

'It depends on whether I want to be helpful. What is it? Don't tell me. Henry blew the coffee money on a dud horse?'

'Claude has committed the unforgivable sin.'

'You mean, adultery? Well, that's something of an achievement. His attempts usually end in all-round frustration.'

'That too, most probably. No. This is what he said in the clerk's room.'

'Go on. Shock me.'

'Kate Inglefield, who's an assistant solicitor in Damiens, heard him say it. And, of course, she was tremendously distressed.'

'Can you tell me what he said?' I wondered. 'Or are you too embarrassed? Would you prefer to write it down?'

'Don't be silly, Rumpole. He asked Henry if he'd seen his fat pupil about recently.'

There followed a heavy silence, during which I thought I was meant to say something. So I said, 'Go on.'

'What do you mean?'

'Go on till you get to the bit that caused Kate Inglefield – not, I would have thought, a girl who distresses easily – such pain.'

'Rumpole, I've said it. Do I have to say it again?'

'Perhaps if you do, I'll be able to follow your argument.'

'Erskine-Brown said to Henry, "Have you seen my fat pupil?"'

'Recently?'

'What?'

'He said recently.'

'Really, Rumpole. Recently is hardly the point.'

'So the point is my fat pupil?'

'Of course it is!'

I took out a small cigar and placed it between the lips. Sorting out the precise nature of the charge against Claude would require a whiff of nicotine. 'And he was referring – I merely ask for clarification – to his pupil Mizz Crump?'

'Of course he meant Wendy, yes.'

'And he called her fat?'

'It was' – Liz Probert described it as though murder had been committed – 'an act of supreme chauvinism. It's daring to assume that women should alter the shape of their bodies just for the sake of pleasing men. Disgusting!'

'But isn't it' – I was prepared, as usual, to put forward the argument for the Defence – 'a bit like saying the sky's blue?'

'It's not at all like that. It's judging a woman by her appearance.'

'And isn't the other judging the sky by its appearance?'

'I suppose I should have known!' Mizz Probert stood up, all her sorrow turned to anger. 'There's no crime so contemptible that you won't say a few ill-chosen words in its favour. And, don't you dare light that thing until I'm out of the room.'

'I'm sure you're busy.'

'I certainly am. We're having a special meeting tonight of the Sisterhood of Radical Lawyers. We aim to blacklist anyone who sends Claude briefs or appears in Court with him. We're going to petition the Judges not to listen to his arguments and Ballard's got to give him notice to quit.'

'Mizz Liz,' I said, 'how would you describe me?'

'As a defender of hopeless causes.'

'No, I mean my personal appearance.'

'Well, you're fairly short.' The Prosecutor gave me the once over. 'Your nose is slightly purple, and your hair – what's left of it – is curly and you're . . .'

'Go on, say it.'

'Well, Rumpole. Let's face it. You're fat.'

'You said it.'

'Yes.'

'So should I get you blackballed in Court?'

'Of course not.'

'Why not?'

'Because you're a man.'

'I see.'

'I shouldn't think you do. I shouldn't think you do for a moment.'

Mizz Probert left me then. Full of thought, I applied the match to the end of the small cigar.

It was some weeks later that Fred Timson, undisputed head of the Timson clan, was charged with receiving a stolen video recorder. The charge was, in itself, something of an insult to a person of Fred's standing and sensitivity. It was rather as if I had been offered a brief in a case of a non-renewed television licence, or, indeed, of receiving a stolen video recorder. I only took the case because Fred is a valued client and, in many respects, an old family friend. I never tire of telling Hilda that a portion of our family beef, bread, marmalade and washing-up liquid depends on the long life of Fred Timson and his talent for getting caught on the windy side of the law. I can't say that this home truth finds much favour with She Who Must Be Obeyed, who treats me, on these occasions, as though I were only a moderately successful petty thief working in Streatham and its immediate environs.

The Defence was elaborate, having to do with a repair job delivered to the wrong address, an alibi, and the fact that the chief prosecution witness was a distant relative of a member of the Molloy family – all bitter rivals and enemies of the Timsons. While Fred and I were drinking coffee in the Snaresbrook canteen, having left the Jury to sort out the complexities of this minor crime, I told him that I'd seen Tony Timson playing the King of the Fairies.

'No, Mr Rumpole, you're mistaken about that, I can assure you, sir. Our Tony is not that way inclined.'

'No, in *Midsummer Night's Dream*. An entirely heterosexual fairy. Married to the Fairy Queen.'

Fred Timson said nothing, but shook his head in anxious disbelief. I decided to change the subject. 'I don't know if you've heard of one of Tony's fellow prisoners. Bob Weaver, a huge fellow. Started off as a boxer?'

'Battering Bob Weaver!' Fred seemed to find the memory amusing. 'That's how he was known. Used to do bare-knuckle fights on an old airfield near Colchester. And my cousin Percy Timson's young Mavis married Battering Bob's brother, Billy Weaver, as was wrongly fingered for the brains behind the Dagenham dairy-depot job. To be quite candid with you, Mr Rumpole, Billy Weaver is not equipped to be the brains behind anything. Pity about Battering Bob, though.'

'You mean the way he went down for the Deptford minicab murder?'

'Not that exactly. That's over and done with. No. The way he's deteriorated in the nick.'

'Deteriorated?'

'According as Mavis tells Percy, he has. Can't hold a decent conversation when they visits. It's all about books and that.'

'I heard he's learnt to read.'

'Mavis says the family's worried desperate. Bob spent all her visit telling her a poem about a nightingale. Well, what's the point of that? I mean, there can't be all that many nightingales round Worsfield Prison. Course, it's the other bloke they put it down to.'

'Matthew Gribble?'

'Is that the name? Anyway, seems Bob thinks the world of this chap. Says he's changed his life and that he worships him, Mr Rumpole. But Mavis reckons he's been a bad influence on Bob. I mean that Gribble's got terrible form. Didn't he kill his wife? No one in our family ever did that.'

'Of course not. Although Tony Timson was rumoured to have attempted it.'

'Between the attempt and the deed, as you well know, Mr Rumpole, there is a great gulf fixed. Isn't that true?'

'Very true, Fred.'

'And Mavis says Bob's been worse for the last three months. Nervous and depressed like as though he was dreading something.' What, I wondered, had been bugging Battering Bob? It couldn't have been the fact that his friend was in trouble for attacking a warden; that had only happened a month before. 'I suppose,' I suggested, 'it was stage-fright. They started rehearsing *Midsummer Night's Dream* around three months ago.'

'You mean like he was scared of being in a play?'

'He might have been.'

'I hardly think a bloke what went single-handed against six Molloys during the minicab war would be scared of a bit of a play.'

It was then that the tireless Bernard came to tell me that the Jury were back with a verdict. Fred stood up, gave his jacket a tug, and strolled off as though he'd just been called in to dinner at the local Rotary Club. And I was left wondering again why Battering Bob Weaver should decide to be the sole witness against a man he had worshipped.

I got back to Chambers in a reasonably cheerful mood, the Jury having decided to give Uncle Fred the generous benefit of a rather small supply of doubt, and there waiting in my client's chair was another bundle of trouble. None other than Wendy Crump, Claude's pupil, clearly in considerable distress. 'I had to talk to you,' she said, 'because it's all so terribly unfair!'

Was unfair the right word, I wondered. Unkind, perhaps, but not unfair, unless she meant it as a general rebuke to the Almighty who handed out sylphlike beauty to the undiscerning few with absolutely no regard for academic attainment or moral worth. 'Of course,' I said, '*I* think you look very attractive.'

'What?' She looked at me surprised and, I thought, a little shocked.

'In the days of Sir Peter Paul Rubens,' I assured her, 'a girl with your dimensions would have been on page three of the *Sun*, if not on the ceiling of the Banqueting Hall.'

'Please, Rumpole,' she said, 'there are more important things to talk about.'

'Well, exactly,' I assured her. 'People have suggested that *I'm* a little overweight. They have hinted that from time to time, but do I let it worry me? Do I decline the mashed spuds or the fried slice with my breakfast bacon? I do not. I let such remarks slide off me like water off a duck's back.'

'Rumpole!' she said, a little sharply, I thought. 'I don't think your physical appearance is anything to do with all this trouble.'

'Is it not? I just thought that we're birds of a feather.'

'I doubt it!' This Mizz Crump could be very positive at times. 'I came to see you about Erskine-Brown.'

'Of course, he shouldn't have said it.' I was prepared, as I have said, to accept the brief for the Defence. 'It was just one of those unfortunate slips of the tongue.'

'You mean he shouldn't have told me about Kate Inglefield?'

'What's he told you about Mizz Inglefield? You mean that rather bright young solicitor from Damiens? She's quite skinny, as far as I can remember.'

'Rumpole, why do you keep harping on people's personal appearances?'

'Well, didn't Claude say . . .?'

'Claude told me that Kate Inglefield had decided never to brief him again. And she's taken his VAT fraud away from him. And Christine Dewsbury, who's meant to be his junior in a long robbery, has said she'll never work with him again, and Mr Ballard . . .'

'The whited sepulchre who is Head of our Chambers?'

'Mr Ballard has been giving him some quite poisonous looks.'

'Those aren't poisonous looks. That's Soapy Sam's usual happy expression.'

'He's hinted that Erskine-Brown may have to look for other Chambers. He's such a wonderful advocate, Rumpole!'

'Well now, let's say he's an advocate of sorts.'

'And a fine man! A man with very high principles.' I listened in some surprise. Was this the Claude I had seen stumbling into trouble and lying his way out of it over the last twenty years? 'And he has absolutely no idea why he is being victimized.'

'Has he not?'

'None whatever.'

'But *you* know?'

'No, really. I have no idea.'

'Well' – I breathed a sigh of relief – 'that's all right then.'

'No, it's not all right.' She stood up, her cheeks flushed, her voice clear and determined. Mizz Crump might be no oil painting, but I thought I saw in her the makings of a fighter. 'We've got to find out why all this is happening. And we've got to save him. Will you help me get him out of trouble? *Whatever* it is.'

'Helping people in trouble,' I assured her, 'has been my job for almost half a century.'

'So you're with me, Rumpole?' She was, I was glad to see, a determined young woman who might go far in the law.

'Of course I am. We fat people should stick together.' Naturally, I regretted it the moment I had said it.

'The Governor says you're a model prisoner.'

'Yes.'

'Well, that's a kind of tribute.'

'Not exactly what I wanted to be when I was at university. I'd just done my first *Twelfth Night*. I suppose I wanted to be a great director. I saw myself at the National or the R.S.C. If I couldn't do that, I wanted to be an unforgettable teacher of English and open the eyes of generations to Shakespeare. I never thought I'd end up as a model prisoner.'

'Life is full of surprises.' That didn't seem too much of a comfort to Matthew Gribble as we sat together, back in the

prison interview room. Spring sunshine was fighting its way
through windows that needed cleaning. I had sat in the train,
trees with leaves just turning green, sunlight on the grass. A
good time to think of freedom, starting a new life and forgetting
the past. 'If we can get you off this little bit of trouble, you
should be out of here by the end of the month.'

'Out. To do what?' He was smiling gently, but I thought
quite without amusement, as he stared into the future. 'I
shouldn't think they'll ever ask me to direct a play for the
Cowshott amateurs. "You'd better watch out for this one,
darling," I can just hear them whispering at the read through.
"He stabbed his wife to death with a kitchen knife."'

'There may be other drama groups.'

'Not for me. Do you think they'd have me back at the poly?
Not a hope.'

'Anyway' – I tried to cheer him up – 'you did a pretty good
job with *A Midsummer Night's Dream*.'

'Shakespeare with violent criminals, deputy-governors' wives
and wardens' daughters. Not the R.S.C. exactly, but I can put
on a good show in Worsfield gaol. Wasn't Bob Weaver
marvellous?'

'Extraordinary.'

'And you know what I discovered? He responds to the sound
of poetry. He's got to know it by heart. Great chunks of it.'
From Battering Bob to Babbling Bob, I thought, treating his
bewildered visitors to great chunks of John Keats. It was
funny, of course, but in its way a huge achievement. Matthew
Gribble appeared to agree. 'I suppose I'm proud of that.' He
thought about it and seemed satisfied. I turned back to the
business in hand.

'Those other cast members in the carpenter's helping make
the scenery – Tony Timson, the young Molloy? Do you think
either of them saw who threw the chisel?'

'If they did, they're not saying. Grassing's a sin in prison.'

'But your protégé Babbling Bob is prepared to grass on you?'

'Seems like it.' He was, I thought, resigned and strangely
unconcerned.

'Have you talked to him about it?'

'Yes. Once.'

'What did you say?'

'I told him to always be truthful. That's the secret of acting, to tell the truth about the character. I told him that.'

'Forget about acting for a moment. Did you ask him why he said you attacked the screw?'

There was a silence. Matthew Gribble seemed to be looking past me, at something far away. At last he said, 'Yes, I asked him that.'

'And what did he say?'

'He said' – my client gave a small, not particularly happy smile – 'he said we'd always be friends, wouldn't we?'

The master–pupil relationship – the instructing of a younger, less experienced person in the mysteries of some art, theatrical or legal – seemed a situation fraught with danger. While Matthew Gribble's devoted pupil was turning on his master with damaging allegations, Wendy Crump's pupil master was in increasing trouble, being treated by the Sisterhood of Radical Lawyers as a male pariah. As yet, neither Erskine-Brown, nor his alleged victim, had been informed of the charges against him, although Mizz Probert and her supporters were about to raise the matter before the Bar Council as a serious piece of professional misconduct by the unfortunate Claude, who sat, brooding and unemployed in his room, wondering what it was that his best friend wouldn't tell him which had led to him being shunned by female lawyers. I learnt about the proposed petitioning of the Bar Council when I visited the Soapy Head of our Chambers in order to scotch any plan to drive the unfortunate sinner from that paradise which is 4 Equity Court.

'There is no doubt whatever' – here Ballard put on his carefully modulated tone of sorrowful condemnation – 'that Erskine-Brown has erred grievously.'

'Which one of the Ten Commandments is it exactly, if I may be so bold as to ask, which forbids us to call our neighbour fat?'

'There is such a thing, Rumpole' – Ballard gave me the look with which a missionary might reprove a cannibal – 'as gender awareness.'

'Is there, really? And who told you about that then? I'll lay you a hundred to one it was Mizz Liz Probert.'

'Lady lawyers take it extremely seriously, Rumpole. Which is why we're in danger of losing all our work from Damiens.'

'The all-female solicitors? Not a man in the whole of the firm. Is that being gender aware?'

'However the firm is composed, Rumpole, they provide a great deal of valuable work for all of us.'

'Well, I'm aware of gender,' I told Soapy Sam, 'at least I think I am. You're a man from what I can remember.'

'That remark would be taken very much amiss, Rumpole. If made to a woman.'

'But it's not made to a woman, it's made to you, Ballard. Are you going to stand for this religious persecution of the unfortunate Claude?'

'What he said about Wendy Crump was extremely wounding.'

'Nonsense! She wasn't wounded in the least. None of these avenging angels has bothered to tell her what her pupil master said.'

'Did you tell her?'

'Well, no, I didn't, actually.'

'Did you tell Wendy Crump that Erskine-Brown had called her fat?' For about the first time in his life Soapy Sam had asked a good question in cross-examination. I was reduced, for a moment at least, to silence. 'Why didn't you repeat those highly offensive words to her?'

I knew the answer, but I wasn't going to give him the pleasure of hearing it from me.

'It was because you didn't want to hurt her feelings, did you, Rumpole? And you knew how much it would wound her.' Ballard was triumphant. 'You showed a rare flash of gender awareness and I congratulate you for it!'

Although a potential outcast from the gender-aware society, Claude hadn't been entirely deprived of his practice. New briefs were slow in arriving, but he still had some of his old cases to finish off. One of these was a complex and not particularly fascinating fraud on a bookmaker in which Claude and I were briefed for two of the alleged fraudsters. I needn't go into the details of the case except to say that the Prosecution was in the hands of the dashing and handsome Nick Davenant who had a large and shapely nose, brown hair billowing from under his wig, and knowing and melting eyes. It was Nick's slimline pupil, Jenny Attienzer, whom Claude had hopelessly coveted. This fragile beauty was not in Court on the day in question; whether she thought the place out of bounds because of the gender-unaware Claude, I'm unable to say. But Claude was being assisted by the able but comfortably furnished (slenderly challenged) Wendy Crump and I was on my own.

The case was being tried by her Honour Judge Emma MacNaught, Q.C., sitting as an Old Bailey judge, who had treated Claude, from the start of the case, to a number of withering looks and, when addressing him in person became inevitable, to a tone of icy contempt. This circus judge turned out to have been the author of a slender handbook entitled 'Sexual Harassment in the Legal Profession'. (Wendy Crump told me, some time later, that she would challenge anyone to know whether they had been sexually harassed or not unless they'd read the book.)

Nick Davenant called the alleged victim of our clients' fraud – a panting and sweating bookmaker whose physical attributes I am too gender aware to refer to – and his last question was, 'Mr Aldworth, have you ever been in trouble with the police?'

'No. Certainly not. Not with the police.' On which note of honesty Nick sat down and Claude rose to cross-examine. Before he could open his mouth, however, Wendy was half standing, pulling at his gown and commanding, in a penetrating whisper, that he ask Aldworth if he'd ever been in trouble with anyone else.

'Are you intending to ask any question, Mr Erskine-Brown?' Judge MacNaught had closed her eyes to avoid the pain of looking at the learned chauvinist pig.

'Have you been in trouble with anyone else?' Claude plunged in, clay in the hands of the gown-tugger behind him.

'Only with my wife. On Derby night.' For this, Mr Aldworth was rewarded by a laugh from the Jury, and Claude by a look of contempt from the Judge.

'Ask him if he's ever been reported to Tattersall's.' The insistent pupil behind Claude gave another helping tug. Claude clearly didn't think things could get any worse.

'Have you ever been reported to Tattersall's?' he asked, adding 'the racing authority' by way of an unnecessary explanation.

'Well, yes. As far as I can remember,' Mr Aldworth admitted in a fluster, and the Jury stopped laughing.

'Ask him how many times!'

'How many times?' Wendy Crump was now Claude's pupil master.

'I don't know I can rightly remember.'

'Do your best,' Wendy suggested.

'Well, do your best,' Claude asked.

'Ten or a dozen times . . . Perhaps twenty.'

I sat back in gratitude. The chief prosecution witness had been holed below the waterline, without my speaking a word, and our co-defendants might well be home and dry.

At the end of the cross-examination, the learned Judge subjected Claude to the sort of scrutiny she might have given a greenish slice of haddock on a slab, long past its sell-by date. 'Mr Erskine-Brown!'

'Yes, my Lady.'

'You are indeed fortunate to have a pupil who is so skilled in the art of cross-examination.'

'Indeed, I am, my Lady.'

'Then you must be very grateful that she remains to help you. For the time being.' The last words were uttered in the voice of a prison governor outlining the arrangements, temporary of course, for life in the condemned cell. Hearing them, even my blood, I have to confess, ran a little chill.

When the lunch adjournment came Claude shot off about some private business and I strolled out of Court with the model pupil. I told her she'd done very well.

'Thank you, Rumpole.' Wendy took my praise as a matter of course. 'I thought the Judge was absolutely outrageous to poor old Claude. Going at him like that simply because he's a man. I can't stand that sort of sexist behaviour!' And then she was off in search of refreshment and I was left wondering at the rapidity with which her revered pupil master had become 'poor old Claude'.

And then I saw, at the end of the wide corridor and at the head of the staircase, Nick Davenant, the glamorous Prosecutor, in close and apparently friendly consultation with the leader of the militant sisterhood, Mizz Liz Probert of our Chambers. I made towards them but, as she noticed my approach, Mizz Liz melted away like snow in the sunshine and, being left alone with young Nick, I invited him to join me for a pint of Guinness and a plateful of steak and kidney pie in the pub across the road.

'I saw you were talking to Liz Probert?' I asked him when we were settled at the trough.

'Great girl, Liz. In your Chambers, isn't she?'

'I brought her up, you might say. She was my pupil in her time. Did she question your gender awareness?'

'Good heavens, no!' Nick Davenant laughed, giving me a ringside view of a set of impeccable teeth. 'I think she knows that I'm tremendously gender aware the whole time. No. She's just a marvellous girl. She does all sorts of little things for me.'

'Does she indeed?' The pie crust, as usual, tasted of cardboard, the beef was stringy and the kidneys as hard to find as beggars in the Ritz, but they couldn't ruin the mustard or the Guinness. 'I suppose I shouldn't ask what sort of things.'

'Well, I wasn't talking about that in particular.' The learned Prosecutor gave the impression that he *could* talk about that if he wasn't such a decent and discreet young Davenant. 'But I mean little things like work.'

'Mizz Liz works for you?'

'Well, if I've got a difficult opinion to write, or a big case to note up, then Liz will volunteer.'

'But you've got Miss Slenderlegs, the blonde barrister, as your pupil.'

'Liz says she can't trust Jenny to get things right, so she takes jobs on for me.'

'And you pay her lavishly of course.'

'Not at all.' Still smiling in a blinding fashion, Nick Davenant shook his head. 'I don't pay her a thing. She does it for the sake of friendship.'

'Friendship with you, of course?'

'Friendship with me, yes. I think Liz is really a nice girl. And I don't see anything wrong with her bum.'

'Wrong with what?'

'Her bum.'

'That's what I thought you said.'

'Do you think there's anything wrong with it, Rumpole?' A dreamy look had come over young Davenant's face.

'I hadn't really thought about it very much. But I suppose not.'

'I don't know why she has to go through all that performance about it, really.'

'Performance?'

'At Monte's beauty parlour, she told me. In Ken High Street. Takes hours, she told me. While she has to sit there and read *Hello!* magazine.'

'You don't mean that she reads this – whatever publication you mentioned – while changing the shape of her body for the sake of pleasing men?'

'I suppose,' Davenant had to admit reluctantly, 'it's in a good cause.'

'Have the other half of this black Liffey water, why don't you?' I felt nothing but affection for Counsel for the Prosecution, for suddenly, at long last, I saw a chink of daylight at the end of poor old Claude's long, black tunnel. 'And tell me all you know about Monte's beauty parlour.'

The day's work done, I was walking back from Ludgate Circus and the well-known Palais de Justice, when I saw, alone and palely loitering, the woman of the match, Wendy Crump. I hailed her gladly, caught her up and she turned to me a face on which gloom was written large. I couldn't even swear that her spectacles hadn't become misted with tears.

'You don't look particularly cheered up,' I told her, 'after your day of triumph.'

'No. As a matter of fact I feel tremendously depressed.'

'What about?'

'About Claude. I've been thinking about it so much and it's made me sad.'

'Someone told you?' I was sorry for her.

'Told me what?'

'Well' – I thought, of course, that the damage had been done by the sisterhood over the lunch adjournment – 'what Claude had said about you that caused all the trouble.'

'All what trouble?'

'Being blackballed, blacklisted, outlawed, outcast, dismissed from the human race. Why Liz Probert and the gender-aware radical lawyers have decided to hound him.'

'Because of what he said about me?'

'They haven't told you?'

'Not a word. But *you* know what it was?'

'Perhaps.' I was playing for time.

'Then tell me, for God's sake.'

'Quite honestly, I'd rather not.'

'What on earth's the matter?'

'I'd really rather not say it.'

'Why?'

'You'd probably find it offensive.'

'Rumpole, I'm going to be a barrister. I'll have to sit through rape, indecent assault, sex and sodomy. Just spit it out.'

'He was probably joking.'

'He doesn't joke much.'

'Well, then. He called you, and I don't suppose he meant it, fat.'

She looked at me and, in a magical moment, the gloom lifted. I thought there was even the possibility of a laugh. And then it came, a light giggle, just as we passed Pommeroy's.

'Of course I'm fat. Fatty Crump, that set me apart from all the other anorexic little darlings at school. That and the fact that I usually got an A-plus. It was my trademark. Well, I never thought Claude looked at me long enough to notice.'

When this had sunk in, I asked her why, if she hadn't heard from Liz Probert and her Amazonians, she was so shaken and wan with care.

'Because' – and here the note of sadness returned – 'I used to hero-worship Claude. I thought he was a marvellous barrister. And now I know he can't really do it, can he?'

She looked at me, hoping, perhaps, for some contradiction. I was afraid I couldn't oblige. 'All the same,' I said, 'you don't want him cast into outer darkness and totally deprived of briefs, do you?'

'Good heavens, no. I wouldn't wish that on anyone.'

'Then, in the fullness of time,' I told her, 'I may have a little strategy to suggest.'

'Hilda,' I said, having managed to ingest most of a bottle of Château Fleet Street Ordinaire over our cutlets, and with it taken courage, 'what would you do if I called you fat?' I awaited the blast of thunder, or at least a drop in the temperature to freezing, to be followed by a week's eerie silence.

To my surprise she answered with a brisk 'I'd call you fatter!'

'A sensible answer, Hilda.' I had been brave enough for one evening. 'You and Mizz Wendy Crump are obviously alike in tolerance and common sense. The only trouble is, she couldn't say that to Claude because he has a lean and hungry look. Like yon Cassius.'

'Like yon *who*?'

'No matter.'

'Rumpole, I have absolutely no idea what you're talking about.'

So I told her the whole story of Wendy and Claude and Mizz Probert, with her Sisterhood, ready to tear poor Erskine-Brown apart as the Bacchantes rent Orestes, and the frightened Ballard. She listened with an occasional click of the tongue and shake of her head, which led me to believe that she didn't entirely approve. 'Those girls,' she said, 'should be a little less belligerent and learn to use their charm.'

'Perhaps they haven't got as much charm as you have, Hilda,' I flannelled, and she looked at me with deep suspicion.

'But you say this Wendy Crump doesn't mind particularly?'

'She seems not to. Only one thing seems to upset her.'

'What's that?'

'She's disillusioned about Claude not because of the fat chat, but because she's found out he's not the brilliant advocate she once thought him.'

'Hero-worship! That's always dangerous.'

'I suppose so.'

'I remember when Dodo and I were at school together, we had an art mistress called Helena Lampos and Dodo absolutely hero-worshipped her. She said Lampos revealed to her the true use of watercolours. Well, then we heard that this Lampos person was going to leave to get married. I can't think who'd agreed to marry her because she wasn't much of a catch, at least not in my opinion. Anyway, Dodo was heartbroken and couldn't bear the idea of being separated from her heroine so, on the morning she was leaving, Lampos could not find the blue silky coat that she was always so proud of.'

When she starts on her schooldays I feel an irresistible urge to apply the corkscrew to the second bottle of the Ordinaire. I was engaged in this task as Hilda's story wound to a conclusion. 'So, anyway, the coat in question was finally found in Dodo's locker. She thought if she hid it, she'd keep Miss Lampos. Of course, she didn't. The Lampos left and Dodo had to do a huge impot and miss the staff concert. And, by the way, Rumpole, there's absolutely no need for you to open another bottle of that stuff. It's high time you were in bed.'

At the Temple station next morning I bought a copy of *Hello!*, a mysterious publication devoted to the happy lives of people I had never heard of. When I arrived in Chambers my first port of call was to the room where Liz Probert carried on her now flourishing practice. She was, as the saying is, at her desk, and I noticed a new scarlet telephone had settled in beside her regulation black instrument.

'Business booming, I'm glad to see. You've had to install another telephone.'

'It's a hotline, Rumpole.'

'Hot?' I gave it a tentative touch.

'I mean it's private. For the use of women in Chambers only.'

'It doesn't respond to the touch of the male finger.'

'It's so we can report harassment, discrimination and verbally aggressive male barrister or clerk conduct direct to the S.R.L. office.'

The S –?'

'Sisterhood of Radical Lawyers.'

'And what will they do? Send for the police? Call the fire brigade to douse masculine ardour?'

'They will record the episode fully. Then we shall meet the victim and decide on action.'

'I thought you decided on action before you met Wendy Crump.'

'Her case was particularly clear. Now she's coming to the meeting of the Sisterhood at five-thirty.'

'Ah, yes. She told me about that. I think she's got quite a lot to say.'

'I'm sure she has. Now what do you want, Rumpole? I'm before the Divisional Court at ten-thirty.'

'Good for you! I just came in to ask you a favour.'

'Not self-induced drunkenness as a defence? Crump told me she had to look that up for you.'

'It's not the law. Although I do hear you work for other barristers for nothing, and so deprive their lady pupils of the beginnings of a practice.'

Mizz Probert looked, I thought, a little shaken, but she picked up a pencil, underlined something in her brief and prepared to ignore me.

'Is that what you came to complain about?' she asked without looking at me.

'No. I've come to tell you I bought *Hello!* magazine.'

'Why on earth did you do that?' She looked up and was surprised to see me holding out the publication in question.

'I heard you read it during long stretches of intense boredom. I thought I might do the same when Mr Injustice Graves sums up to the Jury.'

'I don't have long moments of boredom.' Mizz Liz sounded businesslike.

'Don't you really? Not when you have to sit for hours in Monte's beauty parlour in Ken High Street?'

'I don't know what you're talking about...' The protest came faintly. Mizz Probert was visibly shaken.

'It must be awfully uncomfortable. I mean, I don't think I'd want to sit for hours in a solution of couscous and assorted stewed herbs with the whole thing wrapped up in tinfoil. I suppose *Hello!* magazine is a bit of a comfort in those circumstances. But is it worth it? I mean, all that trouble to change what a bountiful nature gave you – for the sake of pleasing men?'

I didn't enjoy asking this fatal question. I brought Mizz Liz up in the law and I still have respect and affection for her. On a good day she can be an excellent ally. But I was acting for the underdog, an undernourished hound by the name of Claude Erskine-Brown. And the question had its effect. As the old-fashioned crime writers used to say in their ghoulish way, the shadow of the noose seemed to fall across the witness-box.

'No one's mentioned that to the S.R.L.?'

'I thought I could pick up the hotline, but then it might be more appropriate if Wendy Crump raised it at your meeting this afternoon. That would give you an opportunity to reply. And I suppose Jenny Attienzer might want to raise the complaint about her pupil work.'

'What *are* you up to, Rumpole?'

'Just doing my best to protect the rights of lady barristers.'

'Anyone else's rights?'

'Well, I suppose, looking at the matter from an entirely detached point of view, the rights of one unfortunate male.'

'The case against Erskine-Brown has raised strong feelings in the Sisterhood. I'm not sure I can persuade them to drop it.'

'Of course you can persuade them, Liz. With your talent for advocacy, I bet you've got the Sisterhood eating out of your hand.'

'I'll do my best. I can't promise anything. By the way, it may not be necessary for Crump to attend. I suppose Kate Inglefield may have got hold of the wrong end of the stick.'

'Exactly. Claude said "that pupil". Not "fat pupil". Try it anyway, if you can't think of anything better.'

And so, with the case of the *Sisterhood* v. *Erskine-Brown* settled, I was back in the gloomy prison boardroom. When I'd first seen it, members of the caring, custodial and sentencing professions were feasting on sausage-rolls and white wine after *A Midsummer Night's Dream*. Now it was dressed not for a party but for a trial, and had taken on the appearance of a peculiarly unfriendly Magistrates Court.

Behind the table at the far end of the room sat the three members of the prisoners' Board of Visitors who were entitled to try Matthew Gribble. The Chairwoman centre stage was a certain Lady Bullwood, whose hair was piled up in a jet-black mushroom on top of her head and who went in for a good deal of costume jewellery, including a glittering chain round her neck from which her spectacles swung. Her look varied between the starkly judicial and the instantly confused, as when she suddenly lost control of a piece of paper, or forgot which part of her her glasses were tied to.

Beside her, wearing an expression of universal tolerance and the sort of gentle smile which can, in my experience, precede an unexpectedly stiff sentence, sat the Bishop of Worsfield, who had a high aquiline nose, neatly brushed grey hair and the thinnest strip of a dog-collar.

The third judge was an elderly schoolboy called Major Oxborrow, who looked as though he couldn't wait for the whole tedious business to be over, and for the offer of a large gin-and-tonic in the Governor's quarters. Beside them, in what I understood was a purely advisory capacity, sat my old friend the Governor, Quintus Blake, who looked as if he would rather be anywhere else and deeply regretted the need for these proceedings. He had, I remembered with gratitude, been so anxious to see Matthew Gribble properly defended that he had sent for Horace Rumpole, clearly the best man for the job. There was a clerk at a small table in front of the Visitors, whose job was, I imagined, to keep them informed as to such crumbs of law as were still available in prison. The Prosecution was in the nervous hands of a young Mr Fraplington, a solicitor from some government department. He was a tall, gangling person who looked as though he had shot up in the last six months and his jacket and trousers were too short for him.

What I didn't like was the grim squadron of screws who lined the walls as though expecting an outbreak of violence, and the fact that my client was brought in handcuffed and sat between two of the largest, beefiest prison officers available. After Matthew had been charged with committing an assault, obstructing an officer in the course of his duty, and offending against good order and discipline, he pleaded not guilty on my express instructions. Then I rose to my feet. 'Haven't you forgotten something?'

'Do you wish to address the Court, Mr Rumpole?' The clerk, a little ferret of a man, was clearly anxious to make his presence felt.

'I certainly do. Have you forgotten to read out the charges of mass murder, war crimes, rioting, burning down E-wing and inciting to mutiny?'

The ferret looked puzzled. The Chairwoman sorted hopelessly through her papers and Mr Fraplington for the Prosecution said helpfully, 'This prisoner is charged with none of those offences.'

'Then if he is not,' I asked, with perhaps rather overplayed amazement, 'why is he brought in here shackled? Why is this room lined with prison officers clearly expecting a dreadful scene of violence? Why is he being treated as though he were some hated dictator guilty of waging aggressive war? My client, Mr Gribble, is a gentle academic and student of Shakespeare. And there is no reason for him to attend these proceedings in irons.'

'Your client, as I remember, was found guilty of the manslaughter of his wife.' The handsome bishop was clearly the one to look out for.

'For that,' I said, 'he has almost paid his debt to society. Next week, subject to the dismissal of these unnecessary charges, that debt will be fully and finally settled and, as I'm sure the Governor will tell you, during his time in Worsfield he has been a model prisoner.'

Quintus did his stuff and whispered to the Chairwoman. She found her glasses, yanked them on to her nose and said that, in all the circumstances, my client's handcuffs might be removed.

After that the proceedings settled down like an ordinary trial in a Magistrates Court, except for the fact that we were all in gaol already. Mr Fraplington nervously opened the simple facts. Then Steve Barrington, the screw who received the flying chisel, clumped his way to the witness stand and gave the evidence which might keep Matthew Gribble behind bars for a good deal longer. He hadn't seen the chisel thrown. The first he knew about it was when he was struck on the cheek. Gribble had been the only prisoner working with a chisel and he had seen him using it immediately before he turned away to answer a request from prisoner D41 Molloy. Later he took statements from the prisoners, and in particular from B19 Weaver. What Weaver told him led to the present charges against A13 Gribble. What Weaver told him, I rose to point out, had better come from Weaver himself.

'Mr Barrington' – I began my cross-examination – 'you were a teacher once?'

'Yes, I was.'

'And you gave it up to become a prison officer?'

'I did.'

'Is that because you found teaching too difficult?'

'I wonder if this is a relevant question?' Young Fraplington had obviously been told to make his presence felt and interrupt the Defence whenever possible.

'Mr Fraplington, perchance you wonder at this question? But wonder on, till truth make all things plain.'

'Mr Rumpole, I'm not exactly sure what you mean.' The Chairwoman's glasses were pulled off and swung gently.

'Then you didn't see *A Midsummer Night's Dream*? You missed a treat, Madam. Produced brilliantly by my client and starring Prisoner Weaver as bully Bottom. You enjoyed it, didn't you, Mr Barrington?'

'I thought they did rather well, yes.'

'And I don't suppose, as a teacher who gave up the struggle, you could have taught a group of hard-boiled villains to play Shakespeare?'

'Mr Rumpole, I *must* agree with Mr Fraplington. How is this in the least relevant to the charge of assault?' The Bishop came in on the act.

'Because I think we may find, Bishop, that this isn't a case about assault, it's a case about teaching. Mr Barrington, you would agree that my client took Weaver and taught him to read, taught him about poetry and finally taught him to act?'

'To my knowledge, yes, he did.'

'And since this pupillage and this friendship began, Weaver, too, has been a model prisoner?'

'We haven't had any trouble from him lately. No.'

'Whereas before the pupillage, he was a general nuisance?'

'He was a handful. Yes. That's fair enough. He's a big man and . . .'

'Alarming when out of control?'

'I'd have to agree with you.'

'Good. I'm glad we see eye to eye, Mr Barrington. So before Matthew Gribble took him on, so to speak, there'd been several cases of assault, three of breaking up furniture, disobeying reasonable orders, throwing food. An endless list?'

'He was constantly in trouble. Yes.'

'And since he and Gribble became friends, nothing?'

'I believe that's right.'

'So you believe Matthew Gribble's influence on Weaver has been entirely for the good.'

'I said, so far as I know.'

'So far as you know. Well, we'll see if anyone knows better. Now, you questioned the other prisoners, Timson and Molloy, about this incident in the carpenter's shop?'

'Yes, I did.'

'And what did they tell you?'

'They said they hadn't seen anything.'

'And did you believe them?'

'Do I have to answer that question?'

'I have asked the question, and I'll trouble you to answer it.'

'No, I didn't altogether believe it.'

'Because prisoners don't grass.'

'What was that, Rumpole?' The Chairwoman asked for an explanation.

'Prisoners don't tell tales. They don't give evidence against each other. On the whole. Isn't that true, Mr Barrington?'

'I thought they might have seen something, but they were sheltering the culprit. Yes.'

'So Timson might have seen Molloy do it. Or Molloy might have seen Timson do it. Or either of them might have seen Weaver do it. But they weren't telling. Is that possible?'

'I suppose it's possible. Yes.'

'Or Weaver might have seen Timson or Molloy do it and blamed it on Gribble to protect them?'

'He wouldn't have done that.' There was an agitated whisper from my client and I stooped to give him an ear.

'What?'

'He wouldn't have blamed it on me. I know Bob wouldn't do that.'

'Matthew,' I whispered sternly, 'your time to give evidence will come later. Until it does, I'd be much obliged if you'd take a temporary vow of silence.' I went back to work. 'Yes, officer. What was your answer to my question?'

'B19 Weaver had a particular admiration for A13 Gribble, sir. I don't think he'd have blamed him. Not just to protect the other two.'

'He wouldn't have blamed him just to protect the other two, eh?' The Bishop, who seemed to have cast himself as the avenging angel, dictated a note to himself with resonant authority.

Bottom the Weaver towered over the small witness table and the screws that stood behind him. He looked at the Visitors, his head slightly on one side, his nose broken and never properly set, and smiled nervously, as he had stood before the court of Duke Theseus, awkward, on his best behaviour, likely to be a bore, but somehow endearing. He didn't look at A13 Gribble, but my client looked constantly at him, not particularly in anger but with curiosity and as if prepared to be amused. That was the way, I thought, he might have watched Bob Weaver rehearsing the play.

Mr Fraplington had no trouble in getting the witness to tell his story. He was in the carpenter's shop in the morning in question. They were making the scenery. He was enjoying himself as he enjoyed everything about the play. Although he was dead nervous about doing it, it was the best time he'd ever had in his life. A13 Gribble was a fantastic producer, absolutely brilliant, and had changed his life for him. 'Made me see a new world', was the way he put it. Well, that morning when all the others were busy working and Mr Barrington was turned away, he'd seen A13 Gribble pick up the chisel and throw it. It struck the prison officer on the cheek, causing bleeding which he fully believed was later seen to by the hospital matron. He kept quiet for a week, because he was reluctant to get the best friend he ever had into trouble. But then he'd told the investigating officer exactly what he saw. He felt he had to do it. Doing the play was the best day in his life. Standing there, telling the tale against his friend, was the worst. Sometimes he thought he'd rather be dead than do it. That was the honest truth. To say that Battering Bob was a good witness is an understatement. He was as good a witness as he was a Bottom; he didn't seem to be acting at all.

'The first question, of course, is why?'

'Pardon me?'

'Why do you think your friend Matthew threw a chisel at the officer? Can you help me about that?' It would have been no use trying to batter the batterer – he had clearly won the hearts of the Visitors – so I came at him gently and full of smiles. 'He's always been a model prisoner. Not a hint of violence.'

'Perhaps' – Bob Weaver closed one eye, giving me his careful consideration – 'he kind of had it bottled up, his resentment against Mr Barrington.'

'We haven't heard he resented Mr Barrington?'

'Well, we all did to an extent. All of us actors.'

'Why was that?'

'He put Jimmy Molloy on a charge, so he lost two weeks' rehearsal with Puck.'

The Visitors smiled. I had gone and provided my client with a motive. Up to now this cross-examination seemed a likely candidate for the worst in my career so I tried another tack.

'All right. Another why.'

'Yes, sir.'

'If you feel you'd rather be dead than do it, why did you decide to grass against your friend?'

'I don't know why you have adopted the phrase "grass" from prison argot, Mr Rumpole.' The Bishop was clearly a circus judge manqué. 'This inmate has come here to give evidence.'

'Evidence which may or may not turn out to be the truth. Very well then. The Bishop has told us to forget the argot.'

'Forget the what?' Bob looked amicably confused and the Bishop smiled tolerantly. 'Slang,' he translated. 'I should have called it slang.'

'Why did you decide to give evidence against your friend?'

'Let me tell you this quite honestly.' The Batterer turned from me and faced the Visitors. 'Years ago, I might not have done it. In fact, I wouldn't. Grass on a fellow inmate. Never. Might have given him a bit of a hiding like. If I'd felt the need of it. But never told the tale. Rather have had me tongue cut out. But then ... Well, then I got to know Matthew. I'd still like to call him that. With all respect. And he taught me ... Well, he taught me everything. He taught me to read. Yes. He taught me to like poetry, which I'd thought worse than a punch in the kidneys. Then he taught me to act and to enjoy myself like I never did even in the old days of the minicab battles, which now seem a complete waste of time, quite honestly. But Matthew taught me more than that. "You have to be truthful, Bob", those were his words to me. Well, that's what I remembered. So, when it came to it, I remembered his words. That's all I've got to say.'

'You took his advice and told the truth.' The Bishop was clearly delighted, but I was looking at Bob. It had never happened before. It certainly didn't happen when he performed in the *Dream*, but now I knew that he was an actor playing a part.

And then something clicked in my mind. A picture of Dodo Mackintosh at school, not wanting to let her heroine go, and I knew what the truth really was.

'You've told us Matthew Gribble is the friend who meant most to you.'

'Meant everything to me.'

'The only real friend you've ever had. Would you go as far as to say that?'

'I would agree with that, sir. Every word of it.'

'And one who has let you into a new world.'

'He's already told us that, Mr Rumpole.' I prayed for the Bishop to address himself to God and leave me alone.

'It's too true. Too very true.'

'I don't suppose life in Worsfield Category A Prison could

ever be compared to a holiday in the Seychelles, but he has made your life here bearable?'

'More than that, Mr Rumpole. I wouldn't have missed it.'

'And in a week, if he is acquitted on this charge, Matthew Gribble will be free.'

It was as if I had got in a sudden, unexpectedly powerful blow in the ring. Bob closed his eyes and almost seemed to stop breathing. When he shook his head and answered, he had come back, it seemed to me, to the truth.

'I don't want to think about it.'

'Because you may never see him again?'

'Visits. There might be visits.'

'Are you afraid there might not be?' Matthew appeared to be about to say something, or utter some protest. I shot some *sotto voce* advice into his earhole to the effect that if he uttered another sound, I would walk off the case. Then I looked back at the Batterer. He seemed not to have recovered from the punch and was still breathless.

'It crossed my mind.'

'And did it cross your mind that he might move away, to another part of England, get a new job, work with a new drama group and put on new plays with no parts in them for you? Did you think he might forget the friend he'd made in prison?'

There was a long silence. Bob was getting his breath back, preparing to get up for the last round, but with defeat staring him in the face.

He said, 'Things like that do happen, don't they?'

'Oh yes, Bob Weaver. They happen very often. If a man wants to make a new life, he doesn't care to be reminded of the people he met inside. Did that thought occur to you?'

'I did worry about that, I suppose. I did worry.'

'And did you worry that all that rich, fascinating new world might vanish into thin air? And you'd be left with only a few old lags and failed boxers for company?'

There was silence then. Bob didn't answer. He was saved by the bell. Rung, of course, by the Bishop.

'Where's all this leading up to, Mr Rumpole?'

'Let me suggest where it led you, Bob.' I ignored the cleric and concentrated on the witness. 'It led you to think of the one way you could stop Matthew Gribble leaving you.'

'How was I going to do that?'

'Quite a simple idea but it seems to have worked. Up to now. The way to do it was to get him into trouble.'

'Trouble?'

'Serious trouble. So he'd lose his remission. I expect you thought of that some time ago and you waited for an opportunity. It came, didn't it, in the carpenter's shop?'

'Did it?'

'Matthew turned away to fix the grass covering on the mound. No one else was looking when you picked up his chisel. No one saw you throw it. Like all successful crimes it was helped by a good deal of luck.'

'Crime? Me? What are you talking about? I done no crime.' Bob looked at the Visitors. For once even the Bishop was silent.

'I suppose I'm talking about perverting the course of justice. Of assaulting a prison officer. I've got to hand it to you, Bob. You did it for the best of motives. You did it to keep a friend.'

Bob's head was lowered, but now he made an effort to raise it and looked at the Visitors. 'I didn't do it. I swear to God I didn't. Matthew did it and he's got to stay here. You can't let him go.' By then I think even they thought he was acting. But that wasn't the end of the story.

'Why did you do it?' The trial, if you could call it a trial, was over. Matthew and I were together for the last time in the interview room. We were there to say goodbye.

'I told you. What've I got outside? Schools that won't employ me. Actors and actresses who wouldn't want to work with me. What would they think? If I didn't like their performances, I might stab them. They'd be talking about me, whispering, laughing perhaps. And I'd come in the room and they'd be silent or look afraid. Here, they all want to be in my plays. They want to work with me, and I want to work with them. I thought of *Much Ado* next. Won't Bob make a marvellous Dogberry? Then, I don't know, do you think he could possibly do a Falstaff?'

'Become an old English gent? Who knows. You've got plenty of time. They knocked a year and a half off your remission.'

'Yes. A long time together. You were asking me why I threw the chisel?'

He knew I wasn't asking him that. At the end of Battering Bob's evidence I had to decide whether or not to call my client. Matthew had kept quiet when I'd told him to, and I knew he'd make a good impression. He walked to the witness table, took the oath and looked at me with patient expectation.

'Matthew Gribble. We've heard you were a model prisoner.'

'I've never been in trouble here, if that's what you mean.'

'And of all you've done for Bob Weaver.'

'I think it's been a rewarding experience for both of us.'

'And you are due to be released next week.'

'I believe I am.'

I drew in a deep breath and asked the question to which I felt sure I knew the answer. 'Matthew, did you ever throw that chisel at Prison Officer Barrington?'

The answer, when it came, was another punch in the stomach, this time for me. 'Yes, I did. I threw it.' Matthew looked at the Visitors and said it as though he was talking about a not very interesting part of the prison routine. 'I did it because I couldn't forgive him for putting Puck on a charge.' After that, the case was over and Matthew's exit from Worsfield inevitably postponed.

'You know I wasn't asking you why you threw the chisel because you didn't throw it. I'm asking you why you said you did.'

'I told you. I've decided to stay on.'

'You knew Battering Bob did it and he blamed you to keep you here because he thought he needed you.'

'Don't you think that's rather an extraordinary tribute to a friendship?'

There seemed no answer to that. I didn't know whether to curse Matthew Gribble or to praise him. I didn't know if he was the best or the worst client I ever had. I knew I had lost a case unnecessarily, and that is something I don't like to happen.

'You can't win them all, Mr Rumpole, can you?' Steve

Barrington looked gratified at the result. He took me to the gate and, as he waited for the long unlocking process to finish, he said, 'I don't think I'll ever go back to teaching. They seem half barmy, some of them.'

At last the gates and the small door in the big one were open. I was out and I went out. Matthew was in and he stayed in. Damiens sent a brief in a long case to Claude and I told him he had a brilliant pupil.

'I suppose she'll be wanting a place in Chambers soon?' Claude didn't seem to welcome the idea.

'So far as I'm concerned she can have one now.'

'Young Jenny Attienzer is apparently not happy with Nick Davenant over in King's Bench Walk. Do you think I might take her on as a pupil?'

'I think,' I told him, 'that it would be a very bad idea indeed. I'm sure Philly wouldn't like it, and I'd have to start charging for defending you.'

'Rumpole' – Claude was thoughtful – 'do you know why everyone went off me in that peculiar way?'

'Not really.'

But Claude had his own solution. 'It never ceases to amaze me,' the poor old darling said, 'how jealous everyone is of success.'

Six months later I saw a production of *Much Ado About Nothing* in Worsfield gaol with Bob Weaver as Dogberry. I enjoyed it very much indeed.

Rumpole and the Way through the Woods

There are times, I have to admit, when even the glowing flame of Rumpole sinks to a mere flicker. It had been a bad day. I had finished a case before old Gravestone, a long slog against a hostile judge, an officer in charge of the case who seemed to regard the truth as an inconvenient obstacle to the smooth and efficient running of the Criminal Investigation Department, and a client whose unendurable cockiness and self-regard rapidly lost all hearts in the Jury. It had been a hard slog which would have seemed as nothing if it had ended in an acquittal. It had not been so rewarded and, when I said goodbye to my client in the cells, carefully failing to remind him that he might be away for a long time, he said, 'What's the matter with you, Mr Rumpole? Losing your touch, are you? They was saying in the Scrubs, isn't it about time you hung up the old wig and took retirement?' Every bone in my body seemed to ache as I stumbled into Pommeroy's where the Château Thames Embankment tasted more than ever of mildew and Claude Erskine-Brown cornered me in order to describe, at interminable length, the triumph he had enjoyed in a rent application. Leaving for home early, I had to stand up in the tube all the way back. Returning to the world from the bowels of Gloucester Road station, I struggled towards Froxbury Mansions with the faltering determination of a dying Bedouin crawling towards an oasis. All I wanted was my armchair beside the gas fire, a better bottle of the very ordinary claret, and a little peace in which to watch other people in trouble on the television. It was not to be.

When I entered the living-room the lights were off and I heard the sound of heavy and laboured breathing. My first thought was that She had fallen asleep by the gas fire, but I

could hear the clatter of saucepans from the kitchen. I sniffed
the air and received the usual whiff of furniture polish and
cabbage being boiled into submission. But, added to this brew,
was a not particularly exotic perfume, acrid and pervasive,
which might, if bottled extravagantly, have been marketed as
wet dog. Then the heavy breathing turned into the sort of dark
and distant rumble which precedes the arrival of an Underground train. I snapped on the light and there it was: long
legged, overweight and sprawled in my armchair. It was awake
now, staring at me with wide-open, moist black eyes. I put out
a hand to shift the intruder and the sound of the approaching
train increased in volume until it became a snarl, and the
animal revealed sharp and unexpectedly white pointed teeth.
'Hilda,' I called for help from a usually reliable source, 'there's
a stray dog in the living-room.'

'That's not a stray dog. That's Sir Lancelot.' I turned round
and She was standing in the doorway, looking with disapproval
not at the trespasser but at me.

'What on earth do you mean, Sir Lancelot?'

'That's your name, isn't it, darling?' She approached the
animal with a broad smile. 'Although sometimes we call you
Lance for short, don't we?' To these eager questions the dog
returned no answer at all, although it did, I was relieved to see,
put away its teeth.

'Whatever its name is, shall we call the police?'

'Why?'

'To have it removed.'

'Have you *removed*, Sir Lancelot? What a silly husband I've
got, haven't I?' In this, the dog and my wife seemed to be of
the same mind. It settled itself into my chair and she tickled it,
in a familiar fashion, under the chin.

'Better be careful. It's got a nasty snarl.'

'He only snarls if you do something to annoy him. Was
Rumpole doing something to annoy you, Lance?'

'I was trying to budge it off my chair,' I told her quickly,
before the dog could get a word in.

'You like Rumpole's chair, don't you, Lance? You feel
at home there, don't you, darling?' I was starting to feel
left out of the conversation until she said, 'I think we might

make that his chair, don't you, Rumpole? Just until he settles in.'

'Settles in? What do you mean, settles in? What's this, a home of rest for stray animals?'

'Lance isn't a stray. Didn't I tell you? I meant to tell you. Sir Lancelot is Dodo Mackintosh's knight in shining armour. Aren't you, darling?' Darling was, of course, the dog.

'You mean he's come up from Cornwall?' I looked at the hound with new respect. Perhaps he was one of those animals they make films about, that set off on their own to travel vast distances. 'Hadn't we better ring Dodo to come and fetch him?'

'Don't be silly, Rumpole.' Hilda had put on one of her heroically patient voices. 'Dodo brought Lancelot up here this afternoon. She left him on her way to the airport.'

'And what time's she getting back from the airport? I suppose I can wait until after supper to sit in my chair.'

'She's going to Brittany to stay with Pegsy Throng who was jolly good at dancing and used to be at school with us. Of course, she couldn't take Sir Lancelot because of the quarantine business.'

'And how long is Pegsy Throng entertaining Dodo?' I could feel my heart sinking.

'Just the three weeks, Rumpole. Not long enough, really. Dodo did ask if I thought you'd mind and I told her, of course not, Lance will be company for both of us. Come and have supper now, and after that you can take him out on the lead to do his little bit of business. It'll be a chance for you two to get to know each other.'

Sleep was postponed that night as I stood in the rain beside a lamp-post with the intruder. Sir Lancelot leapt to the extent of his lead, as though determined to choke himself, wrenching my arm almost out of its socket, as he barked savagely at every passing dog. Looking down at him, I decided that I never saw a hound I hated more, and yet it was Sir Lancelot that brought me a case which was one of the most curious and sensational of my career.

'What on earth are we doing here, Hilda?' Here was a stretch of countryside, blurred by a sifting March rain so, looking towards the horizon, it was hard to tell at which precise point the soggy earth became the sodden sky.

'Breathe in the country air, Rumpole. Besides which, Sir Lancelot couldn't spend all his time cooped up in a flat. He had to have a couple of days' breather in the Cotswolds. It'll do you both good.'

'Couldn't Sir Lancelot have gone for a run in the Cotswolds on his own?'

'Try not to be silly, Rumpole.'

The dog was behaving in an eccentric manner, making wild forays into the undergrowth as though it had found something to chase and, ending up with nothing, it came trotting back to the path quite unconscious of its own stupidity. It was, I thought, an animal with absolutely no sense of humour.

'Why on earth does your friend Dodo Mackintosh call that gloomy hound Sir Lancelot?'

'After Sir Lancelot of the Lake, of course. One of the knights of the Table Round. Dodo's got a very romantic nature. Come along, Lance. *There's* a good boy. Enjoying your run in the country, are you?'

'Lance,' I told her firmly, 'or, rather, *Launce* is the chap who had a dog called Crab in *Two Gentlemen of Verona*. Crab got under the duke's table with some "gentlemanlike dogs" and after "a pissing while" a terrible smell emerged. Launce took responsibility for it and was whipped.'

'Do be quiet, Rumpole! You always look for the seamy side of everything.' At which point, Lance, in another senseless burst of energy, leapt a stile and started chasing sheep.

'Can't you keep that dog under control?' The voice came from a man in a cap, crossing the field towards us, with a golden labrador trotting in an obedient manner at his side. Hilda and I, having climbed the stile and called Lance, with increasing hopelessness, were set out on a course towards him.

'I'm afraid we can't,' I apologized from a distance. 'The animal won't listen to reason.'

'What did you say its name was?'

'Sir Lancelot,' Hilda boasted.

'Of the Lake. To give him his full title,' I added, trying to make the best of our lamentable attachment.

'Sir Lancelot! Here, boy!' the man in the cap called in a commanding tone and gave a piercing whistle. Whereupon Dodo's dog stood still, shook itself, came to its senses and, much to the relief of the sheep, joined our group. At which, the man in the cap turned, looked me in the face for the first time and said, 'By God, it's Horace Rumpole!'

'Rollo Eyles!'

'And this is your good lady?''

I resisted the temptation to say, 'No, it's my wife.' Rollo was telling Hilda about our roots in history. He had been the Prosecution junior in the Penge Bungalow affair, arguably the classic murder of our time and undoubtedly the greatest moment of triumph in the Rumpole career.

Until they heard my first devastating cross-examination of the police surgeon, legal hacks in the Penge Bungalow case treated me as an inexperienced white-wig who shouldn't be allowed out on a careless driving. A notable exception was young Rollo Eyles, the Prosecution junior, then a jovial, school-boyish young man, born, like me, without any feelings of reverence. He was a mimic, and we would meet after Court in Pommeroy's to drown our anxiety, and Rollo would do his impressions of the Judge, the prosecuting silk and the dry, charnel-house voice of Professor Ackerman, master of the morgues. In the middle of his legal career Rollo inherited an estate, and a good deal of money, from an uncle, and left the busy world of the Old Bailey for, it appeared, these damp fields where he was a farmer, Master of Foxhounds and Chairman of the Bench.

For a while he wrote to me at Christmas, letters in neat handwriting, full of jokes. After a while, I forgot to answer them and our friendship waned. Now he said, 'Why don't you come up to the house and we'll all have a strong drink.' Rollo Eyles always had a sensible solution to the most desperate case. Sir Lancelot, realizing he had met a man he couldn't trifle with, came and joined us with unusual docility.

It was over a large whisky in front of a log fire that I told Rollo where we were staying. Our hotel was a plastic and concrete nightmare of a building conveniently situated for the trading estate outside the nearest town. It had all the joys of piped music in the coffee shop, towels in a thinness contest with the lavatory paper, and waitresses who'd undergone lengthy training in the art of not allowing their eyes to be caught. It was the only place we could find where we were allowed, after slipping a bribe larger than the legal aid fee for a guilty plea to the hall porter, to secretly have Sir Lancelot in the bathroom. There, he was due to spend a restless night on a couple of wafer-thin blankets. Having heard this sad story, Rollo offered us dinner and a bed for the night; Lancelot could be kennelled with the gentlemanlike dogs. Our host said he was looking forward to hearing the latest gossip from the Old Bailey and, in return, we could have the pleasure of seeing the hunt move off from his front drive before we went back to London.

The rain had stopped during the night and the March morning was cold and sunny. Sir Lancelot was shivering with excitement, as if delightedly aware that something, at some time, was going to be killed; although I doubted if, during his peaceful cohabitation with Dodo Mackintosh in Lamorna Cove, he had ever met foxhunters before. However, he leapt into the air, pirouetted at the end of his lead, barked at the horses and did his best to give the impression that he was entirely used to the country sports of gentlemanlike dogs. So there I was, eating small slices of pork pie and drinking port which tasted, on that crisp morning, delicious. Hilda, wearing an old mac and a tweed hat which she'd apparently bought for just such an occasion, was doing her best to look as though, if her horse hadn't gone lame or suffered some such technical fault, she'd've been up and mounted among our dinner companions of the night before.

I looked up with my mouth full of pork pie to join in Hilda's smiles at these new acquaintances who had merged with the children on ponies, the overweight farmers, the smart garage owners and the followers on foot. Rollo was there, sitting in the saddle as though it was his favourite armchair, talking to a whipper-in, or hunt servant, or whatever the red-coated officials may be called. Mrs Rollo – Dorothea – was there, the relic of a great beauty, still slim and upright, her calm face cracked with lines like the earth on a dried-up river bed, her auburn hair streaked with grey, bundled into a hairnet and covered with a peaked velvet cap. I also recognized Tricia Fothergill, who had clung on to the childish way she mispronounced her name, together with the good looks of an attractive child, into her thirties. She was involved in a lengthy divorce and had, during dinner, bombarded me with questions about family law for which I had no ready answer. And there, raising his glass of port to me from the immense height of a yellow-eyed horse, sitting with his legs stuck out like wings, was the old fellow who had been introduced to us as Johnny Logan and who knew the most intimate details of the private lives of all sporting persons living in the Cotswolds. Rollo Eyles, in the absence of any interesting anecdotes from the Central Criminal Court, clearly relied on him for entertaining gossip. 'Roll 'em in the aisles, that's what I call him,' Logan whispered to me at dinner. 'Our host's extremely attractive to women. Of course, he'll never leave Dorothea.'

Now, at the meet in front of Wayleave Manor, Logan said, 'Seen our charming visitors at the end of the drive? You might go and have a look at them, Horace. They're the antis.'

Dorothea Eyles was leaning down from her horse to chat to Hilda in the nicest possible way, so I took Lancelot for a stroll so I could see all sides of the hunting experience. A van was parked just where the driveway met the road. On it there were placards posted with such messages as STOP ANIMAL MURDER, HUNT THE FOXHUNTERS, and so on. There was a small group standing drinking coffee. At that time they seemed as cheerful and excited as the foxhunters, looking forward as eagerly to a day's sport. There was a man with a shaven head and earrings, but also a woman in a tweed skirt who looked like a middle-aged schoolmistress. There was a girl whose hair was clipped like a sergeant-major back and sides, with one long, purple lock left in the middle. The others were less colourful – ordinary people such as I would have seen shopping in Safeway's and there, I thought, probably buying cellophane-packed joints and pounds of bacon. The tallest was a young man who remained profoundly serious in spite of the excited laughter around him. He was wearing jeans and a crimson shirt which made him stand out as clearly, against the green fields, as the huntsmen he had come to revile.

There was the sound of a horn. The dogs poured down the drive with their tails waving like flags. Then came Rollo, followed by the riders. The antis put down their sandwiches, lowered their mugs of coffee and shouted out such complimentary remarks as 'Murdering bastards,', 'Get your rocks off watching little furry animals pulled to pieces, do you?' and 'How would you like to be hunted and thrown to the dogs this afternoon, darling?' – an invitation to Tricia.

Then Dorothea came riding slowly, to find the Crimson Shirt was barring her path, his arms spread out as though prepared to meet his death under a ton of horseflesh. A dialogue then took place which I was to have occasion to remember.

'You love killing things, don't you?' from the Crimson Shirt.

'Not particularly. Mostly, I enjoy the ride.'

'Why do you kill animals?'

'Perhaps because they kill other animals.'

'Do you ever think that something might kill you one fine afternoon?'

'Quite often.' Dorothea looked down at him. 'A lot of people die, out hunting. A nice quick death. I hope I'll be so lucky.'

'You might get killed this afternoon.'

'Anyone might.'

'It doesn't worry you?'

'Not in the least.'

'It's only what you deserve.'

'Do you think so?' Looking down from her horse, I thought she suddenly seemed thin and insubstantial as a ghost, her lined face very pale. Then she pulled a silver flask from her jacket pocket, unscrewed it and leant down to offer the Crimson Shirt a drink.

'What have you got in there?' he asked her.

'Fox's blood, of course.'

He looked up at her and said, 'You cruel bitch!'

'It's only whisky. You're very welcome.' He shook his head and the cobweb-faced lady took a long pull at the flask. Other riders had come up beside her and were listening, amused at first and then angry. There were shouts, conflicting protests, and the Crimson Shirt called out in the voice of doom, 'One of you is going to die for all the dead animals. Justice is sure to be done!'

I saw a whip raised at the back of the cavalcade but the Crimson Shirt had dropped his arm and moved to join his party by the van. Dorothea Eyles put away her flask, kicked her horse's sides and trotted with the posse after her. They were chattering together cheerfully, after what had then seemed no more than a routine confrontation between the hunters and the sabs – rather enjoyed by both sides.

The sound of the horn, the baying of the dogs and the clattering of horses had died away. The van, after a number of ineffectual coughs and splutters, started its engine and went. It was very quiet as Lancelot and I walked back down the drive to join Hilda who was enjoying a final glass of port. We went into the house to wait for the taxi which would take us back to the station.

That evening we were at home at the mansion flat and I had been restored to my armchair. Lancelot, exhausted by the day's excitement, was asleep on the sofa, breathing heavily and, no doubt, dreaming of imaginary hunts. The news item was on the television after a war in Africa and an earthquake in Japan. There were stock pictures of hunters and sabs. Then came the news that Dorothea Eyles, out hunting and galloping down a woodland track, had ridden into a high wire stretched tight between two trees. Her neck was broken and she was dead when some ramblers found her. An anti-hunt demonstrator named Dennis Pearson was helping the local police with their inquiries.

Rollo Eyles had returned to my life, suffered a terrible tragedy and immediately disappeared again. Of course I telephoned but his recorded voice always told me he was not available. I left messages of sorrow and concern but the calls were never answered, and neither were the letters I wrote to him. Tragedy too often causes embarrassment and we didn't visit Rollo in the Cotswolds. Tragedy vanishes quickly, swept on by the tide of horrible events in the world, and I began to think less often of Dorothea Eyles and her ghastly ride to death. Rollo joined the unseen battalion of people whom I liked but never saw.

'Rumpole! I have heard reports of your extraordinary behaviour!'

'Don't believe everything you hear in reports.'

'Erskine-Brown has told me that Henry told him . . .'

'I object! Hearsay evidence! Totally inadmissible.'

'Well well. I have had a direct account from Henry himself.'

'Not under oath, and certainly not subject to cross-examination!'

'You were seen entering the downstairs toilet facility with a bowl.'

'What's *that* meant to prove? I might have been rinsing out my dentures. Or uttering prayers to a water god to whose rites I have been recently converted. What on earth's it got to do with Henry, anyway? Or you, for that matter, Bollard?'

'Having filled your bowl with water, you were seen to carry it to your room.'

'It would be inappropriate to say prayers to the water god in the downstairs toilet facilities.'

'Come now, Rumpole, don't fence with me.' Soapy Sam Ballard was using one of the oldest and corniest of legal phrases, long fallen into disuse in the noble art of cross-examination, and I allowed myself a dismissive yawn. It wasn't the brightest period of my long and eventful practice at the bar. Since our visit to the Cotswolds, and its terrible outcome, briefs had been notable by their absence. I came into Chambers every day and searched my mantelpiece in vain for a new murder, or at least a taking away without the owner's consent. My wig gathered dust in my locker down the Bailey; the ushers must have forgotten me and I looked back with nostalgia on the days when I had laboured long and lost before Mr Injustice Gravestone. At least something was happening then. Now the suffocating boredom of inactivity was made worse by the arrival of an outraged Head of Chambers in my room, complaining of my conduct with something so totally inoffensive as a bowl of water.

'You might as well confess, Rumpole.' Ballard's eye was lit

with a gleam of triumph. 'There was one single word written in large letters on that chipped enamel bowl.'

'Water?'

'No, Rumpole. Henry's evidence was quite clear on this point. What was written was the word DOG.'

'So what?'

'What do you mean, so what?'

'Plenty of people wash their socks in bowls with DOG written on them.'

Before Ballard could meet this point, there was that low but threatening murmur, like the sound heralding the dark and distant approach of a tube train, from behind my desk.

'What was that noise, Rumpole?'

'Low-flying aircraft?' I suggested, hopefully. But at this point the accused, like so many of my clients, ruined his chances by putting in a public appearance. Sir Lancelot, looking extra large, black and threatening, emerged like his more famous namesake – with lips curled, dog teeth bared – eager to do battle in the lists. There was no contest. At the sight of the champion, even before the first snarl, Sir Soapy Sam, well-known coward and poltroon of the Table Round, started an ignominious retreat towards the door, crying in terror, 'Get that animal out of here at once!'

'No!' I relied on my constitutional rights. 'Not until the matter has been properly decided by a full Chambers' meeting.'

'I shall call one,' Ballard piped in desperation, 'as a matter of urgency.' And then he scooted out and slammed the door behind him.

The fact of the matter was that Hilda had been out a lot recently at bridge lessons and coffee mornings, and I, lonely and unoccupied in Chambers, started in a curious way to relish the company of a hound who looked as gloomy as I felt. On the whole, the dog was not demanding. Like many judges, Lancelot fought, nearly all the time, a losing battle against approaching sleep. Water from the downstairs loo, and the dog biscuits I brought in my briefcase, satisfied his simple wants. The sound of regular breathing from somewhere by my feet was company for me as I spent the day with *The Times* crossword.

★

The Chambers' meeting was long and tense. At first the case for the Prosecution looked strong. Henry sent a message to say that he undertook to clerk for a barristers' chambers and not a kennel. He added that the sight of Sir Lancelot peering round my open door and baring his teeth had frightened away old Tim Daker of Daker, Winterbotham & Guildenstern, before he'd even delivered a brief. Erskine-Brown questioned the paternity of Sir Lancelot and when I said labrador loudly, he replied, 'Possibly a labrador who'd had hanky-panky with a dubious Jack Russell.' He ended up by asking in a dramatic fashion if we really wanted a mongrel taking up residence in 4 Equity Court. This brought a fiery reply from Mizz Liz Probert who said that animals had the same rights to our light, heat, comforts, and presumably law reports, as male barristers. She personally could remember the days, not long past, when she, as a practising woman, was treated as though she were a so-called labrador of doubtful parentage. Gender awareness was no longer enough. In Mizz Probert's considered opinion we needed species awareness as well. She saw no reason, in the interests of open government and tolerance of minorities, why a living being should be denied entrance to our Chambers simply because it had four legs instead of two. 'Of course,' Mizz Probert concluded, looking at Erskine-Brown in a way which forced him to reconsider his position, 'if we were to support the pin-striped chauvinists who hated mongrels and women, we should be alienating the Sisterhood of Radical Lawyers, devoted to animal rights.'

I took up her last point in my speech for the Defence and did so in a way calculated to make Soapy Sam's flesh creep. I had seen something of animal rights enthusiasts. Did we really want their van parked outside Chambers all day and most of the night? Did Ballard want a shorn-headed enthusiast with earrings shouting, 'Get your rocks off shutting out innocent dogs, do you?' Could we risk a platoon of grey-haired, middle-class dog-lovers staging a sit-in outside our front door every time we wanted to go to Court? After this, the evidence of a Member of Chambers, to the effect that dogs made him sneeze, seemed to carry very little weight. The result of our deliberations was, of course, leaked and a paragraph appeared in next day's Londoner's Diary in the *Evening Standard*:

Should dogs be called to the Bar? The present showing of the legal profession might suggest that they could only be an improvement on the human intake. Indeed, a few Rottweilers on the Bench might help reduce the crime rate. The question was hotly debated in the Chambers of Samuel Ballard, Q.C. when claret-tippling Old Bailey character Horace Rumpole argued for the admittance of a pooch, extravagantly named Sir Lancelot. Rumpole won his case but then he's long been known as a champion of the underdog.

It was a pyrrhic victory. Dodo came back from holiday a week later and reclaimed Sir Lancelot. She was delighted he had been mentioned in the newspapers but furious he was called a pooch.

Sir Lancelot's trial had a more important result, however. Henry told me that a Mr Garfield of Garfield, Thornley & Strumm had telephoned and, having heard that I was a stalwart battler for animal rights, was going to brief me for a hunt saboteur charged with murder. I was relieved that my period of inactivity was over, but filled with alarm at the thought of having to tell Hilda that I had agreed to appear for the man accused of killing Dorothea Eyles.

Mr Garfield, my instructing solicitor, was a thin, colourless man with a pronounced Adam's apple. He had the rough, slightly muddy skin of the dedicated vegetarian. The case was to be tried at Gloucester Crown Court and we sat in the interview room in the prison, a Victorian erection much rebuilt, on the outskirts of the town. Across the plastic table-top our client sat smiling in a way which seemed to show that he was either sublimely self-confident or drugged. He was a young man, perhaps in his late twenties, with a long nose, prominent eyes and neat brown hair. The last time I had seen him he was wearing a crimson shirt and telling the hunt in general, and Dorothea Eyles in particular, that one of them was going to die for all the dead animals. Garfield introduced him to me as Den; my instructing solicitor was Gavin to my client. I had the feeling they had known each other for some time and later discovered that they sat together on a committee concerned with animal rights.

'Gavin tells me you fought for a dog and won?' Den looked at me with approval. Was that to be my work in the future, I wondered. Not white-collar crime but leather-collar crime, perhaps?

'More than that,' I told him. 'I'm ready to fight for you and win the case.'

'I'm not important. It's the cause that's important.'

'The cause?'

'Den feels deeply about animals,' Gavin interpreted.

'I understand that. I was there, you know. Watching the hunt move off. I'd better warn you I heard what you said, so it's going to be a little difficult if you deny it.'

'I said it,' Den told me proudly. 'I said every word of it. We're going to win, you know.'

'Win the case?'

'I meant the war against the animal murderers. Did you see the looks on their faces? They were going out to enjoy themselves.'

I remembered the words of the historian Lord Macaulay: 'The Puritan hated bear-baiting, not because it gave pain to the bear, but because it gave pleasure to the spectators.' But I wasn't going to be drawn into a debate about fox-hunting when I was there to deal with my first murder case for a long time, too long a time, and I fully intended to win it. I rummaged in my papers and produced the first, the most important witness statement, the evidence to be given by Patricia Fothergill of Cherry Trees near Wayleave in the county of Gloucester.

'I'd better warn you that I met this lady at dinner.'

'I don't mind where you met her, Mr Rumpole.'

'I'm glad you take that view but I had to tell you. All right, Tricia – that's what she calls herself – Tricia is going to say that she saw a man in a red shirt in the driveway of the Eyles's house, Wayleave Manor. She heard you shout at Mrs Eyles. Well, we all know about that. Now comes the interesting bit. At about one o'clock in the afternoon of the day before the meet she'd been out for a hack and was riding home past Fallows Wood – that's where Dorothea Eyles met her death.

She says she saw a man in a red shirt coming out of the wood, carrying what looked like a coil of wire: "I didn't think much of it at the time. I suppose I thought he had to do with the telephone or the electricity or something. There was a moment when I saw him quite clearly and I'm sure he was the same man I saw at the meet, shouting at Dorothea." We can challenge that identification. It was far away, she was on a horse, how many men wear red shirts – all that sort of thing . . .'

'I'm sure you will destroy her, Mr Rumpole.' Gavin was trying to be helpful.

'I'll do my best.' I hunted for another statement. 'I'm just looking . . . Here it is! Detective Constable Armstead searched the van you came in and found part of a coil of wire of exactly the same make and thickness as that which was stretched across the path and between the trees in Fallows Wood.' I looked at my client and my solicitor. Neither had, apparently, anything to say. 'Who drives the van?'

'Roy Netherborn. It's his van,' Gavin volunteered.

'Is he the hairless gentleman with the earrings?'

'That's the one.'

'And did Mr Netherborn pack the things in the van? The tools and so on?'

'He did, didn't he, Den?' Gavin had been answering the questions. When he was asked one, Dennis Pearson was silent.

'Had you taken wire with you before?'

'We'd discussed it,' Den admitted. 'There'd been some talk of using it to trip up the horses.'

'Did you know there was wire in the van that day?' I asked Den the question direct, but Gavin intervened, 'I don't think you did, did you?'

Den said nothing but shook his head.

'Did you know that exactly the same wire was used as a death-trap in Fallows Wood?'

'Den didn't know that. No.' Gavin was positive.

'When did you arrive in Wayleave village? And *that's* a question for Mr Dennis Pearson,' I invited.

'We came up the morning before. We were staying with Janet Freebody who lives in the village. Janet's a schoolteacher.'

'And chair of our activist committee.' Gavin was finding it difficult to keep quiet.

'Where was the van parked?'

'In front of Janet's house.'

'From what time?'

'About midday.'

'You hadn't taken a trip in it to Fallows Wood before then?'

'Den tells me he hadn't.' Once again, Gavin took on the answering.

'Was the van kept locked?'

'Supposed to be. Roy's a bit careless about this, isn't he, Den?'

'Roy's careless about everything,' Den agreed.

There were a lot more questions that required answering, but I didn't want them all answered by way of the protective Gavin Garfield.

'There's one other thing I should tell you,' I said as I gathered up my papers. 'I know Rollo Eyles. I met him when he was at the Bar. And I was staying with him the night before . . . Well, the night before the fatal accident. I'll have to tell him I'm defending the man accused of murdering his wife. If you don't want me to defend you, you know that, of course, I shall understand.' I was giving them a chance to sack me even before my precious murder case had begun. I kept my fingers crossed under the table.

'I'd like you to carry on with the case, Mr Rumpole,' Den was now speaking for himself. 'Seeing what you did for that dog, I don't think I'll cause you much trouble.'

'Oh, why's that?'

'Well, you see . . .' Dennis Pearson was still smiling pleasantly, imperturbably.

Gavin looked at him anxiously and started off, 'Den . . .'

But my client interrupted him, 'You see, I did it.'

'You knew he was going to do that?' Gavin was driving me from the prison to Gloucester station in a car littered with bits of comics, old toys, empty crisp packets and crumpled orange juice cartons with the straws still stuck in them. I supposed that, in his pale, vegetarian way, he had fathered many children.

'I had an idea. Yes,' Gavin admitted it. 'What do we do now?'

'We're entitled to cross-examine the prosecution witnesses and see if they prove the case. We can't call Dennis to deny the charge, so, if the Prosecution holds up, we'll have to plead guilty at half-time.'

'Is that what you'd advise him to do?'

'I'd advise him to tell us the truth.'

'Why do you say that?'

'Because I don't believe he is.'

I wanted to work on the case away from the garrulous Gavin and the uncommunicative Den. I thought that they lurked somewhere between the world of human communication and the secret and silent kingdom of animals, and I didn't feel either of them would be much help down the Bailey. The case seemed to me to raise certain awkward and interesting questions, not to say a matter of legal ethics and private morality which was, not to put too fine a point upon it, devilishly tricky to cope with.

As I sat in Chambers I decided it was better for a legal hack like me to stop worrying about such things as ideas of proper or improper behaviour and concentrate on the facts. I lit a small cigar and opened a volume of police photographs. As I did so, I stooped for a moment to pat the head of the gloomy Lancelot, who had become my close companion, and then realized he was gone, ferreting for disgusting morsels, no doubt, at the edge of the sea while Dodo Mackintosh sat at her easel and perpetrated a feeble watercolour. I felt completely alone in the defence of Den Pearson, who didn't even want to be defended.

I hurried past the mortuary shots of Dorothea and her fatal injuries, and got to a picture of a path through trees. It was a narrow strip hardly wide enough for two people to pass in comfort, so the beech trees on either side were not much more than six feet apart. A closer shot showed the wire, then still stretched between nails driven into the trees. The track was muddy, with patches of grass and the bare earth. I picked up a magnifying glass and looked at the photo carefully. Then I rang little Marcus Pitcher, who, I had discovered, was to be in charge of the Prosecution. 'Listen, old darling,' I said, when I got his chirrup on the line, 'what about you and me organizing a visit to the *locus in quo*?' When he asked me what I meant, I said, 'There was once a road through the woods.'

'A day out in the country?' Marcus sounded agreeable. 'Whyever not. I'll drive you.'

My learned friend was a small man with a round face, slightly protruding teeth and large, horn-rimmed glasses, so that he looked like an agreeable mouse, although he could be a cunning little performer in Court. Marcus owned a bulky old Jaguar and had to sit up very straight to peer out of the windscreen. In the back seat a white bull-terrier sat, pink-eyed and asthmatic, looking at me as though she wondered why I'd come to ruin the day out.

'Meet Bernadette,' Marcus introduced us. 'As soon as she heard about the trip to the Cotswolds, she had to come. Hope you don't mind.'

'Not at all. In fact I might have brought my own dog, but Lancelot's away at the moment.'

At the scene of the crime Bernadette went bounding off into the undergrowth, while Marcus, his solicitor from the D.P.P.'s office, and I stood with the Detective Inspector in charge of the case. D. J. Palmer was a courteous officer who lacked the tendency of the Metropolitan force to imitate the coppers they've seen on television. He led us to the spot where death had taken place. The wire and nails had been removed to be exhibited in the case, and the hoof marks had been rubbed out by the rain.

'"There was once a road through the woods,"' I told the Inspector, '"Before they planted the trees./It is underneath the coppice and heath,/And the thin anemones . . ." But this one isn't, is it, Inspector?'

'I'm not quite sure that I follow you, Mr Rumpole.'

'This road hasn't disappeared so that

> Only the keeper sees
> That, where the ring-dove broods,
> And the badgers roll at ease,
> There was once a road through the woods.'

'It's a footpath here as I understand it, Mr Rumpole.' The
D.I. was ever helpful. 'Mr Eyles is very good about keeping
open the footpaths on his land.' It did seem that the edges of
the path had been trimmed and the brambles cut back.

'Is the footpath used a lot? Did you ever find that out,
Inspector?'

'Ramblers use it. It was ramblers that found Mrs Eyles. A
shocking experience for them.'

'It must have been. Don't know why they call it rambling,
do you? We used to call it going for a walk. So people don't
ride down here much?'

'I wouldn't think a lot. You'd have to be a good horseman to
jump that.'

We had come to a stile at the end of the narrow track. Beside
it there was a green signpost showing that the footpath continued across the middle of a broad field dotted with sheep. The
stile had a single pole to hold on to and a wide step set at right
angles to the top bar. I supposed it would have been a difficult
jump but I saw a scar in the wood. Could that have been the
mark of a hoof that had just managed it?

Marcus Pitcher called Bernadette and she came lolloping
over the brambles and started to root about in the long grass at
the side of the stile.

'You gents seen all you want?' the D.I. asked us.

Marcus was satisfied. I wasn't. I thought that if we waited
we might learn something else about that cold, sunny day in
March when Dorothea died as quickly as she'd said she'd
always wanted to. And then I was rewarded. Bernadette pulled
some weighty object out of the grass, carried it in her mouth
and laid it, as a tribute, at the feet of Marcus Pitcher. I said I'd
like a note made of exactly where we found the horseshoe.

'I don't see what it can possibly prove.' Marcus was doubtful.
'It might have been dropped from any horse at any time.'

'Let's just make a note,' I asked. 'We'll think about what it
proves later.'

So the polite Inspector took charge of the horseshoe and he,
Marcus and Bernadette moved on across the field on their way
back to the road. I sat on the stile to recover my breath and
looked into the darkness of the wood. What was it at night? A

sort of killing field – owls swooping on mice, foxes after small birds – a place of unexpected noises and sudden death? Was it a site for killing people or killing animals? I remembered Dorothea, old and elegant, handing down with a smile to Den what she said was a flask of fox's blood. I thought about the hunters and the antis shouting at each other and Den's yell: 'One of you is going to die for all the dead animals.' And I tried to see Dorothea, elated, excited, galloping down the narrow path and her sudden, unlooked-for near-decapitation. From somewhere in the shadows under the trees, I seemed to hear the sound of hoofs and I remembered more of Kipling, a grumpy old darling but with a marvellous sense of rhythm. I chanted to myself:

> 'You will hear the beat of a horse's feet,
> And the swish of a skirt in the dew,
> Steadily cantering through
> The misty solitudes,
> As though they perfectly knew
> The old lost road through the woods.
> But there is no road through the woods.'

But there was no swish of a skirt. It was Rollo Eyles who came cantering down the track, reined in his horse and sat looking down on me as I sat on his stile.

'Horace! *You* here? I heard the police were in the wood.'

I looked up at him. He was getting near my age but healthier and certainly thinner than me. He was not a tall man, but he sat up very straight in the saddle. His reins were loose and his hands relaxed; his horse snorted but hardly moved. He wore a cap instead of a hard riding-hat, regardless of danger, and an old tweed jacket. His voice was surprisingly deep and there was little grey in the hair that showed.

'I was having a look at the scene of the crime.' Then I told him, as I had to, 'I'm defending the man who's supposed to have killed your wife.'

'Not the man who killed her?'

'We won't know that until the Jury get back. Do you mind?'

'That he killed Dorothea?'

'No. That I'm defending him.'

'You have to defend even the most disgusting clients, don't you?' His voice never lost its friendliness and there was no hint of anger. 'It's in the best traditions of the Bar.'

'That's right. I'm an old taxi.'

'Well, I wish you luck. Who's your judge?'

'We're likely to get stuck with Jamie MacBain.'

'"I was not born yesterday, y'know, Mr Rumpole. I think I'm astute enough to see through *that* argument!"' Rollo had lost none of his talents as a mimic and did a very creditable imitation of Mr Justice MacBain's carefully preserved Scottish accent. 'Why don't you come down to the house for a whisky and splash?' he asked in his own voice.

'I can't. They'll be waiting for me in the car. You're sure you don't mind me taking on the case?'

'Why should I mind? You've got to do your job. I've no doubt justice will be done.'

I climbed over the stile then walked away. When I looked back, he wasn't going to jump but turned the horse and trotted back the way he had come. He had said justice would be done but I wasn't entirely sure of it.

I kept all of this to myself and said nothing to She Who Must Be Obeyed, although I knew well enough that the time would come when I'd certainly have to tell her. As the trial of Dennis Pearson drew nearer, I decided that the truth could no longer be avoided and chose breakfast time as, when the expected hostilities broke out, I could retreat hastily down the tube and off to Chambers and so escape prolonged exposure to the cannonade.

'By the way,' I said casually over the last piece of toast, 'I'll probably be staying down in the Gloucester direction before the end of the month.'

'Has Rollo Eyles invited us again?'

'Well, not exactly.'

'Why exactly, then?' With Hilda you can never get away with leaving uncomfortable facts in a comforting blur.

'I've got a trial.'

'What sort of a trial?'

'A rather important murder as it so happens. You'll be glad to know, Hilda, that when it comes to the big stuff, the questions of life and death, the cry is still "Send for Rumpole".'

'Who got murdered?'

The question had been asked casually, but I knew the moment of truth had come. 'Well, someone you've met, as a matter of fact.'

'Who?'

My toast was finished. I took a last gulp of coffee, ready for the off.

'Dorothea Eyles.'

'You're defending that horrible little hunt saboteur?'

'Well, he's not so little. Quite tall actually.'

'You're defending the man who murdered the wife of your friend?'

'I suppose someone has to.'

'Well! It's no wonder you haven't got any friends, Rumpole.'

Was it true? Hadn't I any friends? Enemies, yes. Acquaintances. Opponents down the Bailey. Fellow Members of Chambers. But *friends*? Bonny Bernard? Fred Timson? Well, I suppose we only met for work. Who was my real friend? I could only think of one. 'I got on fairly well with the dog Lancelot. Of course he's no longer with us.'

'Just as well. If you defend people who kill your friends' wives, you're hardly fit company for a decent dog.' You have to admit that when Hilda comes to a view she doesn't mince words on the matter.

'We don't know if he killed her. He's only accused of killing her.'

'No hair and earrings? You only had to take a look at him to know he was capable of anything!'

'They didn't arrest the one with no hair,' I told her. 'I'm defending another one.'

'It doesn't matter. I expect they're all much of a muchness. Can you imagine what Rollo's going to say when he finds out what you're doing?'

'I know what he thinks.'

'What?'

'That it's in the best tradition of the Bar to defend anyone, however revolting.'

'How do you know that's what he thinks?'

'Because that's what he said when I told him.'

'You told him?'

'Yes.'

'I must say, Rumpole, you've got a nerve!'

'Courage is the essential quality of an advocate.'

'And I suppose it's the essential quality of an advocate to be on the side of the lowest, most contemptible of human beings?'

'To put their case for them? Yes.'

'Even if they're guilty?'

'That hasn't been proved.'

'But you don't know he's not.'

'I think I do.'

'Why?'

'Because of what he told me.'

'He told you he wasn't guilty?'

'No, he told me he *was*. But, you see, I didn't believe him.'

'He told you he was guilty and you're still defending him? Is that in the best traditions of the Bar?'

'Only just,' I had to admit.

'Rumpole!' She Who Must Be Obeyed gave me one of her unbending looks and delivered judgement. 'I suppose that, if someone murdered *me*, you would defend them?'

There was no answer to that so I looked at my watch. 'Must go. Urgent conference in Chambers. I won't be late home. Is it one of your bridge evenings?' I asked the question, but answer came there none. I knew that for that day, and for many days to come, as far as She Who Must Be Obeyed was concerned, the mansion flat in Froxbury Mansions would be locked in the icy silence of the tomb.

During the last weeks before the trial Hilda was true to her vow of silence and the mansion flat offered all the light-hearted badinage of life in a Trappist order. Luckily I was busy and even welcomed the chance of a chat with Gavin Garfield whom, although I had excluded him from my visit to the Cotswolds, I now set to work. I told him his first job was to get statements from the other saboteurs in the van, and when he protested that we'd never get so far as calling evidence in view of what Den had told us, I said we must be prepared for all eventualities. So Gavin took statements, not hurriedly, but with a surprising thoroughness, and in time certain hard facts emerged.

What surprised me was the age and respectability of the saboteurs. Shaven-headed Roy Netherborn was forty and worked in the accounts department of a paper cup factory. He had toyed with the idea of being a schoolmaster and had met Janet Freebody, who was a couple of years older, at a teacher training college. Janet owned the cottage in Wayleave where the platoon of fearless saboteurs had put up for the night. She taught at a comprehensive school in the nearby town where we had fled from the dreaded hotel. Angela Ridgeway, the girl with the purple lock, was a researcher for BBC Wales. Sebastian Fells and Judy Caspar were live-in partners and worked together in a Kensington bookshop, and Dennis Pearson, thirty-five, taught sociology at a university which had risen from the ashes of a polytechnic. They all, except Janet, lived in London and were on the committee of a society of animal rights activists.

Janet had kept Roy informed about the meet at Rollo Eyles's house, and they had taken days off during her half-term when the meet was at Wayleave. The sabbing was to be made the occasion of a holiday outing and a night spent in the country. When they had got their rucksacks and sleeping-bags out of the van, Roy, Angela, Sebastian and Judy retired to the pub in Wayleave where real ale was obtainable and they used it to wash down vegetable pasties and salads until closing-time at three. Janet Freebody had things to do in the cottage, exercise books to correct and dinner to think about, so she didn't join the party in the pub. Neither did Den. He said he wanted to go for a walk and so set off, according to Roy, apparently to commune, in a solitary fashion, with nature. This meant that he was alone and unaccounted for at one o'clock when Tricia was going to swear on her oath that she saw him coming out of Fallows Wood with a coil of wire.

Other facts of interest: Fallows Wood was only about ten

minutes from Wayleave. Roy couldn't remember there being
any wire in the van when they set out from London; it was true
that they had discussed using wire to trip up horses, but he had
never bought any and was surprised when the police searched
the van and found the coil there. It was also true that the van
was always in a mess, and probably the hammer found in it was
his. Den had brought a kitbag with his stuff in it and Roy
couldn't swear it didn't contain wire. Den was usually a quiet
sort of bloke, Roy said, but he did go mad when he saw people
out to kill animals: 'Dennis always said that the movement was
too milk and watery towards hunting, and that what was
needed was some great gesture which would really bring us
into the news and prove our sincerity – like when the girl fell
under a lorry that was taking sheep to the airport.' I made a
mental note not to ask any sort of question likely to produce
that last piece of evidence and came to the conclusion that Roy,
despite his willingness to give Gavin a statement, wasn't entirely friendly to my client, Dennis Pearson.

The placards, a small plantation at the meet, had become a
forest outside the Court in Gloucester. Buses, bicycles, vans,
cars in varying degrees of disrepair, had brought them, held up
now by a crowd which burst, as I elbowed my way towards the
courthouse door, into a resounding cheer for Rumpole. I didn't
remember any such ovation when I entered the Old Bailey on
other occasions. In the robing-room I found Bernadette asleep
in a chair and little Marcus Pitcher tying a pair of white bands
around his neck in front of a mirror. 'See you've got your
friends from rent-a-crowd here this morning, Rumpole.' He
was not in the best of tempers, our demonstrators having
apparently booed Bernadette for having thrown in her lot with
a barrister who prosecuted the friends of animals.

I wondered how long their cheers for me would last when I
went into Court, only to put my hands up and plead guilty. My
client, however, remained singularly determined: 'When we
plead guilty, they'll cheer. It'll be a triumph for the movement.
Can't you understand that, Mr Rumpole? We shall be seen to
have condemned a murderer to death!'

The approach of life imprisonment seemed to have concentrated Den's mind wonderfully. He was no longer the silent

and enigmatic sufferer. His eyes were lit up and he was as excited as when he'd shouted his threats at the faded beauty on the horse. 'I want you to tell them I'm guilty, first thing. As soon as we get in there. I want you to tell them that I punished her.'

'No, you don't want that. Does he, Mr Garfield?' Gavin, sitting beside me in the cell under the Court, looked like a man who had entirely lost control of the situation. 'I suppose if that's what Den has decided . . .' His voice, never strong, died away and he shrugged hopelessly.

'I *have* decided finally' – Den was standing, elated by his decision – 'in the interests of our movement.' For a moment he reminded me of an actor I had seen in an old film, appearing as Sydney Carton on his way to the guillotine, saying, 'It's a far, far better thing I do, than I have ever done.'

'You're not going to do the movement much good by pleading guilty straight away,' I told him.

'What do you mean?'

'A guilty plea at the outset? The whole thing'll be over in twenty minutes. The animal murderers, as you call them, won't even have to go into the witness-box, let alone face cross-examination by Rumpole. Will anyone know the details of the hunt? Certainly not. Do you want publicity for your cause? Plead guilty now and you will be lucky to get a single paragraph on page two. At least, let's get the front page for a day or so.' I wasn't being entirely frank with my client. The murder was serious and horrible enough to get the front pages in a world hungry for bad news at breakfast, even if we were to plead guilty without delay. But I needed time. In time, I still hoped, I would get Den to tell me the truth.

'I don't know.' My client sat down then as though suddenly tired. 'What would you do, Gavin?'

'I think' – Gavin shrugged off all responsibility – 'you should be guided by Mr Rumpole.'

'All right' – Den was prepared to compromise – 'we'll go for the publicity.'

'Dennis Pearson, you are accused in this indictment of the murder of Dorothea Eyles on the sixteenth of March at Fallows

Wood, Wayleave, in the county of Gloucester. Do you plead guilty or not guilty?'

'My Lord, Members of the Jury' – Den, as I had feared, was about to orate. 'This woman, Dorothea Eyles, was guilty of the murder of countless living creatures, not for her gain but simply for sadistic pleasure and idle enjoyment. My Lord, if anything killed her, it was natural justice!'

'Now then, Mr –' Mr Justice James MacBain consulted his papers to make sure who he was trying. 'Mr Pearson. You've got a gentleman in a wig sitting there, a Mr Rumpole, who's paid to make the speeches for you. It's not your business to make speeches now or at any time during this case. Now, you've been asked a simple question: Are you guilty or not guilty?'

'She is the guilty one, my Lord. This woman who revelled in the death of innocent creatures.'

'Mr Rumpole, are you not astute enough to control your client?'

'It's not an easy task, my Lord.' I staggered to my feet.

'Your first job is to control your client. That's what I learnt as a pupil. Make the client keep it short.'

'Well, if you don't want a long speech from the dock, my Lord, I suggest you enter a plea of not guilty and then my learned friend, Mr Marcus Pitcher, can get on with opening his case.'

'Mr Rumpole, I was not born yesterday!' Jamie MacBain was stating the obvious. It was many years since he had first seen the light in some remote corner of the Highlands. He was a large man whose hair, once ginger, had turned to grey, and who sat slumped in his chair like one of those colourless beanbags people use to sit on in their Hampstead homes. He had small, pursed lips and a perpetually discontented expression. 'And when I want your advice on how to conduct these proceedings, I shall ask you for it. Mr Moberly!' This was a whispered summons to the clerk of the court, who rose obediently and, after a brief *sotto voce* conversation, sat down again as the Judge turned to the Jury.

'Members of the Jury, you and I weren't born yesterday and I think we're astute enough to get over this little technical difficulty. Now we don't want Mr Pearson, the accused man here, to start giving us a lecture, do we? So what we're going to do is to take it he's pleading not guilty and then ask Mr Marcus Pitcher to get on with it and open the prosecution case. You see, there's no great mystery about the law. We can solve most of the problems if we apply a wee bit of worldly wisdom.'

I suppose I could have got up on my hind legs and said, 'Delighted to have been of service to your Lordship,' or, 'If you're ever in a hole, send for me.' But I didn't want to start a quarrel so early in the case. I sat quietly while little Marcus went through most of the facts. The Jury of twelve honest Gloucestershire citizens looked stolid, middle-aged and not particularly friendly to the animal rights protesters who filled the public gallery to overflowing. I imagined they had grown up with the hunt and felt no particular hostility to the Boxing Day meet and horses streaming across the frosty countryside. They had looked embarrassed by Dennis's speech from the dock, and flattered when Jamie MacBain shared his lifetime's experience with them. Like him, they hadn't been born yesterday, and worldly wisdom, together with their dogs and their rose gardens, was no doubt among their proudest possessions. As I listened to my little learned friend's opening, I thought he was talking to a jury which, whatever plea had been entered, was beginning to feel sure that Den was as guilty as he was anxious to appear.

The first witness was the rambler, a cashier from a local bank who, out for a walk with his wife and daughter, had been met with the ghastly spectacle of an elderly woman almost decapitated and fallen among the brambles of Fallows Wood.

'Where was the horse?' was all I asked him in cross-examination.

'The horse?'

'Yes. Did you see her horse by any chance?'

'I think there was a horse there, some distance away, and all saddled up. I think it was just eating grass or something. I didn't stay long. I wanted to get my wife and Sandra away and phone the police.'

'Of course. I understand. Thank you very much, Mr Ovington.'

'Is that all you want to ask, Mr Rumpole?' Jamie MacBain looked at me in an unfriendly fashion.

'Yes, my Lord.'

'I don't think that question and answer has added much to our understanding of this case, Members of the Jury. I'd be glad if the Defence would not waste the time of the Court. Yes. Who is your next witness, Mr Marcus Pitcher?'

I restrained myself and sat down in silence 'like patience on a monument'. But my question *had* added something: Dorothea's riderless horse hadn't galloped on and jumped the stile. We learnt more from Bob Andrews, a hunt servant who, when the hunt was stopped, went back to the wood to recover Dorothea's horse which had been detained by the police. I risked Jamie's displeasure by questioning Andrews for a little longer.

'When you got to the wood, had Mrs Eyles's body been removed?'

'It was covered. I think it was just being taken away on a stretcher. I knew the ambulance was in the road. The police were taking photographs.'

'The police were taking photographs – and where was Mrs Eyles's horse?'

'I think a police officer was holding her.'

'Can you remember, had Mrs Eyles's horse lost a shoe?'

'Not that I noticed. I looked her over when I took her from the policeman. He seemed a bit scared, holding her.'

'I'm not surprised. Horses can be a little alarming.'

'Can be. If you're not used to them.'

There were a few smiles from the Jury at this; not because it was funny but as a relief from the agony of hearing the details of Dorothea Eyles's injuries. The Jury, I thought, rather liked Bob Andrews, while the animal rights enthusiasts in the public gallery looked down on him with unmitigated hatred and contempt.

'Mr Andrews,' I went on, while Mr Justice MacPain (as I had come to think of him) gave a somewhat exaggerated performance of a long-suffering judge, bravely enduring terminal boredom, 'tell me a little about the hunt that day. You were riding near to Mr Eyles?'

'Up with the master. Yes.'

'Did your hunt go near Fallows Wood?'

'Not really. No.'

'What was the nearest you got to that wood?'

'Well, they found in Plashy Bottom. Down there they got a scent. Then we were off in the other direction entirely.'

'How far is Plashy Bottom from Fallows Wood?'

'About half a mile . . . I'd think about that.'

'Did you see Mrs Eyles leave the hunt and ride up towards the wood?'

'Well, they'd got going then. I wouldn't have looked round to see the riders behind me.'

'Did you see anyone else – Miss Tricia Fothergill, for instance – leave the hunt and ride up towards Fallows Wood?'

'I didn't, no.'

'He's told us he wasn't looking at the riders behind him, Mr Rumpole.' Jamie managed to sound like a saint holding on to his patience by the skin of his teeth.

'Then let me ask you a question you *can* answer. It's clear, isn't it, that the hunt never went through Fallows Wood that day?'

'That's right.'

'So, it follows that in order to come into collision with that wire, Mrs Eyles had to make a considerable detour?'

'That's surely a matter for argument, Mr Rumpole.' Jamie MacBain did his best to scupper the question so I asked another one, very quickly.

'Do you know why she should make such a detour?'

'I haven't got any idea, no.'

'Thank you, Mr Andrews.' And I sat down before the Judge could recover his breath.

Johnny Logan replaced the whipper-in. He was wearing a dark suit and some sort of regimental tie; his creased and brown walnut face grinned over a collar which seemed several sizes too large for him. He treated the Judge with a mixture of amusement and contempt, as though Jamie were some alien being who could never understand the hunting community of the Cotswolds. Logan said he had heard most of the dialogue between the sabs and the hunters in the driveway of Wayleave

Manor. He also told the Jury that he had seen the saboteurs'
van at various points during the day, and heard similar abuse
from them as he rode by.

'You never saw the saboteurs' van near Fallows Wood?' I
asked when it was my turn.

'We never went near Fallows Wood as far as I can
remember.'

'Then let you and I agree about that. Now, will you tell me
this? Did you ever see Mrs Eyles leave the hunt and ride off in
a different direction?'

'No, I never saw that. I'm not saying she didn't do it. We
were pretty spread out. I'd seen a couple of jumps I didn't like
the look of, so I'd gone round and I was behind quite a lot of
the others.'

'Gone round, had you?' Jamie MacBain, about to make a
note, looked confused.

'Quite a lot of barbed wire about. I don't think you'd have
fancied jumping that, my Lord,' Johnny Logan added with a
certain amount of mock servility.

'Never mind what I'd've fancied. Just answer the questions
you get asked. That's all you're required to do.' It was clear
that the Judge and the witness had struck up an immediate lack
of rapport.

'Did you see anyone else leave the hunt?'

'I don't think so. Well, you mean at *any* time?'

'At any time when you were out hunting, yes.'

'Well, I think Tricia Fothergill left. But that was at the very
end, just before the police arrived and told us that Mrs Eyles
had been – well, had met with an accident.'

'So that must have been after Mrs Eyles's death?' The Judge
made the deduction.

'You've got it, my Lord,' Johnny Logan congratulated him
in such a patronizing fashion that I almost felt sorry for the
astute Scot.

'Why did she leave then, do you remember?'

'I'm not sure. Her horse was wrong in some way, I think.'

'Just one more thing, Mr Logan.'

'Oh, anything you like.' Johnny showed his contempt for us
all.

'It would be right to say, wouldn't it, that Mr Rollo Eyles was devoted to his wife?'

'He would certainly never have left her. Is that what you mean?'

'That's exactly what I mean. Thank you very much.'

As I was about to sit down, the Judge said, 'And what were the Jury meant to make of that last question and answer?'

'They may make of it what they will, my Lord, when they are in full possession of the facts of this interesting but tragic case.' At which point I lowered my head in an ornate eighteenth-century bow and sat down with as much dignity as I could muster.

'Work at the Bar!' little Marcus said. 'Sometimes I think I'd rather be digging roads.'

'Only one thing to be said for work at the Bar,' I tended to agree, 'is that it's better than no work at the Bar.'

It was the lunch adjournment and the three of us – Marcus, Bernadette and I – were in a dark corner of the Carpenters Arms, not far from the Court. There they did a perfectly reasonable bangers and mash. Marcus and I had big glasses of Guinness and Bernadette took hers from a bowl on the floor. The little prosecutor said he was looking forward to going for a holiday with a Chancery barrister called Clarissa Clavering on the Isle of Elba. 'I'd been living for the day, but now it seems likely I'll have to cancel.'

'Why on earth?'

'I can't find anyone to leave Bernadette with. Clarissa only likes cats. And I do love her, Rumpole! Love Clarissa, I mean. She has a lot of sheer animal magnetism for a girl in the Chancery Division.'

'Couldn't you put her in a kennel? Bernadette, I mean.'

'I couldn't do that.' Marcus looked as though I'd invited him to murder his mother. 'Much as I fancy Clarissa, I couldn't possibly do that.'

'Then, there's nothing else for it . . .'

'Nothing else for it.' His little mouselike face was creased with lines of sorrow. My heart went out to the fellow. 'Except cancel the holiday. I won't blame Bernadette, of course. It's not *her* fault. But . . .'

'It's a pity to miss so much animal magnetism?'

'You've said it, Rumpole. You've said it exactly.'

When we arrived back at the Court, there was a certain amount of confusion among the demonstrators. They started with the clear intention of cheering me and Bernadette, who, even if she was part of the prosecution team, was, after all, an animal. They knew they should boo and revile young Marcus, the disappointed lover. Finally, when they saw that I, as well as Bernadette, was on friendly terms with the forces of evil and the prosecutors of sabs, they decided to boo us all.

In the entrance hall the prospective witnesses sat waiting. I saw Tricia Fothergill as smartly turned out as a pony at a show, with gleaming hair, shiny shoes and glistening legs. She was prepared for Court in a black suit and her hands were folded in her lap. On the other side of the hall sat the prospective witnesses for the Defence: purple-haired Angela Ridgeway, Sebastian and Judy from the bookshop, and shaven-headed Roy Netherborn. Janet, the schoolteacher, sat next to Roy, but I noticed that they didn't speak to each other but sat gazing, as though hypnotized, silently into space. Then, as I was wigged and gowned by now, I crossed the entrance hall towards the Court. Roy got up and walked towards me slowly, heavily and with something very like menace. 'What the hell's the idea,' he muttered in a low voice, full of hate, 'of you getting into bed with the prosecution barrister?'

'Little Marcus and I are learned friends,' I told him, 'against each other one day and on the same side the next. We went out to lunch because his dog Bernadette felt in need of a drink. And I didn't get into bed with him. I left that to his girlfriend Clarissa of the Chancery Division. Any more questions?'

'Yes. Haven't you got any genuine beliefs?'

'As few as possible. Genuine beliefs seem to end up in death threats and stopping other people living as they choose. I do have one genuine belief, however.'

'Oh, do you? And what's that when it's at home?'

'Preventing the conviction of the innocent. So, if you will allow me to get on with my job . . .' I moved away from him

then, and he stood watching me go, his fists clenched and his
knuckles whitening.

Tricia had given her evidence-in-chief clearly, with a nice
mixture of sadness, brightness and an eagerness to help. The
Jury had taken to her and Jamie MacBain seemed no less
smitten than little Marcus was with Clarissa, although there
was a great gulf fixed between them and she called him my
Lord, and he called her Miss Fothergill in a voice which can
best be described as a caressing, although still judicial, purr.
She looked, as she stood in the witness-box and answered
vivaciously, prettier than I had remembered. Her nose was a
little turned up, her front teeth a little protruding, but her eyes
were bright and her smile beguiling.

'Tricia Fothergill, you say your name is?' I rose, after Marcus
had finished with her, doing my best to break the spell woven
by the most damaging prosecution witness. 'Why not Patricia?'

'Because I couldn't say Patricia when I was a little girl. So I
stayed Tricia, even when I went away to school.'

'Which, I'm sure, wasn't long ago. Don't you agree, Members of the Jury?' the judge purred and a few weaker spirits in
the jury box gave a mild giggle. Tricia Fothergill, in Jamie's
view, it seemed, *had* been born yesterday.

'I'll call you Miss Fothergill, if I may, if that's your grown-
up name. Or is it? Were you once married?'

'Yes.'

'And your husband's name is . . .?'

'Charing.'

'Cheering, did you say?'

'No, Charing.'

'Are you going deaf, Mr Rumpole?' the Judge raised his
voice to me as though at the severely afflicted.

'Not quite yet, my Lord.' I turned to this witness. 'Are you
divorced from this Mr Charing?'

'Not quite yet, Mr Rumpole,' the witness answered with a
smile and won a laugh from the Jury. The Judge's pursed lips
were stretched into a smile, and the inert beanbag was shaken
up and repositioned in his chair. 'The divorce hasn't gone
through,' Tricia explained when order was restored.

'Yet you call yourself Miss Fothergill?'

'It was such an unhappy relationship. I wanted to make a clean break.'

'Surely you can understand that, Mr Rumpole?' Jamie was giving the witness his full and unqualified support.

'And have you now found a new and happier relationship?'

Little Marcus, the mouse that roared, rose to object, but the learned Judge needed no persuading. 'That was an entirely irrelevant and embarrassing question, Mr Rumpole. Please be more careful in the future.'

'I hope we shall all be careful,' I said, 'in our efforts to discover the truth. So I understand you live alone, Miss Fothergill, in Cherry Trees in the village of Wayleave?'

'That is another entirely improper question. What does it matter whether this young lady lives alone or not?' This time the Judge was doing Marcus's objections for him. 'We'd be greatly obliged, Mr Rumpole, if you'd move on to something relevant.'

'I'll move on to something very relevant. Do you say you saw a man coming out of Fallows Wood carrying wire on the day before the hunt?'

'That's right.'

'What time was it?'

'One o'clock.'

'How do you know?'

'I'd just looked at my watch. I was out for a hack and had to be home before two because my lawyer was ringing me. I saw it was only one and I decided to do the long round through Plashy Bottom. Then I saw the man coming out of the wood, with the coil of wire.'

'When you saw the man with the wire, you were alone?'

'Yes.'

'No one else saw him at that time?'

'Not so far as I know.'

'You say you thought he might have been working for Telecom or the electricity company? Did you see a van from any of those companies?'

'No.'

'Or the van the saboteurs came in?'

'I didn't see the van then, no. Of course it might have been parked on the road.'

'Or it might still have been parked in the village. As far as you know.'

'As far as I know.'

'You saw a man the next day, shouting at Mrs Eyles?'

'That was the same man. Yes.'

'Why didn't you warn everyone in the hunt that you'd seen that man coming out of the wood, carrying wire?'

'I suppose I just didn't put two and two together at the time. It was only when I heard Dorothea had been killed by a wire . . .'

'You put two and two together then?' The Judge was ever helpful to his favourite witness.

'Yes, my Lord. And I was going to say that, in all the excitement of starting out with the hunt, I may have forgotten what I saw, just for a little while.'

'I don't suppose Mr Rumpole knows much about the excitement of the hunt.' Jamie MacBain was wreathed in smiles and seemed almost on the point of laying a finger alongside his nose.

I didn't join in the obedient titters from the Jury, or the shocked intake of breath from the faces in the public gallery. I started the long and unrewarding task of chipping away at Tricia's identification. How far had she been away from the wood? Was the sun in her eyes? How fast was her horse moving at the time? As is the way with such questioning, the more the witness was attacked the more positive she became.

'On your way back to your house in Wayleave, on the day before the hunt, did you pass Janet Freebody's cottage?'

'Yes, I had to pass that way.' Tricia made it clear that she wouldn't go near anything of Janet Freebody's unless it were absolutely necessary.

'Did you see the sabs' van parked outside Miss Freebody's cottage?'

'I think I did. I can't honestly remember.'

'Was it locked?'

'How would she know that, Mr Rumpole?' Jamie put his oar in.

'Perhaps you tried the door.'

'I certainly didn't! I was just riding past.'

'Let me ask you something else. Mr Logan has told us that you left the hunt shortly before the police arrived with the news of Mrs Eyles's death. There was something wrong with your horse. What was it?'

'Oh, Trumpeter had lost a shoe,' Tricia said as casually as possible. 'It must have happened earlier, but I hadn't noticed it. I noticed it then and I had to take him home.'

It was a moment when I felt a tingle of excitement, as though, after a long search in deep and muddy waters, we had struck some hard edge of the truth. 'Miss Fothergill,' I asked her, 'were you riding with Mrs Eyles in Fallows Wood on the day she met her death?'

The Jury were looking at Tricia, suddenly interested. Even Jamie MacBain didn't rush to her assistance.

'No, of course I wasn't.' She turned to the Judge with a small, incredulous giggle which meant 'What a silly question'.

'My Lord. I call on my learned friend to admit that a horseshoe was found by Inspector Palmer near to the stile in Fallows Wood.'

'Perfectly true, my Lord,' Marcus admitted. 'It was found some weeks after Mrs Eyles died.'

'So it might have been dropped by one of any number of horses at any unknown time?' Jamie was delighted to point out. 'Isn't that so, Miss Fothergill?' Tricia was pleased to agree and repeated that she had never ridden through Fallows Wood that day. I was coming to the end of my questions.

'When your divorce proceedings are over, Miss Fothergill, are you going to embark on another marriage?' I asked and waited for the protest. It came. Little Marcus drew himself up to his full height and objected. Jamie agreed entirely and said that he wouldn't allow any question about the witness's private life. So my conversation with Tricia ended, finally silenced by the Judge's ruling.

At the end of the afternoon I came out of Court frustrated, despondent, seeing nothing in front of me but a pathetic guilty plea. Gavin hurried away to see Den in the cells and I heard an urgent voice saying, 'Mr Rumpole! I've got to talk to you.' I looked around and there was Janet Freebody, showing every sign of desperation. I saw Roy and a representative group of the sabs watching us, as well as the hunters who were leaving the Court. I said I'd meet her in the Carpenters Arms round the corner in half an hour.

'It's kind of you to see me. So kind.' I realized I had never looked closely at Janet Freebody before, but just filed her away in my mind as a grey-haired schoolmistress in a tweed skirt. It was true that her hair was grey and her skirt was tweed but her eyes were blue, her eyelids finely moulded and her long, serious face beautiful as the faces on grave madonnas or serious angels in old paintings. At that moment her cheeks were pink and her hands, caressing her glass of gin-and-tonic, were long-fingered and elegant.

'What is it you want to tell me?'

She didn't answer directly, but asked me a question. 'Wasn't it at one o'clock that Dennis was meant to be coming out of that wood, carrying wire?'

'That's what Tricia said.'

'Well, he wasn't. I know where he was.'

'Where?'

'In bed with me.'

I looked at her and said, 'Thank you for telling me.'

'I know I've got to tell that in Court. Den's going to be furious.' And then it all came out, shyly at first, nervously, and then with increasing confidence. She'd had an affair with shaven-headed Roy, who was jealous of Den and now in a perpetually bad temper. She and Dennis had waited until the others went out to the pub to go upstairs, where, it seemed, the solemn Den forgot his duty to the animals in his love for the schoolmistress. Meanwhile, the saboteurs' van was unlocked and unattended outside Janet's front gate.

'You can't go on pretending.'

'Pretending what?'

'Pretending you're guilty, just to help animals. I doubt very much whether the animals are going to be grateful to you. In fact they'll hardly notice. Like Launce's dog, Crab. Do you know *The Two Gentlemen of Verona*?'

'How do they come into the case?'

'They don't. They're in a play. So is Launce. And so is his dog, Crab. When Crab farts at the Duke's dinner party, Launce takes the blame for it and is whipped out of the room. Launce also sat in the stocks for puddings Crab stole and stood in the pillory for geese Crab killed. How did Crab reward him? Simply by lifting his leg and peeing against Madam Silvia's skirt. That's how much Crab appreciated Launce's extraordinary sacrifice.'

There was a silence and then Dennis said, 'Mr Rumpole.'

'Yes, Den.'

'I am not quite following the drift of your argument.'

'It's just that Launce led an unrewarding life trying to take the blame for other people's crimes. Don't be a martyr! And don't pretend to be a murderer.'

'I'm not.'

'Of course you are. And what do you think it's going to get you? A vote of thanks from all the foxes in Gloucestershire?'

'I don't know what you're saying, Mr Rumpole.'

'I'm saying, come out of some fairy-story world full of kind little furry animals and horrible humans and tell the truth for a change.'

'What's the truth?'

'That you didn't kill anyone. All right, you can shout blood-thirsty threats and work yourself into a fury against toffs on horses. But I don't believe you'd really hurt a fly. Particularly not a fly.'

It was early in the morning, before Jamie MacBain had disposed of bacon and eggs in his lodgings, and I was alone with my client in the cells. I hadn't bothered to tell Gavin about this dawn meeting, and he would have been distressed, I'm sure, at Dennis's look of pain.

'I'm thinking of the cause.'

'The cause that can't accept that we're all hunters, more or less?'

'And I told you I was guilty.'

'You told me a lie. That was always obvious.'

'Why? Why was it obvious?'

'Because you had no way of knowing that Dorothea Eyles was going to leave the hunt and gallop between the trees in Fallows Wood.'

'You can't prove it.' For a moment Den was lit up with the light of battle.

'Prove what?'

'That I'm innocent.'

'Really! Of all the cockeyed clients. I've had some dotty ones but never one that didn't want to be proved innocent before.' It was early in the morning and the hotel had only been serving the continental breakfast. I'm afraid that my temper was short and I didn't mince my words. 'I can prove you didn't carry wire out of the wood at one o'clock on the day before the murder.'

'How?'

'Because you were doing something far more sensible. You were making love to Janet Freebody.'

There was a silence. Den looked down at his large hands, folded on his lap. Then he looked up again and said, 'Janet's not going to say that, surely?'

'Yes, she is. She's going to brave the story in the *Sun* and the giggles in her class at the comprehensive, and she's going to say it loud and clear.'

'I'm not going to let her.'

'You can't stop her.'

'Why not?'

'Because you're going to tell the truth also. And because you're going to fight this case to the bitter end. With a little help from me, you might even win.'

'Why should I fight it?' Den looked back at his hands, avoiding my eye. 'You give me one good reason.'

So then I gave him one very good reason indeed. 'You can't tell the story,' I warned Den. 'It can't be proved and you'd be sued for libel. But I promise to tell them what I know.' Later, when I had finished with Den, I went into the robing-room to slip into the fancy dress and there I confronted little Marcus, combing his mouse-coloured hair. 'My learned friend,' I told him, 'I'm serving an alibi notice on you. Only one witness.

You'll be a sweetheart and tell darling old Jamie that you don't want an adjournment or anything awkward like that. I can rely on you, can't I, Marcus?'

'Why on earth' – Marcus looked like a very determined mouse that morning – 'should you think that you can rely on me?'

'Because,' I told him, with some confidence, 'if you behave well, Hilda and my good self might see our way to looking after Bernadette while you're away in the Chancery Division.'

'That' – little Marcus turned back to the mirror and the careful arrangement of his hair – 'puts an entirely different complexion on the matter.'

'What is the single most important fact about this case, Members of the Jury? The fact which I ask you to take with you into your room and put first and last in your deliberations. It's just this: Mrs Eyles met her death half a mile from any point where the hunt had been. If Dennis Pearson intended to kill her, how did he lure her away to that remote woodland path? Did he offer her a date or an assignation? Did he promise to give her the winner of the two-thirty at Cheltenham? Or did he say, "Just gallop along the track in Fallows Wood and you'll probably be killed by a bit of tight wire I stretched there yesterday lunchtime"? How did he organize not only that she should be killed, but that she should go so far out of her way to meet her death? It was impossible to organize it, was it not, Members of the Jury? Doesn't that mean that you must have doubts about Dennis Pearson's guilt?

'Remember, he was seen at various places during the hunt, with the other saboteurs, shouting his usual abuse at the riders. So whoever went off and lured Dorothea Eyles to her death, it certainly wasn't him. And remember this, if he's guilty, the whole hunt would have had to come down that track, and the first to be killed wouldn't have been Mrs Eyles but the Master of Foxhounds himself, or one of the hunt servants. The Prosecution haven't even tried to explain these mysteries and, unless they can explain them, you cannot be certain of guilt.'

Little Marcus was reading a guidebook on Elba and Jamie MacBean was feigning sleep, but the Jury was listening, attentive and, I thought, even interested. The abrupt manner in which the Judge had put an end to my cross-examination of Tricia had, I suspected, aroused their curiosity. What was it that the Judge didn't wish them to know? There are moments when an objection sustained can be almost as good as evidence.

And then Janet Freebody turned out to be a dream witness. When Jamie asked her, in what he hoped were withering tones, if she was in the habit of having sexual intercourse with men at lunch time, she answered, with the smallest of smiles, 'Only when my feelings overcome me, my Lord. And I am dreadfully in love.' The Judge was silent, the Jury liked her, and little Marcus closed his eyes and no doubt thought of Clarissa. I needn't go through all the points I made in my final speech, brilliant as they were. They will have become obvious to my readers who have studied my cross-examination. Jamie summed up for a conviction which, as the Jury were not entirely on his side, was a considerable help to us. They were out for an hour and a half, but when they came back they looked straight at my client and said not guilty. The Judge then threatened to have those cheering in the gallery committed to prison for contempt; however astute he was, and however long ago he'd been born, he had failed to achieve a conviction.

When I said goodbye to Dennis he was hardly overcome with gratitude. He said, 'You prevented me from striking a real blow for animal rights, Mr Rumpole. I came prepared to suffer.'

'I'm sorry,' I said, 'Janet Freebody ruined your suffering for you. And I think she's prepared to give you something a good deal more valuable than a martyr's crown.'

Months later, on the occasion of a long-suffering member of our Chambers becoming a Metropolitan magistrate, he gave his fellow legal hacks dinner at the Sheridan Club. She Who Must was not of the party, having gone off on yet another visit to Dodo and the dog Lancelot on the Cornish Riviera. As I sat trying not to drop off during one of Ballard's lively discussions of the Chambers' telephone bill, I saw, softly lit by candlelight, Rollo Eyles and Tricia Fothergill dining together at a distant table. I remembered a promise unfulfilled, a duty yet undone. I excused myself and went over to join them.

'Horace! Have a seat. What's going on over there? A Chambers dinner? This is the claret we choose on the wine committee. Not too bad.' Rollo was almost too welcoming. Tricia, on the other hand, looked studiously at her plate.

'So' – Rollo was signalling to the waiter to bring me a glass – 'you won another murder?'

'Yes.'

'I suppose the Jury thought another of those revolting antis did it.'

'I don't suppose we'll ever know exactly what they thought.'

'By the way, Horace' – Rollo looked at me, one eyebrow raised quizzically – 'I thought you'd like to know. Tricia and I are going to get married.'

'I thought you would be.'

For the first time Tricia raised her eyes from her plate. 'Did you?'

'Oh, yes. Rollo would never have left his wife, while she was alive. Thank you.' The waiter had brought a glass and Rollo filled it. 'You know my client, Dennis Pearson, was going to take the blame for the crime. He thought, in some strange way, that it might help the animals. He only agreed to fight because, if he was acquitted, the real murderer might still be discovered.'

'The real murderer?' I still didn't believe that Rollo knew the truth. Tricia knew it and I wanted Tricia to be sure I knew it too.

'What made Dorothea ride through Fallows Wood?' I looked at Tricia. 'I think you were riding with her in the hunt and you said something, probably something about Rollo, which made her want to know more. But you rode away and she followed you. When you got on to the track between the trees, you knew where the wire was and you ducked. Dorothea was galloping behind and knew nothing. It was a very quick death. You carried on and jumped the stile, where your horse lost a shoe.'

'You're drunk!' Rollo had stopped smiling.

'Not yet!' I took a gulp of his wine.

Tricia said, 'But I saw the man with the wire.'

'At least we proved you were lying about that. The only person who went into the wood with wire was you. And when you'd done the job, you dumped the coil in the sabs' van. You knew one of them could be relied on to threaten the riders. Dennis said exactly what was required of him.'

'Tricia?' Rollo looked at her, expecting her furious denial. He was disappointed.

'You repeat one word of that ridiculous story, Rumpole' – he was angry now – 'and I'll bloody sue you.'

'I don't think you will. I don't think she'll let you.'

'What are you going to do?' Tricia was suddenly businesslike, matter of fact.

'Do? I'm not going to do anything. I don't know who could prove it. Anyway, I'm not the police, or the prosecuting authority. What you do is for you two to decide. But I promised the man you wanted to convict that I'd let you know I knew. And now I've kept my promise.'

I drained my glass, got up and left their table. As I went, I saw Rollo put his hand on Tricia's and hold it there. Did he not believe in her crime, or was he prepared to live with it? I don't know and I can't possibly guess. I had left the world of the hunters and those who hunted them, and I never saw Rollo or his new wife again, although Hilda did tell me that their wedding had been recorded in the *Daily Telegraph*.

When I got back to our table I sat in silence for a while beside Mrs Justice Erskine-Brown, Phillida Trant that was, the Portia of our Chambers.

'What are you thinking about, Rumpole?' Portia asked me.

'With all due respect to your Ladyship, I was thinking that a criminal trial is a very blunt implement for digging out the truth.'

Some weeks later Ballard entered my room when I was busy noting up an affray in Streatham High Street.

'I'm sending you a memo about the telephone bill, Rumpole.'

'Good. I shall look forward to that.'

'Very well. I'll send it to you then.' Apparently in search of another topic of conversation, the man sniffed the air. 'No dogs in here now, are there?'

'Certainly not.'

'I well remember the time when you had a dog in here.'

'No longer.'

'And we had to call a Chambers' meeting on the subject!'

'That was some while ago.'

'And you assure me you now have got no dog here, of any sort?'

'Close the door behind you, Bollard, when you go.'

As he left, the volume was turned up on the sound of heavy breathing. Bernadette was sleeping peacefully behind my desk.

Hilda's Story

MRS HILDA RUMPOLE TO DOROTHY (DODO) MACKINTOSH

My dear Dodo

This is the story Rumpole will never tell. It's not at all how he would wish to present himself to his audience, his readers, his ladies and gentlemen of the Jury, in the many accounts he has written of his brilliance down at the Old Bailey, and his particular cleverness at enabling assorted scamps and scally-wags to escape their just deserts. Such work Rumpole sees as protecting the liberty of the subject, Magna Carta and the presumption of innocence, and he assumes a look of injured nobility when I tell him that he has become little more than an honorary uncle to the Timson family – that infamous clan of South London villains, whom Rumpole, when under attack, says I have to rely on for my scanty housekeeping allowance. Rumpole also prides himself on his worldly wisdom and the fact that he can see further through a brick wall than anyone else in the legal profession, the entire Bench of Judges, including the Lord Chancellor, the Master of the Rolls and the Lords of Appeal in Ordinary. My reason for writing this account, entirely for my own consumption – and yours, Dodo, as my oldest schoolfriend and one who has seen the best and the worst of Rumpole at quarters which may have been, from time to time, uncomfortably close – is to show that in the case of *R. v. Skelton*, I certainly saw further through a brick wall than he could without having passed a single Bar exam. I pulled off a coup to equal his in that case which he never tires of telling us about, the Penge Bungalow murders.

Rumpole is, I have to tell you, Dodo, a bit of an actor. I don't think you've ever seen him in Court, with his grey wig askew (dirty when he bought it secondhand from the ex-Attorney-General of the Windward Islands, and now even dirtier after fifty years of contact with Rumpole's glistening forehead), his gown tattered (he never asks me to mend it), and his waistcoat gravy-stained (he seldom allows me to take it to the Smarty Pants cleaners, who give a pretty reliable service in the Gloucester Road). He is, of course, acting the part of an inadequately paid and outspoken rebel against authority. And when he's at home, and you've seen this, my dear old Dodo, many times, he is acting the part of a free spirit imprisoned, through no fault of his own, in marriage, just as the clients in his less successful cases are banged up in Wormwood Scrubs.

Dodo, I don't know if you remember the case of Michael Skelton? There was a good deal about it in the *Daily Telegraph* at the time, but I know you object to the amount of quite gratuitous violence there is in crime-reporting these days, and perhaps you were too busy with your splendid watercolours to notice it! Your 'Lamorna Cove on a Wet Afternoon' hangs over the gas fire as I write and I can *feel* the dampness rising. We all know that young people have got quite difficult lately. Since our Nick went off to teach in Florida and married his Erica we have hardly been close but, quite honestly, Dodo, families have got to learn to live together and, although no one knows better than you how completely maddening Rumpole can be at times, it's impossible to imagine Nick ever being tempted to beat his father to death with a golf club, the crime which the Skelton boy was up for. I mean, it simply isn't the way youngsters from nice homes carry on.

You can imagine the poorer sort of people doing it – people on drugs and income support and such like – although I can't really imagine them having golf clubs available in their entrance halls. But young Michael Skelton seemed to have nothing in the world to complain about. His father, Dimitri Skelton, was a very successful surgeon. (I believe there was Russian blood in the family somewhere and, although I can connect the Russians with violence, they don't seem, in the course of history, to have played much golf . . . Just a passing thought, Dodo.) Anyway, the father did cosmetic surgery, I think they call it, which means giving other rich people better bosoms or more youthful faces. I don't know, you and I have lived quite comfortably with our faces since we were a couple of new bugs, all wet around the ears, at Chippenham. And, as for Rumpole's face, it seems to me, it is quite beyond repair – only fit for demolition, I might think sometimes – but I wouldn't say it aloud, Dodo. Apart from the various acts he puts on, he can be quite a sensitive soul at times and I don't wish to cause him pain – unless it's absolutely necessary.

Well, as I was saying, this business of yanking up people's bosoms and tightening their cheeks had provided the Skeltons with an extremely nice converted farmhouse in Sussex, with a marble swimming-pool (there were colour pictures in the *Weekend Telegraph*), a jacuzzi, four cars in the garage, and all the trimmings, which we tell each other we wouldn't want but might quite like if we found them provided for us. Having been sent to Lancing, and then to Cambridge to study medicine and follow in his father's footsteps (or should I say his father's wrinkles, Dodo, if you will forgive a small joke on a serious subject) the boy should have been grateful or, if he couldn't have managed that, at least not beaten his father about the head with a favourite driver.

Late one afternoon – could it have been last July? Anyway, I know it was still light – I came home from my bridge lesson with Marigold Featherstone. She's Lady Featherstone, you know, the Judge's wife, and we both suffer from extremely irritating husbands. Of course she's not an *old* friend like you, Dodo. Marigold and I were never together as new bugs at Chippenham. She is a somewhat younger person but actually not as silly as she quite often sounds. Well, when I got back to Froxbury Mansions, I found Rumpole home surprisingly early. An urgent conference in Pommeroy's Wine Bar over a bottle of Château Fleet Street usually takes up at least two hours at the end of his working day. He had his jacket and waistcoat off and sat in his braces and shirtsleeves in a flat with closed windows, where you might have roasted a chicken without the help of the gas oven.

'You seem to be enjoying that brief, Rumpole,' I said as I

forced open a reluctant window, 'even more than a bottle of your usual third-rate red wine.'

'Are you planning to freeze me to death before I can pull off what promises to be one of my most sensational defences?' he asked in a plaintive sort of voice.

'If you're cold' – when dealing with Rumpole, you have to be merciless – 'there's always your cardigan. Don't tell me you've found another Penge Bungalow murder?'

'Penge Bungalow? What was that exactly? I tell you, *R. v. Skelton* is going to outdo the fame of all my previous triumphs. This is a case which will go down in history. I envisage a final speech lasting at least a day.'

'Why will you be giving the final speech, Rumpole?'

'Because, needless to say, I am doing this case – as I did that rather more trivial affair of the Penge Bungalow – alone and without a leader!'

'Is that because all the leaders realize that Michael Skelton has simply got no defence?'

'It's because my instructing solicitor knows that I am a far greater defender than all those self-important amateurs who wrap themselves in silk gowns and flaunt the initials Q.C. after their names.'

'And who is your instructing solicitor?' I asked to put an end to a speech which, after a lengthy marriage to a permanent non-Q.C., I could repeat by heart. 'Some owner of a South London bucket-shop? Cut-price defences in hopeless murder cases offered to close friends of the Timson family?'

'What nonsense you do talk, Hilda.' Rumpole sighed heavily. 'My instructing solicitor happens to be Daniel Newcombe. To those of us who know him well, and undertake his more difficult cases, he will always be Danny Newcombe.'

'And who is this Danny, anyway?' It seems extraordinary to me now, Dodo, that there was ever a time when I had to ask such a question.

'Hilda, I know you are a complete innocent when it comes to the law, but Newcombe, Pouncefort & Delaney are quite the grandest firm dealing in criminal matters. Danny is the senior partner. I believe that, with me in command, his firm may pull off something sensational.'

'You mean, get a boy off who murdered his father.'

'Who is *alleged* to have murdered his father. Young Michael is as innocent as you are until he's proved guilty.'

'I don't suppose you'd get Nick off if he'd beaten you to death with a golf club.'

'If he'd beaten me to death I'd scarcely be in a position to stand up and defend him.' Rumpole had the intolerable expression he puts on when he thinks he's said something clever, so I ignored this and opened another window.

'And, by the way, Danny's invited me to dine with him at the Sheridan Club next Thursday. He said he wanted to get to know me better.'

'If that's what he wants, he'd be better off talking to me. At least he'd get an unbiased opinion.'

'Oh, you're coming too.'

'You mean, he's invited me?'

'"And do bring your lovely wife." I assume it was you he had in mind.'

'But, Rumpole! You hate going to dinner at the Sheridan Club. You say it is full of pompous bores and . . .'

'Hilda! We all have to make sacrifices if we are to rise to the top in the legal profession, and for the sake of a brief from Newcombe, Pouncefort & Delaney, I would willingly rent a dog-collar and go to dinner with the Archbishop of Canterbury. My God! There's a wind whistling round my knees that must have come straight from the Ural Mountains.'

'I told you, Rumpole. If you're feeling cold, then go and put on warm clothing.'

He left me then, his lips forming those syllables which, I had come to understand, spelt out She Who Must Be Obeyed.

'I'm sorry to drag you to my club, which I'm afraid you'll find desperately dull, Hilda. My excuse is, we need girls like you to lighten the old place up occasionally. Don't we, Horace?' Danny fished the bottle of Chablis out of the ice-bucket and considerately refilled my glass when I was only halfway through the potted shrimps.

'I really don't know.' I think it was the first time I'd known

Rumpole short of an answer to a question. 'I'm not a member here.'

'Not a member here?' Danny seemed genuinely surprised. 'We must do something about that. Or are you against Horace joining the Sheridan, Hilda? Do you want to keep an eye on him at home?'

'I wouldn't mind in the least. Life at home's far more peaceful without him. That's provided he can spare time from his other port of call.'

'What's that?'

'Pommeroy's Wine Bar.'

'I don't know it, I'm afraid,' Danny smiled. 'But it sounds interesting.' I felt a sudden affection for a lawyer who'd never heard of Pommeroy's. 'Is that white Burgundy all right for you?' he was asking Rumpole with what I thought was admirable consideration. To which my husband replied, if you can believe this, Dodo, 'Thanks. If you're asking, I'd rather have a slurp of the red. A couple of slurps, if that's at all possible.' I suppose I should count myself lucky that Rumpole and I don't go out to dinner very much.

When the red wine came Rumpole said thoughtfully, 'From the photographs it's obvious there'd been a hell of a fight in the hall. The grandfather clock was knocked over and stopped at ten forty-five. You noticed that, of course?'

'Horace, please! We didn't come here to talk shop.' Danny put a hand on his Counsel's sleeve and I noticed how clean and well-manicured his fingernails were, something you could hardly say for Rumpole. 'We came here to get to know each other. Thee are some pretty dusty old members here, Hilda. But we do boast of quite decent pictures. There' – he turned to look at the portrait of a man in a wig, smiling in what I thought rather a condescending way, over the mantelpiece – 'Richard Brinsley himself, a true wit like you, Horace, and a man of many love affairs.' Not like Horace, I thought. I began to wonder about Danny . . . I must confess, Dodo, he seemed a great deal more interesting than any other lawyer I'd met. He had come alone, and there had been no mention of a Mrs Newcombe. Later I remember him saying that he dreaded going back to his empty flat. 'Since I lost Deirdre it's been lonely. I mean, you can't have much of a conversation with the television. Television is full of discussion programmes, but you can't discuss anything with it. It's not like a wife. It never answers back.' When Danny said this, I had to fight a curious impulse to put my arm round his shoulder to cheer him up. But, of course, I couldn't do that. Not in the Sheridan Club, not with Rumpole sitting there slurping his claret and asking a really charming Indian waiter if he had anything remotely resembling a toothpick about him.

'And over there,' Danny said, 'is the portrait of Elizabeth Linley, whom Sheridan loved. There's a difference in years, of course, but don't you think, Horace, she has a distinct look of Hilda about her?' Rumpole looked surprised and said, 'No.'

At the weekend Rumpole and I went shopping in Safeway's. I'd honestly rather he'd stayed at home but he'd become strangely attentive since our dinner at the Sheridan and had insisted on coming with me 'to help lug the heavy stuff'. As I wandered round the shelves – I have to tell you, Dodo, I wasn't even comparing prices, I was shopping in a kind of dream – I couldn't help thinking of Danny (whom I no longer thought of as Mr Newcombe). I wondered how old he might be and thought he was timeless, anything from the late fifties to the early seventies. His skin was a healthy pink and as free from wrinkles, apart from laugh lines around the eyes, as it would've been if Michael Skelton's father had been at it, which I was quite sure he hadn't. His eyes had a strange brilliance, an almost unearthly blue, I remembered as I reached for a tin of pineapple chunks which turned out to be Japanese bean shoots when I got them home. Danny's eyes were as blue as the clearest of seas on the sunniest of days. No reflection, Dodo, on the wonderful way you painted a wet afternoon in Lamorna. I thought about the well-cut tweed suit, the highly polished brogues, the silk handkerchief in the breast pocket and the slight whiff of some completely masculine eau de cologne. And I thought of the way he leant towards me, one ear always turned in my direction, seriously interested in anything I might have to say.

And then I saw Rumpole come padding towards me down

the long alleyway between the fancy breads and the pet food, wearing his weekend uniform of a woollen shirt and cardigan, tubular grey flannels and battered Hush Puppies, worn with the feet turned distinctively outwards. He shouted at me from some distance, 'Blood, Hilda! I've been thinking about blood.'

'Stop making an exhibition of yourself, Rumpole! Everyone can hear you,' I rebuked him in my most penetrating whisper as soon as he was in earshot.

'You know why Michael Skelton didn't want to be a doctor like his father?'

'Young people nowadays are always trying to be different from their parents.'

'It was the blood. He couldn't stand the sight of blood.'

'Well, some people *are* squeamish, Rumpole. We all know you're not squeamish about anything. Now, have you achieved that simple little list I gave you?'

'Of course I have. Perfectly painless business, shopping – *if* you've got a system. I can't imagine why women make such a song and dance about it.' At the checkout he returned to his favourite subject. 'The hallway was covered in blood. Splashes on the walls, pictures, everything in sight.'

'I see you forgot the washing powder, Rumpole, and I said frozen potato chips not potato *cakes*. Is that the result of your wonderful system?' The girl at the till was looking a little green and I wanted to shut my husband up. Bloodstains are not the thing to talk about on a Saturday morning in Safeway's.

'How would a boy who couldn't stand the sight of blood commit a murder? Poison, perhaps. An electric fire dropped in the bath, even. Hire a contract killer and he wouldn't have had the embarrassment of taking any part in it. Surely the last thing he'd choose is the way they deal with pigs in an abattoir?'

'Rage, Rumpole,' I told him, 'can drive people to forget squeamishness. Now, give me the list and I'll finish off the shopping properly.'

How would you react, Dodo, to being called a girl? I'm quite sure Mizz Liz Probert, the young radical lawyer in Rumpole's Chambers, would have found it patronizing at best and probably deeply insulting. And yet we *were* girls, weren't we, Dodo, when we passed notes to each other in the back row during Gertie Green's French lesson, or when we used watercolours as experimental make-up in the art room? I don't know how it is with you, but I don't feel that we've changed much over the years. A little stiffer when I wake up perhaps, a lot more weight to push up off the sofa, and a few hopes dashed. Do you remember when I made a desperate plan to marry Stewart Granger – I was going to bump into him, one morning, quite casually, during the Christmas holidays in Cornwall Gardens, where that awful little show-off Dorothy Bliss told us, quite erroneously, he lived at the time. So far as I remember, Dodo, you were after James Mason? So you've ended up unmarried and I'm landed with Rumpole, and sometimes I find myself wondering which of us is more lonely. But I think we're still girls at heart, time has never robbed us of that, and when Danny called me one in the Sheridan, I felt, to be quite honest with you, nothing but pleasure.

All the same, it was a huge surprise as the telephone rang one morning, when I was looking forward to keeping myself company in Froxbury Mansions, and some secretary's voice said, 'Mrs Rumpole? I've got Mr Daniel Newcombe on the line.'

'It must be some mistake. Mr Rumpole's in Court and . . .'

She told me there was no mistake. He'd asked for Mrs Rumpole particularly. I was surprised, Dodo, and even more surprised when I found myself alone with Danny at a corner table at the Brasserie San Quentin, and Danny, who had a meeting with clients in Knightsbridge – a millionaire from Kuwait, who, he told me, was accused of pinching nighties from Harrods – was pouring out Beaujolais for me. He had a double-breasted suit on this time, and gleaming black brogues instead of brown, and some regimental or old school tie, and the same bright blue eyes glittered at me.

'Bit of luck,' he said, 'you happened to be free.'

'It wasn't luck at all. I'm free nearly always.'

'And your husband's in Court?'

'Luckily. When he isn't, you'd think there'd been a death in the family.'

'And when he's busy, it's because there's been a death in

someone else's family?' This was rather neatly phrased, don't you think, Dodo?

'Oh, he doesn't always do murders. It's usually thieving, or something or other indecent. Murder is a rare treat for Rumpole. Of course, he's full of himself because you decided to let him do Skelton alone and without a leader.'

'I didn't want the Jury to think Michael's a poor little rich boy.' Danny looked at me and I saw the wrinkles at the corner of his blue eyes. 'If I'd had a top Q.C., they'd've said, "That's what he does with his father's money!" Your husband, with his gravy stains and torn gown, might make the good citizens of East Sussex feel quite sorry for the lad.'

'Is that the reason?'

'I'm sure I can be honest with you, Hilda.'

'I'm sure you can but I don't think I'll tell Rumpole.'

'It might be more tactful not to.' I don't know why I felt a sort of excitement then, Dodo. It wasn't only because I was drinking wine in the middle of the day – something I never do. It was, I'd better admit it, because Danny and I were sharing a secret, something which Rumpole would never know. I mean, to put it far more bluntly than he'd have liked, it seemed he had been chosen because of the state of his waistcoat.

'Rumpole seems to have found a defence.'

'Good for him. I've been racking my brains.'

'Apparently Dimitri Skelton was desperate for Michael to become a surgeon.'

'Naturally the father wanted his only son to follow in his footsteps. Didn't Rumpole's son . . .?'

'Oh, Nick had seen quite enough of the law to put him off it for ever. It seems that Michael Skelton almost fainted at the sight of blood.'

'So he told me.'

'So how, Rumpole's going to ask, could he have committed such a blood-stained murder?'

Danny didn't answer my question, or Rumpole's question, for a while, but when he did, he was still smiling. 'I suppose money overcomes a lot of finer feelings. A terrible lot of money.'

'You mean . . .?'

'About three million in the estate. New faces can be expensive. And the profits from the beauty treatment had been cleverly invested.'

'So it wasn't just a quarrel about the boy's career?'

'More serious than that. Dimitri's wife died of cancer five years ago. It seems he never got on with her family. Michael was his sole heir. He stood to gain a huge amount of money from his father's death. That's the big hurdle Rumpole's got to get over. I don't envy him that, however much I envy him other things.'

'I can't imagine what sort of other things.'

'Like your companionship.' I have to say, Dodo, I found Danny's answer strangely disturbing. 'By the way, Hilda,' he went on, in quite a businesslike way, to cover my confusion, 'I've got seats at Covent Garden next Thursday. If you happen to have a free evening?'

> *'Underneath these granite crosses*
> *No one counts their gains and losses –*
> *But they whisper underground*
> *All the answers they have found.*
>
> *How else can our quarrels end?*
> *Our enemy become our friend?*
> *The dead around us all reply*
> *Peace be with you – you must die.'*

'What's that, Rumpole? Poetry?'

'Hardly. Not really poetry. Not the sort of stuff that gets into *The Oxford Book of English Verse*, the Quiller-Couch edition.'

'I thought it was quite good. At least it rhymes. Who wrote it?'

'It's called "In a Sussex Graveyard" by Michael Skelton.'

'He's a poet?'

'He wants to be. His father wanted him to be a plastic surgeon. Personally, I don't believe he was suited to either profession. If you're going to be a poet you've got to be able to stand the sight of blood.' This was one of Rumpole's epigrams – or *bons mots*, as Gertie Green used to call them, Dodo. So, as you may imagine, I ignored it. I was more than a little irritated by him. He had a load of new instructions open on the kitchen table so I could hardly get at my chops and mash, and he was slightly above himself, as he always is after he's been to see a customer in prison in an important case, and he seemed to regard his day trip to Sussex as something of a day out.

'A strange young man, Hilda. He seems to think that because he writes poetry he exists in a world of his own, rather above ordinary mortals. Can you believe it, he hardly bothered to answer my questions? He didn't seem nervous or frightened or even especially concerned about the case. Just bored by it. But he's wrong, you know. In my opinion poetry is written by people who live quite ordinary lives and have a way with words:

"Golden lads and girls all must,
    As chimney-sweepers, come to dust."

The man who wrote that went to the pub and worried about his bank account.'

'You must be a poet then, Rumpole. You spend enough time in Pommeroy's Wine Bar. Was that another bit of young Skelton?'

'No, another bit of old Shakespeare.' You know, Dodo, Eng. Lit. was never my strongest subject, but Rumpole needn't have sounded so patronizing.

'You're not telling me this boy killed his father because he wanted to be a poet, are you, Rumpole?'

'I'm not telling you he killed his father full stop. That is a fact which still has to be decided by twelve honest citizens of East Sussex.'

I gave a heavy sigh, signalling that I'd heard quite enough of Rumpole on the burden of proof to last a lifetime. Then I said, 'I should think he probably killed his father for the money.'

'Hilda, have you accepted a brief for the Prosecution?'

'Well, he was his father's sole heir, wasn't he? And I don't suppose cosmetic surgery comes cheap.' In my anxiety to put Rumpole down I had said rather more than I intended.

'How did you know that?' Rumpole gave me his sharp cross-examiner's look.

'I really can't remember. Hadn't the mother died and Michael was the only child? It said that in the *Daily Telegraph*.'

'It's not quite true that he's the sole heir.' Rumpole ferreted about among his papers for a copy of the will. 'Skelton left £100,000 to his secretary – an attractive girl, Michael tells me: "And all the rest and residue of my estate to my son, Michael Lymington Skelton, or if he should predecease me to my cousin Ivan Lymington Skelton, now resident in Sydney, Australia."'

'Well, Michael didn't predecease him, did he? Otherwise you wouldn't be defending him.'

'Oh, Hilda, what a wonderful grasp of legal principles you have!' It was at moments like these that I was strongly tempted to tell Rumpole why he'd been chosen to defend young Skelton alone and without a leader. However, I contented myself with saying, 'I don't really know what kind of defence you've got.'

'The grandfather clock' – Rumpole produced the photograph of the bloodstained hall – 'stopped at ten forty-five. I told you that was important.'

'Why?'

'Michael's got an alibi for ten forty-five.'

'Really. What is it?'

'That poem. He was walking in the beechwoods, about half a mile from the house. Composing it.'

'But you said it wasn't even a good poem.'

'Or convincing evidence. In itself. But there were witnesses.'

'Who?'

'New Age travellers. That's what they call themselves. Sort of politically correct gypsies. They were camping in the woods and Michael stopped to talk to them. He even recited his poem to them, so they might remember him.'

'So have you found these gypsies?'

'Not yet. But today, after we'd seen Michael in Lewes gaol, old Turnbull took me for a walk to the beechwoods near Long Acre, the Skeltons' home.'

'Who's Turnbull?'

'Newcombe's clerk or legal executive – I think that's what they call themselves now. I really don't know what you find so funny, Hilda.'

'Just the thought of you, going for a walk in any sort of wood.'

'One has to make sacrifices – for all-important murders. We found some tyre marks, the remains of a sort of camp-fire and an old shirt bearing the legend LESBIANS WITH ATTITUDE.'

'Talking of Danny Newcombe, Rumpole.'

'I wasn't. I was talking of his clerk.'

'Danny's invited me to Covent Garden next Thursday. He didn't think you'd care for the opera.'

'Opera? Isn't that the stuff Claude Erskine-Brown takes young legal ladies to when he's trying to get off with them? No, Danny's damned right, I wouldn't care for it. I'd rather be stuck before Mr Injustice Graves on a six months' post office fraud. But why on earth has he asked *you*, Hilda?'

'I think, Rumpole' – the time had come to take his mind off his murder case and give him something serious to worry about – 'that Danny Newcombe has taken a bit of a shine to me.'

There was a short silence and then Rumpole said, 'The first thing Danny Newcombe's got to do is to find those New Age travellers.' At that moment he didn't seem to give a hoot whether his instructing solicitor had taken a shine to me or not, and, quite honestly, Dodo, I decided to proceed accordingly.

Well, there I was in the Crush Bar at Covent Garden Opera House, which I had often heard about, but never been crushed in before. It was the first interval and I had sat for an hour and a half in the great gold and plush of the place, letting the music wash over me and getting little clue about the story from the words which occasionally flickered on a screen over the stage. I couldn't really understand what the fuss over Don Giovanni was all about. He was a shortish, stout person, who sweated a good deal, and I would be prepared to say that, as a lady-killer, he didn't rank far ahead of Rumpole. I had bought something new and blue for the occasion from Debenham's and, by an amazing coincidence, Danny was also wearing a dark blue suit with a cornflower-coloured tie which made him look younger and went stunningly with his eyes. There at least, I thought, as he came towards me with two glasses of champagne, was a man who might have made a thousand and three conquests in Spain.

'This is a great treat for me,' he said, as he handed me a glass clouded by the iced wine. 'My favourite opera with a truly sympathetic companion!'

'A treat for me,' I told him, 'to be in a theatre without having to give Rumpole a quick dig with my elbow every time his eyes start to close and the snores threatens to begin.'

'I hope he doesn't mind our going out together?'

'Not at all. He's perfectly happy to be left at home with your murder.'

'Oh, dear. Is he boring you to death with that?'

'I do get rather a lot of the Skeltons. When I was trying to eat my supper the other night he insisted on reading out the father's will . . .'

'Was that interesting?'

'Not really. Rumpole seemed surprised to discover that Michael wasn't the only person to benefit.'

'Oh, you mean the Aussie secretary. We checked up on her. She had gone to a girlfriend's birthday party in Wimbledon and spent the night there. She was celebrating until she went to bed around two in the morning. Anyway, I doubt if she'd be much of a hand with a golf club. You know, looking round this bar, I can see a good many people I've acted for when they were charged with various offences. They all look extremely prosperous and, of course . . .'

'And what?' I asked when he hesitated, smiling.

'Envious. That I'm with such a charming companion. Oh, good evening, Judge.' We were joined, not by one of Danny's clients, but by a woman sent to try them, Mrs Justice Phillida Erskine-Brown, always known to Rumpole (who, for many years, had had the softest of spots for her) as the Portia of his Chambers. In her wake trailed her husband Claude Erskine-Brown, now a Q.C. You will remember, Dodo, that he only achieved what Rumpole calls Queer Customer status when his wife was made up to a scarlet judge, adding beauty and an unexpected degree of serenity to the Bench. 'Hilda Rumpole and Mr Newcombe. Good heavens!' her ladyship delivered judgement. 'It *is* a surprise seeing you two here together.'

'Hilda had a free evening and I was happy to introduce her to my favourite opera.'

'I'm afraid it's not my favourite Leporello.' Claude Erskine-Brown looked as though he'd been invited to a feast and offered a damp sausage-roll. 'Quite the worst "Non voglio piu servire" I've ever heard at the Garden.'

'But, of course, you're not usually listening so carefully, are you, Claude? You're usually far more interested in whomever you happen to have invited. Isn't that true?' The Judge accompanied her question with a sort of humourless laugh, and I remembered that she'd learnt the art of cross-examination from Rumpole.

'How's the Skelton case going?' Claude asked Danny with, I thought, ill-concealed anxiety. 'I only ask because my diary's getting pretty full since I took silk.'

'Oh, I think Danny's going to leave *R*. v. *Skelton* to Rumpole.' I spoke as a person with inside knowledge. 'He's not taking in a leader.'

'Can that be right?' Claude looked seriously concerned, but his wife said, 'Not a bad idea, that. Rumpole's always at his best in a hopeless case.'

'But he'll start attacking the police. He'll try to destroy all the prosecution witnesses. They won't like that sort of thing in East Sussex.' Claude moved closer to Danny in a vain attempt to sell his forensic talents as though they were double-glazing, and Phillida leant forward and asked for a word in my ear. They were a few words and they came as a question, 'Don't tell me you're going out with Danny Newcombe?'

'Well, isn't it obvious?'

'Is it?'

'We're not exactly sitting at home watching television, are we?'

'But, you mean . . . you're actually going *out* with him.'

'Yes, of course. Well, we've only actually done it twice.'

There was what I believe is known as a pregnant pause, and then Phillida said, 'And Rumpole doesn't know?'

'Well, he knows about the opera. I haven't told him about

the other thing.' I had, you will remember, Dodo, kept quiet about the Brasserie San Quentin.

The Judge gave me a long look of deep concern and said, 'I promise you, Hilda, your secret is absolutely safe with me. And if Claude starts blabbering, I'll do him for contempt of Court!'

Before she could explain this urgent but mysterious message, the interval was over and the bell called us to the further adventures of the Don, who, in my honest opinion, Dodo, couldn't hold a candle to Danny Newcombe in the lady-killing department.

In the second interval we saw Phillida and Claude together in the distance, talking to each other with unusual vivacity and studiously avoiding looking in our direction, as though we were tedious relations they hoped they need have nothing further to do with, or people suffering from a contagious disease. I might have taken some offence at this, Dodo, but I was too busy listening to what Danny was saying to me. Although his eyes were still bright and smiling, his voice had become low and unusually serious. He looked at me, Dodo, in what I can only describe as a yearning sort of way and said, 'Sometimes I long for a complete change in my life.'

'I'm sure we all do.'

'I'd love to give up the legal treadmill. Go away to the sunshine. Perhaps with new companions, or a new companion. You know what, Hilda?'

'No, what?' Quite honestly, Dodo, I was feeling quite weak at the knees, and I'm quite sure it wasn't the champagne when he said, '"'Tis not too late to seek a newer world."'

I couldn't look at him, Dodo. I glanced across at the Judge and her husband, and caught them turning hurriedly away. Then I stared down into my glass of champagne and knocked the rest of it back. My mouth was full of air bubbles which made me suddenly speechless, which may have been just as well.

'"Push off, and sitting well in order smite / The sounding furrows;"' Danny went on and I realized that he was reciting poetry, as Rumpole does at important moments. I don't know what you'd've thought, Dodo, but I was quite sure that the words contained some sort of an invitation. Then we were summoned to see the last bit of the opera, where the General's statue comes to supper, and the unfortunate lady's man is sent down to hell.

Some nights later the scene was far less exciting. Rumpole and I were sitting either side of the gas fire in Froxbury Mansions, and I thought I'd discover whether he was noticing me or not, so I asked, 'What are those photographs, Rumpole?'

'Oh, nothing very sensational.' His brief in Skelton was spread out on the floor around him. 'Pictures I got Turnbull to take in the woods. The remains of the gypsy encampment. I'm getting Newcombe to advertise: ANY NEW AGE TRAVELLERS WHO MET A YOUNG MAN WHO READ POETRY TO THEM ABOUT 10.45 ON THE NIGHT OF 12TH MAY ... I thought he should put it in *Time Out*, the *Big Issue* and the *East Sussex Gazette*. Can you think of anything else politically correct gypsies might read?'

'I have no idea *what* gypsies read.' I went back to the *Daily Telegraph* crossword, but Rumpole was in an unusually communicative mood. 'I had the most extraordinary conversation with Claude Erskine-Brown,' he told me. 'By the way, he's prosecuting me in Skelton. Graves is coming down to try it.'

'I thought Claude was busy angling to lead you.'

'Did you hear that at your bridge lesson?'

'Yes.' It was very strange, Dodo, how quickly I took to telling Rumpole some untruths.

'Well, Danny wouldn't brief him, but Ambrose Clough, who was prosecuting, went off with jaundice and Claude got the brief. Oh, yes, and he's leading Mizz Liz Probert. She'll know what paper New Age travellers take in, I'll have to ask her. Anyway, Claude and I were chatting about the case and he suddenly said, "Philly and I are tremendously sorry for you, Rumpole."'

'Why on earth did he say that?' I asked, knowing the answer.

'That's what I asked him. I told him I'd done far more hopeless cases than Michael Skelton, and I thought I'd been able to put up with the funereal Graves in the past and the old Death's Head had no further terrors for me. Furthermore, having Claude for the Prosecution was always a distinct plus for the Defence . . .'

'How very kind of you, Rumpole, to tell him that.'

'And then he said the reason he felt sorry for me had got nothing to do with the case.'

'Well, what on earth had it got to do with?'

'"If you don't want to talk about it, of course, I understand perfectly," Claude said, in a most mysterious way.'

'"Have you been taking lessons from the Sphinx, old thing?" I ventured to ask Claude. "You're speaking in riddles."'

'"It must have come" – the chump Claude looked at me extremely seriously – "like a dagger through the heart."'

'"If you're speaking of my occasional fits of indiscretion I find a quick brandy works wonders," I told him, and then he asked how long you and I had been married.'

'And what did you tell him?'

'That I couldn't remember.'

'Typical, Rumpole. Entirely typical. Well, it's getting along for forty-seven years.' Nearly half a century, and, I wondered, Dodo, if that made it too late to seek a newer world?

'And then Claude said the most extraordinary thing,' Rumpole said, quite seriously. '"It might make it a lot easier if you were thinner."'

'What did he mean?'

'I asked him that and he said, "Positions and all that sort of thing." Can you understand what he meant?'

'No.' That was true, at least, Dodo. Quite honestly I couldn't.

'Do you think anything would be easier if I were thinner?' Rumpole was puzzled.

'Putting on your socks, perhaps.'

'Perhaps *that's* what he meant.' Rumpole thought it over. 'Claude said that a simple diet might make all the difference. Then he gave me a long, sorrowful look and buggered off.' I turned my own long, sorrowful look back to the *Daily Telegraph* crossword, which had managed to defeat me, and silence reigned in Froxbury Mansions until Rumpole said, 'Skelton's fixed for the fourth of next month. It'll be quite an occasion. Danny Newcombe's attending the trial in person. He'll be staying in the same hotel. Rather a drawback, really. I don't want to spend every dinner time getting unhelpful advice from my instructing solicitor.'

'Rumpole . . .' I started, not after I'd thought things over, but after I'd given way to a sudden, irresistible temptation, 'can I come too?'

'Come where?'

'To East Sussex Assizes. To stay in the . . .'

'The Old Bear hotel?'

'Yes.'

'Why on earth would you want to do that?'

'Because it's a long time since I've seen you in action, Rumpole.'

'What *do* you mean, Hilda?'

'I mean, it's a long time since I've seen you in Court.'

'Well, if you really want to. I'll be working most evenings. I mean, I don't suppose it'll be much fun for you.'

'Oh, I think I might like it quite a lot.' And then, after we had sat in silence for another five minutes, I said, 'Rumpole . . .'

'Yes, Hilda.'

'You know the poem you're always reciting: "'Tis not too late to seek a newer world . . . / We are not now that strength which in old days / Moved earth and heaven;"?'

Rumpole's brief was folded and in his lap with his hands over it. He sat back in his chair, his eyes shut and recited:

'We are not now that strength which in old days
  Moved earth and heaven; that which we are, we are;
  One equal temper of heroic hearts,
  Made weak by time and fate, but strong in will
  To strive, to seek, to find, and not to yield.'

'"And not to yield,"' I repeated. 'I'm not quite sure about that.'

It was true, Dodo, I hadn't seen Rumpole in Court for a long time, and I had to admit, reluctantly, that as soon as he took his seat in the second row (the front one is reserved for the

Queer Customers), he was a man in his element. Mr Justice Graves looked just like Rumpole's description – a man on his deathbed about to make a will, cutting out almost everyone he could think of. Claude, opening the case, looked nervous and not always in complete control of his voice, which trilled up into a high note of indignation as he described the peculiar horror of the crime. Liz Probert, sitting behind him, was frowning as though she feared some terrible insult to women was about to be offered in evidence, although I couldn't for the life of me see how the case concerned women at all. Michael Skelton, in the dock, was small, dark, pale and neat, looking absurdly young, like a schoolboy at some important event such as a prizegiving, and not like a murderer at all; although I wondered if there was any particular way of recognizing a murderer, and how many of those old clients Danny recognized in the Crush Bar might have done someone in. Only Rumpole, spreading out his papers, dropping them on the floor, pushing back his wig to scratch his head, or pushing it forward as he yawned heavily and closed his eyes, seemed likely to dominate the courtroom. He looked, I thought, far more at home than he ever does in Froxbury Mansions; and I was in no doubt he would continue his real life in Court whether I was there or not.

I sat with the solicitors, next to Danny. The Court was so full that we had to sit close together and, from time to time, when he moved to look for a statement or pass a note, his arm brushed mine. I could feel the roughness of his sleeve and smell his discreet eau de cologne. On Danny's other side sat Mr Turnbull, a squat, red-faced man with a bull neck who called me madam and already seemed to regard me as attached to his employer rather than to Rumpole.

Well, Dodo, I don't know how much you remember of the Skelton murder trial, and I'm certainly not going to bore you by going through all the evidence that took up one of the strangest and most unnerving weeks of my life. Of course *I* remember every moment of it. But it's difficult for me to write about it without cold shivers and flushes of embarrassment but, as we used to say long ago, if you can live through Gertie's French lessons, you can live through anything, so here goes.

First came the Beazleys who worked for Skelton and lived in a cottage about fifty yards from the back door of Long Acre. Mrs Beazley, a wobbling, panting woman, with a look of perpetual discontent, was the cook–housekeeper, and Mr Beazley, a short, weaselly sort of person, who spoke as though he was always apologizing for something – perhaps working for the deceased plastic surgeon meant always having to say you're sorry – was the driver and handyman.

'I'm afraid Mrs Beazley has quite a taste for old war films, my Lord,' Beazley apologized from the witness stand. 'And we had the one on again about the Yankees fighting over a Pacific island . . .'

'Iwojima,' Claude was helping him, as Rumpole growled, 'Don't lead . . .'

'Iwojima. Thank you, sir. Well. The guns were firing and the bombs dropping and my wife, sir, was thoroughly enjoying herself, and that was it until the film finished. I doubt very much if we'd've heard anything from the house before then.'

'And what time did the film end?' Claude asked.

'I think it was about eleven o'clock time.'

'And what happened after that?'

'Well, I heard someone calling from the house. It was a sort of call for help.' And then Beazley described how he went across to the house and found a scene of bloodstained confusion, and saw Michael Skelton holding a golf club beside the battered body of his father, who appeared to be already dead.

'Now then, Beasley.' Rumpole, it seemed, was prepared to sail into the first prosecution witness with his guns blazing. 'You heard a cry for help and you crossed the yard and went into the house. How long did it take you to get into the hallway from the moment you heard the cry?'

'I might venture to suggest . . . a matter of seconds, sir.'

'You might venture to suggest it, Beazley. And you might well be correct. And when you first saw Mr Skelton Senior, he appeared to you to be dead?'

'He appeared to me to be very dead, sir.'

'So if he was dead, then he's unlikely to have been able to call out for help a few seconds before?'

'That would seem to follow, Mr Rumpole.' A weary and

sepulchral voice came from the Bench, apparently inviting Rumpole to get on with it and not waste time. At which my husband, with elaborate courtesy, said, 'Thank you, my Lord. Thank you for that helpful interruption in favour of the Defence. Now, Beazley, you say you and your wife were watching a war film at ten forty-five?'

'He has already told us that, Mr Rumpole.' Graves was making it clear that he hadn't joined the defence team.

'Any rumpus in the hallway which took place at that time would have been drowned by the battle of Iwojima?'

'Yes, sir.'

'So you heard no voices from the house at that time?'

'No, sir.'

'But when you did hear a voice, we are agreed it could hardly have been that of Mr Skelton Senior?'

'No, sir.'

'It might very well have been the voice of my client, young Michael Skelton?'

'It might have been.'

'Calling for help for the man he's accused of murdering? Is *that* your evidence?'

And without waiting for a reply, Rumpole swathed himself in his gown and sat down in triumph. This gesture had the unfortunate effect of tempting Graves (Mr Injustice Gravestone, I've heard Rumpole call him) to restore the balance by asking the witness if it were also possible that the young man was calling for help because he didn't realize how seriously he had injured his father, a proposition with which the obedient Beazley was delighted to agree.

'The Judge is against us,' Danny turned to whisper to Rumpole.

'So much the better.' Rumpole was indestructibly cheerful. 'We'll make the Jury realize how highly prejudiced the old Death's Head is. That might get us a sympathy verdict.'

But all looks of sympathy seemed to me to drain out of the Jury's faces when Mrs Beazley struggled into the witness-box and described what had happened when she served dinner on that fatal evening. From the first course ('a nice roast beef done with my own horseradish sauce and all the trimmings,' she panted), she'd heard father and son arguing, and the son getting more and more agitated, as Mr Skelton stayed calm and determined. Michael would have to finish his medical course or he wouldn't get another penny, his father told him. And, if he thought he could live on poetry, he was welcome to try it, eked out with a bit of National Assistance, but he wasn't going to live for nothing in his father's house. I thought it was strange of Mr Skelton to tell his son all that with a heavily breathing cook in the room, but perhaps he was one of those people who think their workers are deaf and blind, and probably have no real existence at all.

The evidence was at its worst when Mrs Beazley came back with the treacle tart and cream. 'Mr Skelton always had a sweet tooth, bless him, and I make treacle tart according to my own recipe which, he said, couldn't be beaten.' She had no doubt about what she heard. Michael was standing up and shouting at his father, 'I've got a whole long life to lead and you might die quite soon.' There was a sudden, awful silence and then Mrs Beazley went on. 'They just looked at each other and neither of them said anything. I set the plates for their dessert and just got out as quick as I could.' When she came back to clear away at about nine o'clock, the dining-room was empty and she thought they had probably gone into the drawing-room. (Mr Skelton always liked the coffee served *with* the pudding.) Then she settled down to watch her favourite war film and knew no more until her husband told her that he'd telephoned for the police and an ambulance was on its way.

Rumpole always told me that if a witness was telling the truth you should keep the cross-examination short. I don't know why he told me that, Dodo. He could hardly have thought that I'd ever be in a position to cross-examine anybody. So he was clearly anxious to get Mrs Beazley out of the witness-box as quickly as possible. He established the fact that Michael might have left the house after dinner and not returned until after eleven, and then he let her go. Danny turned his head and whispered in my ear, 'He hasn't even challenged her evidence about Michael saying his father might die quite soon. The strongest evidence against us and Rumpole hasn't even contradicted it!' It seemed to me he spoke more in sorrow than in anger.

I'll spare you all the gory details, Dodo. Rumpole particularly enjoyed himself with the forensic evidence. He seems to regard himself as the greatest living authority on bloodstains. There was blood of his father's group on Michael's hands, his shirt cuffs, on one of his sleeves and on the head of the golf club. Rumpole seemed to be suggesting that the blood got on Michael's clothes when he knelt down to examine his father's wounds, and I thought that he had made a bit of headway with this theory, in spite of the gloomy interventions of the learned Judge. 'I thought your client didn't want to be a doctor, Mr Rumpole,' was one of them. 'I don't know why he would have been so anxious to examine the wounds.' Rumpole also got the scene of the crime officer to agree that the grandfather clock in the hall had fallen over and stopped at ten forty-five, which probably would have been the time of the attack. He also established that it was a Saturday, and that Skelton had been playing golf and had left his bag of clubs in the hall, so his assailant wouldn't have had far to look for a weapon.

At four o'clock Claude got to his feet and asked to raise a matter. He told the Judge that the Defence had filed an alibi notice stating that Michael Skelton was in the woods reading a poem he had written to some New Age travellers. However, Mr Rumpole had failed to give the Prosecution the names of the witnesses they intended to call to support this so-called alibi.

'Well, Mr Rumpole?' Graves asked in a voice as near to doom as he could make it. 'Why has the Defence not supplied the names of their alibi witnesses?'

'Simply because we haven't traced them yet, my Lord.' Rumpole can, when hard pressed to it, manage a disarming smile.

'And what steps have you taken?'

'We have advertised, my Lord, in several publications.'

'Aren't these travellers committing an offence under the new Criminal Justice Act? I imagine they were camping without permission in Mr Skelton's woodland.'

'Even those who commit offences read newspapers, my
Lord. We shall produce the advertisements we placed in *Time
Out*.'

'Time *what*, Mr Rumpole?' His Lordship was making a
note.

'*Out*, my Lord. The *Big Issue* and the *East Sussex Gazette* –
have you got them there?' Rumpole leant forward to whisper to
Danny who, in close consultation with Turnbull, was going
through the file.

'I'm afraid we didn't.'

'You didn't what?'

'I'm sorry, Mr Rumpole.' The red-faced clerk was looking
extremely flustered. 'Pressure of work. I'm afraid the advertising got overlooked.'

'Overlooked! This is a charge of murder, you know, not an
unrenewed dog licence.' I saw Claude and Liz Probert smiling,
enjoying Rumpole's discomfiture, and Danny, as shocked as he
was, told Rumpole, 'I'm afraid there's no excuse for Turnbull.
Of course, I can't deal with every detail personally. I've told
him that.'

Well, Rumpole managed to wipe the anger off his face and
stood up and smiled again. He asked Graves to adjourn the
case so that the advertisements might be published. After
lengthy argument, his Lordship refused to grant an adjournment. The case could take several more days and would be
fully reported in the press. When he left Court, Rumpole said,
'Thank God, he's given us a ground for appeal!' But I could
tell that he was still very angry indeed.

Rumpole was late getting back to the hotel that night, so
Danny and I decided to go in to dinner without him. It was
hardly cheerful in the dining-room, distinctly cold, hung with
sporting prints and heavy with the smell of furniture polish
and overcooked lamb. Whilst we were waiting for the soup,
Danny said, 'I'm seriously worried about your husband,
Hilda.'

'Why?' At that moment I wasn't worrying about Rumpole
particularly.

'He's started off badly, getting on the wrong side of the

Judge. And I'm not at all sure the Jury like the way he's
handling our case. Do you honestly think he wants to win?'

'I honestly think Rumpole wants to win every case he does.
The only thing is . . .'

'What, Hilda?'

'I think he was cross because the advertisements hadn't gone
in the papers.'

'I tore Turnbull off a most terrific strip about that. Not that
I believe it was a particularly hopeful line of country. Can you
imagine any of these travellers turning up? Let's face it, Hilda,
those sort of free spirits spend their time keeping away from
the law.'

The soup came then, beige in colour and not particularly
hot. In spite of these drawbacks, I was enjoying my stay at the
Old Bear, particularly when Danny gave me one of his most
twinkling looks and said, in a confidential sort of way, 'Hilda?'

'Yes.'

'Will you do something for me?'

I don't know why it was, Dodo, that I felt suddenly breathless when he asked me that, but I tried to answer him as calmly
as possible. 'It depends what it is. But I'll try . . .'

'Keep an eye on Rumpole, will you? I know he's not pleased
with me, and he may not tell me what he's got in mind. So if
he's planning to take any sort of peculiar line . . .'

'What sort of peculiar line?'

'I don't know. But if he gets any really strange ideas you will
let me know, won't you?'

'I suppose so,' I found myself saying. 'Well, all right.'

'Thank you, Hilda dear. I knew I could trust you.' And then
he put his hand on mine.

I can see it now in my mind's eye, Dodo. My hand was on
the table and his, slightly suntanned, with the carefully tended
nails and heavy gold signet ring on the little finger was on top
of it, and then I looked up and there was Rumpole standing in
the doorway. I think he must have seen where Danny's hand
was but he never mentioned it; and as for me, well you may be
sure, Dodo, I never asked him whether he had seen it or not.

'I hope you don't mind. We've started without you.' Danny
gave my husband his most dazzling smile.

'Apparently.' Rumpole was far from friendly.

'You haven't been working?' I wanted to sound sympathetic.

'Someone has to. I've been down the cells with Michael.'

'I don't suppose you learnt anything new?'

'As a matter of fact I did. Something he hadn't the sense to tell us before. He said he didn't, out of respect for his father's memory. He's a strange lad. It's almost as though he wants to get himself convicted. Anyway, he gave me the name of the doctor.'

'Which doctor, Rumpole?'

'Fellow called Christie-Vickers. Minds a shop somewhere in Harley Street. Michael isn't sure where. About two weeks before the quarrel . . .'

'You mean the quarrel when Skelton got killed?' Danny interrupted.

'No, I mean the quarrel Mrs Beazley heard at dinner . . . His father told him that Christie-Vickers had diagnosed cancer of the prostate. That's why he said the skin doctor might die soon, and he couldn't expect Michael to live on doing a job he hated.'

'He's only just thought of that?' Danny looked doubtful.

'He's only just decided to tell us. Perhaps he's beginning to realize that even poets can't ignore the evidence against them.'

'It wasn't a particularly nice thing for the boy to say to his father.' I was feeling as sceptical as Danny did about young Skelton.

'He's not accused of not being particularly nice, Hilda.' Rumpole was quite sharp with me, Dodo. 'He's on trial for murder.'

'So you want me to get on to this Christie-Vickers?' Danny got out a little pad in a leather case and made a note with a gold pencil.

'Now would hardly be soon enough.' So Danny went off to telephone and, when the waitress came to take his order, Rumpole astonished me. 'Just a green salad if you can manage it,' he said. 'And perhaps a hunk of cheese. A smallish hunk, I suppose.'

'Rumpole' – I looked at him – 'are you sickening for something?'

'I don't think so,' he said. 'Are you?' We didn't say much more until Danny came back and said he'd found Dr Christie-Vickers in the telephone book and tried his house number but got no reply. He'd ring the Harley Street consulting room in the morning.

That night I honestly thought I must tell Rumpole. Tell him what, you may say after reading this far, which, as a story of illicit love and infidelity, would be considered too uneventful for your average parish magazine and would certainly not get a line in the *Daily Telegraph*. But Danny had invited me, hadn't he, not only to the opera but to share his life? What else was all that stuff about it not being too late to seek a newer world and pushing off and smiting the sounding furrows? I was sitting up in my twin bed in the Old Bear as these thoughts flickered through my mind, looking at the yellowing walls and repeated patterns of daisies on the curtains and bed covers, the elecric kettle and assorted tea bags on a rather unsteady shelf, and hearing the sound, like a whale rising up through the waves and spouting, which was Rumpole cleaning his teeth in the *en suite* bathroom. When he came back with his hair standing on end, in his old camel-hair dressing-gown and striped pyjamas, he looked, I thought, like a small boy to whom something unexpectedly outrageous has suddenly happened. I really don't know why it was, perhaps I wanted to put off telling him for as long as possible, or did I want to justify myself by putting Rumpole in the wrong? Quite honestly, Dodo, I can't be sure why I did it, but I said, 'Danny's worried about the way you're doing the case.'

'Danny? Why do you call him Danny?'

'You said everyone did.'

'Perhaps *everyone* hasn't got a special reason. Have you, Hilda?'

'I told you. He's worried about the case.'

'I expect he has other worries on his mind also. What was that wretched opera you saw? *Don Giovanni*? That bed-hopping Spaniard had a few worries on his plate from what I remember. And didn't he come to a sticky end?'

'Rumpole!' I didn't like the turn the conversation was taking. 'You're going to lose Skelton, aren't you?'

'Why? Am I in the habit of losing cases?'

'It has been known. Danny . . .'

'Let's call him Mr Newcombe, shall we? Now that you've really got to know him.'

'All right. Mr Newcombe says it's obvious Michael did it for the money. Even if you lose and he goes away for ten years, he'll come out and collect three million.'

'Did Newcombe tell you that?'

'He didn't say he couldn't.'

At this point, Rumpole sat down on the edge of my bed and began to talk in a slow and patient sort of way, as though to a child. 'A murderer can't profit as a result of his crime, Hilda. If Michael's convicted of murder he won't be able to benefit from his father's estate. Newcombe knows that as well as I do.'

'Did Michael know?'

'He said he did, when I pointed it out to him.'

'Then he must be an extremely stupid young man.'

'Not at all. He got a scholarship to King's. And he writes poetry, of a sort.'

'So he does the murder in a way which is almost certain to be discovered, hangs about by the corpse and calls for help so that a witness can see him with a bloodstained golf club in his hand – all so that he won't get the money from his father's will. Does that really sound likely?'

Rumpole, who had been looking at me with a mixture of resentment and grief, now spoke with unusual respect. 'Hilda,' he said, 'I don't know how you managed it but you seem to have hit on a better argument than a little queasiness at the sight of blood.'

'Thank you.' I was able to look dignified and aloof. 'You're perfectly at liberty to use it, Rumpole.'

He couldn't quite decide how to reply to that and, instead of raising the difficult subject of Danny Newcombe again, he took off his dressing-gown, hung it up, as usual, on the floor and climbed into his twin bed.

'Perhaps we should go to sleep now. You've got the police interviews tomorrow, remember?' I switched off my light and he switched off his.

'Hilda?' His voice came out of the darkness. 'Have you got anything else to tell me?'

'No, Rumpole. Not now, anyway. Let's go to sleep.'

But I didn't. I lay awake for a long time. And I was surprised to find that I was no longer thinking about pushing off and smiting the sounding furrows. I was remembering the pale, calm face of Michael Skelton and asking myself questions which became more unnerving as I stared into the darkness where familiar objects, such as Rumpole's fallen dressing-gown and the electric kettle, seemed to take on new and surprising shapes.

The next morning, I have to confess, Dodo, was boring. I was sitting in Court, turning over the photographs bound together in a slim volume and marked Prosecution I (you see how used I'm getting to courtroom expressions). Before the Judge sat, Mr Turnbull told us that he'd rung Christie-Vickers's secretary, and the doctor was driving through France with his wife but they'd do their best to find him. Rumpole had received the news fairly calmly, for him, and when the police were reading accounts of their interviews with Michael from their notebooks, he closed his eyes and acted the part of someone enjoying a light doze, in order to show the Jury how unimportant the evidence was. Turnbull had gone off on some errand and I was alone in the front row with Danny, who was also finding it hard to keep his eyes open.

I'm not as squeamish as young Michael, Dodo. You know how we used to open up a frog in biology lessons? And I had no qualms about cutting up a rabbit when we used to eat them after the war. But, I must confess, I flicked over the photos taken on the mortuary slab and the colour close-ups of the head wounds. I enjoyed the exterior views of Long Acre and thought that such a spread would be a step up from Froxbury Mansions. And then I got to the most recent photograph of the beauty doctor when he was alive – the picture the police used for the purposes of identification. He was as handsome as his son, with the same high arched nose, full lips and large, dark eyes and black hair. Only, the surgeon's good looks were more arrogant, more supercilious, and his hair was just starting to turn grey over the ears. I thought it odd that the victim looked more dangerous and even brutal than his killer.

I yawned a little, bit my tongue to keep myself awake, and then looked up to the ceiling of the old courtroom. The public gallery was quite full but there, standing in a doorway at the back of it, I saw Skelton, the murdered man.

I swear to you, Dodo, I saw him clearly. There were no head wounds, of course. In fact he looked remarkably well and suntanned as though, since his death, he'd found time for a Caribbean holiday. Indeed, he looked as though he were still on holiday. His white shirt was open at the neck, he wore a blazer and, I think, fawn-coloured trousers. He seemed to be reasonably interested in the proceedings caused by his death, although I couldn't help noticing, as the police evidence droned on, that he covered his mouth with the back of his hand, politely concealing a small yawn.

I must have given a small gasp, an intake of breath, hardly a cry and certainly not loud enough to stir Rumpole from his simulated sleep. But Danny looked towards where I was staring and it seemed to me that he aged quite suddenly. I had, at my most besotted moments, given him late fifties and now he was middle seventies, without a doubt, in front of my eyes. He got to his feet and, in trying to go quietly, stumbled a little, bowed to the Judge and left the Court.

I made sure that Michael, sitting in the dock, his hands folded in his lap and his head down, couldn't see who was in the gallery immediately above his head, and so he missed the sight of his father returned from the grave and looking extremely well. I also saw that Rumpole wasn't looking. Then I turned my eyes to heaven again and there, by the gallery doorway, Danny Newcombe was whispering urgently to the ghost – for if it wasn't Dimitri Skelton's spirit I had no idea, I promise you, Dodo, what it was. But I was going to find out. I got up, did my best possible bow to the Judge who, as usual, also looked dead, and left the Court. As I left Rumpole opened one speculative eye.

I came out of the courtroom door into the entrance hall and I heard voices from the stairs which lead down from the public gallery. You know what I took into my head to do, Dodo? I hid! You might think I'm not exactly the shape for it now, not sylphlike as I was when we squeezed in behind the dormitory door to jump out and scare that ghastly little show-off, Dorothy Bliss, witless. But the hall was pretty dark and there were some thick stone pillars and I tucked behind them somehow. I was just in time to see Danny and the deceased cross to the main entrance. Danny was talking quietly but his voice echoed across the stone floor. I suppose he might have been speaking to a ghost. 'I told you to keep away,' he was saying. 'I told you to go back down under and never come near me again.' Then he pulled open one of the big glass doors and they both stepped out into the sunlight.

I tried to walk quietly across the hallway then. My footsteps seemed to clatter and echo but there was no one there to notice me. I stood by the doors and looked through to the sunlit car park. I saw the figure that seemed to be Dimitri Skelton get into a car and Danny slammed the door. The car was parked very near the Law Court steps and I could see a sticker for RUDYARD'S CARS, LEWES on the back window. I was even able to notice part of the number: ARB and I think it ended with an S. You see, at that moment, I had stopped being a discontented housewife with longings for a newer world. At that moment, Dodo, I had become a lawyer – or at least a detective.

Oh, when the man with the suntan and the open-necked shirt drove the car away, I made quite sure, Dodo, that he wasn't dead. I've had very little experience of the after-life, but I don't think dead people go driving around East Sussex in a hired car.

I didn't go back to Court that afternoon; I had too much to think about. What was that poem of Michael's? Something about 'The dead around us all reply'? Well, the dead, or someone very like the dead, had brought a message to me which I knew was important although I didn't fully understand it yet. There was a lot still to find out so I took a taxi to Long Acre, about five miles out of the town, and asked the driver to wait for me.

It had obviously been a lovely old farmhouse, Dodo, but there was something rather flashy and obviously false about it,

like a woman who has had too obvious a face-lift and wears a
lot of costume jewellery. Carriage lamps gleamed brassily on
each side of the front door. There were white plastic lounging-
chairs around the pool bar, a lot of chalky-white statues from a
garden centre – cherubs and frogs and things like that – and an
ostentatious burglar alarm. I walked round to the back of the
house and knocked at the Beazleys' door. There was some
noisy shuffling and gasping from inside and then Mrs Beazley
opened it. I introduced myself, said I was just passing and
there was something I wanted to ask her. When I told her that
my husband, one of the lawyers in the case, doted on treacle
tart, and I was never quite sure of the recipe, she invited me in.
She was alone and seemed in need of company.

'Spoonful of black treacle,' she told me, 'to go with the
golden syrup. Three teaspoonfuls of white breadcrumbs and
the grated rind of a lemon. I'll write it out for you if you'd
like.' At which, she sat down heavily at the kitchen table.
'Would you?' I said. 'That would be extremely kind.' While
she made off in the direction of a pencil and paper I carried on,
'Life must seem strange to you, without Mr Skelton?'

'I don't know what's going to happen to us,' Mrs Beazley
gasped. 'I don't know what he's done for us in the will. Mr
Newcombe's not told us about that.'

'Mr Newcombe?'

'The gentleman what's the family solicitor.' She waddled
back to the table and sat down with the pencil and paper which
she forgot about as we moved away from the subject of treacle
tart.

'Yes, of course.' I knew what Dimitri Skelton had done
about the Beazleys in his will – nothing. He didn't seem to
have been a man who cared much for the people who worked
for him but I didn't say that. I said, 'Mr Skelton must have
been very handsome. Such an attractive man, wasn't he?'

'To some people, I suppose.' She spoke as though she had a
considerable contempt for handsome men, this scarcely mobile
woman with a passion for war films. 'To that secretary of his, I
suppose he *was* attractive. That's why we were going to have to
leave anyway. Even if none of this had ever happened.' She
spoke of 'this' – a terrible murder, Dodo – as though it had

been an inconveniently leaking radiator. 'Raymond and I couldn't have stayed after *she* took over.'

'You didn't like Miss – ?'

'Miss Ashton. Miss Elizabeth Ashton. Came into my kitchen and said she'd show me how to cook. Trendy food, she said, like they got in some place up in London. Pasta – that meant spaghetti – but she *would* call it pasta. Well, you don't need much brain to boil spaghetti and I could do that, but she wanted it with scallops and squids in it, and stuff like that. If he wants fish, I told her, what about a nice fish pie? One night she decided to cook for herself and made a terrible mess of my kitchen. Clean out the saucepans? She wouldn't have considered it!'

'Wasn't she Australian?'

'That's no excuse though, is it? Yes, I think he said she'd come from Australia. Mr Skelton had some relation over there, cousin or something, and he'd said she might be suitable for the job. Far too suitable Raymond and I thought he found her. We couldn't have stayed. Not if she were permanent.'

I have to say, Dodo, I felt quite triumphant, when she told me that. You see, I was out on my own and far, far ahead of Rumpole. I thought perhaps that Mrs Beazley had still more to tell me, so I said, 'I did admire the way you gave your evidence. It must have been terrifying standing up there in front of all those people in wigs.'

'Oh, I didn't mind once I got started. And your husband was very nice to me. Nice as pie he was, though they warned me he could be a bit of a terrier with a witness. The trouble was . . .' She hesitated.

'Yes, Mrs Beazley. What was the trouble?'

'Well, you can't tell them everything, can you? You're only meant to answer *their* questions.'

'Is there anything you didn't tell them?'

She panted a little and then said, 'Yes. About Raymond.'

'What about Raymond?'

'Well, he missed a bit of the film, a really good bit he missed, when they was hand-fighting. He had to go to the toilet, if I have to be honest. And he looked out of the window, upstairs.

And in the yard between us and the big house there was a car parked.'

'A strange car?'

'Well, Ray'd never seen it before. He happened to notice the number. I know the first three letters, if you like, because they happen to be his initials.'

'What are your husband's names? Raymond Beazley?'

'Albert Raymond Beazley. We went to Mr Newcombe, you know, and asked if we should say anything about it. But he said it wasn't that important. I think it may have been, don't you?'

'Yes, Mrs Beazley, I think it may have been very important indeed. Now, do you think there's any chance of a cup of coffee while we write out that recipe?' It was a bit of cheek saying that, I knew, in someone else's kitchen. But I felt I'd earned it.

When I got back to the hotel I had some telephone calls to make: one to Rudyard's Cars and another to the house of Dr Christie-Vickers – who, I was not altogether surprised to find, had got back from his holiday trip in France. Then I have to confess, Dodo, that such was my mood that I went straight into the bar and ordered myself a small sherry, and there was the bull-necked Turnbull in conversation with a strange-looking creature. I believe she was a woman, but her hair was clipped and bristly, a sort of stubble all over her head. At first sight, her face seemed beautiful and even young. But when you looked more closely she had lines which, like you or I, Dodo, she made no attempt to conceal. She wore patched jeans and a sort of camouflage jacket over a T-shirt, and enormous earrings. She was smoking what seemed to be a homemade cigarette and talking very quietly, so I couldn't overhear what she was saying. After a while she got up and left. Turnbull finished what looked like a dark and generous whisky and said, 'Good evening, Mrs Rumpole,' on his way out.

'Was that a New Age traveller?' I asked him as though my curiosity was perfectly idle.

'How did you know?'

'I thought that was what they looked like.'

'She'd read about the case in the local paper.'

'And you're going to call her?'

'Hardly. You know what she said?'

'I've no idea.'

'That she knew we needed one of the travellers to give evidence and she'd say anything for a hundred pounds in the hand. Terrible world, isn't it, Mrs Rumpole? They live like pigs and then pervert the course of justice. Good evening to you.'

'Good evening, Mr Turnbull.' I tried my best to look as though I believed what he'd told me. Then, I'm very much afraid, I ordered another sherry. I had hardly finished it when Rumpole came into the Downlands Bar looking tired and not particularly happy. I told him to order a large red wine – a bottle of it, if that would cheer him up – and invited him to sit beside me.

'Hilda, are you feeling well?' He looked, I have to admit, apprehensive. 'Have you something to tell me?'

'A good many things. But first let me ask you something. What do you call down under?'

'Down under?' The poor man looked entirely confused and, when the first glass of wine was put in front of him, he took a quick and consoling gulp. 'What do you mean?'

'I don't mean hell, Rumpole. I don't mean where Don Giovanni ended up. Where else do you call down under?'

'Do you mean Australia?'

'Yes, Rumpole, I mean Australia.' And, of course, that was what Danny meant.

'Hilda, I asked if you were feeling well. Has this trial been too much for you?'

'Not at all. I was afraid it was too much for *you*. So I've found you a defence.'

'I thought you went out shopping.' He gave a distinctly mirthless laugh. 'Where did you get my new defence from, Marks & Sparks? You were out shopping a long time. I was surprised that Mr Daniel Newcombe had the courtesy to stay with me. When he went out of Court this morning I saw you troop after him soon enough.'

'Rumpole' – I hope I smiled tolerantly, as that would have been the most effective way – 'you're never jealous, are you?'

'Jealous? Should I be?'

'No, I really don't think you should. Mr Newcombe and I left the Court because we both saw Dimitri Skelton in the public gallery.'

'Hilda! You're joking . . .' Or delirious, I felt was what he wanted to say.

'It wasn't exactly funny.'

'You mean you saw . . .'

'The man they all say was murdered.'

'I've tried that defence before.' Rumpole was back to his usual patronizing self. 'Witnesses saying they saw the corpse alive after the date of the murder. It has a sort of biblical authority, I suppose, but it never worked particularly well down the Old Bailey. Is that your defence, Hilda?'

'No, as a matter of fact it isn't. We didn't see Dimitri Skelton.'

'Hilda, please . . . I'm tired and unusually depressed.'

'If you're tired, sit back in your chair and listen, Rumpole. I'll tell you who we did see. And then you'd better scoot down to the cells early tomorrow morning and ask your Michael Skelton some pertinent questions.'

'Such as?'

'Such as, how much he knows about Miss Elizabeth Ashton from down under?' He looked at me then and, entirely for his own good, decided to listen quietly. We talked for a while, time enough for Rumpole to get through a bottle of wine, and do you know, Dodo, it was the most serious, even enjoyable, conversation we'd had for a long time. It didn't take him long to get the hang of what I was saying and when he did he knew exactly what to do. When I had told him everything he said, 'I suppose you realize what this means?'

'What it means for Michael Skelton?'

'No. For your friend Danny boy.'

'Yes,' I said, 'I do realize.'

'And you don't mind?'

'No,' I told him, 'I don't think I mind at all.'

Rumpole left very early in the morning to go to the cells and have a further conversation with the non-talkative Michael

Skelton. Dodo, I felt strangely calm. I realized that for the last
few months, ever since that dinner in the Sheridan with Danny
Newcombe, in fact, I'd been nervous, strung up and even, if I
have to say it myself, rather silly. Now I had killed what had
been going on in my mind for a long time. Rumpole always
says that the real murderers he had met – I mean the ones who
had actually done it – were always strangely calm, as though
something had been decided for ever.

Anyway, after Rumpole had gone I had a nice bath, making
full use of the complimentary sachet of Country Garden toilet-
ries in the little wickerwork basket on the glass shelf. I have to
confess that I pinched the verbena shampoo and hollyhock skin
freshener, together with a little packet of sewing stuff. I do find
that staying in hotels brings out everyone's criminal tendencies.
Then I put on the rather nice coat and skirt I had been wearing
in Court and went down to the Sussex-by-the-Sea coffee shop
for the full English breakfast. And there was Danny Newcombe, standing at a table by the door, throwing down his
Financial Times and offering me a seat at his table. I accepted
and sat down.

'So we're going to have the pleasure of your company in
Court again today, Hilda?'

'If you think it's a pleasure, yes.'

'You must have thought it rather strange when I suddenly
bolted out yesterday.'

'I didn't think it strange at all,' I lied.

'I thought I saw someone I knew in the public gallery. Did
you see me go up there?'

'No.' I went on lying.

'It was all a mistake. I mean, it wasn't anyone I knew.'

'Well, that's all right then.'

'Yes.' And then he said, very seriously now, 'I'm afraid
there's not much hope for us.'

I looked at him and said, 'You mean you're afraid there's not
much hope for Michael Skelton?'

'That's what I mean, yes.'

'I don't think you should be so sure of that. You never know
what Rumpole's going to pull out of the bag.'

'You mean you *do* know, Hilda?' He gave me his best

twinkling smile, complete with the wrinkles at the corners of the eyes. 'And you promised to tell me if he had one of his funny ideas, didn't you?' I thought for one dreadful moment that he was going to add 'You naughty girl, Hilda'.

'If I promised that,' I told him, 'I'm afraid I'm not going to keep my promise.'

'Whyever not?'

'Because I don't think Rumpole would like it. Oh, and I'll tell you something else I'm not going to do.'

'What's that?'

'I'm not going to smite the sounding furrows. I have to tell you this, Mr Newcombe. It's far too late to seek a newer world.'

He looked at me then as though he didn't quite understand what I was talking about. I noticed he had dropped a lump of scrambled egg on what he told me was the Sheridan Club tie. I have to tell you, Dodo, that I thought it looked quite disgusting.

'Members of the Jury. Young Michael Skelton may *seem* guilty, kneeling beside the body, his father's blood on his hands, clutching that fatal golf club. But things, Members of the Jury, are not always as they seem. Let us together, you and I, set out to discover the truth behind that strange and terrible apparition. Ladies and gentlemen, look back to the time when you were but twenty years old and consider how you would have felt if you'd had to go into the witness-box and defend yourself on such a serious charge as this. It would be an ordeal for anyone.' And here Rumpole's voice sank to a tone of deep insincerity and he leaned forward and stared at the Jury. 'It must be terrible for the innocent.' Then he straightened up and trumpeted out the summons 'Call Michael Skelton'.

Michael's performance wasn't, of course, anything like as good as Rumpole's. He remained strangely aloof, but he looked pale, proud and vulnerable. He retold his story quite clearly and when Claude came to cross-examine him he seemed suddenly bored, as though he thought it quite unnecessary to go through the whole thing again, and was privately composing a poem. Claude didn't really get anywhere, but when Michael left the witness-box, the Jury probably still thought that he'd killed his father. And then Rumpole surprised everyone, and particularly Danny, by saying, 'My next witness will be my instructing solicitor, Mr Daniel Newcombe.'

Sitting next to me, but as far away as possible now, as though we were a married couple in bed after a quarrel, Danny gave a little gasp of surprise and turned round to Rumpole. 'You don't mean you're calling *me*?'

'That's the general idea. Will you just step into the witness-box?'

Danny had no choice then, but I thought he walked as grimly as a soldier crossing a minefield. When he reached the exposed little platform, he raised the Bible with a great air of confidence and, encouraged by a rare smile from the Gravestone, promised to tell the whole truth and nothing but the truth.

'Mr Newcombe' – Rumpole was quietly courteous – 'you are familiar with the late Dimitri Skelton's will?'

'I should be. I drafted it.'

'He drafted it, Mr Rumpole.' His Lordship did his best to raise a small laugh against Rumpole. Claude even obliged.

'I am aware of that, my Lord.' Rumpole gave a small bow and then turned to Danny. 'Now, in the event of this Jury finding Michael guilty, he won't be able to inherit under his father's will, will he?'

'We all know that, Mr Rumpole, don't we? A murderer can't profit from his crime.' The Judge did his best to patronize Rumpole, who replied with elaborate courtesy, 'Exactly, my Lord! I do so congratulate your Lordship. You have put your finger upon the nub, the very heart, of this case. Now, who is to benefit if my client is found guilty of murder?'

'Well, Elizabeth Ashton will still get her hundred thousand pounds legacy.' Danny looked as though he now felt that the witness-box wouldn't be so dangerous after all.

'Miss Elizabeth Ashton. Remind us. She is Dimitri Skelton's secretary, is she not?'

'That is so, my Lord.' Danny chose to give his answer to the Judge.

'And the residue of the estate?'

'That would all go to the deceased's cousin in Australia, Ivan Skelton.'

'About three million pounds, isn't it?'

'Something like that, yes.'

'Lucky old Ivan.'

The Jury giggled slightly and the Judge looked deeply pained.

'Of course, if Michael Skelton is acquitted,' Danny added in all fairness, 'Ivan doesn't get a penny.'

'So Ivan must be praying for a guilty verdict, mustn't he? This jury comes back and says Guilty, my Lord and, Bingo, the old darling's worth three million.'

'Mr Rumpole' – Graves was deeply distressed – 'is this a subject for joking?'

'Certainly not, my Lord. It is extremely serious. Mr Newcombe, Ivan Skelton is taking a considerable interest in the outcome of this case, isn't he?'

'I imagine he is concerned about it, yes,' Danny had to admit.

'You've met Ivan Skelton, haven't you?'

'Please don't lead.' It was Claude's turn to grumble.

'Very well. Mr Newcombe, have you ever met Ivan Skelton?'

'I met him when he came to England, yes.'

'What does he look like?'

'Well, it's a little difficult to describe . . .'

'It is? Is it? Doesn't he look exactly like this?' At which Rumpole held up the murdered Dimitri's photograph for all to see, and Claude stood up to whinge.

'My Lord, Mr Rumpole is cross-examining this witness.'

'No, I'm not. I'm refreshing his memory. This is a picture of the dead man, isn't it? Does his cousin look almost exactly like him?'

'They are about the same age. Yes. There is a family resemblance.'

'Thank you.' Rumpole began to rummage among his papers and Danny looked only moderately worried.

'Is that all, Mr Rumpole?' Graves sighed.

'Not quite, my Lord.'

'I'm just wondering, Mr Rumpole, how far this line is taking you in your defence?'

'It's taking me to the truth, my Lord. Never mind about the Defence. Now, Mr Newcombe' – he turned to the witness-box, looking far more pugnacious – 'you're the trusted old family solicitor?'

'I'm the family solicitor. And I suppose I'm old . . .'

'Indeed you are! This secretary, Miss Elizabeth Ashton, she comes from Australia, doesn't she?'

'I rather think so.'

'And is she engaged to be married to Ivan Skelton? So he recommended her to his cousin for the job? He's planning to come over later this year and marry her, is he not?'

'I have heard that.'

'Engaged to be married and she spent weekends with his cousin Dimitri and became his mistress?'

'Mr Rumpole' – Mr Justice Graves intruded like the dead general who came to dinner with the Don – 'I wonder what this has to do with the charge against your client?'

'Then wonder on, my Lord, till truth makes all things plain.' I suppose Rumpole was quoting poetry of some sort, as he went on quickly, 'When did you last see Ivan Skelton, Mr Newcombe?'

'I forget . . .'

'Oh, come now. Your memory's not quite as short as that. There are others in Court' – he looked down at me, and I suddenly became others – 'who can tell us, if you don't want to. When did you last see him?' Danny looked at me, I thought sadly, as though I had betrayed him.

'Yesterday.'

'Where?'

'In Court.'

'In this Court?' The Judge raised his eyebrows.

'Yes, my Lord. In the public gallery.'

'No doubt anxious to see if he was going to get his money. And you spoke to him?'

Danny looked at me again, pleadingly. I stared back and he had to answer yes.

'What did you say?'

'Mr Rumpole, that's pure hearsay.' Graves was doing Claude's job for him.

'Of course it is, my Lord. One can always trust your Lordship, with his great experience, to be right on a point of law. Mr Newcombe, I advised your firm to advertise for the New Age travellers and you have not done so?'

'That is right. I'm afraid it got overlooked.'

'You declared that the deceased's doctor couldn't be found and he has been found now, without your help?'

'I'm very glad to hear it.'

'Are you, Mr Newcombe? I shall be calling Mr Beazley to say that a strange car was parked in the yard at Long Acre on the night of the murder. Did you tell him that evidence was irrelevant?'

'My Lord' – Claude was stung into activity at last – 'Mr Rumpole is cross-examining his own witness!'

'Not at all! At the moment I'm making no attack on Mr Newcombe. He may genuinely have thought that the presence of a car hired by the murdered man's cousin was quite irrelevant. And I shall be calling Mr Beazley.'

'I may have said something . . .' Danny was about to agree but Graves did his best to save him. 'Mr Rumpole,' he said, 'I agree that this question is an attack on your own witness. It is quite improper.'

'Then let me ask you a quite proper question. Have you, Mr Daniel Newcombe, been offered a share of Ivan Skelton's winnings to make sure that this young man who stands before us in the dock is convicted of murder?'

'Mr Rumpole.' The pale judge seemed, in his indignation, to be rising in his seat, again, I thought, like some spectre arising from the tomb. He glared at Rumpole with such terrible disapproval that if you or I, Dodo, had been in his place I honestly think we'd have simply collapsed, as we felt like doing when Stalky Sullivan gave us one of her looks and said she'd have to let our unfortunate parents know we were a disgrace to the school. Rumpole just stood there, smiling in an unusually polite way and, I have to say, I rather admired him as Graves went on, 'This cross-examination is going from bad to worse.'

'Oh, I agree with every word that has fallen from your

Lordship.' Rumpole was still smiling. 'We are dealing here with something very bad indeed.'

'Mr Rumpole!' The old Gravestone unclenched his teeth in a vain attempt to call my husband to order. 'Do I understand that you are accusing your own solicitor of entering into a criminal conspiracy to get this young man falsely convicted for murder?'

'Ah, your Lordship puts the matter far more eloquently than I ever could. It is that gift for words that brought your Lordship such success at the Bar.'

In fact Graves hadn't been much of a success at the Bar. I remember Rumpole telling me that he'd got 'his bottom on the Bench thanks to his skill in winning a safe Conservative seat'. I had to admire his Lordship's self-control. The temptation to shout at Rumpole at that point is one which personally I would have found irresistible. 'At least Mr Newcombe is entitled to refuse to answer a question likely to incriminate him, is he not?'

'Of course.' Rumpole got more polite as Graves became more irate. 'As always your Lordship is perfectly right.'

'Then I fully intend to warn him.'

'Your Lordship can take no other course.'

So the Judge warned the witness that he needn't answer this incriminating question. Danny suddenly looked very old – I wondered why I had even put him in his sixties – and much smaller. He was hardly audible when he said, 'My Lord, I prefer not to answer.'

'You prefer not to? That is probably extremely wise.' And Rumpole sat down in triumph, looking meaningfully at the Jury. Danny Newcombe never returned to sit between me and Mr Turnbull but, as soon as he left the witness-box, scuttled out of Court and, to be honest with you, Dodo, I never saw him again. But when I looked up to the public gallery I saw, not Danny talking to Ivan Skelton this time, but a woman with a stubbly head, who looked quite young from a distance, and who had come to tell the truth in spite of Mr Turnbull.

The rest, of course, is history, and I'm sure you read about it in the papers. I don't know whether they gave you Rumpole's final speech or the bit which began so quietly that the Jury had to strain their ears to hear it: 'A young man is walking in the woods, making up poetry and reciting it to some modern-day gypsies when one of Rudyard's Cars drives up to Long Acre. Out of it gets the man who had hired it, Mr Ivan Skelton from Sydney, Australia. Why has he come there? Because he has heard of the love affair between Dimitri Skelton and Elizabeth Ashton whom Ivan was to marry, the girl who came over to work for his cousin and wait for him to join her.

'Nobody heard the quarrel, Members of the Jury. The Beazleys were too busy listening to ancient warfare and the house was empty. Overcome with rage and jealousy did Ivan lift this fatal weapon' – by now Rumpole had the golf club high above his head – 'and strike! And strike! And strike again in the terrible and fatal fight that followed. No one saw Ivan after that fight or gave evidence as to the bloodstains on *him*. But when young Michael came home and found his father dead, and was stained by his father's blood as he knelt beside the body, was it not natural that he should be suspected?

'And how very convenient for Ivan that he was. Because if Michael was convicted, Ivan would inherit a fortune. And remember, he was here with us the other day, Members of the Jury, the man you might think is possibly, quite, quite possibly, even probably, guilty. That man was in the public gallery making sure his inheritance was safe. And then, when he had been warned by my solicitor, did he not slink away, as he had on the night of the murder, in one of Mr Rudyard's hired cars to await the news of that young poet's wrongful conviction?

'If you think that's what *may* have happened, Members of the Jury, let us deny Ivan Skelton his final satisfaction and his undeserved wealth. Let us find young Michael Skelton not guilty of the terrible crime of murdering his father. And, remember, it is *your* decision' – here Rumpole glared at the Judge who, sitting motionless, had closed his eyes as though in pain – 'and not the decision of anyone else in the Court.'

And so the next day we were home again and sitting on either side of the gas fire at Froxbury Mansions in the evening. I'm glad to say there had been no further requests for salad.

Rumpole had done full justice to the shepherd's pie and cabbage I had cooked for him, taken with a great deal of mustard and tomato sauce. Now he said, 'Thank you, Hilda. Thank you for the work you put in to *R*. v. *Skelton*. Some of your ideas were surprisingly helpful.'

'Only some of them?' And, when he didn't answer, I said, 'I have to say you didn't seem able to follow up some fairly obvious clues. At least not until I got on the case.'

'I was distracted,' Rumpole had to admit. 'I was suffering from certain anxieties.'

'What sort of anxieties, Rumpole?'

'Matters of a domestic nature.'

'You mean, you thought it was about time we had the kitchen redecorated? I've been thinking that too.'

'No. I was concerned . . . Well, damn it all, Hilda. I thought you might have grown tired of life here . . . with me.'

'Life with you in Froxbury Mansions? Good heavens, how could anyone be tired of that?'

'You said . . . Well, anyway, you told me . . .' It was the first time in my entire life I had seen Rumpole stumped for words. 'What was all that about Newcombe having taken a shine to you?'

'No, I was wrong about that. He hadn't taken a shine to me. He wanted to win me over so I could be his spy.'

'His *what*?' I had surprised Rumpole.

'So I could spy on you. Tell him if you were getting too near the truth in *R*. v. *Skelton*. And there was something else I didn't like him for.'

'What was that?'

'Well, he called me a girl, which I thought was very patronizing. And I know why he gave you the brief.'

'Well, I do have a certain reputation . . . Ever since that little problem at the Penge Bungalow.'

'He thought because you aren't a Q.C. you wouldn't do the job properly.'

'That's ridiculous!'

'Of course it is.' There was silence for a while. Rumpole considered my extraordinary suggestion and rejected it. Then he said, 'I shan't include *R*. v. *Skelton* in my memoirs.'

'Whyever not? It was one of your greatest triumphs.'

'No, Hilda.' He picked up his brief in a little receiving job at Acton. 'The triumph was yours.'

This is the story that Rumpole will never write. So I'm writing it for you, Dodo, and for you only. It's the truth, the whole truth and nothing but the truth.

Rumpole and the Little Boy Lost

'Whoever did that,' Dot Clapton said, 'deserves burning at the stake!'

'I'm afraid they abolished that a few years ago.' I took the *Daily Trumpet* Dot was offering me across her typewriter. 'Although, given the reforming zeal of the appalling Ken Fry' – I winced as I invariably do when I mention the name of the current Home Secretary – 'we might get it back in the next Criminal Justice Act.'

What I saw was a big photograph, almost the whole tabloid front page. A young woman, wearing a T-shirt and jeans, was looking into the camera, trying to smile; a husband only a few years older, puzzled and frowning, had his arm protectively round her shoulder. Behind them was the blur of an ordinary semi-detached and a small, ordinary car, but they were the victims of an extraordinary crime. Their child had been snatched away from them, hidden among strangers and perhaps ... It was the awful perhaps which made Steve Constant put his arm round his wife and why her smile might turn so easily into a scream. SHEENA CONSTANT TALKS EXCLUSIVELY TO THE TRUMPET, the front page told the world. SEE CENTRE STORY.

'If they catch the old witch who did it, you wouldn't speak up for her in Court, would you? I mean you'd let her hang herself out of her own mouth, wouldn't you, Mr Rumpole?'

I had turned over to the central spread, entirely devoted to the little boy lost. There was an enlarged picture of little Tommy in the strangely metallic washed-out colours in which photographs appear in newspapers: an ordinary, carrot-haired three-year-old with a wide grin, no doubt a singular miracle to the Constants whose first and only child he was. There were

snaps of the family at the seaside, by a swing in the garden of
the semi and a picture of the huge South London hospital,
gaunt and unfriendly as a nuclear power station, from which
Tommy Constant had unaccountably disappeared. As I glanced
over these apparently harmless records of a tragedy, I was
trying to remind Dot of an Old Bailey hack's credo. 'I'm a
black taxi, Dot,' I told her, 'plying for hire. I'm bound to
accept anyone, however repulsive, who waves me down and
asks for a lift. I do my best to take them to their destination,
although the choice of route, of course, is entirely mine.'

'The destination of her who nicked that child' – Dot was
unshakeable in her demand for a conviction, she was not the
sort you'd want called up for jury duty – 'would be burning at
the stake. If you want my honest opinion.'

I have to confess that I wasn't giving Dot my full attention.
There wasn't a long story between the pictures, but what there
was had been written in the simple, energetic style of the *Daily
Trumpet* which, I thought, might be appreciated by a jury.

Twenty-four-year-old Sheena Constant spoke through her tears:
'After he was seen by the doctor, I put him on the kiddies' mechanical donkey in the out-patients assembly. He's been on it before, so I
left him with Steve while I went to the toilet. Steve just crossed
over to buy a packet of Marlboro. He was in sight of Tommy and
only turned away for about a minute. It was during that minute our
little son was stolen off us. He sort of vanished clutching a little
yellow flop-eared rabbit which was his favourite toy!'

Police investigations continue. Who was the pale-faced woman in
a black beret and black plastic mac carrying a toddler away from
out-patients? Police Superintendent Greengross hadn't yet found
her. Where were the social workers? Drinking carrot juice and
knitting pullovers? Where were the hospital managers? Upstairs
with their noses in the trough? Where was hospital security? Out to
lunch? These are the questions the *Trumpet* will be asking during
the coming week.

Tomorrow: WHY MY DAUGHTER'S HEART IS BROKEN. Tommy's
gran talks exclusively to the *Trumpet*.

'We've got her!' Claude Erskine-Brown had entered the
clerk's room in a state of high excitement. 'Got her, at last.'

'The woman who stole little Tommy?' I was still absorbing

the *Trumpet*'s simple story. I had supped full of horrors at Equity Court, but there seemed to be something peculiarly tragic about this young couple's loss.

'Of course not. She didn't steal anything. Can't you get your mind off crime for a single moment? Does the wonderful world of art mean nothing to you? We've got Katerina Regen to sing to us in the Outer Temple Hall.'

'Have you, by God?' I folded the *Daily Trumpet* neatly and put it back on Dot's typewriter. I thought I might have to forget Steve and Sheena Constant and fill my mind with other people's troubles. 'I doubt whether I shall be among those present.'

'She will give us Schubert.'

'So far as I'm concerned, she can keep him.'

'And the Bar Musical Society, of which by a strange quirk of fate I seem to have become president' – here I can only say that Erskine-Brown gave a modest simper – 'will be hosting a small champagne reception afterwards. The eighteenth of this month. Put it in your diary, Horace.'

For a moment my strong resolution wavered. Any invitation to take me to your *lieder* is one which, as a general rule, I have no difficulty in declining. But I have no such fears of a champagne reception. However, the preliminary trills seemed a highish price to pay for a glass or two of bubbles, so I sent an apology. 'I'm sorry but Hilda and I will be entertaining.'

'Entertaining who?'

'Each other. To a couple of chops in Froxbury Mansions. Awfully sorry, old darling, previous engagement.'

That night we were settled in front of the television in the mansion flat when Hilda said, 'I hope you've got the eighteenth marked down in your diary, Rumpole?'

'Yes, I have. I'm staying at home.'

'Oh no, you're not.'

Sometimes the dialogue of She Who Must Be Obeyed becomes strongly reminiscent of the pantomimes my old father used to take me to in my extreme youth. Don't I remember some such witty line having been used by the Widow Twankey?

'Hilda,' I reassured her, 'you don't want to spend a couple of hours on a hard chair in the Outer Temple Hall listening to some overweight diva trilling about departed love.'

'You know nothing, Rumpole,' she told me. (Had she forgotten my encyclopaedic knowledge of bloodstains?) 'Katerina Regen is not only Covent Garden's new Mimi but she's as slender as a bluebell.'

'Who told you that?'

'Claude Erskine-Brown, when he rang up. I told him to put us down for two tickets.'

'How much is he paying us to go?'

'Nothing, Rumpole. *We* are paying. It will be extremely good for you. You have so little art in your life.'

'I have poetry.'

'*Some* poetry. And it's like your jokes, always the same.'

'How much?'

'How much the same? Exactly.'

'No, how much are the tickets, Hilda! Erskine-Brown didn't con you out of a tenner?'

'The tickets were fifty pounds each and that includes two glasses of a really good Méthode Champenoise, which I think's a bargain considering how much you'd pay to listen to Regen at the Garden.'

And considering the happy evenings I might have had at Pommeroy's with the Méthode Fleet Streetoise for half that enormous expenditure. I might have said that but thought better of it. And then my attention was grabbed by the television on which an astonishingly young superintendent was holding a press conference. He sat between Sheena and Steve Constant – he in an ornate pullover, she in what must have been her best outfit, trying not to weep.

'I just want to say . . .' The superintendent had longish fair hair and protruding eyes. He looked as though he'd be much happier sharing jokes with his mates in the pub. However, he managed to sound both serious and sincere. '. . . to whoever's *got* Tommy, we can understand your problems. Maybe you're longing for a little boy of your own and can't have one. Perhaps you even lost a little boy in tragic circumstances. We understand and we're all sympathetic. We think you may need help and we'll see to it that you get it. So will you ring us at the number we'll put up on the screen in a minute and tell us where Tommy is? We're sure he's alive and well. (Here Sheena looked down, a hand to her forehead, covering her eyes.) We're sure you've been looking after him really well. But just tell us where he is, that's all. Give Tommy what he *really* needs: his mum and dad.'

As he talked I remembered some of the old poetry She Who Must Be Obeyed was tired of.

> 'Father! father! where are you going?
> 'O do not walk so fast.
> 'Speak father, speak to your little boy,
> 'Or else I shall be lost.'
>
> The light was dark, no father was there;
> The child was wet with dew;
> The mire was deep, & the child did weep, . . .

Sheena lowered her hand and shook her head bravely, like a diver shaking the water out of her eyes as she emerges from beneath the sea. Steve's teeth were clenched, his jaw set, his face a mask of misery.

I didn't know why I felt so concerned about the Tommy Constant case. Had I fallen a little, perhaps, in love with Sheena's face and looked forward, when the good news came, to seeing it light up with joy? I dreaded the pictures of the police with dogs crossing parkland or rubber-suited figures flopping into canals. I was even more afraid that they might find something. Whatever the reason, I found myself taking the Chambers' stairs like a two-year-old and arrived panting in the clerk's room feeling every day of seventy-four. I could hardly find enough breath to ask Dot for a quick loan of her *Daily Trumpet*.

There was a notable absence of hard news. Mrs Bellew, Sheena's mum, was reminiscing. Sheena had been a model child who did well at school and had a really lovely singing voice and was so pretty that the family hoped she might end up on television. She'd gone in for a few beauty competitions:

'Just local ones. I wouldn't have let her near the Albert Hall.' And a schoolfriend who knew the drummer in Stolen or Strayed (musicians whom I have to confess I'd never heard of) thought she might get her a job singing with the group, but nothing came of it. Tommy, it seemed, had inherited his mother's talents and, although only three, could perform 'Ooh! Aah! Cantona' as a solo number without prompting. Anyway Sheena gave up her chance of becoming famous when she met Steve at a party – a young computer salesman who was going to do very well for himself in the fullness of time. She started going out with him. Tommy's gran had always thought they were an ideal little family: 'Every night in my prayers I thanked God for their luck, until this horrible thing had to happen.' The double-spread was filled out with pictures of Granny Bellew stirring a cup of tea and five-year-old Sheena stumbling across the sands carrying a bigger beach-ball than she could cope with. We also saw Sheena singing in a school production of *Jesus Christ Superstar*, heavily jewelled and wearing an unexpected sari (no doubt to keep the school play ethnically neutral). There was a picture of Stolen or Strayed – a quartet I wouldn't care to have met on a dark night and whose music, I felt sure, would have made an evening of Katerina Regen's trilling sound like the song the sirens sang – and a photograph of the Constant wedding.

Wednesday brought a hard-hitting article entitled NUT-CUTLET LAYABOUTS: THE SOCIAL WORKERS WHO HAVE DONE B–ALL TO HELP FIND SHEENA'S BABY. Thursday was devoted to Steve's family, including his aunt Brenda Constant, who had never married but was gifted with psychic powers, practised as a clairvoyant, and had asked for help and guidance, in finding young Tommy, from the spirit world.

On Black Friday a man from the *Daily Trumpet* had been out with the police and the chilling pictures of frogmen and tracker dogs duly appeared. Young Superintendent Greengross gave a gloomy interview: 'We still hope for the best,' he said, 'and we are pursuing every possible line of inquiry to establish that young Tommy is still alive. But it's no use hiding the fact that, the more the days pass by, the more reason we have to fear the worst.'

On Saturday Chambers was shut and Dot's *Trumpet* was not available. On my way to Safeway's with She Who Must Be Obeyed for shopping duty, I read the posters and crossed the road to buy the paper. I saw a young mother with her face lit up and an apparently unharmed child in her arms. I thought the huge headline surprisingly literary: LITTLE BOY FOUND, it said. I gave a great cry of joy.

'Rumpole!' the captain of my fate called briskly from the other side of the road. 'What on earth are you doing?'

'I am whooping,' I told her, 'whooping with delight. Tommy Constant has been found and all is more or less right with the world!'

I learnt how Tommy had been discovered by reading that day's *Daily Trumpet*, and the following Sunday's papers. Next week the story was retold, in considerable detail, in a long interview with Sheena, which took up more pages of Dot's favourite publication. Later, some time later, I was to learn even more about the great kidnapping case.

It was a hot night in late summer, near midnight apparently, when the Constants got the telephone call. It was too hot, Sheena said, and anyway they were too worried to sleep. When the phone rang, Steve looked at it, frozen, expecting the worst news. Sheena took a deep breath and grabbed it. She said she felt a moment of relief when she didn't hear the voice of Superintendent Greengross. What she heard was much fainter, a woman's voice, with an attempt at disguise, as though the caller were speaking through a handkerchief. 'Nineteen Swansdown Avenue,' was all it said. 'You'd better get there quick.' Later, the call was traced to a phone box at the end of nearby Swansdown Avenue. Later still, Sheena said that she thought she recognized the mystery voice.

The street used to be quiet and well kept, the home of middle managers and owners of small businesses who cleaned their cars on Sunday mornings and decked out their back gardens with oven-ready blooms from the local garden centre. Many of the middle managers had been made redundant and the small businesses gone broke. The houses had been repossessed by the banks and the For Sale notices had grown

weather-stained as the houses decayed. At one end of the
avenue, a speculator was building flats – otherwise the street's
sleep was more or less undisturbed, except when there was an
improvised rave-up in number 19, which had been broken into
so many times that the bank, which had evicted the previous
owners, now hardly bothered to change the locks or mend the
windows.

The Constants drove at high speed to Swansdown Avenue,
less than a mile from their house. They didn't dare to hope,
but couldn't help but fear. The padlock on the front gate was
broken, the back door swung on its hinges. The electricity had
been cut off, but a street light enhanced the moonlight and left
hard shadows in the corners of the rooms. 'The place was a
tip,' Sheena said in her interview. 'There were piles of dis-
carded clothes, stained mattresses with their innards protruding, piles of bottles, half-empty Coke cans all over the place
and cardboard plates of half-eaten takeaways, and needles scattered everywhere.' The couple went from room to room,
Sheena said, fearing what they might see in the shadows, and
for a long while they avoided the garden, terrified of signs of
recent digging.

And then, sickened by the lingering smell of unwashed
bodies and rotting food, Sheena pushed open a bedroom
window and found herself looking down into the rank garden.
She saw more bottles and syringes glistening in the moonlight,
and then she heard a child cry. She had heard it often in her
imagination since Tommy vanished, but now she fancied it was
real and she hoped she was not mistaken. It seemed that he had
been playing quite happily in the dark garden until he stung
his hand on a clump of nettles. He was wearing the same red
anorak and blue jeans and red boots, together with the small
Star Trek T-shirt, which Sheena had put on him to go to the
hospital. In that filthy house he was clean, well-dressed and
seemed in excellent health. He greeted his mother and father
without visible surprise.

A week later Superintendent Greengross told the *Daily Trumpet* that Thelma Ropner of 17 Swansdown Avenue was helping
him with his inquiries. We got little further information about
her, except that she was twenty-six and had recently given

birth to a baby son, who died four weeks later. Later still, she was charged and hurried into the local magistrates court with a blanket over her head. Her defence was reserved and, after a good deal of argument from Mr Bernard, her solicitor, she was granted bail.

'For this song, I am a young peasant girl going to the well in my village. My lover is a soldier who has deserted me and gone away to the wars. I sing, "Oh dear, I wish I could draw my lover back to me on a rope, as easily as I draw water from this well." "Der Brunnen" is the name of this beautiful song.'

There was a polite smattering of applause from the audience assembled in the Outer Temple Hall, among which Erskine-Brown's fevered clapping sounded like a volley of rifle-fire during a church service. The gratified *chanteuse* flashed a healthy set of white teeth in Claude's direction and then leaned for a reviving moment against the grand piano, her hand spread over her chest, her eyes closed, breathing in deeply. During the pause for rest and inspiration, her perky little accompanist suspended his fingers over the keys and sat with his eyes bright and his head on one side like a hen waiting for the egg to drop. Then Miss Regen fixed her smile and the first note rang out among the oak panelling and portraits of dead judges.

She was giving us the sad story once more, but this time with plenty of trills and repetitions, and in German. She was certainly not your standard fat opera singer, but rather beautiful with blonde hair, a suntan and clear blue eyes. Everything was, however, larger than life, not only her teeth but her hands, her eyes and her mouth. She was as tall as most of the men in the audience and, I thought, any lover who tried to escape from her and join the army would have been hauled in rapidly with a rope around his neck. And then, I have to say, my attention wandered.

> He kissed the child & by the hand led
> And to his mother brought,
> Who in sorrow pale, thro the lonely dale,
> Her little boy weeping sought.

I remembered the lines and the mysterious figure of a God dressed in white who returned the child in Blake's poem. I wondered who had made the telephone call to the Constants. Was it a friend, or a contrite enemy? Then I fell into a light doze.

I was woken by the final applause, sufficiently rested to join in the scrum for the champagne-style refreshments. The clapping was renewed when Miss Regen appeared, smiling with immeasurable courage, in spite of her exhaustion, and was immediately pounced on by Claude, who greeted her with such effusive praise that she might have sung her way through the role of Brünnhilde while winning the long-distance Olympic hurdles. Our sensitive Claude seemed to be quivering with excitement, and I thought she undoubtedly had a rope round his neck if ever she wanted to haul him in.

'All through that beautiful music, Rumpole' – Hilda was in a confessional mood – 'I couldn't help thinking of something else.'

'Couldn't you? I was pretty riveted by the girl at the well, as it so happens.'

'I couldn't help thinking of that poor woman who lost her baby.'

'She's got it back now, Hilda.'

'I know. But the person who did it, can you think of a worse crime?'

'Scarcely.'

'Even you couldn't defend a woman like that, could you, Rumpole?'

'Even I might find it difficult; but she hasn't been tried yet.'

'It doesn't matter. She's clearly guilty. It sticks out a mile. And please don't start a long speech about the burden of proof. You're so childish, sometimes, Rumpole. You imagine everyone in the world's as innocent as little Tommy Constant.'

Before I could refresh the memory of She Who Must on the presumption of innocence, our ears were shattered by a yell of, 'Thank you, Fräulein Regen, for bringing sunshine into this dusty old hall. I'm so glad I persuaded my fellow benchers to invite you.' It was Barrington McTear, Q.C. (known to me as Cut Above, because he regards himself as a very superior person), who had approached the diva and, in a gesture which I thought went out with old Scarlet Pimpernel films, kissed her hand. She glowed back at him and these two immense people seemed, for a moment, like the meeting of a male and female giant in some unreadable Nordic saga. Then Cut Above straightened up, patted the hand he had been kissing, and responded to a call of 'Barrington!' from a sharp-featured woman, no doubt his wife, who looked as though she found life with Cut Above no picnic. 'Coming, Leonora.' The ex-rugby football blue of a Q.C. turned reluctantly from the singing star and went bellowing off into the distance. Claude, who had looked somewhat miffed during this encounter, moved to fill the gap left by his fellow Q.C. and started to address the Fräulein in confidential tones. On our way out I heard him mention the fatal word lunch. Whenever Claude speaks of this meal to any female, the consequences are usually dire.

But I had more to worry about than Claude's tentative and no doubt embarrassing romances. That afternoon Bonny Bernard, my trusty instructing solicitor with a thriving practice in the Timson country south of Streatham, had booked a conference in *R*. v. *Thelma Ropner*. I was heavily pencilled in as Counsel for the Defence, and the faggots round the stake were no doubt ready for lighting.

'She's in your room, Mr Rumpole. And she's wearing the black mac.'

That morning Dot Clapton's Botticelli face was set in anger and contempt, a young angel determined to drive the sinners out of the Garden of Eden with a flaming sword.

'It is raining, Dot, as usual.'

'So does she have to wear the *same* mac? Some sort of nerve she must have, mustn't she? But I can't stay chatting, Mr Rumpole. Some of us has got work to do.' And Dot attacked her typewriter as though it were my client's throat.

Some of us did have work – hard, unpleasant work – and the prospect, at some time in the not-too-distant future, of being treated in Court as though we were personally responsible for pinching defenceless infants from hospitals. I pushed open the door of my room and it seemed, in some curious and quite evil way, to be dominated by Miss Thelma Ropner.

Thinking back, it seems absurd to have felt so instantly chilled. Thelma was almost a caricature from a movie and I might even, in other circumstances, have found her appearance comic. She was very pale, with rust-coloured, lank hair, and her features seemed curiously misplaced: her eyes too small, her nose slightly crooked and her mouth turned downwards. She looked both unpleasant and unhappy. And she wore, as Dot had said, with what was either bravado or sheer stupidity, the black beret set at what might have been intended as a cheeky angle, and the unmistakable shiny, crackly, black plastic mac which protected her like the armour of a crustacean. One thing was absolutely certain. She could never have got out of a hospital carrying a child unnoticed.

So vivid was the effect of Miss Ropner that the rest of my room seemed to sink into shadow. Somewhere, dear old Bernard was sorting through the file on his lap and chewing peppermints. Even I, taking my place on the swing chair, felt colourless – an Old Bailey hack quite outshone by the lurid vision of evil in front of him.

'It's all a complete waste of time, Mr Rumpole. I never ever took Sheena's child.' Thelma Ropner spoke in a curiously girlish, high-pitched little voice, as though the possible child-stealer were herself a child, and added, 'I wouldn't want to.'

'You call Mrs Constant Sheena, I couldn't help noticing. Do you know her?'

'Know her. Of course I know her. We were at Cripps together.'

'Cripps?'

'Cripping Comprehensive. I'm sure it was nothing like the academy for the sons of gentlemen you attended.'

'And probably a great deal more comfortable than my draughty boarding-school. Better lunches, too, I should imagine.' She didn't smile. I never saw her smile. What I got was a mood of petulance or a sarcastic sigh. I was in for a difficult trial with a difficult client and wondered if Hilda or Dot Clapton would ever forgive me if I won.

'You mean you were close friends?' Bernard sucked his

peppermint and looked in the statement he had taken for any reference to their friendship, and didn't find it.

'We got on all right. Sheena was quite good fun until she met Steve and lost her femininity.'

'I'm not entirely sure what you mean . . .' I have kept my patience under more trying circumstances. 'She got married and had a baby. Was *that* losing her femininity?'

'Of course it was.' Thelma sighed again at my question. 'She got the one kid and the boring young man in computers, the semi and the Daf – and she was well stuck in a male-dominated rut, wasn't she?'

'Do you think Sheena felt in a rut?' I wondered.

'Of course she did. She was awfully envious of Tina Santos when she got her name in all the papers for bonking some dreadful little government minister. Sheena always wanted to be famous like a telly star or something. Well, I suppose she is now, in a way. Famous.'

'Not in the way she'd like, I'm sure.'

'Probably not.' Miss Ropner turned away from me and looked out of the window, as though she had lost interest in me and Mr Bernard, and the tedious workings of the criminal law.

I renewed my attack, to gain at least a little of her attention. 'You think everyone who has a baby gets stuck in a male-dominated rut?'

She looked at me then and said, 'You mean I had one?'

'So you say in your statement.'

'And they're going to use it against me?'

'What do you mean?'

'They're going to use it against me that Damon died. They'll say it's because my little boy died that I wanted to steal Sheena's. That's what they're going to say, aren't they?'

'I suppose it might provide a motive.'

'Well, let me tell you, Mr Legal-Eagle, that if I'd wanted to nick a child I certainly wouldn't have chosen Sheena's. I'd've found one with a far more interesting father.'

It's not often that I am to be found sitting in a stunned silence, but this was such an occasion. Bernard was also immobile. He had his tube of peppermints open, but didn't lift one to his mouth.

Then I recovered sufficiently to tell the client, 'I have known witnesses sink themselves with one unwise answer, probably more times than you've had hot dinners. But if you say anything like that in Court we might as well plead guilty and start your sentence as soon as possible.'

'I'm so sorry, Mr Lawyer.' Thelma gave a bizarre impression of a little girl's pout. 'So sorry I can't give you all the answers you'd like.'

'Don't bother about what I'd like. It's the jury who've got to like you. And they're fairly ordinary men and women stuck in various kinds of a rut.'

'Well, I'm sorry for them, that's all I've got to say. Now, is there anything you want to ask me?'

'Just a few things. You live at seventeen Swansdown Avenue?'

'That's what it says there, doesn't it?'

'If the uneven numbers are all down one side of the street, nineteen is next door.'

'I can see it from my window.'

'On that moonlit night, did you see Tommy Constant down there among the nettles?'

'Hardly. On that moonlit night I was fast asleep. Or as fast as you can get in the Edmunds's house with Classic FM always on the go and that woman getting up at all hours to feed her unattractive baby on demand.'

'Brian Edmunds is your landlord? A professor?'

'Professor! He teaches Communication Studies at some rotten poly that now calls itself the University of South-West London.'

'The Edmundses.' I picked up another statement. 'Both say that they didn't see you in their house at all during the week Tommy Constant went missing.'

'I was there every night! I've got my own key, you know. I am a grown-up, free and independent spirit, Mr Rumpole. I don't have to report to Mr Brian Edmunds every time I go out or come back. As a matter of fact I avoid them both as much as possible. I don't particularly enjoy conversation with the brain dead.'

'They say they couldn't tell if you slept in your bed during that week.' I thought the Edmundses must be cursing the day they took in Thelma as a lodger. 'Because your bed is hardly ever made, anyway.'

'I've told them not to look into my room.' Thelma clearly felt that her civil rights had been outraged: 'In fact I've expressly forbidden it!'

'What were you doing during that week?'

'I *do* work, Mr Rumpole. I have to work to live. We can't all sit around in nice comfortable rooms in the Outer Temple waiting for someone to get into trouble.'

Thelma Ropner's resentment was like a high-pitched ringing, a perpetual noise in the ear like the disease of tinnitus. I ignored it with an effort. 'Where do you work, Miss Ropner?'

'Anywhere that's interesting, and worthwhile, and exciting. I help out a lot at groups.'

'Such as?'

'The Stick-Up Theatre Company. They're based in Croydon. Friends of the Earth. Animal Rights. Outings – that's an organization for gay and lesbian groups of retired people. I organize events for them. Some of us, Mr Lawyer, think that work should have a social context.'

'Mr Rumpole's work' – my defence came, unexpectedly, from Bonny Bernard, who had sat, up till then, quietly sucking peppermints – 'is done in the interests of justice. I'm sure you understand that, Miss Ropner.'

'It's also done in the interests of meeting this quarter's gas bill and financing Saturday's trip to Safeway's.' I hastened to reassure my client that my interest in her case was not based on any abstract conception. A too fervent attachment to the interests of justice, I began to suspect, might not help me to keep the disagreeable Thelma out of chokey.

'During each night that little Tommy was missing' – I wanted to get her story entirely clear – 'you tell me you were sleeping at the Edmunds's house?'

'Entirely alone, Mr Lawyer. Without even a three-year-old in bed with me.'

'Very well.' I shuffled through the bundle of statements again. 'On the night young Tommy was found in the garden of number nineteen, Mrs Edmunds says she was up with her baby . . .'

'Surprise, surprise.' Thelma Ropner gave a small, mirthless laugh.

'She was looking out of the first-floor bedroom window. "I saw someone under the street lamp in front of number nineteen," I read aloud. '"It looked like a woman in a black plastic mac and a beret. I thought it was Thelma, but she was pushing something, a pram or a pushchair, I couldn't be sure. Then my baby started crying again, and when I looked back the woman had gone."'

'Why didn't she call the police? Everyone was on the lookout for someone in a mac like mine, who'd pinched Sheena's precious little Tommy. If Polly Edmunds thought she'd seen me, why didn't she rush down, or at least call the police?' To my surprise, my client now sounded quite calm and sensible.

'That's a very good point for cross-examination. Thank you.' I was polite enough to let her think I hadn't thought of it.

'That's all right. I'm sure you need a bit of help. Anyway, why didn't she knock on my door if she thought it was me? She'd've found me tucked up with myself, wouldn't she?'

I thought I knew the answer. With a lodger like Thelma Ropner, the Edmundses must have blessed the hours when she was either out or asleep. They wouldn't have gone looking for her. I sorted through a number of police officer's statements and found the description of number nineteen's unlovely garden patch: '"The police found wheel-marks on the wet ground which might have been made by a pushchair. There were plenty of footprints . . ."'

'And body prints too.' Thelma's smile was so chilling that I thought, for a moment, she was talking about death and not the pleasures of sexual conquests in an urban tip. 'You know they came and took my shoes away? Haven't we got any civil rights left? Haven't we?'

'Only a few. And that's because I keep on shouting about them down the Old Bailey.' My strength to be polite to Thelma seemed likely to run out before her resentment. '. . . Prints that fitted a pair of your shoes were found in the garden of number nineteen.'

'Of course they were. I was there the night before. It was pretty muddy then.'

'You went into the garden?'

'Lots of people did.'

'Why?'

'Number nineteen's the only place you meet interesting people. It was the house for free spirits.'

So was that why the three-year-old little boy lost had been dumped there, I wondered. To meet interesting people?

After a session with Thelma Ropner, there was only one place to go and I stumbled towards it as a wounded, thirsty lion might crawl to the water-hole. The first two glasses of liquid hardly banished her chilly memory, but by the third I felt some inner warmth returning. Jack Pommeroy's new and untried barmaid, who seemed a nice girl, gave me a smile of apparently genuine concern and asked unnecessarily if I would care for another. And then a strange voice said, 'Got you, Mr Rumpole. Trapped you in your lair, sir.' At the same time a card was slapped on the bar in front of me bearing the legend: JONATHAN ARGENT, *Daily Trumpet.*

I looked up, expecting to be staring at the craggy features and moist eyes of a tabloid journalist marinated in whisky, a sweat-stained trilby and a dirty mac. I saw what seemed to be an impertinent sixth former who had just, more by luck than hard work, done rather well in his A-levels – the sort of youth who would be in constant minor trouble, but usually forgiven. He had a small, upturned nose, a bang of dark hair that strayed across his forehead, and lips that were fuller and redder than might have been expected. He wore a suit with a rather long jacket and a double-breasted waistcoat, and across a stomach which hardly deserved the name a gold watchchain dangled. Young Mr Argent seemed to see himself as an Edwardian dandy. 'So, this is Fleet Street.' He looked around at the assembled legal hacks, their solicitors, whom they were flirting with energetically, and their secretaries whom they probably intended to flirt with later. 'I wasn't quite sure I'd be able to find it.'

'There was a time,' I told him, 'when your newspaper and

practically every other rag was in this street. That was before you all pushed off to some nightmare electronic city on the Isle of Dogs where you could stay safely away from the news.'

'I thought you'd talk like that,' the infant Argent said.

'Like what, exactly?'

'Like starting every sentence "There was a time".'

'Time was,' I said, rather grandly, I thought – the Château Fleet Street was loosening the throat and somewhat inflating the prose – 'is by now far the longest and most important part of my life.'

'There's an old chap at the *Trumpet* who remembers when it was in Fleet Street. They put him on to the Saturday para Down the Garden Path, but now he's been made redundant.'

Time to come, I thought, is not something I wish to sit here thinking about, taking a quick glance towards the end. Then Argent said, 'Why not ditch that ghastly-looking cough mixture and join me in a bottle of the Dom?'

'Of the what?'

'Dom Perignon? He was an old monk who had a cunning sort of a way with champagne. I don't know if you ever met him round Fleet Street?'

'Why on earth' – I was puzzled by this curious encounter – 'should you want to buy me expensive champagne?'

'Oh, it's not me, sir.' He used the word sir as though he was speaking to a schoolmaster for whom he'd long lost respect. 'The *Trumpet* wants to stand us both a drink. After that peculiar plonk you might be in the mood for a bit of blotting paper, so I'm sure the scandal sheet would run to a couple of cheese sandwiches to go with the bubbles.'

I am, I hope, a fair-minded man and I thought I should consider his offer without prejudice, and come to a fair conclusion. 'I must admit that your paper gave the Tommy Constant case very thorough coverage,' I told him.

'Oh, we want it to be much more serious than that, sir. I think there's an empty table in the corner. Shall I take your arm to steady you?'

'Certainly not' – I was quite brusque with the lad – 'I am perfectly steady, thank you very much indeed.'

Young Argent said when we landed safely at the table, 'I'm

glad you thought we told Sheena's story well, sir. Now we want to do the same for Thelma.'

'Do what?'

'Tell her story.'

'It'll be told in Court.'

'We'd like the *Trumpet* to be on the inside track with Thelma. You've got to admit she's got an even bigger circulation potential than Sheena. Thelma's story has got an added dimension.'

'Oh? What dimension's that?'

'Well, quite honestly, sir, her baby died.' He gave me his candid, boyish look, half amused, as though he had to confess that he planned to raid the tuck shop.

I did my best to suppress rage. 'Do you call that a plus? There should have been a *Daily Trumpet* around in the days of Herod the King. You might have broken all circulation records.'

'We want to do Thelma's story' – Jonathan Argent looked very serious and sincere, his eyes wide and his voice particularly quiet – 'in a way which will be a hundred per cent fair and sympathetic. We all know how women get after childbirth. We've got stuff from a psychiatrist. It's jolly understandable, really.'

Thirty-five years after childbirth, I thought, She Who Must Be Obeyed could still spring some surprises; but I didn't encourage the upper-crust young Jonno by telling him that. 'If Miss Ropner wants to tell you her story when the trial's over, that's entirely up to her.'

'I don't think Miss Ropner's going to be in much of a position to speak to anyone when the trial is over.' Jonathan Argent was smiling.

'Why? Do you assume she's going to be convicted?'

'Surprise me, then. You've got some brilliant defence tucked away under that old hat of yours? Have you, quite honestly, sir?'

How many more people would have to remind me of the burden of proof? I took a generous gulp of the old monk's recipe and said, 'Thelma Ropner is innocent and will be until the Jury down the Bailey comes back with a verdict.'

'You're expecting the thumbs up?'

'We shall see,' I said – champagne after plonk is no recipe for epigrams – 'what we shall see.'

'Quite honestly, Mr Rumpole, it's not so much Thelma we're after.'

'Who are you after, then? You seemed to have squeezed the best out of the Constant family.'

'We're after you.'

He was very young, probably quite silly and looked harmless enough. I don't know why but when he said this I felt, in some curious way, trapped; he spoke modestly, but as though he had an immense power behind him.

'I'm an old taxi' – I embarked on the much-loved speech – 'plying for hire. If the *Trumpet* wants to brief me in some lucrative action, provided it doesn't conflict with the interests of my client, well and good. I make it a rule to represent all riff-raff, underdogs and social outcasts.'

'We don't want to employ you, sir. We want to tell your story.'

'You mean the "Have you anything to say why sentence of death should not be passed against you?" And the chap in the dock says, "Bugger all, my Lord." And the Judge says to his counsel, "What did your client say, Mr Smith?"' My stories, by now, have achieved a pretty wide circulation.

'Not exactly that, sir.' Argent shook his wise young head sadly, unable to understand the wilful old. 'Your story in Tom's case: WHY I'M DEFENDING THELMA ROPNER, THE MOST HATED WOMAN IN ENGLAND. Your taxi bit can come in there: I PUT MY TALENT AT THE DISPOSAL OF THE RIFF-RAFF AND THE UNDERDOG. And then: THE LIGHT AT THE END OF THE TUNNEL. HOW I FOUND A DEFENCE IN A HOPELESS CASE.'

'What are you suggesting I do? Spill all the beans? I can't do it.'

'Whyever not? I'd write it for you.'

'It would be against all the best traditions of the Bar.'

'You might find it extremely profitable.'

'How profitable? I only ask out of idle curiosity.'

The young hack looked around conspiratorially, made sure

no one was listening and then offered me a sum of money, expressed in Ks, which I took to be thousands. I saw myself retiring, moving from icy Froxbury Mansions to a place with a small pool and a microwave on the Malaga coast, sitting in the bar with a group of accountants who had taken voluntary redundancy, drinking sangria. I stifled a huge yawn.

'No thanks,' I told him politely, 'it's too late for all that sort of thing.'

'That isn't the end of the story, sir. With syndication it might be much more.'

I drained my glass. 'In the circumstances I think it best if I pay for the Dom Perignon.'

'There's absolutely no need, sir, for that sort of gesture. It's been a pleasure and a privilege to talk to you.'

I saw the man's point. 'Then I'll be getting back to work.' I rose from the table. He smiled at me as though I had agreed to all his ridiculous propositions. As I was walking towards the door I heard him call after me, 'And we'll keep in very close touch indeed.'

I discovered later, a good deal later, that when I was being given the expensive sauce, and offered all the kingdoms of Southern Spain, by the schoolboy journalist, my learned but incautious friend Claude Erskine-Brown, Q.C., was engaged in his first romantic encounter with the statuesque Regen. The place chosen for this tryst was hardly discreet, no small spaghetti house in the purlieus of Victoria station but the glittering glass and brass 1930s Galaxy Hotel in the middle of Mayfair, where the nomadic diva was pigging it during her Covent Garden visit. By a chance which turned out to be less than happy, she arrived back from shopping just as Claude's taxi drew up and then enjoyed a notable encounter on the marble steps in front of the Galaxy's top-hatted commissionaire and revolving door.

Of course, I wasn't a spectator at this event which assumed an importance rather like Solomon's greeting to the Queen of Sheba, or King David's 'Hallo, there' to Bathsheba. I imagine that Claude was effusive and pathetically grateful that his suggestion of lunch, made at the Outer Temple concert, had

been accepted and that the singing star was a little confused
and perhaps unable to remember who her visitor was. Claude,
however, announced himself in clear and ringing tones and
swooped at her with two kisses on both cheeks, which, he
imagined, would be acceptable to a jet-setting soprano. I believe Katerina Regen made a brisk movement, whether of
greeting or avoidance I'm not altogether sure, and Claude
stumbled on a shallow, marble step, with the result that their
mouths collided in a manner which looked a great deal friend-
lier than it was. This mischance didn't embarrass the singer,
who didn't embarrass easily. She gave a resonant laugh down
the scale of C, put her arm in Claude's and dragged him in
through the revolving door as though she was hauling him
up from a well. And there, for a moment, and for the purpose
of this narrative, we must leave the happy couple.

I decided to visit the scene, or rather the scenes, of the crime –
a stretch of South London which took the place of the lonely
fen in which the little boy was lost in William Blake's strange
poem. We went in Bonny Bernard's unwashed Fiesta which
seems to contain, in a state of unexpected chaos, all the elements
of his life. Files, bulging envelopes, cardboard boxes, were
piled on the back seat, together with a squash racket and a
zipped-up bag of some sort of sportswear which I had never
seen moved.

Our first call was the Springtide General Hospital. At my
direction Bernard parked his motor in a space clearly marked
RESERVED FOR HOSPITAL HEAD OF HUMAN RESOURCES and
joined the throng pouring in at the main entrance, a huge space
which resembled a town centre during late-night shopping
when all the traffic lights are out of order and the local constabulary have gone on holiday.

Visitors sat on benches eating takeaway meals, and patients,
long ago forgotten, were slumped in wheelchairs. Hospital
trolleys rattled past, some heavy with sheeted figures. Other
trolleys stood parked with old persons, belly upwards, staring
hopelessly at the ceiling. A doctor or two, a little posse of
clattering nurses, hugging their cardigans about them, were
somewhere glimpsed. Otherwise, the crowd was notably civil-

ian. The predominant smell was of rubber, disinfectant and popcorn.

We passed a row of shops selling plastic toys, girlie magazines and best-selling paperbacks. In the concourse in front of the out-patients, there was a children's corner: a broken playpen, a huge pink teddy bear and the mechanical donkey on which a small child might enjoy a stationary trip for fifty pence. At that moment, a shaven-headed, earringed nineteen-year-old was sitting astride it, swigging mineral water from a kingsize bottle. As I took in the *locus in quo*, the wonder was not how a child could be stolen there but how a small and adventurous boy could ever be kept safe.

'God protect me' – I shared my prayers with my instructing solicitor – 'from having to die in a place like this.'

'Is there anything you want me to do here?' Bernard was as anxious as I was to get out of this house of healing.

'Find out what was wrong with little Tommy. I mean, why did they take him to the out-patients that morning?' I looked towards the newspaper and tobacconist shop where Steve had turned his back on his son to buy fags, and where great piles of the *Daily Trumpet* were on sale. 'It wasn't an accident. We knew that. Sudden sickness. Sheena says that in her statement. What sort of sickness exactly? Find that out, Bonny Bernard, in the fullness of time.'

'Where to next, Mr Rumpole?'

'Up to Redwood Road, I think. Just for a glance at the matrimonial home.'

In the car park the Head of Human Resources was standing beside his unparked B.M.W. and swearing at us. I smiled sweetly and told him that we were official inspectors sent by Mrs Lavinia Lyndon, the glamorous and lethal Minister of Health, to report on his hospital's efficiency, and that shut him up effectively.

I had seen the semi-detached in Redwood Road before, faintly in that first picture in the *Trumpet*. Now it seemed bigger and brighter than I had expected. The front garden looked as though it had been recently trimmed and rhododendrons and bright azaleas, already in flower, had been brought in from a garden centre. Parked in front of the garage was a

low-lined, bright-red and sporty model with a number Mr
Bernard knew to be recent. If the Constants had come into a
bit of money, I saw no reason, after their week of misery, why
they shouldn't enjoy it. We didn't see little Tommy, or either
of his parents, although we waited for about ten minutes on the
other side of the road. Then a middle-aged women in a bright
yellow dress came out of the house and started to snip a bunch
of early, straight-stalked and military tulips in the front garden.
She had reddish hair, a pale face and a sharp nose. I thought
she condemned the flowers to death in the house without
mercy or regret.

On the way to Swansdown Avenue, threading our way along
streets of identical pink-and-white houses (they looked, I
thought, like carefully packed and identical packets of streaky
bacon), round crescents and across wider roads, we stopped at
traffic lights beside a row of small shops that no doubt were
struggling for existence against the mass attack of the supermarkets and the shopping malls. As I looked idly out of the
window, I saw a shoe mender's, a dry cleaner's with a window
display of wire coathangers and paper flowers, and a shop
called Snappy Print: COPIES MADE AND FAXES SENT. In the
window I saw a poster offering a course in computer and
business studies: ONE WEEK IN A COUNTRY HOUSE NEAR
TUNBRIDGE WELLS CAN PUT YOU ON THE TOP EXECUTIVE
LADDER OF SUCCESS. SALESMANSHIP AND COMPETITIVE MAR-
KETING THOROUGHLY TAUGHT. After the printer's came a
peeling hut with blackened windows and a sign advertising
THERAPEUTIC MASSAGE AND SAUNA. The door was padlocked.
The next shop, so narrow it seemed to have been squashed in
after the rest of the row was finished, had a surprising and
half-broken neon sign. PSYCHIC it must have once said when
all the letters were fully operational. ASTROLOGICAL SIGNS
CHARTED AND CONSIDERED. CLAIRVOYANT ADVICE GIVEN.
The shop window was empty except for a white vase which
contained three wilting tulips and a photograph. It was a
glimpse of that photograph that made me ask Bernard to park,
and I got out and stood examining it and the window display.
In the shadows of the small room behind it I was sure I saw
something of importance to our case. I tried the door but it was

locked and, when I got back to the car, Bernard said, 'What did you want, Mr Rumpole? To know our future in *R*. v. *Thelma Ropner*?'

'I'm afraid,' I told him, 'that we don't need a chart to tell us that the omens are against us. The star sign of the Constants, however, is definitely in the ascendant.' As we drove off towards Thelma's pad, another sporty car turned from under a sparse clump of trees. The driver seemed a very young man and I made sure he was following us.

Swansdown Avenue produced no surprises. The tip in which young Tommy had been discovered lived up to its sordid reputation, and the front garden of number seventeen next door was not much tidier. The grass was uncut, the paths weedy, and there was a pram blocking the front door. The garage doors were open and I imagined that the head of communication studies had taken the car off to the University of South-West London. There was the thin, insistent cry of a baby and I saw an upstairs window from which Mrs Edmunds would have had a clear view of the front gate of number nineteen, which was opposite a street lamp. I imagined the academic's house, and the perpetual smell of milk, vegetable soup and soaking nappies. I decided that my legal team and I couldn't go on much longer without a drink.

We found the Old Pickwick at a crossroads about half a mile from Swansdown Avenue and Dickens's fat hero would have thought it considerably less warm and welcoming than the Fleet Prison. Bernard and I sat in a cavernous bar where banks of electronic games squeaked and flashed and muttered angrily around us. The barmaid, a ferocious girl with a spiky hairdo, was heavily engaged on the telephone and avoided a glance in our direction. At long last she finished her call, switched on her favourite tape, and allowed me to yell a request for two pints of Guinness to a musical accompaniment which sounded like the outbreak of World War III. I had barely put my lips to the froth when I heard a penetrating word in my ear.

'Sherlock Rumpole? Have you brought the magnifying glass and the deerstalker?'

I turned to find young Argent of the *Trumpet* breathing

down my neck. 'I'm here,' I told him rather grandly, 'to consult with my instructing solicitor. Our conversation is, as I'm sure you'll understand, entirely privileged.'

'Kill the karaoke, sweetheart.' The reporter's voice rose high above the music, and to my amazement Miss Spiky smiled sweetly at him and plunged us into silence. 'A word in your ear if I might, a very private word.' Argent ignored Bernard and ordered himself a brandy and soda.

'I have no secrets from my instructing solicitor.'

'Oh, but the lawyer we're going to talk about probably has. And this hasn't got anything to do with little Tommy Constant. Not for the moment, anyway.' Bernard, who could take a hint almost before it was dropped, filtered off to telephone his office and the man from the *Trumpet* opened a slim leather briefcase and laid a glossy photograph on the bar. I didn't look at it.

'Are you offering me money?' I asked him.

'I've already done that. We'd pay you awfully well for the How I'm Defending Baby-snatcher story. Might even run to a new hat, Mr Rumpole. No, what we're offering now is for information.'

'What information?'

'Take a look.'

I glanced down. What I saw was the prize idiot and Queen's Counsel, Claude Erskine-Brown, locked in the sturdy embrace of Ms Katerina Regen, and apparently administering mouth-to-mouth resuscitation to her on the front step of the Galaxy Hotel.

'Top lawyer and judge's husband in afternoon bonk with German nightingale. Not a bad little story for us.'

'They are simply friends,' I hastened to assure him. 'I know he admires her voice.'

'Admires her silver tongue so much that they went up to Room 307 together and didn't emerge from the Galaxy until five-thirty in the afternoon.'

'He probably had nothing on in Court. It often happens.'

'He might try to have something on in Court if we tell him we're publishing this. You wouldn't want us to do that, would you?'

I couldn't believe that after so many disastrously fumbled and frustrated attempts, Claude had actually succeeded in consummating an extramarital romance. 'I don't see why I should care,' I told Argent. 'You're not suggesting I was bonking anyone, I sincerely hope?'

'The honour of your Chambers is at stake, sir. Its reputation for high morals and respectability. And think of the effect on her Ladyship, the learned Judge. Just about blow her wig off, wouldn't you say?'

He was right, of course. Phillida Erskine-Brown would be deeply distressed at seeing her husband splashed across the *Trumpet* as a post-prandial bonker. I will never lose a long and lingering affection for the Portia of our Chambers, now a High Court Judge, and I wanted to spare her pain.

'I can't see that this' – I pushed the photograph back towards Argent – 'is of the slightest interest to your readers.'

'You don't know our readers, sir. They love reading about the great and good bonking. Saves them all the trouble of doing it for themselves.'

'But you won't publish it?'

'That depends.'

'Depends on what?'

'On whether you're going to give us another story: How I Defended Thelma.'

There was a long silence. Miss Spiky was baring her lips to a mirror, seriously examining her teeth. I said, 'When would you want it?'

'Run the first instalment the day before the trial. No desperate hurry.'

'Can I have that picture?' I asked him. 'Of course, you've got the negative.'

'Of course.' He pushed Claude and the diva towards me. I stored them away in an inside pocket before Bernard came back.

'One thing you might do for us,' Argent said, 'if we keep your learned friend off the front page . . .'

'What's that?'

'Couldn't you just give me a little taster? Just a hint, you understand, of your approach to the defence of the wicked witch?'

'Perhaps I'd say that if I were a wicked witch I think I'd be careful not to dress as one. But you can't print that yet.'

'Understood! We'll save it for your first instalment. Anything else?'

'Just that I wonder where Thelma Ropner is meant to have kept Tommy locked up, fed, cleaned and watered for a week.'

'Have you any ideas?'

'Not yet,' I said.

'Let me know when you have. We'll be in constant touch.' Argent drained his brandy and left, leaving me, in spite of all the *Trumpet*'s promises to make my fortune, to pay for it.

'My name coupled with that of Katerina Regen?' Claude Erskine-Brown said, and I detected an unmistakable note of pride in his voice.

'Not only are your names coupled,' I assured him, 'everything about you is said to have been coupled also.'

The chump picked up the photograph and examined it closely. 'Doesn't she look beautiful?' he purred at it. 'And don't you think I'm looking rather young?'

'Positively childlike,' I told him. 'I'm sure Phillida will tell you what a spring chicken you look when she sees the front page of the *Trumpet*.'

'That would not be a good thing.' Claude put the photograph back on my desk and I saw that his hand was now trembling. 'Please put it away, Rumpole. In a sealed envelope, in case the clerk sees it. They won't really publish it, will they? Not in a *tabloid*?'

'If I let them.'

'You have some influence over the *Trumpet*, Rumpole?' Claude's voice was full of hope.

'Perhaps a little.'

'You would act for me in this matter?'

'You obviously need help.'

'On the whole,' he said, after having given the matter deep thought, 'I think it's better that the very beautiful thing Katerina and I have for each other should remain a secret. It would be better for Chambers.'

'And considerably better for you.'

'I'm not in the least ashamed of loving Katerina.'

'But Mrs Justice Phillida Erskine-Brown would condemn you to a long stretch of withering contempt if she got to hear about it.'

'I suppose you're right. Perhaps you'll let me look at this from time to time, though? Just to remember.'

'To remember what?'

'The day I had lunch with Katerina.'

'At the *Trumpet* they don't think that's all that you had.'

'Don't they?' Claude was smiling complacently. He seemed, poor chump, to be deeply flattered. 'It was a wonderful experience.'

'How wonderful exactly?'

'Well, we went into the restaurant.'

'You would do if you were having lunch.'

'And sat down.'

'You amaze me.'

'And talked about Schubert.'

'Please, Erskine-Brown, spare me the embarrassing details.'

'And then . . . Well, I touched her hand and I was about to tell her how much I really fancied her and I hadn't felt so, well, uplifted by any other woman. And then we were interrupted, rather rudely I thought.'

'By her husband?'

'Of course not. She hasn't got one. No. By the waiter who told us about that day's specials.'

'Talkative bloke, was he?'

'Honestly, Rumpole, he went on for what seemed like hours, all about sea bass grilled with aubergines and served with a light pesto and tomato coulis – and that sort of thing.'

'He broke the spell?'

'Exactly. And when I got back in my stride and said I felt my whole life in love and music was simply a prelude to that golden moment, that bloody waiter came back.'

'And interrupted?'

'He said, "Who's having the fish?" '

'Put you off your stroke again.'

'I'm afraid so. But we got very close after that. She asked me up to her room.'

'So you did . . .'

'Well, not exactly. I mean, she asked me up to give me her new CD. Strauss's last songs.' There was a lengthy pause.

'Is that the end of the story?'

'Until the next time.'

'Next time?'

'She said we must have lunch again. I knew exactly what she meant. She said, "I'll have longer for you next time." I think she had another appointment that particular afternoon.'

'The *Trumpet* thinks you strayed till five-thirty when you came out again and kissed.'

'Does it think that?' Erskine-Brown gave me another chance to study his self-satisfied smirk. 'Then it understands exactly how close we are to each other.' He made for the door and, on the way out, had another attack of anxiety. 'I say, Rumpole. About that lovely photograph . . . Of course, it would be a great deal better if Philly didn't see it in the paper.'

'I'm bound to agree with you.'

'So will you act for me in this rather delicate matter, Rumpole?'

'I suppose I'd better. I must say you seem quite incapable of acting for yourself. What time did you leave the Galaxy Hotel?'

'About two-thirty, I think. I went out of the back entrance.'

As soon as the door had closed on him, I forgot Claude and his troubles. I had other things to think of. I thought of them for a long time and then I rang Bonny Bernard and asked him to send round copies of every piece the *Trumpet* had published about Sheena Constant and the Little Boy Lost. There was something in one of them, I felt sure, which was of great importance for me to remember. And then, to complete the story, I told him to get all they had written about Tina Santos.

'Now, when I think about it again, I am sure that the voice I heard on the telephone the night we found Tommy, the voice that told us to go to nineteen Swansdown Avenue, was Thelma Ropner's. I was at school for many years with Thelma and we used to be close friends. I am prepared to give this evidence on oath in Court.' The Prosecution had served Sheena's additional

statement on us and, with considerable reluctance, I had told
Bernard to get Thelma in for another conference.

'Is that what Sheena says?' Miss Ropner laughed, an eerie
and not very comfortable sound. 'Then Sheena is lying.'

'Why would she lie?'

'Because she doesn't like me. She's never liked me since I
told her what a boring little company creep her precious Steve
was.'

Another of Miss Ropner's insults had come home to roost,
but there was no point in going on about it. Instead I said, 'I
just hope *you've* told me the truth. If you haven't, it's going to
make life very difficult for me.'

'Poor old you!' She was still laughing. 'Can't you cope with
difficult cases? Anyway, it's true. I didn't take Tommy.'

'Did you tell us the truth about what you were doing during
the week he went missing?'

'I told you I was sleeping at the Edmundses and working
during the day.'

'Working at what exactly? Will you give Mr Bernard a list,
with dates?'

'Oh, you can't expect me to remember dates.'

'I think you'd better try. And I don't suppose you'll have
any difficulty in telling us where you're working now.'

'Now?' The question seemed to shock her.

'Yes. Where?' I lifted a pencil.

'I told you!' She was making an exaggerated effort to control
her irritation. 'The Stick-Up Theatre Company. We've got a
tour of Welsh community centres at the planning stage.'

'What do you do with a client who won't stop lying to you?'
I asked Bonny Bernard when Miss Ropner had gone off with
no goodbye, only a look of undying resentment. Bernard smiled
sadly, as though the truth was rare and unhoped-for among his
clientele. Then I told him to engage the services of a seasoned,
not to say elderly, private eye to discover exactly what Thelma
had been up to during the week of Tommy's captivity. Ferdinand Isaac Gerald Newton (known to his many grateful
customers as Fig Newton) was well known and respected by
Bernard, who doubted if the legal aid authorities would pay
him and dared we ask Thelma to dig into her handbag because

we seriously doubted her word? 'Try my friends on the *Trumpet*,' I told him. 'If they can afford Dom Perignon, they can afford Fig. I think it's the least they can do for us.'

'I sent for you, Rumpole, as a senior member of Chambers, because I have had some most unhappy news.'

'Then I'll be going. I've got quite enough worries at the moment.'

'Claude Erskine-Brown,' Soapy Sam Ballard rabbited on, 'has dishonoured his silk! He is likely to bring Equity Court into scandal and disrespect.' Pacing the room in a disturbed fashion, he had now blocked my passage to the door.

'He's never pinched the nailbrush from the downstairs loo?'

'These are serious matters, Rumpole. He has broken the Seventh Commandment. He has committed adultery – in the afternoon.'

'Is that so much worse than adultery in the morning?'

'He has been flagrantly unfaithful – to a High Court Judge.'

'That's not his fault.'

'Of course it's his fault.'

'Not his fault that his wife's a High Court Judge.'

'I suppose you'll say it's not his fault he's committed adultery! I suppose you'll put forward some ridiculous defence.'

'Claude's no more capable of adultery than he is of winning a difficult case. His extramarital coitus is perpetually and incurably interruptus. I ask for – no, I demand – a verdict of not guilty.'

'Rumpole! I have it from his own mouth.'

'Then he's an unreliable witness.'

'He has told me that this scandalous liaison is about to be exposed in the national press.'

'In the *Trumpet*?'

'I think that's what he said.'

'Why do you suppose he told you that?'

'I imagine because he sincerely regretted his sin and wanted to throw himself on my mercy.'

'Nonsense! He was boasting.'

'Boasting?' Soapy Sam looked entirely confused.

'Showing off. Bragging, wanting us all to think that he's a

gay young dog, when in truth he's an entirely domesticated animal that's almost never off the lead.'

'Are you saying that people would boast of breaking the Seventh Commandment?'

'They do it on practically every page of the *Trumpet*.'

Ballard sat down then, as though his legs had become weak with amazement. He gasped for breath. 'I have told Erskine-Brown that if this scandal becomes public knowledge, there will be no room for him in Chambers.'

'I thought he'd thrown himself on your mercy.'

'He did.'

'And your mercy wasn't there?'

'God may forgive Erskine-Brown. After repentance.'

'But you won't.'

'I have Chambers to consider.'

'I suggest you leave Chambers alone and get on with your practice, what there is of it.' I rose and made for the door whilst the path to it was unimpeded. 'Oh, and don't worry your pretty little head, Sam. There isn't going to be a scandal.'

'How can you be sure of that?'

'Because if Claude's Don Giovanni, I'm Tarzan of the Apes. No need for you to envy the poor blighter, Bollard. He didn't get around to bonking anybody.'

And I left before he could argue.

The Psychic Shop was open at three the next afternoon when I pushed open the door. What on earth did I think I was doing? When young Argent called me Sherlock Rumpole, had the title completely unhinged me? Was I trying to outdo the incomparable Fig Newton, or was this a mission of such delicacy that I didn't feel I could leave it to him? I had nothing in Court and for the day I was no longer a barrister; in fact I had put on the old tweed jacket, grey flannel bags and comforting Hush Puppies to prove it. I was an anonymous old man after information. If I was rumbled, I had my cover-story pat. I had just dropped in for a clairvoyant reading because I was seriously interested in the future.

A bell pinged faintly as I opened the door, but the shop was empty. I stood for a moment breathing in a smell which seemed to be a mixture of incense, Dettol and drains. There were some printed astrological charts pinned on the walls, otherwise the shop was dim and sparsely furnished. There was no sign of what I had noticed on the day when I had asked Bernard to park his car and stood looking in at the window. There was a bead curtain at the back of the shop. It rattled and a woman entered like a burst of sunlight. She had reddish hair, a bright yellow dress and the fixed, somewhat desperate smile of someone who is constantly in touch with those who have passed over and who has learnt to make the best of it. She was the woman I had seen in the Constants' front garden, snipping tulips, the woman whose photograph was in the window of the Psychic Shop. She was Steve's Aunt Brenda, who'd been in touch with the spirit world for news of the Little Boy Lost.

'Welcome, stranger,' she said. 'Have you come for a reading?'

'If you have time.'

'Perhaps you have an anxiety about your future.'

'Always. An extreme anxiety.'

'And you want your birth chart analysed?'

'That would be extremely helpful.'

'You have an interest in clairvoyancy?'

'A lifetime's interest.'

'Then, if you'll follow me, I'll see if I can fit you in.'

She led me into a sudden blaze of colour. The inner room had huge vivid green leaves on its wallpaper, and bright red, blue and yellow astrological charts. The table was covered with pink formica on which a glass ball on a bright blue stand presumably provided an entrance to a Technicolor spirit world for those with sufficient imagination to switch on to its channel. Death, I thought, in this small and lurid world was an endless soap opera in primary colours. I said, 'You are Miss Brenda Constant, aren't you?'

She was not at all surprised. 'I suppose I've got to get used to the fact that I've become famous.' She was middle-aged, but she giggled like a young girl. 'I can't complain. It's brought me a lot of customers.'

'Because of little Tommy?'

'Because the spirit people were able to tell us who'd got the baby.'

'And who had?'

'Thelma Ropner, of course. She was always jealous of Sheena. Now then, do please sit down and tell me *your* name.'

'Samuel Ballard.' I couldn't help it. It just occurred to me as I sat on a hard and shiny plastic chair and rested my elbows on the pink formica.

'Samuel. That's a very *nice* name.' She unrolled some sort of chart of the heavens and sat opposite me, ready to voyage into the unknown. 'There are plenty of Samuels in the spirit world.'

I told her that didn't surprise me in the least. I was looking past her at a narrow window which seemed to overlook a small, paved strip and a high wooden fence.

'Birth sign?' She was about to fill in a form.

'Cancer, the crab.' I thought that might be appropriate for Bollard.

'Birthdate?'

'The twenty-ninth of June 1940. It was a stormy night and there was a partial eclipse of the moon. Apparently a dead owl fell out of the sky and into my parents' garden in Waltham Cross.' From then on I was inventing and Auntie Brenda was taking copious notes. I didn't have to go on too long before the shop door pinged again. She put down her scarlet Biro, sighed heavily and said, 'Everyone wants a reading since the story came out in the *Trumpet*,' and exited through the bead curtain. I got up and crossed to the window. It was then I saw, on the strip of crazy paving, what I thought I had once seen in the shop, a child's pushchair with something on the seat which, I was sure, could be described as a yellow flop-eared rabbit, much clutched and frequently caressed.

I could hear Auntie Brenda's grand and busy greeting to a prospective customer in the shop. There was a long cupboard built against one wall of the astrological consulting room. I slid back the door as quietly as possible and was surprised, as I often am, by the casual way in which many people preserve evidence. Hanging uncertainly on a wire coat-hanger, I saw a shiny, black plastic mackintosh and, on the shelf above it, a dark beret.

I got the door shut as Auntie Brenda came back to peer into Samuel Ballard's future.

'One last question, Mrs Sheena Constant. Looking back on that telephone call in which you were told to go and look in nineteen Swansdown Avenue, can you now say who you think called you?'

'Don't let's have what she thought, my Lord.' I was up on my hind legs in no time. 'Don't let's have pure speculation.'

'The witness is fully entitled to say who she thinks telephoned her, Mr Rumpole. There is no need to delay this trial with unnecessary objections.' His Honour Judge Pick bore, in my opinion, a singular resemblance to a parakeet. He had a high colour, a small and beaky nose, a bright and malignant eye, and his usual reaction to my contributions to the proceedings was a flurried and resentful squawk.

'I'm quite sure who it was now.' Sheena smiled from the witness-box. 'It was someone I'd known from school.'

'What was her name?'

'Thelma Ropner.'

'The defendant Ropner whom we now see in the dock?' The bird on the Bench rubbed it in quite unnecessarily. My learned friend, Leonard Fanner (known to us down the Bailey as Lenny the Lion because of his extreme nervousness in Court and general lack of roaring power), appearing for the Prosecution, said, 'Thank you very much, Mrs Constant,' and sat down gratefully.

I rose to cross-examine Mrs Constant. 'You say you were at school with my client, Thelma Ropner?'

'Yes.'

'And were you also at school with a girl called Tina Santos?'

'Tina? Yes, I knew her.'

'And did she become the secretary of a local MP called David Bangor, Parliamentary Secretary to the Minister for Enterprise?'

'She worked for a politician. I think that's what Tina did.'

'You know what Tina did, don't you? She had a well-publicized love affair with the Honourable Member.'

'Mr Rumpole!'

I ignored the squawk from the Bench and continued, 'And then told the whole story to the *Trumpet* because he wouldn't leave his wife and marry her.'

Sheena frowned a little and said, 'I think I did read something about it, yes.'

'The whole nation read something about it.' I picked up a cutting: '"I shared a shower with Minister in Commons' bathroom. Skinny-dipping during the debate on Post Office privatization."'

'Mr Fanner, are you not objecting to this cross-examination?' The Judge turned to my learned friend for help.

'I'm not entirely sure where it's leading, my Lord.' Lenny the Lion stood up, magnificent in his indecision.

'Exactly where is it leading, Mr Rumpole? Perhaps you'd be good enough to explain.' The Judge was pecking away at me, but I rose above it.

'It's leading, my Lord, to a vital issue in this case.' I turned to give my full attention to the mother for whom I had felt such sympathy. 'Do you know how much Tina Santos got paid for that story?'

'Mr Rumpole!'

'I think it was quite a lot. A ridiculous lot of money, it was.'

'Exactly. For that parliamentary shower bath, Tina Santos earned thousands of pounds. Wasn't that common knowledge among the old girls of Cripping Comprehensive?'

'She told us she got a lot of money, yes.'

'Easy money, wasn't it?'

'Much too easy, I'd say, for Tina.'

'Mrs Constant, how much did the *Trumpet* pay you for the exclusive rights to the story of your Little Boy Lost?'

Up to then the witness had been quiet, composed, a young woman reliving a painful event with commendable courage. For a moment, I saw another Sheena, hard and angry. 'That's no business of yours, that isn't! I don't have to tell him that, do I?' She turned, for escape, to the Judge, who offered it to her eagerly.

'Certainly not. The question was entirely irrelevant. Members of the Jury, you will ignore Mr Rumpole's last question. I'm looking at the clock, Mr Fanner.'

'Yes, my Lord.' Lenny the Lion confirmed that that was exactly what the old bird was doing.

'I shall adjourn now. Mr Rumpole, by tomorrow morning, perhaps you will have thought of some relevant questions to ask this witness.'

'Tomorrow morning, my Lord, I shall hope to demonstrate that the question I just asked was entirely relevant.'

'I have ruled on that, Mr Rumpole. I trust that the Jury will put it completely out of their minds.'

But I knew the Jury wouldn't.

I emerged from that bout in Court panting slightly, bruised a little, but undaunted, mopping the brow and removing the wig to give the top of my head an airing. The researches of the admirable Fig Newton had allowed me to serve an alibi notice on the Prosecution, and I asked Lenny the Lionhearted if the forces of law and order had been able to check the story it contained.

'I'm not sure, Rumpole. I'll have to speak to the officer in charge of the case.'

'Screw up your courage, old darling, to the sticking point,' I encouraged him. 'And do just that.'

Then, as Lenny went off on his daring mission, I heard a voice at my elbow. 'Well, sir. You seem to know a lot about the *Trumpet*'s money. Are you going to let us pay you a slice of it?'

'I'll meet you in Pommeroy's.' I took young Argent's arm and walked him away from the assembled lawyers. 'Six o'clock convenient?'

'You'll let us in on your defence?'

'It's possible. Oh, you know that picture of Katerina Regen, the Nightingale, arriving at the Galaxy Hotel?'

'For her afternoon bonk?'

'Did your man get a snap of her leaving by any chance?'

'I'm sure he did. I told you, we've got that story sewn up.'

'Probably. But bring a copy of the leaving picture, will you? I'm curious to see it.'

'Right you are, sir.' The boy journalist seemed to be suppressing laughter, his usual problem. 'And you'll tell me what *you've* got up your sleeve?'

'My sleeve,' I promised him, 'will be entirely open to you.'

So I went back to Chambers and had a brief consultation with Bonny Bernard about the events of the day, skimmed through a forthcoming matter of warehouse-breaking by a particularly inefficient member of the Timson clan, and put on my hat for Pommeroy's. On my way out of Chambers, I passed a despondent Claude, who whispered a furtive question about his exposure in the public prints. 'I'm going to meet the journalist in question now. I have high hopes that you will emerge without a stain on your character.' As I left him I couldn't honestly tell if the fellow looked relieved or disappointed.

'You needn't invest in Dom Perignon,' I told Jonathan Argent, when we were established in a discreet table in Pommeroy's, the one under the staircase, and the furthest from the gents, 'until you're quite sure you like what I'm going to tell you.'

'You mean you still haven't thought of a defence in the case of the Little Boy Lost?'

'Not exactly. In fact, my defence is a perfectly simple one. The little boy was never lost at all.'

'You're joking!' But that was one moment when I noticed that young Argent wasn't tempted to suppress a laugh.

'Not really. Tell me how much *did* the *Trumpet* pay Sheena Constant?'

He mentioned a generous number of Ks.

'Not bad money for sending young Tommy to stay at his Great-aunt Brenda's.'

'What on earth are you talking about?'

'What on earth? Dear old Brenda doesn't want to be on earth very much, does she? She wants to be up in the stars, in the spirit world, or on the other side of the wall of death. But she is of the earth, earthy. I wonder what her cut was for a week's babyminding.'

'Do you mind telling me what you're talking about?' Young Jonathan looked, for once, out of his depth.

'I don't mind in the least. I'm talking about fraud, rather an ingenious one to fool sentimental old folks like me and con your hardboiled tabloid out of a considerable amount of cash. Poor old darling, what a soft touch you brilliant journalists are!'

'You mean . . .?'

'I mean Aunt Brenda was hired to put on a black mac with a dashing beret and remove the little boy from the mechanical donkey. Did you ever wonder why he went so quietly? Why he didn't cry or yell out? Because he knew he was safe with his dad's old auntie. She looked after him for a week, sometimes at her house, at least once or twice at her fortune shop. Then she dumped him in the squatters' garden as planned and made the call from a phone box in Swansdown Avenue.'

'But Sheena recognized your client's voice.'

'No, she didn't. That was all part of the plot to frame Thelma. Someone who is far easier to frame than a reproduction of "The Stag at Bay".'

'Why Thelma?'

'Sheena hates her. She'd been rude about Steve, called him a boring little company man and a dreary middle manager. That's why they chose Brenda, because she's got rust-coloured hair like Thelma's. And that's why they tricked Brenda out in Thelma's customary suit of solemn black.'

There was a pause while Jonathan Argent digested the information. Then he asked me if I could prove it.

'We'll see after I've finished cross-examining Sheena. What I *can* prove is that Thelma's innocent.'

'How?'

'She spent that week at a residential business course at a country house near Tunbridge Wells. She had lessons in salesmanship and competitive marketing. She went to school with a lot of ambitious reps and wore her name on a plastic label.'

'Did she tell you that?'

'Of course not. But we found it out, and we've got witnesses to prove it. Thelma's going to be furious when she hears the evidence.'

'Why?'

'Because it'll prove one thing. That she wants to become a

boring little middle manager just like Steve Constant. She's terribly ashamed of that. She'd rather be suspected of kidnapping than admit it. She even took the course under an assumed name. Luckily, one of the tutors recognized her photograph.'

'What did she call herself?'

'Tina Jones. Not Santos. Just the Christian name. It's odd that they all seem to have been jealous of Tina.'

The talkative journalist broke all records for a long and thoughtful silence. At last he said, 'If you tell that story in Court, it's going to make the *Trumpet* look rather foolish.'

'You can't make an omelette without breaking eggs.'

'And you can't expect us to pay you for holding us up to general ridicule.'

'That's why I advised you to save on the Dom Perignon. By the way, did you bring me the diva's leaving photograph?'

He said he had, but it seemed as though Claude's troubles no longer interested him greatly. Suddenly he was a very anxious young journalist.

'Of course,' I said, 'I could go and beard Lenny the Lion in his den and see if he'll drop the case.'

'Could you?' He couldn't help sounding eager.

'I could try.'

He thought it over and then said, 'Why do you call him Lenny the Lion?'

'Because he's such a fearsome prosecutor. Carnivorous, I'd call him. Still, I'm prepared to ask if he'll go quietly, and keep your name out of the papers. I imagine the *Sun* would rather make mincemeat of you.'

'Yes . . .' The thought clearly gave him no pleasure. 'Will you try to settle it?'

'On one condition.'

'You want money?'

'Strangely enough, I don't. But I want you to drop the story about Claude Erskine-Brown.'

'I think we can do that.'

'Anyway, it seems you've got the wrong chap.' I looked down at the photograph. It showed Katerina leaving the Galaxy with her appointment for the afternoon, the man she had no doubt embraced after her lunch with Claude. It was none other

than the huge, booming barrister who had organized her concert in the Outer Temple, Barrington McTear, Q.C., known to
me only as Cut Above.

'We've checked your client's alibi, Rumpole. I had a word with
the officer in charge of the case.'

'That was extremely brave of you. And . . .?'

'It appears to stand up.'

'That's right. It's not a baby any more. It's a big, strong
grown-up alibi.'

We were having coffee in the Old Bailey canteen before Mr
Justice Pick started work for the day. Around us, solicitors and
learned friends, plain-clothes officers of the law and accused
persons trying to look optimistic, were preparing to meet the
challenge of a day in Court. Lenny lowered his voice almost to
a whisper. 'I don't suppose the *Trumpet* wants to look foolish
in public.'

'No, Lenny. I don't believe it does.'

'The paper wouldn't welcome a prolonged investigation.'

'You might get rather a bad press if you go on.'

'Do you know, Rumpole, I've been thinking I might ask to
see the Judge.'

'You always were a brave prosecutor.'

'Tell him that, all things considered, the Prosecution aren't
offering any further evidence against your client.'

'I've always said you were a complete carnivore.'

'No need to subject the Constants and the paper to universal
derision.'

'No need at all.'

'It would serve no useful purpose.'

'None.'

'So I'll tell Pick I'm throwing in my hand.'

'It takes courage to do that.'

'Will that suit you, Rumpole?'

'It will suit me very well indeed.'

'So that's sorted then.'

'Yes.'

'Sorry we couldn't have had a fight.'

'So am I. In a way.'

'Never mind, Rumpole. There'll be other occasions.' He looked at me, I thought, quite gloomily.

'Yes, Lenny. I'm sure there will.'

That didn't seem to cheer him up at all.

It was all over. Thelma sniffed when she was discharged and told me that the whole thing had been a complete waste of her time. I got a little parcel from Jonathan Argent and took it to Claude Erskine-Brown in his room.

'Here's your picture back. And the negative.'

'They're not going to use it in the paper?'

'Don't worry. There'll be no scandal. And Soapy Sam Bollard won't throw you out of Chambers.'

'I might keep this photograph.' Claude took the record of his encounter out of its envelope and looked at it lovingly.

'I strongly advise you not to.'

'In my drawer? Here in Chambers?'

'Wherever you keep it, our Portia's going to find it some time.'

'Perhaps you're right.' He sighed heavily. 'But a memento of what might have been . . .'

'It's all in your mind, Claude. Keep it there.'

'I might have been famous as Katerina Regen's lover.' His voice was full of regret.

'You want me to take that picture round to the *Sun*?'

'Perhaps not. Let it go.' He handed me the package. 'Dispose of it how you will. But I shall think of her, Rumpole. I shall think of her quite often. When I'm alone.'

I took the package from him and looked at Claude with pity. Poor fool! He'd really wanted to get his name in the papers.

Rumpole and the Rights of Man

'A toast to Mr Rumpole, our fellow European.' The faces around me were pink and smiling encouragingly. Glasses of a colourless fluid were raised, which rushed down the throat like a hot wind, took your breath away and left you gasping and more than a little confused. Was I European? I supposed so, although I had never thought of it before.

If I think about it at all, I suppose I'm English. Not British. The Scots, the Irish and in particular the Welsh, although full of charm and excellent qualities, are undoubtedly foreign. I never talk about the U.K., an expression much favoured by politicians and management consultants who have retired to live on the Costa del Crime. Had I been mistaken all this time, I wondered, as the cold beer joined the eau de vie? Was I not just an Englishman abroad but a European who had stayed at home? I looked down at the huge plate of sour cabbage and boiled sausage (in England, I had been tempted to say, we don't boil sausages). The restaurant was in a street of huge, medieval, half-timbered houses, now sheltering boutiques and souvenir shops. We were in France but near that part of Germany where, so my hosts told me, the Rhine maidens and the dwarf and the giants lived through those endless operas Claude Erskine-Brown was so keen on, characters I found so much less interesting than the clients down the Old Bailey, or even my latest quarry, his Honour Judge Billy Bloxham, a new and unwelcome addition to the Judges entitled to try cases of alleged murder.

'And also to you, Mr Rumpole!' The toastmaster, a somewhat rimless man with rimless glasses perched on a long, narrow nose, who spoke with the pursed lips and squeezed vowels of a Nord, raised his glass to me: 'The defender of human rights'.

'Well,' I had to tell them, 'I'm not exactly that. I mean, I spend most of my time defending people.'

'Defending their rights.' Peter Fishlock, my instructing solicitor, who had travelled with me from England, was a great one for rights and for the Society for a Written Constitution, of which he was, as he kept telling me, 'chair'. During our long hours together, in English courts and on the bumpy ride across the sky to Strasburg, I realized how much I missed Bonny Bernard, who was less interested in human rights than in trying to find a decent bit of alibi evidence.

'I'm not so sure about that either.' We had gone through a good many toasts that evening, to the Community of Nations and the Irrelevance of Gender, Freedom from Torture combined with a Common Currency, and so much eau de vie had slipped down the red lane that my courage had become extremely Dutch. 'I'm defending their wrongs quite often. Their errors and foolish ways. I suppose I look on the law as a sort of disease, and I'm the doctor who tries to cure his patient of it as quickly as possible.'

'That is only your English modesty speaking there, Mr Rumpole.' A reassuring female voice sounded somewhere above my head. Betsi Hoprecht, tall and blonde, with a face as smooth and delicately brown as a new-laid egg, a young German lawyer with an encyclopaedic knowledge of the ways of the European Court, had appointed herself my helper, guardian, nurse and general protector for the purposes of the present proceedings. 'We all know how you English wish to conceal your finer feelings under all those layers of clothing you wear. But I think we know where Mr Rumpole's heart is, and I think it's in the right place.' Betsi's speech was in perfect English, although no one English would have made it.

'I propose a toast then.' Govan Welamson, the rimless Swede and Professor of International Law, had his slender glass refilled. 'To Mr Rumpole's heart.'

'Please,' I begged, 'couldn't we drink to something a little less embarrassing. Like the Common Agricultural Policy?'

'Come on, Rumpole. We all know you spend your time defending the underdog.' This came from Jeremy Jameson, Member of the European Parliament, who had a surprisingly young face stuck on the body of a sedentary and spreading politician. He had come with a half-smiling and mostly silent woman with a thin nose and a short upper lip. With her tight curls she had the appearance of an intelligent and attractive sheep. She wore a neat black suit with a few gold ornaments and smelled of the most expensive perfume in the duty free. The Euro M.P. had introduced her simply as Poppy.

Jameson stood, I seemed to remember, in the Liberal interest and had a huge constituency in the West of England, where no one was able to remember his name. He spoke, even when he was at his most polite, with a kind of contemptuous amusement: 'Defending the underdog brought you to Strasburg,' he said. 'To all these perfectly marvellous restaurants, with a side salad of human rights?'

'The great thing about underdogs,' I reminded him, 'is that they're usually on legal aid.'

'But you defend them,' Betsi told me firmly, 'for the sake of your principles.'

'I defend them,' I corrected her, 'for the sake of the rent of the mansion flat and my wife's effort to boost consumer spending every Saturday at Safeway's.'

'Don't know why we wanted to go into Europe anyway,' a deep-voiced woman, her grey hair tousled, her cheeks flushed, who had been chain-smoking over the choucroute, boomed at us. 'All a lot of bloody nonsense. They want us to grow square strawberries! They must be potty.' She had been introduced as Lady Mary Parsloe, the wife of Eddie Parsloe, the neat, pretty-faced man from the consular service who wore, whenever his wife was speaking, a smile of agonized patience. 'Mary,' he told us, 'is more of a gardener than a diplomat.'

'If you'd lost five great-uncles at Passchendaele and a father shot a week before V.E. Day, I don't think you'd be diplomatic, would you, Mr Rumpole?'

'And Mary's direct ancestor lost his leg at Waterloo, didn't he, dear?'

'That was a mere trifle.' She brushed her husband off as though he were a cloud of gnats bothering her weeding. 'Come on, Mr Rumpole, speak up. Don't you think it's potty?'

'I hadn't heard about the square strawberries.'

'Well, you've bloody well heard about them now. You can't be too happy about it.'

'Mr Rumpole is contented because he can enjoy a good dinner and also serve the cause of justice.' Betsi had also appointed herself my official spokesman. 'But there's someone over there who's not so happy, I'm just thinking.'

Our company turned to glance at the man sitting under an elaborate mural depicting an unfortunate and bloodstained moment during the Thirty Years War. I didn't turn. I had seen his Honour Billy Bloxham when he came in; he had stared past me as though he hoped I didn't exist.

'The Judge,' Peter Fishlock said with scarcely suppressed excitement, 'is looking as though he's waiting to be sentenced.'

At which point a waiter, who looked as though his day job was Euro Minister in charge of Strawberry Shapes, came up to point out that to *fumer* was *absolument défendu*.

'Eddie' – Lady Mary made what I felt was a rare appeal to her husband – 'can you tell me the French for piss off?'

It all started at the Bank Underground. It should seem a long time ago, for I have reached the age when every day must be savoured and cherished. In fact, the years flash by like stations at which the train doesn't stop, and the year which it took Amin Hashimi's case to reach the dizzy eminence of the European Court of Human Rights seemed to take up no time at all. I don't know how slowly it went for Mr Hashimi, but then he was in prison for life.

George Freeling was forty-three years old, with a wife and two children in Buckhurst Hill. He worked as a middle manager at Netherbank, a huge glass and concrete tower which dwarfed a Wren church not far from the Mansion House. Each night at approximately five forty-five Mr Freeling joined the population explosion which surged away from their computer screens and, leaving the world's markets to enrich or ruin their clients, struggled down the tube. On the evening in question the platform for the eastbound Central Line resembled the Black Hole of Calcutta. Most of the sufferers at least had a safe journey home but George Freeling, standing on the edge of the platform, fell in front of the train as it rattled out of the darkness on its way from St Paul's. He was found to have been shot in the back: a revolver with a silencer and a single blue glove made of polyester and wool were lying between the lines and beside his dead body.

This method of public assassination had, I later discovered, been copied from a detective story where it attracted less attention. Sandra Atherton, a secretary at Citibank, saw a young man of Middle-Eastern appearance apparently push Freeling in the back before he fell. She lost sight of him in the crowd, but then she saw him again, running towards the exit. She called to the guard, who gave chase, followed by some other passengers who also thought they'd seen Freeling pushed – among them Vernon Wynstanley, a young stockbroker, and Emily Brotherton, a tea-lady. For a very short time these witnesses lost sight of the supposed assassin in the tiled and echoing underground passages, but the guard managed to communicate with ground level. Amin Hashimi was stopped as he was leaving the station and the City police were sent for. The three named witnesses made a positive identification. Later, when Hashimi was examined forensically, fibres similar to those in the blue glove were found, in a microscopic quantity, under the fingernails of his right hand. Peter Fishlock got the case, thanks to a friend in the Magistrates Court, and, as I had just won a rather tricky affray and criminal damage for him, he was wise enough to instruct Horace Rumpole for the Defence. During the complicated course of the proceedings he got the idea of Rumpole as the champion of the underdog, or at least of a student of Middle-Eastern extraction, which led us to the choucroute and the eau de vie – and to my international acclaim in Strasburg.

The case came on before his Honour Judge Bloxham, a person who, I think, deliberately cultivated his likeness to a pallid bulldog. His skin was curiously white and his forehead was perpetually furrowed, as were his jowls. With these similar lines above and below, and his eyebrows matching his moustache, he had one of those faces which could make sense either way up, like the comical drawings that once appeared in children's books.

I can't say I had embarked on the Defence of Mr Hashimi with any high hopes of success. I could only do my poor best, although I have to say, in all modesty, that my poor best is considerably better than the poorer best of such learned friends as Claude Erskine-Brown and Soapy Sam Ballard, Q.C. The most I could do, I thought, was to unsettle the identification evidence, have a bit of harmless fun on the subject of wool and polyester fibres, and point to the great weakness of the Prosecution case: the complete absence of any sort of motive for the alleged assassination of George Freeling.

'You had never met this man Freeling?'

'Never. Never had I spoken to him.'

'Or seen him?'

'Perhaps. Travelling on that Underground line you see many faces. Perhaps his was among them.'

'You use that line every day?'

'Back and forwards. To my college in Holborn, where I take business studies and office management. I am reading during the journey; I don't notice many people.'

'Did you know anything about Netherbank where Freeling worked?'

'I have heard of it, of course. Not much more.' We were sitting in the interview room in Brixton and I thought that Mr Hashimi might appeal to the women on the Jury. He looked young enough to be mothered and his large brown eyes gave him an expression of injured innocence. He had long, pale fingers and, even in the disinfected atmosphere of Brixton, he seemed to give off a faint smell of sandalwood and spices. I told him that I would do my best for him.

'We are in the hands of Allah the Compassionate and Merciful. He ordains life and death and has power over all things.'

'You pray to Allah?'

'Of course.'

'Well, ask him to be particularly compassionate and merciful down the Old Bailey next week, why don't you?'

As the gates of the prison house closed behind us and we squeezed into Peter Fishlock's small Japanese motor, I said, 'We have one bright spot in a rather gloomy prospect.'

'The absence of motive?'

'No. The presence of his Honour Judge Bloxham.'

'I thought Billy Bloxham disapproved of foreign students using the Health Service.'

'Better than that. He's allergic to any sort of alien. Visitors from what was once our far-flung empire bring him out in a nervous rash.'

'How's that going to help Amin?'

'Because if we can get Billy to show his hand, if we can needle the old darling into a quaint little display of racial prejudice, then we can present a bigoted Bloxham to the Jury and they might decline to obey orders. In fact, there's an outside chance, I say no more than that, my fine Fishlock, that we might just scrape home to victory!'

'Of course, their evidence on the fibres is very unconvincing.'

'The fibres are one thing. But Bloxham's prejudices are something else entirely. He never stops talking about being British and living in the U.K. He's a fellow who sings "Rule Britannia" in his bath and wants the Kingdom to be reserved strictly for Bloxham look-alikes, their lady wives and white children. If Allah the Compassionate wants a way for Amin Hashimi to walk, then Billy's going to lead him to it.'

'Miss Atherton. You say you saw a young man of Middle-Eastern appearance push the victim's back as the train was about to stop.'

'I saw the man in the dock do that.'

'That's what I'm trying to test, Miss Atherton. Just bear with me, will you? I suggest the first time you got a good look, face to face, at my client Mr Hashimi was when he was stopped on his way out of the station. You came up then and identified him?'

'I did, yes.'

'Are you quite sure that was the same Middle-Eastern gentleman you saw push the man on the platform?'

'Yes. I'm sure.'

'You had lost sight of him during the chase?'

'For a short while, yes.'

'And might not you and the others have ended up pursuing another Middle-Eastern young man?'

'I don't think so.'

'Come now, Miss Atherton. Don't all Middle-Eastern young men look rather similar to you? Are you sure you could have told the two of them apart?'

'Mr Rumpole.' I smiled towards the Bench, waiting for Billy to let his prejudices show. To my dismay he did nothing of the sort. 'Mr Rumpole,' he said, surprisingly gently, 'this Court is colour-blind! Where in the world this young man came from is a matter of no significance. He's fully entitled to the fair trial which I'm sure this jury is going to give him. I'm also sure that this very intelligent young lady can identify an assailant without going into racist characteristics. Isn't that so, Miss Atherton?'

'Of course I can.' Sandra Atherton was delighted to agree with the not so learned Judge.

'Very well, then. Let us continue, Mr Rumpole. And let us do so without reference to creed or colour.'

My heart sank. I could see the Jury, a mixed bag from the Hoxton area, looking at the pallid Bloxham and rather liking what they saw. He had decided, I now realized, to play a particularly mean trick on the Defence. He was going to give us a fair trial.

Vernon Wynstanley, the stockbroker, and Emily Brotherton were hardly less sure of their identification. Mrs Brotherton, the image of the jolly tea-lady about to be replaced by a mechanical dispenser, was particularly popular with the Jury. I let them both go as soon as possible, but spent a good deal of time cross-examining the fibre expert on the amount of wool and polyester mixture available in London, and the vast number of garments which might have left innocent traces under my client's fingernails. I stopped when I noticed that number three in the jury-box had dropped off to sleep.

In my final speech, given, I had to say, with even more than my usual eloquence, I dwelt on the uncertainty of identification evidence at the best of times, and particularly when the incident took place in an Underground station during the rush hour and must have been a horrific shock to all concerned. I gave the Jury at least twenty minutes on the absence of motive. What was my client, Amin Hashimi, meant to be? A criminal lunatic who killed at random just for kicks? Nothing in his history, his success at his studies and his hitherto unimpeachable behaviour could support such a theory. After I had imitated the Scales of Justice, and put in the ounce of reasonable doubt which would weigh them down on the side of the Defence, I sank into my seat, tired and sweating. I had done my best and I could only hope that Billy Bloxham would put his foot in it.

He didn't. He told the Jury that, although the Prosecution didn't have to supply a motive, they should take full account of all Mr Rumpole had said about the apparent purposelessness of the crime. He told them that identification evidence was often unreliable and they should approach it with great care, but whether they believed the secretary, the stockbroker and the tea-lady was a matter entirely for them. He said they should think about whether the fibres helped prove the case and that they mustn't convict unless they were quite sure. In fact, it was an appallingly fair summing-up.

I said goodbye to my client after Allah the Compassionate, the Merciful, had failed to come up trumps. Amin Hashimi, as calm as ever, thanked me politely and said, 'The hypocrites will not be forgiven. He does not guide the evildoers. And he has knowledge of all our actions. I have nothing to regret, Mr Rumpole, so please give my best wishes to your lady wife.' I had no doubt that, three or four weeks later, he would wake up to the reality of life imprisonment and his soft, brown eyes would fill with tears.

A few weeks later, however, the Compassionate one arranged something that might possibly provide an escape route for my imprisoned client. His Honour Judge Bloxham was invited to a rugby club dinner somewhere near his home in the Midlands, and he was asked to sing for his supper.

END IMMIGRATION TO END CRIME. JUDGE THANKFUL TO HAVE GOT ONE MORE ARAB STUDENT BEHIND BARS. So screamed the headline in Hilda's *Daily Telegraph* which I saw as we sat at breakfast in the mansion flat. 'Your Judge Bloxham,' she said, crunching toast, 'seems to have been rather a Silly Billy.'

'He seems to have said it all a bit too late.' I borrowed Hilda's paper. 'Anyway, he's not my Judge. I want no part of him.'

I suppose it was bad luck in a way. Billy Bloxham had no doubt expected the speech to be a private affair, and in this simple faith he must have let himself go with the pink gin, the claret, the brandy and the port. He stood up to address those used to scrumming down and tackling each other perilously low, and let the real Billy Bloxham bubble to the surface. He wasn't to know that some eager young rugby-playing reporter, fresh from the local *Echo* and anxious to make a name for himself in the world of journalism, was writing shorthand on the back of a menu and would communicate the highlights to the Press Association. The report in the *Daily Telegraph* of what Bloxham had said was fairly full:

A great many of these towel-headed gentry come here as so-called students to escape the tough laws of their own countries. No doubt they find a short stretch of community service greatly preferable to losing a hand if they're caught with their fingers in the till. No doubt they prefer our free Health Service to the attentions of the Medicine Man in the Medina. I don't know how much studying they do, but they certainly have time for plenty of extra-curricular activities. They take special courses in drug-dealing and the theft of quality cars.

Coming from a part of the world where scraps were always breaking out, they are easily drawn into violence. This is not so bad when they do it to each other, but not, repeat not, when a law-abiding subject of Her Majesty gets shot in the Underground. I have to tell you, gentlemen, that when my jury brought in a guilty verdict on the murderer Hashimi, I had a song in my heart. I retired to my room and invited my dear old usher, ex-Sergeant Major Wrigglesworth of the Blues and the Royals, to join me in a glass of sherry. 'Well done, sir,' Wrigglesworth said. 'You managed to pot the bastard.' 'One down,' I replied, 'and thousands left to go.'

When I got into Chambers Fishlock, the human rights solicitor, was already there, cradling a bundle of morning papers as though it were a long-lost child. 'Biased Judge,' he almost whooped for joy. 'Flagrantly biased! No doubt at all about that. So what do we do now?'

'We get whoever was the mole in the rugby club to swear an affidavit and troop off to the Court of Appeal.'

'To tell them the Judge was biased?'

'And has, with any luck, delivered himself into our hands.'

I am not an habitué of the Court of Appeal. It has none of the amenities I'm used to – such as witnesses to cross-examine and juries to persuade. One Judge is bad enough, but the Appeal Court comes equipped with three who bother you with unnecessary and impertinent questions which are not always easy to answer.

Lord Justice Percival Ponting, who presided over the Hashimi appeal, had hooded eyes and the distasteful look of a person who goes through life with a bad smell under his nose. He had never recovered from having achieved a double first at Cambridge and regarded Old Bailey hacks in general, and Horace Rumpole in particular, as ill-educated dimwits who couldn't read the Institutes of Justinian in Latin.

'Mr Rumpole' – the Lord of Appeal in Ordinary pronounced my name as though he regretted having stepped in it – 'will you be so good as to refer us to any passage in the transcript of the trial in which the learned Judge made any sort of biased remark to the Jury concerning your client, Mr Harashimi?'

'*Hashimi*, my Lord, as it so happens.'

'Oh, I'm so sorry. I do beg his pardon. Hashimi then. Well, Mr. Rumpole, will you now refer us to the passages in the transcript.'

'In the transcript of the speech at the rugby club? The Judge couldn't have made his views more absolutely clear . . .'

'Do remind us, Mr Rumpole. The Jury wasn't empanelled to sit in judgement at the rugby club dinner, was it?'

'No, my Lord, but . . .'

'And by the time that event took place, the Jury had reached a verdict, after an unbiased summing-up, had they not?'

'His after-dinner diatribe, his post-prandial peroration, my Lord, shows exactly what the Judge had in mind.'

'Mr Rumpole. We all may have things on our minds. We may have views about the merits of this Appeal which it might be kinder not to express in public. You may have in mind a proper realization of the shallowness of your argument. It's what's said in Court that matters!'

'We don't live our entire lives in courtrooms. What's my client to think now? What's any reasonable man to think? That he was tried unfairly by a biased judge.'

'Is that your best point?'

'Indeed, it is!' I turned up the volume to show I was running out of patience with Ponting, alarming the ushers and causing the little Lord Justice on the left to open his eyes.

'No need to raise your voice, Mr Rumpole. You are perfectly audible. Your first point is that your client was tried by a Judge who successfully concealed his true feelings?'

'And secondly, that he did so deliberately to secure a conviction.'

'You were right, Mr Rumpole.' Percy Ponting smiled down at me from a great height and in a wintry fashion. 'Your first point was the best one.'

'"A great many of these towel-headed gentry came here as so-called students to escape the tough laws of their own countries ... when my jury brought in a guilty verdict on the murderer Hashimi I had a song in my heart." How can you possibly say that's not biased?'

'Words which he didn't utter at the trial?'

'Words which show exactly how he felt at the trial.'

'Mr Rumpole, I think we are now seized of your argument.'

'I don't think you are. I think you are about to ignore my argument.'

'If you have nothing more to add . . .'

'Oh, yes, I have. A great deal more to add.' I added it for another three-quarters of an hour, while Percy Ponting joined the little fellow on his left in carefully simulated sleep. It came as no surprise when we lost, and leave to appeal to the House of Lords was refused. Two days later that august and elevated body also refused leave.

'I'm afraid,' I had to tell Fishlock, 'it looks like the end of the line.'

'Not exactly.' He looked like a man possessed of a well-kept secret. 'What about Article Six of the European Convention on Human Rights?'

'A document,' I hastened to tell him, 'which is my constant bedtime reading.'

'Everyone is entitled to a fair hearing by an independent and impartial tribunal!'

'That is what I had in mind. So we're off to The Hague, are we?'

'*You* may be, Mr Rumpole. But the Court of Human Rights sits in Strasburg.'

'Of course! That's the one I meant. So you're going to brief me in Strasburg, are you? It'll make a change from the Uxbridge Magistrates Court.'

It was then that Peter Fishlock began to talk about Rumpole and human rights being as inseparable as Marks & Spencer, and I speculated on the possible generosity of Euro legal aid.

'I hear you're off to Europe, Rumpole.' Soapy Sam Ballard looked at me with incredulity and distaste, as though I had just won the National Lottery.

'Rather a bore, really.' I lit a small cigar in an offhand manner. The man had entered my room eagerly enough, but now covered his mouth with his fist and coughed as though I had set out to asphyxiate him. 'But you've got to be prepared to travel when you've got an international practice like mine.'

'I understand. And I'm perfectly prepared to travel, Rumpole.'

'Going far? We'll have to do our best to get along without you.'

'I'm coming with you, of course. In a case of this importance, you'll be in need of a leader. Preferably one from Chambers.'

'Oh, I don't think so, old darling. My instructing solicitor is prepared to leave it to me. The Rights of Man, you know, are rather my *spécialité de la maison*. I'm sure you've got enough landlord and tenant stuff to keep you fully occupied.' At which, I blew out smoke and the would-be leader, looking extremely miffed, simulated terminal bronchitis and withdrew from my presence.

So the long journey started which ended up over the choucroute and the water of life in the Grimms' fairytale Kammerzell House in Strasburg. There I was applauded for

my devotion to justice by a fan club of Europeans and his
Honour Judge Bloxham, looking extremely green about the
gills, sat glowering at me with ill-concealed hostility from the
corner of the room.

As Jeremy Jameson collected the bill to put in with his Euro
expenses, I plodded off towards the facilities. As I stood in
front of the porcelain, lit by a sudden and blinding white light,
I was conscious of a shrunken figure at the far end of the row
of stalls. Judge Bloxham turned to face me, zipping up his
trousers; and, looking paler than ever, his eyes dead with
despair, he uttered one word, pronounced like a curse from a
dry throat, 'Rumpole', and shuffled away across the marble
floor.

I gave him time to get away and then returned to the dining-
room, only to discover that, as rare things will, all my newfound
friends had vanished. Betsi Hoprecht and the rimless Professor
of International Law (both of whom had met me at the airport),
the Euro M.P., Poppy, the elegant sheep, and even my instructing solicitor had gone off into the night and the table was being
cleared under the instruction of the Minister for Strawberries.
At that moment I felt I was in Europe, a stranger and alone.

Walking back to the hotel in the moonlight, I looked at my
watch. Almost eleven on a Saturday night. It seemed a long
time since I and Peter Fishlock had been met at the airport by
Betsi Hoprecht, who had stood tall and fair-haired above the
smaller, darker inhabitants of Alsace-Lorraine waiting for their
loved ones. She had taken us in charge, kept us going on a tour
round the monuments, and arranged the dinner at the Kammerzell House at which we were to meet the gallant band who
sat shoulder to shoulder, consuming choucroute and fighting
for the Rights of Man. I had felt safe in Betsi's hands, relieved
of the painful process of decision. Now I was on my own,
crossing the cathedral square, and I decided to see the astro-
nomical clock put on its hourly performance.

The shadowy cathedral was empty, the windows which Betsi
had shown us glowing with coloured sunlight were now blind
and black. Only a few candles, lit for the dead and the dying,

flickered in the cloisters by the side-chapels. In the empty pews only a few heads, the anxious, the insomniac or old, were bowed in prayer and contemplation. I put in a coin and the clock towered above me in golden light with its minarets and huge dials, the signs of the Zodiac, the round sun in a bright blue sky dotted with stars, the columns of gold and black marble, and the figures of Christ and Death waiting for their hourly moment of confrontation.

As I looked up at these wonders, I was conscious of a tallish tourist standing beside me. I thought how badly his clothes went with the wonders of sixteenth-century science and architecture: a red plastic anorak with LES DROITS DE L'HOMME written on it, trousers that looked as though they'd been made in a computer, and a baseball cap which bore the insignia of the Common Market. Then eleven struck. The heavens began to whirr and move at the command of the master clockmaker, the Ages of Man passed in their chariots, the heavenly globe was lit up in front of the perpetual calendar with its statues of Diana and Apollo, and Christ, his hand held up in benediction, chased the skeleton Death. As the slow strokes died away, and all the devices on the clock shuddered to a standstill, a voice with which I was unfortunately familiar said, 'The continentals are clever fellows, aren't they?'

'Bollard! What on earth are you doing here?'

'What on earth? That's rather a good question, Rumpole. What are any of us doing on earth? Our duty, let us hope. To God and our country. And preparing ourselves for a better life *not* on earth. That's the hope we live with.'

'I have to tell you, Bollard, that if the hope you live with is infiltrating yourself into Monday's case as leading Counsel for Amin Hashimi, forget it. Your journey has been entirely unnecessary.'

'I shall be in the case on Monday, as you would know, Rumpole, if you were in the habit of reading your papers before going into Court. But I shall be appearing for a slightly more reputable client than your Mr Hashimi.'

'Oh, really. Who's that?'

'H.M.G., Rumpole.'

'Who's he, when he's at home?'

'Her Majesty's Government. I'm here to support Lord Justice Ponting's opinion in the Court of Appeal.'

'You mean you're for the H.M.G. of the U.K.?'

'Exactly so!' Of course Ballard failed to detect the note of sarcasm in my flight to the acronym.

'But you didn't do the case at the Bailey or in the Court of Appeal. Tubby Arthurian did it.'

'Quite right. But with the international importance this matter has now achieved, with the entire reputation of the U.K. judiciary at stake, it was thought by H.M.G. . . .'

'What was thought?'

'Well' – the man seemed embarrassed, as it turned out he had good cause to be – 'that Counsel should be chosen who would be likely to have some influence over you. To check what H.M.G. described, in a confidential memo to myself, as your worst excesses, Rumpole.'

'Why on earth would you have any influence over me?'

'Well, H.M.G. thought that as I am undoubtedly your Head of Chambers and therefore placed in some position of authority . . .'

'H.M.G. thought *that* might curb my excesses?'

'Naturally.'

'Then H.M.G. must be singularly ignorant of the inner working of our great legal system. H.M.G. should know by now that the sight of you, Bollard, causes my worst excesses to break out like the measles.'

'I had hoped' – Soapy Sam had the good sense not to sound particularly optimistic – 'that we might be able to reach some sort of common approach. We don't want to cause poor old Bloxham public embarrassment, do we?'

'Don't we? I've been looking forward to it for months.'

'Perhaps we could talk over a drink.'

'You can buy me a drink at any time,' I was kind enough to tell him.

'Thank you, Rumpole.' Ballard was now looking anxiously round the cathedral, and a note of fear had come into his voice, 'Hilda's not with you, is she?'

'Mrs Rumpole,' I told him, with some dignity, 'has gone to stay with her friend Dodo Mackintosh in Cornwall.'

'I wouldn't want Marguerite to hear that wives were allowed. I told her this was strictly no spouses.'

Marguerite, I remembered, was the ex-Matron of the Old Bailey, the person once in charge of aspirins and Elastoplast, whom the fearless Ballard had decided to marry. 'How did she take that?'

'Not too well, I'm afraid. But I told her that when you're appearing for H.M.G. confidential matters may arise.'

'Baloney!'

'Well, I have to confess, Rumpole, that the idea of being fancy-free on this agreeable little trip to the Continent did rather appeal to me. I thought I might stay on for a couple of days. I took the opportunity of buying some holiday gear this afternoon.' He looked down at his trousers with incomprehensible pride.

'You mean that rig-out? You look as though you were going in for a bicycle race.'

'You should learn to get with it, Rumpole. An old tweed jacket with leather patches' – the man had the ice-cold nerve to look critically at my attire – 'and grey flannel bags simply don't say *European*.'

'Unlike your plastic anorak? It doesn't seem to be able to stop talking about it.'

'Perhaps you should mix a little more with young people, Rumpole. Perhaps you should learn to approach the millennium. I've got to know some young people. Since I got here, I've got to know what you might call the international set.'

'You must be a quick worker.'

'What?'

'I said you must be a quick worker. Didn't you arrive today?'

'Oh, no. I've been here a few days. Getting used to the atmosphere. I must say, it's all been quite stimulating.'

'A few days?' I raised my eyebrows at a complacently smiling Ballard. 'I'm surprised that Marguerite let you off the leash for so long.'

'I have to confess' – Soapy Sam didn't look at all ashamed – 'I wasn't entirely candid about the date of our *cause célèbre*.'

'You, mean you told her that Hashimi started last Wednesday?'

'Something like that, yes.'

'I bet they've got that written down, in the great charge-sheet in the sky.'

'The God I believe in,' he had the nerve to tell me, 'is deeply understanding of human frailty. You only flew over this morning, did you? That must be exhausting for you, at your age. I expect you're longing for your bed. Well, mustn't keep you.'

'So what are *you* going to do? Hang around until the clock strikes another hour?'

'Never you mind, Rumpole. There are better things to do in Strasburg than to wait for the clock to strike, I'm bound to tell you.'

As I left the cathedral, I saw, in the shadows of an empty pew, a fair head bent in prayer. To my surprise, Betsi Hoprecht was kneeling, no doubt interdenominationally calling on the God of the clock to ally Himself with the Merciful, the Compassionate, for the protection of Amin Hashimi.

It was a short walk to the Hôtel D'Ange Rouge, and from my bedroom I could still hear the odd calls of love from the backpackers who loitered round the cathedral or staggered home singing. I lay in bed reading the written brief to the Court of Human Rights, a somewhat long document prepared by Fishlock with an analysis of all the British cases on bias. The Judges were welcome to it. What I profoundly hoped would stir them out of their international coma would be the Rumpole address, the rallying cry against injustice, the devastating destruction of Billy Bloxham with which I expected to win the day. I heard the cathedral clock strike one and then I turned out my light.

It was a warm spring night and the window on to the little balcony that overlooked the square was open and the curtain flapping. The window of the next room must have been open also, and I heard the sound of a strong woman, who sounded very much like Betsi Hoprecht, laughing. The full and disturbing significance of this was not revealed to me until the next morning, however, when, setting out eagerly for breakfast, I saw none other than Soapy Sam Ballard emerge from the next-door room in question. He was shaved, bathed and, I had a shrewd suspicion, slightly perfumed. He was wearing his *Droits de l'Homme* anorak and looked like the cat that had got at the cream.

It was Sunday, a day of rest and respite before battle was joined between myself, a freelance, and the Government of Her Britannic Majesty, in the person of its improbable champion, Soapy Sam Ballard, Q.C. Breakfast was held in a small, hot room which I found to be crowded. Ballard was at a table in the corner with some unremarkable person I thought to be connected with H.M.G. The only seat I could find was at a table set for three at which the curly-headed Poppy was already installed, smiling vaguely and peeling an orange. I asked if I could sit down.

'Why not? Jeremy won't be here for hours. He's sleeping off the choucroute.'

I put in a request for ham and eggs and looked thoughtfully back towards my Head of Chambers. I tried to see him in a new light: Casanova Ballard, Soapy Don Juan, Lord Byron Ballard, bedroom Ballard, high in the list of the world's great lovers, and then the mind, I have to confess it, boggled. It also failed to come to terms with the idea of that slimmed-down Betsi Hoprecht on her way to Ballard's bed, even though she was kneeling, as though hoping for a miracle, in prayer as a necessary preliminary.

'Bloody Europe!'

I looked around for the source of this condemnation and decided it could only have come from the smiling Poppy, whose orange, by now, was neatly peeled and quartered.

'So you're a Euro-sceptic?' I thought she was, on the whole, preferable to that grumpy group of M.P.s who had appointed themselves the Prosecutors of the Common Market.

'Sceptic's not the word for it! Other people get taken to the Seychelles, or the Caribbean, or even Acapulco.'

'Other people?'

'Other people's girlfriends, I mean. When my daughter starts looking for a lover, I'll say I don't give a toss what he is doing, just so long as he's not a Euro M.P. I wouldn't even mind Jeremy being an M.P. if he took me out in England, but at

home he's always at terrible black-tie dinners where we mustn't
be seen together. He has to go on holiday with his wife and
dear little Sebastian, who has to get postcards from everywhere and last-minute presents at the airport. All I see of the
world is Brussels and Luxemburg and Strasburg, where
there's nothing to do except eat until the brass buttons on
your Chanel suit shoot off like bullets. You've left your wife
at home?'

I had to admit it.

'I thought so! Everyone leaves their wives at home when
they go to Strasburg. Jeremy's wife has taken little Sebastian to
Brighton. God, how I envy them.'

'Aren't we going on a trip round the wine towns?'

'You haven't done that before?'

'No.'

'Jeremy and I've done it almost more times than we've had
sex. Those little half-timbered buildings you wander round as
though you were Hansel and bloody Gretel. And you know
what the aim and object of the whole exercise is? Yes, you're
right. A socking great lunch!'

At which point Betsi Hoprecht strode into the breakfast
room, clapped her hands three times and announced that the
bus would leave from the front entrance in exactly twenty-five
minutes and would we make sure that we were on it. At her
entrance, Ballard smiled in as sickly and ingratiating a manner
as Malvolio in the play. Betsi returned this greeting with what
I thought was an admirably contrived glare of non-
recognition.

The Tokay d'Alsace tasted of grapes, a gentle flavour far
removed from the chemical impact of Pommeroy's Reasonable
White. The sun shone on the restaurant terrace, it glittered on
the glasses and ice-bucket, and was warm on our faces. Around
us the tops of the pinkish, plastered houses bulged like huge
bosoms, kept in place by the ribbons of dark oak. Their steep
tiled roofs were pierced with the eyes of numberless dormer
windows. Flowers clambered round a well in the centre of the
square and, on the slender, sand-coloured church steeple, the
clock stood at half past one. We had filled the minibus and now

occupied another long restaurant table. The rimless professor was there, as was the man in the consular service and his gardener wife. Jeremy Jameson was there, smiling with a mixture of defiance and guilt. He had come downstairs late, buttoning his shirt, which was not satisfactorily tucked into his crumpled linen trousers. Poppy was smiling, sipping Tokay, and reading the *Mail on Sunday*, hot from the morning plane and greeted by her like a missing child.

'Our whole team is here.' I was sitting next to Betsi and she was giving me her full and flattering attention. 'All of us are behind you, Mr Rumpole. Cheering you on!'

'Not that little chap from the consular service, surely? Isn't he on the side of H.M. Government?'

'Well, he should be, of course. That is where his duty lies. But his heart is with us, Mr Rumpole. He has read all of your memoirs, he tells me. Some of them twice over.'

'Is that really so?' I looked down the table at Eddie Parsloe with a new respect.

'"We must be free or die." He says the spirit of your poet Wordsworth breathes through you.'

'Well, that's remarkably civil of him.'

'And Lady Mary, she's what you would call a hoot, isn't she?'

'And do you know your Common Market's only going to allow us three varieties of bloody begonia?' Lady Mary Parsloe was hooting at the unfortunate Nordic professor. 'It's a disgrace. They'll be at our floribunda roses next.'

'What about Samuel Bollard, Q.C.? You didn't think of inviting him?'

'Mr *Ballard*, I have to correct you. Ballard is his name.'

'I know that perfectly well.'

'So why do you call him by the wrong name then?'

'I suppose in the hope of irritating him.'

'But he is a very nice man.' To my distress, a faraway look came into her pale blue eyes. She was wearing a crisp white dress, which showed off her brown arms to advantage. She smelt of clean linen and rustled like a hospital nurse. 'Also, he is your boss, I think.'

'You think wrong,' I had to tell her.

'He is Head of your Chambers?'

'Bollard has made himself responsible for the coffee machine and the paper clips. But I am a free spirit and a freelance advocate.'

'You are not afraid of him?'

'Of course not.' I felt full of courage, though I must confess that we had got through a number of bottles of Tokay with considerable help from me. 'An advocate can't afford to be afraid.'

'So' – Betsi gave me a display of blindingly white teeth – 'you are afraid of nothing or nobody?'

'Except sometimes,' I had to confess, 'She Who Must Be Obeyed.'

'Who is this she?'

'As a matter of fact, my wife, Hilda.'

'And you have to obey?'

'Well. No. Of course not.'

'So why do you call her that? Is it to irritate her?'

'It seems to describe her.'

'I feel it describes certain aspects of your character more. You are very English, Mr Rumpole. That's your characteristic, I think.'

I wanted to ask her if she found Soapy Sam Ballard was a good lover but my courage failed me. In any event we were interrupted by an even louder hoot from Lady Mary.

'That shower running Europe couldn't organize a village fête in Gloucestershire, I have to tell you.'

'You've got to admit, Lady Mary' – Peter Fishlock came galloping to the defence of Europe – 'The Common Market has kept peace in Europe.'

'Oh, yes? Didn't I read somewhere they're blowing each other up in Bosnia – or whatever you call it. Shooting children in playgrounds. Ethnic cleansing. But I suppose Yugoslavia's not in Europe. Where is it? China or somewhere?'

'Worse than that.' Poppy was reading a bit out of her *Mail on Sunday*. 'Saddam Hussein's buying stolen Russian nuclear weapons. We're all going to get blown up.'

There was a sudden, strangely uncomfortable silence, as though we had all been brought face to face with the ending of

the world. And then Betsi leaned across the table and took the
paper out of Poppy's hands. Poppy looked disappointed, as
though deprived of a favourite toy, but said nothing.

'Neither Russia nor Iraq,' my instructing solicitor reminded
us, 'is in the European Common Market.'

Poppy said, 'Lucky old them.' And Betsi, turning the pages
of the paper, said, 'Here's some *really* important news. Your
Princess Fergie is short of cash!' They all relaxed. The world
crisis was clearly over, forgotten in the *important news*.

'You must have got to know Bollard before I arrived?' I said
to Betsi.

'He is a very charming man.'

'Do you really think so? Charming in what sort of way
exactly?'

'Perhaps' – Betsi was thoughtful – 'like all Englishmen, the
charm lies in the innocence.'

'And you say you only got to know him a little?' I remembered the laughter from the bedroom with a certain pang.

'Quite enough to know that he will take a civilized attitude
tomorrow. I think you will find him very reasonable.'

'He asked me to be reasonable too.'

'What did you say?'

'I said I had no intention of being reasonable. I intend to
fight him with every weapon at my command.'

'You know' – Betsi looked at me thoughtfully – 'I asked Mr
Fishlock why he didn't employ a more important barrister than
you, a barrister of the same rank as Mr Ballard.'

'Oh, really?' I did my best to appear cool and hoped that I
didn't sound envious of Soapy Sam. 'And what did Fishlock
say?'

'He said he had every faith in you as a defender of human
rights.'

It was at that point that the bill arrived and was grabbed by
Jeremy Jameson, M.E.P., with a cry of 'I need this for my
expenses.' He slapped his pocket and discovered that he'd left
his credit cards in his other jacket and announced that he was
writing out a cheque and could he borrow a pen from someone.
I lent him mine and happened to see a cheque book of an
unusual mauve variety. I also saw that our lunch was to be paid

for by funds lodged in Netherbank of Queen Victoria Street, London.

Fresh air, Tokay and dislike of myself for feeling jealous of Soapy Sam Ballard ended in exhaustion as I sat in my room and tried to compose a rousing speech about the human rights of Amin Hashimi. I had decided to call it a day, sink into bed and rely in Court on the inspiration of the moment (such moments have rarely let me down), when the telephone rang and what sounded much like a voice from the tomb said, 'Is that you, Horace? This is Billy speaking. I say, could you spare me five minutes, old fellow? I'm in a bar quite near your hotel.'

It was this sudden use of Christian names that startled me about the beleaguered Judge. I didn't want to talk to him. I certainly didn't want to see him. Any contact between us at that moment could only lead to embarrassment. And yet I had to go and meet the old idiot. It was no longer a visit to a Judge; it was almost like the daily duty of a trip down the cells to cheer up an unsuccessful villain facing trial for a serious offence. I put my jacket on, stuffed my back pocket with a handful of francs, and went off to the tryst. I hadn't far to go, a small dark bar in the rue des Juifs close to the cathedral.

'It was good of you to come, Horace. I'd do the same for you, of course.'

'I hope you'll never have to.'

Billy was sitting in the company of a small espresso and a quartet of adolescents who were drinking rum and Coke and playing the fruit machine. Behind the bar a sleepy woman sat longing for us to go home. While Soapy Sam had gone desperately continental, Billy looked like the caricature of an English tourist, wearing a blazer with gold buttons, a Sheridan Club tie and hating being abroad.

'I was entrapped, Horace. You do realize that, don't you? I've complained to the Press Council. I didn't know that little runt of a journalist had sneaked into the rugger club. So far as I know journalists don't play rugger. It was pure bad luck. Could have happened to anybody.'

'Anybody wasn't a Judge who'd just sentenced a foreign student to life imprisonment.'

'I was giving voice to my private opinions. As I'm entitled to do. I didn't say any of that in Court, did I?'

'No, that's what I've really got against you.'

Billy Bloxham looked puzzled. Indeed, during our brief pre-trial meeting he was either angry or puzzled, more often both at the same time.

'You think that might have helped you? If I'd said what I thought about foreigners?'

'I'm damn sure it would.'

'Horace, the very next time you're before me I'll do my best to help you. I'll say exactly what I think.' And then his voice began to break and his hand, lifting the dregs in the tiny coffee cup to his pallid lips, trembled. 'You think there may not be a next time?' he dared to ask.

'It's possible.'

'You mean they may sack me? The Lord Chancellor could do that, couldn't he? I'm not a High Court Judge.'

'I suppose it's on the cards.'

'Horace, you've got a wonderful reputation, down the Bailey, for being on the side of the underdog.'

'And you've become one?'

'In this particular instance, yes.'

'I don't know where everyone got the idea I only act for underdogs.'

Billy was sitting hunched, staring up at me with watery eyes. He looked as though he was prepared to do anything, even bark in a servile fashion and lick my hand. 'Horace, you won't put the case too strongly against me, will you, old boy?'

'I'll do my best,' I said, leaving him in doubt as to whether I was going to do my best to draw it strong or mild.

'You see' – Billy was putting every ounce of emotion into his final speech – 'I have to go on being a Judge. I'm really unfit for anything else.'

'I'm sure there are other things you could do.' I could not, however, imagine what they were.

'No. I know you're only trying to be kind. You see, I couldn't go back to what you chaps do. Arguing with each other. Catching out witnesses. Trying hard to win. I mean, would people give me any work, even if I was allowed back? Would they honestly?'

'I suppose they might.' It was an answer I wouldn't have given under oath.

'I don't believe it. Besides which, I've got used to a certain amount of respect. I like it when you fellows stand up and bow to me. I find that quite delightful. And when I go into the bank, the assistant manager sometimes pops over and says, "How can we help you, Judge?" And they ask me to say a few words at the Rotary and the rugby club dinners. Do you imagine they'd ask a sacked judge to speak at the rugger club?'

'Don't despair.' The sight of the man was beginning to pain me.

'You mean you'll go easy on me?' Billy cheered up a fraction.

'I mean, I may not win.'

'Why? Who's on the other side?'

'Samuel Ballard, Q.C.'

'He doesn't often win.' The Judge was back in the Slough of Despond.

'It's got to happen some time. Anyway, the Euro Judges may not want to upset the British Government.'

'But the British Government's always upsetting them. Do you happen to know who the Judges are?'

'I believe they come from a variety of countries.'

'Foreigners?'

'Bound to be. One's Irish.'

'All foreigners, then.'

'Oh, and one English. Because it's an English case.'

'Who've they got?'

'I think it's Thompson. Used to practise in the Chancery Division.'

'Tradders Thompson?' Billy looked seriously worried now. 'Didn't he marry an Indian?'

'I know nothing,' I assured him, 'about his domestic arrangements.'

'I feel sure I spotted him at an Inner Temple garden party' – Billy was now up to his neck in the Slough – 'with someone in a sari.'

'I've got to get to bed.' I yawned realistically and drained my cognac.

'Written your speech, have you? Couldn't you just water it down a bit, Horace? We Brits should stick together.'

'I haven't written anything.' As I said this, some faint hope returned to the desolate Judge. 'We drank rather a lot of wine at lunch and my eyes won't stay open.'

'Please,' he begged me, 'please have another drink.'

'Not possible.' I stood up then. I was fighting to keep awake. 'Goodnight, Billy. Remember, the trial isn't decided until it's over.' It was the poor crumb of comfort I always kept for my most hopeless of cases.

'I shall wear my Sheridan Club tie.' Billy was down to his last hope. 'Perhaps some of the Judges are members.'

'Oh, I expect so. Get a lot of Slovenes and chaps from Liechtenstein in there, do you?'

So I left him, conscious that my visit to the cells hadn't done much to cheer up the man who might go down in legal history as Lord Bloxham of Bias. I staggered out into the street and started on my way back to the hotel like a sleepwalker.

I hadn't gone far along the rue des Juifs when two things startled me into full wakefulness. First of all I saw an all too familiar red anorak and blue baseball cap moving, not altogether steadily, in the road in front of me. Then I heard the sudden acceleration of an engine behind me and I moved further from the edge of the pavement. An anonymous, dark-blue car thundered past and appeared to be aiming, like a heavy artillery shell, for Ballard's back. Just before it reached him, he skipped with hare-like agility on to the pavement, which the driver mounted. Luckily for Sam, there was a deeply recessed doorway into which he dived and the car, which had braked suddenly, couldn't follow him although he was lit, for a vivid moment, by its headlights, cowering as though from a fatal and expected blow. The car then reversed with a snort of the engine and vanished down the street. I emerged from the shadows as a second shock to my shaken Head of Chambers. 'My God, Rumpole!' he said. 'These continentals are the most terrible drivers!'

*

'I'm not sure about bad drivers, Bollard. It looked to me as if it might have been a deliberate mistake.'

I was ministering to the man, who was still in a state of shock, and I had shown my medical skill by activating the night porter to shuffle off in search of a bottle of eau de vie. I administered a dose of this to Ballard who was still complaining about Alsatian driving skills. 'I shall have to be careful,' he complained, 'now I'll be coming to Strasburg on a regular basis.'

'A regular basis?'

'I've been talking to Betsi.'

'So I understand.'

'And there's a need for Senior Counsel who understand the importance of human rights. She has told me that there will be a great deal of work for a skilled international lawyer who is prepared to stick up for liberty and so on.'

'And that's what you're going to stick up for? Liberty and so on?'

'That's what the work is. According to Betsi.'

'And does Betsi know about your long record as a persecutor? I mean, you're here to protect a biased Judge.'

'I think she knows as well as anyone, Rumpole, that I am an extremely fair man. With liberal opinions.'

'You made that clear to Betsi?'

'I think she knows that about me.'

'I expect she does. And on your future visits to Strasburg, will you be bringing your wife with you?'

'Marguerite is heavily engaged with her first aid classes to the Housewives' League in Waltham Cross.'

'That's all right then.' I poured out a further medicinal glass. 'Bollard, does it occur to you that what happened in the street wasn't an accident?'

'The car was out of control.'

'It seemed very much *in* control to me.'

'What do you mean?'

'Someone may not like you.'

'Who?' The possibility didn't seem to have occurred to the man.

'A jealous husband, perhaps. Or a boyfriend. Someone who took exception to your amorous adventures.'

'Rumpole! I have no idea what you're talking about.'

'Wasn't Betsi in your room rather late last night?'

'Of course she was.'

'Well, then.'

'We were discussing human rights.'

'I suppose that's another way of describing it.' I looked at the man without pleasure and emptied my glass.

It was Monday morning, the day dedicated to the rights of Amin Hashimi who had brought me to Europe and who, except for that moment when I had seen a cheque drawn on Netherbank, I had almost forgotten in a series of expensive and eventful meals.

I wasn't, I have to confess, feeling at my best on the day of the hearing. I have never tasted the bottom of a budgerigar's cage but I imagine it to be as dry as I felt that morning; added to which my head was stuffed with cotton wool penetrated, from time to time, with stabs of pain. Anxious supporters, interested speculators and the representatives of Her Majesty's Government, gathered in the sunshine outside the hotel and a fleet of taxis set off for the Cour Européenne des Droits de L'Homme.

I sat next to Betsi in the back of one taxi and told her that I hoped our driver was more reliable than the madman who nearly ran Ballard over the night before. 'There are some idiots in this town,' she said. 'I heard about that. It was absolutely unnecessary.'

'Unnecessary?'

'To drive so fast. Through the streets of the old town. The idiot was French, I have no doubt. They drive like madmen.'

The Court was a long, grey concrete erection beside a river, with two circular towers like gasworks sawn off crookedly. Inside, we had wandered, uncertain of the way, in what looked like the vast boiler-room of a ship, painted in nursery colours. We went up and down steel and wire staircases, and travelled in lifts whose glass sides let you see more of the journey than made you entirely comfortable. And then I was standing up at a desk in a huge courtroom. Across an expanse of blue carpet, so far away that I could hardly distinguish their features, sat the Judges in black gowns under a white ceiling perforated like a giant kitchen colander. Human rights, it seemed, like the scientific romances of H. G. Wells, had been set in the future and now the future had arrived with a rush and overtaken me before I was quite sure how to address it.

'Mr Rumpole' – the voice of the presiding Judge, a Dutchman, boomed electronically over the vasty hall of death – 'we have read the submission filed on behalf of your client. Would you now speak to your paper?'

'Speak to my paper?' It didn't sound much of an audience. I had been used to speaking to my Jury, so close that I could lower my voice, at dramatic moments, almost to a whisper. Now I was in contact only by microphone with the remote, international platoon of seven Judges: the Austrian, the Finn, the Slovene, the Hungarian, the British, the Irish and the Portuguese. In some glass case halfway between us, lit up like tropical fish, the translators were noiselessly mouthing my words in various languages which some of the Judges put on headphones to catch, and others, either superb linguists or premature adjudicators, didn't bother to fit over their ears.

'I haven't much to say to the paper, my Lords. But I have a point of the greatest importance to make to your Lordships.' I waited in silence for the maximum effect, and because I felt suddenly in need of a rest I leant on the desk in front of me for support. At long last the Irishman was good enough to say, 'And what is your point, Mr Rumpole?'

'My point is' – another stab of pain penetrated the cotton wool – 'that the learned Judge in this case was not only biased but bluffing. Not only prejudiced but perfidious. In fact, he might stand, if your Lordships will allow the phrase, as the personification of Perfidious Albion.'

For some reason I was rather pleased with this opening paragraph. I looked around and there, in an otherwise empty row at the back of the Court, I saw his Honour Judge Bloxham looking at me with ill-concealed hatred.

'Perfidious *what*, Mr Rumpole?' Some sort of panic had clearly affected the translator in the fish tank and the presiding Dutch Lordship asked for clarification.

'Albion, my Lord. An expression once popular on the

continent of Europe, in which you now sit. It described the hypocrisy and slyness of a certain class of Englishman.'

'You are using this expression to describe the learned Judge in this case?' The Finn's English was almost too perfect but he looked extremely interested.

'Indeed I am. We all know the Judge was prejudiced. He was as biased as a crooked roulette wheel. He'd picked up his so-called opinions in the back of a taxi. He hated all foreign students and he made that perfectly clear in his speech to the rugger buggers.' At this, I saw expressions of genuine despair in the fish tank and the presiding Hollander clearly couldn't believe his headphones.

'To the *what*?'

'To the rugby football players' annual dinner. You see, this is the point I wish to impress on your Lordships. We all have prejudices. You may have prejudices. So do I. I have always found, that is until I came here and sampled your excellent Tokay d'Alsace, that all discussions about the European Common Market were about ten points less interesting than watching paint dry. That was my prejudice and I freely and frankly admit it to your Lordships.' Here I looked down and saw the note Betsi Hoprecht had pushed on to my desk: CALL THEM THE COURT. WE DON'T HAVE LORDSHIPS IN EUROPE. 'But did the perfidious Judge admit his prejudices?' I boomed on. 'Did he come into Court and kick off with: "Members of the Jury, I personally cannot stick foreign students. The idea of a foreigner, particularly of the slightly tinted Middle-Eastern variety, makes my gorge rise to a dangerous level. I want that clearly understood. Now let's get on with it, shall we?"'

'And if he had said that?' Far, far away I heard the caressing voice of the Irish.

'If he had, we'd have all known where we were. The Jury could have marked its disapproval of such views by a not guilty verdict. I could have made considerable use of them in my final speech. Justice would not only have been done, but would clearly have been seen to have been done! But what did Judge Bloxham do?' I leant forward and whispered secretly to the Court through the microphone, in tones calculated to make its collective flesh creep. 'He decided to dissemble! He made up his mind to deceive. He set about to defraud. He very deliberately acted the part of a totally unbiased Judge, something which hardly exists in this imperfect world. And so, when he belatedly showed himself in his true colours, what was the unfortunate Mr Hashimi to think? What *could* he think? Except that his trial had been an elaborate charade performed by a Judge with the clear intention of deceiving the Jury, which was bad, and Counsel for the Defence which was, in my humble submission, unpardonable.'

My head had cleared and, as I spoke, I felt healthier, saner – even elated. I gave them my views on the perfidy of the Court of Appeal, only anxious to protect the reputation of a judge at the expense of justice. Peter Fishlock's résumé of the leading cases on bias came back to me and I took them through it. I even touched on the subject of human rights about which I had heard so much since I went into Europe. By the end of it, I thought that I had won over the Irish, although the Portuguese looked doubtful, and the Slovene had laid down his earphones and seemed to have fallen into a light doze. I turned up the volume of my peroration. 'Let us go on,' I told the seven, 'to a community of tolerance, a community which has shut the door on prejudice. To quote a great poet, who, like so many great poets, happened to write in English:

> Forward, forward let us range,
> Let the great world spin for ever down the ringing grooves of
> change.

> Thro' the shadow of the globe we sweep into the younger day:
> Better fifty years of Europe than a cycle of Cathay!

Then I sat down and applied the red-and-white spotted handkerchief to the slightly less fevered brow. Fishlock whispered, 'Well done!' Jameson gave me an admiring look and Betsi's eyes were glowing. And then Soapy Sam Ballard completely ruined my triumph by more or less throwing in the towel.

'Having heard Mr Rumpole,' the faint-heart representing Her Majesty's Government began, 'we cannot argue that the words spoken by the learned Judge at the rugby club dinner wouldn't be considered prejudiced by any reasonable man or woman. This must be borne in mind by the Court when considering if Amin Hashimi received a fair hearing by an impartial tribunal, within the terms of Article Six of the Convention for the protection of human rights . . .'

So there it was. I had taken a battering ram to the door of a castle which had been unlocked by its so-called defenders. It couldn't be called a famous victory. As we stood to bow and the Judges filed out, Betsi said we should get the result in three to six months and there was little doubt what it would be. On the other side of the Court the man from the consular service and Lady Mary were grouped round Billy Bloxham, as though he was the victim of a serious road accident. Sam Ballard, who had been looking gravely downcast, raised his eyes to smile across to Betsi. I noticed that she didn't smile back.

'So, Mr Rumpole. You have fought the good fight!'

'Too easy. Sam Ballard chucked in his hand.'

'He is very conscious of the importance we all attach to human rights. I told him that we need lawyers with such a fine record as you have, Mr Rumpole.'

'And did you tell him that a lot of European cases might come his way if he showed himself a good libertarian?'

Betsi Hoprecht and I were standing by a table in the airport bar. Jeremy Jameson was waiting in line to pay for the last round of European Court drinks, and Poppy had gone off shopping. Now Betsi gave me a smile which I can only describe as conspiratorial and put a brown hand on my arm, a touch so light I hardly felt it. 'He might have thought that. I don't know what went through his mind.'

'You had a good many little chats with Soapy Sam, didn't you?'

'It's always best' – Betsi was still smiling – 'to get to know the opposition.'

'You were in his room at night, weren't you? Painting a rosy picture of his future as an international lawyer.'

'We drank beer out of his refrigerator, certainly.'

'And Article Six of the Convention was your pillow talk?'

'Pillow talk? I think I don't know that phrase. Pillow talk?'

'Were you and Sam' – I put the question direct – 'in bed together?'

'Me and *Mr Ballard*? In bed together? What a ridiculous idea! You must be making a very big joke, Mr Rumpole.' Betsi wasn't just smiling then; she threw back her blonde hair and laughed loudly and clearly enough to scare the dwarf and startle the maidens on the other side of the Rhine. Jeremy Jameson was coming towards us with his hand round three eaux de vie and I felt an immediate need to slip off to the gents.

When I came back the bar was even fuller. I pushed my way towards the table in the corner and saw Betsi and Jameson with their heads together. My hearing isn't altogether what it was, and I can't be sure of this, but I think I heard the M.E.P. say, 'He won't talk now. He'll soon be on his way home.' Then they clinked their glasses together, drank and Betsi turned and saw me. I had the distinct feeling that I wasn't, at that moment, a welcome sight.

'Who won't talk now?' I asked her.

'Oh, no one you know, I think. We were discussing another case altogether.' And then she fell back, as she had with the unfortunate Ballard, on promises. 'But perhaps you will be asked to argue it for us. When the time comes.' Then the crackling, amplified voice of Europe announced that the flight to London Heathrow was boarding immediately from gate number three. I was, I must confess, quite relieved to hear it.

A bright spring turned into a long, wet summer and then, in September, pale sunshine returned. During those months Ballard complained that none of the promised briefs in international cases arrived on his desk, but I had almost forgotten the weekend in Europe until Peter Fishlock rang to say that we had won an almighty success in Strasburg, and Betsi and Jeremy and all our friends sent greetings and congratulations. I sat at breakfast that Saturday morning and felt curiously little elation. Was that because it all seemed so long ago and had none of the immediate excitement of a jury verdict on the last day of the trial? My *joie de vivre* was at a low level that weekend anyway as Hilda's old schoolfriend, Dodo

Mackintosh, was inhabiting the mansion flat in return for the hospitality she had shown to She Who Must in Cornwall during the Hashimi appeal.

'Dodo has suggested a trip to Kingslake, Rumpole. She says the garden has been thrown open to the public.'

'Sounds exciting. I'm sure you'll both have a rattling good time.' I saw a fine prospect of a solo lunch in the pub, and a snooze by the gas fire, opening before me.

'Of course you're coming too, Rumpole. It's about time you got a little fresh air into your lungs. And the herbaceous border at Kingslake will come as a nice change from all those squalid little criminals you spend your time with.'

'I don't suppose Rumpole can tell a mahonia from an azalea, can he, Hilda?' Dodo Mackintosh, with what I took to be an evil glint in her eye, piled on the agony.

'Dodo's going to drive us to Sussex, Rumpole. It's very good of her. So you'd better gulp down that coffee. We're going to make an early start.' I saw it was no time for argument. She has to be obeyed.

Always distrust people who have nicknames for their motor cars and, when my wife and her old schoolfriend were strapped into the front, and I had poured myself into the back, where I found precious little leg-room, Dodo switched on the engine which coughed, spluttered and started, my heart sank when she chirped, 'Buzzfuzz *is* in a good mood this morning.' It remained at a low level during the journey by reason of Dodo's habit of driving very slowly along clear and straight roads, and then accelerating wildly at intersections or dangerous corners.

When, after what seemed a lifetime of alternating bursts of boredom and terror, we got to Kingslake, it proved to be a greenish-grey Regency house in a poor state of repair – and full of draughts, I should imagine – with gumboots in the hallways. Dodo and Hilda had been gossiping about various mistresses and ex-pupils from their old school, and this less than fascinating conversation continued as we paid our duty call to the dahlias and chrysanthemums in the wide herbaceous border. It was around midday and the alcohol content in the Rumpole blood had fallen to a dangerous point. Muttering something about a search for the gents, I stole away through the rose garden and down the gravel paths between the greenhouses which looked in dire need of a lick of paint.

Round a corner I came to what I took to be a back door of the house. It was open and I had a view of a stone passageway, the regulation number of gumboots and pegs for tweed caps, battered panamas and some disintegrating macs. I also saw a wooden table with a tray-like top holding a welcoming collection of bottles, some glasses and a corkscrew. A desperate plan crossed my mind; I would pour myself a large snort, leave a more than adequate supply of money and retreat to a quiet refuge behind the cucumber frames. I had put my hand in my pocket and was advancing on the drinks table when a door opened further down the hallway and a voice boomed, 'The house is not, repeat not, open to the public!' It was Lady Mary Parsloe, looking windblown and armed with what I took to be an extra large gin-and-tonic. She narrowed her eyes, looked at me as though I were a serious blight on the roses and said, 'By God, it's you!'

'I'm sorry. Is this your house?'

'Eddie's house. His family house, as it so happens. He's in London, trying to assess the damage you've done.'

'Damage?'

'Peddling human rights. What human rights? The right to get us all blown up. I suppose that's your idea of freedom?'

'You're talking about the Hashimi case?'

'*And* I'm talking about your friends Fräulein Hoprecht and that dreadful fat Member of the European Parliament. I bet they're celebrating! Why aren't you with them, with your nose in the trough?'

'I thought they were your friends, too. You and your husband were at dinner . . .'

'Eddie was there to see what they were up to. He knew perfectly well, of course. Not that we'll ever prove anything now that your Mr Hashimi has walked away from us. With a life sentence in front of him, Eddie thinks he'd've talked eventually. Oh, you know what I'm talking about.'

'I'm afraid I don't.'

'The bloody great mess you've got us in!' She made an expansive gesture with her hand holding the glass, slopping some of the drink which settled the dust on the stairs of the hallway.

'Can I ask you a question?'

'I suppose so. I don't promise I'll answer it.'

'Can I have a drink?'

She stood looking at me, an old, untidy woman, swaying slightly like an unpruned shrub in a high wind. 'I'll pay for it,' I told her.

'Pay for it? You think that makes it all right, don't you? You think everything's all right if you pay. Or someone pays you. How much did they pay you? The gun-runners?'

'I got legal aid from the Court in Strasburg. Who were the gun-runners exactly?'

'Not guns, was it? Something much more than guns. You honestly don't know?'

'Honestly.'

'Then you should. You should know what you've done to the world.' She moved unsteadily to the table. 'What is it you want?'

'A brandy-and-soda,' I suggested, 'would be very welcome.' If I was going to be operated on, I needed an anaesthetic. I saw her pick up a bottle and wave it vaguely in the air. 'I'll pour it out,' I told her.

'You pour it out,' she said, 'and come into the kitchen. Don't let it go any further. Eddie would kill me, but I think you bloody well ought to know.'

A quarter of an hour later I walked across the garden alone. Should I have guessed? Were there moments that should have told me the truth? Betsi grabbing a newspaper? A car threatening Ballard – an incident Betsi Hoprecht said was 'unnecessary'? A few words overheard in the bar at Strasburg airport? Should these things have told me the truth, and was I getting too old to take the hint?

The sky had darkened as if in warning of a storm but the earth, the grass and the dahlias, golden chrysanthemums and blue Michaelmas daisies were still bright and stood out vividly against the gun-metal grey of the sky. Hilda and Dodo were walking towards me.

'Rumpole! Where on earth have you been?'

'Here and there. I had a look inside the house.'

'You've been drinking.'

'I've been listening.'

'Who to?'

'A woman who owns this garden. I met her when I was doing a case.'

'Oh, was it one you lost?'

'No, I won it. Unfortunately.'

'Dodo knows a place where we can have lunch in Haywards Heath.'

'They do homemade soups.' Dodo opened an unexciting prospect.

Whose fault was it that the truth never emerged and that deadly Russian weapons were still being traded to Iraq? Was it my fault, or Ballard's fault when he was tempted to show his libertarian principles in the hope of future briefs? Was it all because Billy Bloxham let his prejudices show at a rugby club dinner, or because a cub reporter heard what he said? Or because a new Court had been invented to take care of the Rights of Man? Who should I blame – or was I to blame myself?

These questions would never have occurred to me but for an encounter with a half-drunk woman who had thrown her garden open to the public. What she had told me were official secrets, and included the fact that the arms trade was being financed through Netherbank in London, and that George Freeling was an investigator reporting back to some modestly retiring Department of State. So my young Iraqi client, a servant of the arms dealers, among whom Betsi and Jameson were numbered, was chosen to silence him for ever. My job had been to get him out of prison before he decided to talk in exchange for parole. These important facts, like Billy Bloxham's racist opinions, never saw the light in the Old Bailey.

I put down my spoon in the restaurant, which was without a licence and served iced tea with the carrot soup and vegetarian quiche. 'It's Billy Bloxham's fault,' I said. 'He should never have developed a taste for rugby football.'

'*Do* stop thinking about your work, Rumpole,' Hilda rebuked me. 'Can't you enjoy a day out in the country?'

Quite honestly I couldn't. I was looking forward to Monday and a receiving of stolen fish at Acton. It had nothing to do with human rights at all.

Rumpole and the Angel of Death

I have, from time to time in these memoirs, had some harsh things to say about judges, utterances of mine which may, I'm afraid, have caused a degree of resentment among their assembled Lordships who like nothing less than being judged. To say that their profession makes them an easy prey to the terrible disease of judgeitis, a mysterious virus causing an often fatal degree of intolerance, pomposity and self-regard, is merely to state the obvious. Being continually bowed to and asked 'If your Lordship pleases?' is likely to unhinge the best-balanced legal brain; and I have never thought that those who were entirely sane would undertake the thankless task of judging their fellow human beings anyway. However, the exception to the above rule was old Chippy Chippenham, who managed to hold down the job of a senior circuit Judge, entitled to try murder cases somewhere in the wilds of Kent, and remain, whenever I had the luck to appear before him, not only sensible but quite remarkably polite.

Chippy had been a soldier before he was called to the Bar. He had a pink, outdoors sort of face, a small scourer of a grey moustache and bright eyes which made him look younger than he must have been. When I appeared before him I would invariably get a note from him saying, 'Horace, how about a jar when all this nonsense is over?' I would call round to his room and he would open a bottle of average claret (considerably better, that is, than my usual Château Thames Embankment), and we would discuss old times, which usually meant recalling the fatuous speeches of some more than usually tedious prosecutor.

In Court Chippy sat quietly. He summed up shortly and perfectly fairly (that I *did* object to – a fair summing-up is most likely to get the customer convicted). His sentences erred, if at all, on the side of clemency and were never accompanied by any sort of sermon or homily on the repulsive nature of the accused. I once defended a perfectly likeable old countryman, a gamekeeper turned poacher from somewhere south of Sevenoaks, who, on hearing that his wife was dying from a painful and inoperable cancer, took down his gun and shot her through the head. 'Deciding who will live and who will die,' Chippy told him, having more or less ordered the Jury to find manslaughter, 'is a task Almighty God approaches only with caution,' and he gave my rustic client a conditional discharge, presumably on the condition that he didn't shoot any more wives.

The last time I appeared before Chippy he had changed. He found it difficult to remember the name of the fraudster in the dock and whether he'd dealt in spurious loft conversions or non-existent caravans. He shouted at the usher for not supplying him with pencils when a box was on his desk, and quite forgot to invite me round for a jar. Later, I heard he had retired and gone to live with some relatives in London. Later still, such are the revenges brought in by the whirligig of time, he appeared in the curious case of *R.* v. *Dr Elizabeth Ireton*, as the victim of an alleged murder.

The Angel of Death no doubt appears in many guises. She may not always be palely beautiful and shrouded in black. In the particularly tricky case which called on my considerable skills and had a somewhat surprising result, the fell spirit appeared as a dumpy, grey-haired, bespectacled lady who wore sensible shoes, a shapeless tweed skirt, a dun-coloured cardigan and a cheerful smile. This last was hard to explain considering her position of peril in Number One Court at the Bailey. She was a Dr Elizabeth Ireton, known to her many patients and admirers as Dr Betty, and she carried on her practice from a chaotic surgery in Notting Hill Gate.

I'll admit I was rather distracted that breakfast time in the kitchen of our so-called mansion flat in the Gloucester Road. I was trying to gain as much strength as possible from a couple of eggs on a fried slice, pick up a smattering of the events of the day from the wireless and make notes in the case of Dr Ireton, with whom I had a conference booked for five o'clock. My usual calm detachment about that case was unsettled by the discovery that the corpse in question was that of Judge Chippy with whom I had shared so many a friendly jar. There was little time to spare before I had to set off for a banal matter of receiving a huge consignment of frozen oven-ready Thai dinners in Snaresbrook.

Accordingly, I stuffed the papers in my battered briefcase, placed my pen in the top pocket and submerged my dirty plate and cutlery in the washing-up bowl, in accordance with the law formulated by She Who Must Be Obeyed.

'Rumpole!' The voice of authority was particularly sharp that morning. 'Have you the remotest idea what you have done?'

'A remote idea, Hilda. I have prepared for work. I am going out into the harsh, unsympathetic world of a Crown Court for the sole purpose of keeping this leaky old mansion flat afloat and well-stocked with Fairy Liquid and suchlike luxuries . . .'

'Is this the way you usually prepare for work?'

'By consuming a light cooked breakfast and doing a bit of last-minute homework? How else?'

'And I suppose you intend to appear in Court with the butter knife sticking out of your top pocket, having thrown your fountain-pen into the sink.'

A glance at my top pocket told me that She Who Must Be Obeyed, forever eagle-eyed, had sized up the situation pretty accurately. 'A moment of confusion,' I agreed. 'My mind was on more serious subjects. Particularly it was on a Dr Ireton, up on a charge of wilful murder.'

'Dr Betty?' As usual Hilda was about four steps ahead of me. 'She's the most wonderful person. Truly wonderful!'

'You're not thinking of her as Quack By Appointment to the Rumpole household?' I asked with some apprehension. 'She's accused of doing in his Honour Charles Chippy Chippenham, a circuit Judge for whom I had an unusual affection.'

'She didn't do it, Rumpole!'

'My dear old thing, I'm sure you know best.'

'I was at school with her. She was a house monitor and we all simply adored her. I promised you'd get her off.'

'Hilda, I know you have enormous respect for me as a courtroom genius, but your good Dr Betty was apparently a leading light in Lethe, a society to promote the joys of euthanasia . . .'

'It's not a question of your being a genius, Rumpole. It's just that I told Betty Ireton that you'd have me to answer to if you didn't win her case. I know quite well she believes passionately' – and here I saw Hilda watching me closely as I dried the fountain-pen – 'that life shouldn't be needlessly prolonged. Not, at any rate, after old people have completely lost their senses.'

The case of the frozen Thai dinners wound remorselessly on and was finally adjourned to the next day. When I got back to Chambers I found my room inhabited by a tallish, thinnish man in a blue suit with hair just over his ears and the sort of moustache once worn by South American revolutionaries and now sported by those who travel the Home Counties trying to flog double-glazing to the natives. He had soft, brown eyes, a wristwatch with a heavy metallic strap which gleamed in imitation of gold, and all around him hung a deafening odour of aftershave. This intruder appeared to be measuring my room, and the top of my desk, with a long, wavering, metal tape.

'At long last,' I said, as I unloaded the antique briefcase. 'Bollard's got the decorators in.'

'It's Horace Rumpole, isn't it? I'm Vince.'

'Vince?'

'Vince Blewitt.'

'Glad to know you, Mr Blewitt, but you can't start rubbing down now. I'm about to have a conference.' I was a little puzzled; we'd had the decorators in more than once in the last half-century and none of them had introduced themselves so eagerly.

'Rubbing down?' The man seemed mystified.

'Preparing to paint.'

'Oh, that!' Vince was laughing, showing off a line of teeth which would have graced a television advertisement. 'No, I'm not here regarding the paint. I'm just measuring your work-space so I can see if it makes sense in terms of your personal through-put in the organization's overall workload. That's what I'm regarding. And I have to tell you, Horace, I'm going to have a job justifying your area in terms of your contribution to overall Chambers' market profitability.'

'I have no idea what you're talking about.' I sat down wearily in the workspace area and lit a small cigar. 'And I'm not sure I want to. But I assume you're only passing through?'

'Hasn't Sam Ballard told you? My appointment was con-firmed at the last Chambers' meeting.'

'I've given up Chambers' meetings,' I told him. 'I regard them as a serious health hazard.'

'I'm really going to enjoy this opportunity. That Dot Clap-ton. Am I going to enjoy working with her! Isn't she something else?'

'What *else* do you mean? She's our general typist and tel-ephone answerer.'

'And much more. That girl's got a big future in front of her!' Here, the man laughed in a curiously humourless way. 'Oh, and there's another thought I'd like to share with you.'

'Please. Don't share anything else with me.'

'Looking at your own workload, Horace, what strikes me is this: you fight all your cases. They go on far too long. Of course you get daily refreshers, don't you?'

'Whenever I can.' All I could think of at that moment was how refreshing it would be to get this bugger Blewitt out of my room.

'But the brief fee for the first day has far more profitability?'

'If you're trying to say it's worth more money, the answer is yes.'

'So why not accept the brief and bargain for a plea, what-ever you do? Then you'd be free to take another one the next day. And so on. Do I need to spell it out? That way you could increase market share on your personal achievement record.'

'And a lot of innocent people might end up in chokey. You say you've joined our Chambers? Are you a lawyer?'

'Good heavens, no!' Blewitt seemed to find the suggestion

mildly amusing. 'My experience was in business. Sam Ballard head-hunted me from catering.'

'Catering, eh?' I looked at him closely. He had, I thought, a distinctly fishy appearance. 'Frozen Thai dinners come into it at all, did they?'

'From time to time. Do you have an interest in oriental cuisine, Horace?'

'None at all. But I do have an interest in my conference in a murder case which is just about to arrive.'

'Likely to be a plea?' Blewitt appeared hopeful.

'Over my dead body.'

'Well, make sure it's a maximum contributor to Chambers' cashflow.'

'That's quite impossible,' I told him. 'If I don't do this case free, gratis and for nothing, I shall get into serious trouble with She Who Must Be Obeyed.'

'Whoever's that?'

'Be so good as to leave me, Blewitt. I see you have a great deal to learn about life in Equity Court. Things you'd never pick up in catering.'

He left me then, and I thought I wasn't only landed with the Defence of Dr Betty Ireton but the Defence of our Chambers against the death-dealing ministrations of Vincent Blewitt.

After our new legal administrator had left my presence, I refreshed my memory, from the papers in front of me, on the circumstances of old Chippy's death.

It seemed that he had a considerable private fortune passed down from some eighteenth-century Chippenham who had ransacked the Far East whilst working for the East India Company. He had lived with his wife Connie in a large Victorian house near Holland Park until she died of cancer. Chippy was heartbroken and began to show the early symptoms of the disease which led to his retirement from the Bench – Alzheimer's. This is a condition in which the mind atrophies, the patient becomes apparently infantile, incomprehensible and incontinent. Early symptoms are a certain vagueness and loss of memory (such as washing up your fountain-pen? Perish the thought!). After the complaint has taken hold, the victim remains physically healthy and may live on for many years to the distress, no doubt, of the relatives. Whether, although unable to express themselves in words, those with Alzheimer's may still enjoy moments of happiness must remain a mystery.

As he became increasingly helpless, Chippy's nephew Dickie and Dickie's wife, Ursula, moved in to look after him. They kept their ten-year-old son, Andrew, reasonably quiet and they devoted themselves to the old man. He was also cared for by a Nurse Pargeter, who came when the young Chippenhams went out in the evenings, and by Dr Betty, who, according to the witnesses' statements, got on like a house on fire with the old man.

In fact they were such good friends that Dr Betty used to call at least one or two times a week and sit with Chippy. They would drink a small whisky together and the old man had, in the doctor's presence, occasional moments of lucidity, when he would laugh at an old legal joke or weep like a child when remembering his wife. When she left, Dr Betty would, on her own admission, leave her patient a sleeping tablet, or even two, to see him through the night. So far, Dr Betty's behaviour couldn't be criticized, except for the fact that she thought it right to prescribe barbiturates. But, to be fair to her, she was told that these were the soporifics Chippy relied on in the days when he still had all his marbles.

One night the Chippenhams went out to dinner. Nurse Pargeter had been engaged with another patient and Dr Betty volunteered to sit with Chippy. (I couldn't help wondering if her kindness on that occasion included a release from this vale of tears.) When the Chippenhams arrived home Dr Betty told them that her patient was asleep and she left then. The old man died that night with a suddenness that the nurse, who found him in the morning, thought suspicious. In an autopsy his stomach was found to contain the residue of a massive overdose of the sleeping tablets Dr Betty had prescribed and also a considerable quantity of alcohol. Dr Betty was well known as a passionate supporter of euthanasia and she was charged with murder. She was given bail and her trial was due to start in three weeks' time.

'Of course I remember Hilda. She was such a quiet, shy girl

at school.' I looked at Dr Betty, sitting in my client's chair in Chambers, and came to the conclusion that here was a quite unreliable witness. The suggestion of a quiet and shy Hilda was not, on the face of it, one that would satisfy the burden of proof.

'She told me that you don't think life should be needlessly prolonged in certain circumstances. Is that right?'

'Oh, yes.' The doctor, I judged, was in her late sixties but her smile was that of an innocent; her eyes behind her spectacles were shining with as girlish an enthusiasm as when she led her mustard-keen team out on to the hockey field. 'Death is such a lovely thing when you're feeling really poorly,' she said. 'I don't know why we don't all give it a hearty welcome.'

'"The grave's a fine and private place,"' I reminded her, '"But none, I think, do there embrace."'

'How do we know, Mr Rumpole? How can we possibly know? Are you really sure there won't be any cuddles beyond the grave?'

'Cuddles? I hardly think so.'

'We're so prejudiced against the dead!' Dr Betty was almost giggling and her glasses were glinting. 'Rather like there used to be prejudice against women when I went in for medicine. There must be so many really nice dead people!'

'You believe in the afterlife?'

'Oh, I think so. But whatever sort of life goes on after death, I'd be out of a job there, wouldn't I? No one would need a doctor.'

'Or a barrister?' Or might there be some celestial tribunal at which a crafty advocate could get a sinner off hell? Plenty of briefs, of course, but my heart sank at the thought of eternal work before a jury of prejudiced saints. I decided to return to the business in hand. 'Do you think that sufferers from Alzheimer's disease are appropriate candidates for the Elysian Fields?'

'Of course they are! I'd fully decided to send old Chippy off there as soon as I judged the time was ripe.'

My heart sank further. The danger of having a conference with customers accused of murder is that they may tell you they did the deed and then, of course, the fight is over and you have no alternative but to stagger into Court with your hands up. That's why, during such conferences, it's much wiser to discuss the Maastricht Treaty or Whither the Deutschmark? than to refer directly to the crude facts of the charge. It was my error to have done so and now I had to tell Dr Betty that she had as good as pleaded guilty.

'No, I haven't,' she told me, still, it seemed, in a merry mood. 'I'm not guilty of anything.'

'You're not?'

'Of course not! It's true I was prepared to release old Chippy from this unsatisfactory world, when the time came.'

'And it had come the night he died?'

'No, it certainly had not! He was still having lucid intervals. I would have done it eventually, but not then.' I meant to rob the bank, Guv, but not on that particular occasion: it didn't sound much of a defence, but I was determined to make the most of it.

'So do you think' – I threw Dr Betty a lifeline – 'Chippy might have got depressed during the night and committed suicide?'

'Of course not!' I'd never had a client who was so cheerfully anxious to sink herself. 'He was an old soldier. He always told me that he regarded suicide as cowardice in the face of the enemy. He'd have battled on against all odds, until I decided to sound the retreat.'

It hadn't been an easy day and to go straight home to Froxbury Mansions without a therapeutic visit to Pommeroy's Wine Bar would have been like facing an operation without an anaesthetic. So, because my alcohol content had sunk to a dangerous low, I pushed open the glass door and made for the bar. I saw, on top of a stool, a crumpled figure slumped in deepest gloom and attacking what I thought was far from his first gin-and-Dubonnet. Closer examination proved him to be our learned clerk.

'Cheer up, Henry,' I said, when I had called upon Jack Pommeroy to pour a large Château Fleet Street and mark it up on the slate. 'It may never happen!'

'It *has* happened, Mr Rumpole. And I could manage another

of the same if you're ordering. Our new legal administrator has happened.'

'You mean the blighter Blewitt?'

'Tell me honestly, Mr Rumpole, have you ever seriously considered taking your own life?'

'No.' It was perfectly true. Even in the darkest days, even when I was put on trial for professional misconduct after a run-in with a hostile judge and when She Who Must Be Obeyed's disapproval of my way of life meant that there was not only an east wind blowing in Froxbury Mansions but a major hurricane, I could always find solace in a small cigar, a glass of Pommeroy's plonk, a stroll down to the Old Bailey in the autumn sunshine and the possibility of a new brief to test my forensic skills. 'I have never felt the slightest temptation to place my head in the gas oven.'

'Neither have I,' Henry told me and I congratulated him. 'We're all electric at home. But, I have to say, I'm tempted by a handful of aspirins.'

'Messy,' I told him. 'And, in my experience, not entirely dependable. But why this desperate remedy?'

'I have lost everything, Mr Rumpole.'

'Everything?'

'Everything I care about. Dot Clapton and I. Our relationship is over.'*

'Really? I didn't think it ever began.'

'Too right, Mr Rumpole. Too very right!' Our clerk laughed bitterly. 'And my job has gone. What's my future? Staying at home . . .'

'In Bexleyheath?'

'Exactly. Helping out with a bit of shopping. Decorating the bathroom. And my wife will lose all respect for me as a breadwinner.'

'Your wife, the Alderperson?'

'Chairman of Social Services. It gives her a lot of status.'

'You'll have a good deal of time for your amateur dramatics.'

'I have been offered the lead in *Laburnum Grove*. I turned it down.'

---

*See 'Rumpole on Trial' in *Rumpole on Trial*, Penguin Books, 1993.

'But why, Henry?'

'Because I'm losing my job, and I've got no heart left for taking on a leading role!'

Further inquiry revealed what I should have known if I'd had more of a taste for Chambers' meetings. The skinflint Bollard had decided to get rid of a decent old-fashioned barrister's clerk who got a percentage of our takings and to appoint a legal administrator, at what I was to discover was a ludicrously high salary. 'Vince takes over at the end of the month,' Henry told me.

'Vince?'

'He asked me to call him Vince. He said that for us two to be on first-name terms would "ease the process". And what makes me so bitter, Mr Rumpole, is I think he's got his eye on our Dot.' Mizz Clapton is so casually beautiful that I thought she must have many eyes on her, but I didn't think it would cheer up our soon to be ex-clerk to tell him that. Instead I gave him my considered opinion on what I took to be the heart or nub of the matter.

'This man, Blewitt,' I said, 'appears to be a considerable blot on the landscape.'

'You're not joking, Mr Rumpole.'

'One that must be removed for the general health of Chambers.'

'And of me in particular, Mr Rumpole, as your long-serving and faithful clerk.'

'Then all I can tell you, Henry, is that a way must be found.'

'Agreed, Mr Rumpole, but who is to find it?'

It seemed to me a somewhat dimwitted question, and one that Henry would never have asked had he been entirely sober. 'Who else?' I asked, purely rhetorically, 'but the learned Counsel who found a defence in the Penge Bungalow affair, which looked, at first sight, even blacker than the case of the blot Blewitt – or even the predicament of Dr Betty Ireton.'

'Then I'll leave it to you, Mr Rumpole.'

'Many doubtful characters have said those very words, Henry, and not been disappointed.'

'And I could do with another gin-and-Dubonnet, sir. Seeing as you're in the chair.'

So Jack Pommeroy added to the figure on the slate and Henry seemed to cheer up considerably. 'I just heard a really ripe one in here, Mr Rumpole, from old Jo Castor who clerks Mr Digby Tappit in Crown Office Row. Do you know, sir, the one about the sleeveless woman?'

'I do not know it, Henry. But I suppose I very soon shall.'

As a matter of fact I never did. My much-threatened clerk began to tell me this ripe anecdote which had an extremely lengthy build-up. Long before the delayed climax I shut off, being lost in my own thoughts. Did old Chippy Chippenham die in the course of nature or was he pushed? If he had been, would he have felt as merciful to Dr Betty as he had to my rustic client who shot his sick wife?

Had one long, confused afternoon arrived when Chippy muttered to himself, 'I have been half in love with easeful Death'? The sound of the words gave me a lift only otherwise to be had from Pommeroy's plonk and I intoned privately and without interrupting Henry's flow:

> 'Now more than ever seems it rich to die,
> To cease upon the midnight with no pain,
> While thou art pouring forth thy soul abroad
> In such an ecstasy!'

Then Henry laughed loudly; his story had apparently reached its triumphant and no doubt obscene conclusion. I joined in for the sake of manners, but now I was thinking that I had to win the case of Blewitt as well as that of Dr Betty, and I had no idea how I was to emerge triumphant from either.

'We don't call this a memorial service. We call it a joyful thanksgiving for the life of his Honour Judge Chippenham.' So said the Reverend Edgedale, the Temple's resident cleric. Sitting at the back of the congregation, I thought that old Chippy wasn't in a position to mind much what we called it, and wondered if some of the villains he'd felt it necessary to send away to chokey would call it a joyful thanksgiving for his death. Chippy was dead, a word we all shy away from nowadays when almost anything else goes. What would Mizz Liz Probert have said? Old Chippy had become a non-living person. And then I thought how glowingly Dr Betty had talked about Chippy's present position, happily unaware of the length of the sermon – 'Chippy was the name he rejoiced in since his first term at Charterhouse, but you and I can hardly think of anyone with less of a chip on his shoulder' – and the increasing hardness of the pews. I looked around at the assembled mourners, Mr Injustice Graves, and various circuit judges and practising hacks who were no doubt wondering how soon they might expect a joyful thanksgiving for their own lives. I peered up at the stained-glass windows in the old round church built for the Knights Templar, who had gone off to die in the Crusades without the benefit of a memorial service, and then I fell into a light doze.

I was woken up by a peal on the organ and old persons stumbling across my knees, anxious to get out of the place which gave rise to uncomfortable thoughts of mortality. And, when we joined in the general rush for the light of day, I heard a gentle voice, 'Mr Rumpole, how delighted Uncle Chippy would have been that you could join us.'

I focused on a pleasant-looking, youngish woman, pushing back loose hair which strayed across her forehead. Beside her stood an equally pleasant, tall man in his forties. Both of them smiled as though their natural cheerfulness could survive even this sad occasion.

'Dick and Ursula Chippenham,' the tall man bent down considerately to inform me. 'Uncle Chippy was always talking about you. Said you could be a devilish tricky customer in Court but he always enjoyed having you in for a jar when the battle was over.'

'Chippy was so fond of his jar. What he wanted was to ask all his real friends back to toast his memory,' Ursula told me. 'Do say you'll come!'

'I honestly don't think . . .' What I meant to say was that I already felt a little guilty for slipping in to the memorial service of a man when I was defending his possible murderer. Could I, in all conscience, accept even one jar from his bereaved family?

'It's thirty-one Dettingen Road, Holland Park.' Dick Chippenham smiled down on me from a great height. 'Chippy would have been so delighted if you were there to say goodbye.'

As I say, I felt guilty but I also had a strong desire to see what we old-fashioned hacks call the *locus in quo* – the scene of the crime.

It was an English spring, that is to say, dark clouds pressed down on London and produced a doleful weeping of rain. I splurged out on a taxi from the Temple to Dettingen Road and spent some time in it while the approach to number thirty-one was blocked by a huge, masticating rubbish lorry which gave out strangled cries such as 'This vehicle is reversing!' as it tried to extricate itself from a jam of parked cars. Whistling dustmen were collecting bins from the front entrance of sedate, white-stuccoed houses, pouring their contents into the jaws of the curiously articulate lorry and then returning the empty bins, together with a small pile of black plastic bags, given, by courtesy of the council, to their owners. I paid the immobile taxi off and took a brisk walk in the sifting rain towards number thirty-one. As I did so, I saw a solemn boy come down the steps of the house and, in a sudden, furtive motion, collect the black plastic bags from the top of the dustbin, stuff them under his school blazer and disappear into a side entrance of the house. I climbed up the front steps, rang the bell and was admitted by a butler-like person who I thought must have been specially hired for Chippy's send-off. Sounds of the usual high cocktail-party chatter with no particular note of grief in it were emerging from the sitting-room. The wake seemed to be a great deal more cheerful than the weather.

Ursula Chippenham bore down on me with a welcome glass of champagne. 'We're so glad you came.' She moved me into a corner and spoke confidentially, much more in sorrow than in anger. 'Dr Betty got on so terribly well with Chippy. We never thought for a moment that she'd do anything like that.'

'Perhaps she didn't.'

'Of course, Dick and I don't want anything terrible to happen to her.'

'Neither do I.'

'We know you'll do your very best for her. Chippy always

said you were quite brilliant with a jury on a good day, when you didn't go over the top and start spouting bits of poetry at them.'

'That was very civil of him.'

'And, of course, Dr Betty and Chippy became best friends. Towards the end, that was.'

'I suppose you know that she was against ... Well, prolonging life?' Or in favour of killing people, I suppose I would have said, if I were appearing for the Prosecution.

'Of course. But I never dreamt she'd do anything ... Well, without discussing it with the family. She seemed so utterly trustworthy! Of course we hadn't known her all that long. She only came to us when Chippy took against poor Dr Eames.'

'When was that exactly?'

'There are certain rules, Mr Rumpole. Certain traditions of the Bar which you might find it convenient to remember.' Chippy had said that to me in Court when I asked a witness who happened to work in advertising if that didn't mean he'd taken up lying as a career. In his room afterwards he'd said, 'Horace, sometimes I wish you'd stop being such an *original* barrister.' 'Is trying to squeeze information out of a prosecution witness while consuming her champagne at a family wake in the best traditions of the Bar?' he would have asked. 'Probably not, my Lord,' I would have told Chippy, 'but aren't you curious to know exactly how you met your death?'

'Only about six months ago.' Ursula answered my question willingly. 'Eames is a bit politically correct, as a matter of fact. He kept telling Chippy that at least his illness meant that his place on the Bench was available to a member of an ethnic minority.'

'Not much of a bedside manner, this quack Eames?'

'Oh, I don't think Chippy minded that so much. It was when Eames said, "No more claret and no more whisky to help you to go to sleep, for the rest of your life", that the poor chap had to go.'

'Understandable.'

'Dick thought so too.'

'And how did you happen to hear of Dr Betty Ireton?'

'Some friends of mine in Cambridge Terrace said she was an

absolute angel. Oh, there you are, Pargey! This is Nurse
Pargeter, Mr Rumpole. Pargey was an angel to Chippy too.'
The nurse who was wandering by had reddish hair, a long
equine face and suddenly startled eyes. She wasn't in uniform,
but was solemnly dressed in a plain black frock and white
collar. I had already seen her, standing alone, taking care not to
look at the other guests in case they turned and noticed her
loneliness.

Ursula Chippenham drifted off to greet some late arrivals.
'Are you family?' the nurse asked in a surprisingly deep and
unyielding voice, with a trace of a Scottish accent.

'No, I'm a barrister. An old friend of Chippy's . . '

'Mr Rumpole? I think I've heard him mention you.'

'I'm glad. And then, of course, I have the unenviable task of
defending Dr Betty Ireton. Mrs Chippenham says she got on
rather well with the old boy.'

'Defend her?' Nurse Pargeter suddenly looked as relentless
as John Knox about to denounce the monstrous regiment of
women. 'She cannot be defended. I warned the Chippenhams
against her. They can't say I didn't warn them. I told them all
about that dreadful Lethe.'

'Everyone *can* be defended,' I corrected her as gently as
possible. 'Of course whether the Defence is successful is entirely another matter.'

'I prefer to remember the Ten Commandments on the subject. ' Pargey was clearly of a religious persuasion.

Those nicknames, I thought – Pargey and Chippy – you
might as well be in a school dormitory or at a gathering of very
old actors.

'Oh, the Ten Commandments.' I tried not to sound dismissive of this ancient code of desert law. 'Not too closely observed
nowadays, are they? I mean adultery's about the only subject
that seems to interest the newspapers, and coveting other
people's oxen and asses is called leaving everything to market
forces. And, as for worshipping graven images, think of the
prices some of them fetch at Sotheby's. As for Thou shalt not
kill – well, some people think that the terminally ill should be
helped out of their misery.'

'And some people happen to believe in the sanctity of life.

And now, if you'll excuse me, Mr Rumpole, I have an important meeting to go to.'

As I watched her leave, I thought that I hadn't been a conspicuous success with Nurse Pargeter. Then a small boy piped up at my elbow, 'Would you like one of these, sir? I don't know what they are actually.' It was young Andrew Chippenham, with a plate of small brown envelope arrangements made of brittle pastry. I took one, bit into it and found, hardly to my delight, goat's cheese and some green, seaweed-like substance.

'You must be Andrew,' I said. The only genuine schoolboy around wasn't called Andy or Drew, or even Chippy, but kept his whole name, uncorrupted. 'And you go to Bolingbroke House?' I recognized the purple blazer with brass buttons. Bolingbroke was an expensive prep school in Kensington, which I thought must be so over-subscribed that the classrooms were used in a rota system and the unaccommodated pupils were sent out for walks in a crocodile formation, under the care of some bothered and junior teacher, round the streets of London. I had seen regiments of purple blazers marching dolefully as far as Gloucester Road; the exit from Bolingbroke House had a distinct look of the retreat from Moscow.

'How do you like being a waiter?' I asked Andrew, thinking it must be better than the daily urban trudge.

'Not much. I'd like to get back to my painting.'

'You're an artist?'

'Of course not.' He looked extremely serious. 'I mean painting my model aeroplanes.'

'How fascinating.' And then I lied as manfully as any unreliable witness. 'I was absolutely crazy about model aeroplanes when I was your age. Of course, that was a bit before Concorde.'

'Did you ever go in a Spitfire?' Andrew looked at me as though I had taken part in the Charge of the Light Brigade or was some old warrior from the dawn of time.

'Spitfires? I know all about Spitfires from my time in the R.A.F.' I forgot to tell him I was ground staff only. And then I said, 'I say, Andrew, I'd love to see your collection.' So he put down his plate of goat's cheese envelopes and we escaped from the party.

Andrew's room was on the third floor, at the back of the house. In the front, a door was open and I got a glimpse of a big, airy room with a bed stripped and the windows open. When I asked who slept there, he answered casually and without any particular emotion, 'That was Great-uncle Chippy's room. He's the one who died, you know.'

'I know. I suppose your parents' bedroom's on the floor below?' It wasn't the subtlest way of getting information.

'Oh, yes. I'm all alone up here now.' Andrew opened the door of his room which smelled strongly of glue and, I thought for a moment, was full of brightly coloured birds which, as I focused on them, became model aeroplanes swinging in the breeze from an open window. From what seemed to be every inch of the ceiling, a thread had been tied or tacked to hold up a fighter or an old-fashioned seaplane in full flight.

'That's the sort of Spitfire you piloted,' Andrew said, to my silent embarrassment. 'And that's a Wellington bomber like you had in the war.' I did remember the planes returning, when they were lucky, with a rear-gunner dead or wounded and the stink of blood and fear when the doors were opened. I had been young then, unbearably young, and I banished the memory for more immediate concerns.

'Are these all the models you've made?' I asked Andrew. 'Or have you got lots more packed away in black bin bags?'

'Bin bags?' He was fiddling with a half-painted Concorde on his desk. 'Why do you say that?'

'You know, the plastic bags the dustmen leave after they've taken away the rubbish. Don't you collect them? A lot of boys do.'

'Collect plastic bags? What a funny thing to do.' Andrew had his head down and was still fiddling with his model. 'That wouldn't interest me, I'm afraid. I haven't got any plastic bags at all.'

Back in Chambers that afternoon I found Dot Clapton alone in front of her typewriter, frowning as she looked over a brightly coloured brochure, on the cover of which a bikinied blonde was to be seen playing leapfrog with a younger, fitter version of Vincent Blewitt on a stretch of golden sand.

'I'm afraid Henry's just slipped out, Mr Rumpole. I don't know what it is. His heart doesn't seem to be in his work nowadays.' She looked up at me in genuine distress and I saw the perfectly oval face, sculptured eyelids and blonde curls that might have been painted by some such artistic old darling as Sandro Botticelli, and heard the accent which might have been learnt from the Timson family somewhere south of Brixton. I didn't tell her that not only Henry's heart, but our learned clerk himself, might not be in his work very soon. Instead I asked, 'Thinking of going on holiday, Dot?'

She handed me the brochure in silence. On the front of it was emblazoned THE FIVE S HOLIDAYS: SEA, SUN, SAND, SINGLES AND SEX ON THE COSTA DEL SOL. WHY NOT GO FOR IT? 'Quite honestly, is that your idea of a holiday, Mr Rumpole?'

'It sounds,' I had to tell her, 'like my idea of hell.'

'I've got to agree with you. I mean, if I want burger and chips with a pint of lager, I might as well stay in Streatham.'

'Very sensible.'

'If I'm going to be on holiday, I want something a bit romantic.'

'I understand. Sand and sex are as unappealing as sand in the sandwiches?'

'My boyfriend's planning to take me to the castles down the Rhine. Of course, I don't want to upset him.'

'Upset your boyfriend?'

'No. Upset Mr Blewitt.'

'Upsetting Mr Blewitt – I have to say this, Dot – is my idea of a perfect summer holiday.'

'Oh, don't say that, Mr Rumpole.' Dot Clapton looked nervously round the room as though the blot might be concealed behind the arras. 'He is my boss now, isn't he?'

'Not *my* boss, Dot. No one's my boss, and particularly not Blewitt.'

'He's mine then. And he told me these singles holidays are a whole lot of fun.'

'Did he now?' I felt that there was something in this fragment of information which might be of great value.

'I don't know, though. Vince . . . Well, he asked me to call him Vince.'

'And you agreed?'

'I didn't have much choice. Does he honestly think I haven't got a boyfriend?'

'If he thinks that, Dot, he can't be capable of organizing a piss-up in a brewery, let alone a barristers' Chambers.'

'Piss-up in a brewery!' Dot covered her mouth with her hand and giggled. 'How do you think of these things, Mr Rumpole?'

I didn't tell her that they'd been thought of and forgotten long before she was born, but took my leave of her, saying I was on my way to see Mr Ballard.

'Oh, he's busy.' Dot emerged from behind her hand. 'He said he wasn't to be disturbed.'

'Then it will be my pleasure and privilege to disturb him.'

'Have you "eaten on the insane root",' I asked the egregious Ballard, with what I hoped sounded like genuine concern, '"That takes the reason prisoner?"'

'What *do* you mean, Rumpole?'

'I mean no one who has retained one single marble would dream of introducing the blight Blewitt into Equity Court.'

'I thought you'd come to me about that eventually.'

'Then you thought right.'

'If you had bothered to attend the Chambers' meeting you might have been privy to the selection of Vincent Blewitt.'

'I have only a few years of active life left to me,' I told the man with some dignity. 'And they are too precious to be wasted on Chambers' meetings. If I'd been there, I'd certainly have banned Blewitt.'

'Then you'd have been outvoted.'

'You mean those learned but idiotic friends decided to put their affairs in the hands of this second-rate, second-hand car salesman.'

'Catering.' Ballard smiled tolerantly.

'What?'

'Vincent Blewitt was in catering, not cars.'

'Then I wouldn't buy a second-hand cake off him.'

'Horace' – Soapy Sam Ballard rose and placed a considerate and totally unwelcome hand on my shoulder – 'we all know that you're a great old warhorse and that you've had a long, long career at the Bar. But you have to face it, my dear old Horace, you don't understand the modern world.'

'I understand it well enough to be able to tell a decent, honest, efficient, if rather over-amorous, clerk from the dubious flogger of suspect and probably mouldy canteen dinners.' I shrugged the unwelcome hand off my shoulder.

'The clerking system,' Ballard told me then, with a look of intolerable condescension, 'is out of date, Horace. We are moving towards the millennium.'

'You move towards it if you like. I prefer to stay where I am.'

'Why should we pay Henry a percentage when we can get an experienced businessman for a salary?'

'What sort of salary?'

'Vincent Blewitt was good enough to agree to a hundred, to be reviewed at the end of one year. The contract will be signed when the month's trial period is over.'

'A hundred pounds? Far too much!'

'A hundred thousand, Rumpole. It's far less than he would expect to earn in the private sector of industry.'

'Let him go back to the private sector then. If you want to be robbed, I could lend you one of the Timsons. They only deal in petty theft.'

'Vincent Blewitt has been very good to join us. At some personal financial sacrifice . . .'

'Did you check on what his screw was in the canteen?'

'I took his word for it.' Ballard looked only momentarily embarrassed.

'Famous last words of the fraudster's victim.'

'Vincent Blewitt isn't a fraudster, Rumpole. He's a businessman.'

'That's the polite word for it.'

'He says we must earn our keep by a rise in productivity.'

'How do you measure our productivity?'

'By the turnover in trials.'

'In your case, by the amazing turnover in defeats.' It was below the belt, I have to confess, but it didn't send Ballard staggering to the ropes. He came back, pluckily, I suppose. 'Business, Rumpole,' he told me, 'makes the world go round.' Later I discovered he'd got these words of wisdom from some ludicrous television advertisement.

'Rubbish. Justice might make the world go round. Or poetry. Or love. Or even God. *You* might think it's God, Bollard, as a founder member of the Lawyers As Christians Society.'

'As a Christian, Rumpole, I remember the parable of the talents. The Bible points out that you can't fight market forces.'

'Didn't the Bible also say something like Blessed are the poor? Or do you wish it hadn't said that?'

'I've got no time to trade texts with you, Rumpole.' Soapy Sam looked nettled.

I was suddenly tired, half in love, perhaps for a moment, with easeful death. 'Oh, let's stop arguing. Get rid of the blot, confirm Henry in the job and we need say no more about it.'

'I'm sure you'll find Vincent Blewitt a great asset to Chambers, Rumpole. He's a very human sort of person. He likes his joke, I understand. I'm sure you'll have plenty of laughs together.'

'If he stays . . .'

'He *is* staying . . .'

'Then I'll take a handful of pills, washed down with a glass of whisky, and cease upon the midnight with no pain.'

'If you wish to do that, Rumpole' – our learned Head of Chambers sat down at his desk and pretended to be busy with a set of papers – 'that is entirely a matter for you.'

That evening, before the news, Ballard's favourite commercial about business making the world go round came on. Later there were some pictures of a Pro-Life demonstration outside an abortion clinic in St John's Wood. Prominent among those present was a serious, long-faced woman with reddish hair. Nurse Pargey was waving a placard on which was written the words THOU SHALT NOT KILL.

★

'Alzheimer's isn't a killer in itself. Certainly the patient gets weaker and more forgetful. Helpless, in fact. But it would need something more to kill Chippy.'

'Like an overdose of sleeping pills, for instance?'

'Evidently that's what did it.' Dr Betty was one of those awkward clients, it seemed, who felt impelled to tell the truth. And what she went on to say wasn't particularly helpful. 'I might have given Chippy an overdose of something when the time came, but it hadn't come on the night he died. You must believe that, Horace.'

'Whether I believe it or not isn't exactly the point. What matters is whether the Jury believe it.'

'That's for them to decide, isn't it?'

'I'm afraid it is.' At which moment there was a rapid knock on the door which immediately opened to admit Blewitt's head. He took a quick look at the assembled company and said, 'Sorry folks! Mustn't interrupt the workers' productivity. Speak to you later, Horace.' At which, as rare things will, he vanished.

'Who on earth was that extraordinary man?' For the first time Dr Betty looked shaken.

'A temporary visitor,' I told her. 'Nothing for you to worry about. Now tell me about the sleeping pills.'

'I gave him two.'

'And you saw him drink his whisky?'

'A small whisky-and-soda. Yes.'

'And then . . .?'

'Well, I settled him down for the night.'

'Did he go to sleep?'

'He seemed tired and dreamy. He'd been quite contented that day, in fact. But incontinent, of course. Quite soon after he'd settled down, I heard the Chippenhams come home from their dinner-party, so I went downstairs to meet them.'

'What happened to the bottle of pills?'

'Well, that was kept in the house so that the Chippenhams or Nurse Pargeter could give Chippy his pills when I wasn't there.'

'Kept where in the house?'

'I put them back in the bathroom cupboard.'

'Are there two bathrooms?'

'Yes. The one next to the Judge's bedroom. You know the house?' Dr Betty looked surprised.

'I have a certain nodding acquaintance with it. And young Andrew?'

'His mother had sent him up to bed before they went out. But I'm afraid he hadn't gone to sleep.'

'How do you know that?'

'When I went to put the pills back in the bathroom, I saw his light on and his bedroom door open. He was still reading – or playing with his model aeroplanes more likely.'

'Quite likely, yes. Oh, one other thing. Had you ever spoken to Chippy about Lethe?'

'No, certainly not. I told you, Horace. The time had not come.'

'And was anyone else Chippy knew a member of Lethe? Any friends or his family?'

'Oh, no, I'm sure they weren't.'

'I think it might be just worth getting a statement from a Dr Eames.' I turned to Bonny Bernard, my instructing solicitor. 'Oh, and a few inquiries about the firm of Marcellus & Chippenham, house agents and surveyors.'

'David Eames?' Dr Betty looked doubtful.

'He treated Chippy before you came on the scene. He might know if he'd ever talked of suicide.'

Dr Betty once again spurned a line of defence. 'As I told you, I'm quite sure he never contemplated such a thing.'

'So if you didn't kill him, Dr Betty, who do you think did?'

She was looking at me, quite serious then, as she said, 'Well, that's not for me to say, is it?'

'Sorry to have intruded on your conference. Although it may be no bad thing for me to make spot checks on the human resource in the workplace.'

I had hardly recovered from the gloomy prospect of defending Dr Betty when the Blight was with me again. I sat, sunk in thought.

'Cheer up, Horace.' Vince's laugh was like a bath running out. 'It may never happen.' As he said that, I regretted having used the same fatuous words of encouragement to Henry, our condemned clerk. Most of the worst things in life are absolutely bound to happen, the trial of the cheerful doctor, for instance, or death itself.

'I wanted a word or two with you about formalizing staff holidays. You thinking of getting away to the sun yourself?'

'Hardly,' I told him, 'having glanced at the brochure you gave Dot Clapton.'

'Sea, sand and sex, Rumpole. You'd enjoy that. Very relaxing,' Vince gurgled.

'I'm hardly a single.'

'Well, send the wife on a tour of the Lake District or something, and you head off to the Costa del Sol. That's my advice. I mean, when you're invited to a gourmet dinner, why take a ham sandwich?'

I looked at Vincent Blewitt with a wild surmise. Was there no limit to the awfulness of the man? I could imagine no matrimonial situation, however grim, in which I could tell Hilda that she was a ham sandwich.

'I've rota'd Dot early July in the format,' Vince told me. 'I don't think she can wait to join me and assorted singles.'

I thought of telling him that Dot didn't even like the Costa del Sol. That she didn't think that sex and sand made a good mix. That she had a romantic nature and she wanted to drift past the castles on the Rhine listening to the Lorelei's mystic note. Some glimmering hope, a faint idea of a plan, led me to encourage the Blot. 'Considerable fun, these singles holidays, are they, Vincent?'

'You're not joking!' He had now sunk into my client's armchair and stuck out his legs in anticipation of delight. 'First day you get there, as soon as you've got checked in, it's down to the beach for games to break the ice.'

'Games?'

'I'll just tell you one. Whet your appetite.'

'Carry on.'

'The fellas get to blow up balloons inside the girls' bikini bottoms. And then the girls do it vice versa in our shorts. By the time we've played that, everyone's a swinger.'

I looked longingly at the door, thinking how restful the

forthcoming murder trial would be, compared with a quiet chat with our legal administrator.

'It sounds very tasteful.'

'I think you've got the message. I'll rota you for a couple of weeks then. After Dot and I have left the Costa, of course. I never knew you were a swinger, Horace.'

'Oh, we all have our joys and desires.'

'Don't we just!' Vincent looked at me, I thought, with unusual respect. 'Heard any good ones lately?'

'Ones?'

'You know. Jokes. You've got hidden talents, Horace. I bet you know about rib-ticklers.'

'You mean' – I looked at him seriously – 'like the one about the sleeveless woman?'

'Isn't that a *great* story?' Happily Vincent knew this anecdote and he gurgled again. 'Laughed like a drain when I first heard it. Whoever told you that one, Horace?'

I looked him straight in the eye and lied with complete conviction, 'Oh, Sam told me that. It's just his type of humour.'

'Sam?' Vincent was puzzled.

'You know, our learned Head of Chambers, Soapy Sam Ballard.'

I have often noticed that before any big and important cause or matter – and no one could doubt the size and importance of *R. v. Dr Betty* – a kind of peace descends on my legal business. In other words, I hit a slump. I had nothing in Court, not even the smallest spot of indecency at Uxbridge. I had no conferences booked and those scurrying about their business in the Temple, or waiting in the corridors of the Old Bailey, might well have come to the conclusion that old Rumpole had ceased upon the midnight hour with no pain. In fact I was docked in Froxbury Mansions with my ham – no, I will not be infected by Vince's vulgarity – with She Who Must Be Obeyed.

Needless to say, I had no wish to spend twenty-four hours a day closeted with Hilda, so I went on a number of errands to the newsagent in search of small cigars, to the off-licence at the other end of Gloucester Road to purchase plonk, stretch my legs and breathe in the petrol fumes.

I was walking, wrapped in thought, through Canning Place, when I saw the familiar sight of purple blazers marching towards me in strict battle formation, led by a sharp-faced young female wearing a tweed skirt and an anorak, who uttered words of command or turned to rebuke stragglers. I stood politely in the gutter to let them pass, raising my umbrella in a kind of salute when I saw, taking up the rearguard, Andrew Chippenham.

'Andrew!' I called out in my matiest tones, 'how are you, old boy? Marching up with your regiment to lay siege to the Albert Hall, are you? Or on the hunt for bin bags?'

It was not at all, I'm sure you'll agree, an alarming sally. I intended to be friendly and jocular, but when he heard my voice young Andrew stopped, apparently frozen, his head down. He raised it slowly and what I saw was a small, serious boy frozen in terror. Before I could speak again, he had turned and run off after his vanishing crocodile.

I was finding this enforced home leave so tedious that, a few days later, I took a trip on the tube back to my Chambers in the Temple, although I had no business engagements. I was sunk in the swing chair with my feet on the desktop workspace, trying to fathom out the depths of ingenuity to which the setter of *The Times* crossword puzzle might have sunk, when the Blot oozed through the door and defiled my carpet.

'I thought it might be rather appropriate,' he said in the sort of solemn voice people use when they're discussing funeral arrangements, 'if we gave a great party in Chambers to mark Henry's career change.'

'What's that called?' I asked him. 'Easing the passing?'

'At least give him a smashing send-off.'

'I suppose he can live on that as his retirement pension.'

'I'm sure Henry has got a bit put by.'

'He hasn't got a job put by. I happen to know that.' And then some sort of a plan began to take shape in my mind. 'Why does it have to be a *great* party?'

'Because' – and then Vince looked at me in a horribly

conspiratorial fashion as the penny dropped. 'Horace, you're not suggesting?'

'A bit of a singles do, why not?'

'Leave the ham sandwiches at home, eh?'

'Exactly!' I forced myself to say it, although it stuck in my throat.

'I mean, we'd ask Dot Clapton, wouldn't we?'

'Of course,' I reassured him.

'And some of the gorgeous bits that float around the Temple.'

'As many of them as you can cram in. We'll make it a real send-off for Henry.'

'Something he'll remember all his life.'

'Certainly.'

'Only one drawback, as far as I know.'

'What's that?'

'We'll have to ask permission from the Head of Chambers.' Vincent looked doubtful and disappointed.

'The Head of Chambers would be furious if he weren't included,' I assured him, and the gurgling laughter was turned on again.

'Of course. I remember what you told me about Sam Ballard. A bit of a swinger, didn't you indicate?'

'Bollard,' I said, remembering an old song of my middle age, '"swings as the pendulum do". Put the whole proposition to him, Vincent. Put it in detail, not forgetting the balloons blown up in the trousers, and then watch his eyes light up.'

'We're in for a good time, then?'

'I think so. At very long last.'

After the Blot had left me, suitably encouraged, I went home on the Underground. Emerging from Gloucester Road station, I saw the formation of purple blazers bearing down on me remorselessly on what must have been the last route-march of the day. I stood aside to let them pass, but the C.O. halted the column and looked at me, through a pair of horn-rimmed spectacles, with obvious distaste. 'Are you the person who spoke to Chippenham the other day, down at the end of the line?' she asked me. 'The boys told me he had spoken to somebody strange.'

'It just so happened' – I decided to overlook the description – 'that I know the family.'

'Whether you do or you don't' – she frowned severely – 'he was clearly upset by what you said to him. It's most unusual for people to speak to my Bolingbrokers in the street. He was obviously shocked, the other boys said so. Ever since he met you, Chippenham's been away sick.'

'But I honestly didn't say anything,' I started to explain but, before I could finish the sentence, the word of command had been given and the column quick-marched away from me.

When I got back to the seclusion of the mansion flat (there were times when I felt that our chilly matrimonial home was more a mausoleum than a mansion), I found Hilda had gone to her bridge club and left a message for me to ring my instructing solicitor and 'make sure neither of you slip up on Dr Betty's case'. When I got through to Bonny Bernard, he had news which interested me greatly. The puritanical Dr Eames had, it seemed, returned to care for the Chippenham family and, in particular, he was looking after young Andrew, who was suffering from some sort of nervous illness and was off school. As a witness, Bernard told me, Dr Eames was of the talkative variety and seemed to have something he was a strangely anxious to tell me. I hoped he would become even more talkative in the days before the trial.

I discovered that our case was to come before Mrs Justice Erskine-Brown, for so long the Portia of our Chambers and its acknowledged beauty (even now, when she is Dame Phillida and swathed in the scarlet and ermine of a High Court Judge, she is a figure that the unspeakable Vince might well have wanted to lure into a singles holiday on the Costa del Sand and Sex). I had known her since she had joined us as a tearful pupil;* we had been together and against each other, and I had taught her enough to turn her into a formidable opponent, in more trials than I care to remember. She was brave, tenacious, charming and provocative as compared with her husband

* See 'Rumpole and the Married Lady' in *Rumpole of the Bailey*, Penguin Books, 1978.

Claude who, upon his hind legs in any courtroom, could be counted upon to appear nervous, hesitant and unconvincing. I have a distinct fondness for Portia which I have reason to believe, because of the way she behaved during the many crises in Equity Court, is suitably returned. In short, we have a mutual regard, and I hoped she might feel some sympathy for a case which, in other hands, was likely to prove equally difficult for Dr Betty Ireton and Horace Rumpole. There, hopes were dashed quite early on in the proceedings.

'It may be argued on behalf of the Defence . . .' The Prosecutor was the beefy Q.C., Barrington McTear. He had played rugby football for Oxford and his courtroom tactics consisted of pushing, shoving, tackling low and covering his opponents, whenever possible, with mud. Although his name had a Highland ring to it, he spoke in an arrogant and earblasting Etonian accent and considered himself a cut above such middle-class, possibly overweight, and certainly unsporty barristers as myself. For this reason I had privately christened him Cut Above McTear.

Cut Above had massive shoulders, a large, pink face and small, gold half-glasses. They perched on him as inappropriately as a thin, gold necklace on a ham. Now, in a voice that could have been heard from one end of a football field to the other, he repeated what he thought would be my defence for the purpose of bringing it sprawling to the ground in a particularly unpleasant tackle. 'Your Ladyship may well think that Mr Rumpole's defence will be "This old gentleman was on his way out anyway, so Dr Ireton committed an act of mercy and not an act of murder" . . .'

'Such a defence will receive very little sympathy in this Court, Mr McTear.' Portia was clearly not in a mood to fuss about the quality of mercy. 'Murder is murder until Parliament chooses to pass a law permitting euthanasia.'

'Oh, I do so entirely agree with your Ladyship,' Cut Above informed the Bench and probably those assembled in the corridor and nearby Courts, 'so it will be interesting to discover if Mr Rumpole has a defence.'

'May I remind my learned friend' – I climbed to my feet and spoke, I think with admirable courtesy – 'that a prosecutor's job is to prove the charge and not to speculate about the nature of the Defence. If he wishes any further advice on how to conduct his case, I shall be available during the adjournment.'

'I hardly need advice on prosecuting from Mr Rumpole, who hasn't done any of it!' Cut Above bellowed.

'Gentlemen' – Portia's quiet call to order was always effective – 'perhaps we should get on with the evidence. No doubt we shall hear from Mr Rumpole in the fullness of time.'

So Cut Above turned to tell the Jury that they would find the evidence he was about to call entirely persuasive and leading to the inevitable verdict of guilty on Dr Ireton. A glance at Hilda, who had come to support her friend and make sure that I secured her deliverance from the dock, was enough to tell me that She Who Must Be Obeyed didn't think much of my performance so far.

Dick Chippenham was the sort of witness that Cut Above could understand and respect. They probably went to the same tailor and played the same games at the same sort of schools and universities. Dick even spoke in Cut Above's sort of voice, although with the volume turned down considerably. When he had finished his examination Cut Above said, 'I'm afraid I'll have to trouble you to wait there for a few minutes more,' as though there was an unfortunate deputation from the peasantry to trouble him, but it needn't detain him long.

'Mr Chippenham, I'm sure all of us at the Bar wish to sympathize with you in your bereavement.'

'Thank you.' I glanced at the Jury. They clearly liked my opening gambit, one that Cut Above hadn't troubled himself to think of.

'I have only a few questions. Up to six months before he died, your uncle was attended by Dr Eames?'

'That is so.'

'But, rightly or wrongly, your uncle took against Dr Eames?'

'I'm afraid so.'

'That doctor not being convinced of the therapeutic effects of whisky and claret?'

I got a ripple of laughter from the Jury and a smile of assurance from the witness. 'I believe that was the reason.'

'So you then engaged Dr Ireton. Why did you choose her?'

'She was a local doctor who had treated one of my wife's friends.'

'At the time when you transferred to Dr Ireton, did you know that she was a member of Lethe, a pro-euthanasia society?'

'Mr Rumpole admits that she was a member of Lethe.' Cut Above sprang to attention. 'I hope the Jury have noticed this admission by the Defence,' he bellowed.

'I'm sure you can't have helped noticing that,' I told the Jury. 'And I'm sure that, during any further speeches from my learned friend, earplugs will be provided for those not already hard of hearing.'

'Mr Rumpole!' Portia rebuked me from the Bench. 'This is a serious case and I wish to see it is tried seriously.'

'An admirable ambition, my Lady,' I told her. 'And tried quietly too, I hope.' And then I turned to the witness before Cut Above could trumpet any sort of protest.

'When you and your wife got back from the dinner party, it was about eleven o'clock?'

'Yes.'

'And apart from your uncle, the only people in the house were Dr Betty Ireton and your son?'

'That's right. Dr Betty met us in the hall and she said she'd given Chippy his pills and a drink of whisky.'

'At that time, would your uncle have remembered whether he'd taken his pills or not?'

'He probably would have remembered. Dr Betty said she'd given him his pills as usual.'

'When you got upstairs, you went in to see your uncle?'

'We did.'

'Was he asleep?'

'Yes.'

'Was he still breathing?'

'I'm sure he was. Otherwise we'd have called for help immediately.'

'You noticed the bottle of whisky. Was it empty?'

'It must have been, but I can't say I noticed it then.'

'So perhaps it wasn't empty?'

'I can't say for sure, but I suppose it must have been.'

'You can't say for sure. And the bottle of pills had been put away in the bathroom?'

'Yes, I believe it had . . . My wife will tell you.'

'So you can't be sure how many pills were left when you last saw your uncle alive?'

'In the morning I saw the bottle of pills empty.'

'And in the morning your uncle was dead?'

'Yes, he was.'

'Thank you very much, Mr Chippenham.' I sat down with what I hoped was a good deal more show of satisfaction than I felt.

'Dr Betty said she thinks you and that deafening McTear person are behaving like a couple of small boys in the school playground.'

I thought it was perhaps unfortunate that Dr Betty was allowed bail if she was going to abuse her freedom by criticizing my forensic skills. 'She only sees what happens on the surface. Tactics, Hilda. She's no idea of the plans that are forming at the back of my mind.'

'Have you any idea of them either, Rumpole? Be honest. Or have you forgotten that, in the way you forgot to turn out the bathroom light when you'd finished shaving?'

It was breakfast time once again in Froxbury Mansions. I felt a longing to get away from the sharp cut-and-thrust of domestic argument and be off to the gentler world of the Old Bailey. Hilda pressed home her advantage. 'I hope you realize that I am personally committed to your winning this case, Rumpole. I have given my word to Dr Betty.'

Then you'd better ask for it back again, was what I might have said, but lacked the bottle. Instead I told Hilda that Dr Eames was going to give us a full statement which I thought might be helpful. At which, I gathered up my traps, ready to hotfoot it down to the Old Bailey canteen where I had a date with the industrious Bernard.

'You certainly need help from somewhere, Rumpole. And, I don't know if you noticed, you've left me your briefcase and taken my *Daily Telegraph.*' As I made the changeover, he said, 'We've learnt a lot lately, haven't we, about the onset of Alzheimer's disease?'

Dr David Eames was a rare bird, a doctor who liked talking to lawyers. He was tall, bony, with large, capable hands and a lock of fair hair that fell over his eyes, and a serious, enthusiastic way of speaking as though he hadn't yet lost his boyish faith in human nature, the National Health Service and the practice of medicine. I don't usually have much feeling for those who seek to deprive their fellow beings of their claret, but I felt a strange liking for this youthful quack who seemed only anxious to discover the truth about the fatal events which had taken place that night in Dettingen Road.

As we sat with Bernard in the Old Bailey canteen, with coffee from a machine, and went through the medical evidence, I noticed he was strangely excited, as though he had something to communicate but was not sure when, or if indeed ever, to communicate it.

'I'm right in thinking Alzheimer's is not a killer in itself, although those who contract it usually die within ten years?'

'That's right,' Eames agreed. 'They contract bronchitis or have a stroke, or perhaps they just lose their wish to live.'

'There's no evidence of bronchitis or a stroke here?'

'Apparently not.'

'So it seems likely that death was hurried on in some way?'

There was a silence, then Dr Eames said, 'I think that must follow.'

'My old friend and opponent, Dr Ackerman of the morgue, the Home Office pathologist, estimates death as between ten p.m. and one a.m.'

'I read that.'

'At any rate, he was dead by seven-thirty a.m. when Nurse Pargeter came to look after him. Dick Chippenham says that Chippy was alive and sleeping well at around eleven the night before. If Dr Betty had just given him an overdose . . .'

'The pills might not have taken their effect until some time later.'

'I was afraid you'd say that.' I took a gulp from the machine's coffee, which is pretty indistinguishable from the machine's tea, or the machine's soup if it comes to that. 'When you stopped being the Chippenhams' doctor . . .'

'When I was sacked, you mean?'

'If you like. Had you had a row with Chippy? I mean, did *he* sack you?'

'Not really. As far as I remember, it was Mr Chippenham who told me his uncle wanted me to go.'

'There was no question of you having had a row with Chippy about drinking whisky?'

'No. I can't remember anything like that.' The doctor looked puzzled and I felt curiously encouraged and lit a small cigar.

'Tell me, Doctor, did you know Nurse Pargeter?'

'Only too well.'

'And did you like her?'

'Pro-Life nurses can be a menace. They seem to think of themselves as avenging angels.'

'And she didn't care for Dr Betty?'

'She hated her! I think she thought of her as a potential murderess.'

I wondered if that might be helpful. Then I said, 'One more thing, Dr Eames, now that I've got you here . . .'

'What are you up to *now*, Rumpole? Talking to potential witnesses? Is that in the best tradition of the Bar?' Wasn't Stentor some old Greek military man whose voice, on the battlefield, was louder than fifty men together? No doubt his direct descendant was the stentorian Cut Above, who now stood with his wig in his hand, his thick hair interrupted by a little tonsure of baldness so that he looked like a muscular monk.

'I am consulting with an expert witness. A doctor of medicine,' I told Cut Above. 'And for Counsel to see expert witnesses is certainly in the best tradition of the Bar.'

'I'm warning you. Just watch it, Rumpole. Watch it extremely carefully. I don't want to have to report you to her lovely Ladyship for unprofessional conduct.' My opponent gave a bellow of laughter which rattled the coffee cups and passed on with his myrmidons, a junior barrister and a wiry little scrum-half from the D.P.P.'s office.

'Who's that appalling bully?' Dr Eames appeared shocked.

'Cut Above, Q.C., Counsel for the Prosecution.'

'I've known surgeons like that. Full of themselves and care nothing for the patient. Doesn't he want me to talk to you?' I think it was Cut Above's appearance and interruption which persuaded Dr Eames to tell me all he eventually did.

'Probably not. I want to talk to you, though. Aren't you treating young Andrew? He seemed a charming boy!'

'I'm not sure what's the matter with him. Some sort of nervous trouble. Something's worrying him terribly.' Dr Eames also looked worried.

'I spoke to him in the street, and a schoolmistress ticked me off for it. But that couldn't have had anything to do with his illness, could it?'

'I'm afraid you reminded him of something.' I felt a prickle of excitement. Dr Eames was about to reveal some evidence of great importance.

'What exactly?'

'I think I know. It was something you'd said before, when you came to the house. It reminded him of his dream.'

At a nearby table Cut Above was yelling orders to his junior. If Dr Eames hadn't taken such an instant dislike to my opponent he might never have told me about young Andrew's dream.

Without doubt, the Jury took strongly to Ursula Chippenham and I have to say that I also liked her. Standing in the box with her honey-coloured hair a little untidy, a scarf floating about her neck, her gentle voice sounding touchingly brave, yet clearly audible, she was the perfect prosecution witness. She showed no hatred of Dr Betty; she spoke glowingly of her care and friendship for the old Judge; and she was only saddened by what the doctor's principles had led her to do. 'I'm quite sure that Dr Betty was only doing what she thought was right and merciful,' she said. Having got this perfect, and unhappily convincing, answer, even Cut Above had the good sense to shut up and sit down.

If I'd wanted to lose Dr Betty's case I'd've gone in to the attack on Ursula with my guns blazing. Of course I didn't. I started by roaring as gently as any sucking dove, showing the Jury how much more polite and considerate I could be than Cut Above at his most gentlemanly.

'Mrs Chippenham, I hope it won't offend you if I call the deceased Judge, Chippy?'

'Not at all, Mr Rumpole.' Ursula's smile could win all hearts. 'We both knew and loved him, I know. I'm sure he would have liked us to call him that.'

'And that's how he was affectionately known at the Bar,' Portia added to the warmth of the occasion.

'And Chippy was extremely ill?'

'Yes, he was.'

'And, entirely to your credit, you and your husband looked after him? With medical help?'

'We did our best. Yes.'

'He was unlikely to recover?'

'He wasn't going to recover. I don't think there's a cure for Alzheimer's.'

'Can we come to the time when Dr Betty started to treat Chippy? Was Nurse Pargeter coming in then?'

'Yes, she was.'

'And Nurse Pargeter strongly disapproved of Dr Betty's support for legalizing euthanasia?'

'She warned us about Dr Betty, yes.'

'And you discussed the matter with your husband?'

'Oh, yes. We thought about it very carefully. And then I had a talk about it with Dr Betty.'

'Did you?' I looked mildly, ever so mildly, surprised. 'Was your husband present?'

'No, I didn't want it to be too formal. We just chatted over coffee, and Dr Betty promised me she wouldn't give Chippy ... Well, give him anything to stop keeping him alive, without discussing it with the family.'

I looked around at the dock where Dr Betty was shaking her head decisively. So I was put in the embarrassing position of having to call the witness a liar.

'Mrs Chippenham, I have to remind you that you said nothing about this conversation with Dr Betty in your original statement to the police.'

'Didn't I? I'm afraid I was upset and rather flustered at that time.' Ursula turned to the Judge, 'I do hope you can understand?'

'Of course,' Portia understood, 'but can I just ask you this, Mrs Chippenham? If Dr Ireton had come to you and recommended ending Chippy's life what would you have said?'

'Neither Dick nor I would have agreed to it. Not in any circumstances. We may not go to church very much, but we do believe that life is sacred.'

'"We do believe that life is sacred.",' Portia repeated as she wrote the words down, and we all waited in respectful silence. 'Yes, Mr Rumpole?'

'We've heard that it was Nurse Pargeter who found Chippy dead.'

'Yes, she called for me and I joined her.'

'And it was Nurse Pargeter who reported the circumstances of Chippy's death to the police?'

'She insisted on doing so.'

'And you agreed?'

'I think I was too upset to agree or disagree.'

'I see. Now, that morning, when the nurse found Chippy dead, the whisky bottle was almost empty and the bottle of sleeping pills empty. You don't know how that came about?'

'I assumed that Dr Betty gave Chippy the overdose and the whisky.'

'You assumed that because she's a well-known supporter of euthanasia?'

'Well, yes, I suppose so.' Ursula frowned a little then and looked puzzled, but as attractive as ever.

'Because she believes in euthanasia, she's the most likely suspect?'

'Isn't that obvious, Mr Rumpole?' Portia answered the question for the witness.

'And because she was the most likely suspect, is that why you decided to ask her to look after Chippy?' I asked Ursula the first hostile question with my usual charm.

'I'm not sure I understand what you mean?' Ursula smiled in a puzzled sort of way at the Jury, and they looked entirely sympathetic.

'I'm not sure I understand either.' Portia sounded distinctly unfriendly to Counsel for the Defence.

'I'll come back to it later, if I may. Mrs Chippenham, we've got a copy of Chippy's will. Nurse Pargeter does quite well out of it, doesn't she? She gets a substantial legacy.'

'Twenty thousand pounds. She did a great deal for Chippy.'

'And let me ask you this. Your husband's in business as an estate agent, is he not?'

'Marcellus & Chippenham, yes.'

'It's going through a pretty difficult time, isn't it?'

'I think the housing market is having a lot of difficulty, yes.'

'As we all know, Mr Rumpole.' The Erskine-Browns were trying to get rid of a house in Islington and move into central London, so the learned Judge spoke from the heart.

'Let's say that the freehold of the house in Dettingen Road and the residue of Chippy's estate might solve a good many of your problems. Isn't that right?'

The Jury looked at me as though I had suggested that Mother Theresa was only in it for the money and Ursula gave exactly the right answer. 'We were both extremely grateful for what Chippy decided to do for us.' Then she spoilt it a little by adding, 'When he made that will, he understood it perfectly.'

'And I am sure he was conscious of all you and your husband were doing for *him*?' Portia was firmly on Ursula's side.

'Thank you, my Lady.' Ursula didn't bob a curtsey, but it seemed, for a moment, as if she was tempted to do so.

'Mrs Chippenham, you know the way the Lethe organization recommends helping sufferers out of this wicked world?'

'I'm afraid I don't.'

'Are you sure? Didn't Nurse Pargeter give you a pamphlet like this when she was trying to persuade you not to engage Dr Betty?' I handed her the Lethe pamphlet which Bonny Bernard had got me and it was made Defence Exhibit One. Then I asked the witness to turn to page three where a recipe for easeful death was set out. I read it aloud: '"The method recommended is a large dose of sleeping pills which are readily obtainable on prescription and a strong alcoholic drink such as whisky or brandy. When the patient is asleep, a long plastic bin-liner is placed over the head and pulled over the shoulders.

Being deprived of air, the sleep is gentle, painless and permanent." Did you read that when Nurse Pargeter gave you the pamphlet?'

There was a silence and the courtroom seemed to have become suddenly chilly. Then Ursula answered, more quietly than before, 'I may have glanced at it.'

'*You* may have glanced at it. But I suggest that someone in your house remembered it quite clearly when old Chippy was helped out of this troubled world.'

Of course there was an immediate hullabaloo. Cut Above trumpeted that there was no basis at all for that perfectly outrageous suggestion, and Portia, in more measured tones, asked me to make it clear what my suggestion was. I said I was perfectly prepared to do so.

'I suggest someone woke Chippy up, around midnight. He hadn't remembered taking his pills, of course, so he was given a liberal overdose, washed down with a large whisky. One of the long black bin-liners that your dustmen provide so generously was then made use of.'

Ursula was silent, but Counsel for the Prosecution wasn't. 'I hope, my Lady, that Mr Rumpole will be calling evidence to support this extraordinary charge?'

I didn't answer him, but asked the witness, 'Your son Andrew hasn't been well lately?'

'I'm afraid not.' Ursula recovered her voice, thinking I'd passed to another subject.

'Mr Rumpole' – Portia was clearly displeased – 'the Court would also like to know if you are going to call evidence to support the charge you have made.'

'I'm happy to deal with that, my Lady, when I've asked a few more questions.' I turned back to the witness. 'Is Dr Eames treating young Andrew?'

'Yes, Dr Eames has come back to us.'

'Is Andrew's illness of a nervous nature? I mean, has he become worried about something?'

'I don't know. He's had sick headaches and we've kept him out of school. Dr Eames isn't sure what the trouble is exactly.'

'Is Andrew worried by something he might have seen the night Chippy died? Remember, he sleeps with his door open and Chippy's room is immediately opposite. He saw something that night which has worried him ever since. Perhaps that's why he collects the plastic bags from the dustbins and hides them away. Is it because he knows bin bags can cause accidents?'

Ursula's voice slid upwards and became shrill as she asked, 'You say he saw . . . What did he see?'

'He thought it was a dream. But it wasn't a dream, was it?'

'My Lady, are we really being asked to sit here while Mr Rumpole trots out the dreams of a ten-year-old child?' Cut Above boomed, but I interrupted his cannonade.

'I'm not discussing dreams! I'm discussing facts. And the fact is' – I turned to Ursula – 'that you were coming out of Chippy's room that night, perhaps to take the empty bottle of pills back to the bathroom. It was then Andrew saw Chippy propped up on the pillows. Shrouded, Mrs Chippenham. Suffocated, Mrs Chippenham, with a black plastic bag pulled down over his head.'

The Court was cold now, and silent. Ursula looked at the Judge who said nothing, and at the Jury who said nothing either. Her beauty had gone as she became desperate, like a trapped animal. I saw Hilda watching and she appeared triumphant. I saw Dr Betty lean forward as though concerned for a patient who had taken a turn for the worse. When Ursula spoke, her voice was hoarse and hopeless. She said, 'You're not going to bring Andrew here to say that about the plastic bag, are you?'

I hated my job then. Chippy was dying anyway, so why should either Dr Betty, or this suffering woman, be cursed for ever by his death? I felt tired and longed to shut up and sit down, but if I had to choose between Ursula and Dr Betty, I knew I had to protect my client. So I took in a deep breath and said, 'That entirely depends, Mrs Chippenham, on whether you're going to tell us the truth.'

To her credit she didn't hesitate. She was determined to spare her son, so she turned to Portia and said quietly, 'I don't think he suffered and he would have died anyway. When I thought of doing it, I got Dr Ireton to treat Chippy so she would be blamed. That's all I have got to say.' Then she stood, stunned, like the victim of an accident, as though she didn't yet understand the consequences of any of the things she'd done or said.

When I came out of Court, I felt no elation. Cut Above, almost, for him, pianissimo, had offered no further evidence after Ursula's admission, and the case was over very quickly. I had notched a win, but I felt no triumph. I saw the Inspector in charge of the case talking to Dick and Ursula, and when I thought of their future, and Andrew's, I hated what I had done. The merciful tide of forgetfulness which engulfs disastrous days in Court, sinking them in fresh briefs and newer troubles, would be slow to come. Then I saw Hilda embrace Dr Betty and give her one of She Who Must Be Obeyed's rare kisses. My wife turned to me with a look of approval which was also rare; it was as though I were some sort of domestic appliance, a food blender perhaps, or an electric blanket, she had lent to an old friend and which, for once, worked satisfactorily. They asked me to join them for coffee and went away as happy as they must have been when young Betty Ireton led the school team to another victory. Bonny Bernard went about his business and I stood alone, outside the empty Court.

'Rumpole, a word with you, if you please, in a matter of urgency.'

Soapy Sam Ballard had paused, wigged and gowned, in full flight to another Court. He looked pale and agitated to such an extent that I was about to greet him with a quotation I thought might be appropriate: 'The devil damn thee black, thou cream-fac'd loon! Where gott'st thou that goose look?' Before I could speak, however, Soapy Sam started to burble. 'Bad news, I'm afraid. Very bad news indeed. We shall not be entering into a contract of service with Vincent Blewitt.'

I managed to restrain my tears. 'But Bollard,' I protested, 'didn't you think he was the very man for the job?'

'I did. Until he came to me with an idea for a Chambers' party. Did you know anything about this, Rumpole?' The man was suddenly suspicious.

'He told me he wanted to give Henry some kind of a send-off. I thought it was rather generous of him.'

'But did he tell you exactly what sort of send-off he had in mind?'

'A Chambers' party, I think he said. I can't remember the details.'

'He described it as a singles party. At first, I thought he was suggesting tennis.'

'A natural assumption.'

'And then he asked me to leave my ham sandwich at home – I wondered what on earth the man was talking about. I mean, it's never been my custom to bring any sort of sandwich to a Chambers' party. Your wife's friend, Dodo Mackintosh, usually provides the nibbles.'

'Have you any idea, Ballard' – I looked suitably mystified – 'what he meant?'

'I have now. He was talking about my wife Marguerite.'

'Marguerite, who once held the responsible position of matron at the Old Bailey?'

'That is exactly whom he meant.'

'Who was known, even to the red judges, as Matey?'

'Marguerite got on very well with the Judiciary. She treated many of them.'

'Can I believe my ears? Vincent Blewitt called your Marguerite a ham sandwich?' I was incredulous.

'I can't imagine what she would have to say if she ever got wind of it.'

'All hell would break loose?'

'Indeed it would!' Ballard nodded sadly and went on, 'He said we'd all have more fun if I left her at home. And the same applied to your Hilda.'

'Ballard, I can see why you're concerned.' I sounded most reasonable. 'It was a serious error of judgement on Blewitt's part, but if that was the only thing . . .'

'It was not the only thing, Rumpole.'

'You mean there's worse to come?'

'Considerably worse!' Ballard looked around nervously to make sure he wasn't overheard. 'He suggested that the party should start . . . I don't know how to tell you this, Rumpole.'

'Just take it slowly. I understand that it must be distressing.'

'It is, Rumpole. It certainly is. He thought the party should start . . .' Soapy Sam paused and then the words came tumbling out. '. . . By the male Members of Chambers and the girl guests blowing up balloons inside each other's underclothes. Rumpole, can you imagine what Marguerite would have said to that?'

'I thought Marguerite was to be left at home.'

'There is that, of course. But he wanted Mrs Justice Erskine-Brown to come. What would she have said if Blewitt had approached her with a balloon?'

'She'd have jailed him for contempt.'

'Quite right too! And then to top it all . . .'

'He topped that?'

'He said he knew I liked a good story, and wasn't that a great joke about the sleeveless woman?'

'What on earth was he talking about?' I looked suitably mystified.

'I have no idea. Do you know any story about a sleeveless woman?'

'Certainly not!' I replied with absolute truth.

'So then he told me about a legless nun. It was clearly obscene but I'm afraid, Rumpole, the point escaped me.'

'Probably just as well.'

'I'm afraid I shall have to tell Chambers. I'm informing you first as a senior member. We shall not be employing Vincent Blewitt or indeed any legal administrator in the foreseeable future.'

'It will be a disappointment, perhaps. But I'm sure we'll all understand.'

'Henry may have had his faults, Rumpole. But he calls me Sir and not Sam. And I don't believe he knows any jokes at all.'

'Of course not. No, indeed.'

The case of *R.* v. *Ireton* had not, so far as I was concerned, ended happily. *Rumpole* v. *Blewitt*, on the other hand, was an undoubted victory. Win a few, lose a few. That is all you can say about life at the Bar.

Henry decided, in his considerable relief, that he should have a Chambers' party to celebrate his not leaving. All the wives came. Hilda's old schoolfriend Dodo Mackintosh provided the cheesey bits and, perhaps because he had a vague idea of what I had been able to do for him, our clerk laid on a couple of dozen of the Château Thames Embankment of which I drank fairly deep. The day after this jamboree, I was detained in bed with a ferocious headache and a distinct unsteadiness in the leg department.

In a brief period of troubled sleep about midday, I heard voices from the living-room and then the door opened quietly and the Angel of Death was at my bedside. 'Mr Rumpole,' she smiled and her glasses twinkled, 'I hear you're not feeling very well this morning.'

'Really?' I muttered with sudden alarm. 'Whatever gave you that idea? I'm feeling on top of the world, in absolutely' – and here I winced at a sudden stabbing pain across the temples – 'tiptop condition.'

'And Hilda tells me the dear old mind's not what it was?' Dr Betty smiled understandingly. 'The butter knife in the top pocket, is that what she told me? Dear Mr Rumpole, do remember I'm here to help you. There's no need for you to suffer. The way out is always open, and I can steer you gently and quite painlessly towards it.'

'I'm afraid I must ask you to leave now,' I told the Angel of Death. 'Got to get up. Late for work already. As I told you, I never felt better. Full of beans, Dr Betty, and raring to go.'

God knows how I ever managed to climb into the striped trousers, or button the collar, but when I was decently clad I hotfooted it for the Temple. There, I sat in my room suffering, my head in my hands, determined at all costs to keep myself alive.

FOR THE BEST IN PAPERBACKS, LOOK FOR THE

The Rumpole Books

"Rumpole is one of the immortals of mystery fiction."
—*San Francisco Chronicle*

FOR THE BEST IN PAPERBACKS, LOOK FOR THE

In every corner of the world, on every subject under the sun, Penguin represents quality and variety—the very best in publishing today.

For complete information about books available from Penguin—including Puffins, Penguin Classics, and Arkana—and how to order them, write to us at the appropriate address below. Please note that for copyright reasons the selection of books varies from country to country.

In the United Kingdom: Please write to *Dept. JC, Penguin Books Ltd, FREEPOST, West Drayton, Middlesex UB7 0BR.*

If you have any difficulty in obtaining a title, please send your order with the correct money, plus ten percent for postage and packaging, to *P.O. Box No. 11, West Drayton, Middlesex UB7 0BR*

In the United States: Please write to *Consumer Sales, Penguin USA, P.O. Box 999, Dept. 17109, Bergenfield, New Jersey 07621-0120.* VISA and MasterCard holders call 1-800-253-6476 to order all Penguin titles

In Canada: Please write to *Penguin Books Canada Ltd, 10 Alcorn Avenue, Suite 300, Toronto, Ontario M4V 3B2*

In Australia: Please write to *Penguin Books Australia Ltd, P.O. Box 257, Ringwood, Victoria 3134*

In New Zealand: Please write to *Penguin Books (NZ) Ltd, Private Bag 102902, North Shore Mail Centre, Auckland 10*

In India: Please write to *Penguin Books India Pvt Ltd, 706 Eros Apartments, 56 Nehru Place, New Delhi 110 019*

In the Netherlands: Please write to *Penguin Books Netherlands bv, Postbus 3507, NL-1001 AH Amsterdam*

In Germany: Please write to *Penguin Books Deutschland GmbH, Metzlerstrasse 26, 60594 Frankfurt am Main*

In Spain: Please write to *Penguin Books S. A., Bravo Murillo 19, 1° B, 28015 Madrid*

In Italy: Please write to *Penguin Italia s.r.l., Via Felice Casati 20, I-20124 Milano*

In France: Please write to *Penguin France S. A., 17 rue Lejeune, F-31000 Toulouse*

In Japan: Please write to *Penguin Books Japan, Ishikiribashi Building, 2–5–4, Suido, Bunkyo-ku, Tokyo 112*

In Greece: Please write to *Penguin Hellas Ltd, Dimocritou 3, GR–106 71 Athens*

In South Africa: Please write to *Longman Penguin Southern Africa (Pty) Ltd, Private Bag X08, Bertsham 2013*